Richard Laymon wrote over thirty novels and seventy short stories. In May 2001 *The Travelling Vampire Show* won the Bram Stoker Award for Best Horror Novel, a prize for which Laymon had previously been shortlisted with *Flesh*, *Funland*, *A Good, Secret Place* (Best Anthology) and *A Writer's Tale* (Best Non-fiction). Laymon's works incude the books of the Beast House Chronicles: *The Cellar*, *The Beast House* and *The Midnight Tour*. Some of his recent novels have been *Night in the Lonesome October*, *No Sanctuary* and *Amara*.

A native of Chicago, Laymon attended Willamette University in Sale , Oregon, and took an MA in English Literature from Loyola Uni sity, Los Angeles. In 2000, he was elected President of the Horror W rs Association. He died in February 2001.

L. mon's fiction is published in the United Kingdom by Headline, nd in the United States by Leisure Books and Cemetery Dance lications. To learn more, visit the Laymon website at: http:// b.net

u've missed Laymon you've missed a treat' Stephen King

Laymon's books, blood doesn't so much drip drip as explode, splatter coagulate' *Independent*

apable of writing a disappointing book' *New York Review of Science tion*

one writes like Laymon and you're going to have a good time with thing he writes' Dean Koontz

ne of the best, and most underrated, writers working in the genre ay' *Cemetery Dance*

is author knows how to sock it to the reader' *The Times*

The Beast House Trilogy:

The Cellar

and

The Beast House

and

The Midnight Tour

headline

THE CELLAR first published in Great Britain in 1980 by New English Library

Published in 1989 by Star Books

Reprinted in this edition in 1991 by HEADLINE BOOK PUBLISHING

THE BEAST HOUSE first published in Great Britain in 1986
by New English Library

This edition published in 1994 by HEADLINE BOOK PUBLISHING

THE MIDNIGHT TOUR first published in Great Britain in 1998
by HEADLINE BOOK PUBLISHING

First published in this omnibus edition in 2006
by HEADLINE BOOK PUBLISHING

A HEADLINE paperback

6

ISBN 978 0 7553 3167 3

Typeset in Janson by Avon DataSet Ltd, Bidford on Avon, Warwickshire

Printed and bound in Great Britain by
CPI Antony Rowe, Chippenham, Wiltshire

Headline's policy is to use papers that are natural, renewable and recyclable
products and made from wood grown in sustainable forests. The logging and
manufacturing processes are expected to conform to the environmental
regulations of the country of origin.

HEADLINE PUBLISHING GROUP
A division of Hodder Headline
338 Euston Road
London NW1 3BH

www.headline.co.uk
www.hodderheadline.com

The Cellar

To Clayton Matthews

Prologue

Jenson grabbed the radio mike. His thumb froze on the speak button. He looked again at the upstairs window of the old, Victorian house across the street, and saw only the sheen of the moon on the glass pane. He lowered the mike to his lap.

Then a beam of light again flashed inside the dark house.

He raised the mike to his mouth. He forced his thumb down on the button. 'Jenson to headquarters.'

'Headquarters, go ahead.'

'We've got a prowler in Beast House.'

'Ten-nine, Dan. What's the matter with you? Speak up.'

'I said we've got a prowler in Beast House!'

'Jeezus! You'd better go in.'

'Send me a back-up.'

'Sweeny's ten-seven.'

'So *phone* him, for Christsake! He never eats anyplace but the Welcome Inn. Phone him.'

'Just go in, Jenson.'

'I'm not going inside that fucking place alone. You get Sweeny out here, or we can forget the whole thing.'

'I'll try to raise Sweeny. You stay put, and keep an eye on the place if you're too yellow to go in. And watch your language on the airways, buddy.'

'Ten-four.'

Patrolman Dan Jenson put down his radio mike and looked at the distant upstairs window. He saw no sign of the flashlight. His eyes moved to other windows, to the hooded darkness of the balcony over the porch, to the windows of the room with the peaked roof, then back again.

There, in the nearest window, the slim white beam of a flashlight made a quick curlicue and vanished. Jenson felt his skin shrivel as if spiders were scurrying up his back. He rolled up his window. With his elbow, he punched down the lock button of his door. The spiders didn't go away.

*   *   *

Inside the house, the boy was trying hard not to cry as his father pulled him by the arm from one dark room to the next.

'See? Nothing here. Do you see anything?'

'No,' the boy whimpered.

'No ghost, no boogie man, no monster?'

'No.'

'All right.'

'Can we go?' the boy asked.

'Not yet, young man. We haven't seen the attic yet.'

'She said it's locked.'

'We'll get in.'

'No. Please,'

'The monster might be waiting for us in the attic, right? Now where *was* that?' He pulled open a hall door and shined his flashlight inside. The beam illuminated an empty closet. Roughly, he pulled the boy behind him towards a door farther up the narrow corridor.

'Dad, let's go home.'

'Afraid the beast will get you?' The father laughed bitterly. 'We're not stepping outside this cruddy old house until you admit there *is* no beast. I won't have a son of mine cowering and whimpering his way through life, jumping at shadows, afraid of the dark.'

'There *is* a beast,' the boy insisted.

'Show it to me.'

'The guide, she said . . .'

'The guide handed us a load of bull. That's her job. You've gotta learn to know bull when it smacks you in the face, young man. Monsters are bull. Ghosts and goblins and witches are bull. And so is the beast.' He grabbed a knob, jerked open the door, and swung the beam of his flashlight inside. The staircase was a steep, narrow tunnel leading upward to a closed door.

'Come on.'

'No. Please, Dad.'

'Don't *no* me.'

The boy tried to free his arm from his father's grip, but couldn't. He began to cry.

'Stop blubbering, you little chicken.'

'I want to go home.'

The man shook him violently. 'We-are-going-up-those-stairs. The sooner we get into the attic and look for this monster of yours, the sooner we'll leave here. But not a minute earlier, do you hear me?'

'Yes,' the boy managed.

'Okay. Let's go.'

At his father's side, he started up the stairs. The wooden steps groaned and squeaked. The flashlight made a bright, small disc on each stair as they climbed. A halo surrounded the disc, dimly lighting their legs and the walls, and the next few stairs.

'Dad!'

'Quiet.'

The disc of light swung up the stairway and made a spot on the attic door high above them.

The boy wanted to sniff, but was afraid to make a sound. He let the warm fluid roll down to his upper lip, then licked it away. It tasted salty.

'See,' the father whispered. 'We're almost . . .'

From above them came a sound like a sniffing dog.

The man's hand flinched, squeezing pain into his son's arm. The boy took a single step backward, probing for the stair behind him as the attic door swung slowly open.

The flashlight beam pushed through empty darkness beyond the door.

A throaty laugh crept through the silence. It sounded to the boy like the laughter of a very old, dry man.

But it wasn't an old man who leapt through the doorway. As the flashlight dropped, its beam lit a snouted, hairless face.

When the scream came, Dan Jenson knew he couldn't wait for Sweeny. Pulling his 12-gauge Browning off its mount, he threw open the patrol-car door and leapt to the street. He dashed across it. The ticket booth was lighted by a streetlamp. The big wooden sign above it spelled 'BEAST HOUSE' in dripping letters meant to resemble blood.

He shoved the turnstile. It held fast, so he vaulted it.

More screams came from the house, screams of pain torn from a child.

Sprinting up the walkway, Jenson took the porch steps two at a time. He tried the door. Locked. He pumped a cartridge into the shotgun chamber, aimed at the lock face, and pulled the trigger. The 00 shot slammed a hole through the door. He kicked. The door whipped back. He stepped into the foyer.

From above came tearing sounds and breathless animal grunts.

Enough moonlight poured through the front windows. to show him the foot of the staircase. Grabbing the bannister post, he swung himself on to the stairs. Blackness swallowed him. With one hand on the railing to guide him, he climbed. At the top of the stairs, he stopped and listened. Grunting, snarling sounds came from the left.

Cocking the shotgun, he jumped into the hallway and whirled to the right, ready to fire.

All was dark except for a puddle of brightness spilling across the hall floor. It came from the end of a flashlight.

Jenson wanted that flashlight. Needed it. But it lay far down the hall, close to the black centre of the quick, loud, gasping sounds.

Shotgun pointed up the hallway, he dashed towards the flashlight, his shoes pounding echoes, his own sharp breaths masking the rasp of the other breathing. Then his foot came down on something round like a club, but soft. Maybe an arm. His other foot kicked a hard object, and he heard its teeth clash shut as he stumbled headlong into the darkness. The shotgun mashed his fingers against the floor.

Stretching his right arm, he reached the flashlight. He swung its beam in the direction of the grunts.

The creature loosed its teeth from the nape of the boy's neck. It turned its head. The skin of its face was white and puffy like the belly of a dead fish. It seemed to smile. It writhed, freeing itself from the boy.

Jenson dropped the flashlight and tried to raise the shotgun.

He heard soft, dry laughter, and the beast took him.

Chapter One

1.

Donna Hayes put down the telephone. She rubbed her trembling, wet hands on the covers, and sat up.

She had known it would happen. She had expected it, planned for it, dreaded it. Now it was upon her. 'I'm sorry to disturb you at this hour,' he'd said, 'but I knew you'd want to be informed immediately. Your husband was released. Yesterday morning. I just found out, myself . . .'

For a long time, she stared into the darkness of her bedroom, unwilling to swing her feet down to the floor. Darkness began to fade from the room. She could wait no longer.

The Sunday morning air was like cold water drenching her skin as she stood up. Shivering, she bundled herself into a robe. She stepped across the hallway. From the slow breathing inside the room, she knew that her twelve-year-old daughter still slept.

She went to the edge of the bed. A small shoulder, covered with yellow flannel, protruded from the top of the covers. Donna cupped it in her hand and gently shook it. Rolling on to her back, the girl opened her eyes. Donna kissed her forehead. 'Good morning,' she said.

The girl smiled. She brushed pale hair away from her eyes and stretched. 'I was having a dream.'

'Was it a good one?'

The girl nodded seriously. 'I had a horse that was white all over, and so big I had to stand on a kitchen chair to get on him.'

'That sounds awfully big.'

'It was a giant,' she said. 'How come you're up so early?'

'I thought you and I might just pack our bags, get in the Maverick, and take ourselves a vacation.'

'A vacation?'

'Yep.'

'When?'

'Right now.'

'Wow!'

It took nearly an hour to wash up, dress, and pack enough clothes for a week away from the apartment. As they carried their luggage down to the carport, Donna fought a strong urge to confide in Sandy, to let the girl know that she would never return, never spend another night in her room or another lazy afternoon at Sorrento Beach, never see her school friends again. With a sense of guilt, Donna kept quiet about it.

Santa Monica was grey with its usual June morning overcast as Donna backed on to the road. She looked up and down the block. No sign of him. The prison authorities had left him at the San Rafael bus depot yesterday morning at eight. Plenty of time for him to arrive, look up her address, and come for her. But she saw no sign of him.

'Which way do you want to go?' she asked.

'I don't care.'

'How about north?'

'What's north?' Sandy asked.

'It's a direction – like south, east, west . . .'

'Mom!'

'Well, there's San Francisco. We can see if they've painted the bridge right. There's also Portland, Seattle, Juneau, Anchorage, the North Pole.'

'Can we get there in a week?'

'We can take longer, if we want.'

'What about your job?'

'Somebody else can do it while we're gone.'

'Okay. Let's go north.'

The Santa Monica Freeway was nearly deserted. So was the San Diego. The old Maverick did fine, cruising just over sixty. 'Keep an eye out for Smokey,' Donna said.

Sandy nodded. 'Ten-four, Big Mama.'

'Watch that "Big" stuff.'

Far below them, the San Fernando Valley was sunny. The smog's yellow vapour, at this hour, was still a barely noticeable smudge hanging low over the land.

'What can your handle be?' asked Sandy.

'How about "Mom"?'

'That's no fun.'

They nosed down towards the valley, and Donna steered on to the Ventura Freeway. After a while, Sandy asked permission to change the radio station. She turned it to 93 KHJ and listened for an hour before Donna asked for an intermission, and turned the radio off.

The highway generally followed the coast to Santa Barbara, then cut inland through a wooded pass with a tunnel.

'I'm sure starving,' Sandy said.

'Okay, we'll stop pretty soon.'

They stopped at Denny's near Santa Maria. They both ordered sausage and eggs. Donna sighed with pleasure as she took her day's first drink of coffee. Sandy, with a glass of orange juice, mimicked her.

'That bad?' Donna asked.

'How about "Coffee Mama"?' Sandy suggested.

'Make it "Java Mama," and we've got a deal.'

'Okay, you're "Java Mama."'

'Who are you?'

'You have to name me.'

'How about "Sweetie-Pie"?'

'*Mom!*' Sandy looked disgusted.

Knowing they would have to stop for gas within an hour's driving, Donna allowed herself three cups of the dark hot coffee with breakfast.

When Sandy's plate was clean, Donna asked if she was ready to leave.

'I have to make a pit stop,' the girl said.

'Where'd you pick *that* up?'

Sandy shrugged, grinning.

'Uncle Bob, I bet.'

'Maybe.'

'Well, I have to make a pit stop, too.'

Then they were on the road again. Just north of San Luis Obispo, they pulled into a Chevron station, gassed up the Ford, and used the toilets. Two hours later, in the bright heat of the San Joaquin Valley, they stopped at a drive-in for Cokes and cheeseburgers. The valley seemed to go on forever, but finally the freeway curved upward to the west, and the air lost some of its heat. The radio began to pick up San Francisco stations.

'Are we almost there?' Sandy asked.

'Where?'

'San Francisco.'

'Almost. Another hour or so.'

'That long?'

'Afraid so.'

'Will we spend the night?'

'I don't think so. I want to go far, don't you?'

'How far?' Sandy asked.

'The North Pole.'

'Oh, *Mom.*'

It was after three o'clock when Highway 101 sloped downward into a shadowy corner of San Francisco. They waited at a stoplight, turned, watched for signs marking 101, and turned again: up Van Ness Avenue, left on to Lombard, finally up a curving road to the Golden Gate.

'Remember how disappointed you were the first time you saw it?' Donna asked.

'I'm still disappointed. If it isn't golden, they shouldn't say it is. Should they?'

'Certainly not. It is beautiful, though.'

'But it's orange. Not golden. They ought to call it the Orange Gate.'

Glancing out towards the open sea, Donna saw the front edge of a fog mass. It looked pure white in the sunlight. 'Look at the fog,' she said. 'Isn't it lovely?'

'It's okay.'

They left the Golden Gate behind.

They passed through a tunnel with a mouth painted like a rainbow.

They sped by the Sausalito off-ramp.

'Hey, can we go to Stinson Beach?' Sandy asked, reading the sign for the turn-off.

Donna shrugged. 'Why not? It won't be as fast, but it'll be a lot prettier.' She flicked on her turn signal, followed the curving ramp, and left 101 behind.

Soon they were on the Coast Highway. It was narrow: far too narrow and far too crooked, considering the steep drop just across the left-hand lanes. She drove as far to the right as the road would allow.

The fog lay just offshore, as white and heavy as cotton batting. It seemed to be moving slowly closer, but was still a good distance away from shore when they reached the town of Stinson Beach.

'Can we spend the night here?' Sandy asked.

'Let's keep going for a while. Okay?'

'Do we have to?'

'You've never been to Bodega Bay?'

'No.'

'That's where they filmed that movie *The Birds*.'

'Oooh, that was scary.'

'Should we try for Bodega?'

'How far is it?' the girl asked.

'Maybe an hour.' She ached, especially in her back. It was important, though, to keep going, to put more miles behind them. She could stand the pain for a while longer.

When they reached Bodega Bay, Donna said, 'Let's keep going for a little while.'

'Do we have to? I'm tired.'

'*You're* tired. *I'm* dying.'

Soon after they left Bodega Bay, fog started to blow past the windshield. Fingers of it began reaching over the lip of the road, sneaking forward, feeling blindly. Then, as if they liked what they felt, the whole body of fog shambled on to the road.

'Mom, I can't see!'

Through the thick white mass, Donna could barely make out the front of the hood. The road was only a memory. She stepped on the brakes, praying that another car hadn't come up behind them. She steered to the right. Her wheels crunched gravel. Suddenly the car plunged down.

2.

An instant before the stop threw Donna into the steering wheel, she flung an arm across her daughter's chest. Sandy folded at the hips, knocking the arm away. Her head hit the dashboard. She started to cry. Donna quickly turned off the engine.

'Let's see.'

The soft dashboard had left a red mark across the girl's forehead.

'Are you hurt any place else?'

'Here.'

'Where the seat belt got you?'

She nodded, gulping.

'Good thing you had it on.' Her mind pictured Sandy's head breaking through the windshield, jagged glass ripping her body, then the last of her disappearing into the fog, forever lost.'

'Wish I hadn't.'

'Let's undo it. Hold on.'

The girl braced herself against the dash, and Donna unlatched the seat belt.

'Okay, let's get out now. I'll go first. Don't do anything until I say it's all right.'

'Okay.'

Climbing out, Donna slipped on the fog-wet grassy covering of the slope. She clung to the door until she found her footing.

'Are you okay?' Sandy asked.

'So far, so good.' Holding herself steady, she peered through the fog. Apparently the road had curved to the left without them, and they had nose-dived into a ditch. The rear of the car remained at road level: unless the fog was too thick, it would be visible to passing cars.

Donna worked her way carefully down the slippery embankment. The Maverick's front bumper was buried in the ditch. Steam hissed from the crevices of the hood. She crawled across the hood, got down on the other side, and climbed the slope to Sandy's door. She helped the girl out. Together they slid and stumbled to the bottom of the ditch.

'Well,' Donna said, in a voice as cheerful as she could muster, 'here we are. Now let's have a look at your wounds.'

Sandy untucked her plaid blouse and lifted it out of the way. Donna, squatting, lowered the girl's jeans. A wide band of red crossed her belly. The skin over her hip bones looked tender and raw, as if layers had been sandpapered off. 'I'll bet that stings.'

Sandy nodded. Donna began to lift the jeans.

'I've gotta go.'

'Well, pick a tree. Just a second.' She climbed up to the car and took a box of Kleenex from the glove compartment. 'You can use these.'

Carrying the box of tissue with one hand and holding up her jeans with the other, Sandy walked along the bottom of the ditch. She vanished in the fog. 'Hey, here's a path!' she called.

'Don't go far.'

'Just a little ways.'

Donna heard her daughter's feet crushing the forest mat of dead twigs and pine needles. The sounds became faint. 'Sandy! Don't go any farther.'

The footfalls had either stopped, or faded so completely with distance that they blended with the other forest sounds.

'Sandy!'

'What?' The girl sounded annoyed, but her voice came from far away.

'Can you get back all right?'

'Geez, Mom.'

'Okay.' Donna leaned back until the seat of her corduroy pants pressed against the car. She shivered. Her blouse was too thin to keep out the cold. She would wait for Sandy, then get jackets out of the back seat. Until the girl's return, she didn't want to move. She waited, staring into the grey where Sandy had gone.

Suddenly, the wind tore away a shred of fog. 'That was a longer-than average pit stop,' Donna said.

Sandy didn't answer, or move.

'What's the matter, hon?'

She just stood there, above the ditch, motionless and mute.

'Sandy, what's wrong?'

Feeling a prickling chill on the back of her neck, Donna snapped her head around. Nothing behind her. She looked back at Sandy.

'My God, what's wrong?'

Pushing from the car, she ran. She ran towards the paralysed, silent figure at the forest edge. Ran through the grey, obscuring murk. Watched the shape of her daughter twist into a crude resemblance as the fog thinned until, a dozen feet away, nothing remained of Sandy but a four-foot pine sapling.

'Oh, Jesus,' Donna muttered. And then she shrieked, 'Sandy!'

'Mom,' came the distant voice. 'I think I'm lost.'

'Don't move.'

'I won't.'

'Don't move. Stay right where you are! I'm coming!'

'Hurry!'

A narrow path through the pines seemed to point in the voice's direction. Donna hurried.

'Sandy!' she shouted.

'Here.'

The voice was closer. Donna walked quickly, watching the fog, stepping over a dead pine trunk blocking the path.

'Sandy?'

'Mom!'

The voice was very close now, but off to the right.

'Okay, I've almost reached you.'

'Hurry.'

'Just a minute.' She stepped off the path, pushing between damp limbs that tried to hold her back. 'Where are you, darling?'

'Here.'

'Where?'

'Here!'

'Where?' Before the girl could answer, Donna shoved through a barrier of branches and saw her.

'Mom!'

She was clutching the pink box of Kleenex to her chest as if it would somehow keep her from harm.

'I got turned around,' she explained.

Donna hugged her. 'That's all right, honey. It's all right. Did you take care of business?'

She nodded.

'Okay, let's go back to the car.'

If we can find it, she thought.

But she found the path without difficulty, and the path took them to the opening above the ditch. Donna kept her eyes down as she stepped past the pine sapling she had mistaken for Sandy. Silly, she knew, but the thought of seeing it frightened her; what if it looked like Sandy again, or like someone else – a stranger, or *him?*

'Don't be mad,' Sandy said.

'Me? I'm not mad.'

'You look mad.'

'Do I?' She smiled. Then the two of them climbed down the slope of the ditch. 'I was just thinking,' Donna said.

'About Dad?'

She forced herself not to react. She didn't gasp, didn't suddenly squeeze her daughter's hand, didn't let her head snap towards the girl in shock. In a voice that sounded very calm, she said, 'Why would I be thinking about Dad?'

The girl shrugged.

'Come on. Out with it.'

Ahead of them, the dark bulk of the car appeared through the fog.

'I was just thinking about him,' Sandy told her.

'Why?'

'It was scary back there.'

'Is that the only reason?'

'It was cold, like that time. And I had my pants down.'

'Oh God.'

'I got afraid he might be watching.'

'I bet that was plenty scary.'

'Yeah.'

They stopped at the side of the car. Sandy looked up at Donna. In a very small voice Sandy said, 'What if he gets us here? All by ourselves?'

'Impossible.'

'He'd kill us, wouldn't he?'

'No, of course not. Besides, it can't happen.'

'It might, if he escaped. Or if they let him out.'

'Even if they did, he'd never find us here.'

'Oh yes he would. He told me so. He said he'd find us wherever we went. He said, "I'll sniff you down."'

'Shhhh.'

'What?' Sandy whispered.

For a moment, Donna held to the hope that it was only the sound of the ocean surf beating the rocky shore. But the surf was across the road, and far down the cliff. Besides, why hadn't she heard it before now? The sound grew.

'A car's coming,' she muttered.

The girl's face went pale. 'It's *him!*'

'No, it's not. Get in the car.'

'It's him. He escaped! It's him!'
'No! Get in the car. Quick!'

3.

She first saw the man in the rear-view mirror, hunched over the back of the car, turning his head slowly as he looked in at her. His tiny eyes, his nose, his grinning mouth, all seemed far too small, as if they belonged to a head half the size of this one.

A gloved fist knocked on the rear window.

'Mom!'

She looked down at her daughter crouched on the floor below the dashboard. 'It's okay, honey.'

'Who is it?'

'I don't know.'

'Is it *him?*'

'No.'

The car rocked as the stranger's hand tugged the door handle. He knocked on the window. Donna turned to him. He looked about forty, in spite of the deep lines carved in his face. He seemed less interested in Donna, than in the plastic head of the lock button. He pointed a gloved finger at it, pecking the window glass.

Donna shook her head.

'I'll come in,' he called.

Donna shook her head. 'No!'

The man smiled as if it were a game. 'I'll come in.' He let go of the door handle and leapt to the bottom of the ditch. When he hit the ground, he almost fell. Steadying himself, he glanced over his shoulder as if to see whether Donna had appreciated his jump. He grinned. Then he started hobbling along the ditch, limping badly. The fog nibbled at him. Then he was gone.

'What's he doing now?' Sandy asked from the floor.

'I don't know.'

'Did he go away?'

'He's in the ditch. I can't see him. The fog's too thick.'

'Maybe he'll get lost.'

'Maybe.'

'Who is he?'

'I don't know, honey.'

'Does he want to hurt us?'

Donna didn't answer. She saw a dark shape in the fog. It slowly became distinct, became the strange, limping man. In his left hand he carried a rock.

'Is he back?' Sandy asked.

'He's on his way.'

'What's he doing?'

'Honey, I want you to sit up.'

'What?'

'Get up in your seat. If I tell you to, I want you to jump out and run. Run into the woods and hide.'

'What about you?'

'I'll try to come, too. But you go when I say, regardless.'

'No. I won't go without you.'

'Sandra!'

'I won't!'

Donna watched the man climb up the embankment to the car. He used the door handle to pull himself up. Then he thumped the window, like before, pointing at the lock button. He made a smile. 'I'll come in,' he said.

'Go away!'

He raised the grey, wedge-shaped rock in his left hand. He tapped it lightly against the window, then looked at her.

'Okay,' Donna said to him.

'Mom, don't.'

'We can't stay in here,' she said quietly.

The man grinned as Donna reached over her shoulder.

'Get ready, hon.'

'No!'

She flicked up the lock button, levered the door handle and thrust herself against it. The door swung, jolted, and knocked into the man. With a yelp of surprise, he tumbled backward, the rock flying from his hand. He did a crooked somersault to the bottom of the ditch.

'Now!'

'Mom!'

'Let's go!'

'He'll get us!'

Donna saw him motionless on his back. His eyes were shut. 'It's all right,' she said. 'Look. He's knocked out.'

'He's playing possum, Mom. He'll get us.'

Hanging on to the open door, one foot down on the slippery grass, Donna stared at the man. He certainly *looked* unconscious, the way his arms and legs were splayed out in such strange, grotesque ways. Unconscious, or even dead.

Playing possum?

She raised her foot inside the car, pulled the door shut, and locked it. 'Okay,' she said, 'we'll stay.'

The girl sighed, and lowered herself, once again, to the floor in front of the seat.

Donna managed a smile for her. 'You okay?'

She nodded.

'Cold?'

Another nod. Awkwardly, Donna turned and stretched an arm over the back of the seat. She reached Sandy's coat first, then her own.

Curled against the passenger door, Sandy used the coat to cover all but her face.

Donna got into her blue windbreaker.

The man outside hadn't moved.

'It's almost dark,' Sandy whispered.

'Yeah.'

'He'll come for us when it's dark.'

'Do you have to say that kind of stuff?'

'I'm sorry,' the girl said.

'Besides, I don't think he's coming for anybody. I think he's hurt.'

'He's pretending.'

'I don't know.' Bent forward with her chin on the steering wheel, Donna watched him. She watched for the movement of an arm or leg, for a turn of the head, an opening eye. Then she tried to see if he was breathing.

In his fall, the sweatshirt under his open jacket had pulled up, leaving his belly exposed. She watched it closely. It didn't seem to be moving, but the distance was enough that she could easily miss the subtle rise and fall of his breathing.

Especially under all that hair.

He must be a mass of hair from head to toe. No, the head was shaved. Even the top. There seemed to be a bristly crown of dark stubble on top, as if he hadn't shaved it for several days.

He ought to shave his belly, she thought.

She looked at it again. Still, she couldn't see any movement.

His grey pants hung low on his hips, showing the waistband of his underwear. Baggy boxer shorts. Striped. Donna looked down at his feet. His sneakers were soiled grey, and held together with tape.

'Sandy?'

'Hmmm?'

'Stay inside.'

'What are you doing?' Fright in the girl's voice.

'I'm going out for a second.'

'No!'

'He can't hurt us, honey.'

'Please.'

'I think he might be dead.'

She opened the car door and climbed out carefully. She locked the door. Shut it. Tried it. Fingering the side of the car for balance, she eased herself down the slope. She stood above the man. He didn't move. She zipped her windbreaker, and knelt beside him.

'Hey,' she said. She jiggled his shoulder. 'Hey, are you okay?'

She pressed a hand flat against his chest, felt its rise and fall, felt the light throbbing of his heart.

'Can you wake up?' she asked. 'I want to help you. Are you hurt?'

In the growing darkness, she didn't notice the moving, gloved hand until it grabbed her wrist.

4.

With a startled yelp, Donna tried to twist free. She couldn't break the man's stiff grip.

His eyes opened.

'Let go. Please.'

'It hurts,' he said.

His hand squeezed more tightly. His grip felt strange. Glancing down, Donna saw that he was holding her with only two fingers and the thumb of his right hand. The other two glove fingers remained straight. With a vague stir of revulsion, she realized there were probably no fingers inside those parts of the glove.

'I'm sorry it hurts,' Donna said, 'but you're hurting me, now.'

'You'll run.'

'No. I promise.'

His tight grip eased. 'I wasn't going to hurt you,' he said. He sounded as if he might cry. 'I just wanted in. You didn't have to hurt me.'

'I was frightened.'

'I just wanted in.'

'Where are you hurt?'

'Here.' He pointed at the back of his head.

'I can't see.'

Groaning, he rolled over. Donna saw the pale shape of a rock on the ground where his head had been. Though the night was too dark to be certain, there didn't seem to be blood on his head. She touched it, feeling the soft brush of his hair stubble, and found a lump. Then she inspected her fingers. She rubbed them together. No blood.

'I'm Axel,' the man said. 'Axel Kutch.'

'I'm Donna. I don't think you're bleeding.'

'Dah-nuh.'

'Yes.'

'Donna.'

'Axel.'

He got to his hands and knees and turned his face to her. 'I just wanted in.'

'That's okay, Axel.'

'Do I have to go now?'

'No.'

'Can I stay with you?'

'Maybe we can all go away. Will you drive us somewhere for help?'

'I drive good.'

Donna helped him to stand. 'Why don't we wait for the fog to lift, then you can drive us somewhere for help.'

'Home.'

'Your home?'

He nodded. 'It's safe.'

'Where do you live?'

'Malcasa Point.'

'Is that nearby?'

'We'll go there.'

'Where is it, Axel?'

He pointed into the darkness. North.

'We'll go home. It's safe.'

'Okay. But we have to wait for the fog to lift. You wait in your car, and we'll wait in ours.'

'Come with me.'

'When the fog lifts. Good-bye.' She feared he would try to stop her from getting into the car, but he didn't. She shut the door and rolled down the window. 'Axel?' He limped closer. 'This is my daughter, Sandy.'

'San-dee,' he said.

'This is Axel Kutch.'

'Hi,' Sandy greeted him, her voice soft and uncertain.

'We'll see you later,' Donna said. She waved goodbye and rolled up the window.

For a few moments, Axel stared silently in at them. Then he climbed the slope and was gone.

'What's wrong with him?' the girl asked.

'I think he's . . . slow.'

'You mean a retard?'

'That's not a nice way to put it, Sandy.'

'We've got them like that at school. Retards. Know what they're called? Special.'

'That sounds a lot better.'

'Yeah, I guess. Where'd he go?'

'Back to his car.'

'Is he leaving?' Sandy's voice was eager with hope.

'Nope. We'll wait for the fog to thin out, then he's going to drive us out of here.'

'We're going in his car?'

'Ours isn't going any place.'

'I know, but . . .'

'Would you rather stay here?'

'He scares me.'

'That's just because he's strange. If he wanted to do us harm, he's had plenty of opportunity. He certainly couldn't find a better location for it than right here.'

'Maybe, maybe not.'

'Anyway, we can't just stay here.'

'I know. Dad'll get us.' The girl's eyes were black holes in the oval of her face. 'Dad's not in prison anymore, is he?'

'No, he's not. The district attorney . . . remember Mr Goldstein? . . . he telephoned this morning. They let Dad out yesterday. Mr Goldstein called to warn us.'

'Are we running away?'

'Yes.'

The girl on the floor lapsed into silence. Donna, resting against the steering wheel, closed her eyes. At some point, she fell asleep. She was awakened by a quiet sob.

'Sandy, what is it?'

'It won't do any good.'

'What won't?'

'He'll get us.'

'Honey!'

'He *will!*'

'Try to sleep, honey. It'll be all right. You'll see.'

The girl became silent except for an occasional sniff. Donna, leaning on the steering wheel, waited for sleep. When it finally came, it was a tense, aching half-sleep feverish with vivid dreams. She stood it as long as she could. At last, she had to get out. If the rest of her body could endure the torment, her full bladder couldn't.

Taking the box of Kleenex from the floor beside Sandy, she climbed silently from the car. The chilly air made her shake. She breathed deeply. Rolling her head, she tried to work the stiffness out of her sore neck muscles. It didn't seem to help much. She locked the door and pushed it quietly shut.

Before letting go of its handle, she looked over the top of the car. On the shoulder of the road, less than twenty feet from the rear of the Maverick, was a pick-up truck.

Axel Kutch sat on the roof of its cab, legs hanging over the windshield. His face, turned skyward, was lighted by a full moon. He seemed to be staring at it, as if entranced.

Silently, Donna crept down the slope. From the bottom of the ditch, she could still see Axel's head. She watched it as she opened her corduroys. The huge head was still tilted back, its mouth gaping. She crouched close to the car.

The breeze was cold on her skin.

I was cold, like that time. And I had my pants down.

Everything will be fine, she thought.

He'll sniff us down.

When she finished, Donna climbed the slope to the roadside. Axel, sitting on the roof of his truck cab, didn't seem to notice.

'Axel?'

His hands flinched. He looked down at her and smiled. 'Donna,' he said.

'The fog's gone. Maybe we can leave now.'

Without a word, he jumped down. When he hit the asphalt road, his left leg buckled, but he kept his balance.

'What's going on?' Sandy called to them.

'We're leaving.'

The three of them unpacked the Maverick and transferred the suitcases to the bed of the pick-up truck. Then they climbed inside, Donna sitting between Axel and her daughter.

'Help me remember where the car is,' she told Sandy.

'Will we come back for it?'

'We sure will.'

Axel steered his truck on to the road. He grinned at Donna. She grinned back.

'You smell good,' he said.

She thanked him.

Then he was quiet. On the radio, Jeannie C. Riley sang about the

Harper Valley PTA. Donna fell asleep before the end of the song. She
opened her eyes, sometime later, saw the truck's headlights opening a
path through the darkness of the curving road, and shut them again.
Later, she was awakened when Axel started to sing along in his thick,
low voice, with 'The Blind Man in the Bleachers.' She drifted again into
sleep. A hand on her thigh woke her up.

Axel's hand.

'Here we are,' he said. Lifting the hand away, he pointed.

The headlights lit a metal sign: 'WELCOME TO MALCASA
POINT, pop. 400. Drive with Care.'

Looking ahead through the bars of a wrought-iron fence, Donna
saw a dark, Victorian house: a strange mixture of bay windows, gables,
and balconies. At one end of the roof, a cone-shaped peak jabbed at the
night. 'What's this place?' she asked in a whisper.

'Beast House,' said Axel.

'*The* Beast House?'

He nodded.

'Where the murders were?'

'They were fools.'

'Who?'

'They went in at night.'

He slowed the truck.

'What are you . . .?'

He turned left on to an unpaved road directly across from the ticket
booth of Beast House. Ahead of them, perhaps fifty yards up the road,
stood a two-story brick house with a garage.

'Here we are,' Axel said.

'What *is* this?'

'Home. It's safe.'

'Mom?' Sandy's voice was like a moan of despair.

Donna took the girl's hand. The palm was sweaty.

'It's safe,' Axel repeated.

'It doesn't have windows. Not a single window.'

'No. It's safe.'

'We're not going in there, Axel.'

5.

'Isn't there some place else we can spend the night?' Donna asked.

'No.'

'Isn't there?'

'I want you here.'

'We won't stay here. Not in *that* house.'

'Mother's here.'

'It's not that. Just take us some place else. There has to be some kind of motel or something.'

'You're mad at me,' he said.

'No, I'm not. Just take us some place else, where we can stay till morning.'

He backed the pick-up on to the road, and drove through the few blocks of Malcasa Point's business section. At the north end of town was a Chevron station. Closed. Half a mile beyond it, Axel pulled into the lighted parking lot of the Welcome Inn. Overhead, a red neon sign flashed the word 'VACANCY.'

'This is just fine,' Donna said. 'Let's just unload our luggage, and we'll be all set.'

They climbed from the truck. Reaching into the back, Axel pulled out the suitcases.

'I'll go home,' he said.

'Thanks a lot for helping us like you did.'

He grinned and shrugged.

'Yeah,' said Sandy. 'Same here.'

'Wait.' His grin became very big. Reaching into a hip pocket, he pulled out his billfold. The black leather looked old, shiny with a dull gloss from so much use, and ragged at the corners. It flopped open. He spread the lips of its bill compartment, which was bloated more with a thick assortment of papers and cards than with money. Holding the billfold inches from his nose, he searched it. He began to mutter. He looked at Donna with a silent plea for patience, then made a quick, embarrassed smile at Sandy. 'Wait,' he said. Turning his back to them, he ducked his head and bit the fingertps of his right-hand glove.

Donna glanced at the motel office. It looked empty, but lighted. The coffee shop across the driveway was crowded. She could smell french fries. Her stomach rumbled.

'Ah!' Glove hanging from his teeth, Axel swung around. In his hand – or what there was of a hand – he held two blue cards. The skin of his hand was seamed with scars. Half-inch stumps remained of the two missing fingers. The tip of his middle finger was gone. Two flesh-coloured bandages wrapped his thumb.

Donna took the card, smiling in spite of the heavy thickness she suddenly felt in her stomach. She started to read the top one. 'COMPLIMENTARY' was printed in block letters. The small type beneath it was difficult to see in the lights of the parking lot, but she struggled with it, reading aloud. 'This ticket entitles the bearer to one free, guided tour of Malcasa Point's infamous, world-renowned Beast House . . .'

'Is that the scary old place with the fence?' Sandy asked.

Axel nodded, grinning. Donna saw that his glove was on again.

'Hey, that'd be neat!'

'I work there,' he said, looking proud.

'Is there really a beast?' the girl asked.

'Just at night. No tours after four.'

'Well, thank you for the tickets, Axel. And for driving us here.'

'Will you come?'

'We'll try to see it,' Donna said, though she had no intention of touring such a place.

'Are you the tour guide?' asked Sandy.

'I clean. Scrub-a-dub-dub.' Waving at them, he climbed into his truck. Donna and Sandy watched it roll out of the parking lot. It disappeared down the road towards Malcasa Point.

'Well.' Donna took a deep breath, relishing the relief she felt at Axel's departure. 'Let's get registered, and then we'll grab a bite to eat.'

'A bite won't be enough.'

'We'll buy the joint out.'

They picked up their suitcases and walked towards the motel office.

'Can we take the tour tomorrow?' Sandy asked.

'We'll see.'

'Does that mean no?'

'If you want to go on the tour, we'll do it.'

'All right!'

Chapter Two

Roy rang the doorbell of Apartment 10 and waited. He heard nothing from inside. He jammed the button five times, quickly.

Goddamn bitch, why wouldn't she open up?

Maybe she's not home.

She has to be home. Nobody's out on a Sunday night, not at eleven-thirty.

Maybe she's asleep.

He pounded the door with his knuckles. Waited. Pounded again.

Down the hallway, a door opened. A man in pyjamas looked out. 'Knock it off, would you?'

'Go fuck yourself.'

'Look, buddy . . .'

'You want me to kick the shit out of you, just say one more word.'

'Get out of here, or I'll call the cops.'

Roy started towards him. The man slammed the door. Roy heard the rattle of a guard chain.

Okay, the guy's probably dialling right now.

It'd take the cops a few minutes to get here. He decided to use those minutes.

Bracing himself against the wall opposite Apartment 10, he threw himself forward. The heel of his upraised shoe caught the door close to the knob. With a crash, the door shot open. Roy ducked, slid up his right pants leg, and unsheathed the Buck knife he'd bought that day at a sporting goods store. Knife out, he entered the dark apartment.

He turned on a lamp. Crossed the living room. Rushed down a short hallway. The bedroom on the left, probably Sandy's room, was deserted. Same with the one on the right. He opened its closets. Most of the hangers were bare.

Shit!

He ran out of the apartment, down the stairs, and out the back way to the alley. Across the alley was a row of garages. He ran past the end garage and found a gate. He pushed it open. A walkway led down the side of an apartment building. He followed it to the street.

No cars coming.

He dashed across.

This block had houses instead of apartment buildings. Much better. He crouched behind a tree and waited for a car to pass. When it was gone, he started along the sidewalk, inspecting each house, looking for the one that seemed most promising.

He chose a small, stucco house that was dark at the windows. He didn't choose it because of the darkness, he chose it because of the girl's-style bicycle he saw in the front yard.

Careless, leaving it there.

It could've been stolen. Maybe they thought the little fence would protect it.

The fence wouldn't protect anything.

Roy reached over the gate and carefully lifted the latch. The gate squeaked as he pushed it open. He shut it gently and hurried up the walkway to the front stoop. The door had no peephole. That would make things easier.

He knocked hard and fast. He waited a few seconds, then hit the door three more times.

Light appeared in the living-room window.

'Who's there?' a man asked.

'Police.' Roy backed away and crouched slightly, right shoulder towards the door.

'What do you want?'

'We're evacuating the neighbourhood.'

'What?'

'We're evacuating the area. A gas main broke.'

The door opened.

Roy lunged. The guard chain, snapped taut. It's mounting shot from the doorjamb. The door slammed into the man, knocking him backward. Roy dived into him, covered his mouth, and jabbed the knife into his throat.

'Marv?' a woman called. 'What's going on out there?'

Roy shut the front door.

'Marv?' Fear in her voice. 'Marv, are you all right?'

Roy heard the whirr of a spinning telephone dial. He ran to the hall. Near the end, light shone through an open door. He rushed towards it. He was almost there when a girl stepped out of a dark doorway, glanced at him, and gasped. Roy grabbed her hair.

'Mommy!' Roy called. 'Hang up the phone or I cut your daughter's throat.'

'God in heaven!'

'Let me hear it.' He yanked the girl's hair. She cried out.

The phone clattered. 'It's down! I put it down!'

Roy twisted the girl's hair, making her turn around. 'Walk,' he said. Knife blade poised across her throat, he walked behind her to the far bedroom.

The woman stood next to her bed, stiff and trembling. She wore a white nightgown. Her pale arms were crossed tightly as if she were trying to warm herself.

'What . . . what did you do to Marv?'

'He's all right.'

Her eyes lowered to Roy's knife hand. He glanced down. His hand was shiny red. 'So I lied,' he said.

'God in heaven! O merciful God!'

'Shut up.'

'You killed him!'

'Shut up.'

'You killed my Marv!'

He shoved the girl roughly towards the bed and ran at the hysterical woman. Her mouth gaped wide to scream. Clutching the front of her nightgown, he jerked. her forward and punched the knife into her stomach. She sucked air as if her wind had been knocked out. 'Gonna shut up now?' Roy asked, and stabbed again.

She started to sag, so Roy let go of the nightgown. She sank to her knees, both hands pressing her belly. Then she slumped forward.

The girl on the bed didn't move. She just stared.

'Now, you don't want to get stabbed, too, do you?' he asked her.

She shook her head. She was trembling. She looked ready to scream.

Roy glanced down at himself. His shirt and pants dripped blood. 'I guess I'm a mess, aren't I?'

She said nothing.

'What's your name?'

'Joni.'

'How old are you, Joni?'

'I'll be ten.'

'Why don't you come along and help me clean up?'

'I don't want to.'

'Do you want me to stab you?'

She shook her head. Her lips trembled.

'Then come with me.' Taking her hand, he pulled her off the bed. He led her down the hallway until he found the bathroom. He turned on its light, and pulled her inside.

The bathroom was long, with a sink and counter close to the door, a space, and then the toilet. The bathtub, set into the wall opposite the toilet, had frosted shower doors.

Roy led the girl to the toilet. The seat was already down. Its green, fuzzy cover matched the carpet. 'Sit there.'

Joni obeyed.

Kneeling in front of her, Roy unfastened the buttons of her pyjama top. She sobbed. 'Knock that off.' He slipped the pyjamas down her arms. 'We'll get good and clean,' he said. He unsnapped the waistband, tugged the pants out from under her, and down her legs. She clamped her knees together. Arms crossed over breasts no more developed than a boy's, she bent far down, bringing her shoulders almost to her knees.

Roy turned on the hot water. As it splashed into the tub, he undressed himself. When all his clothes lay heaped on the floor, he plugged the bathtub drain. He adjusted the water so it was hot, but not scalding.

Joni still sat on the toilet seat, hunched over and hugging her knees.

Roy grabbed her arm. She tried to pull free, so he slapped the side of her head. She yelped, but didn't move. Standing in front of her, Roy grabbed both arms and jerked her to her feet. She cried, 'No!' as he swung her into the bathtub. Her feet whipped. She kicked the metal spout and cried out in pain. Roy nearly lost his grip but managed to keep from falling backward. She splashed the water, rump first. Roy climbed in, facing her.

He knelt in the water. 'I've about had it,' he warned. 'Sit still.'

She kicked. Her heel caught him in the thigh.

'Okay.'

Clutching her ankles, he lifted her legs and pulled her forward. Her head slipped underwater. Her eyes and mouth were puckered shut. Her hands slapped the sides of the tub, reached up blindly for something to hold, found nothing, and splashed water. Roy watched the frantic girl, enjoying the struggle, excited by the sight of her skinny body and the cleft at the hairless joining of her legs.

He let her ankles down. The girl's face broke the surface, eyes and mouth gaping as if surprised. She gasped air. Roy let her sit up.

'No more trouble,' he said.

She sniffed, and wiped her runny nose with the back of her hand. Then she crossed her arms and bent forward.

Roy twisted sideways. He turned off the cold faucet, and let just the hot water run for a while. The water level rose. Soon it was good and hot and deep. He turned off the water.

'Let's switch places,' he said. Standing, he stepped over her. She scooted forward, her rump squeaking on the enamel. Roy sat down, leaned against the cool back of the tub, and stretched out his legs on each side of her.

'Now we'll get all clean,' he said.

He lifted a bar of soap from its tray and began to rub her back. When that was slick, he eased her closer so she was reclining against him. Reaching over her shoulders, he soaped her chest, her belly. Her skin was warm, pliant, slippery. He pulled her more tightly against him. He put the soap in the tray. He reached down between her legs.

That's when the mother staggered up to the tub, raising a butcher's knife. Roy's left hand rammed the sliding door shut. The knife point thumped the door, and scraped down it. Roy shoved the girl forward. He kneed her away. Pressing the edge of the door to keep it. shut, he got his feet under him. The mother lurched sideways. Her left hand let go of her sopping, bloody nightgown and reached for the rear half of the sliding door. Roy held it shut with his other hand. As if there were no door, the women plunged the knife towards Roy's face. It's point hit, shaking the door. She stabbed again and again. The sound from her throat was part growl, part an outcry of pain or frustration.

Joni gripped Roy's leg and started to pull.

'Bitch! Let go!'

He released the right-hand door long enough to bat Joni's face with the back of his fist. Her head jerked with the impact. It thudded the tile wall.

The mother reached for the free door. Roy got to it first and held it shut. Growling with rage, she grabbed the top runner of the doors. She climbed and pulled herself until she was standing on the tub's edge. Her face appeared above Roy, eyes wild. She swung her right arm down, slashing towards him. He ducked below the knife's arc.

Inches from his eyes, the mother's red, clinging nightgown smeared blood on the door. She was pressed tightly to the door, her bare feet on the rim of the tub.

She grunted. The blade *whished* above him. She propped her left knee on the towel bar halfway up the door.

Shit, she's climbing it!

Roy jerked the door. It slid open, slamming the wall at the front of the tub. Reaching forward with both hands, he clutched the woman's right ankle. He pulled. His hands slipped on the bloody skin, but he kept his grip. With a cry of horror, she flopped backward. She hit the floor first with the back of her head. She went limp. Still holding her right ankle, Roy climbed out of the tub. He picked up her other leg and swivelled her away from the tub.

He picked up her knife. He cut her throat with it, then returned to the tub.

Joni, sitting sideways, looked up at Roy with blank eyes.

He squatted in the tub. The water felt tepid. He turned on the hot water. When the temperature felt hot enough, he turned the water off and stepped to the rear of the tub.

He sat and leaned back.

Taking Joni under the arms, he slid her close between his spread legs until he could feel the press of her against his penis.

'Now,' he said, and picked up the soap. His throat was tight. This was what he'd wanted for so long, so long. This was what he'd always wanted. 'Now,' he said, 'we're all set.'

Chapter Three

1.

The Nubian guards, dressed like pimps, came at Rucker from all sides. Their black faces were glossy with sweat, their big teeth white and shiny. Some aimed handguns at his face, other began spraying him with automatic fire from AK-47 assault rifles. He cut them down, but more came running, shrieking, brandishing cutlasses. His American 180 stitched holes across their bright shirts. They fell, but more came.

Where the hell are they coming from? he wondered.

From Hell.

He kept firing. One hundred and seventy rounds in six seconds. A mighty long six seconds.

They still came. Some had spears. Some, now, were naked.

He dropped the ammo drum, stuffed another into place, and kept firing.

Now all of them were naked, their black skin shimmering in the moonlight, their smiles big and white. None had guns. Only knives, swords, and spears.

I've killed all the pimps, he thought. Who're these? The reserves. When I get them, I'll be home free.

But stark fear whispered a message of death in his ear. Looking down, he saw the alloy barrel of his rifle droop, melting.

Oh Jesus, oh Jesus, they're gonna get me now. They'll lay me low. They'll cut off my head. Oh Jesus!

Gasping, heart racing, he bolted upright. He was alone in the bedroom. A trickle of sweat slid down his back. He ran a hand through his wet hair and wiped it dry on the sheet.

He looked at the alarm clock.

Only five past midnight. *Damn.* This was a lot earlier than usual. When the nightmares got him at four or five, he could go out for breakfast and start the day. When they got him this early, it was bad.

He got out of bed. The sweat on his naked body turned cold. In the bathroom, he dried himself with a towel. Then he put on a robe and went into the living room of the apartment. He turned on all the lights. Then the television. He flipped through the channels. *The Bank Dick* was on. It must've started at twelve. He got a can of Hamms from the refrigerator, a can of peanuts from the cupboard, and returned to the living room.

As he reached for the flip-tab, he watched his hand shake.

It never shook on a job.

Judgement Rucker's got balls of brass.

If they could only see him now.

It's those damned nightmares.

Well, those would ease off. They always did. Just a matter of time.

Watch the movie.

He tried.

When he ran out of beer, he went into the kitchen for another. He popped its tab and looked out the window. Moonlight made a silver path on the water. Across the bay, fog matted the hills above Sausalito as white as a bank of snow. Fog wrapped most of the Golden Gate Bridge, too. All but the top of its northern tower, with its red flashing light, was hidden in fog. Probably the other tower was poking through, too, but Belvedere Island blocked that part of his view. He listened to the low groan of a foghorn, then carried his beer into the living room.

He was about to sit on the couch when a harsh, male scream of horror slashed the stillness.

2.

Jud listened at the door of Apartment 315. From inside came the sound of a man taking quick gasps of air. Jud rapped the door quietly.

At the end of the hallway, a woman in curlers peered out her doorway. 'Let's keep it down, huh? You can't keep it down, I'll call the cops. Do you know what time it is?'

Jud smiled at her. 'Yes,' he said.

The anger pinching her face seemed to let go. She made a tentative smile. 'You're the new tenant, aren't you? The one in 308? I'm Sally Leonard.'

'Go to bed now, Miss Leonard.'

'Something the matter with Larry?'

'I'll take care of it.'

Still smiling, Sally pulled her head back inside her apartment and shut the door.

Jud knocked again on 315.

'Who is it?' a man asked through the door.

'I heard a scream.'

'I'm sorry. Did it wake you?'

'I was already up. Who screamed?'

'Me. It was nothing. Just a nightmare.'

'You call that nothing?'

Jud heard the slide of a guard chain. The door was opened by a man in striped pyjamas. 'You sound as if you know nightmares,' the man said. Though his sleep-tangled hair was as white as the fog, he seemed to be no older than forty. 'My name's Lawrence Maywood Usher.' He offered his hand to Jud. It was bony, and damp with sweat. The feeble grip had a weariness that seemed to sap strength from Jud's hand.

'I'm Jud Rucker,' he said, entering.

The man shut the door. 'Well, Judson . . .'

'It's Judgement.'

Larry immediately perked up. 'As in Judgement Day?'

'My father's a Baptist minister.'

'Judgement Rucker. Fascinating. Would you care for some coffee, Judgement?'

He thought about the open can of Hamms in his apartment. What the hell, he could use it tomorrow for cooking. 'Sure, Coffee'd be great.'

'Are you a connoisseur?'

'Hardly.'

'Nevertheless, this should be a treat for you. Have you ever tasted Jamaican Blue Mountain?'

'Not that I know of.'

'Well, opportunity has knocked. Your ship has come in.'

Jud grinned, astonished at the new liveliness of the man who'd screamed.

'Will you join me in the kitchen?'

'Sure.'

In the kitchen, Larry opened a small brown bag. He tilted its opening towards Jud's face. Jud sniffed the sharp coffee aroma. 'Smells good,' he said.

'It ought to be. It's the best. What line of work are you in, Judgement?'

'Engineering,' he said, using his usual cover.

'Oh?'

'I'm with Brecht Brothers.'

'Sounds like a German coughdrop.'

'We build bridges, power plants. How about you?'

'I teach.'

'High school?'

'God forbid! I had my fill of those rude, insolent, foul-mouthed bastards ten years ago. Never again! God forbid!'

'What do you teach now?'

'The elite.' He cranked, grinding down the coffee beans. 'Upper division, mostly, at USF. American Lit.'

'And they're not foul-mouthed?'

'The oaths are not directed at *me*.'

'That would make a difference,' Jud said. He watched the man spoon coffee grounds into the basket of a drip machine and turn it on.

'*All* the difference. Shall we sit down?'

They went into the living room. Larry took the sofa. Jud lowered himself into a recliner, but didn't recline.

'I'm certainly glad you dropped by, Judgement.'

'How about Jud?'

'How about Judge?'

'I'm not ever a lawyer.'

'From your looks, however, you are a good judge. Of character, of situations, of right and wrong.'

'You can tell all that from my looks?'

'Certainly. So I'll call you Judge.'

'All right.'

'Tell me, Judge, what possessed you to come knocking at my door?'

'I heard the scream.'

'Did you realize it was inspired by a nightmare?'

'No.'

'Perhaps I was being murdered.'

'That occurred to me.'

'But you came, nonetheless. And unarmed. You must be a fearless man, Judge.'

'Hardly.'

'Or perhaps you've known such fear that the possibility of being confronted by a mere murderer seemed trifling.'

Jud laughed. 'Sure.'

'Nonetheless, I'm certainly glad you came. For terrors of the night, there's no antidote like a friendly face.'

'Do you have your terrors often?'

'Every night for the past three weeks. Not quite three weeks – that would be twenty-one nights, and I've only had the nightmares for the past nineteen. Only! I must tell you, it seems like years.'

'I know.'

'Sometimes, I wonder if there ever was a time before the nightmares. Of course, there was. I'm not loony, you realize, just upset. Nervous, very very dreadfully nervous I had been and am; but why *will* you say that I am mad?'

'I didn't.'

'No, of course not.' He grinned with one side of his mouth. 'That's Poe. "The Tell-Tale Heart." About another distressed fellow. Distressed to the point of madness. Do I look mad?'

'You look tired.'

'Nineteen nights.'

'Do you know what triggered your nightmares?' Jud asked.

'Let me show you.' From beneath a *Time* magazine on the coffee table, he took a newspaper clipping. 'You may read this while I see to the coffee.' He got up from the sofa and handed the news article to Jud.

Alone in the room, Jud eased back on the recliner and read:

THREE SLAIN IN BEAST HOUSE

(MALCASA POINT) – The mutilated bodies of two men and an eleven-year-old boy were found late Wednesday night in Malcasa Point's grisly tourist attraction, Beast House.

According to local authorities, police patrolman Daniel Jenson entered the house at 11:45 P.M. to investigate possible prowlers. When he failed to contact headquarters, a car was dispatched to the location. With the aid of the volunteer fire department, officers cordoned off the area and entered the mysterious house.

The body of Patrolman Jenson was found in the upstairs corridor, along with the bodies of Mr Matthew Ziegler and his son, Andrew. All three were the victims of apparent knife assault.

According to Mary Ziegler, wife of the deceased, Matthew was angered by their son's frightened reaction to a public tour of Beast House earlier in the day, and vowed to 'show him the beast.' Shortly after 11 P.M. Wednesday night, he drove the boy to Beast House with the intention of breaking in and forcing young Andrew to 'face up to' his fears.

Beast House, built in 1902 by the widow of Lyle Thorn, leader of the infamous Thorn Gang, has been the scene of no fewer than eleven mysterious killings since the time of its construction. The present owner, Maggie Kutch, moved out of the house in 1931 after her husband and three children were 'torn asunder by a raving white beast' that reportedly entered the house through a downstairs window. Shortly after the brutal slayings, Mrs Kutch opened the house for daylight tours.

No further incidents were reported until 1951, when two twelve-year-old boys, residents of Malcasa Point, entered the house after dark. One boy, Larry Maywood, escaped with minor injuries. The mutilated body of his friend, Tom Bagley, was found at dawn by investigators.

Commenting on the most recent slayings, the seventy-one-year-old owner of the house explained, 'After dark, it belongs to the beast.' According to Malcasa Point Police Chief Billy Charles, 'No beast is responsible for the deaths of Patrolman Jenson and the Zieglers. They were slain by a man wielding a sharp instrument. We expect to apprehend the perpetrator in short order.'

Beast House tours have been suspended for an indefinite period, pending completion of the homicide investigation.

Jud sat forward in the recliner and looked at Larry's nervously smiling face as the man brought two cups of coffee into the room. He accepted one of the cups. He waited for Larry to sit down. Then he said. 'You introduced yourself as Lawrence Maywood Usher.'

'I've always been a great admirer of Poe. In fact, I suppose, it was largely his influence that inspired me to explore Beast House that night with Tommy. It seemed only fitting, when I finally decided a new name was essential for my emotional survival, to take the name of Poe's haunted Roderick Usher.'

3.

Lawrence Maywood Usher sipped coffee from his fragile, bone-china cup. Jud watched him hold the liquid in his mouth like wine, savouring it before swallowing. 'Ah, delicious.' He looked eagerly at Jud.

Jud lifted his cup. He liked the heavy aroma, and took a sip. It tasted stronger than he preferred. 'Not bad,' he said.

'You're a master of understatement, Judge.' Concern furrowed the gaunt man's face. 'You *do* like it?'

'It's fine. Very good. I'm just not used to this kind of thing.'

'Never become *used* to anything you love. It blunts the edge of appreciation.'

Jud nodded and took another drink. This time the coffee tasted better. 'Are your nightmares about Beast House?' he asked.

'Always.'

'I'm surprised it took a newspaper story to start them, considering what you must've gone through at the time.'

'The story, more or less, reactivated the nightmares. I had them constantly for several months following my ... encounter. Doctors suggested psychiatric treatment, but my parents wouldn't hear of it. Perceptive people that they were, they considered psychiatry to be the pursuit of fools and madmen. We moved away from Malcasa Point, and my nightmares rather quickly lost their intensity. I've always considered it a victory of common sense over quackery.' He smiled, apparently delighted by his wit, and indulged himself in another taste of coffee.

'Unfortunately,' he continued, 'we weren't entirely able to leave the incident behind. Every now and then, an eager journalist would track us down for a story on the miserable tourist attraction. That would always start the nightmares again. Every major magazine, of course, has done the story.'

'I've seen a couple of them.'

'Did you read them?'

'No.'

'Lurid bunk. Reporters! Do you know what a reporter is? "A writer who guesses his way to the truth and dispels it with a tempest of words." Ambrose Bierce. The single time I did allow one of those scavengers to interview me, he twisted my words so that I appeared a gibbering idiot. He concluded that the encounter had unhinged me! After that, I changed my name. Not one of those bastards has tracked me down, so far, and I've been free of nightmares about the beast until now . . . now that it's killed again.'

'It?'

'Officially, since the time of the attack on the Thorns, it's been a *he*, a knife-wielding maniac, something on the order of Jack the Ripper. Each attack, of course, is a different killer.'

'And it's not?'

'Not at all. It's a beast. Always the same beast.'

Jud didn't try to conceal the expression of doubt he knew was beginning to appear on his face.

'Let me refill your cup, Judge.'

4.

'I don't know what the beast is,' Larry said. 'Perhaps nobody knows. I've seen it, though. With the exception of old Maggie Kutch, I'm probably the only living person who has.

'It is not human, Judge. Or if it *is* human, it's some kind of unspeakable deformity. And it is very, very old. The first known attack occurred in 1903. Teddy Roosevelt was President then. That's the year the Wright brothers flew at Kitty Hawk, for heaven's sake. The beast killed three people that year.'

'The original owner of the house?'

'She survived. That was Lyle Thorn's widow. Her sister, though, was killed. So were Lilly's two children. The authorities blamed the atrocity on a mental defective they found on the outskirts of town. He was tried, convicted, and hanged from the house balcony. Even then, apparently, cover-up was the order of the day. They *had* to know the fellow was innocent.'

'Why did they have to know that?'

'The beast has claws,' Larry said. 'They're sharp, like nails. They shred the victim, his clothes, his flesh. They pierce him to hold him down, while the beast . . . violates him.' The cup began to clatter against its saucer. He set it down on the table and folded his hands.

'Were you . . .?'

'My God, no! It never touched me. Not *me*. But I saw what it did to Tommy there in the bedroom. It was too . . . overcome . . . to bother with me. It had to finish with Tommy, first. Well, I put one over on it! The window gave me some nasty cuts, and I broke my arm in the fall, but I got away. I got away, goddamn it! I lived to tell the tale!'

He managed another drink of coffee. His trembling hand set the cup back down on the table. The drink seemed to help restore his calm. In a quiet voice, he said, 'Of course, no one believes the tale. I've learned to keep it to myself. Now I suppose you think I'm mad.' He looked at Jud, despair in his weary eyes.

Jud pointed towards the newspaper clipping. 'That says eleven people have died in Beast House.'

'Its facts are correct, for a change.'

'That's a lot of killing.'

'Indeed.'

'Somebody should put a stop to it.'

'I'd kill it myself, if I had the courage. But God, to think of entering that house at night! Never. I could never do it.'

'Has anybody gone in after it?'

'At night? Only a fool . . .'

'Or a man with a very good reason.'

'What kind of reason?' Larry asked.

'Revenge, idealism, money. Has a reward ever been offered?'

'For killing it? Its existence isn't even *admitted*, not by anyone but old Kutch and her crazy son. And they certainly don't want it harmed. That goddamned beast, and its reputation, is their sole source of income. It's probably all that keeps the town afloat, for that matter. Beast House is no Hearst Castle or Winchester House, but you'd be surprised how many people will pay four bucks a head for a guided tour of an old place that not only boasts a legendary monster but that also was the scene of eleven brutal murders. They come from all over California, from

Oregon, from every state in the union. A family driving through California can't pass within fifty miles of Malcasa Point without its kids screaming to tour Beast House. Tourist dollars are the lifeblood of the town. If somebody were to kill the beast . . .'

'Think of the tourists its carcass would bring,' Jud suggested, grinning.

'But the mystery would be gone. The beast is the heart of that house. The house would die without it. Malcasa Point would follow close on its heels, and the people don't want that.'

'They'd rather have the killing continue?'

'Certainly. An occasional killing does wonders for business.'

'If the town is that way, it doesn't deserve to live.'

'A perceptive man your father was, naming you Judgement.'

'You said you would kill the beast yourself, if you could.'

'If I had the courage, yes.'

'Have you ever thought of hiring someone to do it for you?'

'Who could I hire for a job like that?'

'Depends on what you're willing to pay.'

'What's a good night's sleep worth, eh?' The grin on his hollow face looked grotesque.

'You might look upon it as a contribution to humanity,' Jud said.

'I assume you know someone who might be willing, for a large sum of money, to enter the house at night and dispatch the beast?'

'I might know someone,' Jud told him.

'What would it cost?'

'That depends on the risk involved. He'd have to know a lot more before making a firm commitment.'

'Can you give me a rough idea?'

'His minimum would be five thousand.'

'His maximum?'

'No maximum.'

'My funds aren't bottomless, but I believe I'd be willing to invest a considerate portion of them, if necessary, in a project of that type.'

'What are you doing tomorrow?'

'I'm open to suggestions,' Larry said.

'Why don't the two of us drive up the coast, bright and early, and pay a visit to Beast House.'

5.

The two cups of coffee didn't keep Jud awake when he got back to his apartment. He fell asleep at once, and if he dreamed at all, he remembered none of it when the alarm clock blared at 6 A.M. Monday.

Chapter Four

Roy woke up in a king-sized bed. Next to him, face down with her hands tied behind her back, lay the girl Joni. She was naked. A short length of clothesline led from her wrists to Roy's right hand. He untied his hand, then both of hers.

He rolled Joni on to her back. Her eyes were open. She looked up at him, through him, past him. Almost as if she were blind.

'Sleep well?' he asked.

She didn't seem to hear.

He placed a hand on her chest, feeling the steady beat of her heart, and the rise and fall of her breathing.

'Where's your spirit?' he asked, and laughed.

She didn't blink or move. Not when he pinched her. Not when he stroked her body, nor sucked it, or bit it. Not when he entered her. Not when he shuddered with an orgasm. Not when he pulled out and got off the bed.

He tied her again, anyway.

He dressed in the father's clothes. He made coffee. While it percolated, he prepared six slices of bacon, three eggs over easy, and two pieces of toast. He carried them into the living room and turned on the television.

The phone rang. He picked it up.

'Hello?' he asked.

'Hello?' The woman's voice sounded confused. 'May I speak to Marv, please?'

'He isn't here. Can I take a message?'

'This is Esther. His secretary?'

'Oh. You must be wondering why he didn't show up at work.'

'He didn't even call in.'

'Oh, well, no. He had a heart attack last night. Early this morning, actually.'

'No!'

'I'm afraid so. Last I saw, they were loading him into an ambulance.'

'Is he . . . is he alive?'

'Last I heard. I'm staying with Joni. You know, babysitting. I haven't heard a thing since they left.'

'What hospital was he taken to, do you know?'

'Let me think. Gee, you know, I'm not really sure. Everything was so confused.'

'Could you let us know when you hear any word of his condition?'

'I'd be glad to.'

She gave him the office telephone number. He didn't copy it. 'I'll be sure to get back to you,' he said, 'the minute I get any news.'

'Thank you so much.'

'You're welcome.'

He hung up, went back to the couch, and began to eat. His breakfast was still warm.

When he finished it, he searched for the telephone book. He found it in a kitchen drawer under a wall extension. He poured himself another cup of coffee and returned to the living room.

First, he looked up Hayes. No Hayes, Donna. Only the Hayes, D., that he had checked last night. It had been her apartment, no question about that. He'd recognized some of the furniture.

He wondered if she still worked for that travel agency. What was its name? Had a catchy slogan. 'Let Gold be your guide.' Not gold, Gould. Gould Travel. He thumbed through the white pages, found it, and dialled.

'Gould Travel Service, Miss Winnow.'

'I'd like to speak to Mrs Hayes, please.'

'Hayes?'

'Donna Hayes.'

'We have no Donna Hayes at this number. This is Gould Travel Service.'

'She works there, or she *did*.'

'Just a moment, please.' He waited for almost a minute. 'Sir, Donna Hayes left our employ several years ago.'

'Do you know where she went?'

'I'm afraid not. May I be of service to you? Were you thinking of a cruise, perhaps? We have some marvellous cruises . . .'

'No thank you.' He hung up.

He looked up Blix, John. Donna's father. Her parents would know where she'd gone, for sure. He copied the address and phone number.

Shit, he didn't want to see them. They were the last people he wanted to see.

What about Karen? He grinned. He wouldn't mind seeing Karen, at all. In fact, he wouldn't mind seeing a lot of her. Maybe she'd know where to find those two bitches.

Worth a try.

Even if she didn't know, a visit could still turn out worthwhile. He'd always liked the looks of her.

What was the name of that guy she'd married? Bob something. Something like a candy bar. Milky Way? No. Mars Bar. Bob Mars Bar. Marston.

He looked up Marston, found a Robert, and copied the address and telephone number.

He'd pay them a nice visit. Not now. He didn't want to leave quite yet. What was the hurry? He might as well stick around for a while, enjoy himself.

He went into the bedroom. 'Hi there, Joni. What you been up to?'

She stared at the ceiling.

Chapter Five

1.

Sunlight and screeching seagulls woke Donna. She tried to fall asleep again, but the narrow bed, sway-backed with age, made it impossible. She got up and stretched her stiff muscles.

Sandy was still asleep on the other bed.

Quietly, Donna crossed the cool wood floor to the front window. She raised the blind and looked out. Across the courtyard, a man weighted down with suitcases was leaving a small, green-painted cabin. A woman and a matching pair of children waited for him inside a station wagon. Half the cabins of the Welcome Inn had either a car or a camper parked in front. Somewhere nearby, a dog barked. She pulled the blind.

Then she looked for the telephone. The room didn't have one.

While she was dressing, Sandy woke up.

'Morning, honey. Did you sleep well?'

'Fine. Where are you going?'

'I want to find a telephone and call Aunt Karen.' She tied her sneakers. 'I don't want her worrying about us.'

'Can I come?'

'You can stay here and get dressed. I'll only be a minute, then we'll go get some breakfast.'

'Okay.'

She buttoned her plaid cotton blouse and picked up her handbag. 'Don't open the door for anyone, right?'

'Right,' the girl said.

Outside, the morning air was fresh with the scent of pine, a smell that reminded her of warm, shadowed trails in the Sierra where she used to backpack with her sister. Before Roy. The way Roy acted in the mountains, she quickly lost the taste for the wilderness. Once she was rid of him, she should have taken up backpacking again. Maybe soon . . .

She climbed steps to the porch of the motel office and saw a telephone booth at the far end. She headed for it. The wood groaned under her feet, sounding like the weathered planking of an aged pier.

She stepped into the booth, dropped coins into the telephone slot, and dialled Operator. She charged the call to her home phone. The call went through.

'Hello?'

'Morning, Karen.'

'Uh-oh.'

'Is that any kind of greeting?'

'Don't tell me, your car broke down.'

'You're clairvoyant.'

'Do you need a lift?'

'No, I'm afraid I'll have to beg off, for today.'

'Poor loser.'

'It's not that.'

'They changed your days off? And we were having such good times on Mondays. What've you got now, Friday-Saturday, Tuesday-Wednesday?'

'Your clairvoyance has slipped.'

'Oh?'

'I'm calling from the glamorous resort town of Malcasa Point, home of the infamous Beast House.'

'Are you crocked?'

'Sober, unfortunately. As near as I can figure, we're about a hundred miles north of San Francisco. Give or take fifty.'

'Christ almighty, don't you know?'

'Not exactly. I'm sure, if I could see a map . . .'

'What are you doing way the hell-and-gone up there, anyway?' Before Donna could answer, Karen said, 'Oh God, is he out?'

'He's out.'

'Oh my God.'

'We thought we'd better make ourselves scarce.'

'Right. What do you want me to do?'

'Let Mom and Dad know we're okay.'

'What about your apartment?'

'Can you have our stuff put into storage?'

'Sure, I guess.'

'Call Beacon, or someone. Let me know what it comes to, and I'll send you a cheque.'

'How am I gonna let you know anything?'

'I'll keep in touch.'

'Are you ever coming back?'

'I don't know.'

'How could they let him *out*? How *could* they?'

'I guess he behaved himself.'

'Christ!'

'It'll be all right, Karen.'

'When am I gonna *see* you again?' She sounded close to tears.

'This'll blow over.'

'Sure it will. If Roy happens to drop dead of a coronary, or drives into a bridge abutment, or . . .' A sob broke her voice. 'Christ, this sort of thing . . . how can they let it happen?'

'Hey, don't cry. Everything'll be fine. Just tell Mom and Dad we're okay, and we'll be in touch.'

'Okay. And I'll . . . take care of your apartment.'

'Take care of yourself, while you're at it.'

'Sure. You too. Tell Sandy hi for me.'

'I will. Goodbye, Karen.'

'Bye.'

Donna hung up. She breathed deeply, fighting for control of her own shaken emotions. Then she crossed the porch. As she started to climb down, she heard the squeak of an opening door.

'Lady?'

She looked around at a teenage girl standing in the office doorway. Probably the owner's daughter. 'Yes?'

'Are you the lady with the car trouble?'

Donna nodded.

'Bix from the Chevron called. Him and Kutch went after it. Bix said he'd see you when he gets back.'

'They don't have the keys.'

'Bix doesn't need 'em.'

'Did he want me to do anything?'

The girl shrugged one shoulder. It was bare except for the strap of her tank top. She was obviously wearing no bra, her nipples pressing dark and turgid against the thin fabric. Donna wondered why the girl's parents allowed her to dress that way.

'Okay. Thanks for the message.'

'Any time.'

The girl spun away. Her cut-off jeans were slit up the sides, revealing tawny leg almost to the hip.

The girl's going to get herself raped, Donna thought. If Sandy ever dressed like that . . .

Donna climbed down the porch steps and crossed the parking area to their cabin. She had to wait while Sandy finished in the bathroom.

'Do you want to eat here at the Inn?' Donna asked. 'Or should we try our luck in town?'

'Let's go into town,' Sandy said, her voice eager. 'I hope they've got Dunkin' Donuts. I'm dying for a doughnut.'

'I'm dying for a cup of coffee.'

'Java Mama.'

They went outside. Sandy, squinting, opened her denim handbag and took out her sunglasses. Their round lenses were huge on her face. Donna, who rarely wore sunglasses, thought they made her daughter look like a bug – a *cute* bug, bit still a bug. She was careful never to mention the resemblance.

'What did Aunt Karen say?' Sandy asked.

'She said to tell you hi.'

'Were you gonna play tennis today?'

'Yep.'

'I bet she was surprised.'

'She understood.'

They reached the roadside. Donna pointed to the left. 'Town's that way,' she said. They started towards it. 'From the way Aunt Karen sounded, I don't think she'd ever heard of Malcasa Point. It is a beautiful place, though, isn't it?'

Sandy nodded. Her sunglasses slipped down her nose. With a forefinger, she poked them into place. 'It's pretty around here, but . . .'

'What?'

'Oh, nothing.'

'No, tell me. Come on.'

'How come you told Aunt Karen?'

'Told her what?'

'Where we are.'

'I thought she ought to know.'

'Oh.' Sandy nodded, and adjusted her glasses.

'Why?'

'Do you think it was a good idea, telling her? I mean, now she knows where we are.'

'She won't tell anyone.'

'Not unless he *makes* her.'

They stepped off the roadside and waited on the rutted shoulder until an approaching car whooshed by.

'What do you mean, "*makes* her"?' Donna asked.

'Makes her tell. Like he used to make you tell things.'

Donna walked in silence, no longer enjoying the cool, piny air. She imagined her sister stretched naked on a bed, tied firm, Roy beside her using a cigarette lighter to heat the shaft of a screwdriver.

'You never saw what he did to me, did you? He always locked the door.'

'Oh I never saw *that*. Not what he did in the bedroom. Just when he hit you. What *did* he do in the bedroom?'

'He hurt me.'

'It must've been awful.'

'Yeah.'

'How did he hurt you?'

'Lots of ways.'

'I bet he does that to Aunt Karen.'

'He wouldn't dare,' Donna said. 'He wouldn't dare.'

'When can we leave here?' the girl asked nervously.

'As soon as the car's ready.'

'When'll that be?'

'I don't know. Axel went out there this morning with a man from the service station. If it doesn't need repairs, we can go as soon as they get here with it.'

'We'd better,' Sandy said. 'We'd better get out of here fast.'

2.

They chose to eat breakfast at Sarah's Diner across from the Chevron station. After seeing the selection of doughnuts displayed on a counter-top cake stand, Sandy decided against them. She ordered bacon and eggs, instead.

'This place is gross,' she said.

'We won't eat here from now on.'

'Ha ha.'

Sandy put a hand underneath the table, and crinkled her nose with disgust. 'There's *gum* under the table.'

'There's always gum under tables. Some of us have sense enough to keep our hands off it.'

Sandy sniffed her fingers. 'Gross.'

'Why don't you go wash your hands?'

'I bet the John is *really* the pits,' she said, and got up from the table as if eager to verify her theory.

Smiling, Donna watched her step smartly towards the far end of the diner. The waitress came and filled Donna's heavy, chipped cup with coffee.

'Thank you.'

'Welcome, sweetie.'

She watched the waitress head for another table. Then the opening door caught her eyes.

Two men entered the diner. The emaciated one seemed far too young to have white hair. Though nicely dressed in a blue leisure suit, he had a harassed look like a refugee. The man beside him might have been his keeper. With deep blue eyes in a face that made her think of carved, highly polished wood, he had the confident look of a cop. Or a soldier. Or the guide in Colorado, many years ago, who led her and Karen on a deer hunt with their father.

The two men sat at the counter. The strong one had light brown hair neatly clipped above his shirt collar. His wide back filled the tan shirt, pulling it taut. The black belt looked stiff and new in jeans so old that one of the belt loops hung loose, dangling over his rear pocket. His rubber-soled hiking boots looked older than the jeans.

As if attracted by the intensity of her gaze, the man looked over his shoulder. Donna fought an urge to turn away. She met his eyes for a moment, then glanced at the next man, then on down the counter casually. She lifted her coffee cup. Steam no longer rose from the coffee. An oily film on the dark surface reflected swirling colours like a rainbow, or spoiled roast beef. She drank, anyway. Setting down the cup, she allowed herself another glance at the man.

He was no longer watching her.

Disappointment shadowed Donna's relief.

She drank more coffee and watched him. His head was turned as he listened to the nervous, white-haired man. A shoulder blocked her view of his mouth. She saw a slight rise on the ridge of his nose, apparently from an old break. A scar slanted from the corner of his eyebrow down to his cheekbone. She looked back into her coffee, afraid she might again attract attention.

When she heard quick, familiar footsteps, she saw the man's head turn. He glanced at Sandy, then Donna, then looked back at his friend.

'All clean?' Donna asked, perhaps too loudly.

'They didn't have anything to dry my hands on,' Sandy told her, and sat down.

'What'd you use?'

'My pants. Where's the food?'

'Maybe we'll be lucky and it won't come.'

'I'm starved.'

'I guess we can give it a try.'

The waitress soon came, bringing plates of eggs, sausage links, and hash browns. The food looked good, oddly enough. As Donna sliced into her sausage, her stomach rumbled loudly.

'Mother!' Sandy giggled.

'Must be a thunderstorm on the way,' Donna said.

'Can't trick me. That was your gut.'

'Gut isn't polite, honey.'

The girl grinned. Then, with an expression of wrinkled distaste, she picked a sprig of parsley off her hash browns and flicked it over the edge of the plate.

Donna glanced at the man. He was drinking coffee. As she ate and talked with Sandy, she looked up at him often. She realized that he wasn't eating. Apparently he and his friend had only come into Sarah's for coffee. Soon they got up from the counter.

The man reached into his hip pocket as he headed for the cash register. His nervous friend protested, and lost. After he paid the bill, he took a thin cigar out of his shirt pocket. He unwrapped it. As he wadded its cellophane wrapper into a tiny ball, he scanned the area near the counter, probably searching for a trash container. Finding none, he stuffed the ball into his shirt pocket. He clamped the cigar between his teeth. His eyes swung suddenly towards Donna. They fixed upon her, held her stunned like a doe in headlights. They eyes stayed on her while the man struck a match and sucked its flame to the tip of his cigar. He shook out the match. Then he turned, and pushed through the door.

Donna let out a deep, trembling breath.

'You okay?' Sandy asked.

'I'm fine.'

'What's wrong?'

'Nothing. Everything's fine.'

'You don't look so fine.'

'Are you about done eating?'

'All done,' Sandy said.

'Ready to go?'

'*I* am. Aren't you gonna finish?'

'No, I don't think so. Let's be on our way.' She picked up the bill. Her hand shook as she reached into her purse. She tucked three quarters under the edge of her plate, and got up quickly.

'What's wrong?'

'I just want to get outside.'

'Okay,' the girl said doubtfully as she followed Donna to the cash register.

Outside, Donna looked down the sidewalk. A block off, an old woman with a poodle was stepping awkwardly off a curb. No sign of the two men from the cafe. She checked the other direction.

'What're you looking for?' Sandy asked.

'Just trying to decide which way looks best.'

'We've already been that way,' the girl said, and nodded towards the left.

'Okay.' So they turned right, and began walking.

'Do you think we can leave this morning?' Sandy asked.

'I don't know how long it'll be. I think we're a good hour or so from where we left the car. The girl at the motel didn't say what time Axel went to get it.'

'If we aren't gonna leave right away, can we go see Beast House?'

'I don't know, honey.'

'It's half-price for me.'

'Are you certain you really want to see a place like that?'

'What is it?'

'It's supposed to be the home of a horrible beast that kills people and tears them up. It's where those three people were murdered a few weeks ago.'

'Oooh, *that* place?'

'Yes indeed.'

'Wow! Can we see it?'

'I'm not sure I'm up to it.'

'Oh come on. We're almost there. Please?'

'Well, it wouldn't hurt to see what time the tours start.'

3.

Standing at the northern corner of the wrought-iron fence, Donna looked at the bleak, weathered house and felt a reluctance to approach it.

'I'm not sure I want to do this, honey.'

'You *said* we can check on the tours.'

'I'm not sure I want to go in there, at all.'

'Why not?'

Donna shrugged, unwilling to put words to her dark chill. 'I don't know,' she said.

She moved her eyes from the slanted bay window to the veranda with its balustraded balcony overhead, past a gable to a tower at the south end. The tower windows reflected emptiness. Its roof was a steep cone: a witch's cap.

'Afraid it'll gross you out?'

'Your language is enough to gross me out.'

Sandy laughed, and adjusted her slipping sunglasses.

'Okay, we'll have a look at the tour schedule. But I'm not guaranteeing anything.' They started towards the ticket booth.

'I'll go alone, if you're scared.'

'You will not go in there alone, young lady.'

'It's half-price for me.'

'That's not the point.'

'What *is*?'

You might never come out, Donna suddenly thought. She took a deep breath. The air, scented like high mountain pine, calmed her.

'What is the point?'

Donna made her grin as evil as she could, and muttered, 'I don't want the beast to eat you.'

'You're awful!'

'Not as awful as the beast.'

'Mother!' Laughing, Sandy swung her denim handbag.

Donna blocked it with her forearm, looked up, and saw the man from the cafe. His eyes were on her. Smiling at him, Donna fought off another assault by her daughter.

She saw a blue ticket in his hand.

'Okay, honey, that's enough. We'll go on the tour.'

'Can we?' she asked, delighted.

'Shoulder to shoulder, we'll confront the awful beast.'

'I'll smash it with my purse,' Sandy said.

As she approached the line at the gate, Donna saw the man turn casually to his nervous friend and start talking.

'Look.' Sandy pointed at a wooden clockface near the top of the ticket booth. The sign above it read, 'Next tour departs at,' and the clock indicated ten. 'What time is it now?'

'Almost ten,' Donna said.

'Can we do it?'

'All right. Let's get in line.'

They stepped behind the last person in line, a pudgy teenage boy whose hands were folded judiciously across his belly. Without moving his feet, he swivelled enough to cast a critical eye at Donna and Sandy. He made a quiet 'Humph,' as if insulted by their presence, and swung his shoulders towards the front.

'What's *his* problem?' Sandy whispered.

'Shhh.'

Waiting, Donna counted fourteen people in line. Though eight seemed to be children, she only saw two who might qualify for the 'children under twelve' discount. If none of the others had complimentary tickets, she figured the tour would net fifty-two dollars.

Not too shabby, she thought.

The man from the cafe was three from the front.

A young couple with two blond girls stepped up to the ticket booth.

'That makes sixty-four,' Donna said.

'What?'

'Dollars.'

'What time is it?'

'Two minutes to go.'

'I hate waiting.'

'Look at the people.'

'What for?'

'They're interesting.'

Sandy looked up at her mother. Even with sunglasses hiding most of her face, Sandy's scepticism was obvious. But she sidestepped out of line to check the people more closely.

'Fiends!' someone shrieked from behind. 'Ghouls!'

Donna swung around. Crouched in the middle of the street, a thin pale woman pointed at her, at Sandy – at all of them. The woman was no older than thirty. She had the trim, short hair of a boy. Her sleeveless yellow dress was wrinkled and stained. Dirt streaked her white legs. Her feet were bare.

'You and you and you!' she screeched. 'Ghouls! Grave sniffers! Vampires, all of you, sucking the blood of the dead!'

The ticket-booth door slammed open. A man ran out, his gaunt face scarlet. 'Outta here, damn you!'

'Maggots!' she shouted. 'All of you, maggots, paying to see such filth. Vultures! Cowards!'

The man jerked his wide leather belt free of its loops, and doubled it. 'I'm warning you!'

'Corpse fuckers!'

'That about does it,' he muttered.

The woman scampered backward as the man rushed her, belt high and ready. Stumbling, she fell hard on to the pavement. 'Go ahead, maggot! The ghouls love it! Look at 'em gawk. Give 'em blood! That's what they're here for!' Rising to her knees, she ripped open the front of her dress. Her breasts were huge for a woman so small. They swung over her belly like ripe sacks. 'Give 'em a show! Give 'em blood! Tear my flesh! That's what they love!'

He raised the belt overhead, ready to bring it down.

'Don't.' The word shot out, quick and sharp.

The man looked around.

Turning, Donna saw the man from the cafe step out of the line. He walked forward.

'You just stay put, bud.'

He kept walking.

'We don't have need of interference.'

He said nothing to the man with the belt, but walked past him to the woman. He helped her to her feet. He lifted the dress, covering her shoulders, and pulled it gently shut in front. With a shaking hand, the woman held the torn edges together.

He spoke quietly to her. She thrust herself against him, kissed him wildly on the mouth, and sprang away. 'Run! Run for your lives!' she yelled. 'Run for your souls!' And then she dashed away down the street.

A few people in the crowd laughed. Someone mumbled that the madwoman was part of the show. Others disagreed. The man from the cafe came back and stood silently beside his friend in the line.

'Okay folks!' called the ticket man. He walked towards them, threading his belt through its loops. 'We 'pologize for the delay, though I'm sure we can all appreciate the gal's dilemma. Three weeks back, the beast took her husband and only child, tore 'em to ribbons. The experience unhinged the poor gal. She's been hangin' around here the past couple days, since we started doin' the tours again. But now here's another woman, a woman who passed through the purifyin' fire of tragedy, and came out the better for it. This woman's the owner of Beast House, and your personal guide for today's tour.' With a grand, sweeping gesture, he led the eyes of the crowd towards the lawn of Beast House where a stooped, heavy woman hobbled towards them.

'Do you still want to do it?' Donna asked.

Sandy shrugged. Her face was pale. She had obviously been shocked by the hysterical woman. 'Yeah,' she said, 'I guess so.'

Chapter Six

1.

They passed through the turnstile, and gathered on the lawn in front of the old woman. She waited, ebony cane planted close to the side of her right foot, her flowered dress blowing lightly against her legs. In spite of the day's warmth, she wore a green silken scarf around her neck. She fingered the scarf briefly, then spoke.

'Welcome to Beast House.' She said it reverently, in a low, husky voice. My name's Maggie Kutch, and I own it. I began showing the house to visitors way back in '31, shortly after tragedy took the lives of my husband and three children. You may be asking yourselves why a woman'd want to take people through her home that was a scene of such personal grief. The answer's easy: m-o-n-e-y.'

Quiet laughter stirred through the group. She smiled pleasantly, turned, and limped up the walkway. At the foot of the porch stairs, she wrapped a spotted hand over the newel post and pointed upward with the tip of her cane.

'Here's where they strung up poor Gus Goucher. He was eighteen at the time, and on his way to San Francisco to join his brother working at the Sutro Baths. He stopped here on the afternoon of August 2, 1903, and split firewood for Lilly Thorn, the original owner of the house. She fed him a meal in payment, and Gus was on his way. That very night, the beast struck for the first time. No one, but only Lilly, lived through the attack. She ran into the street screaming as if she'd met the devil himself.

'Right away, the town got up a posse. It searched the house from cellar to attic, but no living thing was found. Only the torn, chewed bodies of Lilly's sister and two little boys. The posse tromped through the wooded hillside yonder and found young Gus Goucher fast asleep.

'Well, some of the townspeople recalled seeing him by the Thorn place that afternoon, and figured this was their man. They gave him a trial. Weren't no witnesses with everybody dead but Lilly, and her raving. They judged him guilty quick enough, though. A mob broke him outta the old jail, that night. They dragged the poor lad to this very spot, whipped a rope over the balcony post up there, and hoisted him.

'Course, Gus Goucher didn't kill no one. It was the beast done it. Let's go in.'

They climbed six wooden stairs to the covered porch.

'You can see this is a new door, here. The original got shot up, three weeks back. You probably saw it on the news. One of our local police shotgunned the door to get inside. He'd of been better off, course, staying out.'

'Tell me,' asked the critical boy, 'how did the Zieglers get inside?'

'They got in like thieves. They broke a window out back.'

'Thank you.' He cast a smile towards the rest of the group, apparently pleased with the service he'd performed.

'Our police,' Maggie Kutch continued, 'spoiled an antique lock we had on the door here. But we did preserve the hinges and the knocker.' She tapped the brass knocker with her cane. 'It's supposed to be the paw of a monkey. Lilly Thorn stuck it here. She was partial to monkeys.'

Maggie opened the door. The group followed her inside. 'One of you get the door, if you would. Don't want the flies to get in.'

She pointed her cane. 'Here's another monkey for you.'

Donna heard her daughter groan, and didn't blame the girl a bit. The stuffed monkey, standing by the wall with its arms out, seemed to be snarling, ready to bite.

'Umbrella stand,' Maggie said. She dropped her cane into the circle of the monkey's arms, then snatched it up again.

'Now I'll show you the scene of the first attack. Right this way, into the parlour.'

Sandy took Donna's hand. Sandy looked up nervously at her mother as they entered a room to the left of the vestibule.

'When I came into this house, way back in '31, it was just the same as Lilly Thorn left it the night of the beast attack twenty-eight years before. Nobody'd lived in the house since then. Nobody'd dared.'

'Why did *you* dare?' asked the chubby, critical boy.

'My husband and I were duped, pure and simple. We were made to believe that poor Gus Goucher did the dirty work on the Thorn people. Nobody let on about no beast.'

Donna glanced at the man from the cafe. He was standing ahead of her, next to his white-haired friend. Donna lifted her hand. 'Mrs Kutch?'

'Yes?'

'Is it definitely known, now, that Gus Goucher was innocent?'

'I don't know how *innocent* he was.'

Some of the people laughed. The man looked around at her. She avoided his eyes.

'He might've been rowdy and a sneak and a no-good. He was surely a stupid man. But everyone in Malcasa Point knew, the minute they dapped eyes on the poor man, that he didn't attack the Thorns.'

'How could they tell?'

'He didn't have claws, sweetie.'

A few in the group tittered. The chubby boy arched an eyebrow at Donna and turned away. The man from the cafe still looked at her. She met his eyes. They held her, penetrated her, set warm fluid spreading in her loins. He didn't look away for a long time. Shaken, Donna tried to recover her composure. She finally returned her attention to the tour.

'. . . through a window out in the kitchen. If you'll just step around the screen here.'

As they moved to the front of a three-panelled papier-mâché screen that partitioned off a corner of the room, someone screamed. Several members of the group gasped with shock. Others mumbled. Some groaned with repugnance. Donna followed her daughter around the screen, glimpsed an outstretched bloody hand on the floor, and stumbled as Sandy bolted back.

Maggie chuckled at the group's reaction.

Donna led Sandy around the end of the screen. Lying on the floor, one leg propped high on the dusty cushion of a couch, was the form of a woman. Her shiny eyes gazed upward. Her bloody face was twisted in a grimace of terror and agony. Tatters of her stained linen gown draped her body, covering little except her breasts and pubic area.

'The beast tore down the screen,' said Maggie, 'and leapt over the back of the couch, taking Ethel Hughes by surprise while she was reading *The Saturday Evening Post*. This is the very magazine she was reading at the time.' Maggie stretched her cane across the body and poked the magazine. 'Everything is just as it was on that awful night.' She smiled pleasantly. 'Except for the body, of course. This replica was created in wax by Mssr Claude Dubois, at my request, way back in 1936. Every detail is guaranteed authentic, down to the tiniest bite mark on her poor neck. We used morgue photos.

'Of course, this is the gown that Ethel actually wore that night. These dark places are made by her blood.'

'Was there sexual assault?' the white-haired man asked in a strained voice.

Magie's pleasant eyes hardened, flicking towards his face. 'No,' she said.

'That's not what I heard.'

'I can't be responsible for what you heard, sir. I only know what I know, and I know more about the beast of this house than any other person, living or dead. The beast of this house has never carnally abused its victims.'

'Then I apologize,' he said in a cold voice.

'When the beast was done with Ethel, it rampaged through the parlour. It knocked this alabaster bust of Caesar off the mantle, breaking the nose.' The nose rested on the fireplace mantle beside the bust. 'It dashed half a dozen figurines into the fireplace. It upset chairs. This fine rosewood pedestal table was thrown through the bay window. The racket, of course, awakened the rest of the household. Lilly's room was right up there.' Maggie pointed towards the high ceiling with her cane. 'The beast must've heard her stirring. It went for the stairs.'

Silently, she led the group out of the parlour and up a broad stairway to the second floor hall. They turned to the left. Maggie stepped through a side doorway and into a bedroom.

'We're now above the parlour. Here's where Lilly Thorn was sleeping the night of the beast attack.' A wax figure, dressed in a lacy pink gown, was sitting upright, staring fearfully over the brass scrollwork at the foot of the bed. 'When the commotion woke Lilly up, she dragged the dressing table from there' – she pointed her cane at the heavy rosewood table and mirror beside the window – 'to there, barricading the door. Then she made her escape through the window. She jumped to the roof of the bay window below, then to the ground.

'It's always been a wonder to me that she didn't try to save her children.'

They followed Maggie out of the bedroom.

'When the beast found that he couldn't get into her room, he came down the hall this way.'

They passed the top of the stairs. Ahead, four Brentwood chairs blocked the centre of the corridor. Clothesline was strung from one chair to the next, closing off the centre space. The members of the group squeezed between one of the lines and the wall.

'This is where we'll put our new display. The figures are already on order, but we don't expect to have them much before spring.'

'That's a shame,' the man with the two children told his wife in a sarcastic voice.

Maggie entered a door to the right. 'The beast found this door open,' she said.

The windows of the room faced the wooded hillside behind the house. The room's two brass beds looked much like the one in Lilly's room, but the covers were heaped in disarray. A rocking horse with faded paint stood in one corner, next to the wash stand.

'Earl was ten,' Maggie said. 'His brother, Sam, was eight.'

Their wax bodies, torn and chewed, lay sprawled face down between the two beds. Both wore the remains of stripped nightshirts that concealed little except their buttocks.

'Let's go,' said the man with the two children. 'This is the most crude, tasteless excuse for a voyeuristic thrill I've ever come across.'

His wife smiled apologetically at Maggie.

'Twelve bucks for this!' the man spat. 'Good God!' His wife and children followed him out of the room.

A trim woman in a white blouse and shorts took her teenage son by the elbow. 'We're going, too.'

'Mother!'

'No argument. We've both seen too much already.'

'Aw geez!'

She tugged him out the door.

When they were gone, Maggie laughed quietly. 'They left before we got to the best part,' she said.

Nervous laughter whispered through the remaining members of the group.

2.

'We lived sixteen nights in this house before the beast struck.' She led them through the corridor, past the blocking chairs and past the stairway. 'My husband, Joseph, he had a distaste for the rooms where the murders happened. That's partly why we left 'em well enough alone, and settled ourselves elsewhere. Cynthia and Diana weren't so squeamish. They stayed in the boys' room we just left.'

She took the group through a doorway on the right, across from Lilly's bedroom. Donna hunted the floor for wax bodies, but found none, though a four-panelled papier-mâché screen blocked one corner and window.

'Joseph and I were sleeping here. The night was the seventh of May 1931. That's more than forty years back, but it's burned in my mind. There'd been a good deal of rain that day. It slowed down after dark. We had those windows open. I could hear the drizzle outside. The girls were fast asleep at the end of the hall, and the baby, Theodore, was snug in the nursery.

'I fell asleep, feeling all peaceful and safe. But long about midnight, I was awakened by a loud crash of glass. The sound came from downstairs. Joseph, who also heard it, got up real quiet and tiptoed over here to the chest. He always kept his pistol here.' Opening a top drawer, she pulled out a Colt .45 service automatic. '*This* pistol. It made a frightful loud sound when he worked its top.' Clamping her cane under one arm, she gripped the black hood of the automatic and quickly slid it back and forward with a scraping clamour of metal parts. Her thumb gently lowered the hammer. She returned the gun to its drawer.

'Joseph took the pistol with him and left the room. When I heard his footsteps on the stairs, I stole out of bed, myself. Quiet as I could, I started down the hall. I had to get to my children, you see.'

The group followed her into the corridor.

'I was right here, at the top of the stairway, when I heard gunshots from downstairs. I heard a scream from Joseph such as I'd never heard before. There were sounds of a scuffle, then scampering feet. I stood right here, scared frozen, listening to footsteps climb the stairs. I wanted to run off, and take my children to safety, but fear held me tight so I couldn't move.

'Out of the darkness below me came the beast. I couldn't see how it looked, except it walked upright like a man. It made kind of a laugh, and then it leapt on me and dragged me down to the floor. It ripped me with its claws and teeth. I tried to fight it off, but of course I was no match for the thing. I was preparing myself to meet the Lord when little Theodore started crying in his nursery at the end of the hall. The beast climbed off me and ran to the nursery.

'Wounded as I was, I chased after it. I *had* to save my baby.'

The group followed her to the end of the corridor. Maggie stopped in front of a closed door.

'This door stood open,' she said, and tapped it with her cane. 'In the light from its windows I saw the pale beast drag my child from the cradle and fall upon him. I knew that little Theodore was beyond my power to help him.

'I was watching, filled with horror, when a hand tugged at my nightdress. I found Cynthia and Diana behind me, all in tears. I took a hand of each, and led them silently away from the nursery door.'

She took the group again past the rope-connected chairs.

'We were just here when the snarling beast ran out of the nursery. This was the nearest door.' She opened it, revealing a steep, narrow staircase with a door at the top. 'We ducked inside, and I got the door shut only a second ahead of the beast. The three of us ran up these stairs as fast as our legs could carry us, stumbling and crying out in the darkness. At the top, we passed through that door. I bolted it after us. Then we sat in the musty blackness of the attic, waiting.

'We heard the beast come up the stairs. It made laughing, hissing sounds. It sniffed the door. And then, somehow, with such quickness we couldn't move, the door burst open and the beast sprang among us. In the first moments, it killed Cynthia and Diana. Then it leapt on to me. It held me down with its claws, and I waited for it to tear out my life.

But it didn't. It just stayed on top of me, breathing its foul breath against my face. Then it climbed off. It scampered down the attic and vanished. I have never seen the beast since that night. But others have.'

3.

'Why didn't it kill you?' asked the girl whose round face bloomed with acne.

'I've often wondered that. Though I'll never know, this side of the grave, I sometimes think the beast let me stay alive "to report its cause aright to the unsatisfied," as the dying Hamlet asked Horatio to do. Maybe it didn't want another Gus Goucher strung up for its crimes.'

'It seems to me,' said the white-haired man, 'that you give this beast a great deal of credit.'

'Let's see the attic,' said the chubby, critical boy.

'I don't show the attic. I keep it locked – always.'

'The nursery, then.'

'I never show that, either.'

'You don't have more dummies?'

'There're no wax figures of my kin,' she said.

With arched eyebrows, the boy scanned the group as if looking for others who shared his disdain for the woman's selective presentation of history. 'Well, what about those other two guys? They weren't your kin.'

'The *two guys* this young man refers to, they're Tom Bagley and Larry Maywood.' She shut the door to the attic staircase and led the group back down the corridor to her bedroom. 'Tom and Larry were twelve years old. I knew both of them well. They came along on several tours, and probably knew more about Beast House than just about anyone.

'Lord knows why they didn't have more sense than to come in here at night. They weren't ignorant like those Ziegler characters: they knew good and well what to expect. But they come breaking in, anyhow. This was back in '51.

'They were in the house a long spell, nosing around. They tried to pick the locks of the nursery and attic, but couldn't. They were snooping through this room when the beast came.

'It took down little Tom Bagley, and Larry Maywood ran for the window.'

Maggie pulled aside the papier-mâché screen that blocked the window and several feet of floor space in front of it. Some of the group jumped back. The girl with acne whirled away, gagging. A woman muttered, 'Really,' her voice rich with disgust.

The wax figure of Larry Maywood, trying to raise the window, was looking back at the same mangled body as the other spectators in the room. Its clothes were shredded, leaving it bare except for the buttocks. The skin of its back was deeply scored. Its head lay half a foot from the pulpy neck, face up, eyes open, mouth twisted wide.

'Leaving his friend at the mercy of the beast, Larry Maywood jumped from . . .'

'I'm Larry Maywood!' cried the white-haired man. 'And you are lying! Tommy was dead! He was dead before I jumped. I saw the beast twist off his head! I'm no coward! I didn't leave him there to die!'

Sandy squeezed Donna's hand tightly.

One of the children began to cry.

'This is slander! Out-and-out slander!' Spinning away, the man marched out of the room. His friend from the cafe followed.

'I've seen about enough,' Donna whispered.

'Me too.'

'That concludes our tour for this morning, ladies and gentlemen.' Maggie left the room, followed by the group. 'We do have a gift shop on the first floor, where you can purchase an illustrated booklet on the history of Beast House. You can also purchase 35 mm colour slides of the house, including the murder scenes. We have Beast House T-shirts, bumper stickers, and all sorts of fine souvenirs. The Ziegler display will be ready next spring. You won't want to miss it.'

Chapter Seven

1.

'Imagine the gall of that hag, suggesting I ran out on Tommy to save my own skin! That miserable bag of guts, that abomination! I'll take legal action!'

'I wish you hadn't leaked your identity.'

'Well, I'm sorry.' He shook his head, frowning in misery. 'But *really*, Judge, you heard what she said about me.'

'I heard.'

'The contemptible vial of swamp gas!'

'Excuse me!' a woman's voice called from behind.

'Oh dear,' Larry muttered.

They looked around at the woman hurrying up the sidewalk towards them, a blond girl in tow. Jud recognized them both.

'We'll make a run for the car,' Larry whispered.

'I don't think that's necessary.'

'Judge, please! She's undoubtedly a reporter or some other species of uncouth snoop.'

'She looks couth to me.'

'Oh for heaven's sake!' He stamped his foot. 'Please!'

'You go to the car, and I'll check her out.' Jud held out the keys. Larry snatched them away and hurried off several paces ahead of the woman. 'He has a healthy fear of the press,' Jud told her.

'I'm not the press,' she said.

'I didn't think so.'

She smiled.

'But if you're not the press, why did you chase us?'

'Afraid you'd get away.'

'Oh?'

'Yes.' Head tilted to one side, she shrugged. 'I'm Donna Hayes.' She offered a hand. Jud held it lightly. 'This is my daughter, Sandy.'

'I'm Jud Rucker,' he said, still holding her hand. 'What can I do for you?'

'We saw you at breakfast.'

'*I* didn't,' Sandy said.

'Well, I did.'

Jud frowned, enjoying himself and still holding her hand. 'Oh yes,' he finally said. 'You were at the table behind me, weren't you?'

Donna nodded. 'We were on the tour, too.'

'Right. Did you enjoy it?'

'*I* thought it was dreadful.'

'*I* liked it,' the girl said. 'It was so gross.'

'It was gross, all right.' He turned his eyes to Donna and stayed quiet, waiting.

'Anyway,' she said. She took a deep breath. In spite of her smile, she looked worried.

'How'd you like that crazy woman before the tour?' Sandy asked him.

The worry suddenly vanished from Donna's face. In a voice thick with sincerity, she said, 'That's why I wanted to see you, why I ... chased you the way I did.' She smiled shyly. 'I wanted to tell you how refreshing it was, the way you stuck up for that woman. The way you helped her. It was such a thoughtful thing to do.'

'Thank you.'

'You should've given that turkey a knuckle sandwich,' Sandy told him.

'I gave the matter lots of thought.'

'You should've punched out his lights.'

'He backed off.'

'Sandy has a taste for violence,' Donna said.

'Well,' said Jud. He let the single word stand like a period, ending his part of the conversation.

'Well,' Donna echoed. Though she kept her smile, Jud could see her start to deflate. 'I just wanted to let you know . . . how much I admired the way you helped the woman.'

'Thank you. Nice to meet both of you.'

'Nice to meet you,' Sandy said.

Donna started to pull her hand away, but Jud tightened his grip. 'Do you have time for a Bloody Mary?' he asked.

'Well . . .'

'Sandy,' he said, 'how about a Coke or 7-up?'

'Sure!'

'How about it?' he asked Donna.

'Sure. Why not?'

'I think the Welcome Inn should have what we're looking for. Are you on foot?'

'We've been on them all morning,' said Donna.

'In that case, I'll personally chauffeur you to the door.' He walked beside them to his Chrysler, and found it locked. Larry grinned out at him, brimming with satisfaction. Jud made a cranking motion. With a humming sound, the passenger window opened.

'Yes?' Larry asked innocently.

'They're friends.'

'Maybe *your* friends.'

Jud turned to Donna. 'Charm him.'

She bent beside the car. At eye level with him, she said, 'I'm Donna Hayes.' She reached a hand into the window. Larry met it with his hand and shook it briefly, making a smile that seemed to strain his face.

'Admit it,' he said. 'You're a reporter.'

'I'm a passenger-service agent with TWA.'

'You're not.'

'I am.'

'She is,' said Sandy.

'Who asked you?' he snapped.

Sandy began to giggle.

'Who's she?'

'That's Sandy, my daughter.'

'Daughter, eh? Then you're married?'

'Not anymore.'

'Ah-ha! A feminist!'

Sandy turned away, laughing out of control.

'Don't you like feminists?' Donna asked him.

'Only with Béarnaise sauce,' he said.

When Donna laughed, the corners of Larry's mouth began to tremble with concealed mirth. 'I suppose . . .' He swallowed. 'I suppose I'll be relegated to the back seat with Little Miss Giggles.' He unlocked the door and climbed out.

Donna stepped into the car. She scooted to the middle of the front seat. 'Miss Giggles can manage the back seat on her own.'

'A *lady*! I've met a *lady*!' Larry got in beside her. She unlocked the driver's door for Jud, while Larry reached behind him to get the lock of the back door.

'Where to?' Larry asked, slapping his thighs.

'The Welcome Inn,' said Jud. 'For drinks and lunch.'

'Wonderful. A party. I love parties.' He looked over his shoulder. 'Don't you love parties, Miss Giggles?'

'I find them enchanting,' replied Sandy, and burst into a new fit of hysteria.

As they were passing the Chevron station, Sandy called out, 'There's our car!'

'Is it sick?' Larry asked.

Donna said, 'We had a little accident last night.'

'Nothing serious, I hope.'

'Just bruises and scrapes.'

'Would you like me to stop?' Jud asked.

'Would you mind?'

He pulled into the station. Larry climbed out to let Donna through. Then he got back in and shut the door.

'I suppose it's never difficult for a woman to demolish a car,' Larry said, looking around at the girl. 'How did your mother accomplish it?'

Jud didn't listen to the girl's reply. All his attention was focused on Donna: on the way the sun shimmered in the flow of her brown hair, on the inward curve of her back and how the mounds of her buttocks shifted under her corduroy pants as she walked. In front of the office, she met a man wearing coveralls and a smirk. They talked. Donna tossed her rump to the left and slid a hand down her rear pocket. She nodded. With a graceful pivot, she followed the man to her car, where he opened the hood and shook his head.

Jud watched her hair sweep down the side of her face as she ducked to look under the hood. She straightened up, talking.

'Uh-oh,' he heard Sandy say.

The man slammed the hood shut.

Donna talked to him, and nodded while he spoke. She pushed both hands into her hip pockets, and shifted again to her left leg. Then she swung around. She walked with long strides towards Jud's car, shrugged, made a face to show exasperation, and smiled.

Larry climbed out to let her in.

'Well,' she told Jud, 'it's still among the living. He has to send to Santa Rosa, though, for a new radiator.'

'It'll take a couple of days, won't it?'

'He said we might be able to leave tomorrow.'

'Tomorrow?' Sandy sounded worried.

'There's no way around it, honey.'

'Do you need to get somewhere in a hurry?' Jud asked, and pulled on to the road.

'No, not especially. Two days in this town is just about two days longer than we'd planned on, that's all.'

'I spent twelve years in this marvellous berg,' said Larry. 'You'd be amazed at the variety of activities available to you.'

'What sort of things?' asked Sandy.

'The most popular sport, by far, is sitting at the corner of Front and Division to watch the traffic lights change.'

'Oh boy.'

'Do you have a place to stay?' Jud asked.

Donna nodded. 'We've got a room at the Welcome Inn.'

'Why, isn't that a joyful coincidence!' Larry proclaimed. 'So do we! Do all of us play bridge?'

'Never touch the stuff,' Jud said.

'Don't *brag!*'

'Besides, we've already got plans for tonight.'

'Oh.'

'We have some business to take care of,' he told Donna.

'Are you just in town for today?' she asked.

'We may be around for a few days. It's hard to say, at this point. Depends on how things go.'

'What sort of business are you in?'

'We're with . . .' He suddenly knew that he didn't want to lie. Not to this woman. The need to retain a cover wasn't as great as usual, and not worth the loss. 'I'd rather not go into it,' he said.

'Oh. Fine. I'm sorry if I pried.'

'No, don't . . .'

'I'd be happy to tell you our business.'

'Larry!'

'We're going to . . .'

'Don't!'

'Kill the beast.'

'What?' Donna asked.

'Wow!' cried Sandy.

'The beast. The monster of Beast House. Judgement Rucker and I are going to lay it low!'

'Are you?' Donna asked, turning to Jud.

'Do you believe there is a beast?' he asked.

'Something killed all those people, I guess.'

'Or some*one*,' Jud said.

'The killer of Tom Bagley was *not* human,' Larry insisted.

'What was it?' asked Sandy.

'We'll show you its cadaver,' Larry said, 'and you may decide for yourself.'

'What's a cadaver?'

'It's a corpse, honey.'

'Oh, gross.'

'What we plan to do,' Jud said, 'is find out what – or who – killed the people in that house. Then we'll deal with it.' He smiled at her. 'Bet you didn't realize you were riding with a couple of lunatics. Are you still up to a Bloody Mary?'

'Now I may need two.'

2.

'Excuse me,' Donna said. She scooted back her chair. 'If the drinks come while I'm gone, don't wait on me.'

'I'll come, too,' said the girl.

Jud watched them walk across the crowded dining room. Then he leaned close to Larry. In a low voice, he said, 'You screwed up real good, back there. If one more person finds out what we're doing in this town, it's all over. I keep my advance, drive back to San Francisco, and that's the end of it.'

'*Really*, Judge. What possible harm . . .?'

'One more person.'

'Oh, all right. If you must be that way.'

'I must.'

Nobody spoke of Beast House during cocktails or lunch. As they were finishing, Larry told of a footpath that led down a gorge to a beach.

After lunch, they all went to the motel office and registered for another night. Then the two groups split up, giving Donna and Sandy a chance to put on their swimsuits. Jud relaxed on his bed, ankles crossed, hands folded behind his head. He fell asleep.

'There they are!' Larry announced, waking him. The nervous man left the window and inspected himself in a mirror over the dressing table. 'How do I look?'

Jud glanced at the red-flowered shirt and white shorts. 'Where's your Panama hat?'

'I could hardly pack everything on such short notice.'

They left their cabin. Larry rushed ahead to meet the two women, but Jud hung back to have a long look at Donna. She wore a blue shirt with sleeves rolled up her forearms. Below the hanging shirt tails, her legs were slim and dark. No trace of a swimsuit was visible.

'I do hope you're not *au naturel* under that blouse,' Larry said.

'You'll have to wait and see.'

'Oh please, give us a peek. Just a teensy one.'

'Nope.'

'Oh please.'

Sandy lunged forward laughing, and swung her denim handbag at Larry. He spun away, ducking. The bag whunked his back. 'Cruel midget!' he cried out.

The girl started to swing again.

'That's enough, honey.'

'But he's weird,' Sandy gasped, laughing.

'Is he always this way?' Donna asked Jud.

'I only met him last night.'

'Is that true?'

'Judgement never lies,' Larry said.

They got into Jud's Chrysler, and Larry gave directions that took them down Front Street past the Chevron station, past Sarah's Diner, and down two more blocks of shops. Beast House loomed ahead, on the left. The talking and laughter abruptly stopped, but nobody mentioned the house.

Larry broke the silence. 'Turn right on this dirt road.'

Jud made the turn.

'Is that where Axel's mother lives?' Sandy asked, pointing to the brick house.

'That's the place,' said Donna.

Jud looked at the brick house to his left and saw that it had no windows. 'Strange,' he muttered.

'Indeed,' said Larry. He asked Donna, 'How do you know Axel?'

'He gave us a ride into town last night.'

'There's a weird duck.'

'He's retarded,' Sandy explained.

'Who wouldn't be, with a mother like Maggie Kutch?'

'What?' asked Sandy.

'Axel's mother is Maggie Kutch, the owner of Beast House, the tour guide.'

'Her?'

'Yes indeed.'

'Did she remarry after the killings?' Donna asked.

'Keep to the right, Judge. No, she did have visitors, though. Town speculation had it that Wick Hapson fathered Axel. He's been working with Maggie from the start, and they live together.'

'The man in the ticket booth?' Donna asked.

'Right-o.'

'Charming family,' Jud said. 'It looked like the house didn't have any windows.'

'It doesn't.'

'How come?' Sandy asked.

'So the beast can't get in, of course.'

'Oh.' The girl sounded as if she regretted asking.

The dirt road widened and ended.

'Ah, we're here! Just park anywhere, Judge.'

He turned the car around so it headed out, and parked off to the side of the road.

'You'll absolutely adore this beach,' Larry said, getting out.

Before opening his door, Jud watched Donna. As he'd assumed, she was wearing a swimsuit under the shirt: the bottom part of one, at least. Its blue fabric shined at him when she bent to climb out.

He joined the others beside the car. The wind felt good, cutting the heat like a cool spray.

'Are we off?' Larry asked Donna.

'We off?' she asked Jud.

'I'm ready. You ready, Sandy?'

'You're *all* weird.'

They walked single file along a narrow trail that angled downward between two sandy hills. Jud squinted into the wind. It fluttered in his ears, batting away all but the loudest words as Larry told of a childhood experience at the beach.

After they rounded a curve in the trail, the ocean came into view. Its choppy blue was frothing with rows of whitecaps. Waves slammed against a rocky point. Just this side of the point, the waves washed quietly on to a stretch of sand. Jud could see nobody down there.

'Ah wonderful!' Larry yelled, spreading his arms and sniffing a deep breath. 'Last one to the beach is a rotten egg!' He began to run. Sandy chased after him.

Jud turned to Donna. 'Don't you feel like racing?'

'Nope.' Wind threw strands of hair across her face. Jud brushed them away. He couldn't look away from her eyes.

'I bet I know why,' he said.

'Why?'

'You're afraid I'll beat you.'

'Is that it?' Her eyes were amused, but serious, as if she wouldn't permit herself to be distracted by his banter.

'That's it,' he said.

'Is your name really Judgement?'

'It really is.'

'I wish we were alone, Judgement.'

He put his hands on her shoulders and drew her against him, feeling the press of her body, the light touch of her hands against his back, the smooth, moist opening of her lips.

'We're not alone,' she said after a while.

'I guess we'd better quit, huh?'

'While the quitting's good.'

'I wouldn't say it's good,' Jud said.

'Me neither.'

Holding hands, they walked down the trail. Below, Sandy was running across the beach just ahead of Larry. She splashed into the water. Larry stopped at the water's edge and dropped to his knees. The girl waved for him to come in, but he shook his head. 'Come on!' Jud heard through the noise of the wind and surf.

Sandy pranced in the water, crouched and splashed at Larry.

'We'd better hurry,' Donna said, 'before my charming daughter gets carried away and drags him in.'

Even as she said it, the girl ran ashore and began to tug one of Larry's arms.

'Leave him alone, Sandy!'

Larry, still on his knees, managed to look around. 'It's really all right, Donna,' he called. 'She's nothing I can't handle.'

Letting go of his arm, Sandy circled behind him and leapt on to his back. 'Giddyap!' she shouted.

He lunged and twisted, scrambling through the sand on hands and knees, making a noise that sounded, at first, like the whinny of a horse. Then he was on his feet. Sandy, clutching him tightly around the neck, looked back at Donna and Jud. Though she said nothing, her face showed fear. Larry swung himself in a circle, tugging at the girl's arms, and Jud saw terror in his wide eyes. His whinnies were ragged gasps of panic. He pranced and bucked, trying to tear himself free.

'Oh my God!' Donna cired, and broke into a run.

Jud raced past her towards the girl now screaming in horror.

'Larry, stop!' he yelled.

The man didn't seem to hear. He kept jumping and writhing, pulling frantically at the girl's arms.

Then Sandy was falling backward, her legs still hugging Larry's hips but her arms loose and flailing. One of her small hands clutched Larry's collar. The shirt split down his back, and he screamed. Jud caught the falling girl. He pulled her free.

Larry spun, looking at them, his eyes wild. He began backing away. He fell. Propping himself on an elbow, he still gazed at them. Slowly, the strangeness left his face. His harsh breathing grew calm.

Jud left Sandy in her mother's arms and went to him.

'She shouldn't . . . have jumped on my back.' His voice was a high whine. 'Not on my *back*.'

'It's all right now,' Jud said.

'Not on my back.' He lay on the sand, covering his eyes with his forearms, and wept silently.

Jud knelt beside him. 'It's all right, Larry. It's all over.'

'It's not over. It'll never be over. Never.'

'You gave the kid a terrible scare.'

'I kno-o-o-w,' he said, stretching the word like a groan of misery. 'I'm sor-ry. Maybe . . . if I apologize.'

'Might help.'

He sniffed, and wiped his eyes. When he sat up, Jud saw the scars. They criss-crossed his shoulders and back in a savage tracery more white than his pale skin.

'They're not from the beast, if that's what you think. I got them from my fall. The beast never touched me. Never.'

Chapter Eight

Roy made certain, once again, that Joni was securely tied. Probably it didn't matter. She'd obviously lost her marbles. But Roy wanted nothing left to chance.

In the living room, he bent down and lit the candle. He patted the newspaper wads to make certain, once again, they were touching the candle stick. Then he headed for the kitchen, stepping high, his feet crushing the newspaper wads and clothes he'd scattered along the floor.

The fire might not destory all the evidence, but it couldn't hurt.

He put on sunglasses and a faded Dodger cap that had belonged to Marv, and went out the back door. Pulling it shut, he twisted his hand to smear prints on the knob. He trotted down three steps to the patio, then hurried to the driveway. Looking towards the street, he saw that a gate blocked the driveway. He walked casually to it, unlatched it, and opened it.

The neighbour's house was very close. He watched its windows, but saw nobody looking out.

He walked up the driveway to the garage. A two-car garage, with two doors separated by a beam. He raised the left-hand door. Inside was a red Chevy. He climbed into it, glanced at the three sets of keys he'd brought from the house, and easily found the Chevrolet keys.

He started the car and backed out of the garage. He stopped close to the kitchen door. Then he got out and opened the trunk. He brought Joni out of the house, set her inside the trunk, and slammed the lid shut.

The trip to Karen's house took less than ten minutes. He'd expected to recognize, the house, but it didn't look familiar at all. He checked the address again. Then he remembered that she and Bob moved just before the trial. This was the right house.

He parked in front. He checked his wristwatch – Marv's wristwatch – his now. Nearly two-thirty.

The neighbourhood seemed very quiet. He looked up and down the block as he walked to the front door. Four houses to the right, a Japanese gardener was whacking limbs from a bush. To the left, a lawn away, a lone tabby cat crouched, stalking something. Roy didn't bother trying to spot its prey. He had some prey of his own.

Grinning, he rang the doorbell. He waited, and rang again. Finally he decided nobody was in.

He headed around the side of the house, took two steps past the rear corner, and stopped abruptly.

There she was. Maybe not Karen, but *some* woman on a chaise longue, listening to music from a transistor radio. The longue was facing away, so its back blocked Roy's view of all but her slim, tanned legs, her left arm, and the crown of her hat. A white hat, like a sailor's.

Roy scanned the yard. High shrubbery enclosed its sides and rear. Good and secluded. Bending low, he raised his pants leg and slipped the knife from its sheath.

Silently, he stepped closer until he could see over the back of the longue. The woman was wearing a white bikini, its straps hanging off her shoulders. Her skin was glossy with oil. She held a folded magazine in her right hand, keeping it off to the side so it wouldn't cast a shadow on her belly.

Her hand jerked, dropping the magazine as Roy clutched her mouth.

He pressed the knife edge to her throat.

'Don't make a sound, or I'll open you up.'

She tried to say something through his hand.

'Shut up. I'm gonna take my hand away, and you're not gonna make a sound. Ready?'

Her head nodded once.

Roy let go of her mouth, flung the sailor's hat off her head, and clutched her brown hair. 'Okay, stand up.' He helped by pulling her hair. When she was up, he jerked her head around. The tanned face belonged to Karen, all right. He could tell that, even through the sunglasses. 'Not a word,' he muttered.

He guided her to the back door.

'Open it,' he said.

She pulled open the screen door. They stepped into the kitchen. It seemed very dark after the sunny yard, but Roy couldn't spare a hand to take off his sunglasses. 'I need rope,' he said. 'Where do you keep it?'

'You mean I'm allowed to talk now?'

'Where's some rope?'

'We don't have any.'

He put pressure on the blade. 'You'd better hope you do. Now, where is it?'

'I don't . . .' She gasped as he yanked her hair. 'We have some with the camping gear, I think.'

'Show me.' He lifted the knife off her throat, but kept it half an inch away, his wrist propped on her shoulder. 'Move.'

They went out the kitchen, and turned left down a hallway. They walked past closed doors: closets, probably. Past the bathroom. Into a doorway on the right. The room was a study with bookshelves, a cluttered desk, a rocking chair.

'Any kids?' Roy asked.

'No.'

'Too bad.'

She stopped at a door beside the rocker. 'In there,' she said.

'Open it.'

She pulled open the door. The closet held nothing but camping gear: two mummy bags suspended from hangers, hiking boots on the floor, backpacks propped against the wall. A metal-tipped walking stick hung from a hook. Beside it were two soft felt hats. Yellow foam-rubber pads, strapped neatly into rolls, stood upright beside the packs. On the shelf was a long red stuffbag, probably containing a mountain tent. On hangers were outdoor clothes: rain ponchos, flannel shirts, even a pair of grey leather Liederhosen.

'Where's the rope?'

'In the packs.'

He let go of her hair. He took the knife away from her throat and touched the point to her bare back. 'Get it.'

She stepped into the closet and knelt down. She flipped back the red cover of a Kelty pack. She tipped the pack forward, reaching into it, and rummaged through it. Her hand came out with a coil of stiff, new clothesline.

'Is there more?' He took it from her and tossed it behind him.

'Isn't that enough?'

'Look in the other pack.'

She turned to it without closing the first one. As she peeled back its cover, her arm seemed to freeze.

'Don't.' Roy slipped the blade through Karen's hair until its point stopped against the back of her neck. She sucked a quick breath. Keeping the knife at her neck, Roy bent down. He reached over her shoulder and lifted the hand axe out of the pack. Its haft was wood. A leather case enclosed its head. He tossed the axe behind him. It thumped heavily on the carpeted floor.

'Okay, now get the other rope.'

She searched inside the pack and brought out a coil of clothesline much like the first, but grey and soft with wear.

'Get up.'

She stood.

Roy swung her around to face him. 'Hands out.' He pulled the rope away from her. He slid his knife under his belt and tightly bound her hands together. He stepped away from her, paying out rope. Then he picked up the hand axe and the spare coil. Pulling the rope, he led her out the doorway and into the hall. He found the master bedroom at the end of the hall. He pulled her into it.

'Guess what happens now,' he said.

'Aren't I too old for you?'

He grinned, remembering Joni. 'You're way too old for me,' he said. He led her across the carpeted room to a closet. He opened its door halfway and shoved Karen against the wall. With the door between them, he passed the rope over its top and pulled.

'Damn it!' she muttered.

'Shut up.'

'Roy!'

He yanked the rope. The door knocked against him as Karen hit its other side. He saw her fingertips over its top. No doorknob on the inside. Shit! He ran the taut line down to the bottom of the door. Crawling, he brought it under the edge to the front. He lifted one of Karen's feet. She kicked at him. He punched her behind the knee, making her cry out. Then he brought the rope up between her legs and crossed it over her right leg. He tied it to the knob, next to her hip.

He stepped back and admired his work. Karen stood pressed to the door, arms stretched to the top. The rope appeared at the bottom of the door, near the centre, and angled to the right, passing over her leg to the doorknob.

'Now tell me what I want to know.'

'What's that?'

'Where're Donna and Sandy?'

'At their place?' she asked. In spite of her situation, her voice maintained a sarcastic edge.

Roy sliced through one shoulder strap of her bikini, then the other. 'They aren't there, and you know it.'

'They aren't?'

He cut through its back. He reached to her side, and tugged the bikini top from between her body and the door. 'Tell me where they are.'

'If they aren't at home, I wouldn't . . .'

He sliced through the left side of her bikini pants. The edges flopped away. She clamped her legs shut to keep the pants from slipping down.

'What time does your husband get home?'

'Soon.'

'What time?' He pulled the pants down to her ankles.

'Maybe four-thirty.'

'It's only three now. That gives us lots of time.'

'I don't know where they went.'

'Oh?' He laughed. 'You may be able to take a lot of pain. I'll be happy to give it to you. But let me tell you something: if you love that husband of yours, you'll tell me what I want to know before he gets home. When you tell me where they are, I'll leave. I won't hurt you, I won't hurt your husband. If I'm still here when he gets home, though, I'm going to kill you and him both.'

'I don't *know* where she is.'

'Sure you do.'

'I don't.'

'Well then, that's too bad for both of you, isn't it?'

She said nothing.

'Where did they go?'

Crouching, he drew a question mark on the white flesh of her left buttock, and watched it bleed.

Chapter Nine

1.

From his position on Front Street near the south corner of the wrought-iron fence, Jud watched half a dozen people leave Beast House. The final tour of the day was over. He looked at his wristwatch. Almost four.

Maggie Kutch left the house last, and locked the door. She made her way slowly down the porch steps, leaning heavily on her cane. The strain of guiding tourists showed plainly in the weariness of her walk.

At the ticket booth, she met Wick Hapson. They finished locking up. Then, taking her arm, Wick walked with her across Front Street. They went slowly up the dirt driveway and finally disappeared into the windowless house.

Jud slid a cigar out of his shirt pocket. He tore the wrapper off, crumbled it into a tiny ball, and flipped it onto the car floor. Then he took a book of matches from the same pocket. He lit the cigar and waited.

At four twenty-five, and old pick-up truck backed out of the garage beside the Kutch house and came down the driveway trailing a cloud of dust. It turned on to Front Street and headed towards Jud. He pretended to study a road map. The truck slowed and swung across the street.

Looking up from his map, Jud saw a man leap to the ground and hobble towards the fence. At the corner was a wide gate, chained shut and padlocked. The short, heavy man opened the lock, unwound the chain, and pushed the gate open. He drove through, then locked the gate again.

Jud watched the truck move over tyre tracks worn into the lawn, and park at the side of Beast House. The driver climbed out. He let down the truck's tailgate and hopped into its bed. Bending down, he slid a board ramp to the ground. Then he rolled a power lawnmower down the ramp.

As soon as the man started the mower, Jud made a U-turn. He drove slowly, studying the left side of the road. Two miles south of Malcasa Point, he found a fire road leading into the forest. Nothing closer. It was no good. He used it to turn around, and headed back toward town.

A hundred yards behind the spot where he'd parked to watch the house front, he pulled completely off the road. He got out of his car. Nothing was in sight except the bending road and wooded slopes. He stood motionless for a few seconds, making sure.

He heard the far-off motor of the lawnmower. He heard the wind stirring leaves high overhead, and the sounds of countless birds. A fly buzzed near his face. He waved it away and opened the trunk of his car.

He put on the parka, first. Then he hooked a web belt around his waist under the coat, and made sure the holster flap was snapped shut. He lifted out a backpack, and put it on. He took out his rifle case. Then he shut the trunk.

His trek through the pathless woods took him up the side of a hill, over rock clusters and fallen trees, and finally into the sunlight of a clearing at the top. He rubbed sweat out of his stinging eyes. He drank tepid water from his canteen. Then he started down the left side of the hill, seeking an outcropping of rock that he'd noticed that morning through the back windows of Beast House.

He finally saw the rocks ahead. He made his way forward and easily climbed the outcropping, hopping from one rock to the next. When he peered over the top, a clear view of Beast House lay below him.

The short, limping man, apparently finished with the front lawn, was now mowing the back. Jud watched him slowly walk the yard, disappear behind a weathered gazebo, and reappear.

It would be a long wait.

But he didn't intend to do it this way, crouched and peeking over a ledge of rock. Too damned uncomfortable. He backed off. He found a level area between a pair of midget pines several feet from the top. There he set down his rifle case. He shrugged the pack off his shoulders and propped it against one of the pines. Then he removed his coat. The breeze cooled his sweaty shirt. He took the shirt off, used it to wipe his face, and spread it out on a rock to let the sun dry it.

Next, he opened his pack. He pulled out his binoculars case, and a sandwich from a paper bag. Donna had made the sandwich for him earlier in the afternoon.

They'd returned to the Welcome Inn after the scene with Larry at the beach. Donna and Sandy had changed out of their swimsuits, and Larry had wandered off, presumably to have a drink in the motel bar. Then Jud, accompanied by the two women, had walked into town. He bought the sandwich ingredients at a grocery store near Sarah's Diner. Back in Donna's cabin at the inn, she put the sandwiches together. Four of them. When she asked where he would spend the night, he told her only that he would return in the morning.

With the binoculars and sandwich, he scouted for a suitable watching place. Crouching at the top, he found it: a level area halfway down the face, protected by a shield of upthrust rock.

Before moving down to it, he unwrapped his sandwich, a sourdough roll packed with mayonnaise, jack cheese, and salami. He ate, looking across the distance at the back of Beast House.

The guy was still mowing.

Jud watched through his Bushnell binoculars. The man's hairless head was shiny with perspiration. In spite of the heat, he wore a sweatshirt and gloves. Occasionally he wiped a sleeve across his face.

Poor bastard.

Jud looked down at the sweaty man, appreciating his own comfort: the feel of the breeze on his bare skin, the piny smell of the air, the taste of his sandwich, and the good solid knowledge that he'd found a woman, today, who mattered to him.

Done with the sandwich, he climbed down to the flat area where he'd left his pack and rifle. His shirt was still damp. He loaded it into the pack, along with his binoculars and parka, then returned to his observation point.

2.

After the pick-up left the grounds of Beast House, nothing moved inside the perimeter of the fence – nothing within the area visible to Jud, at least. That included the entire back of the house, and its southern side.

Jud wasn't much concerned about the front. In the Thorn and Kutch killings, the assailant had apparently entered by breaking rear windows. He must've come across the yard from the woods behind the house.

If anyone entered tonight, Jud would get a look at him.

But not a shot at him.

That would have to wait. You don't take down a bastard just because he goes into a house at night, or because he's wearing a monkey suit. You've gotta be sure.

He scanned the area with his binoculars. Then he ate another sandwich, washing it down with canteen water.

When the sun was too low to keep him warm, he put on his shirt. It was dry, now, and slightly stiff. He tucked it into his jeans.

Lighting another cigar, he leaned back against the steep rock face. The protective uprise of rocks at the front of his ledge blocked some of his view. The entire backside of the house was still visible, though. He would settle for that. A fair exchange, so he wouldn't have to squat or crouch his way through the night.

After watching the house for an hour, he folded his parka and sat on it. Its thickness not only padded the hard ground but also gave him extra height, improving his view.

As he watched, he thought of many things. He concentrated on what he'd learned of the beast, searching for the most plausible explanation of its identity. Always, he came back to the time element: the first killings in 1903, the most recent in 1977. That certainly seemed to rule out the possibility that one man had performed all the killings.

Yet he couldn't buy the idea that the killer was some ageless, clawed monster. In spite of what Larry had said. In spite of Maggie Kutch's stories.

In spite of the scars on Larry's back?

A human could have made those scars. If not with fingernails, then with the claws of artificial paws. A human dressed up in a monkey suit – or a beast suit.

What about the time element, then? Almost seventy-five years.

Okay, several humans in beast suits.

Okay, who and why?

Suddenly he had a theory. The more he puzzled over his theory, the better it looked. As he began to reflect on ways to gather proof, however, he noticed that darkness had come.

He crawled forward quickly to the stone lip. The house was black. Its lawn was a dark expanse, empty of detail like the surface of a lake on a cloudy night. Reaching into his pack, Jud pulled out a leather case. He opened its snap and removed a Starlight Noctron IV. Putting it to his eye, he made a quick scan of the house and lawn. In the eerie red light generated by his infrared scope, nothing seemed out of place.

When his legs ached from squatting, he backed away from the front. He lowered the Starlight long enough to put on his coat. Then he stood, leaning back against the rock face, and continued his surveillance.

If this theory was correct, he had nothing to gain by spending a cold night up here. He wouldn't see any beast.

Well, it couldn't hurt to stick around.

We should've put somebody inside the house. Bait.

Who'd go in?

Me, that's who.

Too early in the game for that. This is time for surveillance, a good look from a safe distance. Learn the nature of the enemy.

If nothing else, I learn that the enemy didn't enter the house tonight from the rear.

The scope was growing heavy. He put it down and removed the final sandwich from his pack. As he ate it, he watched without the aid of his expensive scope, and could see little except darkness. He finished the sandwich quickly and returned to using the scope.

After a while, he knelt and rested his elbows on the ledge of the rock. He scanned the yard, the edges of the forest, the gazebo, even the windows of the house, though their glass would block most heat that the scope might pick up.

Leaving the scope in place on the rock, he stepped around his backpack and urinated into the darkness.

He returned to the scope. He swept the grounds. Nothing. He glanced at his wristwatch. Just after ten-thirty. He settled down, then, and watched for nearly an hour without changing position.

During that time, he thought about the beast. Thought about his theory. Thought about other nights he'd spent alone with a Starlight and a rifle. Thought a lot about Donna.

He thought about the way she looked that morning in her corduroys and blouse, hands tucked into the hip pockets of her pants. They became his hands, stroking the warm smooth curves of her rump. Then he saw his hands unfastening the buttons of her blouse, slowly parting it, touching breasts he had never seen but could vividly imagine.

Hard, his penis strained against the front of his pants.

Think about the beast.

Into his mind came the fat, black face of General Field Marshal and Emperor for Life Euphrates D. Kenyata. One of the big, round eyes vanished as a bullet ripped through it and took out the back of the Emperor's skull.

The Beast of Kampala was dead.

And so was Jud's erection.

The guards – if they'd caught him. But they hadn't. They hadn't even come close. No closer than he'd allowed for, at least. Still, if they'd caught him . . .

There!

Just this side of the fence.

He held the scope steady. Though something – probably a bush – blocked portions of the heat mage, he could see that the crouching figure had the basic shape of a human.

It lay down flat. It shoved something forward, apparently through a gap beneath the fence. Then it squirmed under the fence, itself. On the other side, it picked up the object and stood upright on two legs. It looked both ways, turning.

In profile, it had breasts.

It ran to the back of the house, climbed stairs, and disappeared into a porch.

A few seconds passed. Then Jud heard a quick, faint crash of breaking glass.

3.

When Jud reached the fence, gasping and hurting from his rush down the dark hillside, he didn't take time to find the burrow. He tossed his flashlight through the bars of the fence, leapt up, and grasped the high crossbar with both hands. He flung himself upward. Stiff-armed, he braced himself above the bar. A muffled scream came from the house. His weight shifted forward too much, and he felt the point of a spike prod his belly. He leaned back, and kicked up his left leg. His foot found the bar. He shoved hard upward, letting go. His right leg cleared the spikes. He fell for a long time. When he hit the ground, he tumbled, rolled to his feet, and retrieved the flashlight. Then he sprinted to the back of the house.

As he rushed up the porch steps, he unholstered his Colt .45 automatic. He wondered briefly if he should change clips – exchange the standard seven-shot magazine for the twenty-shot oversize he kept in his parka. Hell, if he couldn't get it with seven . . . *it?*

Inside the porch, the house door stood open. One of its glass panes was broken.

He entered. He flicked on his flashlight, swung its beam. The kitchen. He ran through a doorway into a narrow hall. Ahead, he saw the stuffed-monkey umbrella holder, and the front door. He shined his light over his left shoulder. It lit the staircase bannister. He rushed to the foot of the stairs, checked to the left and right, then swung his beam up the stairway.

Halfway up, it lit the red of a gasoline can lying on its side. He climbed to the can. Its caps were still in place. A three-foot length of rope had been passed through its handle and knotted, forming a sling. Liquid sloshed inside the can as he set it upright. He holstered his pistol and unscrewed one of the caps. He dropped it into his shirt pocket and sniffed the opening. Gasoline, all right. As he reached into his pocket for the cap, he heard breathing above him. Then a sound of parched laughter.

His beam climbed the stairs, lit a bare leg running blood, a hip, a mauled breast, a face. Hair hung down the face. Blood trickled from its chin. A flap of forehead skin hung down, hiding one eye.

More laughter came, as if trickling from her open mouth along with blood.

'Mary?' Jud called quietly up the stairs. 'Mrs Ziegler?'

She came forward in a strange, gliding way, her arms swinging loosely, her legs barely seeming to move.

Jud lowered his flashlight enough to see that her feet were two inches off the floor.

'Oh God,' he muttered, and started to reach for his pistol.

The body flew down at him.

He dropped to a crouch, bracing himself. The body struck him, rolled over his back with soft liquid sounds, and fell away. It thudded, hitting the stairs below him.

Then something else hit his back.

He shot his elbow into soft flesh and heard an explosion of breath. Gagging at the sour stench, he drove his elbow backward once more and twisted his body. Something sharp raked his shoulder, tearing his parka and skin as the heavy weight left his back. In pain, he dropped his automatic.

He clawed at the stairs, trying to find it. He found the gas can instead. He grabbed it. From below came grunting, snarling sounds.

Swinging the can, he splattered gasoline into the darkness. A pale shape appeared, hunched and climbing. He heard gas spatter it. Its arms flailed, and it shrieked. It knocked the can from Jud's hands. He backed up the stairs, reaching into his shirt pocket. Behind the cigar box was a book of matches.

Claws tore his thigh.

He ripped a match free, still climbing backward. He scratched it across the abrasive strip and saw a blue splutter.

The match didn't light.

But the thing was in midair, vaulting the bannister.

It grunted, hitting the floor far below. Then it scampered away towards the kitchen.

Jud searched the stairs until he found his flashlight and gun. Then he sat down, somewhere above the ravaged body of Mary Ziegler, and listened to the house.

Chapter Ten

Roy ached. Especially his shoulders and back. He felt as if he'd been driving forever. Only seven hours, though. He shouldn't feel this bad, not after only seven hours.

He reached into the bag beside him and felt the heat of the Big Macs. He started to pick one up. Then he set it down again. He could wait. He'd be stopping for the night, soon. That would be the time to eat.

As he drove across the Golden Gate, he glanced to the right at Alcatraz. Too dark. He couldn't see much except the signal light. Just as well. What did he want to see a fucking prison for, anyway?

It's not a prison, he reminded himself.

Sure it is. Once a prison, always a prison. It could never be anything else.

If he stayed on 101 another ten minutes, he'd be able to see San Quentin. Shit, as if he hadn't seen enough of that scumhole.

He didn't want to think about it.

He went ahead and took out a Big Mac. He unwrapped it. He ate slowly, watching the freeway signs. As he swallowed the last bite, he flicked on the turn signal and steered the Pontiac Grand Prix up the Mill Valley exit.

Smooth. He liked the way it handled. Bob Mars Bar had good taste in cars.

Mill Valley hadn't changed much. It still had the feel of a small, country town. The Tamalpias Theater marquee was dark. The old bus depot looked the same as always. He wondered if it still had all those paperbacks. Over to the left, the old buildings had been replaced by a huge, wooden structure. The place was changing, but slowly.

A big dog, part Lab, wandered into the intersection. Roy stepped on the gas and swerved to hit it, but the damn thing leapt out of range.

At the end of town, he turned on to a road to Mount Tamalpais, Muir Woods, and Stinson Beach. It meandered into the wooded hills. For a while, he passed scattered, dark houses. Then they were gone. He drove deeper into the woods, sometimes slowing almost to a stop as he took the tight curves.

When he came to a dirt turn-out, he pulled on to it and stopped. He shut off the headlights. Darkness wrapped the car. The dome light came on when he opened the door. He opened the back door and pulled a red Kelty backpack off the seat. After taking a flashlight from one of its side pockets, he shouldered the pack. He shut the car doors and stepped to the edge of the woods.

The ground sloped gradually upward. Bushes caught at his jeans as he climbed. Soon after leaving the road, he tripped over a low strand of barbed wire. A barb punctured his pants, scratching his shin. He jerked his pants leg free and continued upward.

At the top of the slope, he searched through the evergreens. They seemed closely packed. He was about to give up his search when the beam of his flashlight swept through a space that seemed fairly open. He stepped towards it and grinned.

The clearing, about twenty feet around, had a good flat area for his sleeping bag. A circle of rocks remained where someone else had made a campfire. Inside the circle were half a dozen charred cans. Kneeling, Roy touched one of them. Cold.

He scanned the area with his flashlight. All around the clearing, the forest seemed dark and silent.

This would do fine.

He lowered the backpack and opened it. On top was a plastic ground cloth. He spread it out. Then he took out a blue stuff bag, slipped the drawstring loose, and pulled out Bob's mummy bag. He put it on top of the ground cloth.

Should've brought one of those rubber pads, he thought. If only he'd thought of it.

He wandered into the trees, gathering firewood. He picked up handfuls of kindling, and brought them to the circle of rocks. Then he gathered armloads of dead limbs until he had formed a high pile. He tossed the burned cans into the trees.

With toilet paper from the pack, he started the fire. He fed it twigs. It grew, crackling and spitting. Its flames warmed his hands and cast fluttering light through the clearing. He added larger twigs. As the wood caught, he added more.

'Now, there's a healthy fire,' he muttered.

Three good fires in one day. He was getting a lot of practice.

He stood over the fire, watching its flames leap and curl, feeling its heat on the front of his body. Then he stepped back, out of its heat. He picked up the flashlight.

Once in a while, as he worked his way back through the thick woods, he looked over his shoulder. He could see the fire for a long time, its brightness shimmering on leaves over the clearing. By the time he reached the slope overlooking his car, no trace of the fire was visible.

He climbed down slowly, carefully, to the car. From the front seat, he took the sack from McDonald's. Then he stepped back to the trunk. He unlocked it. The lid swung up.

Joni squinted when the light beam hit her eyes. She was lying on her side, covered by a plaid comforter.

'Hungry?' Roy asked.

'No,' she said in a pouty voice.

The other times he'd opened the trunk, once every hour after leaving Santa Monica, she'd neither spoken nor moved. In fact, she hadn't said a word since last night in the bathroom.

'So, you're not crackers after all.' He pulled the comforter. Joni tried to hold on to it, but couldn't. It jerked out of her hands.

She curled herself more tightly.

'Climb out of there,' Roy said.

'No.'

'Do it, or I'll hurt you.'

'No.'

He reached under her pleated skirt and pinched her thigh. She started to cry. 'What'd I tell you? Now, get out of there.'

On hands and knees, she climbed over the edge of the trunk, and lowered herself to the ground.

Rou shut the trunk. He took the girl's hand. 'We're gonna have a nice camp-out,' he said.

He climbed the slope, pulling Joni behind him. From her struggles and cries, he knew the undergrowth was punishing her bare legs. 'Do you want me to carry you?' he asked.

'No.'

'I'll carry you piggyback, and the bushes won't hurt.'

'I don't want you to. You're bad.'

'I'm not bad.'

'Yes you are. I know what you did.'

'I didn't do anything.'

'You . . .'

'What?'

'You . . .' And suddenly she was making a loud, grating, 'Whaaaaa!' like a baby.

Roy muttered, 'Shit.'

Noisy sobs sometimes interrupted the droning wail, but it would only start again. There was no sign of a let-up. Not until Roy backhanded her cheek. That stopped the bawling. Only stifled sobs remained.

'Sit down,' Roy ordered when they reached the campsite.

Joni dropped to the mummy bag and hugged her knees to her chest. She rocked back and forth on her rump, sniffing.

Roy broke sticks across his knees and built up the fire. When it was high and snapping, he sat down beside Joni. 'This is pretty nice, huh?'

'No.'

'Have you ever been camping before?'

She shook her head.

'Know what I've got in here?' He lifted the white McDonald's sack towards her face. She turned away quickly, but not before Roy saw the craving in her eyes. He sniffed the sack. The aroma of french fries was overwhelming. He reached in, touched the fries, and pulled one out.

'Look what I've got here,' he said.

He held it high, wiggling it like a pale worm. 'It's all yours. Open up.'

She pressed her lips tight and shook her head.

'Suit yourself.' Roy tipped back his head, opened his mouth wide, and dropped it in. It tasted very salty.

He took a can of beer from the pack. The can was dry and warm. He remembered how cold the cans had felt when he took them out of Karen's refrigerator, how they'd left his hands wet. Well, warm beer was better than no beer. When he opened the can, beer sprayed Joni. She flinched, but didn't bother to dry her face. Roy drank, washing the saltiness out of his mouth.

'Have a french fry,' he said, and offered her another one. 'No? Okay.' He ate it. He took the entire bag of fries out of the larger sack. 'There's a Big Mac in here. It's for you.' He chewed the fries, and washed them down. 'I'm not gonna eat it. It's yours.'

'I don't want it.'

'Sure you do.'

'I don't.'

'I bought it for you. You're going to eat it.'

'You're not my father.'

Dangerous territory. He didn't want her bawling again. 'Suit yourself. It's yours, if you want it.'

'Well, I don't. You probably poisoned it.'

'I didn't poison nothing.' He ate more fries, drank more beer. He finished the fries and the beer at the same time. He tossed the oily bag into the fire, and watched the flames take it. Then he got himself another beer. This time he shook the can and aimed it towards Joni, intentionally shooting the spray into her face. She bit her lower lip. Beer dripped from her nose and chin. Roy laughed. 'You should see yourself.'

He took the remaining Big Mac out of the sack and unwrapped it. 'Want it?'

'No.'

He raised it. He opened his mouth wide. Joni's eyes flashed towards it, then away. 'You do want it.'

She shook her head.

'Yes you do. Here.' He held it towards her face. She tightened her lips. 'Open wide.'

Again, she shook her head.

Roy brushed the burger against her closed mouth, leaving a wet trail of juice and dressing. Then he lowered it and waited to see her tongue sneak out.

Her mouth stayed shut.

'Come on, open up.' Again, he rubbed the burger on her closed mouth. 'Do what I say.'

'Mmmm-mmm.'

Roy put down his beer can. He got to his knees.

'Eat, Joni.'

She shook her head.

With his left hand, Roy pinched her nostrils shut and pushed her backward. He held her down tightly against the sleeping bag. For along time, she kept her mouth shut. Finally, with a gasp, she opened up. Roy stuffed in the hamburger: twisting it, breaking it, mashing it into her mouth and chin and nose. When she started to choke, he let go. He flung the remains of the hamburger towards the trees.

Joni sat up, coughing. Her fingers scooped wads of beef and bun out of her mouth.

'Don't get crap on the sleeping bag,' Roy warned. He shoved her forward.

On hands and knees, head close to the fire, she coughed and spit.

Roy watched the rear of her short, pleated skirt, and remembered dressing her that morning. He'd chosen a fresh white blouse, and green skirt. Joni, on the bed, had neither struggled nor cooperated. It had been like dressing a doll. Only different. This doll had real parts, and he'd enjoyed the feel of them. He hadn't put underwear on her. He liked the idea of nakedness under the skirt.

The choking had stopped, but Joni stayed there on her hands and knees, crying.

Roy patted the back of her leg. His touch made her go rigid. He slid his hand up and down, enjoying the curve of the leg and the cool smoothness of the skin. He moved his hand higher. She turned and knocked it away.

Grabbing her arm, Roy pulled her to him. Her mouth was dripping. He wiped it dry with his handkerchief, and threw the handkerchief into the fire.

She hit at his hands as he unbuttoned her blouse. He ignored it. Then she hit his nose. That hurt. He grabbed her hair and twisted it tightly so the pain made her gasp. He kept hold of the hair. She didn't srike him again. When the blouse was off, he let her go. She hugged herself, shivering, while he folded the blouse and set it inside the pack.

'Cold?'

She said nothing.

Roy crawled behind her. He stroked her shoulders and back. He unbuttoned her skirt and lowered its zipper.

'Stand up.'

She shook her head.

Roy pinched her back. 'Stand up.'

She did. Roy pulled the skirt down.

'Keep standing.'

'I'm cold,' she murmured.

'Stand closer to the fire.'

She seemed reluctant to step off the smooth nylon cover of the sleeping bag, but she did. She moved close to the dwindling fire.

'Put more wood on it, if you want.'

He watched her bend down, lift sticks from the pile, and toss them on to the fire. He watched the flames rise. He watched the fluttering orange glow they cast on her skin. He watched her crouch down close to the fire, giving him only a side view of her body.

He unlaced his hiking boots. Pivattas. Bob had good taste in camping gear. He pulled off the boots.

'Stand on the other side,' he said. 'Facing me.'

That's when she ran.

Roy slid up his cuff, pulled his knife. Flipping it, he caught the blade between his thumb and forefinger. He hurled the knife. It whipped end over end, its blade flashing firelight.

The girl almost reached the dark border of the clearing when the knife hit her. Roy heard the thud of its impact. He heard the girl's startled gasp and saw her tumble forward.

Roy took his time pulling on his boots. He didn't bother lacing or tying them. He simply tucked the loose lace ends under the tongues, and got to his feet.

Twigs and pine needles crushed under his soles as he walked towards the sprawled, white body of the girl.

Chapter Eleven

1.

A quiet knocking on the door woke Donna. Raising her face from the pillow, she saw that the window was wrong: off to the side instead of directly over the bed. Strange room. Still dark outside. Somebody knocking. Fear made an uneasy flutter in her belly.

Then she recognized the room, and remembered.

Jud. It must be Jud.

She rolled out of bed. Cold. No time, in the darkness, to find her robe. She stepped quickly to the door and opened it a crack.

Larry stood there in striped pyjamas, hugging himself against the chilly wind.

'What is it?' she whispered, alarm knotting her stomach.

'Judge. He's back. He's been hurt.'

She glanced over her shoulder at Sandy's bed, and decided not to wake the girl. Twisting the handle button, she locked the door. She stepped out, pulled the door shut, and made sure it was secure.

Following Larry across the parking area, she felt the cold breeze and the sway of her breasts inside her nightgown as if she were naked. It didn't matter. Only Jud mattered. Besides, she could borrow something over there to put on.

'How bad is he?' she asked.

'The beast got him.'

'Oh my God!' She remembered the wax figures, shredded and bloody. But he couldn't be like that. Not Jud. He's hurt, but not dead. He'll be fine.

Larry opened the door of Cabin 12. A lamp was on between the beds, but both beds were empty. One had obviously not been slept in. Donna surveyed the room. 'Where is he?'

Larry shut the door and locked it.

'Larry?'

She saw how he looked down her body as if surprised and distracted by the way it showed through the nightgown.

'He isn't here,' Donna said.

'No.'

'If you think you can . . .'

'What?' Larry asked, and looked up from her breasts. His eyes were vague.

'I'm leaving.'

'Wait. Why? I'm sorry if I embarrassed you. I . . . I was just . . .'

'I know what you were just doing. You just thought you'd use Jud as a pretext to lure me over here so you could . . .'

'Oh heavens no. Good heavens.' He laughed nervously. 'Judge asked me to get you.'

'Well, where *is* he?'

'Over here.'

She followed him across the room.

'Judge didn't want to leave blood on the bed, you see.'

He opened the bathroom door. Donna saw a pile of clothes on the floor. Then she saw Jud sitting on the empty tub. Blood sheathed his back and stained the rear of his Jockey shorts. He finished taping a wide bandage on to his thigh.

'That takes care of that,' he said, and looked up at Donna.

She dropped to her knees, leaned over the side of the tub, and kissed him. She pushed a hand through his damp hair.

'You look awful,' she said.

'You should've seen me before I showered.'

'Do you always shower in your shorts?'

'I didn't want to shock you.'

'I see.' She kissed him again, longer this time, taking pleasure in the warm spread of desire through her loins, and wishing Larry would go away.

'I wouldn't spend all night smooching,' Larry said. 'After all, the man *is* bleeding.'

'Would you like to bandage my shoulder?' Jud asked her.

'Sure.'

'Larry's too squeamish.'

'Blood nauseates me,' Larry said, and left the bathroom.

When Donna squeezed a washcloth above the shoulder wounds, water spilled down, rinsing off blood. 'The *beast* did that?'

'Something did,' he told her.

'They look like claw marks.'

'That's how they feel, too.'

She patted them gently with the washcloth.

'Pour on some hydrogen peroxide,' Jud said. 'It's probably by your knees.'

She let it spill over his cuts, fizzing and foaming. Then, with a large gauze pad from the first-aid kit on the toilet lid, she covered the wounds. 'You sure come prepared,' she said, taping the pad in place.

'Mm-hmmm.'

'Any place else need fixing?'

'That should do it. Thank you.'

'Now let's clean you up. Can you keep your leg dry, if we run water?'

'If it isn't too deep.'

She plugged the drain and turned on the water. With his knee up, Jud kept his thigh bandage above the rising water level. Donna shut off the faucets, and began to scrub his back with a soapy washcloth.

'Did you go into the house?' she asked.

He nodded.

'Boy, that's the height of something.'

'You don't approve?'

'You might've been killed.'

'I came fairly close.'

'How did you get away?'

'I threw gas on him. I guess he was afraid he'd go up in flames.'

Jud's back was clean and slick. Leaning over the side of the tub, she kissed it. The skin made her mouth wet. All done,' she said.

'Thank you, ma'am. Could you hand me a towel?'

She gave him one, and watched him press it against his upper leg, to keep water from running on to the bandage as he stood.

'I'll be out in a minute,' he said, climbing from the tub.

'Will you?' she asked, smiling at him and trying to look as if she didn't know he was asking her to leave the bathroom.

'Oh, you prefer to stay?'

She nodded. Reaching behind her, she pulled the door shut. Its handle made a snapping sound as she locked it.

'This isn't the most comfortable place in the world,' Jud said.

'It's fine with me.'

Hands brushing her shoulders, Jud slipped the straps of her night-gown down. She let the nightgown fall. The effect on him was immediate. Dropping to one knee, Donna freed the erect penis from his shorts and tugged the shorts down his legs. Then she stood naked in front of him. First, his eyes caressed her. Then his hands traced the curves of her shoulders, the slopes of her breasts. He pulled her against him, the stiff penis prodding her belly.

As they kissed, Donna's hands explored the dips and rises of his back, the firm globes of his buttocks. She moved a hand to the front, and fingered his scrotum, the long smooth shaft of his penis. She felt his fingers down low between her legs, and moaned as they stroked.

Jud kicked the pile of clothes aside. He spread two bathtowels on the floor, and Donna lay back on them, knees high and parted. Jud knelt over her.

She felt the light touch of his tongue, first on one nipple, then on the other. Then came the slippery pushing. He went deep inside her.

Gasping through her open mouth, she tried to stay quiet. Didn't want Larry to hear. But her breath was coming louder now, and she couldn't help the trembling sound of it. Then she no longer cared. There was only Jud on top of her, inside her, filling her, stroking her to an unbearable urgency that tightened and tightened and finally broke. He muffled her outcry with his mouth.

2.

'For heaven's sake, what took you so long?' Larry asked, looking up at them from the television.

'I thought it was rather quick,' Donna said, smiling.

Jud, wearing only a towel and his bandages, took a robe from the room's closet. He put it on and removed the towel.

'So,' Larry said. 'Now that we're both here and you're nicely patched up, would you be good enough to tell us what happened to you?'

'Do you want to stay?' Jud asked Donna.

'I want to know,' she said. 'I'm chilly, though. May I?'

'Help yourself.'

She pulled back the covers of the bed that had not been slept in. She sat on it, propped the pillow against its headboard, and leaned back. 'All set,' she said, and pulled the blankets shoulder high.

Jud told them what had happened: He told of watching the house from the hillside, of seeing the woman enter, of following her inside, of finding the gasoline can on the stairway.

'Ah,' Larry said. 'Good woman. She was going to reduce the filthy place to ashes.'

'I wonder why she waited so long,' said Donna.

'Could be a lot of things. She probably left town after the killings, to bury her husband and boy. Do you know where they're from?' he asked Larry.

'Roseville, out near Sacramento.'

'It'd only take a few days to bury them and get back here. What was she doing the rest of the time?'

'Trying to figure out how to take her revenge, maybe. Then planning for it, making preparations. When I left there tonight, I used a hole under the fence. I think she probably dug that hole, herself. Once her preparations were made, she probably had to work herself up to actually getting in there and doing the job.'

Larry frowned. 'Why, for heaven's sake, did you try to stop her?'

'I didn't go inside to stop her. I went in to find out who she was, and what she was up to. Until I heard the scream.'

'Oh my God.' Donna could feel a chill, in spite of the covers. 'How badly was she hurt?'

'She was dead.'

'The same as the others?' Larry asked.

'The same as the gal in the parlour. Ethel? This one was in fairly much the same shape, if the wax figure was accurate. I gave her a close look, after the . . . killer . . . got away.'

'Could you tell if she'd been sexually molested?' Larry asked.

Jud nodded. 'It was fairly obvious.'

The thought of it made Donna press her legs tightly together. She became aware that she could still feel Jud inside her, as if he had left an imprint. Her fear and repulsion subsided. She wondered, for a moment, how she might arrange to be alone with him again.

'I knew she'd been molested,' said Larry. 'The beast . . . that's its motive. Sexual gratification. Of course, I should be glad, I suppose. That's what saved my life. The creature was more interested in satiating its lust with Tommy . . .'

'I don't think sex is the main thing.'

'Oh?' Larry sounded sceptical.

'Let me give you my theory. I think this beast is a man.'

'Then your theory's shit.'

'Just listen. It's a man in a costume. The costume has claws.'

'No.'

'Listen, damn it. You too, Donna, and see what you think. The original killings, the Thorn lady's sister and kids, were done by Gus Goucher, the man they hanged.'

'No,' Larry said.

'Why not?'

'They were torn apart with claws.'

'According to whom?'

'According to morgue photos?'

'Have you seen those photos?'

'No, but Maggie Kutch has.'

'If you believe her. Who has possession of the photos?'

'Maggie, I suppose.'

'Maybe we can get a look at them.'

'I rather doubt it.'

'Okay, we'll let that go for the time being. It's not that important. Gus Goucher's jury must've seen the photos, must've heard testimony . . .'

'According to the old newspaper accounts, they did.'

'And what the jury heard was sufficient for them to condemn the man.'

'Granted.'

'We ought to check this, but I have the impression that, until the Kutch murders thirty years later, Goucher was pretty much accepted as being the Thorn killer.'

'It was made to look like he was. They needed a scapegoat.'

'No. They needed a suspect. He was a likely one. And he was, quite possibly, the guilty one.'

'They hanged Goucher,' Donna said. 'So he certainly wasn't responsible for the attack on Maggie Kutch and her family.'

'In a way, he might have been. Look at what Maggie did after the killings. She moved out of the house, took in Wick Hapson, and opened Beast House for tours. I think she and Wick decided they'd be happier without Mr Kutch, killed him using an MO similar to the Thorn murders, and cooked up this business about a beast to cover themselves. When they saw how much interest there was in this fictional beast of theirs, they decided to profit from it by opening the house for tours.'

Larry shook his head and said nothing.

'One thing,' Donna said. 'I can't see a woman murdering her own children.'

'That part threw me, too. It still throws me, in fact. For their beast story to hold up, though, the kids had to go.'

'She wouldn't do it. No mother could do that.'

'Let's say it's unlikely,' Jud corrected. 'Mothers have been known to murder their own children. What's more likely, though, is that Wick took care of the kids.'

'Your theory is ridiculous,' Larry said.

'Why?'

'Because there is a beast in that house.'

'The beast is a rubber suit with claws.'

'No.'

Donna frowned. 'Do you think it was Wick Hapson tonight?'

'If it was Wick, he's damn strong for a man his age.'

'Axel?'

'It can't be Axel. He's too short, too broad in the shoulders, too awkward in his movements.'

'Then who?'

'I don't know.'

'It's the beast,' Larry explained. 'It's not a man in a rubber suit, it's a beast!'

'Just tell us why you're so sure.'

'I know.'

'How?'

'I know. The beast is not human.'

'Will you believe me when I show you its costume?'

Smiling strangely, Larry nodded. 'Of course. You do that. You show me its costume, and I'll believe.'

'How's tomorrow night?'

'Tomorrow night will . . .' He was silenced by a knocking on the door.

3.

Donna watched Jud cross to the door and open it. 'Well hello,' he said.

'Is my mother here?'

'Sure she is. Come on in.'

Sandy, hair rumpled from sleep and her blue robe a bit too small on her, stepped into the room. When her eyes met Donna's, Sandy sighed with exaggerated relief. 'So there you are. What are you doing in bed?'

'Keeping warm. What are you doing *out* of bed?'

'You were gone.'

'Just for a few minutes.' She looked at Jud. 'I guess I'd better get back now.' She climbed out of bed, and moved with Sandy towards the door. Jud opened it for them. She wanted to kiss him good night, wanted to hold him tightly, feeling his strength and warmth against her body. Not in front of Sandy, though. Not in front of Larry.

'See you in the morning,' she said.

'I'll walk you back.'

'That isn't necessary.'

'Sure it is.'

He walked beside Donna, not touching her. Sandy ran ahead of them. She opened the door and waited.

'You go on in,' Donna told her. 'I'll just be a second.'

'I'll wait.'

'Shut the door, honey.'

The girl obeyed.

Standing against the door, Donna held out her arms to Jud. He stepped close and embraced her. He smelled faintly of soap. 'Cold out here,' she said. 'You're so warm.'

'This morning, you told Larry you're not married.'

'Divorced,' she said. 'How about you?'

'I've never married.'

'Hasn't the right girl come along?' she asked.

'There've been a few "right" ones along the way, I guess. My line of work, though . . . it's too chancy. I didn't want to inflict that kind of life on anyone.'

'What line of work is it?'

'I kill beasts.'

She smiled. 'Is that so?'

'Yep.' He kissed her. 'Good night, now.'

Chapter Twelve

1.

A frightened outcry startled Jud awake. He looked through the darkness at Larry. 'You all right?'

'No!' The man sat forward and hugged his knees against his chest. 'No. I'll never be all right. Never!' And he began to cry.

'Once this thing is settled,' Jud said, 'you'll be fine.'

'It'll never be settled. *You* don't even believe there is a beast. A lot of good you are.'

'Whatever it is, I'll kill it.'

'Will you?'

'That's what you're paying me for.'

'Will you cut off its head for me?'

'None of that.'

'I want you to. I want you to cut off its head, and its cock, and . . .'

'Knock that off, will you? I'll kill it. Nothing else. None of that dismemberment shit. I've seen enough of that.'

'You have?' The voice in the darkness sounded surprised and interested.'

'I did some work in Africa. Saw a lot of heads lopped off. One fellow kept them in his freezer, and liked to shout at them.'

Jud heard quiet laughter from the other bed. The laughter had a strange sound that made him nervous. 'Maybe I ought to take you back to Tiburon tomorrow. I can finish the job alone.'

'Oh no. No you don't.'

'We might both be better off, Larry.'

'I've got to be here when you kill the beast. I've got to see it die.'

2.

At six o'clock, Jud's alarm clock woke him up. The alarm didn't seem to disturb Larry. Climbing from bed, Jud stood on the cool floor and removed his leg bandage. The four parallel lacerations were dry, dark marks about three inches in length. They hurt, but they looked as if they would heal without much problem. He went into the bathroom, dropped the blood-sodden bandage on top of his clothes heap, and put a new bandage on his leg. In the mirror, he checked his shoulder bandage. Some blood showed through, but it looked dry. Maybe later he could get Larry or Donna to change it.

He washed up. After he dressed in clean clothes, his suitcase was nearly empty. He tossed its few remaining contents on to the bed, and took the suitcase into the bathroom. There, he piled his torn, bloody clothes into it. He dropped the old bandage in and latched the suitcase. Then he carried it outside.

The morning was quiet, as if nothing were awake yet except a few birds. He glanced at Cabin 9. Donna would be in there, probably asleep. It was a beautiful morning, and he wanted her to be with him. But he wouldn't try to wake her.

He put the suitcase into the trunk of his car and quietly shut the trunk. Then he returned to his cabin. With a washcloth and bar of soap, he carefully scrubbed up every visible trace of blood in the bathroom. The white towels looked okay. So did the other washcloth. The one in his hand was pink with blood.

He peered into the bathroom wastebasket. Its plastic lining held bits of tape and gauze, bandage wrappings, bloody toilet paper. He dropped the dirty washcloth into it and removed the lining.

He carried his first-aid kit and the garbage bag out to his car. Nobody around. He put them in the trunk.

Then, done with the clean-up, he sat on the cabin step and lit a cigar. It tasted fine, the flavour of its smoke blending with the scent of fresh, piny air.

He leaned back, propping his elbows on the stair above him, and grinned. In spite of his wounds, he felt exceptionally fine.

When he was done with the cigar, he drove down Front Street. The town was quiet. He slowed to give a shaggy brown dog time to amble out of his way. A blue-and-white police car was parked in front of Sarah's Diner. The only moving car he saw was a Porsche that approached slowly, as if struggling to stay within a reasonable proximity to the town's thirty-mile-per-hour speed limit.

To his left, Beast House looked barren. To his right, nothing stirred on the property of the house without windows. He slowed when he could see the outcropping of rocks on the hillside behind Beast House. He would have to get up there soon and retrieve his equipment.

But not now.

Beyond town, he made a U-turn and came back. He passed the two houses. On the next block, he parked in front of a closed barber shop. He walked to the Beast House ticket booth.

On its walls, newspaper clippings were framed in glass. Some told of the murders. Others focused on the tours. He read several of the articles. He wanted to read them all, but that would have taken too long. He didn't want to draw too much attention to himself.

He gazed up at the clock face above the ticket window. Then he checked his watch. The first tour wouldn't start for nearly three hours, at ten o'clock.

Stuffing his hands into his front trouser pockets, he strolled farther down the sidewalk. He paused to look at the weathered Victorian house, then started up again, trying his best to look like a tourist with time on his hands and a preference for morning walks.

When he passed the bend, he stepped into the trees and made his way back.

Several yards from the fence, he found an opening that gave him a view of the front of Beast House, but offered good concealment.

Crouching, he began to wait.

3.

Just after nine-thirty, a camper van parked on Front Street. A man climbed out, checked the ticket booth, and returned to the van. Out came a woman and three children. Soon a young couple arrived in a VW.

Jud made his way to the road, and walked up to the ticket booth. It was still deserted.

So was the house, unless someone had entered before Jud began his surveillance: nobody had gone in the front while he'd been watching.

As Jud waited near the ticket booth, more people arrived. He watched the windowless house across the street. Its door was shut. The green pick-up truck was still parked in front of the garage.

Finally, ten minutes before the tour was to start, Jud saw Maggie and Wick leave the house. Braced against Wick, she carried her cane but didn't use it. It took them a long time to reach Front Street. They waited for a station wagon to pass, then they crossed.

Wick helped her up the curb, and let go of her arm. She leaned heavily on her cane. 'Welcome to Beast House,' she called out, her voice low but clear. 'My name's Maggie Kutch, and I own it. You may purchase your tickets from my assistant.' She swung her cane towards the ticket booth. Wick was unlocking its door. 'The tickets run four dollars per adult, only two dollars per child under twelve for the experience of a lifetime.'

The people had listened, quiet and motionless. When Maggie stopped talking, those who were not in line already headed for the ticket booth.

Maggie unlocked the turnstile and pushed through it.

'Back for seconds, eh?' Wick asked when Jud reached the ticket window.

'I can't seem to stay away.' He slid a five-dollar bill under the glass.

'Guess your lady friend didn't show up.'

'Who's that?'

'Your lady friend. The gal that cavorted in the street there, showing off her titties.' Wick gave him the ticket and change.

'I wonder where she is,' Jud said.

'More 'n likely in the loony bin.' Wick chuckled, showing his crooked brown teeth.

Jud went through the turnstile. When the entire group was gathered on the walkway, Maggie began to speak.

'I started showing my house to visitors away back in '31, right after the beast struck down my husband and three darling children. You may be asking yourselves why a woman'd want to take people through her house, when it was the scene of such personal tragedy. Well, the answer's easy: m-o-n-e-y.'

A few of the people laughed uneasily.

Maggie limped up the walkway to the foot of the porch stairs. She pointed her cane upward at the balcony. 'Here's where they lynched Gus Goucher.'

Jud listened carefully to the story of Gus Goucher, checking each detail against his theory that the man had, indeed, been guilty. Nothing she said contradicted his view. He followed Maggie up the porch steps. She told of the old door being shot open by Officer Jenson. She pointed out the monkey-paw knocker. Then she unlocked the door and pushed it open.

The pungent odour of gasoline filled Jud's nostrils.

'I must ask your forgiveness for the smell,' Maggie said, entering. 'My son spilled gas yesterday. It won't be so bad, once we're away from the stairs.'

Jud stepped inside.

'You can see how it stained the carpeting there.'

He manoeuvred around others in the group until he had a clear view of the stairway. Nothing. Where Mary's body should have been, there was only a dark stain. All the blood had been nicely scrubbed before someone doused the carpet with gasoline.

Chapter Thirteen

1.

Sunlight on his face woke Roy. He lifted his head off his rolled jeans, and propped himself up with his elbows. The campfire was out. A sparrow, near the campfire remains, was plucking bread from a clump that Joni had probably spit out. The backpack stood upright, closed and safe.

In daylight, the clearing didn't seem nearly as secluded as it had in the dark. The trees surrounding it were farther apart, the spaces between them offering a wider view than he'd thought. Worse, a hillside over-looked the area.

As he looked up at the hillside, he heard an engine. He saw the blue roof of a car rush by.

'Oh shit,' he muttered.

He unzipped the side of the mummy bag and crawled out. Standing, he unrolled his jeans. He reached into them and pulled out his Jockey shorts. Balancing on one foot, then the other, he stepped into them.

He heard voices.

'Oh shit oh shit.'

He sat down quickly on the mummy bag and started pulling on his jeans.

Two hikers, a young couple, came striding along the hillside just above his camp. They wore soft felt hats, like the ones he'd seen in Karen and Bob's closet.

They came closer and closer.

Lifting his rump, he pulled up his jeans. Zipped them. Buckled them. The couple stepped into the clearing.

He couldn't believe it! The fucking trail ran right past his mummy bag!

'Oh hello,' said the man of the pair. He seemed pleasantly surprised to meet Roy.

'Hi,' said the girl with him. She seemed no older than eighteen.

'Hello,' Roy answered. 'You almost caught me with my pants down.'

The girl grinned. She had a big mouth for smiling, and huge teeth. Also huge breasts. They did a lot of swinging inside her tight, green tank top. She wore white shorts. Her legs looked tanned and powerful.

The man pulled a briar pipe from a pocket of his shorts. 'You camped smack in the middle of the trail,' he said, as if he found it amusing.

'I didn't want to get lost.'

He slipped a leather pouch out of his rear pocket and started filling his pipe. 'What'd you use for water?'

'I did without.'

'There's a public campground about a mile that way.' He pointed his pipe stem at the hill. 'Faucets there, toilets.'

'That's good to know. Maybe I'll head up that way.'

He lit a match and sucked its flame down into his pipe. 'Illegal camping here, you know.'

'I didn't know that.'

'Yep. Anywhere but the public sites.'

'I can't stand those places,' Roy said. 'They're too crowded. I'd rather stay home.'

'They are awful,' agreed the girl.

'Yep,' the man said, and puffed.

'Where are you headed?' Roy asked, hoping to get them on their way.

'Stinson Beach,' said the man.

'How far's that?'

'We plan to get there by noon.'

'Well,' Roy said, 'have a good hike.'

'That's some nice equipment you've got. Where'd you outfit yourself?'

'I'm from LA,' he said.

'That so? Been over to Kelty's in Glendale?'

'That's where I bought most of my stuff.'

'I've been there. Bought my boots there, in fact. Back about six years ago.' He looked down fondly at them.

'Who's that in your sleeping bag?' the girl asked.

Roy's stomach clenched. He thought about his knife. It was rolled inside his shirt, within easy reach of his right hand.

'It's my wife,' he said.

The man grinned, gripping the pipe in his teeth. 'You both fit in the same bag?'

'It's cosy that way,' Roy said.

'Do you have room to manoeuvre?' asked the man.

'Enough.'

The man laughed. 'We ought to try that, huh, Jack?'

Jack, the girl, didn't look amused.

'Our bags zip together,' the man. 'You ought to try it that way. Gives a lot more room.'

'What's wrong with her?' Jack asked.

'Nothing, why? 'Cause she doesn't come out? She's a pretty heavy sleeper.'

'Can she breathe in there?' asked the man.

'Sure. She always sleeps that way. Far down like that. She doesn't like her head getting cold.'

'Yeah?' The girl named Jack looked sceptical.

'Well, we'd better be off,' said the man.

'Have a nice hike,' Roy told him.

'You too.'

They walked past him. He watched until they disappeared into the trees, then he unrolled his shirt. He raised his pant leg, and slipped the knife into the sheath taped to his calf. Then he put on his shirt.

He took Joni's blouse and skirt out of the pack, and knelt at the head of the mummy bag. He scanned the trees. Nobody around.

Joni groaned as he pulled her out by the arm. She opened one eye, and closed it again. Roy arranged her face-up on top of the bag.

The sight of her sunlit, naked body excited him.

Not now.

Shit, not now.

He pulled the dress up her legs, and fastened it. Then he raised her to a sitting position, and worked the blouse up her arms. He let her fall back. Quickly, he buttoned her blouse.

'Wake up,' he said. He slapped her.

Her eyes squeezed tight at the sudden pain, then fluttered open.
'Get up.'

Slowly, she rolled over and got to her knees. Her hair was bloody and matted to the back of her head where the knife hilt had bludgeoned her.

Breaking camp seemed to take a long time. While he worked, he watched Joni closely. He listened for voices. He kept glancing up the hillside at the trail and the road. Finally, everything was loaded in the pack. He swung it to his shoulders, grabbed Joni's hand, and led her down to the lower road.

A Ford van passed.

He waved and smiled.

When the road was deserted again, he opened the Pontiac's trunk. 'Climb in, honey.'

2.

As Roy drove, he heard radio reports about a house fire and double murder in Santa Monica. They didn't give the victims' names, but mentioned a missing eight-year-old girl. He heard nothing about Karen and Bob Marston.

That worried him.

He went over it in his mind: how Karen had spilled the beans about Malcasa Point; how surprised she was when, instead of leaving, he gagged her and really got down to business until she died; how he had waited, hidden in the hall, for Bob to come home; the way Bob shook his head and moaned when he stepped into the bedroom and saw his wife hanging on the door; the sound of Bob's head splitting under the ax; the candle placed carefully in a circle of paper wads, just the way he'd done it at the other place.

Maybe a visitor dropped by and stopped the fire.

Maybe, somehow, the candle blew out.

If the candle blew out, maybe the bodies hadn't been discovered yet.

He couldn't take that chance. He'd better just act as if the car is hot, and get himself a new one.

He swung it on to a dirt turn-out, the tyres flinging up clouds of yellow dust. He got out, opened the hood, and leaned under it, waiting.

Soon he heard the sound of an approaching car. He stayed under the hood and reached towards the fan belt. The car sped past. It kept going. He tried the same tactic with two more cars. Neither stopped.

The next time he heard an engine, he leaned under the hood until the car was close, then stood up and made a frustrated face, and waved. The driver shook his head. His face said, 'Not a chance, buddy.'

Roy yelled, 'Fuck you, too!'

When the next car came, he simply stuck out his thumb. He saw the woman passenger shake her head at the driver. The car kept going. So did the next.

He slammed the hood.

As he stepped to the car's rear, a van approached. A sunburst was painted on its front. The driver was a woman with straight, black hair. She wore a headband, and a leather vest. He saw her right arm point him out. He waved. He liked the looks of her.

But he didn't like the looks of the man who called out the passenger window. 'Car trouble?' The man's voice was raspy. He wore a faded, sweat-stained cowboy hat, sunglasses, and a black, shaggy moustache. His blue Levi's jacket was sleeveless. His upper arm bore the tattoo of a dripping stiletto.

'No trouble,' Roy called. 'I just stopped to take a leak.'

'Power to you.' The man saluted him with a clenched fist, and the van pulled away.

Roy waited until it was out of sight, then opened the trunk. Joni looked up at him. The hot dog he'd bought at Stinson Beach and tossed into the trunk earlier that morning was gone. The can of Pepsi lay open on its side, empty. Must've been tricky, he thought, drinking it in the trunk.

'Climb out,' he said.

He helped her and shut the trunk.

Joni looked around as if wondering where they had stopped, and why. She didn't seem to find the answer. She looked up at Roy.

'We need a new car,' he said. 'You're gonna help us get it.'

He led her along the roadside. When they were fifty or sixty feet from the rear of his car, he told her to lie down in the northbound lane.

Joni shook her head.

Just as well. He really couldn't trust her, anyway. She would probably try to run.

He tried to think of a way to do this without hurting his hand: a rock, a club of wood, or his knife handle would do fine. Maybe too fine. He didn't want to take a chance on killing her. Not yet. So he decided on his hand. Gripping the neck of her blouse, he jerked her forward. As she stumbled towards him, he slammed his right fist against her temple. Her legs went out. He dragged her partway into the road, and set her down. Quickly, he arranged her arms and legs so she looked awkwardly sprawled. Then he returned to his car, ducked into the nearby trees, and waited.

The wait was short.

He grinned, amazed by his good fortune as he watched a black Rolls-Royce round the corner. A man was driving; a woman passenger sat beside him.

The car swerved to miss Joni, then slowed, and pulled behind Roy's Pontiac. The driver stepped out. Leaving the door open, he walked quickly back towards Joni. He was a big man, well over six feet tall, and at least two hundred pounds.

A goddamn football player!

Shit.

The big man knelt beside Joni. He touched her neck, probably trying to find a pulse. The Rolls was about twenty feet from Roy. All the windows were up. The woman, turned away, was looking through the rear window.

The man began to pull off his sports jacket.

Roy lunged from behind the trees. His boots crushed underbrush. The man glanced over his shoulder. The woman began to turn her head. Leaping, Roy's boot thudded on to the hood of the Rolls. The car lurched under his weight. The man was standing. Roy jumped down between the side of the car and the open door. The woman screamed as he thrust himself on to the driver's seat. He pulled the door shut, and locked it a moment before the man arrived.

The screaming woman threw her shoulder towards the passenger door. Roy jerked the neck of her blouse. It ripped, but it stopped her long enough for Roy to grab her hair. He pulled her towards him. Her cheek hit the steering wheel. He forced her head down to his lap, then chopped her neck with the edge of his hand.

The man's face pressed the window, rage in his eyes, fists pounding the glass.

Roy realized that the car was still running. He shifted into reverse and stepped on the gas pedal. The car shot backwards. The big man, staggering after a quick leap aside, looked at him through the tumbling cloud of dust.

He seemed to know.

Roy shifted to drive. As the Rolls sped forward, the man jumped on to the Pontiac's trunk. Roy braced himself. He hit the Pontiac hard. The man's legs flew out. He dropped heavily on to the hood of the Rolls. With a quick shift to reverse, Roy jerked the Rolls backwards and tumbled the man off.

Right off the front.

He sped forward. The car made a satisfying bounce, passing over the man.

Easy as rolling over a log. Roy grinned.

The grin stopped at once.

What if another car comes along?

The woman across his lap was unconscious, maybe dead.

He left the car running, and got out. The man's body lay conveniently close to the rear of the Pontiac. Roy opened its trunk. He didn't want to look closely at the body, much less touch it – not with the way the head had been mashed. But he had no choice. Something made splashy, plopping sounds as he lifted the body. He dropped it into the trunk, and vomited on to it. Then he slammed the trunk shut.

Running back to the girl, he looked down at himself. His shirts and pants were dripping gore. Though he gagged, he kept running. He lifted Joni, smearing her with the dead man's blood, and carried her to the Rolls. He set her down on the back seat. He ran to the Pontiac, grabbed his backpack, and threw it into the Rolls beside Joni. Then he climbed into the front and swung the car on to the road.

3.

Roy drove the Rolls for nearly an hour before he found a side road he liked. It led over bare hills to the left. He was sure it would take him to the ocean, so he turned on to it.

Joni was conscious in the back seat, but so far she had just stayed there, lying on her side, staring forward. The woman in the front seat was dead. Roy didn't like the way her head lay on his lap, but he decided against trying to set her upright: though there was no blood, the struggle for air had left her face hideously contorted. Her skin had a grey-blue tint. If he had her sitting up, people might notice. So he simply accepted the repulsive weight of her head on his lap, just as he accepted the blood on his hands and shirts and pants. He had to accept them, at least until he could find a deserted stretch of shoreline.

This up ahead looked promising.

The road ended a hundred yards from the shore. He parked in the shade. There were no cars in sight. A few cows grazed on the hillside. He got out. Just to the left of the road, the ground slanted down, forming a gorge choked with heavy bushes. A footpath along the edge of the gorge led to a beach.

He would like to get the woman's body into the water, tow it far out, and let it go. But carrying it to the water would be tough. Dangerous, too. Forget it.

He would roll her into the gorge.

Not now, though. Not until he and Joni were cleaned up and ready to leave. In the meantime, he couldn't just leave her in the front seat. Someone might come along.

He thought of the trunk.

Then he got a better idea. Checking once again to be certain he was unobserved, he got out and pulled her across the front seat. Her feet hit the road, knocking off one of her platform shoes. He dragged her in front of the car. There, he stretched her out lengthwise on the dirt shoulder. Her arms and legs were a little stiff, but he managed to straighten them. With her legs together and her arms flat against her sides, Roy went back to the car.

He drove slowly forward.

Over the top of the black hood, he watched as the car seemed to swallow her.

He stopped and climbed out. He had to get down on his hands and knees to see her in the darkness beneath the car.

A great hiding place.

He pulled Joni out of the back seat. Together, they walked down the footpath to the beach.

4.

The water, cold at first, quickly lost the shock of its chill and felt almost warm to Roy. Joni still stood on the shore. Only the largest waves reached far enough to wash over her feet.

Roy took off his shirt. He scrubbed the cloth with his knuckles, trying to wash it. Waves caught him, lifted him, turned him. When they carried him too far from Joni, he swam closer. He held up his blue shirt and studied it in the sunlight. If blood remained on it, which he didn't doubt, at least the stains were barely noticeable.

'Come on in, Joni, and wash up.'

She shook her head. She stepped backwards, farther from the water, and sat down on the sand.

'You know what happens,' Roy called, 'when you don't do like I say.'

She looked down the beach, where a point of rocks jutted into the water. Breakers smashed against the rocks, splashing white froth high. She looked up in the beach. In that direction, the shoreline curved inward and disappeared. 'Don't try it,' Roy yelled, wading forwards.

She stood up and walked into the water. It wound around her ankles. She kept moving. A high wave came, wetting her to the waist, sticking the pleated skirt to her skin. She stopped there. The water receded. Bending, she splashed it on to the bloodstains on her blouse. She rubbed the stains. A wave came, knocking her backwards. She fell, and the white water swirled over her head.

Roy went to her. He lifted her. He kissed her forehead. Then, wrapping his hand in his shirt, he scrubbed the bloodstains on her blouse. They grew faint, but wouldn't vanish altogether. Finally he gave up.

He pulled her deeper into the water, and did his best to wash the blood from her hair. Whenever he touched the sensitive wound left by the knife's hilt, she jerked her head away. Finally her hair was clean enough to suit him. He led her out of the water.

On the beach, he removed her blouse and skirt. He spread them on the sand to dry. Then he took off his own clothes, and spread them next to hers.

They sat down on the sand. It was hot under Roy, almost burning.

'Try to sleep,' he said.

Joni lay back and shut her eyes.

Roy looked at her. Water made tiny points of her eyelashes. Her skin was lightly tanned, except where a two-piece bathing suit had left it pale. Just like a little lady.

Beads of water rolled down her skin, glinting sunlight. He wished he had oil. Suntan oil, or baby oil. He would rub her all over with it. Her skin would be slick and hot.

He lay on his side, and propped himself up on an elbow to look at her. Her eyelids fluttered. She was only pretending to sleep, of course.

She opened her eyes when he touched her.

She turned her head and stared at him. He wondered, briefly, if she looked so sad because of what happened to her parents, or because of what he'd been doing to her.

Not that he gave a shit.

Inching closer, he kissed her on the mouth. His hand began moving down her sun-hot skin.

Chapter Fourteen

1.

'We oughtta be getting it in today, lady. That's all I can tell you. When we get it in, I'll install it.'

'Do you think the car will be ready today?' Donna asked.

'Like I say, depends when the radiator gets here.'

'How late are you open?' she asked.

'Till nine.'

'Can I pick up my car, then?'

'If it's done. Stu'll let you take it. I go off at five, though. Stu's no mechanic. If it doesn't get done by five, it doesn't get done till tomorrow.'

'Thank you.'

She found Sandy nearby, eyeing a vending machine. 'Can I get some potato chips?' the girl asked.

'Well . . .'

'Please? I'm starving.'

'We'll eat pretty soon. Why don't you wait, and have potato chips with your meal?'

'Where can we eat around here?' she asked, leaving the machine behind.

'I'm not sure,' Donna admitted.

'Not that place we went yesterday. It was so gross.'

'Let's try this way.' They started walking south on Front Street.

'When's the car gonna be ready?'

'Who knows?'

'Huh?' Sandy wrinkled her nose. When she unwrinkled it, her huge sunglasses slipped forward. She shoved them into place with a forefinger.

'The guy at the station wasn't up to telling me when it'll be ready. But I have a feeling we'll still be here tomorrow.'

'If Dad doesn't get us first.'

The mention of him jolted Donna. Somehow, after meeting Jud, fears of her ex-husband had been pushed into a dark corner of her mind and forgotten. 'He doesn't know where we are.'

'Aunt Karen does.'

'Tell you what, let's give Aunt Karen a call.' Looking around, she saw a phone booth at the corner of the Chevron station they had just left. They backtracked to it. 'How much are the potato chips?'

'Thirty-five cents.'

She handed Sandy a dollar bill. 'You'll have to get change from the man.'

'You want anything?'

'No thanks. But you go ahead.'

She watched her daughter leave, then she stepped into the telephone booth. Her coins rang inside the machine. She dialled Operator, and asked for the call to be charged to her home phone. When the call went through, she heard the ringing of her sister's phone. It was picked up after the second ring. Donna waited for Karen's voice. She heard only silence.

'Hello?' she finally said.

'So.'

'Bob?' she asked, though the voice didn't sound much like his. 'Bob, is that you?'

'Who is this, please?'

'Who is *this?*'

'Sergeant Morris Woo, Santa Monica Police Department.'

'Oh my God.'

'So. Your business, please, with Mrs Marston?'

'I was just . . . she's my sister. Has something happened to her?'

'Where are you calling from, please?'

How do I know you're a cop? she asked herself. And she answered, I don't. 'I'm calling from Tucson,' she told him.

'So.'

In her mind, she saw him hang up and turn to Roy, grinning that he'd obtained the information so easily. But he didn't hang up.'

'Please, what is your name?'

'Donna Hayes.'

'So. Address and telephone number?'

'What's happened to Karen?'

'Please. Does your sister have relatives in the Los Angeles area?'

'Damn it!'

'So. Mrs Hayes, I regret your sister met with death.'

Met with death?

'She and her husband, Robert Marston, met with death yesterday night. So. If there are relatives . . .'

'Our parents.' She was numb. 'John and Irene Blix.'

'Blix. So, Mrs Hayes, may I have please their address?'

She told him their address and phone number.

'So.'

'They were . . . murdered?'

'Murdered, yes.'

'I think I know who did it.'

'So?'

'What do you mean, *so?* Damn it, I know who killed them!'

'So. You tell me, please.'

'It was my ex-husband. His name is Roy Hayes. He was released yesterday – I mean Saturday. Sometime Saturday.'

'So. Released from what?'

'San Quentin.'

'So.'

'He was in six years for raping our daughter.'

'So.'

'So he must've killed Karen to find out where I am.'

'Did she know, please?'

'Yes, she knew.'

'So. You are in danger. Describe your Roy Hayes, please.'

As she gave the man a description of her ex-husband, she saw Sandy returning with a bag of potato chips. The bag was open. Sandy was pinching chips, one at a time, and pushing them sideways into her mouth.

'So. He drives?'

'Yes, but I don't know what. He may have taken one of Karen's cars. They've got a yellow Volkswagen and a white Pontiac Grand Prix.'

'So. The years?'

'I don't know. She looked at her daughter munching potato chips outside the booth. Turning away, Donna began to cry.

'Please, Mrs Hayes. Are the cars new?'

'The VW, it's a '77. I don't know about the other. A '72, '73.'

'So. Very good, Mrs Hayes. Very good. Now, if I may suggest, call the Tucson police, so, and inform them of your situation. Perhaps an escort to the airport.'

'Airport?'

'So. Your parents are not to be alone during this time of tragedy.'

'No. You're right. I'll get there as soon as I can.'

'So.'

'Thank you, Mr Woo.' She hung up. Sandy knocked on the plastic wall of the booth. Ignoring her, Donna searched her purse for coins. She found them, and made another call.

'Santa Monica Police Department,' said a woman. 'Officer Bleary speaking. May I help you?'

'Do you have a Morris Woo?'

'Just a moment, please.'

Donna heard a telephone ring. It was picked up. 'Homicide,' said the man. 'Detective Harris.'

'Do you have a Morris Woo?'

'He's not in just now. May *I* help you?'

'I talked to a man on the phone.' She sniffed, and rubbed her nose. 'He claimed to be a Sergeant Morris Woo. I just wanted to make sure he's really a police officer.'

'So?'

2.

After a brief, tearful call to give her parents the news, she hung up and left the booth. 'Let's go back to the motel.'

'What's wrong?' Sandy was crying. 'Tell me!'

'Aunt Karen and Uncle Bob. They've been killed.'

'No they haven't!'

'I just talked to a police officer, honey.'

'No!'

'Come on, let's go back to the motel.'

Instead, the girl threw herself against Donna, hugging tightly as she cried.

Chapter Fifteen

1.

When Jud climbed out of his car, he saw Donna sitting on a front step of her cabin and he knew that something was wrong. He went towards her. She saw him, and stood. He took her in his arms, and she began to cry softly, quietly, her back trembling under his hand. Jud stroked the back of her head. Her cheek was wet against his face. He held her for a long time.

Then Donna looked up at him. She sniffed, smiled an apology, and rubbed her face with her sleeves. 'Thanks,' she said.

'Are you okay?'

She nodded, her lips pressed tightly shut. 'Can we go for a walk?' she asked.

'I know a nice place. We'll have to go in the car, though.'

'Before we go, I'd better get registered for tonight.'

'Good idea,' Jud said. 'I'll have to do that, too.'

Together, they went to the motel office. They registered. They then returned to Jud's car. 'Where's Sandy?' he asked.

'Sleeping.'

'She seems to do a lot of that, doesn't she?'

'It's a good way to escape.'

'Is she all right?'

'No. Probably not.'

They climbed into the Chrysler, and Jud drove out to Front Street.

'We saw your car in town this morning,' Donna said in an obvious attempt to change the subject.'

'I took the tour again.'

'You mean they *had* a tour? I would've thought the police . . .'

'The police don't know about the killing, apparently. The body's gone. So's the blood. It looks like somebody did a nice clean-up job.'

'Scrub-a-dub-dub.' Donna met his glance, and frowned. 'That's what Axel does. He's in charge of cleaning the place.'

'Axel's in this thing up to the armpits. So's his mother. They all are. It's a family enterprise. All it takes is a murder, now and again, to keep the tourists coming.'

'If the body's gone, though . . .'

'I think they got nervous, killing someone so close to the other three. Nervous enough to pretend it didn't happen.'

'Why did they kill her – they? Now you've got me believing it. Why did they kill her, if they didn't want the publicity?'

'She was gonna burn the place down.'

'I guess that's a good enough reason. What's your next step? Do you try to find her body?'

'That wouldn't do us much good. What we've gotta find is the man in the monkey suit.'

'Then what?'

'If I have to, I'll kill him.'

'You *intend* to kill him, don't you?'

'I doubt if he'll give me a choice.'

They were silent as they drove past Beast House. After they rounded the bend, Donna said, 'Have you killed very many people?'

'Yes.'

'Do you . . . think about it much?'

He glanced at her, then steered on to the shoulder of the road and stopped. 'You mean, does my conscience bother me?'

'I guess that's what I mean.'

'I never killed a guy who didn't have it coming.'

'Who judges that?'

'Me. I judge him and sentence him.'

'How can you?'

'I hear voices.'

She smiled. 'I'm serious.'

'So am I. I hear a voice. It's usually mine saying, I'd better nail this bastard before he nails me.'

'You're awful.'

He laughed softly. And then he felt a cold tightness inside him. He swallowed. 'Sometimes what I hear are the voices of the dead. People I never knew. People I saw in news photos, or with my own eyes. They say to me, "I'd be alive today if this bastard hadn't cancelled my ticket." Then I look at the living and they say, "That bastard's gonna kill me tomorrow." And then I judge him and then I execute him if I can. I figure I'm paying him back for the dead, and I'm saving a few lives. Maybe this sounds terrible, by my conscience is pretty happy with itself.'

'Do you kill for money?'

'If he's the kind of guy I'm willing to kill, there's always someone who's glad to pay me for it.'

They got out of the car. Jud took Donna's hand and led her across the road. 'Do you mind a work-out?'

'Okay by me.'

They entered the forest. Jud went first, seeking out ways through the tightly grouped pines and around impassable areas of rock or fallen trees. Twice, he stopped to let Donna rest.

'You didn't tell me this was an obstacle course,' she said at one point.

The last few yards were steep, and Jud looked back at Donna. Her face was determined. She backhanded a drop of sweat off the end of her nose. Wet hair clung to her forehead. 'Almost there,' he said, and reached down a hand to her. He pulled her to the top of a dead trunk, then they both hopped down. 'Made it.'

They walked easily along the level crest of the hill and came to a windy clearing.

Donna stretched, spreading her arms. 'Ah, that breeze feels good.'

'You can wait here. I've got to pick up a few things down below.'

'So that's your game!'

She accompanied Jud to the edge of the clearing, when he pointed down to the outcropping. 'I left some equipment in those rocks, he told her.

'That's where you were last night?'

'That's the place.'

'I'll go with you, okay?'

Together, they climbed downhill. Then they made their way up the rocks to the top, where they looked down at the back of Beast House.

'I can't imagine going in that place at night,' Donna said. 'It's bad enough in daylight.'

'I'll climb down and get my gear,' Jud said.

'Fine. I'll wait.'

As Donna sat on a ledge of rock, Jud worked his way down to the recess with its two small pines. His pack and rifle and Starlight seemed just as he had left them last night when he rushed downhill to stop the woman. He put the scope in its case and loaded it into the pack. He strapped the pack shut. Then he slung it on to his shoulders. He picked up the rifle case and climbed to the top.

'Let's go up to the clearing again,' Donna said.

'Sure.'

'I don't much like staring that house in the face.'

'That's actually the back of its head,' Jud told her.

'Whatever.'

They climbed to the grassy clearing. Jud put down his rifle and pack. Donna, stepping close, placed her open hands against his chest and looked up at him. 'Can we talk some more?' she asked.

'Sure.'

'About killing?'

'If you want.'

'What happened today . . .' She lowered her eyes. 'What happened was, I found out my . . . sister . . .' Her voice broke. She turned away. With her back turned, she took a deep breath. Jud put his hands on her shoulders. 'My sister was killed!' she blurted, and broke into tears.

Jud turned her around and held her tightly.

'I *killed* her, Jud. I killed her. I ran away. He wouldn't have done it. He wouldn't have had to. God! I didn't know. I didn't *know!* I killed them. I killed them both!'

2.

After a while, Donna settled down. She stopped talking, and only cried. Jud lowered her to the grass. Sitting against his pack, he held her. Her tears made the front of his shirt wet. Finally she stopped.

'We'd better get back,' she said. 'Sandy. I don't want to leave her alone too long.'

'We'll leave when you tell me what's going on. Who killed your sister, Donna?'

'My ex-husband, Roy Hayes.'

'Why?'

'Partly to get at me, I guess. Mostly, though, to make her tell where I am.'

'Why would he want to know that?'

'He's been in prison. He . . . raped Sandy. She was just six, and he took her out riding on his dirt bike . . . and raped her. He'd done things to me, before. Vicious things.

'I knew they'd let him out, someday. I figured we'd drop everything, and take off. So that's what we did Sunday morning when I found out he was loose.

'It never . . . it just didn't occur to me he'd go to Karen. I don't know what I thought. But I never . . . God, I never thought he'd go to Karen or anyone, and . . . he must've tortured her. God, and it was all because of me!

'We shouldn't have run. We should have stayed. I should have got myself a gun, maybe, and just waited for him to come. But it never even occurred to me. I just thought we'd leave town, and maybe change our name, and everything would work out fine. But it didn't happen that way. And now he knows where we are.'

'Where did your sister live?'

'In Santa Monica.'

'What's that, ten or twelve hours from here?'

'I don't know. Something like that, probably.'

'Do you know when your sister was killed?'

'Sometime last night.'

'Early, late?'

'I don't know.'

'He could be in town right now.'

'I guess so.'

'What does he look like?'

'He's thirty-five, about six-foot-two. Very strong, or he always used to be. He weighed about two-ten.'

'Have you got a picture of him?'

She shook her head. 'I destroyed them all.'

'What colour's his hair?'

'Black. He always wore it short.'

'Anything else about him?'

She shrugged.

Jud got up and helped her to stand. 'Are you convinced,' he asked, 'that running away doesn't work?'

'He convinced me.'

'Then let's go back to the inn and wait for him.'

'What'll we do?'

'If I have to, I'll kill him.'

'I should be the one to handle him.'

'Not a chance. You're stuck with me.'

'I don't want you to kill anyone . . . not for me.'

'I wouldn't be doing it for you. It'd be for myself. And for the voices.'

Chapter Sixteen

1.

'Larry and I have to go out for a while,' Jud said as he walked Donna across the parking lot after lunch. 'I want you and Sandy to stay in our cabin until we get back.'

'Okay.'

No arguments. No questions. Her complete trust gave Jud a good feeling.

He watched her turn to Sandy, who was lagging behind with Larry. Instead of making a rift, yesterday's incident at the beach had created an intimacy between the girl and Larry. During lunch, they had talked like best friends. Jud found their closeness peculiar under the circumstances, but convenient.

'Sandy,' Donna said, 'we'll be spending a while in Jud and Larry's room. Do you want to get your cards, or a book, or something to keep you busy?'

The girl nodded.

'We'll be right out,' Donna said. They went into their cabin, leaving its door open.

Larry, in a quiet voice, said, 'The poor child has been devastated.'

'It's gonna be rough.'

'Rough indeed. She'll be scarred all her life. That miserable brute ought to be shot.'

'He probably will be.'

'I certainly hope so.'

'Tonight, if we're lucky.'

'Tonight?'

'There's a good chance he'll show up sometime today. If he does, I'm going to be there with a gun.'

'What about Beast House?'

'It can wait another day.'

'I suppose you're right, though I *would* feel better if we were finished once and for all with . . .'

'I can't let this guy get his hands on Donna and Sandy. He's hurt them enough, already.'

'Certainly. I'm not suggesting we abandon them. Not at all.'

'Besides, going after the beast tonight would be premature.'

'How so?' Larry asked.

'I want to know more. That's why we're going to visit the Kutch place this afternoon.'

'Beast House?'

'No. The other one. The one without windows.'

2.

As soon as Jud was certain that Donna could handle his rifle without difficulty, he and Larry drove away. He turned right off Front Street, taking the narrow dirt road that led to the beach. In an area sheltered by trees, he parked.

As Jud took his .45 automatic from the trunk, Larry said, 'That, of course, won't stop the beast.'

Jud tucked the automatic under the belt at the back of his pants, and covered it with his shirt tail. 'What makes you think we'll run into the beast? Doesn't it confine its rampages to Beast House?'

'Nevertheless.'

He watched Larry lift a machete out of the trunk. 'Nevertheless what?'

'One never knows, does one?'

Jud shut the trunk. 'You can stay in the car, if you want.'

'No. It's quite all right. I'll come along. I can hardly resist an opportunity to see inside this curious house. And you're right, of course: we should be perfectly safe from the beast.'

Jud checked his wristwatch. 'Okay, the one-o'clock tour should just be staring. Let's go.'

'What about Axel?'

'If he's home, I'll take care of him. You just stick close beside me.'

'I certainly hope you know what you're doing.'

Jud didn't answer that. He led the way through the trees until they ended. Then he dashed across an open space to the back of the garage. Larry followed.

'Do you know if there's a back door?'

'I'm not certain.'

'Let's find out.' He walked towards the rear, careful to keep the garage between him and the ticket booth of Beast House, a hundred yards away. When he was even with the rear of the brick house, he rushed across to it.

The back of the house was solid brick.

'No door,' Larry said.

Jud walked through the overgrown yard to the far corner. He peered around it. No door there, either: just the grey metal box of the house's ventilation system. Across Front Street, the south part of Beast House's fence and lawn were visible, and deserted. 'Stay close to the wall,' Jud said. He wiped sweat off his brow and moved forward.

At the front corner of the house, he stopped. Signalling Larry to stay back, he looked at the ticket booth across the street. The side that faced the street had a closed door, but no windows. As long as Wick Hapson stayed inside, he wouldn't be able to see Jud.

Beyond the ticket booth, the tour group was clustered near the Beast House porch, probably hearing about Gus Goucher. Jud waited for them to file inside.

'Stay here till I signal.'

'Is Axel home?'

'His pick-up's here.'

'Oh dear.'

'That's all right. It might make things easier.'

'For heaven's sake, how?'

'If he's a trusting soul, the door won't be locked.'

'Wonderful. Marvellous.'

'Wait here.' Jud again checked the ticket booth, then walked swiftly across the front lawn to the door.

The inner door stood wide open. Jud pressed his face to the screen door, trying to see inside. He couldn't see much. Except for the light from the doorway, the interior was dark. Quietly, he pulled open the screen door, and entered.

He moved quickly away from the lighted area. For at least a full minute, he stood motionless, listening. Convinced he was alone, he patted the walls near the door and found a switch. He flicked it. A lamp came on, its bulb filling the entryway with dim, blue light.

Directly ahead, stairs led to the upper floor. To the right was a closed door, to the left a room. He stepped into the room. By the faint light from the foyer, he found a lamp. He turned it on. More blue bulbs.

Dark carpeting covered the floor. Pillows and cushions littered it. A lamp stood in a back corner. There was no other furniture.

Jud went to the screen door. Looking through it, he checked the area near the ticket booth for Wick Hapson. No sign of the man. He opened the door a crack and waved to Larry.

Before Larry reached the door, Jud pressed a forefinger to his own lips. Larry nodded and entered.

Jud pointed out the room with the cushions. Then he stepped to the closed door at the right of the entrance. He pushed it open and found a light switch. It turned on a chandelier over a dining-room table. The chandelier bulbs were blue.

Except for the lighting, Jud found nothing unusual about the dining room. A china cabinet stood in one corner. A large mirror occupied the far wall above a buffet. The table had six chairs, but formal dining tables often had that many. He saw two more matching chairs beside the highboy.

Beyond the head of the table was another door. Jud went to it and pushed it open. The kitchen. He entered it, careful to walk quietly on the linoleum floor. He looked in the refrigerator. Even its interior light was blue. Pointing at the botom shelf, he grinned at Larry. The shelf held at least two dozen cans of beer.

Next to the refrigerator was a door.

As he began to pull it open, Jud saw light on the other side. Blue light. He opened it farther and looked down a steep flight of stairs to the cellar.

He shut it quietly. Stepping around Larry, he went to the dining room. He brought one of the straight-backed chairs into the kitchen and tipped it against the door, bracing its back under the knob.

Then he motioned for Larry to follow.

They went from the kitchen to the foyer and silently climbed the stairs. Just off the hallway at the top was a large bedroom. They entered it, and Jud turned on its blue overhead light. Larry flinched, and slapped the hilt of his machete. Then he laughed quietly, nervously, 'How exotic,' he whispered.

Mirrors ran the length of the walls, and one was attached to the ceiling directly above the large bed. There were no blankets on the bed, only blue satin sheets.

As Larry knelt to look under the bed, Jud checked the closet. The hangers held nothing except robes and more than a dozen nightgowns. He pulled out one of the nightgowns and it filled with air, swaying as if it had no weight at all. Dainty pink bows at the shoulders and hips were all that connected the front and back of the gown. Through the sheer fabric, Jud could see Larry stepping over to the bureau. Jud put the nightgown away.

'Oh dear!' Larry muttered.

Jud rushed over to Larry. The open drawer held four pair of handcuffs. Looking in another drawer, he and Larry found a pile of steel chain with padlocks. In another was an assortment of bras and panties, garter belts, and nylons. Two of the drawers contained only leather: leather slacks and jackets, brief leather bikinis, vests, and gloves. From a hook at the side of the dresser hung a riding crop.

They shut all the drawers and left.

The bathroom smelled of disinfectant. They quickly searched it, finding nothing unusual except for the sunken bathtub. It was large, perhaps seven feet by four, with several metal rings fixed into the tile walls at head level.

'What are those for?' Larry asked.

Jud shrugged. 'They look like handles.'

At the far end of the hall, they entered a small room with bookshelves, a desk, and a stuffed chair. By the blue overhead light, Jud made his way to a lamp behind the chair. He turned it on.

'Ah, light,' Larry whispered as white light filled the room. He began to inspect the book titles.

Jud checked the desktop, then the drawers. The drawer on the upper left was locked. Kneeling, he removed a leather case from his pocket. He took out a pick and tension bar, and worked on the lock. It gave him no trouble at all.

The drawer was empty except for a single leatherbound book. A strap with a lock held it shut like a diary. He quickly picked that lock and opened the book to its title page. 'My Diary: Being a True Account of My Life and Most Private Affairs, Volume 12, in the year of our Lord 1903.' The name beneath the inscription was Elizabeth Mason Thorn.

'What do you have there?' Larry asked.

'The diary of Lilly Thorn.'

'Good heavens!'

He thumbed through the pages. Three quarters of the way through, he found the final entry. August 2, 1903. 'Last night, I waited until Ethel and the boys were asleep. Then I carried a length of rope down cellar.' He shut the diary. 'We'll take it,' he whispered. 'Now let's have a look in the other room and get out of here.'

The door of the room across the hallway was shut. Jud twisted the knob. He inched it open.

Larry clutched his arm.

From inside the room came a strange, windy sound. Jud listened closely, ear to the crack. He heard hisses, sighs, a blowing sound like the wind makes coming down a canyon. He silently closed the door.

When they got downstairs, Larry whispered, 'That was the beast. It was in there sleeping.'

'I think it was just Axel.'

'Axel, my foot!'

'But he wasn't alone,' Jud said.

'Indeed not!'

'I heard at least three people in that room. Let's get out of here.'

'Marvellous suggestion. I'm with you 100 per cent.'

Chapter Seventeen

The green, metal sign read, 'WELCOME TO MALCASA POINT, pop. 400. Drive with care.' Roy slowed down to 35 miles per hour.

He saw a dozen people lingering near a ticket booth in front of an old Victorian house. He glanced at the sign. Its red lettering wobbled and dripped like wet blood. BEAST HOUSE. He grinned, and wondered what the hell it was.

Slowing, he studied the faces of the people near the ticket booth. None looked at all like Donna or Sandy, not even with the changes six years might bring. He kept moving.

He watched the sidewalks for them; he watched the road and parking spaces for their car. A blue Ford Maverick, Karen had said. She wasn't lying. At that point, she had been beyond lying.

When he saw a blue Maverick parked at a Chevron station, he couldn't believe his luck. Karen had mentioned car trouble, but that shouldn't take so long to repair: he'd expected Donna to have a day on him, at least.

He stopped beside a row of gas pumps. A skinny, sneering man approached his window. 'Fill 'er up with Supreme,' Roy said, and wondered if Supreme was what the Rolls took. He decided the gas jockey would've made a remark if it didn't. The guy'd said nothing.

Roy climbed out. It felt good to stand and stretch. His jeans were still damp in the pockets. He scratched his itchy skin and stepped to the rear of the car.

'That Maverick over there,' he said. 'It wouldn't belong to a woman travelling with her daughter, would it?'

'Might.'

'The woman's thirty-three, blond, a real fox. The kid's twelve.'

The guy shrugged.

Roy pulled a ten-dollar bill from his wallet. The man eyed it for a moment, then took it and stuffed it into his shirt pocket.

'What's the woman's name?' Roy asked.

'I can check.'

'Is it Hayes? Donna Hayes?'

He nodded. 'That's her. I remember the Donna.'

'And she had a kid with her?'

'Little blond gal.'

'How long you been working on the car?'

'Couple days. We brought her in Monday morning. That's yesterday. Busted radiator. We had to send over to Santa Rosa for a new one, just got it in.'

'So they're staying in town?'

'I don't know where else they'd be.'

'Where are they?'

'Only one motel. That's the Welcome Inn, about a half mile up the road, on your right.'

Roy gave the man another five dollars. 'That's to keep your mouth shut.'

'How come you're looking for her?'

'I'm her husband.'

'Oh yeah?' He laughed. 'She run out on you?'

'That's right. And I'm aiming to fix her for that.'

'Don't blame you a bit. She's a choice piece, that gal. I'd be pissing steam if she run out on me.'

Roy paid for the gas, then drove half a mile up the road. He saw the restaurant first, a rustic building shaded by evergreens. 'Welcome Inn's Carriage House. Fine Dining.' A short distance beyond it was a coffee shop. Then a driveway led into a courtyard with about half a dozen cabins on each side. Just past the driveway entrance stood the motel office. The red tubing of the neon 'Vacancy' sign was lit.

Roy kept driving, suddenly nervous.

So close. He didn't want to blow it, now. He needed time to think.

He drove up the road until he found a wide shoulder. There, he pulled off and shut down the engine. He checked his wristwatch. Nearly three-fifteen.

Donna's car is at the Chevron station, he thought. Okay. If she picks it up today, she either leaves right away, or spends the night. If she leaves, she'll drive past here. He could simply wait and stop her somehow.

What if she heads south? No, she wouldn't do that. Not after making a beeline north like this.

Still, she might.

Or she might stay another night at the Inn.

That'd be easy enough to find out. Just check in the motel office. If she's planning to stay over, she would've registered by now.

He couldn't check the office, though. She might find out.

Well, not necessarily. He could go to the office, get her cabin number, and drive right to her door before she had a chance to find out anything, take precautions, call the cops. He could bust in, grab her and the kid, get out before anyone knows what hit.

Not a chance. People would see. There'd be cops after them so quick. . . .

Why take them anywhere? Just go in, shut them up, and stay inside. Plenty of privacy. Even beds. Stay as long as he felt like it.

What if they're out?

If they're out, they might ask at the office, and find out he'd been there asking.

'Shit,' he muttered, seeing his plan fall apart.

Okay, getting the number from the office is out. That leaves one way to learn which cabin is theirs: stake the place out. Watch for them.

He spent a few moments wondering about the best way to keep watch on the cabins, then climbed out of the car. He took his pack from the back seat and slipped his arms through the straps. Then he opened the trunk. Joni was conscious. He lifted her out by the arms.

They walked along the roadside until Roy saw the office of the Welcome Inn about fifty yards ahead. Then he led Joni into the trees. The twigs and pine cones of the forest floor hurt her bare feet, and she started to cry.

'Stop that.'

'It hurts.'

'Do you want me to carry you?'

She nodded.

Roy grinned, remembering how she'd refused a similar offer, just last night. Maybe she was beginning to trust him. He bent down. She wrapped an arm around the back of his neck, as if she'd had a lot of practice. Roy hooked one arm under her back and the other behind her knees. He lifted, and began to walk with her through the trees.

He enjoyed carrying Joni this way. She was light enough so it caused little, strain. Her arm reaching around his neck seemed almost friendly, though he knew she only did it for her own security. Her face was close to his. With a slight forward shift of his head, he could brush his cheek against the softness of her hair. The backs of her legs were bare against his right arm. As he walked, he caressed the velvety side of her thigh. Her free hand made no effort to stop him.

Soon a row of cabins came into view. They were painted like redwood, with slanted roofs. They had windows in back, but no doors.

Staying far away from the cabins, Roy worked his way past the end one. A break in the trees gave him a view of the parking area. It curved slightly southwards between the cabins. From its angle, he figured that the windows of the nearest cabin on the left should give him a view of all the other cabin fronts.

He made a wide sweep through the woods, and came up directly behind it. He grinned. The angle of the cabin's rear side shielded it from the other cabins. He set Joni on to her feet.

'What are you doing?' she whispered.

Whispered. He liked that.

'I'm getting us a place to stay.'

The window sill was level with Roy's head. The window was shut.

'I'm gonna lift you up,' he whispered. 'Tell me who's inside.' He put down his backpack and patted his shoulder.

Joni climbed on to his shoulders. She held the top of his head. Gripping her knees, Roy slowly stood until her eyes were level with the bottom of the window.

'Closer,' she said. She leaned forward, thighs pressing the sides of his head. Hands cupped to her eyes, she peered into the window screen. 'Higher,' she whispered.

He raised her. 'Who's there?'

'Nobody.'

'Are you sure?'

'Huh?'

'Is anyone there?'

'No.'

'You're sure?'

'Yes.'

He lowered her to the ground, and she climbed off.

'You're not lying, are you?'

'I don't tell lies,' she said solemnly.

'OK. You'd better not.'

'I'm hungry.'

'We'll eat when we get inside.'

'What?'

'I've got lots of stuff in the pack. But first we have to get in there.'

'How?'

He didn't answer. He led her to the right side of the cabin. There were two windows on the side, but they could be seen from the cabin across the parking area. He didn't want to chance being seen. They returned to the single rear window.

He could only get in by breaking it.

That would mean noise.

What were the alternatives? He could walk to the door of an occupied cabin, knock, and knife his way in. Someone might see him, though. And if he screwed it up there might be a scream. That'd be worse, by far, than a little breaking glass.

Maybe he should go under the cabin and watch for Donna from there. Kneeling, he looked into the crawlspace under the elevated floor. It was a couple of feet high. Plenty of room. He ought to have a good view from the front.

It would be filthy, though. All kinds of bugs and spiders. Slugs. Maybe even rats. No telling how long he would have to wait: maybe hours. And what would he do with Joni? The hell with that.

With his knife, he pried loose the two lower clamps of the window screen. He worked the screen loose and propped it against the wall.

Reaching into the pack, he took out his flashlight. 'OK,' he said, 'onto my shoulders.'

Joni climbed on.

Roy handed the flashlight to her. He straightened up.

'See up there? Where the window ends?'

'Here?' She pointed to the wood crossbeam at the bottom of the upper window.

'Right. Break the glass just above that, then you can undo the latch. Use the end of the flashlight. Hit it hard.'

'Here?'

'A little more to the left.'

'Here?'

'Yeah. Now hit it hard so it breaks the first time.'

Holding him across the forehead with one hand, she swung. Roy heard the loud slam of the flashlight striking glass. The glass didn't break. 'Hard!' he muttered. 'Hit it hard! Hard as you can.' He waited. 'Go ahead, damn it!'

The flashlight crashed down on his head. Again. Again. Pain streaked through his skull. He put a hand up. The flashlight struck his fingers.

Ducking, he rammed Joni into the wall. She cried out and dropped the flashlight. Roy reached up. He grabbed her blouse and tugged. The girl tumbled over his head. Her back slammed the ground.

'Hey!'

Roy looked towards the corner. A teenage girl stood there, holding towels in her arms.

'What the hell are you doing?' she demanded. She sounded more angry than afraid.

In an instant, Roy had his knife out. He pressed it to Joni's belly. 'I'm gonna kill this little girl if you don't come over here.'

'You wouldn't dare.'

'Run or yell, and I'll gut her like a catfish.'

The girl began to shake her head. 'You're sick,' she said.

'Come here.'

With short, hesitant steps, the girl began to approach him. Her eyes watched him closely, as if trying to figure him out.

He watched how the late-afternoon breeze ruffled her hair. He watched how her small breasts jiggled seductively inside her white T-shirt. He watched her lean, tanned legs.

'What're you doing here?' he asked.

'I might ask you the same thing.'

'Just answer.'

'I own the place.'

'You?'

'My family.'

'Then you've got keys,' he said, and grinned.

Chapter Eighteen

1.

Over the sound of the television, Donna heard a car drive up. Sandy looked at her, worried. Putting down the newspaper, Donna climbed off the bed and went to the window. A dark green Chrysler pulled to a stop just outside the door. 'It's Jud and Larry,' she said. She opened the door for them.

'Any sign of him?' Jud asked.

Donna shook her head. 'No. How'd you do?'

'Not too bad.'

'Not too bad, indeed!' said Larry. 'We got away scotfree, slick as thieves, and cast your eyes on *this*.' He waved a leather-bound book. '*This* is the diary of Lilly Thorn. Her own words. Good heavens, what a find!' He went to the edge of the bed and sat down beside Sandy. 'How was *your* afternoon, my little lady bug?'

Donna turned to Jud. 'Did you find the beast suit?'

'No.'

'What about Mary Ziegler's body?'

'Not that, either. There were a couple of places we couldn't search, though.'

'Did someone come back?'

'No. One of the rooms was already occupied, and we didn't check the cellar because there was a light down there.'

'Then somebody was home?'

'Several somebodies, by the looks of it.'

'There's only Maggie, Axel, and Wick,' she said.

'And two were over at Beast House running the tours.'

'So who was in the house?'

'Axel, I suppose. And at least two others.'

'But who?'

'I don't know.'

'That's a little spooky.'

'Yeah. I wasn't too happy about it, myself.'

They sat on the side of Jud's bed. 'What was the house like?' Donna asked.

She listened closely, intrigued by what he told her of the blue lights, the living room with no furniture except pillows, the bathtub with its strange handles. Most of all, she was fascinated by the bedroom.

'You wouldn't think Maggie Kutch was the type. And Hapson! That guy's an old weasel. It's hard to picture them making love at all, much less under mirrors. The bondage part I'll buy, though. The sadism. Did you see the look on his face when he went after Mary Ziegler with his belt?'

Jud nodded.

'I always thought they were a bunch of sickoes. I mean, you have to be, don't you, living on tours of a place like Beast House?'

2.

Except for a half-hour walk up a hill that overlooked the ocean, they spent the afternoon in Cabin 12. Larry read the diary in less than an hour, at times shaking his head in disbelief, and muttering. Sandy watched television. Donna sat next to the window with Jud.

At four-thirty, Donna mentioned that she'd like to find out about her car. The four of them walked to the Chevron station. As they approached it, she saw her blue Maverick along with three other cars parked beside the garage. 'I bet he hasn't touched it yet,' she said.

Jud walked with her to the office, where the bony mechanic was busy on the telephone. They waited outside until he was done.

'All set lady,' he announced, coming out.

'You mean it's ready?' Donna asked, unwilling to believe the surprising news.

'Sure is. Radiator came in around noon.' He walked ahead of them to the car and raised the hood. 'There she is. I test-drove her, and she runs sweet as a pie.'

They returned to the office. He showed her the bill, pointing out the cost of parts and labour. 'That be cash or charge?'

'Charge.' She searched her purse for the proper credit card.

'Where are you staying?' he asked.

'Over at the Welcome Inn.'

'That's what I figured. No place *else* to stay.' He took her credit card. 'That's what I told the fella looking for you.'

The words hit her hard. She stared at the man, stunned, until Jud's firm grip on her elbow brought her back. 'Who?' she asked.

'A fella come driving up in a '76 Rolls, says he knows your car. He find you?'

She shook her head.

'Do you always give out information about your customers?' Jud asked.

'Don't come up that often.' His eyes narrowed. 'You folks in some kind of trouble?'

'No,' Jud said, 'but you may be.'

The man handed the credit card back to Donna, then gave her the charge slips to sign. Slowly, he turned to Jud. 'Piss off, mister, before I kick your fucking ass from here to Fresno.'

'Shut up!' Donna shouted into his face. 'What right did you have to tell that man anything . . . *anything* . . . about me?'

'Hell, lady, I didn't tell him nothing. He had your name. He was gonna find you. Like I say, no place *to* stay but the Inn. He was gonna find you, anyway.' The mechanic flicked a hard glance at Jud, then looked back at Donna. 'Gonna step out on your husband, lady, you gotta be more careful.' He grinned and walked away.

'Let's go!' Donna called to her daughter and Larry. They were across the street looking in store windows. As they started back, Donna said, 'I don't want Sandy to know, OK?'

'She'll be more careful if she knows.'

'She's terrified of that man. And after what she's already been through, today . . .'

'We won't tell her. But we'll have to be damned careful from now on. Especially back at the Inn.'

Donna took his hand, and found confidence in his eyes. She met Sandy and Larry with a smile. 'Miracle of miracles,' she said. 'The car's fixed.'

3.

On the way back to the Welcome Inn, Donna watched for a Rolls-Royce but didn't see one. There was no Rolls in the parking lot, either.

'Park in front of your cabin,' Jud said.

She did. Then Jud led them across the asphalt to his cabin. He entered first, and made a quick search before allowing them inside. 'I need to go to the office,' he said. 'I'll be back in a minute.'

He was back in less than five. With a slight shake of his head, he let her know that nobody had been asking about her at the office. 'Why don't we have supper now?' he suggested.

'I'm starving!' Sandy blurted.

'You're a bottomless pit,' Larry told the girl. 'An abyss.'

'*You're* the pit,' she said, laughing.

'Sandy,' Donna warned, 'don't use that kind of language.'

'*He* did.'

'That's different. He didn't mean "pit" the way you did.'

'I most certainly did not.'

As they walked to the motel restaurant, Donna put her arm around Jud's back. Her hand touched a hard, jutting object just above his belt. She fingered the outline.

'So that's why your shirt tail's out.'

'Actually, it's out because I'm a slob.'

'A well-armed slob, at that.'

The dining room was nearly deserted. As the hostess led them among the tables, Donna checked every face. Roy wasn't there.

'We'd like a corner table, please,' Jud said.

'How's this?' asked the hostess.

'Just fine.'

Jud took a seat, Donna noticed, that would give him a wide view of the dining room.

A young, blond waitress came. 'Cocktails?'

Donna ordered a margarita.

Sandy asked for a Pepsi.

'I'd like a double martini,' Larry said. 'Very dry. Bone dry. In fact, dispense with the vermouth entirely.'

'So that's a double gin, straight up, with an olive.'

'Precisely. You're a gem.'

'And you, sir?' she asked Jud.

'I'll have a beer.'

'Budweiser, Busch, or Michelob?'

'Make it Bud.'

'An incorrigible snob,' Larry muttered.

Donna laughed. She laughed very hard, harder than the remark deserved, but it seemed like a long time since anything had struck her as funny, and the laughter felt good. In a moment, a giggle escaped from Larry. That triggered Sandy. Soon the three of them were convulsed with mirth. Jud grinned at them, but his eyes kept sweeping the room.

During the whole dinner, Jud kept watch as if he weren't part of the group, but their guard. Then he insisted on paying the bill.

When they were leaving, Donna, caught his arm and stopped him from following Sandy and Larry outside.

'What's . . .?'

'Thank you for dinner.' She hugged him tightly and kissed him. She could feel him begin to relax, to open, to let emotion into his kiss. Then he forced her away.

'We'd better stick close to Sandy,' he said, tearing down her good feeling so that she wanted to cry.

Chapter Nineteen

From the window of the end cabin, Roy watched Donna, Sandy, and two men enter Cabin 12. Her car was parked in front of 9. He guessed that 9 was her place, and 12 the men's.

That simplified matters. Sometime during the night, Donna and Sandy would return to their cabin alone. Maybe in five minutes. Maybe not for hours. But sometime. Regardless, he would wait until after dark.

He looked around at the two beds, at the two girls tied to them and gagged. The older one, the owner's kid, was still sniffing. He figured she was sixteen, maybe seventeen. He didn't know her name. She'd been good, though. She'd been wet and slippery, and Roy suspected that she'd enjoyed herself. He'd spent nearly an hour with her after the four had walked off, probably for dinner. She hadn't started crying until afterwards. Guilt, more than likely.

He wondered why no one had come around looking for her. Maybe her folks were used to her disappearing.

Roy lifted an edge of the curtain, and looked again at Cabin 12. The door was still shut.

He looked around at the girls. Right now, he didn't want either of them. Still, they were nice to look at, lying there naked and powerless in the darkening room.

Later, maybe he could find time to take one of them.

Which?

Hell, he had lots of time to think about that. Lots of time.

He got up. The older girl's eyes watching him closely as he approached her. He bent over the bed. He traced a circle around her right nipple, watching the dark skin pucker and grow rigid. 'Like that?' he whispered, smiling down at her.

Then he jerked the pillow out from under her head, took it to the chair beside the window, and used it to cushion the straight wooden back. He sat down and leaned against the pillow. That felt much better.

He inched open the curtain and continued his watch.

Chapter Twenty

1.

Leaving the others inside his cabin, Jud walked the perimeter of the Welcome Inn. He saw no Rolls-Royce nor any sign of a six-foot-two man who might be Donna's husband. He returned to his cabin. He motioned for Donna to come outside.

'Now,' he said, 'we'll go over to your place and wait for him.'

'What about Sandy?'

'Her, too.'

'Does she have to? I'd rather . . . I don't want her to see him, if it's possible.'

'Here's the problem. He doesn't seem to be around right now, but he might be. I could've missed him. If he's watching, he'll know we've left Sandy in 12. He might try for her.'

'Suppose she's with us,' Donna said, 'and Roy comes and somehow he . . . gets by you. Then he's got Sandy. If we leave her with Larry and that happens, she'll still be all right.'

'Whichever way you want it.'

'Do you think he'll know, if we leave her in 12?'

'He might,' Jud admitted.

'But there's a good chance he won't.'

'I'd say so.'

'Okay. Let's leave her in 12 with Larry.'

'Fine.'

He instructed Larry to stay inside, to keep the door locked and the curtains pulled, and, at the first sign of trouble, to fire a signal shot and lock himself and Sandy in the bathroom. Low in the tub, they should be safe from bullets. Jud would come running. He'd be there five seconds after the first shot.

'Perhaps,' Larry said, 'I can pot the bugger with my signal shot.'

'If he gives you a clean shot, take it. But don't hang around waiting. You'll be fairly safe once you're in the tub with the bathroom door locked.'

Jud left him the rifle. He picked up Lilly Thorn's diary. Then he and Donna crossed the shadowy parking area to Cabin 9.

He went in first, and searched it. When Donna was in, he locked the door and made sure the window curtains were completely shut. He turned on the lamp on the nightstand between the two beds.

'Where do you want me?' Donna asked.

'I'll be on the floor here between the beds, so I'm out of sight. You might as well take one of the beds. Maybe this would be best,' he said, patting the one farthest from the door.

'Looks good to me. What'll we do while we wait?'

'You can watch TV, if you want. Doesn't matter I want to see what Lilly's got to say.'

'Can't I?'

'Sure.'

'Why don't I read it to you?'

'All right.' He smiled. He liked that idea. He liked it a lot.

Donna took off her sneakers. Her socks were white. Her feet looked very small to Jud. He watched her climb on to the bed and sit upright, bracing her back against the headboard.

He sat down on the floor between the beds. With a spare pillow, he padded the front of the nightstand, and leaned back. He placed his Colt .45 automatic on the floor beside him.

'All set?' Donna asked.

'All set.'

' "My Diary," ' she began to read. ' "Being a True Account of My Life and Most Private Affairs." '

2.

' "January 1," ' she read. 'I guess this whole thing's 1903. "This being the first day of the new year, I devoted myself to solemn meditation. I gave proper thanks to the Lord for his bounty in providing me two fine boys, and the wherewithal to meet our needs. I asked Him to forgive my transgressions, but most of all to look kindly upon my dear Lyle, who had a fine noble heart and strayed from the path of righteousness only because he loved his family to a fault." '

'He was a bank robber,' Jud said

'But he had a noble heart.'

'Maybe you can skip some of this.'

'And get to the good part?' She slowly flipped the pages, scanning them. 'Oh, here's something. 'February 12. I was sick at heart, today. The Lord continued to remind us that we are outcasts in this town. Several of the local youngsters attacked Earl and Sam as they were returning from school. The cowards wounded my boys with stones, then fell upon them, further bludgeoning them with fisticuffs and sticks. I know not the reason for their cruelty, only that its source lies in the reputation of the boys' father." '

Donna turned more pages. 'Looks like she went around town for a few days, telling the parents what their kids had done. They were polite to her, but cold. She no sooner got done making the rounds than her boys got beaten up again. One had a bad knock on the head, so she went to a Dr Ross. "Dr Ross is a kindly, cheerful man of forty-odd years. He appears to bear no grudge against myself or the children because of our kinship to Lyle. On the contrary, he looks upon us with the kindliest eyes I have seen in many months. He assured me that I need not fear for Earl's condition. I invited him to take tea, and we delighted in one another's company for the better part of an hour." '

Jud listened to the whisper of the turning pages.

'Looks like she's seeing Dr Ross almost every day. She's started calling him Glen. "April 14. Glen and I took a picnic basket to the hilltop behind the house. Much to my surprise and delight, he produced from his medicine case a bottle of the finest French Burgundy. We enjoyed ourselves marvellously, feasting upon chicken and wine, and upon each other's company. As the day progressed, our passion rose. I was hard put to restrain the man. Though he kissed me with an ardour that stole my breath away, I allowed him no further liberties."'

Donna stopped reading. She looked down at Jud, smiled, and sat down beside him on the floor. 'I'll allow you the liberty of a kiss,' she said.

He kissed her gently, and she pressed her mouth to his as if hungry for the taste of it. When he put a hand on her breast, she pushed it away.

'Back to Lilly,' she said.

Jud watched her skim the pages. She was sitting shoulder to shoulder with him, the book propped against her upraised knees. The soft downy hair on her cheek looked golden in the lamplight. The closeness and smell of her excited Jud so he stopped caring much about Lilly Thorn.

'She doesn't get very specific, but I think she's well beyond the kissing stage, at this point. She's hardly writing about anything, now, except Glen.'

'Mmmm.' Jud put a hand on Donna's leg, feeling the heat of her thigh through the corduroy.

'Ah-ha! "May 2. Last night, long after the children were abed, I stole outside at the appointed hour and met Glen in the gazebo. After many protestations of love, he asked for my hand in marriage. I accepted his offer without hesitation, and he joyously clutched me to his bosom. Through much of the night, we embraced and planned our future. At length, the chill became too great for us. We stole into the parlour. There, on the couch, we held one another tenderly, blessed by the fullness of the moment."'

Donna shut the diary, keeping place with her forefinger. 'You know,' she said, 'it makes me feel kind of . . . dirty, reading this. Like a peeping Tom, or something. It's so private.'

'It might tell us who killed her family.'

'It might. I'll go on with it. Only . . . I don't know.' She lowered her head and began turning the pages. 'They've set a date for the wedding. July 25.'

Jud put his arm across her shoulders.

' "May 8. We held another rendezvous in the gazebo, last night, meeting at the stroke of one. Glen had the presence of mind to bring a comforter. With the chill of night vanquished, our ardour burst upon us without restraint. We were caught as in a tide. Powerless to resist its pull, we allowed the tide to buoy us upon its bosom and sweep us into blissful delight such as I have never known." I guess,' Donna said, 'that means they screwed.'

'Christ, I thought their raft had capsized.'

Laughing, Donna pounded his leg. 'You're awful.' She faced him, and he kissed her. 'Awful,' she said into his mouth.

He brushed his fingertips along the smooth skin of her cheek, traced the outline of her jaw and throat. She put the book down. Turning so a breast pushed against Jud's side, she plucked at his shirt, unbuttoning it. Then she slid her hand beneath it, stroking his belly and chest.

Jud pulled her down, away from the nightstand. Lying on his side, with the length of her pressed against him, he pulled her shirt tail free and slipped his hand down the back of her corduroys, feeling the cool smooth curves of her buttocks. He moved his hand up her back to unhook her bra.

'Wait,' she said.

'What's wrong?'

'The floor was last night,' she said, pushing away from him. She stood up.

With her eyes fixed steadily on Jud and a slightly apprehensive look on her face, she unbuttoned her blouse. She tossed it on to the bed near the door. She shrugged off her bra, and tossed it. Sitting on the side of the bed, she pulled off her socks. She stood, tugged open her belt, and unfastened her pants. They dropped to her ankles. She stepped out of them. Now she wore only brief panties. The dark of her pubic thatch was visible through sheer blue nylon. She slipped the panties off.

'Stand up,' she said. Jud noticed a tremor of fear or excitement in her voice.

He pulled off his shoes and socks. He set his Colt .45 beside the lamp. Then he stood, taking off his shirt. While he unbuttoned it, Donna unbelted his pants. She lowered them, kneeling. Then she slid the underpants down his legs. Her tongue licked and she took him in, sucking.

He moaned. As Donna stood, he brought her tightly against him. For a long time, he held her there between the beds, kissing her, exploring the slopes and crevices and orifices of her body, stroking and probing while she did the same with him.

Then they parted. Donna pulled back the covers, and they lay on the bed.

They didn't hurry.

Part of Jud's mind remained cautious, listening and alert like a guard standing watch. The rest of him joined Donna. He became part of her smoothness, her hair, the quiet sounds she made in her throat, her dry places and her slippery places, the many smells of her, the tastes. And finally the slick scabbard that took him, taunted him until he ached for release.

Arching his back, he thrust deeper, deeper than ever. Again. Crying out, Donna lurched up and grabbed him. He fell on her, ramming and ramming, and all the tight ache blasted out of him.

They lay together afterwards for a long time. They talked softly; they said nothing. Donna fell asleep holding his hand. Finally, Jud got up. He dressed, and resumed his position on the floor between the beds, the .45 automatic next to his leg.

3.

'Was I asleep long?' Donna asked.

'Half an hour, maybe.'

She pulled herself to the edge of the bed and kissed Jud. 'Want to get back to Lilly?' she asked.

'I've been waiting for you.'

'I really conked out.'

'Yeah.'

She smiled. 'All your fault.' She reached down a bare arm for the book.

'Maybe you'd better get dressed.'

'Mmmm.' She sounded as if she didn't care much for the idea.

'If we have a visitor . . .'

'God, did you have to remind me?'

He stroked the side of her face. 'You get dressed, and I'll look in on Sandy and Larry.'

'Okay.'

She covered herself with a sheet when Jud opened the door.

Sometime during their lovemaking, darkness had come. Light showed through the window of Cabin 12. Jud stood beside Donna's Maverick and searched the parking area. A woman with two children came out of Cabin 14. They got into a camper van. He waited for the van to leave, then he crossed to Cabin 12 and knocked lightly on the door. 'It's Jud,' he said.

'Just a sec.'

A moment later, Larry opened the door. Jud looked in. He saw

Sandy sitting cross-legged in front of the television, looking over her shoulder at him.

'Everything okay?'

'Until you frightened the heebie-jeebies out of me a second ago, everything was marvellous.'

'Okay, I'll see you later.'

He went back to Donna's cabin. She was sitting on the floor between the beds, dressed in her cords and blouse, the diary resting against her upthrust knees. He sat down beside her, and put his .45 next to his right leg. 'They're fine,' he said.

'Okay. Back to Lilly. If you remember, her boat has just capsized.'

'Right. And she was drowned in waves of passion.'

'Which gave you the idea of making waves of your own.'

'Is that what happened?'

'I think so.'

Jud kissed her quickly, and she smiled.

'None of that,' she said. 'Back to Lilly.'

'Back to Lilly.'

'Okay, after she made it with Glen that first night, they "indulged their passion" on a regular basis. Almost every night, in fact. I don't suppose you want to hear about that.'

'In my present condition, not especially.'

'Okay, let's see what's next.' She turned several pages as she skimmed them. ' "May 17. Today, I posted a letter to Ethel, requesting her attendance at the nuptials. I am hoping she will, at long last, journey down from Portland . . ."' Donna read the rest to herself and flipped the page. She remained silent. Looking up at her, Jud saw her eyes moving over the words. Her lips were pressed tightly together.

'What is it?' he asked.

Her eyes met Jud's. 'Something's happened,' she muttered.

' "May 18. A most disturbing sight greeted me, this morning, when I went down cellar to fetch a jar of apples from among those I'd put up last autumn. In the light of my gas lamp, I saw that two of my canning jars lay broken on the floor. Another was open as nice as can be, and empty. My first inclination, naturally, was to blame the boys. However, the label of the empty jar told me it had contained beets, a vegetable abhorred by both boys. That discovery chilled me to the heart, for I knew that a stranger had trespassed within my house and I knew not the nature of his intentions. Resisting my impulse to run upstairs and have done with it, I searched the confines of the cellar.

' "In a corner near the east wall, hidden from view behind half a dozen bushel baskets, I discovered a hole in the dirt floor – a hole large enough to permit the passage of a man or large animal. I quickly fetched my canned apples, and fled the cellar.

' "May 19. I gave much thought to informing Glen of the stranger's visit to my cellar. At length, I decided to leave him in ignorance, for I know that his protective instincts would call upon him to destroy the visitor, I could hardly abide such a stern measure. The visitor, after all, has thus far harmed no one.

' "I resolved to settle the matter myself, by covering the entrance hole. To accomplish this task, I fetched a spade from the tool shed. I went down to the cellar. Two more jars of preserves lay open and empty on the floor. This time, the visitor had indulged himself upon my peaches. Gazing down upon the empty jars, I felt a sudden warmth of compassion in my heart.

' "The visitor, I realized, meant me no harm. His only wish was to stave off the ravages of hunger. Perhaps he was an unfortunate lad, one of society's outcasts. I have known the pains of being an outcast. I have known the loneliness and the fear of it. My heart went out to the luckless, desperate soul who had dug into my cellar for a few mouthfuls of my preserves." I vowed to meet him, and help him if I can.

' "May 30." That's an eleven-day gap, Jud.'

'Yeah.'

' "May 30. I hesitate, I tremble, at the thought of committing my deeds to paper. To whom can I confide, however? Reverend Walters? He would only confirm that which I know already, that my deeds are foul in the eyes of God and I have condemned my soul to everlasting flames. I surely cannot tell Dr Ross. I know not what terrible vengeance he would certainly visit upon me and Xanadu.

' "On May 19, I resolved to meet and attempt to help the visitor to my cellar. Glen came by, after the children were abed. He used me after his usual fashion." What became of the surging tides?' Donna asked. She immediately continued reading. ' "When he was done with me, we chatted idly for a time. At length he departed.

' "I went to the pantry, and silently opened the cellar door. There in the darkness, I waited, listening. Not a sound issued from the cellar. I descended the stairs, feeling my way cautiously, though I carried an unlighted lamp.

' "When I felt the dirt floor of the cellar under my bare feet, I sat down upon the lowest step and continued my wait.

' "My patience, at length, was rewarded. A muffled sound of one breathing heavily with exertion rose from the vicinity of the hole. Soon came faint sounds such as a body might make dragging itself over hard earth. Then I saw a head appear above the bushel baskets.

' "The darkness concealed its features. I could only discern the head's pale shape. Even that was far from distinct. I judged it from the paleness to be the head of a man foreign to the blissful rays of the sun.

' "He rose to his full height, and I was filled with dread, for this was no man. Nor was he an ape.

' "As he drew near, I resolved to discover his identity more fully, even at hazard to my safety. To this purpose, I struck a match. It flared, giving me a momentary view of his hideous countenance before he cowered away, snarling.

' "While he was thus turned, I beheld his back and hindquarters. Whether he was one of God's exotic creatures, or an ill-made perversion vomited forth by the devil, I know not. His ghastly appearance and nudity shocked me. Yet I was drawn, by an irresistible force, to lay my hand upon his misshapen shoulder.

' "I allowed the match to die. In the darkness, totally without sight, I felt the creature turn. His warm breath on my face smelled of the earth and wild, uninhabited forests. He lay his hands upon my shoulders. Claws bit into me. I stood before the creature, helpless with fear and wonder, as he split the fabric of my nightgown.

' "When I was bare, he muzzled my body like a dog. He licked my breasts. He sniffed me, even my private areas, which he probed with his snout.

' "He moved behind me. His claws pierced my back, forcing me to my knees. I felt the slippery warmth of his flesh press down on me, and I knew with certainty what he was about. The thought of it appalled me to the heart, and yet I was somehow thrilled by the touch of him, and strangely eager.

' "He mounted me from behind, a manner as unusual for humans as it is customary among many lower animals. At the first touch of his organ, fear wrenched my vitals, not for the safety of my flesh but for my everlasting soul. And yet I allowed him to continue. I know, now, that no power of mine could have prevented him from having his will with me. I made no attempt to resist, however. On the contrary, I welcomed his entry. I hungered for it as if I somehow presaged its magnificence.

' "Oh Lord, how he plundered me! How his claws tore my flesh! How his teeth bore into me! How his prodigious organ battered my tender womb. How brutal he was in his savagery, how gentle in his heart.

' "I knew, as we lay spent on the earthen cellar floor, that no man – not even Glen – could ever stir my passion in such a way. I wept. The creature, disturbed by my outburst, slipped away into his hole and disappeared."'

4.

' "The following night, when I descended the cellar stairs, I found him waiting for me. I disrobed immediately to save my gown from the ravishment of his claws. I embraced him, savouring the slick heat of his skin. Then I went to my hands and knees, and he took me with no less fervour than on the previous night. When the delirium was past, we lay about until I recovered.

' "At length, I showed him my lamp. I indicated for him to turn around to protect his eyes. Then I lit the lamp, and covered it with an indigo hood I had devised during the day. The blue-shaded lamp was kind to his delicate eyes, while it provided sufficient light for my purpose.

' "I saw, as I studied him, that he was a curiously shaped creature, indeed. Several of his odd features accounted, no doubt, for his magnificence as a lover. His lengthy, spearlike tongue was one of these. His sexual organ, without question, was the most singular and wondrous of his features, accounting as much for his ardour as for my own. Not only was it staggering in size and in its unusual contours and ridges, but also its orifice was unlike that of any creature known to me. The orifice, was hinged like a jaw, possessed a tongue like member with a two-inch extension." '

'Bullshit,' Jud said. 'What the hell is she trying to hand us?'

'A penis with a mouth?' Donna suggested.

'It's not such a bad idea?' Jud said, and laughed tersely.

'As long as it hasn't got teeth,' said Donna.

'Good Christ, how much of this is she making up?'

'What do you think?'

'I don't know. A lot of what she says – the claws and slippery skin, the reaction to light – they fit what I've seen.'

'What about the penis?'

'I didn't notice. Of course, the house was dark. I could hardly see anything.'

'I'll go on. "This orifice and tongue, I am certain, enabled him not only to titillate me in the extreme, but also heighten his ardour by the taste of my juices." '

'Good God!' Jud muttered, shaking his head.

' "After I satisfied my curiosity regarding his body, he explored me with much the same intensity. We then surrendered to a new tide of passion.

' "When we finished, I presented him with an assortment of food. He ate cheese with great delight. He nibbled the roll, and discarded it. He rejected the beef with barely a sniff. As I would later learn, only raw meat suited his palate, and this had been well cooked. He lapped water from a bowl, then sat down on his haunches, apparently satisfied.

' "Lying upon my back, I opened myself to him. He appeared confused, for he was accustomed to having his way in the manner of lower creatures. I urged him down upon me, however, so that I could look upon the strange beauty of his face and feel his slick flesh against my breasts as he ravished me.

' "When we were done, I watched him slide into the hole behind the bushel baskets. I crawled to the edge of the hole. I listened, hearing him deep inside. I called out quietly to him. I knew not what his name might be, so I called him Xanadu after the strange and exotic land described by Mr Coleridge in his unfinished masterpiece. He was gone, but I knew he would return the following night.

' "I have been with Xanadu every night, making my way very silently down cellar after the children are asleep. We indulge our passions with a frequency and intensity that knows no bounds. Each morning, before dawn, Xanadu returns to his hole. I know not why, nor. where he goes. It is my belief that he is a creature of the night, who spends his days in sleep. I have become much that way myself.

' "Daylight finds me weary through every fibre. This has not gone unnoticed by Earl and Sam. I explain to them, with some truth, that I have found sleep difficult of late.

' "Glen Ross was my chief worry, in the beginning. He immediately expressed concern over my lassitude. He demanded to examine me for a physical ailment, but I resisted him to the point of rudeness. He surrendered his demand, and gave me sleeping powders.

' "His nightly demands for amorous attention aggravated and frightened me beyond telling. His embrace made me shudder. His kisses were repugnant to me. Yet I would have borne these tortures and allowed him liberties only to allay his suspicions had it not been for the visible evidence left on my body by Xanadu: the bruises, the scratches and cuts from his claws, the bite marks. Below my neck, hardly an inch of my body had not been wounded in the passion of our love. In the presence of my children and Dr Ross, I wore a highnecked blouse with long sleeves, and a full skirt. Even these were not sufficient covering. Upon one occasion, I attributed scratches on my hands and face to a tomcat flying into a rage when I picked it up.

' "Three nights ago, Dr Ross called on me and demanded to know the meaning of my icy rejections. Though I had long expected such an outburst, I was hard put to the answer in a manner that would bring no suspicion of the truth. At length, with a show of modesty and shame, I divulged that our sins of fornication placed our souls in jeopardy and I could no longer abide such evil. To my astonishment, he suggested that we marry at once. I said I could not live with a man who has brought such a fall upon me. With derisive laughter, he pointed out that I had been satisfied enough, living with a bandit and a murderer. I used this slur upon my deceased husband as a pretext to usher Dr Ross from the house. I do not think he will return.

' "Yesterday, I posted a letter to Ethel. I informed her that Dr Ross had taken back his marriage proposal, and that I was heartsick. I asked that she keep Sam and Earl for two weeks, so that I might make a restorative trip to San Francisco. I am now eagerly awaiting her reply. With the boys far off in Portland, I will be able to abandon my tiring pretences. Xanadu and I will have free reign of the house.

' "June 28,"' Donna read. 'That's what, almost a month after the last entry? "Tomorrow the children are due to return from Portland in the company of Ethel, who wishes to visit for an unspecified period. I have been looking forward with pain to their return.

' "For close on to three weeks, Xanadu and I have been alone in the house. With the arrival of others, he must return to the cellar. I know not whether my heart will bear such separation.

' "July 1. Last night while Ethel and the children slept, I visited the cellar. Instead of greeting me with an embrace, Xanadu glowered from the corner near his hole. He took the raw beef I offered him. Clamping it in his jaws, he crawled into the hole and disappeared. Though I waited until dawn, he did not return.

' "July 2. Xanadu has not returned.

' "July 3. Again tonight, he stayed away.

' "July 4. If he is trying to destroy me by his absence, he is succeeding. I know not what I will do if he does not return soon.

' "July 12. Ten nights have passed, and I fear he has no intention of returning. I know, now, that I was a fool to allow him up from the cellar. He grew accustomed to the comfort of the house, and my constant presence. How could he understand the necessity of his return to the cellar? How could he view it as anything other than rejection?

' "July 14. Last night, instead of keeping my vigil in the cellar, I wandered the wooded hills behind the house. Though I found no sign of Xanadu, I shall search again tonight.

' "July 31. My night time searches of the hillside have accomplished nothing. I am so weary. With the loss of Xanadu, all joy has passed from my life. Even in my children, I take no happiness. I resent them, with all my heart, for they were the instruments of my loss. I would certainly have torn them unborn from my womb, had I known the agony their presence would bring.

' "August 1. I spent last night in the cellar, hoping for Xanadu's return. I would have prayed, but I dared not insult the Lord in such a manner. I determined, at length, to end my life.

' "August 2. Last night, I waited until Ethel and the boys were asleep. Then I carried a length of rope down to the cellar. Lyle had often spoken to me of execution by hanging. It was a style of dying he dreaded until the day he was gunned down. I would have chosen a different way to end my life, but none seemed so sure as the hangman's noose.

' "I worked long on the rope, but was unable to devise a proper hanging knot. A simple loop, I decided, would make do. The pain of suffocation would be great, but only for a time.

' "I managed, after a great deal of trouble, to throw the loop over one of the cellar's support beams. I fixed the rope's loose end to the centre post. Then I climbed upon a chair that I had brought down cellar for that purpose. With the loop around my neck, I prepared myself for the end.

' "At length, I knew that I could not depart this life without making one final attempt to see my beloved Xanadu.

' "To this end, I stepped down from the chair and walked close to the mouth of his earthen hole. I knelt at its edge. I called out to him. Hearing no response after a wait of several minutes, I determined to seek him out. If I should perish in the attempt, so be it. Such an end would only save me from the pain of hanging.

' "Shedding my clothes, I climbed head-foremost into the hole, much as I had seen him do on so many occasions. The earth was cold and moist against my bare flesh. Its blackness was complete. The close confinement of the hole rendered crawling impossible, so I inched forward like a snake, flat on my belly. I know not how I struggled to writhe my way deeper. The walls of the tunnel seemed to tighten around me, bearing down as if to crush the breath from my lungs. Yet I forced myself onward.

' "When I could move no more, I cried out to Xanadu. I cried out in all the pain of my love and desperation. I cried out again and again, though every breath burned my lungs, for I loathed to die without bidding farewell to my lover.

' "At length, I heard the welcome sound of his slick flesh gliding through the clay. I heard the hiss of his breath. He pushed his snout against my face, moaning and licking.

' "Clenching my hair with his massive jaws, he propelled himself backward, dragging me. The pain of it was welcome to my dazed senses. When finally he released my hair, I found no more walls pressing in upon me. The air tasted fresh. I learned, later, that he had brought me to his underground dwelling, a hollowed-out space only large enough for him to stand upright and lie down, located just beyond the limit of my property and several feet beneath the earth's surface. The fresh air came from a concealed opening overhead, and other tunnels that led up the hillside. I learned all this in the morning, however. At the time Xanadu brought me to his dwelling, I was barley conscious, and trembling with chill. In my lover's embrace, the chill departed. I was wrapped in blissful sleep.

' "He woke me, sometime before dawn. I was much recovered. Xanadu entered my body, and loved me more gently than ever before, though not without an extreme of passion. When we were done, he led me to an opening. From the manner of our parting, I know that he will come to me tonight.

' "I made my way across the dewy grass, alone and naked in the early-morning grey.

' "I spent the morning in solitude, planning. Shortly before noon, my thoughts were interrupted by a young man named Gus, who wished to work for a meal. Firewood required splitting, so I gave him the job. For much of the afternoon, I heard the ring of his sledge. All the while, I planned.

' "It is evening, now. Gus took supper with us, and left. The children sleep. Ethel has not yet retired, but that is no matter. Xanadu waits. I shall allow him up from the cellar, and we will again have full reign of the house.'

'That's it?' Jud asked.

Donna nodded.

Chapter Twenty-one

Anytime, now.

In the dim light filtering through the curtain, Roy dressed. He got up and looked at the girls. Their skin seemed very dark against the white of the sheets.

He wanted to start a fire. It would take care of the girls, and whatever evidence he might be leaving behind. A fire would be perfect. But not without a delayed start.

He had no candles.

A cigarette or cigar might work as a delaying device, but he didn't have one.

Maybe the girl.

Crouching over her small pile of clothes, he lifted the T-shirt. It had no pockets. He picked up the cut-off jeans and searched their pockets. Nothing.

Shit!

He couldn't just set the room on fire and run: he had to give himself time. Time to get into Cabin 12, time to get into 9, time to get a good distance away in Donna's car.

Wait.

Shit, he'd have to burn 9 and 12, too.

Forget it.

Forget the whole thing.

He suddenly smiled. Without a delayed fire ready to set this place ablaze, he wouldn't have to rush. He could take his time, enjoy himself.

What he'd do, he'd wipe the place clean, make sure he left no prints.

He wandered the room with the girl's T-shirt, rubbing all the surfaces he remembered touching. Somehow, it seemed pointless. He wasn't sure why, but he felt a hollow ache in his stomach as if something had gone very wrong. Something he'd forgotten about.

He dumped the backpack on to the floor. Along with the ground cloth and sleeping bags, four cans of chilli and spaghetti rolled out.

He should've eaten. That's what made the ache.

He rubbed the cans with the T-shirt.

No, it wasn't just hunger. Something else was wrong.

He rubbed the aluminium tubing of the pack frame.

Shit!

Karen and Bob's place! He'd never found out, for certain, whether or not it had burned.

That morning, on the radio, they'd only mentioned the one fire. If Karen and Bob's place didn't go up, then the cops would have all the proof they'd need.

Okay, maybe it went up, and he just hadn't heard. He should still be careful with this place.

Not leave evidence.

Not leave witnesses.

He swept the room with his eyes, wondering if he'd missed anything. When he was satisfied the place was clean, he went into the bathroom and urinated. He came out. Bending down, he raised his cuff and slipped the knife from its sheath.

A single clean slash across the throats would do it. He'd stand back to stay out of the spray.

Knife in hand, he stood.

He took one step towards Joni's bed and realized she was gone.

Impossible!

Rushing to the bed, he slid his hands across its sheets to be certain his eyes and the darkness hadn't deceived him. No, the bed was empty. She'd somehow worked the rope loose.

He glanced down between the beds. No sign of her.

Under the bed?

The doorknob rattled. Roy looked, saw the small girl reaching, pulling. The door flew open for a moment, and shut.

'Oh fuck!' Roy muttered.

He ran to the door, swung it open, and stepped out. He shut it silently. Except for a few lighted cabin windows, the parking lot was dark. Roy looked to the left, thinking she would head for the office. No sign of her. He glanced to the right. Still nothing. Maybe she'd run around back.

'Okay,' he whispered. 'Okay.'

He would just finish off the other one, first.

He tried to twist the knob. It resisted, as if frozen.

Locked out. Keys inside.

Roy drew a deep, shaky breath. He wiped the sweat off his hands, then hurried around the corner of the cabin. Ahead was only darkness. Woods. The night sounds of crickets.

He wanted his flashlight.

He'd left it inside.

Walking quietly, he entered the darkness to find Joni.

The little bitch!

His hand ached, gripping the knife so hard.

He'd rip her! God, he would rip that little bitch! Up one side, down the other.

'Where are you?' he muttered. 'Think you can hide from me, little bitch? I know your smell. I'll sniff you down.

Chapter Twenty-two

1.

'That's it,' Donna said. 'Lilly let the beast into the house, so it would kill the children and Ethel.'

'That's how it looks,' Jud agreed.

'It's not the way Maggie told it on the tour. Maggie had her barricaded in the bedroom, remember?'

'I think,' Jud said, 'that Maggie lies a lot.'

'Do you suppose she lied about Lilly going mad?'

'I doubt it. That's too easy to check on. We just need to see a local newspaper from the time to verify that. Lilly probably did flip out. If she was really behind the murder of her own children, that could send her over the edge. From the sound of it, she wouldn't have needed more than a nudge, at that point.'

'And watching Xanadu kill the children gave her the nudge.'

'Likely.'

'I wonder what Xanadu did after she was gone. Do you think he stayed in the house?'

'He might've. Or maybe he went off, and continued the way he'd lived before Lilly.'

'But he did come back,' Donna said, 'when Maggie and her family moved in. Maybe he was waiting, all that time, for Lilly to return. When he finally saw someone living there, he must've thought she'd come back.'

'I don't know,' Jud said. 'I really don't know what to think about any of this. The diary sure throws a monkey wrench into my theory about the beast. Assuming the diary is authentic. And I think we *have* to assume it's authentic, at least to the extent that Lilly Thorn wrote it. Nobody else had any reason to tell a story like that.'

'What about Maggie?'

'She kept it locked up. If she'd written it herself, faked it, she would've used it somehow: had it published, sold copies on the tour, something. I think she kept it for her own personal . . .'

A knock on the door silenced Jud. He picked up his automatic. 'Ask who it is,' he whispered.

'Who's there?'

'Mommy?' The girl's voice was choked with fear.

'Open it,' Jud said.

As Donna got to her feet, Jud lay down flat in the space between the beds.

He watched her unlock the door and pull it open. Sandy was standing in the darkness – standing on tiptoes to ease the pain of her pulled hair, tears shiny in her eyes, a six-inch blade pressed to her throat.

'Aren't you glad to see me?' a man asked, and laughed. He pushed Sandy ahead of him into the room, and kicked the door shut.

'Tell your friend to come out,' he said.

'There's no one.'

'Don't shit me. Tell him to come out, or I'll start cutting.'

'She's *your daughter*, Roy!'

'She's just another cunt. Tell him.'

'Jud!'

He pushed his pistol under the bed, and slowly stood, hands out to show they were empty.

'Where's your piece?' the man asked.

'Piece?'

'Everybody's playing dumb. Cut the fuckin' dumb show, and tell me where's your gun.'

'I don't have a gun.'

'No? Your buddy did.'

'Who?'

'Shit.'

'Who're you?' Jud asked.

'Okay, knock it off. Both of you, get your hands on top of your head and interlace your fingers.'

'Donna, who is this guy?'

'My husband,' said Donna, looking confused.

'Jesus, why didn't you tell me? Look, fella, I didn't even know she was married. I'm sorry. I'm really sorry. You think *you're* mad, my wife's gonna kill me. You aren't gonna tell her, are you? Why don't you put down that blade, man? The kid didn't do nothing. She didn't know from Adam. We just stuck her on this guy, gave him a couple of bucks to babysit while we . . . you know, had a good time.'

'Get over against the wall, both of you.'

'What're you gonna do? You're not gonna . . . hey, we didn't even *do* nothing! I didn't even touch her. Did I touch you, Donna?'

Donna shook her head.

'See?'

'Face the wall.'

'Oh Jesus!'

'That's good. Now both of you brace yourselves against it. That's right. Lean. So your weight's on your hands.'

'Oh sweet Jesus!' Jud muttered. 'He's gonna kill us. He's gonna kill us!'

'Shut up!' Roy snapped. He made Sandy lie face down on the floor. 'Now don't move, kid, or I'll gut your mom.'

'Oh sweet Jesus!' Jud cried.

'You shut up.'

'I didn't touch her. Just ask her. Donna, did I touch you?'

'Shut up,' Donna said.

'Jesus, everybody's turning on me!'

'He's already killed at least two people,' Donna said, 'and we're gonna be next if you don't shut up.'

'He *killed* somebody?' Jud looked over his shoulder at the man stepping towards him with a knife. 'You really killed somebody?'

'Face front.'

'He killed my sister and her husband.'

'You did?' Jud asked, looking again.

The man's grin told how much he had enjoyed it.

Jud began to turn, asking, 'Why'd you . . .?'

'Face front!' Roy reached forward to shove Jud into position. As his hand thrust Jud's shoulder, Jud reached back with his right hand, pressed Roy's hand flat against his shoulder, and spun out. Roy yelped as his wrist snapped. Jud, still pivoting, smashed a forearm into the back of Roy's head, slamming him against the wall. In the same swift motion, he hammered his knee into Roy's spine. The knife dropped to the floor. Roy fell backward, groaning, panic in his eyes.

'Take Sandy over to 12,' Jud said. 'See what happened to Larry.'

2.

Outside, Donna crouched and hugged her crying daughter. 'Did he hurt you, honey?'

She nodded.

'Where did he hurt you?'

'He pinched me here.' She pointed to her left breast, a barely noticeable rise through her blouse. 'And he put his finger down here.'

'Indeed?'

She nodded and sniffed.

'He didn't rape you, though?'

'He said later. And he used the bad word.'

'What did he say?'

'The bad word.'

'You can tell me.'

'He said later. He said later he'd F me till I can't walk straight. And then he was gonna F you. And then he was gonna gut us like catfish.'

'Bastard,' Donna muttered. 'The stinking bastard.' She held Sandy gently, stroking the girl's head. 'Well, I guess he won't get a chance to do any of that, will he?'

'Is he dead?'

'I don't know. But he can't hurt us now. Jud took care of that.' She stood. 'Okay, let's see about Larry.'

'Larry's okay. I tied him real good.'

'*You* tied him?'

'I had to. Daddy was gonna kill him.'

They started walking across the parking area.

'I told Daddy, if he killed Larry, I'd scream. He said he'd kill me if I did, and I said I didn't care. I said, if he didn't kill Larry, I'd do anything he wanted. He wanted me to pretend so he could make you open the door.'

'How did he get *Larry* to open the door?'

'He pretended to be a policeman.'

'Great,' Donna muttered, wondering how Larry could be that stupid. She tried the door of Cabin 12. It wasn't locked. She pushed it open.

'Where is he?'

'In the bathtub. It was Daddy's idea.'

She found Larry facedown in the empty tub, a shirt tied around his mouth for a gag. His hands were bound together behind his back, and knotted to the ankles of his upraised feet.

'We got him!' Sandy announced.

Larry answered with a grunt.

Sitting on the edge of the tub, the girl leaned forward and picked at the knots. In a few moments, she had them loose. Larry pushed himself to his knees. He tugged the knotted shirt down from his face, and plucked a black sock out of his mouth. 'Dreadful man,' Larry muttered. 'A total barbarian. Are both of you all right? Where's Judgement? What happened?'

Donna explained what Jud had done, and that she didn't know how badly he'd injured Roy.

'Perhaps we should find out.'

They crossed through the darkness to Cabin 9 and found Jud sitting on the bed. On the floor between the beds, Roy lay face down. His hands were tied behind his back. A pillowcase covered his head, strapped tightly around his neck with a leather belt. Except for his breathing, he was motionless.

'I see you have matters well in hand,' Larry said.

Sandy, looking down at her father, squeezed Donna's hand tightly. Donna sat down beside Jud. They moved sideways to make room for the girl.

'What shall we do with the cad?' Larry asked, lowering himself daintily on to the empty bed.

'He's not a cad,' said Jud. 'He murdered Donna's sister. He murdered her brother-in-law. He sexually abused Sandy. God knows what else he's inflicted on Donna and Sandy. But we all know what he intended to do. That's not a cad, in my book. In my book, that's a beast.'

'What do you propose we do with him?' Larry asked.

'Put him where he belongs.'

'In jail?' Sandy asked.

Donna, feeling a chill scurry up her back, said, 'No, honey. I don't think that's what Jud has in mind.'

Larry suddenly understood. Shaking his head, he muttered, 'Oh dear God.'

Chapter Twenty-three

Donna started the engine of the Chrysler. Beside her sat Sandy. Roy, his head still hooded by the pillowcase and his hands still bound, sat in the back between Jud and Larry. Jud held a .45 against Roy's chest. Larry held a machete across his lap, its curved head pressing Roy's side.

'Once you let us off,' Jud said, 'I want you to drive back to the motel. Give us half an hour, then come back for the pick-up. If we're not waiting, don't stick around. Take off, and come back every fifteen minutes until we show. Any questions?'

'Can't I just park somewhere close, and wait? Then I can signal if someone comes.'

'The car might attract notice.'

'Are they really going in Beast House?' Sandy asked, as if it were a joke everyone was in on except her.

'I guess so,' Donna answered.

'That's crazy.'

'It certainly is,' Larry agreed. 'I concur 100 per cent.'

'You don't have to come,' Jud said.

'Oh, but I do. You are planning to rid the world of Lilly's beast, I take it?'

'I'm planning to.'

'Well, if I'm to bear the expense of the operation, I certainly want to see it carried out. Besides, you may need a hand with our friend here.'

'Are you taking Daddy in there, too?'

'Yes,' Jud said, and didn't explain.

'What for?'

'Punishment.'

'Oh. You're gonna give him to the beast?'

'That's right.'

'Wow! Can we go in too?' she asked Donna. 'I want to see.'

'No, we can't.'

'Why not?'

'It's dangerous.'

'But Jud and Larry are going in.'

'That's different.'

'I want to. I want to see the beast get Daddy in its claws and rip him up.'

'Sandy!'

'I want to see it!'

'Take my word for it,' Larry said. 'You don't want to see the beast do that to a man. I know.'

'We're almost there,' Donna said.

'Okay. Drive on past it, then hang a U.'

'Here?'

'Go a bit farther, so we're past the bend.'

Donna slowed.

'This'll be fine.'

She tried to swing the big car into a U-turn, saw that she couldn't make it, and had to back up before finishing the turn.

'Okay,' Jud said. 'Now kill the lights.'

She pushed the headlight knob, and the road ahead went dark except for patches of moonlight. The road was less dark than the woods on either side, so she had little trouble staying on it. Around the curve, the woods ended. The moon spread pale, creamy light over the road.

'Pull up in front of the ticket booth,' Jud said, his voice a tense whisper.

Donna stopped.

'I'll need the keys for a second.'

She switched off the ignition. Turning in her seat, she handed the key case to him. 'Jud?' she said.

His features were barely visible.

'Shouldn't we just take him to the police?'

'No.'

'It's not that I . . . Can't we shoot him, or something?'

'That'd be murder.'

'It'll be murder giving him to the beast.'

'Then the beast is the perpetrator, not us.'

'I don't want you going in that house again. Not at night. Christ, Jud!'

'It's all right,' Jud said quietly.

'It's *not* all right. You could get killed. It's not fair. We've only had two days.'

'We'll have plenty more,' he said, and climbed from the car. He dragged out Roy, who stumbled and dropped to his knees. 'Keep him here,' Jud told Larry.

Donna followed Jud to the trunk.

'Please,' he said, 'get in the car.'

'One kiss.'

'All right.'

She pressed herself tightly against him, squeezing him hard, hoping that somehow their bodies might fuse and she could stop him from leaving. But after a moment, he forced her gently away.

She watched him take his torn parka from the trunk and put it on. He picked up two flashlights and a road flare. Then he quietly shut the trunk and handed the keys to her.

'What time does your watch say?' he asked.

'Ten forty-three.'

He set his. 'Okay. Meet us here at eleven-fifteen.'

'Jud?'

'Go. Please. I want to get this done.'

She went back to the car, started it, and drove away without looking back at the three men she'd left along the roadside.

Chapter Twenty-four

1.

'It's a turnstile,' Jud said. 'Climb over it.'

Roy shook his head.

Jud prodded him with the knife, and Roy swung a leg up. Larry, on the other side, helped him over by pulling one of his tied arms. Jud heard an approaching car. He vaulted the turnstile, grabbed Roy, and pulled the big man to the ground. The three of them lay close to the ticket-booth wall.

Jud heard the car slow. Its tyres crunched gravel. Crawling forward, he peered around the corner of the ticket booth.

A police car.

It was stopped across the road, but Jud could hear the quiet idle of its engine. A few moments passed. Then it made a U-turn, drove slowly by the ticket booth, and headed off.

They dragged Roy to his feet and led him up the lawn. They hurried alongside the house to the back. There, they climbed the porch stairs.

The broken glass in the back door had neither been replaced nor boarded over. Sliding the knife into his pocket, Jud reached through the opening. He lowered his fingers down the door crack until he found a bolt. He tried to draw it back. It was stuck. He jerked. It snapped back with a clatter that filled the silence.

'That probably woke it up,' Larry whispered.

Jud pushed open the door. He stepped inside, pulling the hooded man. Larry, following, shut the door without a sound.

'Where to?' he whispered.

'Let's take this off, first.' Jud removed the belt from Roy's neck, then pulled off the pillowcase. The man's head jerked as he looked quickly around.

'This is Beast House,' Jud told him.

He made noises through his nose.

'I'll take off the gag. You'll live a bit longer, though, if you stay quiet.'

Roy nodded.

Jud tore the adhesive tape off Roy's mouth, and pocketed it. He strapped the spare belt around his waist, and tucked in the pillowcase so it hung at his side like a white sash. He planned to leave nothing behind.

Nothing but Roy.

'Let's go upstairs,' he whispered.

'That's where the *monster* lives?' Roy asked, and laughed.

'That's where it usually attacks,' Jud said.

'Yeah? You believe that shit?'

'Shhhh.'

Jud stepped out of the kitchen. He flicked on his flashlight. Ahead was the entrance hall, its stuffed-monkey umbrella holder guarding the front door like a grotesque sentry. He put his light away. With his left hand, he reached under the back of his shirt and pulled the Colt automatic from his belt.

'What're you guys, trying to scare me?'

'Shhh,' Larry repeated.

'Shit.'

At the foot of the stairs, Roy said, 'I smell gas.'

'That's from last night,' Jud whispered.

'Yeah?'

'A woman was killed,' Larry said.

'No shit? You guys do this all the time?'

'Shut up,' said Jud.

'I was only making conversation.'

They started up the stairs, and last night's horrors filled Jud's mind: Mary Ziegler, dead, diving down at him; the liquid sounds she made rolling across his back; the awful stench of the beast. He looked towards the top of the stairs, half afraid he would see her there again.

'Anybody got a smoke?' Roy asked.

'Shut up.'

They reached the top of the stairs.

'Okay,' Jud said, 'lie down.'

'What?'

'Lie face down on the floor.'

'Fuck you.'

With a sudden kick, Jud knocked the left leg out from under Roy. The man sat down hard.

'Fuckin' bastard.'

'Face down.'

Roy obeyed.

'You just wait, motherfucker. I'll gut you like a catfish. I'll cut off your cock and jam it down . . .'

'In there,' Jud whispered to Larry, pointing to the door several feet from Roy.

'Alone?'

'Just a second.' Jud knelt. 'Okay, Roy. You just lie here quietly. I tell you what: if you make it to dawn alive, I'll turn you over to the cops.'

'Fuck you.'

'But the only way you've got a chance is to stay real still, and real quiet. Maybe you'll be lucky, and the beast won't notice you.'

'Fuck you.'

'We'll be right over there, where we can keep an eye on you. If you try to sneak off, I'll have to dump you. Any questions?'

'Yeah. What's your name? I like to know a guy's name before I gut him.'

'My name is Judgement Rucker.'

'Shit.'

Jud went to the door where Larry waited. Jud opened it. He flashed his light up its narrow stairway, to the door high overhead. 'This'll be good,' he whispered. 'We can sit on the stairs.'

They stepped inside. Jud put his flashlight away. He pulled the door towards him until only a crack remained. Eye close to the crack, he could see the shape of Roy lying on the dark corridor floor.

Jud switched the automatic to his right hand. With his left, he removed Roy's knife from the pocket of his parka. He patted the parka, feeling the good weight of his spare ammo clips.

'Judge?' Larry whispered. 'Will we actually let the beast have him?'

'Shhh.'

2.

Donna wanted to turn around, wanted to go back to Beast House and wait there for the men to finish. As she was about to make the turn, however, car headlights flashed on her rear-view mirror. The car drew quickly closer. Donna thought she could see a light rack on its roof. She checked her speedometer. No, she wasn't speeding.

Sandy looked back. 'Uh-oh,' she said.

'Yeah.'

'Are you gonna pull over?'

'Not unless he wants me to.'

'Why's he so close?'

'He hasn't got manners.'

The police car stayed on their tail all the way to the Welcome Inn. It followed them through the entrance, then angled left and parked beside the restaurant.

Sandy made an exaggerated, 'Whew!'

'I guess he was just hungry,' Donna said. She pulled into the parking space of Cabin 12. 'Let's give him a minute to get inside.'

'Then what?'

'We'll go back for Jud and Larry.'

'Jud said half an hour.'

'We'll be a little early.'

She backed up and headed out of the parking lot. With a glance at the police car, she saw it was empty. The policeman was nowhere in sight. She turned left.

'If we're early,' Sandy said, 'can we go in?'

'Are you out of your tree?'

'Maybe we can help Larry and Jud.'

'They'll be fine without our help.'

'I'm not scared of the beast.'

'Well, you *should* be.'

'We can take Jud's rifle in with us.'

'Bullets can't hurt it. Weren't you listening on the tour?'

'Sure.'

'Maggie said her husband shot it.'

'Hunh-uh. She only said she heard shots. He probably just missed.'

'Well regardless, we're not going anywhere near that house.'

The town seemed empty as Donna drove through it. A few cars sat in front of closed stores, as if deserted by drivers seeking shelter from the darkness. Street lights cast their glow on barren corners. The traffic light blinked a steady yellow caution.

Donna swung left across the road and pulled into a parking space in front of Arty's Hardware. The head-lights glared off the display window. She shut them off. 'Can you see the house?' she asked.

Sandy peered out of the side window. 'Just the front yard.'

Donna, looking out the far side of the car, could see little except the front of the fence and the ticket booth. 'I guess I'll get out,' she said.

'Me too.'

'Okay.'

They shut the doors silently and met in front of the car. Their tennis shoes were quiet on the sidewalk. At the corner of the hardware store, they came to the wrought-iron fence.

Between the wall and the fence, a narrow walkway ran to the rear of the hardware store. A low picket gate blocked entry. Donna opened it, and they stepped into the gap. Close to the store wall, she felt well hidden from the street.

Sandy took hold of her hand.

Across the lawn, Beast House stood silent. Its board siding, washed by moonlight, looked as pale and dead as driftwood. Where overhangs and balconies dropped shadows, the black made caverns deep into the house.

Donna looked at the dark bay windows. She lifted her eyes to Lilly Thorn's bedroom windows, then along the bone-grey wall to Maggie's window, the one Larry had used for his escape so many years ago. In her mind, she could see the wax figure just inside, struggling to raise the window.

'What time is it?' Sandy whispered.

Donna tipped the face of her wristwatch to catch the moonlight. 'Eleven-twenty.'

'They're late.'

'That's all right.'

'What if they don't come out?'

3.

'Fuckin' shit!' Jud heard panic in Roy's voice. 'Holy fuckin' shit, there's someone coming! Guys? Damn it, you guys!'

Jud knelt, leaving space above him for Larry to see through the crack. Shifting the pistol to his left hand, he wiped his sweaty palm on a leg of his jeans. Then he pulled out his flashlight.

'Guys!' As if giving up on them, he muttered in a low voice, 'Oh Jesus.'

Jud heard a stair creak.

'Hey, who are you.? Huh? Can you help me? There's these two guys, they tied me up. I mean, I'm not trespassing. I been kidnapped. Can you give me a . . . oh shit. *Oh shit!* GUYS!'

Jud heard soft, brittle laughter.

'Oh God.' Roy was starting to cry. 'Oh God, sweet Jesus!' He sobbed. 'Oh Jesus, get it away! Get it away!'

Behind Jud, Larry moaned in horror.

Roy shrieked as the beast sprang. Its pounce seemed to knock out his wind, cutting his outcry short.

Jud shoved the door open. He aimed his flashlight. Flicked it on. The white, snarling thing on Roy's back snapped its head around to look. Bleeding flesh hung from its teeth.

Behind him, Larry screamed.

Before he could raise his automatic, Larry shoved him. He tumbled into the corridor. Larry, still screaming, leapt over him. Jud raised his flashlight. He shined it into the slitted eyes of the beast as Larry rushed it. He saw Larry swing. Saw the machete flash. Heard the thud of it and saw the white, hairless head tumble into the darkness. Blood spouted from the neck stump. The torso flopped on to Roy's back. Jud heard the muffled thumps of the head dropping from one stair to the next.

'I killed it,' Larry whispered.

Jud got to his knees.

'I killed it. Dead!' Larry swung the machete down like an axe, chopping into the dead creature's back. 'Dead!' He hacked it again. 'Dead dead dead!' After each word, he struck.

'Larry,' Jud said softly, standing up.

'I killed it!'

'Larry, we're done in here. Let's get out . . .' Behind him, Jud heard a savage snarl. He whirled. His flashlight reached up the attic staircase. The door at the top stood open. He dropped his beam to the massive, white back of a creature plunging down the stairs.

He snapped the trigger. His Colt roared, flashing as it bucked. A howl tore his ears. The beast took him backward, slamming him to the hallway floor. He jammed the gun muzzle against its side and shot. Another screaming howl. Then the weight was off him. He rolled to his stomach. The flashlight was still in his left hand. He found the white thing lunging at Larry, though two holes in its back poured blood. Larry raised the machete high. A sweeping arm caught the side of his face and raked the skin off. The machete fell.

Dropping the flashlight, Jud pulled the knife he'd taken from Roy. He scurried forward. In the dark, he saw the dim figure of the beast swing around, clutching Larry. Jud sidestepped. As his foot passed through space, he knew that he'd overstepped the top of the stairway. He dropped his knife and tumbled into the darkness.

4.

Donna listened, aghast, to the muffled outcries and gunshots coming from the house. She glanced down at Sandy. The girl stood transfixed, mouth gaping. At the crash of glass, she swung her eyes to the house in time to see a window of Maggie's bedroom explode as a body burst through it, head first.

No, not a body. The wax figure of Larry Maywood.

But it's screaming!

Moonlight glowed on the white hair of the plunging man. Another figure tumbled through the window. She watched it spin, its arms and legs frozen, and knew this one was only wax. Larry's scream stopped with the first thud of impact.

Without a word, Donna shoved open the low wooden gate and pulled Sandy behind her to the car. 'Inside. Get inside.'

'But Mom!'

'Do it!'

As Sandy got into the car, Donna hurried to the rear. She opened the trunk. Leaning in, she pulled a road flare out of its wrapper. She stuffed it into her rear pocket. Then she unzipped a leather case and slipped out Jud's rifle. She slammed the trunk lid. Pushing the rifle bolt forward, she watched a long, pointed cartridge slide into the chamber. She forced the bolt down and rushed to Sandy's window.

'Keep the doors locked and windows up till I get back.'

The girl gazed as if her mind were far away, but she locked the door and began rolling up her window.

Donna ran for the ticket booth.

5.

Halfway down the stairs, where Jud lay clutching a baluster, he heard the smash of glass and Larry's scream. Jud started climbing. The white creature appeared above him. It leapt. He fired one, point blank, before the claws hit his hand and tore the gun away. With an anguished screech, the creature shoved past Jud. It staggered down the stairs. Leaning over the bannister, Jud saw its pale shape moving towards the kitchen.

He hurried to the top of the stairs. Patting the floor near the bodies of Roy and the first beast, he found his flashlight. He turned it on. By its light, he found Larry's machete. He ran up the corridor to Maggie's bedroom. His light showed a broken window beyond the toppled, papier-mâché screen. Then it picked up a headless torso. He was crouching over the body when he realized it was only the wax figure of Tom Bagley, Larry's boyhood friend.

Jud ran to the window and looked down. Two sprawled bodies on the ground. A woman kneeling by one.

Donna.

'Is he alive?'

Donna's face tilted up. 'Jud are you okay?'

'Fine,' he lied. 'Is Larry alive?'

'I don't know.'

'For God's sake, get help. Get him a doctor. An ambulance.'

'Are you coming down?'

'I'm going after the beast.'

'No!'

'Get Larry help.' He pushed himself away from the window and crossed the room to the dresser. Shoving the machete under his belt, he tugged the top drawer open. The dead husband's Colt .45 automatic was just where Maggie had left it. Depressing a button, he dropped its empty clip. He took the oversized, twenty-shot clip from his pocket and rammed it up the handle. It locked into place. Priming a cartridge into the chamber, he ran from the room.

In the corridor, he stepped over the bodies and rushed downstairs. He ran into the kitchen. His flashlight picked up blood on the floor. He followed its trail to the pantry, through an open door, and down a flight of steep wooden stairs to the cellar.

The moist cellar air was chilly and smelled of earth. Sweeping the area with light, he saw stacks of bushel baskets, shelves laden with dusty canning jars. Out of curiosity, he abandoned the trail of blood and stepped closer to the baskets. Behind them, just as described in Lilly Thorn's diary, he found a hole in the dirt floor.

He returned to the dark blood spots on the dirt and followed them to the right where they stopped in front of an upright steamer trunk set flush against the wall. He saw quickly that the trunk was latched shut. The beast couldn't have hidden itself inside.

Two gunshots came, faint with distance. For a moment, he worried. Then he realized that Donna must've fired the rifle to draw attention, to draw the police and help for Larry.

Setting his flashlight on the dirt floor to the right of the trunk, he tucked the Colt into a pocket of his parka. He slipped his fingers between the trunk and the wall, and pulled. With a gritty scraping sound, the trunk came away from the wall. A rope handle dangled from the back of the trunk. The rope was dark with wet blood.

Where the wall should have been, Jud found a tunnel. Picking up the flashlight, he entered it.

6.

Realizing that Larry was dead, Donna ran to the front door of the house. She used two shots to blast apart the lock of the door. Even then, she had to throw her shoulder against the solid wood several times to smash it open. She stepped into the entry hall. 'Jud?' she called.

She heard no answer. She heard no sound at all. She called him again, louder this time. Still, no answer came.

Slinging the rifle over her shoulder, she slid the road flare out of her rear pocket. She twisted off its cap. Reversing the cap, she rubbed its striking surface against the end of the flare. At first, there was only a spark. On the second stroke, the flare sputtered to life, its brilliant blue-white tongue casting a glow that lit the entry hall and much of the stairway. Slowly, she climbed the stairs. She continued climbing, even when the light of her flare illuminated the bodies at the top: Roy face down, the nape of his neck mauled to red pulp; a strange white creature on Roy's back. When she saw the stump of its neck, she gagged. Turning away, she threw up.

Then she resumed climbing. She reached the top of the stairs and stepped over the bodies. She walked down the corridor to Maggie's bedroom, took one step inside, and called out, 'Jud!' She crossed the hall to Lilly's room, and again she called to him. Again, she got no answer.

She returned to the head of the stairs. Even with the beast lying dead at her feet, she felt an icy reluctance to venture down the corridor to the other rooms. 'Jud!' she yelled. 'Where are you?'

When no answer came, she walked quickly down the narrow hall. She shoved aside two of the Brentwood chairs marking the future Ziegler exhibit. At the far end, she stepped into the room to her left. The flare cast fluttering light on the walls, the rocking horse, the twin beds, and the wax figures of Lilly Thorn's slaughtered children. 'Jud?' she asked quietly. Nothing in the room stirred.

Crossing the hall, she twisted the knob of the nursery door. When it didn't give, she remembered Maggie saying it was always kept locked. She kicked it twice. 'Jud?' Then she muttered, 'Damn it.' She looked for a safe place to put the flare. Crouching, she propped it against the wall. The wallpaper began to blacken and curl. Standing, she unslung the rifle and shot through the crack where the lock tongue entered the jamb. She recocked it. Then she nudged the door with her shoulder. Feeling it give, she picked up the flare. She slung the rifle over her shoulder and shoved open the nursery door.

'Jud?' she called. She stepped into the room. Her flare lit an empty cradle, a playpen, a doll house nearly as high as her waist. It also lit buckets, a mop, three brooms, a carpet sweeper, and a table littered with sponges, rags, furniture wax, cleaning fluid, and window polish. Apparently, the nursery had been taken over by Axel for storage.

Donna backed out. She hurried through the corridor, past the Brentwood chairs, and stopped near the bodies.

She gazed at the door to the attic. It stood wide. 'Jud?' she called up the stairs.

She began climbing the stairs. They were very steep. The walls seemed close, as if they were pressing in on her. She hurried. Above her, the door stood open. She climbed to it, and hesitated before stepping inside. 'Jud, are you in here? Jud?'

She ducked through the low doorway. In the circle of light cast by her flare, she saw a rocking chair, a pedestal table, several lamps, and a sofa. She stepped away from the door. Moving sideways, she squeezed between the table and sofa. Ahead stood a weaver's loom. She skirted to the left of it, swung a leg over the high roll of a rug, and stumbled to keep from stepping on a hand. Catching herself against a chair she whirled around, saw wild hair, wide-open eyes, torn shoulder and breasts.

Not Jud, thank God.

Mary Ziegler.

From ankle to hip, little except bones remained of Mary's right leg. Donna turned away, doubled over, and vomited. Her stomach, already empty, kept convulsing, wracking her with pain. Finally, it stopped. She wiped the tears from her eyes and started back towards the door.

She stepped over the rolled rug. She pressed sideways between the table and the sofa. Then, just ahead of her, the door slammed shut.

Chapter Twenty-five

1.

Jud made his way farther into the tunnel, crouching beneath its low ceiling, trying to fight off the sense of suffocation caused by its narrow walls. In places, the earth was shored up with boards. The work of humans.

Wick Hapson, maybe. Or Axel Kutch.

Jud knew, even before stepping into the tunnel, where it would lead him. But he hadn't realized it would be this far. For some reason, the tunnel was not straight. It meandered like an old river, with twists and loops, and hairpin turns. At one point, it split into a Y. Jud went left. The tunnel curved, rejoined the other branch, and continued towarf the west.

At every turn, his finger tensed on the pistol trigger ready for an abrupt assault by the wounded beast. But rounding each, he saw only more tunnel and another bend.

Soon he began to wonder if he had somehow passed the opening he'd expected to find. He remembered the Y. Perhaps the right-hand branch led past the house entrance before curving back to join the one he'd taken.

That seemed unlikely. Still . . .

He stepped around a bend, and the tunnel opened. With a sweep of his flashlight, he found himself in a cellar. Pillows and cushions, like islands, littered the floor's blue carpet. In a far corner was the beast.

Jud walked towards it. The creature lay on its back, white arms clutching a pillow to its chest. Its long, pointed tongue hung from a corner of its mouth. Kneeling beside it, Jud pushed its snout with the gun barrel.

Dead.

Its lower body was sheathed with blood. He quickly checked, and saw that Lilly Thorn's description of the sex organ had been accurate. Amazed and disgusted, he backed away.

He climbed the wooden stairs and entered the kitchen of the window-less house.

2.

Axel Kutch, hunched like a wrestler in front of the attic door, grinned at Donna. His bald head gleamed in the light of her flare. Curly hair matted his bulky shoulders, his arms and chest and belly – but his penis stood hairless, thick and shiny and tilted high. He limped towards her.

'Stay back.'

He shook his head.

Threatening him with the flare, Donna tried to unsling her rifle.

A two-fingered hand grasped her wrist. It twisted sharply. The flare dropped, but he didn't stop twisting. Donna spun sideways, off balance, and. fell to her back. Still clutching her wrist, Axel kicked her in the side. He dropped to his knees. Picking up the flare, he jammed its unlighted end into a crack between the sofa cushions above Donna's head. Then he threw a leg over her. He sat on her belly, pinning her arms to the floor.

'You're beautiful,' he said.

She struggled, trying to free her arms.

'Stay still,' he said.

'Get off!'

'Stay still!'

Bending, he pushed his mouth against hers. She bit his lip, tasting the salty warmth of his blood, but he didn't stop kissing her. She bit again, savagely tearing the flesh of his lip. With a grunt, he pulled away. The back of his hand clubbed her face.

Weak from the blow, she tried with her free arm to shove him away.

He knocked her arm down, then punched her twice in the face.

Each blow was a stunning explosion of pain. Barely holding on to consciousness, she knew that he was tearing open her blouse. She heard buttons skitter across the floor, then felt the rough touch of his hands. Though her arms were free, she couldn't find strength to lift them. He pulled at her bra. When it wouldn't come off, he broke the shoulder straps. Donna felt the looseness, then the chilly bareness of her breasts. Axel squeezed them. The pain helped clear her mind. She felt the suck of his mouth. Then he was tugging at the belt of her corduroys.

She realized she could lift her arms. Opening her eyes, she saw Axel kneeling between her legs, head down as he worked to open her pants.

She reached behind her head. Stretched her arm. Grabbed the shaft of the flare. In a single swift motion, she plunged its sputtering head into Axel's eye. He shrieked as the room went dark. She shoved the flare harder. A warm wetness spilled on to her hand as the flare slid deep. Axel's rigid body bucked with convulsions. She pushed him off and rolled away from his body.

3.

Ahead of Jud, blue light glowed from the living room. He approached silently. He peered around the corner. The sight staggered him. Glancing to his left, he saw the front door. It was no more than six feet away.

Maggie and the creatures were probably thirty feet from him. One underneath her, would be slow getting free. The beast at her rear wouldn't be able to see him. But the one at her head was facing his way. He couldn't possibly make the door without it noticing him.

He pressed himself to the wall, out of sight. For several seconds, he listened to the grunting and the slippery smacking sounds. Maggie was gasping. From the violence of the sounds, he guessed that they would soon be done.

Once they were finished, his chance of escape . . .

Escape?

Christ, he'd almost forgotten what he'd come here to do.

He'd come here to kill the beast.

He'd come to stop it from murdering again.

Except it's not one beast, it's five. Maybe more. That doesn't change the purpose of the mission. It doesn't change the need for them to die. If anything, it increased the urgency of the task.

Lunging away from the wall, Judgement Rucker crouched and fired. A beast shrieked as the bullet crashed through its head. It stumbled backward, penis sliding from Maggie's mouth, ejaculating on to her face and hair.

The one behind her looked. Caught a bullet in its right eye. Slumped on to Maggie's back.

Jud held fire, watching Maggie struggle. The dead beast on her back fell away. She rolled off the live one, and lay on her side so that her body protected it from a shot by Jud.

Slowly, she stood up, being careful to shield the beast with her body. It got to its feet behind her. She began walking towards Jud.

'Bastard,' she muttered. 'Who do you think you are, bastard? Sneaking in here? Shooting us up? Killing my darlings?'

She kept limping towards him, dragging a leg that looked as if it had been chewed many years ago, and healed badly. Her ancient, swaying breasts were lined with scars and recent cuts, some bleeding. Blood dropped from her scarred shoulders and her neck. Jud knew why she wore a scarf in public.

'Stop,' he said.

'Bastard!'

'Damn it, I'll drop you!'

'No you won't.'

Suddenly, he heard snarling on the stairway behind him. He pivoted and fired at the darting shape. It shrieked but didn't stop. The claws of the beast with Maggie slashed across Jud's back. He lurched forward, turning, jerking the machete out of his belt. The claws swiped again. This time, he lopped off the creature's arm. He shot it once in the chest, then turned his gun to the beast leaping from beside the bannister post. His snapping finger blasted three holes into it. It fell.

Maggie dropped to her knees beside it. She hugged the white body, crooning, 'Oh Xanadu, Xanadu. Oh Xanadu!'

Her back was a disfigured mass of scar tissue and bleeding cuts.

'Oh Xanadu,' she sobbed, cradling the dead beast's head.

'Are there more?' Jud asked.

Maggie didn't answer. She didn't seem to hear.

Stepping around her and the body of Xanadu, Jud approached the stairway. He saw dim blue light in the upstairs hallway. Silently, he began to climb.

4.

Donna staggered down the front porch stairs. She slumped against the newel post, hugging it to keep from falling. The rifle strap slipped off her shoulder. She heard the walnut stock batter the railing. Probably put a scratch on the stock.

She wondered, vaguely, if the scratch would anger Jud. Men could be funny about that kind of thing.

God, would she ever see Jud again?

Where could he . . .?

A distant popping noise interrupted her question, and answered it. She raised her head. She heard more of the strange, low popping sounds, and she knew it was gunfire.

Gunfire muffled by the brick walls of the house without windows.

Watching the house, she heard another shot. Then three quick ones.

She started to run. The hanging rifle slapped her leg. Without slowing, she gripped the sling and swung the rifle in front of her. She gripped it solidly with both hands.

She glanced at the Chrysler, far to the right. Sandy's head was visible. The girl was locked in, safe.

Donna climbed awkwardly over the turnstile. She sprinted across the road. Then up the dirt driveway. She tried to remember if the rifle was cocked. Couldn't remember. As she ran, she worked the bolt. The ejected cartridge spun up and hit her face, its point jabbing her upper lip. Blinking tears away, she rammed another cartridge into the chamber.

Approaching the front of the dark house, she slowed to a trot. She shifted the rifle to her left hand. Heavy. She propped its butt against her hip and pulled open the screen door. She tried the knob. Locked. The screen door swung back, bumping her shoulder.

Damn!

She aimed at the door crack next to the knob.

It's getting to be a habit, she thought.

The thought didn't amuse her.

5.

Cautiously, Jud stepped into the main bedroom. The mirrors exposed every corner. No beast. He looked inside the open closet. Satisfied that nothing would jump out at him, he stepped closer to the bed.

Wick Hapson, naked except for a leather vest, lay face down on the sheet. Chains anchored his wide-spread arms and legs to the bedposts. His face was turned to the left.

Kneeling, Jud looked into his eyes. They were wide with fear. His lips were trembling. 'Don't kill me,' he said. 'Christ it ain't my fault. I just gone along. I just *gone along!*'

As Jud left the room, he heard the blast of a gunshot downstairs.

6.

Donna drew back the bolt. As the shell spun out, she saw that the ammunition clip was empty. Her mind flashed a memory of the live cartridge stabbing her face and falling to the dirt driveway. No chance of finding it.

Okay, nobody had to know the rifle was empty.

She shouldered open the door and lurched back at the sight of two hideous beasts lying sprawled near the foot of the stairway. Their shiny flesh looked pale blue. The severed arm of one lay near the wall.

Stepping around them, she glanced into the living room. Two more. 'Jud?' she called.

'Donna? Get out of here!'

His voice came from upstairs.

7.

Damn it! his mind screamed. What was Donna doing here?

He ran towards the last room, the room where he and Larry had heard strange breathing sounds that afternoon. The door was open slightly. Through the gap, he saw a blue light. He kicked the door, lunged into the room, and aimed at a pale figure crouched in a corner.

He held fire.

In the dim light, he saw dark hair hanging to her shoulders. She cradled something in her arms. An infant. It's snout, clamped on her dug, was sucking loudly.

Groaning, Jud backed towards the doorway.

8.

Donna, reaching the top of the stairs, saw the naked, ravaged form of Maggie Kutch limping towards the far end of the hall.

'Mom!'

Her head snapped to the side. Sandy, in tears, stood in the foyer looking up at her.

Donna looked again down the corridor. Maggie glanced back. Donna saw a butcher knife in the old woman's right hand. Donna shouldered the empty rifle.

'Drop it!' she shouted.

9.

Jud turned, faced Maggie, and started to raise his pistol. The knife plunged.

He was astonished.

He couldn't believe it.

That shiny, wide blade was actually vanishing into his chest.

She can't do this, he thought.

He tried to pull the trigger.

His hand didn't work.

She can't!

Chapter Twenty-six

In the cold darkness of the crawlspace beneath the last cabin, Joni lay on her side. She hugged her knees close to her chest. She kept her teeth clenched tight to keep them from chattering.

The man would never find her here.

Never.

A long time ago, when she first got away, he hadn't even looked under the cabin. Maybe he would come back, though.

She didn't dare to move.

The dirt rocks dug into her skin, but she didn't move. Sometimes, itchy bugs crawled on her. She made believe they were caterpillars and lady bugs, and let them crawl.

The cold was worse than anything. It made her shake. If she shook too much, maybe the man would hear her, and catch her again.

A long time went by.

Then she heard something move nearby. An animal.

She held her breath.

Then she heard a quiet, 'Meeeow.'

The cat came up against her legs in the darkness, furry and warm and purring like a motor.

'Kitty,' she whispered.

She stroked its head and back.

The cat let her hold it. She held it lightly against her chest. Its purr was so loud she worried the man would hear it and find her.

Soon she was no longer shaking.

A sound from above startled the cat. It leapt away and disappeared. Joni listened closely. Footsteps on the cabin floor.

She heard the door swing open. She saw bare feet on the stairs at the front of the cabin.

'Girl?' she called.

The legs stopped at the bottom of the stairs.

'Girl?'

The legs turned. The girl crouched and looked through the darkness of the crawlspace. 'You under there?' she asked.

'Yeah.'

'You gonna stay there all night?'

'Is he gone?'

'Yeah, I think so. It's been hours. Took me that long to get untied.'

Getting to her hands and knees, Joni began to crawl through the darkness towards her waiting friend.

Epilogue

'When will they take the chains off?'

'When they figure we won't run away,' Donna said.

'I wouldn't run away.'

Donna, squinting through dark, could see only a white blur where her daughter sat among the pillows. 'I would. I'd run away in a second.'

'Why?'

'We're prisoners.'

'Don't you like it?' Sandy asked.

'No.'

'Don't you like Rosy?'

'No.'

'I do. Except she's ugly like Axel.'

'They're twins, she ought to be.'

'She's a retard.'

'Yeah.'

'Who do you like better, Seth or Jason?'

'Neither.'

'I like Seth better,' Sandy said.

'Oh.'

'Aren't you gonna ask me why?'

'No.'

'Come on, Mom. Just 'cause you're mad they killed Jud. Besides, they didn't even kill him, Maggie did. And he deserved it, too.'

'Sandy!'

'Look how many of them he murdered. Six! God, he deserved it. He deserved a lot worse.'

'Damn it, shut up!' And then she was ashamed for using such language on her daughter.

'At least he didn't get Seth and Jason,' Sandy said.

'Too bad he didn't.'

'You're just saying that. You're just saying that to spoil things. You like them I know you do. I'm not deaf, you know.'

'Well, I don't like being chained up in the dark. I don't like that at all. And the food stinks.'

'Maggie might let you start cooking, if you ask her. Wick told me I can drive with him to Santa Rosa, one of these days, and pick up groceries. Once they trust us more, we can do all kinds of stuff.'

'I'd sure like to see the sun again.'

'Me too. Mom?'

'Yes?'

'Do you still think you're pregnant?'

'I think so.'

'Who's baby do you think it is? Jason, I bet.'

'I don't know.

'I'd like to have Seth's baby.'

'Shhh. I think they're coming.'

The Beast House

March 31, 1979

Mr Gorman Hardy, author
Baylor and Jones Publishing Co
1226 Ave. of the Americas
New York, NY 10020

Dear Mr Hardy,

I am writing to you because I have just read your book, <u>Horror at</u>
<u>Black River Falls</u>, which I know was a best seller and must have made
you a fortune. As the book is supposed to be a true story, I am
wondering whether or not you might want to write a story I know of. It
is also a true story. It is even more horrible than what you wrote in your
other book. Let me tell you, it makes my hair stand up just thinking
about it, and I don't scare so easy.

It is about a haunted house in the town where I live, except the
house isn't literally haunted if you mean ghosts. It is haunted by some
kind of a <u>thing</u> that's slaughtered maybe fifteen or more people over the
past hundred years. I mean slaughtered. It makes mincemeat out of
them.

I think it would make a terrific book for you to write.

If this sounds interesting to you, please let me know right away as
I'll find someone else otherwise. I happen to think this is right up your
alley. You can call it <u>Horror at Malcasa Point</u>, which is where I live and
where the house is that the monster lives in, which is known as Beast
House. Maybe you have heard of it.

Here is where I come in. Last Summer, I got my hands on this really
ancient diary that was written in 1903 by Lilly Thorn. I work at my
parents' motel, and found the diary under mysterious circumstances in
one of the rooms I was cleaning. Nobody knows I have it. (Except now
you know. You must promise to keep this a secret, as I would be in
deep trouble if words of it got to certain people. I mean seriously. We
are talking here about my life.)

Anyhow, this diary I found is <u>hot stuff</u>. Lilly Thorn, the woman that
wrote it, was the very first person ever to live in Beast House, and she
goes into all kinds of details about where the monster came from, and
what it's like, and everything. I mean <u>everything</u>. If you can believe
this, she even had sexual intercourse with it. I don't mean once, but
constantly like she was obsessed. It's steamy stuff, as you can see from
the xerox of the page I'll attach. The diary also goes into the first

murders and let me tell you, this sure is not the way they tell it on the tour!

So if you are interested in another best seller, I think you should let me know and maybe we can split the take.

Sincerely,

Janice Crogan
The Welcome Inn
Malcasa Point, CA 95405

PS This thing here makes your ghost in Black River Falls look like a sissy.

From Diary I Found

He moved behind me. His claws pierced my back, forcing me to my knees. I felt the slippery warmth of his flesh press down on me, and I knew with certainty what he was about. The thought of it appalled me to the heart and yet I was somehow thrilled by the touch of him, and strangely eager.

He mounted me from behind, a manner as unusual for humans as it is customary among many lower animals. At the first touch of his organ, fear wrenched my vitals, not for the safety of my flesh but for my everlasting soul. And yet I allowed him to continue. I know, now, that no power of mine could have prevented him from having his will with me. I made no attempt to resist, however. On the contrary, I welcomed his entry. I hungered for it as if I somehow presaged its magnificence.

Oh Lord, how he plundered me! How his claws tore my flesh! How his teeth bore into me! How his prodigious organ battered my tender womb. How brutal he was in his savagery, how gentle in his heart.

I knew, as we lay spent on the earthen cellar floor,

PS See what I mean?

GORMAN HARDY
PO Box 253
Cambridge, Mass. 03138

June 3, 1979

Miss Janice Crogan
The Welcome Inn
Malcasa Point, CA 95405

Dear Janice,

I must begin by offering an apology for the lengthy delay in answering. Unfortunately, my publisher was rather slow in forwarding your letter of March 31.

Since the publication of *Horror at Black River Falls*, I have been bombarded by fan letters, not a few of which offered ideas guaranteed to inspire another blockbuster. Most such suggestions, of course, were utter tripe. Yours, however, did arouse my curiosity.

Unfortunately, my preliminary research has turned up very little about 'Beast House'. I was able to determine, through various traveler's guides of California, only that such a place does exist in the town of Malcasa Point, that several murders allegedly took place there, and that guided tours of the house are available. While this information is rather paltry, it does substantiate several of the claims made in your letter.

I found myself most intrigued by the photocopy you enclosed of the diary page. If the diary proves to be authentic and if it contains sufficient material along the lines you suggest, it might very well provide a launching pad for a study of 'Beast House'.

Naturally, I must read the diary in its entirety before making any commitment. Enclosed find my check in the amount of twenty dollars to cover copying and mailing expenses.

Very truly

Gorman Hardy

Gorman Hardy

June 11, 1979

Gorman Hardy
PO Box 253
Cambridge, Mass. 03138

Dear Mr Hardy,
   Enclosed is your check for twenty dollars. I am really glad
you are interested and I am sure your not trying to pull something, but
no way am I going to send you the whole
diary because where does that leave me? Maybe I am paranoid, but I
need to have an agreement about my split before you can see any more
diary. I think fifty-fifty would be fair, as its all my idea and you can't do
anything without the diary.

                    Sincerely,

                    Janice Crogan

                    Janice Crogan

GORMAN HARDY
PO Box 253
Cambridge, Mass. 03138

June 16, 1979

Miss Janice Crogan
The Welcome Inn
Malcasa Point, CA 95405

Dear Janice,

Naturally, I am disappointed by your response concerning the diary. I do, however, understand your reluctance to place trust in a total stranger. As a professional writer for nearly twenty years, I have frequently been 'stabbed in the back', not only by strangers but by those I deemed friends. One can never be too cautious.

While I do not feel that the situation, at this time, warrants an agreement of any kind, I want to assure you that I remain interested in pursuing the project.

During the last weekend in August, I will be addressing a convention of the National Library Association in San Francisco. If you are agreeable to the arrangement, I will visit Malcasa Point following the convention, prepared to discuss terms with you, read the diary, and embark on such research as will be necessary to get the project under way.

Very truly,

Gorman Hardy

Gorman Hardy

1

'What you need,' Nora said, 'is a good fucking.'

'I see.'

'Look around you, take your pick. You're the best-looking gal here.'

Tyler didn't look. Instead, she took a sip of her Baileys.

'I'm serious,' Nora said.

'You're plastered.'

'Plastered but lucid, hon. You need a good fucking. You've been pissin' and moanin' ever since we got to San Francisco. Shit, if you didn't want to come to the convention, you should've stayed home.'

'I didn't know it'd be this bad,' Tyler said.

'What'd you expect, Ringling Brothers? These things are always a drag. What do you want from a bunch of librarians?'

'It's not that.'

'What is it?'

'The city.'

'What's wrong with the city? It's gorgeous.'

'I know.'

'You pissed 'cause the cable cars aren't running?'

'Sure,' Tyler said. She tried to smile, but couldn't.

'Come on, what's wrong? Cough it up.'

'I just feel rotten, that's all.'

'Rotten how?'

'Rotten lonely.' Tyler lowered her gaze from Nora's shadowy face. She stared at the candle in front of her. Its flame streaked and blurred as tears came to her eyes. She backhanded the tears away, and took a drink of her Irish cream. 'It's this damn city,' she said. 'Being here again. I thought I'd be okay, but . . . everywhere I go, everywhere I look, they're all places I've been with him.'

'A guy.'

Tyler nodded. 'He even brought me up here once to see the revolving bar. We had margaritas. Then we walked down to North Beach and went to the City Lights and that second-hand bookstore across the alley I showed you yesterday.'

'When was all this?'

'About five years ago. I was a senior at San Francisco State. Dan –
that was his name – Dan Jenson. He lived in Mill Valley, over in Marin.
I met him on the Dipsey Trail.'

Nora made a face. 'The Dipsey Trail?'

'It goes from Mill Valley, up into the hills around Mount Tam, and
finally ends up at Stinson Beach. Anyway, that's where we met. I was
hiking it with my roommate, and he was running it to get in shape for
the annual race . . .'

'And it was love at first sight?'

'He knocked me on my can,' Tyler said. The memory of it forced a
smile. 'I gave him hell for running me down. Not exactly love at first
sight. That came later – five, six minutes later.'

'Was it onesided?'

'I think he loved me, too.'

'So what went . . . oh no.' Nora suddenly looked stricken with pity.
'He died?'

'Hardly. I was accepted for graduate school at UCLA and he had a
job in Mill Valley. I wouldn't give up grad school, he wouldn't give up
his job. Simple as that.'

'Jesus, I don't believe it. You just threw each other away like that?'

'We both wanted our careers. I told him he could be a cop anywhere,
but . . . he was very stubborn. So was I.'

'That was the end of it?'

'I wrote him a letter. He never . . . The way he looked at it, the whole
mess was my fault. I was supposed to drop everything and marry him.'

'Oh Christ, he actually *proposed* to you?'

'He actually did.'

'Brother.'

'And you know what else?'

'What?'

'I'm twenty-six, I've got a job half the people at this convention
would kill to get, and I'm thinking I made the biggest mistake of my life
when I left Dan.'

'This just occurred to you?'

'It occurred to me a long time ago. I just figured, you know, I'd meet
someone else.'

'And you haven't.'

'Nobody I love.'

'What're you gonna do about it?'

'What *can* I do? I made my choice five years ago. I just have to live
with it.'

'Not necessarily.'

'Yeah. There's always the Golden Gate. Conveniently located.'

'Don't even joke about that,' Nora said.

'I really feel . . . oh shit,' she muttered as she started weeping again. 'I really feel . . . sometimes . . . like I threw my life away.'

'Hey, hey.' Nora reached across the table and took her hand. 'It's not the end of the world. What I was gonna suggest – you feel so strongly about this, why not give him another shot? We're how far from Mill Valley? Not very far, are we?'

Tyler shrugged and sniffed. 'I don't know, half an hour.'

'So drive over tomorrow and look him up.'

'I can't do that.'

'Why the hell not?'

'It's been *five years*! He's probably already married . . . He might not even live there anymore.'

'If that job was so important he let you slip out of his fingers, he'll be there.'

'I can't, Nora.'

'Why not take a shot? What've you got to lose? For all you know . . .'

'No.' The thought of it made her sick with dread.

'If you need some moral support, I'll come with you.'

Tyler said, 'We have to drive back tomorrow.'

'What for? We've got two more glorious weeks of summer vacation before the rat race starts. What's so important you have to get home? 'Fraid your house-plants'll croak? Let's drive over to Marin, first thing in the morning, and try to find this Dan of yours. If it doesn't work out, what've we lost? An hour or so? We can still make it to LA by dark.'

'I don't know. I want to think about it.'

'What's to think about? Go for it.'

'I don't know.' Tyler finished her Baileys. She rubbed her face. 'I . . . feel so confused. I'm going back to my room. Are you gonna stay here?'

Nora nodded. 'Night's young. I'll leave the connecting door unlocked. Wake me up at first light, okay?'

'First light? Sure thing.'

In her room on the sixth floor, Tyler flopped onto the bed. The ceiling seemed to be revolving slowly like the bar she'd just left.

She'd had too many drinks.

How many? Let's see. Three vodka tonics at the cocktail party before the banquet. God knows how much wine with dinner. Three or four glassfuls, maybe. Then two snifters of Baileys Irish Cream in the bar with Nora. No wonder the ceiling wouldn't stand still.

No wonder she'd blabbed.

If she'd been sober, she would've kept all that about Dan to herself. Nothing like a few drinks to loosen the tongue, make you say things you wish you hadn't.

Let Nora put down a few more, maybe she won't remember and they can drive on back tomorrow the way they'd planned.

Fat chance.

I can always tell her no. Put my foot down.

Her legs were hanging off the side of the bed. Her feet, resting on the floor, felt cramped. With an effort, she lifted one across her knee and pulled the shoe off. She sat up to take off the other, then remained motionless while a wave of dizziness passed.

At least she didn't feel nauseated. Just a little tipsy.

Tipsy's the word for it, all right, she thought, and let herself tip over. She drew her legs up and lay on her side, a bent arm cushioning her head.

What'll I do?

Stir your bones and take some aspirin and a few glasses of water or you'll really feel like hell in the morning.

The morning. God, the morning. What'll I do?

Tell Nora no. No, no, Nora, I don't want to go.

Why not?

Because, damn it, it would hurt too much to see him again – even to try. He'll have a wife, and she could've been me. You don't know he's married. He might be single and lonely. He might still want you.

Sure thing.

Why did I open my mouth to Nora? Because I drank too much. And if I fall asleep like this, I'll be sorry. Rolling onto her back, she drew up the skirt of her sheath dress. She raised a leg, and started to unfasten a stocking from her garter belt.

Dan hated pantyhose. To please him, she'd stopped wearing the things. She'd never gone back to them.

She'd never gone back to smoking pot, either.

And she still wore her hair short, the way he liked it. Makes you look like Peter Pan, he'd said. Peter Pan's a boy, she'd reminded him, and added that perhaps the hairstyle appealed to his latent homosexuality. Oh yeah? he'd said. Come here and we'll see if I'm a fag.

Big macho cop.

God, she missed him.

She pulled the garter belt out from under her. She slipped her panties down, and kicked them off. Then she stretched, enjoying the feel of the cool bedspread against her buttocks and legs. She could doze off right now, so easily. With a deep sigh, she sat up. She struggled with the zipper at the back of her dress, pulled the dress over her head, and removed her bra. She climbed off the bed and started to gather her clothes.

While she'd kept her hair the same, stayed away from pantyhose and pot, changed very little about herself since leaving Dan, there was one major difference. She'd been chubby, then. In her first term at UCLA, she'd dropped fifteen pounds. As if she'd left her appetite with Dan. Though the appetite had eventually returned, she'd had no trouble keeping the weight off.

She took her nightgown from the suitcase, but didn't put it on. She stepped in front of the mirror. Her eyes looked a little funny. That was the booze. She drew a forefinger over her cheekbone. For all Dan knew, she didn't have cheekbones. Or a waist. Or hip-bones.

She grinned at the Tyler Moran he'd never seen.

He'll go ape, she thought.

Her heart started thudding, for she suddenly realized she would be making that trip tomorrow. No matter the pain, no matter the outcome. If she didn't, she would always wonder about Dan, about the second chance thrown away, and she would never stop regretting it.

Her racing heart made her head throb.

She put the nightgown on. In the bathroom, she took three aspirin and drank three full tumblers of cold water.

Then she went to bed.

She lay in the darkness, remembering the look and feel and voice of Dan Jenson, wondering how he might have changed, worrying about what she might find tomorrow in Mill Valley, hoping.

Tyler smiled the next morning when she saw the Mill Valley bus depot through her windshield. 'That used to be the best place for paperbacks in the whole town,' she said. 'Wish I had a buck for every hour I spent in there.'

'How're the nerves?' Nora asked, grinning at her from the passenger seat.

'Holding out. But just barely.' She wiped her sweaty hands on the legs of her corduroys. The nerves, in fact, were not good. Her heart was beating fast, her mouth was dry, and the armpits of her blouse felt sodden.

'A quaint little burg,' Nora said.

'It used to be quainter.' She drove slowly along Throckmorton, past brightly painted shops. The road curved. To the left was a wooded area. 'Here's where the old mill used to be. The Dipsey Trail starts over there.'

'The famous Dipsey Trail.'

She turned right onto a sideroad, and stopped at the curb.

'This it?'

'This is it,' Tyler said. She took a deep breath and let it out slowly. 'It's that apartment house across the street.' Ducking, Nora looked out of the window. 'Rustic,' she said.

'Quaint and rustic.'

'Can you hack it?'

'We came this far,' Tyler told her, and tried very hard to smile.

'Do you want me to wait here?'

'Are you kidding?'

They climbed from the car. While Tyler waited, Nora took her sweater off and tossed it on her seat. 'Won't be needing that,' she said. She stepped around the rear of the car. She was wearing short culottes and tennis shoes, and without the sweater it was plain that she wore no bra. The powder blue T-shirt clung to her breasts. Her nipples made the fabric jut as if fingers were pushing it out. Tyler wished Nora had kept the sweater on, and she had second thoughts about her friend coming along.

What if Dan . . .? No, that's ridiculous.

He probably doesn't even live here anymore.

They crossed the street and climbed a slanted walkway toward the weathered wood-frame apartment house. Nora's breasts jiggled slightly with each step.

Dan won't notice. *Of course he will.*

Even dressed modestly, Nora drew men like iron filings to a magnet. Her size must be part of it. She was five eleven barefoot. She dwarfed most other women, Tyler included. She was slender, but not at all gawky. Though her face was a bit too long, her teeth too prominent, her chin not quite prominent enough for real beauty, her blue eyes had an intensity that made the imperfections less noticeable. And there was something erotic about her wide mouth, her full lips.

Nora radiated sexuality. Not only men noticed it. So did women, and many seemed to resent it.

Tyler was not very happy about it herself, as they stepped into the shadowed entryway.

Don't worry, she told herself. I'm the one Dan loved. Besides, Nora won't try anything. She's my best friend. She knows how I feel.

Yeah. Outclassed.

Forget it.

Tyler stepped close to the panel of mailboxes. 'He was in number four,' she said.

The name, embossed on a strip of red plastic above the mail slot, was B. Lawrence. They checked the other labels. 'No Jenson,' Nora said. 'You sure you've got the right building?'

'Positive.' She felt a tug of disappointment, but it was mixed with relief. Her voice sounded shaky as she said, 'I knew it'd be a waste of time.'

Nora squeezed her shoulder. She looked determined. 'It's not over yet, hon. You're with Nora Branson, ace reference librarian. What I don't know, I find out. Just a matter of research. First we check on B. Lawrence, then the manager. If they don't pan out, there's the telephone directory. If that doesn't work, we'll pay a visit to the local constabulary. If Dan's not with them anymore, they'll probably know where he went. He'll have friends in the department, not to mention a personnel file that'll tell where they sent his references.'

'Maybe we should just forget it.'

'No way. This is your life we're talking about. You obviously love the guy. One way or another, we're gonna find him for you. Where's number four?'

Tyler sighed. 'Upstairs.'

She followed Nora up the wooden stairway to a balcony that stretched the length of the building front. They stopped at the first door to the right. Five years ago, it had been stained wood. Since then, someone had applied bright, lime green paint. The trim was orange. A wind-chime of clay pipes, suspended just above the door, clinked softly in the breeze.

Tyler knew that Dan didn't live here anymore, but her heart thudded wildly when Nora rang the doorbell. She took deep breaths, trying to calm herself.

The door opened. A short, chubby woman in a *muumuu* and curlers smiled out at them. 'Greetings,' she said. 'What can I do for you?'

Before Tyler could answer, Nora said, 'We're looking for Dan Jenson. Apparently he used to live here.'

'Righto. Steely Dan the cop. My old bud. You friends of his?'

Nora darted a thumb at Tyler. 'They're old buds.'

'Ah ha!' Nodding, she studied Tyler with one eye half shut, and shook a forefinger at her. 'I *knew it*, knew I'd seen your face. Knew it the minute I looked at you. You're the girl in the picture. That eight by five he kept over the fireplace. Sure. That was you, wasn't it?'

Tyler shrugged. She didn't know the picture, but Dan had always been snapping photos of her. He liked to catch her unaware – for the 'natural look', as he called it. He'd even taken a shot, once, as she stepped out of the shower. She blushed at the memory. Obviously, that hadn't been the picture he'd blown up for the mantel.

'The girl he called Tippy, am I right?'

Tyler nodded.

'Tippy?' Nora asked.

'Short for Tippecanoe,' she explained. 'Tippecanoe and Tyler, too.'

'That's Dan. Always one for the nicknames. I was always Barbie Doll. I lived down in number one, back when he was here. He used to have me up for pizza. Oh, he made luscious pizza.'

'My recipe,' Tyler muttered. She felt an ache like homesickness. 'I showed him how to make it.'

'Oh, I'm drooling at the thought of it. How I miss his pizza.'

'I could send you the recipe.'

'Would you?' She snatched Tyler's hand and squeezed it. 'You're such a dear. It's no wonder at all Dan was that stuck on you. He'll be tickled to death to see you again. You will be . . .?'

'Then you know where he is?' Nora asked.

'Why, sure.'

Tyler's heart lurched.

'He left here . . . oh, better than two years ago. I moved right in. My old apartment was so cramped, it was like living in a closet. This is two bedrooms, you know. Gives me some space to spread out. A girl needs her elbow room.'

'Is Dan still in Mill Valley?' Nora persisted.

'Oh no. He took a job on the force up at Malcasa Point. Said he wanted to get out of the Bay Area, though I can't imagine why. You know Malcasa? No? Let me tell you, it's the sticks. I can't feature *anyone* living there. But different strokes, am I right? Not even a decent restaurant, much less a movie theater. I doubt there's a shopping mall within fifty miles. When I say sticks, I mean sticks. But that's what he wanted and that's what he got.'

'Malcasa Point?' Nora asked.

'Hang on a sec, I'll get the address.' As she stepped over to a lamp table, she kept talking over her shoulder. 'I'll admit, now, I haven't heard from him in a year or better. Got a card from him last Christmas – no, that was two Christmases ago, not long after he moved. Seemed to like it fine up there.' She took an address book from the lamp-table drawer, and came back. 'I sent him a postcard from Naples this past December. Spent the holidays there. Oh, a marvelous city, Naples.' She flipped through the pages of her book. 'Ah, here we be. Jenson, Dan. Ten Seaside Lane, Malcasa Point.'

Tyler's hand trembled badly as she scribbled the information on a notepad. 'Why don't you give me your name? Is it Lawrence?'

'Righto. Barbara Lawrence. That's Barbara with three a's, not like

Streisand. Can you imagine, Bar-bra? Sounds like a steel brassiere, am I right?'

'When Dan wrote to you,' Nora said, 'did he say anything about being married?'

'Not a word. Single, far as I know.' She winked at Tyler. 'Now you will send me that recipe, won't you?'

'Absolutely.'

'How far is this Malcasa Point?' Nora asked.

'Oh, you can make it in, I'd say, maybe three hours.

That's if you don't dawdle. You go straight up the Coast Highway, on a good piece past Bodega. You have a map?'

'In the car.'

'Well, you can't miss it. Now, make sure you give Dan regards from Barbie Doll.'

'We'll do that,' Tyler assured her.

'And for the love of Mike, whatever you do up there, don't miss the Beast House tour. Tacky tacky. You'll love it. It's a scream.'

2

After five minutes on the narrow, twisting Coast Highway with its cliff only yards away and the ocean far below, Tyler fastened her seatbelt.

'Might be better off without it,' Nora told her.

'You're right.' She opened the buckle. 'It'd hinder my leap.'

'I'm just glad we're on the inside lane.'

'We won't be, coming back.'

'Let's take an inland route.' Nora picked up the map and studied it for two or three minutes. 'Maybe take 128 over to 101.'

'Whatever,' Tyler said. 'We can worry about it when the times comes.'

'I think we'd better plan on spending the night in Malcasa. It'll be mid-afternoon by the time we get there.'

'Let's just play it by ear.'

'Wonder what it's got in the way of motels.' She opened the glove compartment and pulled out the Automobile Club tour guide for California and Nevada. 'Let's see here. We already know there're no decent restaurants, much less a movie theater.' She flipped through the pages. 'Here we go. Los Gatos, Madera, Mommoth Lakes. Whoops, no Malcasa Point. Maybe we won't spend the night.'

'Every town has a motel. There must be at least one.'

'I hope so. Nothing Triple-A-approved, though. Maybe a fleabag or two. Let's see what the little burg's got in the way of attractions.' She turned toward the front of the book. 'Malcasa, Malcasa,' she mumbled as she searched. 'Ah-ha! It's actually here, can you believe it? Malcasa Point, altitude thirty-four feet. Such height! Hope I don't get nose-bleeds. Only one entry for the place. Beast House. Not to be confused with *Animal House*.' She chuckled at her little joke, then began to read aloud from the guide book. "Beast House, 10 Front Street. Claimed to be the scene of several grisly murders, this Victorian relic was built in 1902 by the widow of the notorious outlaw, Lyle Thorn. Featured are displays of the murder scenes with lifelike wax figures depicting the victims. Tours daily ten till four; closed holidays. Adults four dollars, under twelve, two dollars." Maybe we can take it in while we're there.'

'Barbie Doll thought highly of it,' Tyler said.

'Right. Tacky tacky.'

In the rearview mirror, Tyler saw a Porsche closing in fast. She held her breath as it swung out and roared alongside. It shot by. It swerved back into the lane, missing their front bumper by inches, just in time to avoid a head-on with an approaching station wagon.

'Asshole,' Nora muttered. 'Porsches, VW bugs, and pickup trucks. Gotta watch out for 'em. They've all got maniacs behind the wheel.'

'Not to mention the big rigs,' Tyler said. 'At least there's none of them along here. Nothing like an eighteen-wheeler tailgating you.'

'They're murder. Somebody ought to build a truckers museum and fill it with wax figures depicting their victims.'

'Call it Peterbilt House.'

They stopped for lunch at a restaurant overlooking the water of Bodega Bay. Nora drank Dos Equiis with her plate of fried clams. Tyler, nervous about the twisting road ahead, had a glass of Pepsi with her cheeseburger.

'Look familiar?' she asked, nodding at the expanse of glinting water beyond the window.

'Should it?' Nora asked.

'Remember *The Birds*?'

'The film?'

She nodded, and bit into her burger. Juice dribbled down her chin. She mopped it off with a napkin. 'Yeah,' she said. 'Way across there? That peninsula's where Rod Taylor lived.'

'No kidding?'

'Remember? Tippi Hedren took a motorboat across to it, and that bird divebombed her?'

'Sure. So that's where it happened. I'll be damned. I saw that film three or four times.'

'The schoolhouse is around here someplace, I think.'

'How about the Bates Motel?'

'Wrong movie.'

'That's probably up at Malcasa Point. The one Triple A won't approve.'

'Actually, it's at Universal Studios.'

'I know that, dimbo. Just making a little joke.'

On the way out of Bodega, they drove past a small, wood-frame schoolhouse. 'Bet that's the one they used,' Tyler said.

'Where's the jungle gym?'

Tyler shrugged.

'They probably had to junk the thing after all those birds crapped on it.'

They left Bodega behind. In a short while, Nora was asleep, slumped down in her seat with her knees against the dashboard, her head tilted sideways, her mouth drooping open. Tyler felt a little groggy herself. She lowered her window to catch the fresh ocean breeze on her face.

Thoughts of Dan filled her mind, memories of their times together. She could hardly believe that in just a couple more hours she might actually be seeing him again.

He'd kept a photo of her above the fireplace. He wouldn't have done that unless he still cared. And he'd talked to Barbie Doll about her.

Barbie Doll. What an awful nickname.

He used to invite her up for pizza. Had they . . .?

Tyler felt a tightness inside.

Not Barbie Doll. Why not? Because she's a good ten years older than Dan, and fat? I wasn't exactly svelte and it didn't bother him. At least he never complained.

And so what if Dan did have something going with Barbie? Why not?

Hell, they were probably just friends.

Five years. Face it, he's been with plenty of women since me. Some of it must've been serious.

She wiped her sweaty hands on the legs of her corduroys.

What's the good of thinking about it?

But she couldn't stop. With a sick feeling of despair, she wondered how many women he'd taken to bed. Who were they? Did some remind him of her, and make him miss her? Maybe he never thought about her at all anymore, her image erased by a new love.

Stop this!

At least he's not married. Or he wasn't as of two Christmases ago. Or he had been married by then, but didn't mention it in his card to Barbie. Anything was possible. He might even have moved again. Might've left Malcasa. Wouldn't that be . . .

She was shocked from her thoughts as she rounded a curve and faced a green pickup truck. It was just ahead passing an RV, speeding straight at her. She hit the horn and brakes.

Nora lurched awake. 'Holy shit!'

Tyler swung wide to make room, her right-hand tires spraying up dirt and gravel on the road's shoulder.

The driver of the pickup smirked and saluted the brim of his cowboy hat as he shot past.

Nora gave him the finger. 'Asshole!' she yelled.

Tyler steered her car back onto the road.

'Christ,' Nora gasped. She clutched her chest as if to keep her heart from jumping out. 'Fuckin' redneck scum-butt!'

Tyler took a deep breath. Her own heart was sledging. Her legs felt hot and weak.

'Fucker woulda killed us,' Nora said. 'What'd I tell you? Pickup trucks! Put a bastard in a pickup, he thinks he's King Shit.'

Moments later, a green pickup appeared in the rearview mirror. Tyler groaned. 'He's coming back.'

'You're kidding.' Nora looked over her shoulder. 'Oh, shit.'

'Maybe it's not him.'

'It's him. Oh, shit. Guess I shouldn't have flipped him the bird.'

The truck bore down on them. Then it was tailgating, speeding along no more than a yard from their rear bumper, its horn blasting. Nora faced forward and shrank down in her seat. She made a sick-looking smile at Tyler. 'What do you think, is he pissed or horny?'

'I don't want to find out,' Tyler said. She searched the area ahead. For as far as she could see, the two-lane strip of road was bordered by brown, desolate hills and a slope dropping away to the shoreline. No gas stations where she might stop for help. No shops or cafés. No dwellings of any kind.

'Where's the highway patrol when you need it?' Nora muttered. 'Where's civilization when you need it?'

Tyler eased down on the gas pedal. The pickup fell away as the speedometer needle climbed from fifty-five to sixty to sixty-five. Then she was pushing seventy. She was on a straightaway, but she could see a bad curve in the distance – maybe a mile ahead. And the pickup was gaining fast.

'No way,' she muttered. She took her foot off the accelerator. Their speed dropped quickly. She gazed at the rearview, trying to fight her growing panic as the truck raced closer. It didn't seem to be slowing. She braced herself for the impact. At the last instant, the pickup swung into the southbound lane and pulled alongside. Its horn blared like someone screaming into Tyler's ears. Instead of passing, it kept even. The road ahead was clear, at least for now. She half expected the pickup to swerve and bump her, sending the little Omni careening into the hillside. Her foot hit the brake pedal. The pickup shot by, cut in front, and slowed. She mashed the brake. With a glance at the rearview mirror, she saw a Mustang bearing down fast. She was doing twenty, then fifteen, the pickup blocking her way.

'Oh, Christ!' she cried. She pulled onto the bumpy shoulder and stopped. The pickup swung over. The Mustang to the rear crossed the center line and sped past. The pickup backed up until it almost touched the Omni's front bumper.

With a trembling hand, Tyler cranked her window. She elbowed the lock button. Through the rear window of the pickup's cab, she watched the man take off his cowboy hat.

'You wouldn't happen to have a gun handy?' Nora asked.

'Oh, sure.'

'I didn't think so.'

The man scooted across the front seat. He opened the passenger door and climbed down. He didn't look at them. He scowled at the ground as he ambled closer.

He was a big man, maybe thirty years old, with eyes that seemed too small for his massive face, and thick bulging lips. His jaw looked broader than his forehead.

'Fucking Neanderthal,' Nora muttered.

He suddenly looked up. His tiny eyes flicked from Nora to Tyler. His lips curled into a grin. He raised his middle finger and twisted his hand slowly as if screwing it in. Tyler pressed her knees together.

'Pig,' Nora said.

Using his middle finger, he gestured for them to come out.

Nora leaned close to the windshield. 'Not on your life, shithead!' she yelled.

'For Christsake!' Tyler gasped.

Smirking, the man snapped off the Omni's radio antenna. He swung it like a riding crop. Tyler flinched as it lashed the windshield.

'Shove it up your ass!' Nora yelled.

Tyler punched her shoulder. 'Stop that! It's bad enough! Christ, don't antagonize him.'

He struck the windshield again. Tyler rammed the shift to reverse and sped backward, the car bouncing over the rough ground of the shoulder. She wanted to swing out onto the road, but a huge camper van was rushing in from the rear. Steering away to avoid it, she felt the car tip. She hit the brakes. The RV roared past, close enough to make the Omni shudder with its buffeting wind. She shifted to first, stepped on the gas pedal and let out the clutch. She heard a rear tire spin. But the car didn't move.

The man, jogging toward them, stopped to pick up a rock the size of a softball.

Nora shoved her door open. She leaned out and glanced back and shut the door and locked it. 'We're hanging over the ditch,' she reported.

'Oh, great.'

'That rock, he can bash his way in.'

'I know, I know!'

The man hurried closer, rock in one hand, antenna in the other.

Tyler tried again to make the car move.

'Look,' Nora said, 'he'll just demolish a window and get in anyway.' She opened her door again.

'Don't!'

She climbed out and stepped toward the front of the car.

'Nora!'

She leaned back, rump against the hood, and folded her arms across her chest. The man stopped jogging. One side of his mouth twisted up. He tossed the rock away, shifted the antenna to his right hand, and walked slowly toward her, switching the air.

With a groan, Tyler turned off the engine. She set the emergency brake and got out. Her legs felt rubbery as she walked to the front of the car. She rested against the hood, shoulder to shoulder with Nora.

About four feet away, the man stopped. His gaze roamed slowly down Nora's body, then slid over to Tyler. She felt cold and sick inside. She tried not to squirm.

Nora said, 'Like what you see, liver-lips?'

With a snarl, he whipped the antenna. It whistled by their faces.

'I'm shaking,' Nora said.

He pointed the antenna at a cluster of bushes beyond the ditch. 'Get going,' he said.

'It can talk,' Nora said.

'Move!'

'What've you got in mind?'

'Gonna fuck your asses.'

'No fooling. With what?'

He lashed her shoulder. She flinched and gritted her teeth. 'I'm gonna take you down, buddy,' she muttered, and lunged at the man. He rammed a knee into her belly, doubling her, and flung her sideways. As she tumbled into the ditch, Tyler drove a fist at the man's face. She felt his nose smash under her knuckles. He blinked and shook his head. Blood gushed from his nostrils. Snarling, he clutched Tyler's throat and shoved her backward. The front of the car collapsed her legs. He slammed her down on the hood. His other hand tore at her blouse. Blood spilled onto her face. She punched the side of his head. She kicked, but he was between her legs, leaning down on her, mashing her against the hood. Blinking his blood out of her eyes, she saw his fist rise like a hammer about to strike. Then he looked over his shoulder. He thrust himself off her and whirled around. Raising her head, Tyler saw his pickup racing toward them.

'Hey!' the man yelled.

Tyler sat up, slid forward, and got her feet on the ground as the truck skidded to a stop. She glanced to the side. Nora was scurrying up out of the ditch, hair in her eyes.

The truck's passenger door flew open. A lean man in white pants and a polo shirt jumped down. He nodded to someone inside. The truck rolled forward. It veered to the right. The other door swung open. A man leaped out, windmilling as he caught his balance.

'No!' the big man roared as his pickup nosed down the slope of the ditch. It stopped abruptly with a crunch of metal, a tinkling shatter of headlights. The man covered his ears. He fell to his knees as Nora, coming up behind him, lashed his back with the antenna.

Now that the truck was out of the way, Tyler saw a blue Mustang parked a distance up the road.

Nora tossed the antenna aside. She nodded at the pair of strangers who were standing just in front of the cowering man. 'Are you ladies all right?' asked the one in the polo shirt. He looked from Nora to Tyler.

Tyler pulled her blouse shut, and nodded.

'Too bad about the truck,' said the one who had crashed it, shaking his head and sounding extremely sincere as he stared at the man. He was shorter than his friend, with a crewcut and a chubby boyish face. His neck was thick. His T-shirt was stretched taut over his broad shoulders and bulging chest. The brass buckle of his belt read Colt. He wore blue jeans that looked brand new. Their cuffs were rolled up about three inches. He wore scuffed cowboy boots with pointed toes. Tyler figured he must be gay. That would mean his friend was, too.

The friend squatted down, bringing his face close to the kneeling man. 'Now here's the plan,' he said in a calm voice. 'You get to your feet and apologize to the ladies. You pay them for the antenna. Then you go back to your pickup and stay there.'

'What if I don't?' he muttered.

The man patted his shoulder. Gently, he said, 'I'll let Jack rip your face off.'

They stood up. The big man turned to Nora and Tyler. He kept his head down. He rubbed a sleeve across his mouth to wipe the blood away. He made gasping, sobbing sounds as he reached into a rear pocket and took out his wallet. He pulled out a ten-dollar bill and held it out to Tyler with a shaking, red-stained hand. Jack leaned in close, and eyed the bill. 'Cheap bastard,' he said. He snatched away the wallet. He plucked out a twenty, took the ten from the man, and gave them both to Tyler. Then he handed the wallet back.

'Now apologize,' said the lean one.

'Sorry,' he murmured without looking up.

'It's quite all right,' Nora said. She took a step toward him, arms stiff at her sides, and shot a fist into his groin. His breath exploded out. He dropped to the ground clutching himself, and Nora slammed a knee into his bleeding nose. The blow knocked him backward. The lean man hopped out of his way. The blocky one named Jack grinned at Nora and began to clap.

3

'Nora Branson.' She offered her hand to the musclebound man.

'Jack Wyatt,' he said, shaking it.

'Tyler Moran,' Tyler said, and shook hands with the lean one.

'Abe Clanton.'

'Names like a couple of gunslingers,' Nora said, shaking with Abe as Tyler squeezed Jack's hand. She was surprised by his gentle grip.

'Yup,' Jack said. 'We're mean *hombres*.'

Looking past Abe, Tyler saw the big man stagger down the side of the ditch and climb into his pickup.

'I guess this was our lucky day,' Nora said.

'We saw him force you off the road,' Abe explained. 'We were right behind you.'

'Good thing. That was great of you guys to stop. A lot of people would've kept on going.'

'Yes,' Tyler said. 'We sure appreciate it.'

Abe nodded slightly. He looked into her eyes with a steady, probing gaze. It made her nervous. She wanted to look away, but couldn't. 'Did he hurt you?'

Tyler shook her head. 'Not much.'

'That's *his* blood, I hope.'

'I think so.'

'Look,' Nora said, 'you guys are heading north? Why don't we all stop somewhere, we'll buy you a drink?'

The suggestion made Tyler's pulse quicken. She glanced down at her torn, bloody blouse. 'I can't go in anywhere like this.'

'So change,' Nora said.

'I guess I could.'

'How about it, fellas?'

'Fine by me,' Abe said.

Jack rubbed his hands together. 'All *right*.'

'Why don't you follow us?' Nora asked. 'First decent place we spot, we'll pull in.'

'It's a deal.'

'Whoops,' Nora said. 'One second. We're stuck here.' She nodded toward the rear of the car.

'Gotcha,' Jack said.

Abe leaned over the driver's seat. He released the emergency brake. He gripped the steering wheel and open door, and pushed while Jack shoved the rear end. The little Omni rolled away from the ditch. Abe reset the brake. 'Okay,' he said. 'We'll wait up ahead for you.'

'See you in a bit,' Nora said.

As the men started toward their car, Tyler knelt on the passenger seat and took a plastic container of Wet Ones from the glove compartment. She crawled out. Plucking one of the moist towels from the pack, she scrubbed her face. The paper came away smeared brown-red. 'Did I get it?'

'Most of it.'

'God.' She gave the pack to Nora.

They went to the rear of the car. While she opened the hatchback and unfastened her suitcase, Nora cleaned herself. Her arms were dirty and grass-stained and scraped from her fall into the ditch. The knee she'd driven into the man's face was smudged with his blood.

Tyler waited for a car to pass, then took off her blouse. She stuffed it into a corner of the trunk. 'Damn,' she muttered, seeing the blood spots on her white bra. Well, she couldn't change into a clean one – not here by the road. Her skin, too, was stained as if sunburnt in splotches. Taking a towelette from Nora, she cleaned most of it off her shoulders and chest and belly. She turned to Nora. 'Is that it?'

'Under your chin.'

'God.' She rubbed.

'That's got it. Shit, he bled like a stuck pig.'

'Pig is right,' Tyler said. She made sure her hands were clean, then took a fresh yellow blouse from her suitcase and put it on.

'How am I?' Nora asked, turning round.

Tyler brushed some dirt and bits of weed from the back of Nora's T-shirt. 'Okay,' she said.

She shut the suitcase and hatchback. They hurried to the front and climbed in. A van sped by. Then the lane was clear. She pulled out and glanced at the pickup as they passed it. The cab was low in the ditch, blocked from view by the tailgate. She was glad she couldn't see the man inside.

'Asshole's gonna need a tow truck,' Nora said. 'Not to mention a new set of nuts.' She waved at the Mustang as they drew alongside it.

Abe nodded. He was at the wheel. He pulled out behind them.

'Not bad, huh?' Nora asked. 'An escort.'

Tyler picked up speed. The blue Mustang kept pace, staying several car lengths back.

Nora rubbed her shoulder.

'Hurt?'

'Not like the knee in the guts, the bastard.'

'You got him pretty good.'

'We both did. Scares me, though. If Jack and Abe hadn't come along, he would've had our asses on a plate.'

'Yeah, probably.'

'That Jack's a hunk, isn't he?'

'He must lift weights,' Tyler said.

'You suppose they're gay?'

'They're nice guys, regardless.'

'Yeah. Well, there's nice and there's *nice*.'

'I don't think they're gay. I mean, I sort of wondered at first . . .'

'Yeah. But that Abe sure looked you over.'

Tyler felt heat rise to her skin.

'Still, two guys travelling together.'

'*We're* travelling together.'

'Right!' She snorted. 'They're probably wondering right now if we're a pair of dykes. Ha ha.' She rubbed her belly. 'How about that Abe? I wouldn't kick him out of bed, either. Did you hear how he talked to that bastard? "Now here's the plan. First you apologize . . ." Sounded like Dirty Harry, didn't he? More to that guy than meets the eye, I tell you that much right now.'

'What do you mean?'

'He's a way you don't get in ballet school. Hard eyes. They *both* had hard eyes, did you notice that? Except when old Abe was checking you out. Then they got very soft.' She chuckled. 'And maybe someplace else got *un*soft, if you know what I mean.'

'Nora.'

'You're right. I don't think they're fags. God, I hope not.'

'I don't see what difference it makes,' Tyler said. 'It's not like we'll be dating the guys. We're just gonna buy them drinks, right? We'll probably never see them again.'

'You never know, hon. You just never know.'

4

'Wonderful! Fabulous! Swing over, Brian, get some shots. Too good to be true, wouldn't you say? *Beast* House. What do you think?'

'Nice,' Brian said.

'Nice? It looks positively dripping with evil.'

The Mercedes moved slowly past the small, roadside shack that appeared to be a ticket booth. On its wall, a sign weathered to the dirty gray of the driftwood read BEAST HOUSE in crimson block letters that dripped as if recently painted with blood. Looking over his shoulder, Gorman Hardy saw a girl inside the booth's open window, a blonde of fourteen or fifteen. She held an open paperback on the counter shelf.

Gorman, who had celebrated his fifty-sixth birthday by hurling an empty bottle of Chivas Regal into his mirror to destroy the fat, gray-haired man looking back at him, still had eyes sharp enough to spot his own book covers at a hundred paces. The book in the girl's hands was not *Horror at Black River Falls*.

Several cars were parked along the walkway fronting the grounds. Brian eased into a space between a Datsun and a grimy station wagon with a tail end like a family album of stickers. Glancing over the array of red hearts, Gorman gathered that the clan had loved Hearst Castle, the Sequoia National Park, Muir Woods and the Winchester Mystery House. It had left its heart in San Francisco, and it wanted the world to know that one nuclear bomb could ruin the entire day. That one, he thought, should sport a bleeding heart. A Beast House bumper sticker, if such were available, might very well add a dripping valentine to the collection.

'You getting out?' Brian asked.

'I'll wait here. Try to keep a low profile.'

'Just a tourist with a Nikon,' he said, and climbed out.

As the door thumped shut, Gorman opened the glove compartment. He took out his Panasonic microcassette recorder. Holding it near his lap, out of sight in case someone might be watching, he said, 'Preliminary observations on Beast House, August 1979.' He turned and stared out the open car window as he spoke.

'The house, set back about fifty yards from the main street of Malcasa Point, is surrounded by a seven-foot fence of wrought-iron bars, each bar tipped with a lethal point to keep intruders out, or perhaps to keep the beast inside.' He smiled. 'Good one. Use that.' In ominous tones, he repeated, 'Perhaps to keep the beast inside.

'The only access appears to be through an opening behind the ticket booth, where a lithe teenaged girl is engaged, even now, in reading my previous book, *Horror at Black River Falls*.' Why not? he thought.

'In contrast to the lush green of the wooded hills that rise up beyond the fence, the grounds of Beast House appear singularly flat and dreary. No trees or flowers bloom inside the fence, and even the grass is mottled. with brown patches as if the earth itself has been poisoned by the evil contagion of the house.'

Now we're cooking, he thought. Lay it on, lay it on!

'Though the day is cloudless and bright, a sense of insufferable gloom chills my heart as I gaze at the bleak building.' He nodded. Not bad. Rather Poe-ish. 'The Victorian structure seems a monument to things long dead. Its windows, like malevolent eyes, leer out at the quiet afternoon as if seeking a victim.' Nonsense, of course. The windows were simply windows. From the rather rundown appearance of the house, Gorman was surprised that none was broken. The owners, obviously, were taking some care of the place. The lawn could use more water, and the weathered wooden siding could use a good coat of paint. Such improvements, however, would take away from the aura of deterioration they probably wished to cultivate.

'Especially unnerving,' he continued, 'are the small, attic windows that look out from three gables along the steeply slanting roof, draped in shadow from eaves like brooding eyelids. Peering up at them, wondering what might lurk inside, I feel a chill creep up my spine. If I don't look away soon, I know that a dim, ghastly face will appear at one of the windows.' Such eloquence, he thought – such nonsense. But he suddenly found himself staring at the farthest attic window. A chill had indeed crept up his spine. The skin at the back of his neck felt tight and tingly. *If I don't look away soon . . .*

He lowered his eyes to the gray metal recorder. He listened to its quiet, reassuring hum for a few moments, then looked again toward the house, taking care to avoid the high window.

'At the far end of the roof,' he said, 'is a tower. It has a cone-shaped top. A widow's peak . . . no, a witch's cap, that's what it's called. There are windows under . . .' He switched off the recorder.

Twisting around, he eased his head out the car window and looked back. Brian wasn't in sight. He pulled in his head, turned the other way, and spotted the younger man through the rear window. Camera to his eye, Brian was standing on the other side of the road directly across from the ticket booth. Gorman reached to the steering wheel. He gave the horn a quick beep. Brian lowered the camera, nodded, and returned to the car. Instead of opening his door, he ducked and peered in at Gorman.

'Are you about finished?'

'Any time. I got some sweet ones. Found out they're running another tour in forty-five minutes.'

The news didn't please Gorman; it gave him a chilly, liquid feeling in the bowels. 'Not today,' he said. 'I'd prefer to wait until we've talked to the girl.'

'Fine by me,' Brian said, and climbed in. 'The motel's just a couple of miles up.' He swung out from behind the station wagon. 'The gal said it's on the right, we can't miss it.'

'The girl in the ticket booth?'

'She's the one. Name's Sandy. Very cooperative.'

'Have you ever met a young woman who wasn't?'

'Very few,' Brian answered. A smile creased his lean cheeks, and he gave Gorman a sample of the sincere, penetrating gaze that made him such a hit with the ladies.

'Watch where you're driving,' Gorman said, unable to keep the bitterness out of his voice. After four years of almost daily contact with Brian, he still found himself, at times, seething with envy. The thick blond hair, the pale blue eyes, the flawless skin and trim young body seemed to mock Gorman, make him look by comparison like an aged and overweight bulldog. It hardly seemed fair.

'Wonder what they do for kicks in this burg,' Brian said.

'Our friend Janice will provide you with some distractions.'

'Hope she's not a dog.'

'Dog or not, you'll abide by the game plan.'

'Sure, sure.'

After a few blocks of souvenir shops, cafés, sporting-goods stores, bars and gas stations, they reached the far end of town. The road curved into a forest. Gorman looked back, wondering if they'd somehow passed the Welcome Inn.

'Don't worry,' Brian said. 'We didn't miss it.'

'Sandy told you we couldn't.'

'Should be just ahead.'

And it was.

On the right, looking cool in the shade of pines, stood the Welcome Inn's Carriage House, a quaint-looking restaurant with bright white siding and green trim, an antique buggy adorning its lawn. A walkway led from the entrance to an auto court where a dozen bungalows surrounded a parking area. Except for two cars, the lot was deserted.

'Looks like they're not full up,' Brian observed.

'Very astute,' Gorman said.

Just beyond the entrance to the court, the road flared out for parking in front of the office. Brian slowed and swung over. He pulled up close to the front porch. 'Want to wait in the car?' he asked.

'I hardly think that would be appropriate.'

'Thought you might want to make notes.'

While Gorman put his recorder into the glove compartment, Brian twisted the rearview mirror and patted down the sides of his windblown hair. Then they both climbed from the car. They mounted the wooden steps to the porch. Gorman pulled open the screen door and entered first.

With light pouring in from the door and windows, the office seemed bright and cheerful. He saw no one, but through the half-open door behind the registration desk he heard the voices and music of a television. Stepping up to the desk, he tapped the plunger of a call bell. He turned around. Brian had wandered over to a rack of travel brochures.

'If there's a Beast House, grab a few.'

Brian nodded without looking back.

Gorman scanned the calico curtains, the pine paneling of the walls, the glossy green and yellow body of a fish mounted above the entry, the couch resting beneath one of the windows, its tweedy green fabric faded from the sunlight. A few magazines were neatly stacked on an end table.

Hanging on the far wall was an enormous map labeled MALCASA POINT AND ITS ENVIRONS, VACATION PARADISE with over-sized cartoon characters enjoying the various activities: a little man surf-fishing; a family sunbathing and swimming at a beach; a boat offshore full of cheery anglers one of whom had managed to hook a scuba diver. The diver had exclamation points trapped inside his air bubbles. Back on land, the map depicted an array of hikers and campers in the wooded hills, a man in waders fly-fishing in a stream, rafters riding the rapids. At the center of the map loomed the Welcome Inn, shown in detail and larger than the entire town of Malcasa Point. Gorman's eyes followed the main road downward to a drawing of Beast House. Over its roof hovered a white apparition twice the size of the house. In spite of fangs and claws, the creature bore a marked resemblance to Casper the Friendly Ghost. The word 'BOOO!' was scrawled across its belly.

'Sorry to keep you waiting.'

Turning, Gorman smiled at the girl. 'Quite all right,' he said.

She pushed the door to the living quarters shut. The latch clacked into place. She glanced toward Brian, then fixed her eyes on Gorman. 'Mr Hardy,' she said.

'Janice?'

Her head bobbed a bit.

She was not a dog, which must please Brian. Nor did she appear to be underage, a possibility which had worried Gorman. From the correspondence, he had assumed her to be a teenager but had never pinpointed her age. He guessed, now, that she must be eighteen or close to it.

She was slim and attractive, with golden bangs brushing her forehead, hair flowing down the sides of her face to her shoulders. The white of her bra showed through the thin white cotton of a T-shirt that read Welcome to The Welcome Inn.

Brian, he thought, must be quite pleased indeed.

The girl glanced over her shoulder as if to reassure herself that the door was firmly shut. Then she looked again at Brian, who was staring at her. In his hand were a few brochures.

'He's with me,' Gorman explained.

He came forward as if summoned.

'Janice, I want you to meet Brian Blake – my research assistant, photographer, chauffeur.'

He reached over the counter. Janice, her face puzzled and wary, shook the offered hand. From the letters, she must have assumed Gorman would come alone. Was she wondering if this man's presence would affect her share?

In rich, sincere tones, Brian said, 'Pleased to meet you, Janice.' He kept his hold on her hand. 'Very pleased.'

A blush tinted her cheeks. Her mouth opened as if to speak, but no words came out. Suddenly, her eyes widened. 'Bri . . . *the* Brian Blake?' she blurted. Her stunned expression brought a smile from Gorman. She looked as if she were gawking at a movie star, awestruck and a little frightened. 'My God,' she muttered.

'Nothing to be afraid of,' Brian said. 'I left the spook back in Wisconsin.'

'God, I don't believe this.'

Brian relinquished her hand. It dropped, limp, to the counter. She continued to stare at him.

'As you may remember,' Gorman said, 'Mr Blake and I worked very closely together on *Horror*. He not only recounted the tragedy during our tape sessions, he also was responsible for the photographs used in the book. I've kept him on as an associate ever since. He's really an invaluable asset.'

Janice nodded. She still looked a trifle dazed. 'Must've been awful for you,' she said, her eyes fixed on Brian's.

'It's like Nietzsche says.'

'Huh?'

'What doesn't kill us makes us stronger.'

'Yeah. Yeah, I guess so.'

'Besides, it was a long time ago. I suppose I'll never be over it completely, but . . . I'm coping.'

'Well . . .'

'This,' Gorman interrupted, 'is probably not the ideal place to talk.' He nodded toward the closed door behind which, he assumed, her parents were busy with other matters. 'Why don't you check us in to our rooms? Then we'll make arrangements to meet later, after we've had a chance to rest up from the drive.'

'Good idea,' she said. She made a shaky smile and licked her lips. 'Will you be together or . . .'

'Separate rooms,' Brian told her.

'Very good.' She snapped a pair of guest registration cards down on the counter. 'Would you each fill out one of these?' she said in a firm, practiced voice. Obviously embarrassed by her earlier loss of composure, she was trying to appear businesslike. This delighted Gorman. From the tone of her letters, he'd been prepared to face a rather tough, cynical bitch, an operator. Now, he realized she wouldn't be the obstacle he had feared. The toughness was no more than a thin shell, easily cracked.

He finished filling in his card.

'All our units,' Janice said, 'are equipped with queensized double beds, color TV, and complimentary coffee.'

'Magic fingers?' Brian asked.

A slight frown drew her brows together. She studied him as if trying to figure something out, then seemed to give up. With a shake of her head, she told him, 'I'm afraid not.'

'Well, shit.'

A grin split her face.

'I could just shit, couldn't you, Gorman?'

Now she was softly laughing.

Brian gave her a pitiful look. 'I can't sleep without Magic Fingers.'

'Aw, poor boy.' One of her hands lifted as if to pat him on the head. She caught herself, and lowered the hand behind the counter. 'You'll just have to suffer,' she said. She smiled at Gorman. 'Is he always this way?'

'Just around beautiful women.'

Her face went red as if magically sunburned. 'Any-way.' She took a deep breath. 'How long do you expect to be staying with us?'

'I believe two nights should be sufficient, don't you?'

'Depends, I guess. What're you planning on?'

'Why don't we discuss that in the privacy of our rooms?'

'Yeah, that'd be better.' She glanced at Brian, and quickly looked away. She picked up the two registration cards. 'Will this be cash or charge?'

'Do you take Visa?'

'Yes, we do.'

Gorman used his card to pay for both rooms. After he signed the receipt, Janice turned over the card to compare signatures. 'I'm no imposter, young lady.'

'Huh? Oh. Just force of habit. I know you're Gorman Hardy.'

'The paperback edition didn't have a photo.'

'I saw you on the *Today* show.'

'Ah. Am I even more handsome in person?'

'Oh yes. A lot more handsome.'

'Why, thank you. You have an endearing quality about you, Janice.'

She shrugged, muttered thanks, and reached under the counter. She came up with two keys, each attached to a tab of green plastic. 'I'll put you in five and six. They're together with a connecting door.' She swung an arm out behind her. 'Just drive through, they're the third-duplex on the left. The ice machine's just outside the office here, and there's a soft-drink vending machine beside it.'

Gorman nodded. Leaning against the desk, he asked in a quiet voice, 'When would you be able to join us?'

'I can usually get away. Mom'll be over at the restaurant most of the time, and Dad's pretty loose. I just tell him I want to go out, and he takes over the office.'

'Excellent. Now, as I understand it, they know absolutely nothing about our purpose here.'

'Right. Nobody knows but me.'

'It's imperative that we keep it that way. At least for the present,' he added.

'I'm not gonna tell anyone,' Janice said. 'Are you kidding? It's my neck.'

Brian peered closely at her neck. She met his eyes, blushed and looked back at Gorman.

'Would one of our rooms be a convenient meeting place?' he asked.

'Sure. Good as any. I'll bring in some clean towels, just in case, but nobody's even gonna notice me.'

'Very good. Say room six, then, in an hour?'

'I'll be there.'

'And bring the diary along.'

5

'*Voilà!*' Nora blurted, startling Tyler. She jabbed a finger against the windshield.

Just ahead, on the left, was a white-painted adobe restaurant with a red tile roof. The sign in front, hanging from a miniature lighthouse, read Lighthouse Inn.

Tyler checked the rearview. The Mustang was a hundred yards back. She signaled for a turn. A moment later, the Mustang's turn light began to flash. She swung across the road, into the paved parking lot.

Nora leaned over, twisted the mirror and studied her reflection. She started brushing her hair. Tyler pulled into a space and stopped the car. She waited for Nora to finish, then turned the mirror toward herself. Her blonde hair was slightly mussed, but she thought it looked all right. She checked her face for blood. She couldn't see any.

The Mustang eased in beside them. Tyler grabbed her handbag off the back seat, and climbed out. The ocean breeze felt cool and good. It tossed her hair. It flipped open the bottom of her untucked blouse as she stepped around the car, exposing her tanned belly to Abe's stare. She had neglected to fasten the last button. She closed it now, and Abe lifted his gaze to her face.

Not hard eyes, she thought. But probing, maybe a little amused.

'Bet you're surprised we found a place,' Nora said.

'I was beginning to wonder.'

'Boondocks, USA.'

Jack hurried ahead and pulled open the dark wood door. He held it while the others stepped into the dimly lighted foyer. A blonde girl in a turtleneck and kilts came forward, clutching menus to her chest. Abe told her that they'd come in for cocktails, and she led them through a nearly deserted dining room to a table by the windows. Abe pulled out a chair for Tyler. Jack did the same for Nora. 'A waitress will be by for your orders,' the girl said, and left them.

'Nice joint,' Jack said.

'We picked it special,' Nora told him.

'Come here often?' Abe asked, raising an eyebrow at Tyler.

'Whenever we're in the neighborhood.'

'We're from LA,' Nora said. 'How about you?'

'Here and there,' Jack said.

'These are a couple of very evasive guys,' Nora said.

'What are you, bank robbers?'

Jack grinned. 'Now there's a thought, huh, Abe?'

'I guess you might say we're itinerants.'

'Farm workers? What do you hear from Caesar Chavez?'

Jack laughed. It was more of a giggle, high-pitched and quiet, an odd sound to come from such a powerfully built man but, Tyler thought, somewhat appropriate to his baby face.

A waitress came. Nora ordered a vodka martini, Tyler a margarita. Abe asked for a Dos Equis, was told there was no Mexican beer in stock, and settled for a Michelob. Jack ordered the same.

'So,' Nora said, 'you're not on the lam?'

Smiling slightly, Abe shook his head. 'Actually, we just got ourselves mustered out of the Marine Corps.'

'Ah-ha! Leathernecks.' She grinned at Tyler 'What'd I tell you? Tough guys.'

'You just got out?' Tyler asked.

'We've been civilians since Monday.'

'In since '67,' Jack added.

'Holy shit. That's what, twelve years?'

'We liked it,' Jack said.

'But not enough to re-up again,' Abe added.

Jack wrinkled his nose, shook his head. 'Gets to be a drag when you haven't got a shooting war.'

'Are you kidding?' Nora asked.

'Not that we particularly enjoy combat,' Abe said.

'Speak for yourself,' Jack told him.

'But the peacetime corps is a lot of dull routine, and after the last fiasco we're not going to see any real commitment of ground forces for some time. Not much point being a soldier without a war. So we thought we'd get out and see how the other half lives.'

'What'll you do?' Tyler asked.

'As little as possible,' Jack smiled.

'Right now, we're busy playing tourist. Left Camp Pendleton on Monday, took the Hearst Castle tour at San Simeon, came up through Monterey and Big Sur, stayed a few days in San Francisco. Just seeing the sights.'

'Hanging loose,' Jack said.

The waitress brought the drinks.

'To fortunate encounters,' Nora toasted.

'Hear, hear,' Jack said.

'And thanks for helping us,' Tyler said.

Abe smiled. 'Our pleasure.'

They drank. After a few swallows, Jack sighed loudly.

'Ah,' he said. 'That do hit the spot.'

'You ladies are from Los Angeles,' Abe said. 'What brings you up here?'

'Just . . .' Tyler started.

Nora broke in. 'We're hunting up one of Tyler's old flames.'

Why did she have to say that? Tyler felt herself blushing. 'Well, we were in the area anyway for a conference in San Francisco. We just thought we'd look him up, see how he's doing.'

Abe looked at her. Was that disappointment in his eyes? Or just interest, curiosity?

Tyler shrugged. 'We used to be . . . very good friends. I haven't seen him in five years.'

'Hoping to rekindle things?'

She stared down at her margarita. 'Something like that, I guess.'

'He's supposed to be living up in Malcasa Point,' Nora said. 'That's about an hour more up the road. We'll be spending the night there.'

'Now there's a coincidence,' Jack said. 'So are we.'

Abe looked at his friend and raised his eyebrows.

'Remember in the car? Not half an hour ago. I say, "How about stopping the night at that Malcasa Point?" And you say, "Sounds good to me."'

'That's right,' Abe said.

'Maybe we'll run into you gals up there.'

It was Abe's turn to stare at his drink. He turned the bottle slowly, looking down its neck.

'Who knows?' Jack continued, grinning broadly. 'It's a small world.'

'And a very small town,' Nora added.

'If we just should happen, somehow, to run into you gals, maybe we might buy you dinner.'

'Maybe they'd rather we didn't,' Abe said.

Tyler scooted down in her seat. 'I don't know,' she muttered. 'I might . . . have other plans. I mean, if I find Dan.'

'If she finds Dan,' Nora said, 'I'll be all alone in a strange town with nothing to do.'

'We'll take care of that,' Jack told her.

Nora squeezed his thick forearm. 'You've got a deal. Look, why don't you guys follow us up so you won't get lost, and we'll have us a fancy Marine escort if we run into more weirdos?'

'You bet,' Jack said.

6

Brian, sitting on the edge of a bed, saw Janice stride past the front of the rented Mercedes. She saw him watching through the window, and smiled. She had changed into a sleeveless yellow sundress, sashed at the waist, its breeze-blown skirt pressed to her thighs. She carried a stack of white towels. From the crook of her elbow hung a tote bag. 'Here she comes,' he said, and took a sip of his martini.

Gorman rushed to open the door. With a slight bow, he said, '*Entrez.*'

Janice stepped in. Balanced on one foot, she used the sole of a white sneaker to push the door shut behind her. Gorman lifted the towels from her arms. He set them on the dressing table, and smiled at her like a gracious host. 'Pull up a bed, my dear.'

'Thanks,' she said in a thin voice. She sounded very nervous. She gave Brian a quick, tight-lipped smile, and sat on a corner of the other bed, her knees pointed away from him. After lowering her bag to the floor, she sat up straight and rigid. She smoothed the skirt against her thighs. She licked her lips. 'Is . . . are the rooms okay?' she asked, glancing from Brian to Gorman.

'They're charming,' Gorman said. 'Would you care for a cocktail?'

She nodded, her bangs stirring against her forehead.

'Sure, okay.'

'Should we card her?' Brian asked.

She let out a quiet, uneasy laugh. 'I confess. I'm only eighteen.'

'Close enough,' Brian said. 'Just don't tell on us.'

This time her laughter was not so strained. She turned her head to watch Gorman pour two fingers of martini into one of the motel tumblers. He set down the glass shaker, skewered an olive with a cutlass toothpick, and plopped it into her drink. He handed the glass to Janice, freshened Brian's drink and his own, then swung out a chair and sat facing her. He raised his glass to eye level. 'Let me propose a toast. To Beast House, our partnership, and our imminent prosperity.'

They clinked the rims of their glasses, and drank. Janice took a small sip. She grimaced and smiled, then tried another sip and nodded as if this one was an improvement.

'Too much vermouth?' Gorman asked.

'No, it's fine. Just fine.'

'Now shall we, as they say, talk turkey?'

'Fine.'

'I've given much thought to your proposal of a fifty-fifty split and while it does seem rather steep, there would, as you pointed out, be no book without your cooperation. It is, after all, your idea. And you are the one, after all, in possession of the diary. Therefore, I've concluded that your request is reasonable.'

Her eyebrows lifted, disappearing under the curtain of bangs. 'That means you'll go for it?'

'That means I'll go for it.'

'Great.'

'Brian?'

Brian set aside his drink and snapped open the latches of an attaché case beside him on the bed. He raised the top, removed a manila file folder, and slipped out two neatly typed papers. He handed both sheets to Janice.

'I took the liberty,' Gorman explained, 'of writing up an agreement. It spells out, basically, that I'll be sole owner of the copyright, that you'll be free of any liability in connection with the proposed work, and that you'll receive a fifty percent share of the proceeds from any and all sales. It also stipulates that your participation in the project shall be kept secret. I added that for your benefit, since you seemed to believe you might be in some danger if your involvement became known.'

Nodding, she read the top sheet. When she finished, she slipped the other one over it.

'They're identical,' Gorman said. She scanned it. 'Well, they look fine to me.'

Leaning forward, Gorman held out his gold-plated Cross pen. 'If you'll sign and date both copies . . .'

She pressed the papers against her thigh, and scribbled her signature and the day's date at the bottom of each contract. Both had already been signed by Gorman Hardy two weeks ago.

'One's for you and one's for us,' Brian said. She handed one of the sheets to him. She returned the pen to Gorman. She folded her copy into thirds, and slipped it into her tote. Reaching down beside a folded sweater, she pulled out a thin, leatherbound volume. A brass lock-plate was set into its front cover, but the latch hung loose by the strap on the back.

'The diary?' Gorman asked.

'It's all yours.' She gave it to him, and took a hefty swallow of martini.

Gorman opened the book to its first page. ' "My Diary",' he read aloud, ' "Being a True Account of My Life and Most Private Affairs, Volume twelve, in the year of our Lord 1903. Elizabeth Mason Thom." Fabulous,' he muttered, and riffled through the pages.

'It's pretty boring stuff till you get into April,' Janice said. 'Then she gets into it pretty hot and heavy with the family doctor. Around May eighteenth is when she starts with the beast. She called it Xanadu.'

'Xanadu? As in *Kubla Khan*? "In Xanadu did Kubla Khan a stately pleasure dome decree, where Alph the sacred river ran through caverns measureless to man – down to the sunless sea." '

'I guess,' Janice said. 'That's what she called him, anyway. Xanadu. It gets pretty far out, the diary, and I would've figured she made it up, you know, but it pretty much explains what's behind the killings in Beast House. I mean, those murders really happened, no question.'

'Mmhmm.' Gorman opened the diary at random, and began to read. ' "His warm breath on my face smelled of the earth and wild, uninhabited forests. He lay his hands upon my shoulders. Claws bit into me. I stood before the creature, helpless with fear and wonder, as he split the fabric of my nightgown." '

Brian whistled softly.

Janice glanced at him, and made a slightly lopsided smile. The drink, he figured, was getting to her.

' "When I was bare," ' Gorman continued, ' "he muzzled my body like a dog. He licked my breasts. He sniffed me, even my private areas, which he probed with his snout." '

Janice eased her knees closer together.

'Well,' Gorman said, shutting the book, 'it appears that this little memoir does, indeed, live up to your reports. How exactly did it come into your possession?'

'Like I said in my letter, I found it in one of the rooms here.'

'Could you be more specific?'

She drained her martini, and nodded.

'Refill?' Gorman asked.

'Sure, okay,' She opened her eyes wide as if to test how well the lids were still working. Gorman took her glass, poured in an inch of the clear liquid, and handed it back to her. She took a small drink. 'Anyway . . .'

'Would you mind if I record you?'

A puzzled look crossed her face. 'Aren't I not supposed to be in the book?'

'That's true. None of what you say need find its way into the work, but we'll be on safer ground with a statement regarding the manuscript's origin. You may not be aware of it, but there were accusations regarding the veracity of our previous book.'

'Huh?'

'*Horror at Black River Falls*,' Brian told her. 'Some people accused us of making up the whole damn story.'

Janice frowned. 'No, you didn't do that. Did you?'

'No way,' Brian said. 'But we didn't have much proof to back up our claims. That's why we want to tape what you say. Then, if somebody gets on our case, we've actually got a recorded statement to prove the conversation happened.'

'Ah.' She nodded. 'I see. Okay.'

Gorman lifted his small recorder off the dresser top. He switched it on. 'The following is a statement by Janice Crogan of Malcasa Point, California, in which she explains how she came into possession of the diary of Elizabeth Thorn.' Leaning forward, he placed the device on the bedspread by her hip.

'Okay,' she said. 'I'm Janice Crogan. My folks own the Welcome Inn here in Malcasa, and I help them with it. I found the diary in room nine, one day last summer. In June. Late June. We haven't got any maids here. Dad says that's the kind of overhead that kills you. Me and my mom – my mom and I – we do all the cleaning. That's how I found the diary. It was under one of the beds. In room nine. Did I already say that? Anyway, it was in nine. One of the guests must've lost it there.'

'Do you have any idea who that might have been?' Gorman asked.

She shook her head. Her left cheek bulged out as she pushed it with her tongue. She frowned at her drink and took another sip. 'Could've been under there a while. I don't know. But there was a woman and her kid in nine a couple days before. That was when . . . uh . . . this guy . . .'

Suddenly, Janice's face crumpled. Her eyes squeezed shut and her mouth twisted into a parody of a smile as tears spilled down her cheeks. Sobbing loudly, she pressed one hand across her eyes. Her other hand shook, sloshing her drink up the walls of her glass.

Brian took the glass from her. She hunched over, burying her face in both hands. He sat down beside her and wrapped an arm around her quaking back. 'Hey, it's all right,' he said in a soothing voice. 'It's all right, Janice.' He squeezed her shoulder.

'I'm sorry,' she blurted between sobs. 'You must . . .'

'Shhh.' Gently, he stroked her hair. He caressed her back. It bounced under his hand, but he liked the warm feel of her skin through the fabric.

Slowly, she regained control of herself.

Gorman gave her a Kleenex. She blotted her wet cheeks, wiped her eyes, blew her nose. Then she sat up straight and took a deep breath that sounded shaky as she let it out.

'Better?' Brian asked.

'Better.' She sniffed. She shook her head as if ashamed of her behavior. 'I'm sorry. I . . . I thought I was over it. Guess I'm not, huh?' She made a feeble smile. 'See . . . This guy I was telling you about, he . . . *God*.'

Brian's hand slowly roamed her back. 'It's all right,' he said.

'I caught him trying to break into one of the cabins,' she said quickly, as if to get it over with. 'He had this girl with him, a little kid named Joni. He'd killed her parents and kidnapped her, and – God, the awful things he did to her! We found out all about it later. But this guy, his name was Roy, he grabbed me and he tied us both up in one of the rooms and . . . messed with us. Raped us.'

'How awful,' Gorman said.

'Yeah. He . . . he was a . . . so horrible.' She shut her mouth tightly, jaw muscles bunching, and took a hissing breath through her nose. 'Anyway, that was two days before I found the diary. I don't know if it has anything to do with it. Joni got loose, and ran off, and the guy took off after her. That was the last I ever saw of him. He just vanished, and so did four of our guests. All five of them . . .' She shrugged. 'Like they fell off the face of the earth.'

She lifted her glass off the floor, and took a sip. 'Something else strange, too. These people – they were in nine and twelve – they left all their luggage and stuff behind. A car, too. That stuff was still around that night. But when morning came, everything was gone. Except the diary, which I found the day after. Whether they left it or not, I haven't got the slightest idea. It could've been under that bed for days, a week, no telling how long. Anyway, that's about all there is on how I found the diary.'

'And you didn't tell anyone about finding it?' Gorman asked.

'No. I was alone in the room. Vacuuming. I looked inside the thing, and knew right away it had to do with Beast House. I recognized the woman's name – Thorn. She's the one that built the place, and her kids and sister were the first victims. She wound up in a nut-house someplace. I knew all of this from the tour. I used to go on the tour all the time. Not that I enjoyed it much, but I mean it's kind of a major attraction around here so whenever we had visitors from out of town – like relatives and stuff – it's a place we always took them to. So I was pretty familiar with the story you get on the tour and my eyes nearly fell out when I read the diary. Anyway, I hid it in my room and read the whole thing later on. It gave me a pretty good scare.'

'Why is that?' Gorman asked.

'Read it, you'll find out. I mean, I knew *someone* had murdered all those people, but I figured it was ... I don't know what, but not a monster, for Godsake. I figured that was all bullshit till I read the diary. Then also I got a little nervous about just having the thing. If certain people found out ...'

'Which people?'

'Well, like Maggie Kutch. She's the old bag that owns the place. Beast House. You'll see her if you take the tour. And there's this slime, Wick Hapson. He's like her flunky. He's the one sells the tickets.'

'A young lady,' Gorman said, 'was in the ticket booth when we stopped there earlier this afternoon.'

Janice shrugged. 'I don't know who she'd be. I've been trying to keep my distance from the place. I mean, you can't help going by it some-times, but I haven't been on the tour since I read the diary. And I don't intend to, either. Maybe they hired some kid. I wouldn't know.'

'After reading the diary, what did you do?'

'Nothing. I kept it hidden. I thought a lot about throwing it away. It made me nervous just having it around. But then I got to thinking it might be valuable. When I read your book last March, that's when I realized there might be a book in it. That's when I decided to write you a letter.'

Leaning forward, Gorman picked up the recorder. 'Is there anything else you'd like to add?'

'That's about all, I think.'

He switched it off.

Janice drank the remains of her martini. She set the empty glass on the bedspread. 'What now?' she asked.

'Now,' Gorman said, 'I shall read the diary. Tomorrow, we'll take the tour. Would you care to join us?'

'I don't think so. I don't know. Maybe. I'll think about it.'

7

Pacific Coast Highway had curved inland soon after they left the Lighthouse Inn. Now they were passing through an area of wooded hills. The briny, fresh smell of the ocean was gone, replaced by a sweet scent of pine. The blue Mustang vanished as they rounded a bend. Tyler eased off the gas until it reappeared in the rearview mirror.

'There,' Nora said.

A sign reading MALCASA POINT, 3 MI, pointed at a sideroad to the left. Tyler slowed and signaled the turn, and swung sharply across the empty lane.

'Wait for 'em,' Nora said.

She slowed to a crawl until the Mustang made the turn, then picked up speed again. The road curved along a shadowy hillside, sloping gradually downward. Not far ahead, a squirrel scampered over the pavement, bushy tail up like a question mark. Tyler touched the brake. The squirrel finished its crossing in plenty of time.

As the hill to the left fell away, she glimpsed the ocean through the trees along its crest. The breeze coming in her window suddenly turned slightly cool and smelled again of the sea.

'Almost there,' Nora said.

Tyler's stomach lurched. Almost there. Her hands were slippery on the wheel. She rubbed them, one at a time, on the legs of her corduroys. 'Let's find a place to stay before hunting Dan up,' she said.

Nora agreed.

At the foot of the hill, the road curved to the right. A sign by the ditch read WELCOME TO MALCASA POINT. POP. 400. DRIVE WITH CARE. Tyler took a deep breath. Her lungs seemed to tremble.

She gazed ahead. The road led flat and straight through the center of town. The town ahead was small, no more than a few blocks long, with shops lining both sides of the street before the road turned in the distance and vanished into the woods.

'The sticks, all right,' Nora said. 'I hope it does have a motel. And I hope *that* isn't it,' she added, looking to the right.

Tyler glanced that way. Through the bars of a wrought-iron fence beside the road, she saw a two-story Victorian house with weathered sides, bay windows, a peaked tower.

Nora said, 'Here, we thought the Bates house was at Universal Studios.'

'Maybe they moved it.'

'Gee, should we stop for the tour?'

'That's just what I'd like to do,' Tyler said, and kept on driving. The Mustang stayed a short distance behind them as they moved through town.

Nora, leaning toward the windshield, studied the road-side businesses. 'Where's the Holiday Inn?' she asked. 'Where's the Howard Johnson, the Hyatt?'

'There's gotta be some kind of motel.'

'I sure don't see one. Maybe you'd better pull in at this gas station and we'll ask.'

'We can use a fill-up anyway,' Tyler said. She signaled well in advance, then swung over and eased the car up beside the row of full service pumps. Killing the engine, she looked over her shoulder. The Mustang stopped at the self-service island, and Abe climbed out. He nodded a greeting, then turned away to open his gas tank.

Tyler pulled her hood release as a lean, sourlooking man stepped around the front of her car. He crouched by her window. The name patch on his shirt read Bix. He peered inside as if sizing them both up, and one side of his mouth stretched over. 'Ladies,' he said.

'Hi. Fill it up with unleaded, please.'

He gave the window sill a pat, then ambled around to the other side.

'Guess I'll make a pit stop,' Nora said. 'Go while the going's good.' She left the car, eased past the pumps, and headed for the station building.

Tyler climbed out. She stretched, feeling good as her muscles strained. The breeze off the ocean smelled fresh. Mixed with the subtle aroma of pines was a faint, pungent odor of gasoline. The breeze chilled the sweaty back of her blouse. Reaching around, she plucked the clinging fabric away from her skin.

Abe was watching the pump as he filled his tank.

She turned to Bix as he approached.

'Check under the hood for you?' he asked.

'Please.'

He nodded. His eyes strayed to her breasts and paused there for a moment before shifting away. Then he stepped past her. He bent over the hood and felt under its lip for the catch.

Tyler glanced down to make sure her blouse was buttoned. It was. 'Is there a place to stay around here?' she asked.

'A motel, like?'

'Yes.'

He licked his lower lip. He stared at her breasts as if the answer were written there. 'Only one,' he finally said. 'That'd be the Welcome Inn, about half a mile up the road, on your right.'

'Thank you,' she said.

He raised the hood. Tyler was glad to be hidden from his view. She considered asking the location of Seaside Lane, but wanted as little as possible to do with him. She could find Dan's place without the help of this lech.

Abe was still bent over the rear of his Mustang, pumping in gas. She walked over to him. He looked at her and smiled. 'What's up?' he asked.

'The guy says there's a motel about half a mile up the road.'

'I was starting to wonder if we'd find one.'

'Apparently there is only one. The Welcome Inn.'

'Clever.'

'He says it's on the right.'

'Fine. We'll follow you in.' The feed clicked off. He pulled the spout out of his tank and stepped backward, holding it away from himself so gasoline wouldn't drip onto his Nikes. He hung up the nozzle. Then he sniffed his fingers. He caught Tyler grinning. 'Stinky,' he said.

She laughed. 'We've got some Wet Ones in the car.'

'Thanks,' he said. 'I'm a big boy. I can live with it.' He screwed the gas cap on.

'Oil's half a quart low,' Bix said, coming up behind her.

'Thanks,' she said. 'See you later,' she told Abe, and returned to her car. Watching from the window, she saw him pay cash. He pushed the wallet into his rear pocket. It made a small bulge. The other pocket apparently empty, curved smoothly over his right buttock.

The passenger door swung open. 'Hi ho,' Nora said, climbing in.

'Everything come out all right?' Tyler asked.

'Right as rain. Did you ask Clyde about a motel?'

'Bix. Yeah. Dead ahead.'

'Terrific.'

Tyler found her credit card as Bix approached.

'Eleven-fifty,' he said.

She gave him the card. He left with it. 'What a turkey,' she said.

'Yeah?'

'Like this.' She leered at Nora's breasts, wiggling her eyebrows and running her tongue across her lips.

'Ask him for a date. Definitely.'

'Right.'

A moment later, he stepped in front of the car. He jotted down the license plate number and came back to Tyler's window. She took the plastic clipboard from him, and started to sign the receipt.

'You with those guys?' he asked.

Tyler didn't answer.

'They're our Secret Service escort,' Nora said.

'Yeah? Who you trying to shit?'

Tyler plucked her card from its slot.

'You don't recognize Amy Carter when you see her?'

She ripped off the top copy of the receipt.

'Well, now,' Nora went on. 'I guess you wouldn't. She's incognito.'

Tyler handed out the clipboard. Bix yanked it from her hand. He crouched and stared in at Nora. 'You're a real laugh.'

Tyler started the engine. She released the emergency brake and shifted to first.

'Wi— . . .'

She popped the clutch. The car lurched forward.

'I didn't catch that!' Nora yelled, turning in her seat.

'I did,' Tyler said.

'What did he call me?'

'A wise-ass cunt,' Tyler said, and pulled onto the road.

'Did he?'

'Please. Don't flip him the bird. He knows where we'll be staying.'

'Ah. Well, all right. Coward.'

'That's me.'

'Seaside?' repeated the pleasant, bald man behind the registration desk. 'Did you come in by way of town?'

'Yes,' Tyler said.

'What there was of it,' Nora added.

The man chuckled. So did Jack Wyatt, who was waiting behind them with Abe.

'Well,' the man said, 'you want to head back through what there is of town.

Just this side of the monster palace, you'll see a dirt road on your right.'

'Just this side of Beast House?' Tyler asked.

'Yep. The monster palace. The road's called Beach Lane. It'll take you to the beach parking, but you don't want to go that far. Just about a hundred yards in, you'll come to Seaside. That'll be to your right. Doesn't go to the left.'

'Thank you,' Tyler said.

'Where's the best place for dinner?' Nora asked.

'You're there. Right next door. The Carriage House. Of course I'm partial as I run the place. But you can't do better. Fine steaks and seafood and ambience at moderate prices.' He checked his wristwatch. His arm, unlike his head, was matted with hair. 'If you're after something to cut the thirst, our Happy Hour's just started. Two drinks for the price of one, and free hors d'oeuvres. Runs till six.'

'Hey, all right!' Nora said. She turned around. 'Maybe see you guys there. Say in an hour or so?'

'I'll be there,' Jack assured her.

Abe nodded. He met Tyler's eyes. 'Are you going off now to look up your friend?'

'Yeah, I guess so.'

'Good hunting,' he said.

'Thanks.'

He frowned at his shoes, then looked again into her eyes. 'That offer for dinner's still open. Have him join us.'

'Right,' she said. 'He and his wife.'

'The eternal pessimist,' Nora said.

'Anyway, good luck.'

'I'll need it.'

Abe and Jack stayed in the office to check in. Nora followed Tyler outside. 'You sure you still want to find Dan?' she asked.

'What does that mean?'

'Looks to me like our friend Abe is more than a little interested in you.'

Tyler trotted down the porch stairs and got into the car. Nora climbed into the passenger side. 'He's gorgeous,' she added.

'I hardly know him.'

'Ah, but admit it, he makes your little heart go pittypat.'

'You're imagining things,' Tyler said, and started the engine. She headed for the courtyard entrance. 'You don't have to come along. If you'd rather stay here and clean up, or . . .'

'Do I smell?' Nora sniffed her armpits.

'I don't want to keep you from the Happy Hour.'

'No sweat,' she said. 'Hey. Ritzy clientele.'

'Yeah.' Tyler drove slowly past the gray Mercedes, and pulled to a stop in front of the next duplex over. 'Really,' she said, 'you don't need to come.'

'You telling me I'm not wanted?'

'No. I just thought you might prefer to stay behind, that's all. The way you were trying to talk me out of it.'

'I was only pointing out there's no law you have to go looking for Dan. It's obvious you're nervous about it, and it's also obvious you've got eyes for Abe.'

'I don't have "eyes" for anyone,' she protested.

'Uh-huh. Sure.'

'Come on, let's get our stuff in the rooms.'

A few minutes later, after throwing her suitcase onto one of the beds, washing up, putting on fresh lipstick and brushing her hair, she stepped to the connecting door. 'Ready,' she called.

'Meet you at the car,' Nora answered.

She left her room. Abe's Mustang was parked in front of a bungalow just across the courtyard.

As she stepped around the front of her Omni, Nora's door opened. Tyler watched her friend hop down the steps, breasts jiggling inside her T-shirt. For just a moment, she felt threatened and wary.

A faint scent of perfume entered the car with Nora. 'Loins all girded?'

'My loins are fine,' Tyler said.

'You okay?'

'Just a little nervous.'

'Let's went, Queeksdraw.'

Rounding a bend, they left the wooded hills behind. The service station appeared just ahead.

'Pull in,' Nora said. 'I want to give Clyde a piece of my mind.'

'Bix.' Tyler glanced to the left, saw the man crouching to check the air in a Honda's tire, and pressed harder on the accelerator.

'Wonder if he's related to the asshole we met on the road. You oughta see the welt that sucker raised on me with that aerial.'

'Must have hurt.'

'He'll think twice before he pulls that kind of shit again.' A few minutes later, Nora said, 'Better slow down, here comes the monster palace.'

Tyler glanced ahead at the old house. Its windows, catching the late afternoon sunlight, looked plated with gold.

'This might be it.'

She took her foot off the gas pedal. As the car lost speed, she swept her eyes along the roadside to the right. Just past a five-and-ten was a vacant, wooded lot. The trees stopped at a dirt road. She flicked the arm of her turn signal.

'That's it,' Nora confirmed. 'Beach Lane.'

Tyler eased down on the brake, and swung onto the narrow, rutted road.

'Your Dan believes in roughing it.'

'So it seems.' The area to the right, where his house must be, was thick and shadowy with trees. By comparison, the rolling, weed-choked field to the left looked bare. Off in that direction stood a two-story house of red brick, alone except for a separate garage.

'That's unusual,' Nora said.

'What?'

'How many actual brick houses do you ever see in California?'

'Maybe it was built by eas— . . .'

'I'll be damned. Look at that. No windows.'

Tyler looked again. Sure enough, the only visible wall was an unbroken expanse of brick. 'Maybe on the other sides . . .'

'Guess they're not very view-conscious.'

Tyler laughed.

Nora shook her head and faced the windshield. 'Ah, here comes Seaside.'

Tyler stopped by a row of mailboxes lined up along a raised shelf. The gray metal hoods were labeled two, four, eight, and ten. She rolled past them, and peered down the narrow lane. 'Maybe we'd better walk,' she said. 'Can't be too far.'

'You don't want to block traffic,' Nora said, flashing a smile.

'God forbid.'

Tyler drove past the entrance to Seaside. Not far ahead, the road widened into a parking area. She stopped against a log. A wedge of ocean glinting sunlight showed through a break in the low hills ahead. A footpath curved along one of the slopes.

'Nuts,' Nora said. 'We should've brought our suits.'

They climbed from the car. A stiff breeze tugged at Tyler's hair, molded her blouse to her body. When she turned away from the ocean, it pushed at her back as if urging her to rush.

Nora met her behind the car. She was slipping her arms into the sleeves of her red sweater. Her face was wrapped with tendrils of blowing hair. As they walked along, she buttoned the sweater.

Thank you, wind, Tyler thought.

They hurried to Seaside. There, the trees shielded them from the wind but also kept out the sunlight. They walked in silence through the deep shadows.

Tyler shivered – partly from the chill, mostly from the knowledge that she might, in minutes, be face to face with Dan Jenson. What were the chances, after five years, that he would welcome her, that they could pick up where they left off? Slim, she thought. Minuscule. But she had come this far. There was no turning back. She clenched her teeth to stop her jaw from shaking.

From a cottage on the left, a dog began to yap. A gaunt man appeared behind the screen door. Nora raised a hand in greeting. The man stood motionless, a dim shape through the screen, staring out at them.

'Charming,' Nora muttered. 'Let's hear some "Dueling Banjos."'

They passed a clapboard shack with boarded windows, then came upon a wheelless bus propped up on cinder blocks. They paused to stare at the mural painted on its side: a ghost ship with tattered sails becalmed on a glaring sea. A human skeleton clung to the helm. A giant albatross floated before the ship, an arrow in its breast. Above the bus's door hung a sign carved in driftwood: CAPTAIN FRANK.

'Interesting neighbors your Dan has,' Nora said.

They continued down the gloomy road to its end, where a path led toward a small, green-painted cottage with a screened porch.

'That must be it,' Nora said.

Tyler's heart pounded hard. 'I don't see a car anywhere.'

'Maybe he's not home yet.'

They walked down the path. Tyler followed Nora up the porch steps. Nora knocked on the door, then pulled it open. Except for a swing suspended from its ceiling, the porch was empty. That seemed odd to Tyler. Similar cottages she'd known as a child while vacationing with her parents always had porches cluttered with gear: fishing rods, a tackle box and minnow bucket, a fishnet, an old Coleman lantern, a refrigerator well stocked with soda and beer, hooks on the walls draped with rain slickers and beach towels. There was none of that.

'No doorbell,' Nora whispered. 'I'll let you do the knocking.' She stepped away from the door and sat on the swing. Its chains creaked and groaned as she pushed it into motion.

Tyler rapped lightly on the door. She waited, then struck harder. 'I don't think he's home.'

'It's only about four thirty,' Nora said from the swing.

Tyler cupped her hands to a glass pane in the door, and peered inside. She could see no more than the kitchen. 'Maybe Barbie Doll gave us the wrong address,' she said.

'I doubt it. She was flaky, but not stupid.'

'Well, nobody's home.'

'Shall we wait, or try again some other time?'

Tyler shrugged. Though disappointed, she also felt relieved; her eagerness to meet Dan was mixed with such anxiety that she was almost glad they had failed. 'It might be a long wait,' she said. 'Cops have weird hours. He could've just started a shift, or something.'

'Then you want to leave?'

'We don't want to keep you from the Happy Hour.'

'I'm perfectly willing to wait.'

'No, let's go.'

They left the porch and walked up the path to the dirt road.

'Maybe,' Nora said, 'we can check a phone directory when we get back, make sure we do have the right address. You might even give him a ring, unless you're intent on making a surprise appearance.'

'Yeah, that's an idea.' A phone call, she thought, would be much easier on the nerves. That way, at least, she might find out how he stood. They could arrange to meet, regardless. Even if he was married or engaged or there was some other reason not to renew their relationship, she still would like to see him again.

'Ahoy there!' a man called.

Seated on a lawn chair atop the strangely painted bus, a beer can raised in greeting, was a white-bearded man. He wore a ragged straw hat, a Hawaiian shirt, and plaid Bermuda shorts.

'Captain Frank?' Nora asked.

'At your service, mateys.'

'We're looking for Dan Jenson,' Tyler called up to him. 'He lives at the end of the road?'

'Not anymore.' Captain Frank chuckled softly. 'No indeed.'

'He moved?'

'You might say that.'

'Do you know where we can find him?'

'Can't find him anywhere tonight. Try tomorrow, if you're of a mind.'

'Where?'

He tilted the beer can to his mouth, then crumpled it and tossed it down. It landed on the layer of pine needles beside his bus. 'Oh, Dan's not far off. No, indeed. Just down the road a spell. Can't miss it. A place called Beast House.'

'He *lives* there?' Tyler asked.

'I wouldn't say that, not exactly. Go on by in the morning. Tell him Captain Frank sent you, and give Danny boy my regards.' He waved them away.

'Thanks,' Tyler called.

They started walking.

'He must work as a guard there,' Nora said.

'Yeah. I suppose. But he must live someplace.'

Nora shrugged. 'You can ask him all about it tomorrow.'

'I guess this means we'll have to take the tour.'

'You'll love it. Tacky tacky.'

'I can't wait,' she muttered.

'Let's get back to the inn and get tanked.'

8

Tyler pulled to a stop in front of their bungalow at the Welcome Inn. 'It'll take me a while to get cleaned up and changed,' she said. 'You can go on ahead to the restaurant, if you'd like.'

'Fine,' Nora said. 'Meet you there.'

They climbed from the car.

Alone in her room, Tyler checked a drawer of the night stand between the beds. She found a Gideon Bible and a telephone book. She looked up Jenson, Daniel in the directory. The address listed after his name was 10 Seaside Lane.

According to Captain Frank, he didn't live there now. Not anymore. No indeed.

She flipped the directory shut. The date on its cover was February 1978, making the book more than a year and a half old.

She considered dialing information.

Maybe later. Right now, she had neither the energy nor the desire. She sat motionless on the edge of the bed, the phone book resting on her thigh, and stared into space. She felt weary. Her mind seemed out of focus. In the pit of her stomach was a tiny knot of fear.

She wished that she was home in her own apartment, her life untouched by Barbie Doll, the horrible man on the highway, the leering Bix, the man who stared out like a specter from his cottage on Seaside, or Captain Frank on top of his grimly painted bus. Give Danny boy my regards.

And then she thought, Why not leave in the morning? First thing. As Nora pointed out, there's no law you have to go looking for Dan.

Just get in the car, tomorrow, and bid farewell to all this. Tyler suddenly felt better, as if realizing she could leave had lifted an oppressive weight from her spirits. The knot of fear in her stomach loosened. She *could* leave. Nobody would force her to seek out Dan. Nobody would force her to take the Beast House tour.

If I don't want to, she thought, I won't.

She put away the telephone directory, pulled the curtains across the windows, and took off her clothes. Inspecting her bra in the dim light, she doubted she could ever remove the bloodstains entirely. Even if she succeeded, she would never forget this was the bra she had worn when the man attacked her. It would always be a reminder. So she took it into the bathroom and dropped it into the waste basket.

Standing by the road, she had cleaned most of the blood from her skin. But she hadn't taken off her bra. Some blood had soaked through it, leaving faint rust-colored blotches on her breasts.

In the shower, she lathered her body with a thin bar of motel soap and used a washcloth to scrub her face and neck, her shoulders, her arms, her breasts – every inch of skin that had been touched by the man or his blood. She rinsed. She turned her back to the spray and looked down. Her breasts were tawny to the tan line, then creamy white to the darker flesh of her nipples. No trace of the blood stains remained. Nevertheless, she soaped the washcloth and scoured herself once more before leaving the tub.

The bath towel was threadbare and half the size of her towels at home. After drying herself, she wrapped it around her waist and left the steamy bathroom. She turned on a lamp. The towel pulled loose as she sat down at the dressing table. She left it draping her lap and brushed her hair. Only the fringes at her neck were damp from the shower. With the short length, she had no trouble fixing her hair up enough to look presentable.

Leaning against the table's edge, she studied her face in the mirror. Her eyes needed help. Definitely. They looked haggard and slightly dazed. With a conceal stick from her makeup bag, she covered the smudges under each eye. She darkened her feathery lashes with mascara, then brushed her lids with light blue shadow. A vast improvement.

As she put on lipstick, she wondered why she hadn't bothered to do all this before driving out to look for Dan. Well, she'd been in a hurry. And nervous. Maybe it was something else, though. Maybe it was simply that she thought he wouldn't mind her scruffy appearance. Or maybe, deep down, she had somehow known she wouldn't find him.

She got up from the table. Its edge had left a crease like a long red scar just below her rib cage. She rubbed it as she carried the towel into the bathroom.

She had already decided what to wear. Though she would have preferred slacks because of the chill outside, she'd made up her mind to wear a skirt instead. Rummaging through her suitcase, she took out what she needed. She stepped into fresh panties, hooked her garter belt around her hips, and sat on the bed to put on her nylons. She'd selected a blue tweed skirt. It wasn't very summery but then, neither was the weather. Not at night, anyway. With the skirt on, she slipped into a wispy bra. Its silken feel made her nipples rigid. She drew a white cashmere sweater down over her head. It wasn't thick enough to hide the jut of her nipples completely, but her only other white bra was in the bathroom waste basket. A black one might show through the sweater.

'What the hell,' she muttered.

With Nora at the same table, who would be looking at her anyway? Abe, that's who.

She felt a rather pleasant, nervous tremor. It stayed with her as she stepped into her heels, put a few necessities into a clutch purse – including her room key – and approached the connecting door.

'Nora?' she called. 'Left yet?'

'Five minutes ago,' came the answering voice, followed by a guffaw. 'Want to come through? My side's already open.'

Tyler pulled open her door. The room was a twin of her own. Nora was seated at the dressing table, changing her earrings. 'I'm just about set,' she said. She had on the same green gown she had worn to last night's banquet. With her low neckline and spaghetti straps, she looked considerably more formal than Tyler.

'Going to a prom?' Tyler asked.

Nora eyed her, grinning. 'My, don't *you* look preppy. Going to a frat dance?'

'Call me Muffin.'

'I just figured I might as well give the boys something to look at.'

'Where's Jack going to pin your corsage?'

'To my boobie, darling.' Finished with her earrings, she took a white, cable-knit shawl off the bed, wrapped it around her shoulders, and picked up a purse that matched her gown. 'Shall we be off?'

Outside, the breeze was mild. The sun felt much warmer than Tyler had expected. It hung above the distant tree-tops, blazing into her eyes. She lowered her head and watched her shoes move over the courtyard's asphalt. 'What time is it?' she asked.

'About five thirty. The tail end of the Happy Hour.'

'I hope Abe and Jack are the patient type.'

'We're well worth waiting for.'

'Right.' She hesitated. 'I've been thinking.'

'What?'

'I'm not sure about all this business . . . looking for Dan, digging up the past. Maybe it'd be better to call it off.'

'Getting the jitters?'

'I've had the jitters all along. But nothing's been going right, you know? It's almost as if I'm not meant to find him.'

'Meant? That's a cop-out.'

'And if I do find him, and if he's not married or something, who's to say we're still . . . I don't know, the same people? I know I'm not. He's probably changed, too.'

'No harm in giving it a shot.'

'Isn't there? I don't know.'

Nora frowned at her, looking concerned. 'What *is* it?'

'I just . . . it didn't seem like such a bad idea, last night. But after everything today . . .' She shook her head. 'I have this kind of sick feeling about it.'

'Just nerves.'

'No, it's more than that. I have this feeling that if I do find Dan, I'm going to be very sorry. I'm going to wish I hadn't.'

They crossed the entry drive to a shaded walkway.

'It has been one hell of a day,' Nora agreed. 'I can't blame you for feeling a bit down. But maybe you'll feel different in the morning.'

'Maybe,' Tyler said.

Nora pulled open one of the double doors, and they entered the restaurant. The hostess's desk, with a gooseneck lamp shining down on the reservation list, was deserted. No one was seated in the dining area to the right, but the tables were set. A woman in an ankle-length dress was bent over one, lighting the chimney candle of its centrepiece. From the left came the sounds of quiet conversation and clinking glass.

They stepped past the desk, past the partition behind it, and entered the cocktail lounge. Several people were seated at the bar: a lone man joking with the bartender, a middle-aged redhead with her hand on the thigh of the man beside her, a husky gray-haired man sitting with a blond fellow. Tyler turned her eyes to the tables. She spotted Abe and Jack in a corner booth, and Jack waved. 'They're over . . .'

'That's Gorman Hardy,' Nora said. She was leaning sideways as if to get a better look at someone down the bar.

'The one with the other guy?'

'That "other guy" is Brian Blake.'

Tyler could only see the back of the older man, but the blond one was talking, head turned enough to show the side of his face. 'You might be right,' she said.

'Of course I'm right. Let's go over and say hi.'

'Must we?'

'He's not such an asshole.'

'I never said he was.'

'Effete, arrogant, and slimy – same difference. Come on, don't abandon me.'

'What the hell.'

Nora waved at Abe and Jack, then lifted a forefinger to signal they would be over in a minute. Tyler, smiling toward Abe, shrugged and shook her head like an unwilling accomplice. She followed Nora down the bar.

The younger man looked over his shoulder as they approached. He was indeed Brian Blake, whose ghastly experiences had been the subject of Hardy's bestseller. He didn't appear to recognize either Tyler or Nora, but then, his eyes had barely settled on their faces before sliding down to check out the rest. Apparently pleased by what he found, he bestowed a smile.

Hardy swiveled himself sideways. 'Ladies?'

'Mr Hardy,' Nora said. 'We met you at the NLA.'

For just an instant, he looked wary. He covered it quickly with a smile. 'Oh, yes. Certainly.' His gaze shifted from Nora to Tyler. 'We spoke briefly at the cocktail party, I believe.'

'I didn't have the pleasure,' Blake said.

'I'm Nora Branson. This is Tyler Morgan.'

'Pleased to meet you,' he said, and shook hands with both of them. 'I didn't attend the party, but I suppose you caught my talk.'

'It was fascinating,' Nora said. 'Horrifying.'

'Thank you.'

'You almost made a believer out of me.'

He looked amused. 'Almost?'

'I don't think I'll ever quite believe in ghosties till one goes bump into me.'

'*Touché*,' said Hardy. He laughed and picked up his martini. 'I suppose you were also skeptical of the book. You did read the book?'

'I don't know anyone who hasn't.'

'Neither do I, my dear, neither do I.'

'Could we buy you ladies a drink?' Blake asked.

'No, thank you,' Tyler said. 'We're with some others. In fact, we shouldn't keep them waiting.'

Nora snapped her fingers. 'You're the Mercedes, I'll bet. We're neighbors.'

'In that case, perhaps we'll be seeing you again.'

'Are you just passing through, or . . .' Her eyes suddenly widened. 'You're here for Beast House! You're going to do a book on it. That's the "secret project" you referred to at the party.'

'Oh, no,' Hardy said. 'Not at all. We're on our way up to Portland for another speaking engagement.'

'We do plan to take a look at the place,' Blake added. 'Of course. We could hardly pass through this area without stopping in for the famous Beast House tour.'

'When'll you be doing it – tomorrow?'

'First thing in the morning,' Blake said.

Nora grinned. 'Maybe we'll see you there.'

Tyler's stomach tightened. 'We'd better get going,' she said.

'Yeah, we'd better.'

'Our loss,' Blake said, and winked at Nora. *Winked.*

'*Ciao*,' Hardy said.

Tyler winced. 'Bye,' she said.

'See you later,' said Nora.

Finally, they were heading for the corner booth. 'Isn't that incredible!' Nora said in a hushed voice.

'Brian Blake?'

'Him, too. No, I mean that they're gonna be doing Beast House.'

'They aren't.'

'That's what he said, but that doesn't make it true. They just don't want word getting out, or some damn rip-off artist will beat them to the punch with a Beast House book.'

'Maybe.'

'Maybe? I'd bet on it. And we can be there when they take the tour. It'll be like being part of literary history. *We were there when Gorman Hardy first stepped inside Beast House!*'

'*You* were there.'

'Aw, you'll . . .'

'Sorry we kept you waiting,' Tyler interrupted.

'No problem,' Abe said, rising to his feet. He had changed into gray slacks and a blue blazer. He wore no tie. His yellow shirt was open at the throat. 'Did you run into some friends?'

'Not friends,' Tyler said. She slipped into the booth and sat down beside him.

Nora sat across the table. She patted Jack's forearm through the sleeve of his flashy plaid sport jacket. 'Those two at the bar,' she explained, 'are Gorman Hardy and Brian Blake.'

'Brian Blake?' Jack asked. He looked at Nora with the eagerness of an enthralled child. 'Sure. The middle-weight contender out of Pittsburg.'

'No,' Abe said. 'That's Byron Blake.'

'Well, who's this guy?'

Abe signaled to the barmaid. As she approached, Nora said, 'Do you know that book, *Horror at Black River Falls*?'

'Saw the show.' He looked at Abe. 'They ran it at the post last month. That haunted house flick where blood came out of the faucets and the gal ended up opening her wrists.'

'I saw it,' Abe said. He didn't sound impressed.

The barmaid arrived. After they gave their orders, she cleared off the table and left.

Leaning forward, Jack peered at Nora. 'This Blake, he's the pretty one? I don't remember him in the movie. Who'd he play?'

'He wasn't in the movie,' Nora told him. She spoke cheerfully, without any hint of reproach. 'It was about him. It was his house in real life, and his wife's the one who committed suicide.'

'Bullshit,' Jack said.

'What's bullshit?'

'It never happened. Who are they trying to kid? Okay, maybe the guy's wife pulled the plug on herself, but ghosts? Blood spurting out of the faucets? All those dirty words showing up on the walls? An ax flying at the guy? All that stuff really happened? No way.'

'You could ask him,' Nora suggested.

'Do *you* believe it?'

'I don't know. I've heard him talk on the subject, and he sure sounded convincing.'

'Nobody sounds more convincing than a guy with a good con.'

'The other fellow,' Abe said. 'He's actually Gorman Hardy, the author?'

'He is,' Tyler said.

'I've read some of his books. Including his ghost story.'

'Did you believe it?'

'I didn't disbelieve it.'

Jack's face contorted. 'For Chistsake, Abe.'

'More things in heaven and earth, Horatio . . .'

'Ghosts?'

'Remember Denny Stevens?'

'Not Denny Stevens again. You were hallucinating.'

'The whole platoon was hallucinating?'

'Mass hysteria.'

Abe arched an eyebrow at Jack, then glanced from Nora to Tyler. His hands were folded on the table. He looked down at them. 'Stevens was on point. This was in the jungle near the Vu Gia River, back in '67. He stepped on an anti-personnel mine. When we got to him, his right leg was gone. He was already dead from loss of blood. The femoral artery . . .' He shook his head. 'A couple of hours later, we came to a village. According to our intelligence, the VC had cleared out. The village was supposed to be safe, right? We stayed on our toes, just in case, but we didn't expect trouble. We were about fifty yards from the first huts when Denny Stevens came walking out from behind one. He came walking right toward us, just as if he had both legs.'

'Which he did,' Jack added.

'He was carrying his right leg. Had a hand under the boot, the thigh propped against his shoulder.'

'God Almighty,' Nora muttered.

'We were all . . . slightly stunned. We just stood there, gazing at Stevens. He used his free hand to wave us off, then he kind of melted into a puddle and vanished. We took cover as if every one of us knew for a fact that he'd come back to warn us. Just about then, all hell broke loose. We got chopped up pretty good, but it would've been a wipe-out except for Stevens.'

'You'll have to forgive Abe,' Jack said. 'He's usually not insane.'

'Every survivor of that firefight will tell you the same story.'

'You oughta tell that guy Hardy about it,' Jack said. 'Maybe he'll put you in a book.'

The barmaid came with a tray of drinks. There were two of each. She distributed them, and Abe paid. 'I'll be right back with more hors d'oeuvres,' she said and took away the tray.

Abe twisted his fingers around the lip of a Dos Equiis to clean it and raised the bottle. 'Which is why,' he said, 'I don't disbelieve Hardy's book. But I don't necessarily believe it.'

'Nora thinks he's in town to write about Beast House.'

'He denies it, of course,' Nora said. 'But I'm onto him. I'm gonna be there tomorrow when he goes on the tour. Even if I have to go alone.'

'Want company?' Jack asked.

'You betcha.'

Abe looked at Tyler. 'Did you have any luck finding your old friend?'

'No. Well, we went to his place, but he doesn't live there anymore.'

'We found out he works at Beast House,' Nora said. 'Hey, maybe if we play our cards right he can get us in free.'

'I don't know,' Tyler said.

'Butterflies,' Nora explained.

9

Alone in his room, Brian Blake picked up the telephone and dialed the office. A man answered, but he was prepared for that. 'I'm sorry to bother you, but I don't seem to have an ice bucket.'

'I'll send one right over to you.'

'Appreciate it,' he said and hung up.

He went to the connecting doors and opened his side. Gorman, rereading the diary, looked up at him.

'She's on the way,' Brian said. 'I hope.'

'Excellent. Enjoy yourself, but handle her carefully. We certainly don't wish to alienate her.'

'Trust me.'

'Do I have a choice?'

Laughing, Brian shut the door. He removed a tan jacket from his suitcase, and slipped his arms into the sleeves. He was fastening the buttons when he heard a gentle knock. 'Room service?' he called.

'Your ice bucket.' Janice's voice. Brian smiled.

He opened the door.

'I filled it for you,' she said.

'Thank you.' He took the plastic container. 'Come on in for a minute.'

She stepped inside, and looked around the room as if expecting to find Gorman. She had changed into blue jeans and a powder blue sweatshirt.

'How are you feeling?' Brian asked as he shut the door.

'You mean the gin? I'm okay now, but I sure conked out. I almost missed supper.'

He belted his jacket. 'How about an adventure?'

She looked intrigued. 'What do you mean?'

'Gorman asked me to check on something. You want to come along?'

'Where to?'

'I won't tell.'

'Do we walk or ride?'

'Ride, then walk.'

'How long'll it take?'

'An hour or so. It all depends.'

'On what?'

'Whether we get lucky.'

'It sounds so mysterious.'

'You game?'

She shrugged one shoulder. 'I got nothing better to do. I'll tell Dad I'm going for a walk.'

'Will he buy that?'

'Sure. I take a lot of walks. Just pull off the road and wait for me.'

Brian gave her a head start, then took his camera out to the Mercedes. He drove slowly through the courtyard, turned toward town, and stopped along the roadside. There was no traffic. He killed the headlights. Looking back, he saw Janice leave the motel office and trot down the porch stairs. She walked quickly with a bounce in her step as if eager to run. As she crossed the road, Brian flipped a switch to unlock the passenger door.

'All set,' she said, climbing in. As she swung the door shut, Brian noticed a pleasant, faint scent.

He smiled. He hadn't noticed this aroma in the room. Had she actually taken time to put on cologne for their 'adventure'?

'*Now* will you say where we're going?' she asked.

He put on his headlights and eased onto the road. 'Beast House,' he said. He watched her mouth fall open.

'Not me. At night? You're out of your tree.'

He laughed.

'You are kidding, right?'

'Right. Half kidding.'

'Only half?'

'We'll stay outside the fence. What I want to do is go around behind the place and scout around.'

'What for?'

'The hole.'

'The *beast* hole? For Godsake, what for?'

'To see if it's there.'

'Oh, man, I'm not sure about this.'

'Do you want me to take you back?'

She sighed. 'You weren't kidding about an adventure, were you?'

'Should be fun, huh?'

'Jesus.'

'Chances are, we won't find the thing anyway. If it exists at all, it's probably well hidden. It may have even collapsed by now. But if we *do* find it, you know what that means?'

'I guess it means the diary's not a fake.'

Rounding a bend, they left the dark stretch of road behind. The main street of town was lighted with lampposts.

'It might also mean,' Brian said, 'that we would have access to the house.'

'Now I know you're crazy.'

He slid his gaze down her slim body. 'You might be just about the right size . . .'

'No way, José.'

Brian laughed. 'Actually, I only want to locate the hole and get some shots of it. The tunnel to the house is probably blocked by now, anyway. Unless the beast still uses it.'

'You just had to say that, didn't you? You're having a great old time.'

'Wonderful.'

She laughed softly as she stared out the windshield. Then she looked at him. 'I guess you must've read the diary, huh? What did you think?'

'That Thorn gal either had a very active fantasy life, or she ran into something a bit odd in her cellar.'

'A bit odd?'

'More than a bit.'

'I'll say.'

'It's too bad she didn't describe the thing in more detail.'

'As far as I'm concerned, she described more than enough.' Janice pressed her knees together. 'Look, there's the Kutch house.' She nodded to the right.

Brian glanced at the brick house set back a distance from the road.

'See anything funny about it?'

'No.'

'No windows. That's where Maggie lives. The one who owns Beast House? They say she built it without windows to keep the creature out.'

'Seems excessive,' Brian said. Turning his head, he watched Beast House as he drove slowly by. Its windows caught the moonlight. Its dull gray walls were smudged with shadows. 'Must be pleasant in there at night.'

'It's bad enough in daylight. Are you sure that wouldn't be a better time to go looking for this hole?'

'We don't want to attract attention.'

'The thing's nocturnal, you know.'

'Worried?'

'I just think you'd have a better chance finding the hole in daylight.'

'Well, it's worth a try.'

'How come Mr Hardy didn't come along?'

'He's chicken.'

'Smart man.'

'I'll protect you,' Brian said, and patted her knee.

'Gee, thanks.'

He steered around a bend, and the distant lights of Malcasa's main street vanished from the rearview mirror. The road curved upward through wooded hills. He drove farther than he wanted, looking for a shoulder wide enough to accommodate the Mercedes. When he found one, he turned out and killed the headlights.

'Oh, man,' Janice muttered.

'What?'

'It's dark.'

'All the better for sneaking around, my dear.' He slung the camera strap around his neck and climbed out. While Janice scooted across the seat, he opened the back door. He lifted a blanket and flashlight off the floor.

'What's the blanket for?' Janice whispered.

'In case we want to make out.'

She looked at him. She said nothing.

They started across the road, Janice staying close to his side. 'Actually,' he said, 'it's in case we do find the hole. I'll want to get some shots of it, and we can use the blanket to shield the flashes.'

'Clever.'

'Disappointed?'

'Oh, sure.'

They walked along the edge of the road, heading down the slope toward town. Janice's cowboy boots sounded loud on the pavement. When the wind rushed through the trees, it seemed to Brian like the noise of an approaching car. He often looked over his shoulder.

'Nervous?' Janice asked.

'I don't want to get run over.'

'Fat chance of that.'

'You get careful,' he said, 'after you've had a close one.'

'Did you . . .?' she suddenly turned her face to him. 'My God, that's right. I forgot about that. Must've been pretty hairy.'

'You see your own car speeding at you without anyone at the wheel – yeah, I'd say it's pretty hairy.'

'Awful,' she said. 'God, you've been through a lot. I don't know how you stood it.'

He shook his head slowly. 'I came very close . . . to taking Martha's way out. When I found her in the tub, and all that blood . . .'

Janice patted his forearm, gave it a gentle squeeze.

'Well,' he said, 'it was a long time ago.'

'You must still miss her.'

'Not a day goes by when I don't . . . Hey, let's not get maudlin here and spoil the fun.'

'Fun?'

'I'm all right. Honest.'

She let go of his arm, and nodded. Her face was a dim blur in the darkness. Brian brushed her chin with his forefinger. 'Let's find that hole,' he whispered.

Near the bottom of the road, with the corner of the Beast House fence in sight, they crossed a shallow ditch and started along the slope. Brian led the way through the underbrush, ducking beneath low branches, climbing or descending to bypass trees and thickets, always staying roughly parallel to the fence. When he came to a cluster of rock, he climbed onto it and found a smooth surface. He sat down to rest. Janice settled down beside him. He put a hand on her back. 'How you doing?'

'Okay.'

With no trees blocking the view, Brian could see the rear corner of the fence not far below. The lawn of Beast House was pale with moonlight. Just in back of the house stood a small enclosure of lattice-work. 'The famous gazebo,' he said, 'where Elizabeth and Dr Ross had their "blissful delights".'

'Guess so,' Janice said. 'Do you really think we're gonna find that hole?'

'Should be over there,' he answered, pointing toward the hillside directly behind the house. 'Just outside the fence.'

'It could be anywhere.'

'Elizabeth wrote that the tunnel came out just beyond the property line.'

'But I don't remember she said in which direction. It might've been along the back, or it might've been along this side. For all we know, we already passed it.'

Brian grinned. 'Or it might be *right behind us!*'

'Creep,' she muttered, and nudged him with her elbow. He struck back, tickling her side. She squirmed and yelped.

'Shhh. It'll hear you.'

She clamped her arm down, pinning Brian's hand against her side. 'Gotcha,' she said. 'No more tickling, okay?'

'I promise.' He slipped his hand free. 'Why don't you wait here and relax a minute? I'll be right back.'

'Not a chance. Where you go, I go.'

'Fine with me. Pick a tree.'

'Oh. In that case. Stay close, though, okay?'

He climbed over the top of the outcropping. After only a few steps, he turned around. The back of Janice's head was a shaggy silhouette in the darkness. 'Don't peek,' he warned.

'I won't.'

He unzipped his pants and relieved himself. Then he climbed over to Janice. 'Ready to go?' he asked

'All set.'

He picked up his flashlight, tucked the folded blanket under one arm, and led the way down the rocks. The hillside slanted down to a shallow ravine, then curved as if to follow the line of the fence. Though there were few trees here to give them cover, Brian felt certain that they couldn't be spotted from the distant road. Only someone looking out a rear window of Beast House would be able to see them crossing the slope.

The windows were all dark.

He waited for Janice. 'Anyone in there at night?'

'I doubt it.'

'Just the beast, huh?'

'Very funny.' She didn't sound amused. 'As a matter of fact, they say it wanders the house at night.'

'Looking for Elizabeth?'

'Looking for victims.'

'Let's hope it stays away from the windows.'

Janice lagged behind, staring at the house, then hurried to catch up. 'Maybe we ought to get out of here,' she whispered.

'We haven't even started searching for the hole.'

'C'mon, what are the chances we'll find it? You said yourself that we probably wouldn't.'

'What're you so worried about?'

'I'm not worried, I'm scared shitless.'

'What for?'

She waved toward the house. 'It can *see* us.'

Turning to Janice, he shook his head. He let the blanket and flashlight fall to the ground, and put his hands on her shoulders. He could feel her trembling. 'There's nothing to be afraid of,' he said.

'I'm sorry. Really. But . . .'

'That business with Elizabeth was more than seventy years ago,' he said in a calm, soothing voice. 'Even if the stuff in her diary is true, which I strongly doubt, that creature would be ancient by now. Decrepit. Probably dead. At any rate, nobody's been killed since that kid almost thirty years ago.'

'What do you mean? It killed three people last summer.'

Brian frowned. 'There's nothing about that in the travel brochure.'

'Well, it's outdated.' She glanced at the house. 'They were killed up there, in a corridor on the second floor.'

'The police must've investigated.'

'Sure, but they couldn't come up with an answer. They don't think the beast had anything to do with it – at least that's what they say. They said it must've been a nut.'

'They're probably right.'

'They just *said* that. They can't admit there's some kind of a goddamn monster in the house.'

'There is no monster, Janice. I mean, that's nonsense.'

'No, it's not. You read the diary.'

'Thorn was crazy.'

Janice stared up at him. She smiled slightly. 'If she was crazy, what the hell are we doing out here looking for the goddam hole?'

Brian let out a quick laugh. '*Touché*,' he said.

'Let's leave.'

'Gorman thinks there might be a hole. He's more gullible than me.'

'Let him come and look for it.'

'What'll I tell him?'

'Just say we couldn't find it.'

'That would be fibbing.'

She glanced to each side. 'I don't see the hole. Do you see the hole?'

Brian laughed. 'You're really something, Janice.'

'Am I?' She put her hands on his sides, and stared into his eyes. 'What kind of something?'

'Later. We've got to get out of here, remember?'

'No. Come on, you started it.'

'You're funny,' he said. 'And crafty. And cute.'

'Cute? Hamsters are cute.'

'Okay, how about beautiful?'

She tilted her head. 'That's nice. Now we can leave.' But her hands didn't leave Brian's sides.

He eased her close and she pressed herself tightly against him, arms wrapping his back, mouth opening, sucking in his tongue. She squirmed and moaned in his embrace.

Brian slid his hands under the back of her sweatshirt. Caressing her, he pictured himself gloating as he described it all to Gorman. *Nothing to it, really. I just worked on her emotions, played on her fears till she needed some reassuring, gave a comforting pat here and there, a little wit to break the tension. Worked on her sympathy by leading into some sad talk about my poor departed Martha. Tried to keep a sexual undertone going, joked that I'd brought the blanket for making out, even took a leak out there so she'd have to think about my dick. Stayed close enough so she could hear the piss splatter.*

Masterful job, Gorman would say.

He unhooked the back of Janice's bra. She didn't object. On the contrary, she stepped back enough to make a space between their bodies so Brian could lift the cups away and caress her breasts. Her nipples felt like rubber posts. She arched her back as he thumbed them.

'Shouldn't we leave?' he asked.

Her mouth hung open, but she didn't speak. She shook her head wildly from side to side, making her hair fly.

He slid the sweatshirt up above her breasts, crouched, and used his tongue. Her trembling fingers pushed through his hair, urged his mouth hard against her breast.

Actually, Gorman, it was a cinch. She was as hot to trot as they come.

No, he shouldn't admit that. Let Gorman think he's a superstud.

Which, of course, I am.

As he sucked first on one breast, then on the other, his hands plied her firm rump through the seat of her jeans.

I took it slow, he would say. Didn't want to spook her.

He brought a hand to the front. The crotch of her jeans felt warm and moist. He pressed against it, feeling the jut of her mons through the heavy fabric. She writhed on his rubbing fingers as if she wanted them in.

Straightening up, he pulled her sweatshirt over her head. The bra came off with it. He caressed her bare neck and shoulders as she feverishly unfastened his jacket and shirt. When they were open, she squeezed herself against him. Her breasts, slicked with Brian's saliva, felt cool at first, then warm. Her hands went to his shoulders. They pulled the shirt and jacket down his arms. The chilly night air made him flinch, but her hand took his mind off the cold as it pushed inside his pants and curled around his erection.

'Let's put the blanket down,' she whispered, her fingers gliding. 'That's what you brought it for.'

'It is?'

Grinning, she gave his scrotum a gentle squeeze. Then she took out her hand. They spread the blanket nearby. It was puffy from the weeds beneath it. She walked on the blanket, her moonlit breasts jiggling as she stomped it down.

Lying on her back, she crossed each leg to pull off her boots and socks. She opened her jeans, lifted her buttocks off the blanket long enough to tug the pants out from under her, and raised her feet. 'Give me a hand?'

Brian gripped the cuffs and slid the jeans off her legs. The panties were around her thighs, very white below the dark triangle of her pubic thatch. Crouching beside her, Brian drew the flimsy garment down to her ankles and off.

While he shed the rest of his own clothes, he watched Janice squirm slowly, caressing herself. She had her knees up, her heels dug in to keep her from sliding down the gradual slope.

Her legs spread wide for him when he knelt. He kissed her inner thighs, nibbled and licked, easing lower until his mouth found her wet center. She jerked as his tongue darted. 'God, Brian,' she murmured. He pushed his tongue deep into her hugging warmth. She thrust against him, moaning.

Then he moved up her body. His tongue flicked into her navel while his hands glided up cool skin to her breasts. He squeezed and massaged them. Then he let them go and braced himself above Janice and kissed each breast and eased higher until he met her mouth.

As she sucked his tongue into her mouth, Brian slid his penis into her.

Mission accomplished, he thought.

Half accomplished, but the rest would be easy after this. Just get her into his room tomorrow night for round two and keep her busy. Talk her into showering with him so Gorman would have a chance to snatch her key. Gorman would have the tough part, sneaking into her place to find the contract and exchange it for the phoney that gave her nothing. Brian's part would be a cinch. And fun.

Better than this.

In spite of the blanket, the ground was brutal on his knees. But he kept at it, kept driving into Janice. She was going wild, thrashing around and shoving up to meet his thrusts and tugging his buttocks to force him deeper.

She would drool at the chance for an all-night fucking session.

Why don't you sneak over after your folks are asleep?

She would absolutely drool. At both ends.

She was gasping under him, eyes squeezed shut, head jerking from side to side. A few more good thrusts . . .

Something cold and slippery smashed down on Brian's back. His knees shot out from under him. He slammed flat against Janice. Her breath blasted against his face.

Brian thought, *Who in hell . . .?*

Then the teeth clamped his neck.

10

Tyler took Abe's hand as they left the Carriage House 'That was a delicious dinner. Thank you.'

'My pleasure.'

'So,' Jack said, 'should we try that place?'

'The Last Chance sounds like a dive,' Nora said

'We could look for someplace else,' Abe offered.

'The waitress seemed to think it's fine,' Tyler said.

'Hell, I love dives.'

'Nora's an expert on dives.'

'Especially the triple back somersault.'

Jack nudged her with an elbow. Giggling, she stumbled sideways toward the hedge. Jack grabbed her, and she wrapped an arm around his back.

'Anyhow,' she said, 'I am inappropriately attired for a dive of any ilk and must therefore retire to my boudoir for a change of habiliment.'

'She wants out of her prom dress,' Tyler translated.

'Need a hand?' Jack asked.

Nora swatted his rump.

'I'll want to get a jacket,' Tyler said.

They agreed to meet at Abe's car in five minutes, and left the men. Tyler entered the room after Nora. Even as she shut the door, Nora's gown swirled to the floor.

'Aren't they great?' she asked. Stepping out of it, she staggered and dropped onto the bed, her breasts bouncing.

'Are you all right?' Tyler asked.

'Fine and dandy.' Flopping backwards, she smiled at the ceiling. Her pubic hair was matted flat by her pantyhose.

'You aren't going to pass out on us, are you?'

Nora rolled her eyes. 'Hardly. I'm fine. Are you fine?'

'I'm fine.'

'So am I.' With a sigh, she sat up and started to pull her shoes off.

Tyler went through the connecting doors and slipped into her windbreaker. She brushed her hair and put on fresh lipstick. When she returned to Nora's room, her friend was on the mattress, legs hoisted in the air as she pulled on a pair of white jeans. The pantyhose lay on the floor. 'So what do you think?'

'About what?' Tyler asked.

'My lily-white ass. *Abe. Honest Abe.*'

'I like him.'

She raised her bare rump and pulled up the jeans. 'Like him a lot?'

'Very much.'

Nora sat up. She started to put on socks and loafers. 'So, gonna fuck him?'

'For godsake.'

'Take your mind off Dan.'

'Sure. Let's have a foursome.'

'I could go for that.'

'You've got sex on the brain.'

'And proud of it.' Laughing, Nora stood and slipped into a plaid shirt. She buttoned it only halfway up, and tucked it into her jeans. 'If I were you,' she said, 'I'd go for it.'

'I know you would.'

'You only go around once.'

'My life is not a beer commercial.'

With a laugh, Nora zipped her fly. 'Let's went, Queeksdraw.'

'Jacket?'

'And hide my considerable charms? Bite thy tongue, wench.'

They went outside. Abe and Jack were waiting in the Mustang. Leaning across the seat, Abe opened the door. Nora climbed in back with Jack.

'You look good in your dive habiliments,' Jack told her.

'I look better without 'em.'

'Bet you do.'

Tyler slid onto the bucket seat and pulled her door shut.

'No funny stuff back there,' Abe said as he started the car.

'Far be it from us,' Nora said with a giggle.

'Are you sure you two are librarians?' he asked.

'Nora's a librarian. I'm a media specialist. That's their five-dollar term for a school librarian.'

'*I'm* a school librarian,' Nora protested.

'Don't look like one,' Jack said.

'She's college,' Tyler said. 'I'm high school. They don't fool around that much with projectors and . . .'

'Just when I'm horny,' Nora said.

Though there were no other cars in sight, Abe signaled his right-hand turn before swinging onto the road. The headlights bore pale tunnels into the darkness. 'If this place turns out too sleazy,' he said, 'we can always try somewhere else.'

'Let's hear it for sleaze!' Nora called out. She and Jack clapped and whistled.

'Do we want to be seen with these two?' Abe asked, smiling at Tyler.

'I think we're stuck with them.'

'He's trying to pull the wool over Tyler's eyes,' Jack whispered loudly. 'Point of fact, Abe's an animal. Tell you the time he pissed on Colonel Lockridge? Jesus jumping Christ.'

'Jack!'

'You . . . urinated on a colonel?' Tyler asked.

'Just on his legs. He had it coming.'

'Right in the fuckin' officers' club.'

'In the restroom?'

'Right in the fuckin' officers' club,' Jack repeated, louder. 'After that, they called him "Whizzin' Abe".' Abe, laughing softly, shook his head. 'It was a long time ago. My manners have improved.'

'Two years ago.'

'You're asking for it, Jack.'

'What did this Lockridge do?' Tyler asked.

'Changed his pants,' Jack answered.

'No, I mean . . .'

'He'd insulted a friend,' Abe explained.

'Remind me never to insult your friends.'

'You've nothing to fear.'

'Whizzin' Abe is a gentleman with the ladies,' Jack said. 'Usually. Though I do remember that time . . .'

'And here we are,' Abe said. 'The Last Chance Bar.'

The sign, just ahead, lit up the darkness with red neon letters. An upper corner sported the outline of a tipping cocktail glass. 'What do you want to bet,' Nora said, 'the other side says First Chance Bar?'

As if to satisfy her curiosity, Abe drove past the sign before turning onto the gravel lot.

'It does, it does!' Nora blurted. Someone back there slapped someone's bare skin.

The tires crunched over gravel as Abe drove along behind several parked cars. The building, a squat adobe box, had neon beer signs in both its front windows. Tyler heard muffled sounds of music from inside: Waylon Jennings singing 'Luckenbach, Texas'. Abe pulled to a stop beside a pickup truck, and they climbed out.

He took Tyler's hand. The music stopped as they entered the bar. Through the noise of voices and laughter came the jingle of a pinball machine, the clack of pool balls. The warm air was thick with swirling ribbons of smoke. As they made their way toward a table, Tyler saw a few heads turn to inspect them. One of the faces, ruddy and white-bearded, belonged to Captain Frank. He stared at her, one eye squinted almost shut. She nodded a greeting. A corner of his mouth pulled crooked, and he turned back to the bar.

'Know him?' Abe asked.

'We ran into him when we were looking for Dan.'

Abe pulled out a chair for her. She sat at the table, her back to the wall, and saw Captain Frank glance over his shoulder. Then Nora blocked her view of the man.

A barmaid came. As she cleared away a couple of beer mugs and mopped some wet rings and puddles off the table, Nora eyed her costume: cowboy boots, blue denim short-shorts, and a blouse in the pattern of a red bandanna. The blouse was knotted in front, leaving her midriff bare. 'What'll it be, folks?'

'I like your outfit,' Nora said.

'Do you? It's my own creation. Gives the fellas something to look at.' She winked at Abe. ' 'Course, Charlie says it's shameless.' She laughed. ' "Struttin' your wares like a floozy." He goes on and on, but we bought us a brand new twenty-nine-inch Sony TV from my tips, and I don't hear him squawk about that, do I?'

'Men are just weird,' Nora pronounced.

'Can't live with 'em, can't live without 'em. You folks on vacation?' Nora nodded.

'Well, that's real good. Hope you're having a ball. Now, what can I fetch you?'

They discussed it for a moment, then Abe ordered two pitchers of beer.

'I'll be right along with 'em, and I'll bring along a nice bowl of popcorn to keep you wanting more.'

When she was gone, Nora said, 'I wonder if they've got any openings.'

'You just want to strut your wares,' Tyler told her.

With a prolonged stare at Nora's cleavage, Jack said, 'She's already at it.'

'Get in there!' yelled a man at the pool table. 'All *right*!'

From the juke-box at the far end of the room came the voice of Tom T. Hall singing 'I Like Beer'.

'Reminds me of Le Du's joint in Saigon,' Jack said, looking across at Abe.

'Does at that,' Abe said. 'Le Du was a great lover of the old West,' he explained. 'Found himself a pair of woolie chaps somewhere, and he wore them no matter how hot it was in that bar of his. He had a ten-gallon hat that must've been nine gallons bigger than his head.'

'Was he a half-pint?' Tyler asked.

Abe laughed. 'That, and then some.'

'He got what he had coming,' Jack said, grinning mysteriously.

'Oh, no.' Nora wrinkled her nose. 'Was he a sympathizer?'

'Yup,' Abe said. 'A sympathizer with Hoppy, Gene and Roy.'

'Don't forget Randolph Scott. That was his favorite.'

'Last we heard, Le Du's the proprietor of the Hole in the Wall saloon in Waco, Texas.'

'Hope he's improved his costume,' Jack added as the barmaid approached with a laden tray.

She set out the pitchers, the frosty mugs, and a bowl of popcorn. When Abe reached for his wallet, she said, 'It's already been taken care of. Compliments of Captain Frank.'

Abe looked perplexed. 'Who?'

'The fella over there.' She nodded toward the bar. Captain Frank had swiveled around on his stool to face them. 'Said the girls are old mateys.'

'Did he?' Nora asked. 'That's sweet. Why don't we ask him to join us?'

Tyler felt a tightening in her stomach.

'That okay with you guys? He's probably lonely.'

Shaking her head, the barmaid walked away.

'It's all right with me,' Abe said.

'Long as he doesn't try to move in on us,' Jack added. 'Can't have that.'

'I'll go get him.' Nora stood, and made her way toward the bar.

'Who *is* this guy?' Abe asked.

'Captain Frank,' Tyler said. 'Just an old guy who fancies himself a seaman.'

Abe frowned. 'What's wrong?'

'Nothing, I guess. I just find him a little . . . strange. You ought to see his bus.'

'If he makes you nervous . . .'

'Too late, now.'

Nora, holding onto the old man's arm, was steering him toward the table. He drank from a half-empty mug as he walked. He had on the same faded Hawaiian shirt and Bermuda shorts he'd been wearing that afternoon. His scrawny legs looked out of place beneath his massive torso. He moved with a list.

When they neared the table, Nora found an empty chair for him, and placed it next to Abe. ' 'Preciate it, mate,' he told her, and sat down.

Nora made introductions.

As Abe filled the man's mug from one of the pitchers, everyone thanked him for buying. 'My pleasure,' he said in a low, thick voice. 'My penance.' He raised his mug, winked and drank, and wiped his mouth with the back of a liver-spotted hand. 'Sins of our fathers,' he mumbled.

'You're a seafarer?' Abe asked.

'Fair and foul. A seafarer. Yes, indeed. That's me, Captain Frank, old salt. Me and my father before me.' He leaned forward and stared with bleary eyes at Tyler. 'God forgive him, he brought it here.'

Tyler, unsettled by his gaze, looked down at her beer.

'Brought what?' Nora asked.

'The beast.'

'The Beast House beast?' Jack asked.

'Aye, the filthy spawn of hell.'

'You're saying that your father brought it to Malcasa Point?'

'That he did, and I'm here to tell you the curse of it's a heavy burden to bear. Heavy indeed.' He took another drink.

Nora and Jack exchanged a glance as if they thought the man a lunatic. Abe was frowning.

'The guilt.' Captain Frank held up his thick, calloused hands. 'Do you see the blood? I do. I see the blood of its victims, and God alone knows how many. They don't tell it all on the tour. No indeed. Is my father there in wax? Is my sister Loreen, slain by the fiend seven years before I came wailing into this dreary world? No. You won't find them on the tour. You won't hear their names. How many others? Ten? Fifty? A hundred and fifty? Only God knows. God and the beast. People vanish. See their blood?' he asked, slowly turning his hands.

'You think it killed your father and sister?' Nora asked.

'Oh yes. Yes indeed. Little Loreen first. She was a child of three when he brought it home from some nameless forsaken island off the Australian coast. He was first mate, then, on the *Mary Jane* out of Sausalito. The summer of 1901, it was. They were becalmed, not a breath of wind, day after day, to fill the sails. The food went bad. The water casks emptied. They all thought surely they would die, and it's a shame they didn't. But on the thirteenth day of their travail, they spotted land. A volcanic island it was – all hills and jungle.

'A party went ashore. Fresh water was gathered from a spring. Fruit and berries were plentiful, but the men craved meat and found none. Now what kind of jungle is that that has no wildlife? It's none such as I have ever seen, or any of the men from the *Mary Jane*. It worked on their nerves, and many were anxious to return to the ship before nightfall. Even my father, as stout-hearted a fellow as ever walked a deck, confessed he greeted the sunset, that night, with unholy dread. But he wouldn't abandon the island, not until he was certain it bore no wildlife.'

Captain Frank swigged down some beer. He leaned forward, elbows on the table, and stared into Tyler's eyes as if she were alone with him. The noise of the bar – the talk and laughter, the clink of glasses, the clatter of pool balls, the pinging of the pinball machine, Willie Nelson's clear voice from the juke-box – all seemed strangely distant to Tyler.

'When darkness fell,' he continued, 'they surrounded the water hole. Men concealed themselves among the bushes and climbed into trees. Every last mother's son of them was armed, ready to slay any animal that might come to drink.

'The strategy worked. Near midnight, the creatures came. Twelve or fifteen of them wandered out of the jungle and waded into the pond to drink. My father admits he thought they were humans at first – some primitive tribe – but then he saw their faces in the moonlight. Their snouts. He knew they weren't human, but loathsome, unearthly beasts. He ordered the men to fire. Every last one of the creatures fell. Not a one of them got away. My father's face went ghastly pale when he told me of the slaughter, and what happened afterwards – how some of the men had their way with the female carcasses . . .'

'Frank,' Abe said.

The old man flinched as if startled from his dark reverie.

'I don't think we want to hear all this.'

'I do,' Nora protested. 'It's fascinating.'

'I don't mind,' Tyler said. She was trembling. She hated the story, but she had to hear the rest of it, and even resented Abe's interruption. She took a long drink of beer. Abe gave her a quizzical look, and refilled her glass from the pitcher.

'Go on,' Nora said.

Captain Frank looked to Abe for permission.

'Doesn't bother *me*,' he said.

'Then I'll . . . the slaughter . . . When it was done, my father found a survivor, an infant creature beneath one of the females – its mother, no doubt. Her body had shielded it from the storm of bullets. Father took this infant into his care.

'The others, the bodies, were . . .' He glanced uneasily at Abe. 'They provided sufficient nourishment to see the crew safely to Perth.'

'They ate them?' Nora asked.

'My father claimed they tasted rather like mutton.'

'Charming.'

'He named his creature Bobo, and though he was never fond of it he considered the filthy thing a great curiosity and kept it with him in a cage on the journey home. My mother, rest her soul, thought Bobo appalling. She begged him to get rid of it, but little Loreen found the creature delightful and spent hours behind our home, talking to it through the bars of its cage as if it were a playmate. At last, Mother prevailed upon him to dispose of it. He agreed to transport it to San Francisco, where he hoped to sell it for a good price to a circus or zoo. Alas, Loreen must have overheard the talk, for she opened the cage, the very next morning, and Bobo fell upon her. My folks heard her awful screams, but she was past helping when they reached her. The beast, small as it was, had torn her asunder, and was having . . .' Captain Frank glanced at Abe, and shook his head.

'My father beat it senseless with a spade. He thought he'd killed it. He put the remains in the flour bag, and dragged it up into the hills behind the Thorn house. The place was under construction, then. Lilly

Thorn was just having it built. He buried the creature up there.'

'But it wasn't dead?' Nora asked.

'Not much more than a year went by, and there were three dead in the Thorn house: Lilly's two sons and her sister. Lilly escaped, but she was never right afterward and they carted her off to a sanitarium. The blame fell on a luckless chap name of Goucher, a handyman who'd stopped by, the day before, to chop wood. But my father'd seen the bodies. He had his suspicions, and spoke up for Goucher, claiming a wild animal must've got into the house, but he kept shut about Bobo, not wanting to bring blame on himself. Well, the crowd wouldn't listen. They lynched poor Goucher, strung him up from a porch beam.

'I wasn't born till six years later, that's 1909. I 'spect I'm what you'd call an accident, for I believe my folks were loath to have another child after what happened to Loreen. Oh, they treated me like royalty, but there was always a gloom in their eyes. The Thorn house, all the time I was growing up, stood deserted at the end of town. Nobody'd go near the place. It was said to be haunted. Every now and then, though, we'd have someone disappear. Then, in '31, the Kutch family moved in.

'They came from Seattle, and scoffed at warnings about the house, but they weren't settled in more than a couple of weeks before the husband and kids were slaughtered. Maggie was scratched up bad, but . . . she'll tell you all about it if you take the tour. What she won't tell you – what maybe she doesn't know – is that my father, the night after the funeral, took his Winchester and went off to kill the beast.

'He was sixty-two at the time. He'd been living with the guilt for better than thirty years, and he told me that morning he couldn't abide it any longer. It was then I heard the whole story for the first time, and how he knew it must be Bobo, still alive, behind the murders. I begged him to let me come along, but he just wouldn't hear of it. He wanted me to stay behind, and look after Mother. It was as if he knew he would never come back, and he didn't. He was a good shot. I 'spect Bobo must've snuck up on him, caught him from the back.' Captain Frank raked the air, fingers hooked like claws, and knocked over his mug. Tyler flinched as it pounded onto the table. Beer flew out, splashing Abe, sliding in a sudsy spill across the wood. 'Oh, I'm . . .' The old man shook his head, mumbling, and swept at the puddle with his open hand. 'Oh. I'm . . . I shouldn't of . . . oh damn.'

The barmaid rushed up with a towel. 'We have a little accident here?' she asked, mopping the table.

'Nothing serious,' Abe said.

'If Frank's being a nuisance . . .'

'No. It's fine.'

'I should've warned you,' she said, casting a peeved glance at Captain Frank. 'Going at his Bobo story, I bet. He'll talk your ears off once he's soaked up a few. We've had folks get up and walk out. Haven't we, Captain?'

He stared down at his shirt. 'The tale must be told,' he muttered.

'Gives the place a bad name.'

'Pretty interesting stuff,' Nora said.

'Just don't believe a word of it,' the barmaid said. 'Come on, Frank. Why don't you go on back to the bar and leave these nice folks in peace.' She took his arm and helped him stand up.

'Hang on a second,' Abe said. He lifted a pitcher and filled the old man's mug to the brim.

'Thank you, matey. Let me tell you.' He met the eyes of everyone at the table. 'The hours of the beast are numbered. One night, Captain Frank shall stalk it to its lair and lay it low. The souls of the dead cry out for its blood. I am the avenger. Mark my words.'

'We'll be pulling for you,' Jack called after him.

'Jesus,' Nora said, and rolled her eyes.

Grinning, Jack shook his head. 'The old fart waits much longer, he'll be stalking it from a wheelchair.'

'He'll never do it,' Abe said. 'A guy talks it out that way, he doesn't act on it.'

'Did you believe it?' Tyler asked. 'About the beast?'

'He didn't *dis*believe it,' Jack put in.

'Hey,' Nora said. 'We've gotta tell Gorman Hardy about this guy. Maybe he'll put us in the Acknowledgment. "My gratitude to Nora Branson, Tyler Moran, Jack Wyatt, and Abe Clanton, whose valuable assistance led me to the true story of Bobo the beast." I ask you, would that not be terrif?'

'That,' Tyler said, 'would be almost *too* exciting.'

11

A sharp pounding on the door startled Gorman Hardy awake. He bolted upright and scanned the dark room, wondering where he was. Then he remembered.

It must, he thought, be Brian at the door. But why the frantic knocking?

Perhaps he had lost his key.

'I'm coming,' Gorman called.

The knocking continued.

He swung his legs to the floor and squinted against the brightness as he switched on a bedside lamp.

'I'm coming,' he called again.

The knocking didn't stop.

Something, he thought, must have gone wrong. More than a lost room key. Something bad enough to panic Brian.

He felt on the verge of panic, himself, as he stood up.

For the love of God, what had happened?

He was naked. He put on a satin robe, tied it shut, and opened the door.

Brian was not there.

On the dark stoop waited a man and a woman. The man was about forty and bald. He wore a blue windbreaker. His fists were clenched at his sides. Gorman had never seen him before. The woman, an attractive blonde, looked familiar. She wore jeans and a checkered blouse and an open leather jacket. She looked like an older version of Janice. Gorman realized he had seen her at the Carriage House where she'd been performing hostess duties.

These people are Janice's parents.

He felt a little sick.

'Mr Hardy?' the man asked in a taut voice.

'Yes.'

'I'll try to be civilized about this, but it's two o'clock in the morning and our daughter is missing. Is she here?'

'No, of course not. Come in and see for yourselves.' He stepped away from the door to let them enter. The woman shut the door and backed against it as if to prevent Gorman from escaping.

The man, after a glance at the beds, stepped into the bathroom and turned on a light. He came out a moment later, and checked the closet. He looked at the connecting door, then at Gorman. 'What about Mr Blake?'

'I really can't answer for him.'

'You're together. You paid both rooms.'

'He is my associate, yes. But I have no idea why you suspect either of us might be harboring your daughter.' As he spoke, he walked past the man to the connecting door. He rapped it with his fist. 'Brian?' he called. He opened his side and tried the knob of Brian's door. Fortunately, it didn't turn. With any luck, if the girl was in the room, she would have time to get out. 'Brian?' he called again.

'Let's have a look,' the man said, striding forward.

'He drove her someplace,' the woman said, speaking for the first time.

'I'll take a look anyhow.'

Gorman stepped out of his way. He watched Janice's father insert a key and unlock the door. A lamp was on. Relieved, Gorman saw that both the beds were made. He waited while the man entered to search. Turning to the woman, he said, 'Is the car gone?'

She nodded. Her face was grim, lips pressed together in a tight line, eyes glaring at Gorman.

'I honestly don't know what to say,' he told her. 'You suspect that she and Brian went off together?'

'You wouldn't know anything about that,' she said, her voice bitter.

'I'm afraid not.'

The man came back into the room. 'Okay, buster, where'd they go?'

'I have no idea. I don't even *know* your daughter. Would she be the young lady who registered us?'

'She would be.'

'I haven't seen her since then.'

'Don't lie to us!' the woman suddenly blurted. She rushed to her husband's side. 'Show him, Marty. Show him!'

He pulled a folded sheet of paper from his back pocket. It shook in his trembling hands as he opened it. 'We found this in Janice's room,' he said, and held it out.

Gorman took the sheet. He stared at it. The bitch, he thought. Oh, the bitch! She was supposed to hide it! Brian's fault. Where is he? What could've possessed him to keep her out so late and allow this to happen? He's ruined it. He's ruined everything!

'What do you say to that, Mr Hardy?' the woman said, almost snarling.

He managed a smile as he handed back the contract. 'Janice planned to surprise you,' he said. 'If the proposed book is as successful as my previous one, this agreement will likely earn her in the neighborhood of a million dollars.'

The news had its desired effect. Janice's parents looked at each other, then at the contract. They seemed to soften, as if their pent-up rage was melting away.

'Is this on the level?' Marty asked. He sounded suspicious, but a hint of excitement glittered in his eyes.

'It most certainly is. The agreement gives Janice fifty percent of all earnings from the book. This includes the advance and all royalties. We're talking here about a hardbound sale, book club and paperback sales, foreign sales, probably a movie deal. So far, my previous book has brought in over three million dollars. I suspect the Beast House story will do as well, or better. And Janice will receive half of it all.'

And she will, he thought. Good Christ, she will. Now there was no chance of tricking her out of it. He felt sick.

The woman raised her eyes from the contract. She looked wary. 'What did Janice have to do for this?'

'The book was her idea. She initiated the contact with me. And she provided me with a resource that gives invaluable insight into the subject.'

'What's that?' Marty asked.

'Janice doesn't wish that known, but since you're her parents, I see no harm in telling you that she found a diary written by Elizabeth Thorn, the lady who . . .'

'Where is Janice now?' the mother asked. 'I realize this puts a somewhat different light on the subject, but where *is* she? Does it have something to do with this?' She nodded at the contract.

'I honestly don't know. When did you last see her?'

'Around nine,' Marty answered. 'She said she was going for a walk. This was right after she came back from delivering an ice bucket to Mr Blake – which, by the way, he didn't need in the first place. I saw two in there.'

'I can only suppose,' Gorman said, 'that Brian invited her to accompany him. Perhaps she lied to you, thinking you might disapprove of her traipsing off with one of the motel guests.'

Marty and his wife exchanged a glance.

'I take it she's done such things before.'

'Wherever they went,' Marty said, 'they should've been back long ago.'

The woman said, 'There's no excuse for this.'

'I quite agree,' Gorman told her.

'Where did he take her?' Marty asked.

'We have no proof that she went with Brian at all, but he left with the intention of exploring an area behind Beast House. He was hoping to locate and photograph a hole near the rear fence.'

'A *hole*?'

'It's mentioned in the Thorn diary. Allegedly, an underground tunnel leads from the hillside to the house's cellar. If Brian finds the opening, it lends a certain credence to the . . .'

'Janice wouldn't go anywhere near that place,' her mother said.

'Well, perhaps she didn't. I'm simply pointing out the purpose of Brian's search. That's where he intended to go.'

'She must've gone with him, Claire.'

Claire shook her head. She looked resigned, rather weary. 'I guess I wouldn't put it past her,' she admitted. 'This Brian, I saw him at the restaurant. He's a very attractive man.'

Marty put a hand on Claire's back. In a gentle voice, he said, 'I'll drive out and bring her home.'

'I'm sure she'll be right along,' Gorman said.

'We've been waiting up for hours, Mr Hardy. Have you got any idea what goes through a parent's mind when your kid's out at this time of night and you don't know where she is, what's happened to her? You tell yourself she'll walk through the door any minute, and all the time you're wondering if maybe some lunatic got hold of her, if maybe you'll never see her again.'

'I can assure you, Brian's no lunatic.'

'Why isn't she home?' Marty demanded. He sounded a little frantic.

Claire sighed. 'She probably got carried away and forgot the time.'

'I'll remind her of the time,' Marty snapped, 'when I get my hands on her.' He frowned at Gorman. 'Where, exactly, is this hole supposed to be?'

'If you'd like, I'll accompany you. I'm rather concerned, myself, at this point.'

'We'll all go,' Claire said.

'Just give me a minute to get dressed,' said Gorman.

They found the Mercedes just above the curve leading into town from the south. Marty swung in behind it. He took a flashlight with him, and shone it through a side window. With a shake of his head, he came back down the road to Claire and Gorman. 'Nobody there,' he said.

'That young lady has a lot of explaining to do,' Claire muttered.

'So does Brian,' Gorman said. A million dollars worth, he thought.

They followed the road to the bottom of the hill, then crossed a ditch to the corner of the Beast House fence. Marty took the lead, trudging through the underbrush alongside the fence, playing his flashlight beam over the wooded slope on the right. 'Janice!' he yelled.

Claire tugged his shoulder. 'Don't,' she said.

'Janice!'

'I wish you wouldn't *do* that!'

'There's nobody to hear it but them.'

Gorman saw the woman look through the fence bars at the house. 'I just think we should be quiet about this.'

Now Gorman found himself looking at the house – at the darkness of the porch but especially at the windows. It seemed to have so many:

a bay window directly across the yard from him, a casement farther along the side, three sets on the second story, a single high attic window just below the peak of the roof, a pair beneath the tower's cap. All were moonless and black. Malevolent eyes, he thought, recalling the words he'd spoken into his recorder that afternoon. He'd been waxing eloquent, then – spewing drivel. But now it was three o'clock in the morning and he suddenly wished he were back at the inn, snug in bed, because the windows did, in fact, seem to be watching him.

He forced himself to look away from them. He stared at the weeds ahead of his feet, at Claire's back, at the beam of Marty's flashlight sweeping over bushes and rocks and trees on the slope. And he felt like a man walking down a dark street, stalked by stealthy footsteps, afraid of what he might find sneaking up on him if he should dare to glance over his shoulder. He had to look. He searched the windows. Though nothing showed through their blackness, his skin went tight and crawly.

Tomorrow, if he took the tour, he would have to go inside. The thought of it chilled him. Perhaps he should forget about it, simply abandon the project. After all, tonight's disaster had diminished his and Brian's possible returns by half.

Half of a gold mine, he told himself, is considerably better than no gold mine at all. The book would be a winner, he had no doubt of that. After *Horror*, his reputation alone would insure tremendous sales. But the Beast House story had tremendous potential. It could easily surpass the success of *Horror*. He was a fool to consider giving it up. He would simply have to keep a stiff upper lip and take the tour.

In daylight, the house wouldn't seem quite so forbidding. Besides, Brian would be along. Probably several sightseers, as well. And certainly there couldn't be any danger involved.

'Marty!' Claire gasped.

The man had suddenly broken into a run. He raced around the corner of the fence. Claire took off, chasing him. 'Marty!' she called. 'What is it?'

He didn't answer.

Gorman hurried after them both, reaching the corner with a few strides, then slogging along the rear section of fence.

What craziness is *this*? he wondered.

But he certainly did not want to be left behind. As he tried to catch up, he felt a familiar but long-forgotten mingling of despair and humiliation. The residue of childhood 'games' in which he had too often been the victim. Hey, let's ditch him! Let's ditch Gory! C'mon, let's lose him! And off his pals would go, trying their best to leave him behind, lost and alone.

Gorman knew in this case that he was not being ditched. Marty had seen something. But the awful, desperate feelings remained and tears blurred his vision as he struggled to keep up with the runners. 'Wait up!' he gasped.

They didn't wait.

But suddenly they stopped.

Gorman grabbed a bar of the fence to halt himself. Gasping, he wiped the tears from his eyes.

'Jesus H. Christ,' Marty muttered.

Claire staggered away, bent over, and started to vomit. Marty was aiming his flashlight upward. Gorman followed its beam to the top of the fence.

Brian's legs hung down, one on each side. He was naked. He was on his back. The body looked as if it had been slammed down hard onto the pointed uprights. Gorman's sphincter went cold and tight as he saw where one of the spikes had penetrated. The other bars had entered in a straight line, the final one piercing the back of his skull. His left arm drooped strangely. Gorman realized it had been broken backwards at the elbow.

Marty's light skittered down the length of the fence. Gorman followed its quick course. There was not another impaled body. The man turned toward the hillside. 'Janice!' he yelled. His beam swept over the weeds and bushes, and stopped on something about thirty feet up.

A rumpled blanket. Scattered clothes.

Claire shrieked out her daughter's name and lunged toward the slope. She scrambled up it, falling to her knees, crawling, getting her feet under her and scurrying higher. Marty raced after her.

Gorman stayed where he was. He watched them for a moment, then turned his gaze to the body. He ached as if he could feel the spikes in himself. He wanted badly to run, but the thought of fleeing, all alone in the dark, filled him with dread. He was shaking. He clutched a bar of the fence to steady himself. The cold iron was wet and sticky. He jerked his hand away and stared at it. The smears looked black in the moonlight. He raised his eyes to Brian's body. Suddenly, he didn't feel so terrified.

With his clean right hand, he reached into a pocket and took out his cassette recorder. He switched it on. 'I am standing, as I speak, beneath the body of Brian Blake – my friend, my associate, the man who survived the horror at Black River Falls only to meet a hideous death at the hands of the Malcasa beast. He met his fate in the dead of night, while . . .'

'Hardy! Goddamn you, get up here!'

He nodded, and backed away from the fence. Before starting up the slope, he slipped the recorder into his pocket without turning it off. If only he'd had the presence of mind to record everything from the moment Marty and Claire entered his room! Of course, he'd had no way of knowing at the time that the encounter would lead to such a marvellous tragedy.

Brian slaughtered by the beast. And in such a grisly fashion. It was almost too good to believe. The book would skyrocket!

Not only that, but Brian wouldn't be around to collect his share of the proceeds.

Incredible!

Now, if only Janice's body is up here, nicely mutilated . . . The parents will demand her half of the profits, but perhaps their claim wouldn't stand up in court.

'Look at this, you bastard!' Marty snapped, shining his light on the ground. Gorman recognized Brian's jacket and Hush Puppies. He saw garments all over the ground: a sweatshirt and brassière, cowboy boots, jeans, panties. The tangled blanket was dark with blood.

'Apparently,' Gorman said, 'they must have been . . .'

'Shut up!'

Claire was a distance away, sobbing as she searched through bushes.

'I'm sorry,' Gorman said. 'Honestly, though, I had no idea they. . .'

'You got her into this, goddamn you! I'll kill you if she . . .'

'Perhaps she's all right. She might have fled.'

'You'd better pray she did.' Turning away, Marty shouted up the hillside. 'Janice! Jaaan – nice!'

Gorman crouched and picked up Brian's camera. The flash attachment was in place. He peeled off the lens cap, and raised the camera to his eye. Peering through the viewfinder, he aimed at the blanket. The girl's jeans and panties were also in frame. He snapped a shot. In the quick burst of light, he saw that the panties were pink, the blue jeans faded, the blue blanket splashed with crimson. The automatic film advance buzzed.

The *Horror* photos had been printed in black and white. For this book, Gorman would insist on color plates. At least a few for the hardcover edition.

He turned the camera toward Janice's boots. They were close together, one standing at a slant, propped up by the sole of the other.

Fabulous.

She died with her boots off.

As his fingertip sought the shutter release, Marty blocked the view and drove a fist into Gorman's belly. The blow smashed his wind out, knocked him backwards. The camera flew from his hands. His back hit the slope. He skidded downhill. His legs flipped high and he somer-saulted. The earth pounded his knees, his belly. He clutched at weeds to stop his slide. Through his loud gasps for breath, he heard Claire shouting for Marty to stop.

The man came charging down.

'No!' Gorman cried.

Still in motion, Marty kicked at his head. Gorman shoved his face into the weeds. He felt the breeze of the passing shoe. Looking up, he saw that the momentum of the kick had thrown the man off balance. Marty flailed his arms and fell backwards. He landed on his rump. As he slid, the edge of a shoe scraped Gorman's ear.

Gorman grabbed the shoe and twisted it sharply. He heard a crackly sound of tearing cartilage. Marty flinched with pain. His mouth sprang open and he let out a cry.

'Marty!' Claire yelled. She started down.

In seconds, Gorman would have her to contend with. Two against one. It's not fair!

He tugged Marty's foot. When the groaning man was close enough, Gorman punched him in the groin.

'Leave him alone!' Claire shouted. 'Don't touch him, you bastard!'

She was only a few yards away.

Gorman found a rock the size of a coconut, and slammed it down on Marty's forehead. He felt the skull crush under its impact.

A whiny sound came from Claire. She was climbing the slope backwards, shaking her head from side to side with tight little jerks, her arms batting the air for balance.

Gorman got to his knees. 'It's all right,' he told her. 'Don't be frightened. We'll get him to a doctor.'

Claire suddenly whirled around and bolted up the hillside.

Gorman went after her. 'Don't run!' he called. 'We can't help Marty if you run. Wait up!'

She kept going.

'Goddamn it, wait! I won't hurt you!'

Her foot landed on one of Janice's boots. She stumbled, but didn't fall.

Gorman hurled the rock. It caught her between the shoulder blades and bounced off. She went down, sprawling flat, and scurried to get up again. Gorman pounced on her back. His weight smashed her to the ground. Clutching her hair, he tugged her head toward him and stretched his right arm out past her shoulder and brought his fist back sharply to strike her face. The position was awkward. He couldn't get much power behind the punch. But he pounded her face again and again, very fast. She was crying and attempting to turn her face away. When she managed to grab his wrist, he yanked it free and drove his elbow down hard on her shoulder. That sent a shudder through her body, so he kept hammering down with his elbow, each blow making her cry out and squirm, until finally he somehow struck his crazy bone. His arm went tingly and numb.

Keeping his grip on her hair, he raised himself off her back. He sat on her rump. Her feeble writhing didn't worry him. He knew he'd taken the starch out of her. But he wasn't quite sure how to finish her off. As he shook his arm and waited for its weakness to pass, he scanned the moonlit ground. He saw no rocks close enough to reach.

She twisted under him.

'Stop it,' he snapped. He gave her hair a savage tug. 'And stop that sobbing.'

In a moment, his arm felt better. He raked his fingers through the weeds alongside Claire's body, and found a stick. It was slightly larger than a pencil, and neither end had much of a point. But perhaps it would do.

Clutching it like a knife, Gorman scooted up her back and rammed it at her neck, just below her right ear. The stick skidded down her skin, clawing a furrow. Screaming, Claire bucked and twisted in a frenzy. Gorman struck again. This time, a couple of inches broke off the stick, leaving a decent point. The third blow penetrated. Her shriek leaped to a higher pitch. She thrashed wildly as he forced the stick deeper. Then he pulled it out and stabbed again. He kept plunging the stick into her neck long after the screams stopped and she lay motionless beneath him.

Then he climbed off her. The sleeve of his jacket was sheathed with blood. He wiped his hand on the seat of her jeans.

Patting his pockets, he made sure he hadn't lost his wallet or cassette recorder during the struggles.

The recorder. He took it out. Good God, it had been running throughout the killings. He would have to destroy the tape.

He would also have to get rid of his clothes. Every stitch. But that could wait.

Down the slope, he picked up Brian's pants. The underwear fluttered out. He dug into the pocket and removed the car keys. Wandering along the hillside, he found the camera. Finally, he knelt over Marty's body. The contract was in a pocket of the shirt. He took it out. Though he wasn't precisely sure why, at that moment, he also took Marty's keys.

Then he rushed down to the fence. With a final glance at Brian's impaled body, he ran.

12

The air felt chilly on Tyler's face, but the rest of her body was snug under the covers. Rolling over, she pushed her face into the soft warmth of the pillow.

The chirp and warble of birds sounded peaceful, stirred memories of distant summer mornings when she lay in bed, so comfortable she didn't want to get up, but was eager to get outside. Adventures beckoned: today the comic book stand (she'd make a fortune!), today the careers tournament with Sally and Huss and Loretta, today a picnic at the lake, today exploring.

Exploring was maybe the best – taking off, on bike or foot, to follow that road, that forest path, those train tracks, farther than she'd ever gone before.

Later came the mornings, almost painful with excitement, when she couldn't wait to get up and take the bus to the public pool where Skip Robinson would be practicing his backstroke and this time he might notice her. Finally, he did. And he was so shy. And he always smelled like Coppertone.

Abe smells like Brut. She squirmed against the bed, remembering the feel of his body as he embraced her last night. There on the stoop like a couple of teenagers while Nora led Jack into her room. If she'd asked Abe to come in, he would be next to her now. Instead, they'd gone alone to their rooms. Tyler had regretted it even then, feeling the loss like an empty ache.

I hardly know the man, she thought.

But Dan had been in her mind. She'd come here to find Dan, and it would've been some kind of vague betrayal to make love with Abe.

She wished she had.

She owed nothing to Dan. They'd made their choices five years ago and even if she found him today (in Beast House?) it was probably over for good. She shouldn't have let thoughts of Dan stop her.

More than that had stopped her. It was also wanting Abe so badly and knowing she might never see him again after today. He and Jack would head north; she and Nora would head south. And if she'd made love with Abe, the parting would be worse.

Thinking about it now, she felt the loss as if he were already gone.

We have today, she told herself.

They had agreed, last night, to meet for breakfast. And after that? The Beast House tour? Nora seemed determined to try it, and if Abe and Jack would go along ... at least they'd be together that much longer.

Abe, I want you to meet my old friend, Dan Jenson. Dan, Abe Clanton.

Tyler? I can't believe it's really you. My God, let me look at you. You're beautiful! Lost a few pounds have you?

Jealous sparks from Abe's eyes as Dan sweeps her into his arms. Abe starts walking away. No, wait!

Too upset now to enjoy the luxury of the bed, Tyler got up. She parted the curtains slightly and looked outside. Her heart jumped. Seated on the stoop directly across the courtyard, elbows resting on his knees, eyes down, was Abe. The morning breeze stirred his hair. He was frowning as if deep in thought. Thinking about me? she wondered.

Sure thing. You flatter yourself.

But he might be.

God, he looks so lonely and troubled.

Astonished by her boldness, Tyler stepped away from the window. She put on a robe over her nightgown and went to the door. As she opened it, Abe looked up. His frown melted into a smile. 'Morning,' Tyler called.

'Good morning.'

'Been up long?'

'Not long.'

'How about a cup of coffee?'

'How can I refuse?' He stood and brushed off the seat of his blue jeans. The jeans were old, worn pale at the knees, frayed a little at the cuffs. He wore new-looking boots. His white T-shirt hugged his torso, taking on the curves of his muscles.

Tyler was suddenly very aware that she was naked under her robe and nightgown.

That's hardly naked, she thought.

But she could feel the cool breeze curling up her legs, sliding between them. Her nipples pushed into the slick fabric of her nightgown. She was slightly breathless as she stepped back from the doorway to let Abe enter.

'So,' she said, trying to sound calm, 'did you sleep well? No nightmares about Bobo, I hope.'

He studied her face. 'I slept fine. How about you?'

'Like a log.' She broke from his gaze and turned away. Her knees were shaky as she crossed the room. She took the coffee pot down from the mounted hotplate, and carried it into the bathroom. She filled it and brought it back. As she plugged in the dangling cord, Abe walked up behind her. She turned to face him. 'It'll probably take a few...' Her voice fell away. She stared into his eyes.

His open hand caressed the side of her face. 'I missed you,' he whispered.

Tyler tried to speak but her throat was tight. She stepped into his arms, and kissed him.

Abe held her tightly, more tightly than last night, as if they'd been away from each other a very long time and he needed the feel of her body to know she was with him again. After a moment, his embrace loosened. His hands slid up and down her back.

Tyler wished he would hike up her robe and nightgown so she could feel his hands on her bare skin. But he patted her rump, and eased away.

Tyler untied her cloth belt. She parted her robe. She took him by the wrists and lifted his hands to her breasts. His hands were warm through the filmy nightgown. Her breath trembled as he caressed and gently squeezed. Then he shut the robe. Gripping its lapels, he pulled her forward and kissed her lightly on the mouth. He smiled. 'You trying to seduce me?' he asked.

'It crossed my mind.'

'Shameless hussy,' he said.

'That's me.'

'What about your friend, Dan?'

Her stomach tightened. 'What about him?'

'You came all this way to find him.'

'I know, but...'

'If I'm going to lose you to this guy, I'd rather not ... get in any deeper. I want you too much already. Don't make it any tougher on me.'

'Oh, Abe,' she whispered. His face blurred as tears filled her eyes. She stepped against him and held him tightly.

'There you go again,' he said, stroking her hair. 'Now why don't you get dressed, and I'll fix the coffee. You invited me in for coffee, remember?'

Tyler nodded. She wiped her eyes.

'Don't try undressing in front of me, either.'

She managed a smile. 'Darn, that was my plan.'

'I must be psychic.'

'Don't you want to see what you're missing?'

'That's it, rub my face in it.'

'You *must* be psychic. That would've been phase two.'

Abe laughed softly and shook his head.

Tyler stepped past him. He watched as she bent over the spare bed to search her suitcase. 'I thought you were going to fix the coffee.'

'Do you take anything in it?'

'Just black.'

But he didn't turn away. Tyler took out her corduroys, her yellow blouse, the filmy bra she'd worn last night, and a fresh pair of panties. She held up the garments for Abe to see. 'Do these meet with your approval?'

'Very nice.'

She gave him a coy smile. 'Dan never cared much for these,' she said, and let the bra flutter to the bed.

'You have a definite cruel streak,' Abe said.

'Do I?' She took the rest of the clothes into the bathroom. 'Ta ta,' she said, and shut the door. She leaned against it. Shutting her eyes, she could still feel his arms around her, the firm pressure of his body, his eager lips, the way he'd touched her breasts. *I want you too much already.* My God, had he really said that? He had, he had! She found herself smiling and weeping. *If I'm going to lose you to this guy . . .*

No need to worry about that, Mr Abraham Clanton.

Tyler Clanton.

She whispered the words.

Good Christ, don't get crazy.

But she felt crazy: joyous and guilty and confused. *He wants me, but how much? What's next?*

Breakfast is next. Take it one step at a time. Breakfast, then the tour of Beast House and confronting Dan (Jesus, what'll I say to him?), then what? Lunch, maybe. What happens when it's time to leave? Don't think about that. Not yet. Cross the bridges as you come to them. Maybe we can all stay one more night. Or two. Or . . .

'The coffee's ready,' Abe called through the door.

'I'll be right out,' she said. Quickly, she shed her robe and nightgown. She used the toilet, washed, brushed her teeth, rolled deodorant under her arms, and dressed. It made her feel daring and sexy to wear the gauzy blouse without a bra. Luckily, there was a pocket over each breast. She tucked it in, leaned close to the mirror, and studied herself. 'Lookin' good,' she whispered. She unfastened another button to allow a glimpse of cleavage.

Nora would open still another.

She considered it for a moment, then shook her head.

Abe smiled when she stepped out. 'Lovely,' he said.

She glanced down at her blouse. 'Dan always liked me in yellow.'

Abe gave her a strange look. *He must suspect. Wasn't her teasing a dead giveaway? Well, she would just let him wonder. At least for a while.*

He gave her a plastic cup. Steam was still rolling off the coffee. 'Nora knocked while you were changing. They're just about ready to go.'

Tyler sipped the coffee, and wrinkled her nose.

'What can I say? It's instant.'

'At least it's hot.' She took her cup to the dressing table, sat down, and drank as she brushed her hair. Abe stood behind her, watching. 'Was Jack there?' she asked, and saw him nod in the mirror.

'Lucky Jack,' he said.

'Lucky Nora.'

Abe put down his cup. He rubbed her shoulders, and she moaned.

Then came a quiet knocking. He let go of her, crossed the room, and opened the connecting door.

'All set and rarin' to go?' Nora asked. She entered, followed by Jack. 'We thought it'd be fun to go in town for breakfast. That sound good to everyone?'

'Sure,' Tyler said, getting up.

Nora was wearing a tube-top that left her bare to the tops of her breasts. A faint red line marked her shoulder where the man, yesterday, had struck her with the radio antenna. Her skin had a rosy glow, and her hair looked damp. She must've recently taken a shower, Tyler thought. Jack, too, was slightly flushed. Had they showered together? Made love under the hot spray?

Abe and I could've . . .

'Got your room key?' Abe asked her.

Nodding, she picked up her purse.

They went outside into the cool morning shadows, and Tyler slipped a hand around Abe's back.

'I think,' Nora said, 'I could go for pigs in a blanket.'

13

Gorman dreamed they were after him. He was running down a sunlit slope, laughing at first and waving the paper – the contract – overhead to taunt them. 'You can't catch mee,' he sang. He knew they couldn't. He was fleet of foot while Marty and Claire were staggering after him like sleep-walkers. No, like zombies. It suddenly struck Gorman that they were, indeed, zombies. That notion took away some of the fun:

what if they *should* catch him? Zombies would likely treat him to a horror or two.

Though he knew they were after him, they were somewhat preoccupied. Marty was busy ripping to shreds a pair of pink panties while Claire was digging out one of her eyes with a blunt stick.

I never did *that*, he thought. You're doing *that* to yourself, sweetypie.

Looking forward, he saw Brian wave at him from on top of the fence. Janice was up there, too, straddling the spike – one of them *in* her – writhing passionately on it while she sucked Brian's cock. She saw Gorman and sat up. 'Hey,' she shouted, 'that's *my* contract!'

'Finders keepers, losers weepers!' he yelled back, flapping it at her.

'Forget it,' Brian told her. 'You've got me.'

With a shrug, she leaned down again and took him into her mouth.

Gorman turned away and raced alongside the fence. Looking back, he saw Marty and Claire. They were close behind him, which didn't make much sense because he was running and they were shambling along slowly. Marty was stuffing bits of the shredded panties into his mouth. Claire, beside him, had one eyeball dangling over her cheek and was working on the other, trying to pry it out with her stick. Let her get that one, Gorman thought, and she won't be able to see worth shit.

Then he tripped over the end of a bathtub. He fell toward the water. The water was red. A naked woman, reclining in the tub, stretched out her arms to catch him. Her wrists were crossed-hatched with slashes. Martha! He fell toward her, and fell, and fell. 'Leave me alone!' he shrieked, and lurched awake.

The room was bright with daylight. Gasping for breath, he stared at the ceiling. He used the pillow to mop the sweat off his face.

Good Christ, he thought. What a nightmare.

He glanced at his travel clock. Nine twenty. He'd been in bed no more than three hours. But he'd had some sleep before Marty and Claire came knocking.

God, if only that had been nothing but a dream.

He crawled to the edge of the bed and sat up. The bruise on his stomach where Marty had punched him (*he* started it) looked like a smudge of dirt. There were a few minor scratches on the backs of his hands, but his knuckles weren't even skinned from rapping Claire's face. He walked to the mirror above the dressing table, and peered at his own face. Except for the bloodshot eyes, it looked fine.

He went into the bathroom. Kneeling beside the tub, he looked closely for traces of blood on the enamel, especially around the drain.

The tub looked fine. It should – he'd bathed in the ocean before returning to the room and showering.

He turned on the shower, adjusted the temperature, and stepped beneath its hot spray. As he washed himself, his mind went over every detail. Had he overlooked anything?

The contracts. He had burned them both and flushed the ashes down the toilet.

The tape. He'd pried open the plastic cassette, stripped out the tape, and held it dangling over the toilet while it burned, making greasy black smoke.

The recorder. Since he'd touched its casing with his bloody hand, it had to go. It went into the ocean.

The camera. Same problem. Same solution.

His clothes. After tearing off the tags, he'd weighted each garment with a rock and hurled each into the surf. The shoes hadn't required rocks.

The cars. In Gorman's estimation, his solution to that problem had been brilliant and daring. At the time he'd taken Marty's keys, he hadn't known why he wanted them. But the scheme must, even then, have been brewing in his subconscious. Not until he reached the cars did the plan come fullblown to his mind.

Since he couldn't risk leaving even a minute trace of Claire's blood in the Mercedes, he left it untouched and drove Marty's car to the beach. He'd been very lucky finding the beach; the very first road leading west had taken him within a couple of hundred yards. He'd simply followed a moonlit path along a hillside and *voilà* – the ocean.

Farewell to the cassette player, the camera, and his clothes. The worst part was washing his body in the ocean. No, perhaps the worst part was the trek back to Marty's car, naked and wet and freezing, and frightened half to death that someone might see him. The area was desolate, though, and the only building with a view of the parking area appeared to have no windows.

He'd found a rag under the car's front seat. He'd used it to wipe the seat and steering wheel before climbing in, just in case some blood remained on them. Later, after parking behind the Mercedes, he'd used the same rag to wipe the car for fingerprints. When he'd finished, he wiped its outside handles and flung the keys far up the wooded slope. Then he had simply climbed into the Mercedes and driven it back to the motel. Stark naked. Right through the center of town. But he hadn't seen a living soul, thank God, and all the bungalows of the Welcome Inn were dark when he arrived.

Looking back on it now, he was amazed that he'd succeeded in carrying it off – amazed, indeed, that he hadn't allowed the panic of the situation to overwhelm and destroy him. For he would have been destroyed if he'd simply fled without taking elaborate precautions.

As matters now stood, even if suspicion should fall on Gorman, he was confident that he'd left no evidence connecting him to the crimes. And he had a marvelous bonus in his favor: investigators would naturally assume that the same perpetrator had dispatched Brian, Marty and Claire. It would be obvious to anyone that Gorman was physically incapable of impaling Brian on a seven-foot fence.

Only one possibility worried him – that he may have been seen. Janice was unaccounted for. If she'd been alive on the hillside and witnessed the murders . . . Possible, but highly unlikely since she neither appeared nor called out during the search. More than likely, she was dead. But Gorman had committed the murders within view of Beast House. Someone watching from a window could have watched it all. If that had been the case, however, and his crimes reported, certainly the police would have intercepted him at the cars. Since the police didn't show up, he could assume that either he wasn't seen or the witness had crimes of his own to hide – such as the murders of Brian and Janice.

The thought that he might have been watched by their killers sent a chill through Gorman. He suddenly felt squirmy. His scrotum tightened and his penis drew in as if to hide.

Who could have done such a thing to Brian? The strength it must've taken!

Perhaps, he thought, there is a beast.

He was no longer enjoying the hot spray of the shower. He finished rinsing the soap from his body, and climbed out. To perk himself up, he concentrated on his good fortune as he dried and got dressed.

The killer, whether man or beast, had done him a splendid service. Gorman may or may not be able to use the incident in his book, depending on the outcome of the investigation. Regardless, all the proceeds would now come to him. Every last cent. Even if Janice should miraculously reappear, the contracts were destroyed. The initial correspondence implied no commitment (perhaps he could find those letters and destroy them . . . awfully risky . . . why had he thrown away Marty's keys?) but basically Janice wouldn't have a leg to stand on without the contract itself.

Besides, she's dead.

Please, let her be dead.

As he finished buttoning his sport shirt, he heard a knocking on the door – a light, tentative rapping but it made his stomach lurch. It came from Brian's room. He took a deep breath, cautioned himself to remain calm, and stepped through the connecting doors. Both of Brian's beds were intact. He rushed silently to the closer bed, raked back its cover and sheet, and mashed the pillow. Then he opened the door.

'Good morning, Mr Hardy,' the woman said in a cheerful voice.

She was young and attractive, rather tall and nicely put together, looking fresh and altogether sexy in yellow shorts and a green tube-top that left her shoulders bare and hugged her sizable breasts. Gorman knew that he had met her before. Then he remembered where. The cocktail lounge. Yesterday evening. One of those librarians.

'Oh,' he said, smiling. 'Nina, is it?'

'Nora.'

'How are you this fine morning, Nora?'

'Just terrific. How about you?'

'Couldn't be better.' He took a deep breath. The warm air had a pine aroma. 'A gorgeous day to be alive,' he said.

'Every day's good for that,' Nora said. 'Anyway, the reason I dropped by, you mentioned you might be going on that tour today. Beast House?'

'Yes, I intend to.'

'Well, my friends and I are also going over there in a while. They've got a ten-thirty tour. We were wondering if you and Mr Blake might want to come along with us.'

Gorman glanced at his digital wristwatch. Nine fifty-two. It would be comforting, he thought, to take the tour with acquaintances. Far better than entering that awful house with a group of strangers. 'I would be delighted,' he answered, 'though I'm not certain about Brian. He seems to have wandered off, and I have no idea when he might be back.'

Nora glanced at the Mercedes. 'You think he went for a walk?'

'Apparently.' Gorman shrugged. 'Too bad for him. I'd be glad to . . .' He snicked his tongue. 'Oh, I do have an errand to run first. Suppose I meet you and your friends at the ticket booth?'

'Fine. Great.'

'At ten thirty, correct? I'd best get moving.'

Nora nodded, smiling. 'Okay, we'll see you there.'

She turned and started away. Gorman watched for a moment, enjoying the way her buttocks moved in the tight shorts.

Back in his own room, he uncapped his gin bottle and took a swallow. He found a telephone directory in a drawer of the night stand. Nursing the bottle, he searched the yellow pages. Under the heading PHOTO-GRAPHIC EQUIPMENT AND SUPPLIES – RETAIL were several listings. Most of the shops seemed to be located elsewhere; the book covered a county-wide area. Only Bob's Camera and Sound Center was in Malcasa Point. On the three-hundred block of Front Street. 'Marvelous,' Gorman muttered. He took a final swig of gin, and hurried out to the car.

Five minutes later, he drove past the store. He noted its location, and continued down Front Street, passing the dirt road he'd taken to the beach only a few hours earlier, then turning his eyes towards the grounds of Beast House. His gaze followed the rear fence until the building got in the way. On the other side, he picked it up again. He turned his head, watching the fence until the hillside rose up to block his view. From the two angles, he was almost certain he'd seen the entire length of the fence. Brian's body was gone. He hadn't noticed the other two, either, but of course their bodies wouldn't be easy to spot at this distance.

He'd half expected to find a gathering of police, but the region back there looked deserted.

Perhaps they had already completed their on-scene investigation and departed. That seemed unlikely, though. Surely there would still be officers scouring the area for evidence.

He continued up the road. Marty's old Plymouth, shrouded by morning shadows, was still parked on the shoulder where he'd left it. No police cars there. No coroner's van.

He rounded a bend, then made a U-turn. Coming back down the road, he kept his gaze on the wooded slope. The instant the rear fence appeared, he raced his eyes along it. From this vantage point, he could see almost to its far corner.

His doubts vanished.

The bodies had been removed.

But by the police? He didn't think so.

14

Janice rolled in her sleep and tumbled. Shards of pain tortured her awake. She lay motionless on her side, gasping, eyes squeezed shut.

Oh God, she thought, it hurts.

She whimpered from a searing rush of pain inside, and curled up. Her knees pushed against something soft and yielding.

What happened to me? her mind screamed.

Clutching her belly, she felt tape. She explored it with shaky fingers. It seemed to be holding a pad in place. A bandage? It ended just below her ribs. Moving her hands higher, she touched strips of tape on the underside of her left breast. The bandage started just above her nipple, covered the top of her breast and wrapped over her shoulder. The flesh beneath it felt burning. Her other shoulder was bandaged, too. Her right breast was bare, but tender as if bruised. Another bandage ran along her side to the hip. There, she found an elastic belt. She traced it to her groin and fingered the thick pad of a sanitary napkin.

What happened to me?

Raped. She must've been raped. The awful hurt inside. What did he use, for Christsake, a tree?

She started to sob, and the jolting spasms sent blasts of pain through her.

Who *did* this to me? God, why?

Brian? Did Brian? She remembered being with him, but . . . had he gone nuts or something?

Where am I, a hospital?

It didn't smell like a hospital, it smelled like a zoo. And she knew she wasn't on a bed. She was on the floor, a soft nap of carpet against her bare skin.

She opened her eyes. In the dim blue light, she saw a heap of pillows beside her. She must have been lying on that until she rolled off.

Blue light. Pillows.

Where am I?

Gingerly, gritting her teeth as pain ripped through her, Janice got to her hands and knees. She forced herself to stand. She swayed, and raised her arms for balance. Then she turned slowly.

Nobody here. Just me.

The room was slightly smaller than her own bedroom. Looking up, she saw that the ceiling was covered by mirrors. Except for the carpet and pillows, the room was bare. No furniture, no windows . . .

No windows!

The Kutch house?

'Oh God,' she whispered.

Flinching with each step, she staggered to the single door. She reached out an arm, slapped the jamb, and tried to brace herself. The arm folded. She fell against the door. But she grabbed the knob and held on tightly until the worst of the pain subsided. Then she tried to twist the knob. It wouldn't budge.

I'm locked in.

It came as no great surprise.

Still, she rattled the knob and yanked it, shaking the door in its frame.

Finally, she gave up.

She was out of breath, shuddering with pain.

She sank to her haunches. The bandage on her breast had pulled loose at the bottom. Blood was trickling from under it. She tried to press the tape down, but it wouldn't stick. Her skin was too slippery. Raising the bandage like a thick blue flap, she blinked sweat and tears from her eyes and stared at the wounds.

Her shoulder was torn and raw as if she had been gnawed by a dog. Below that, her flesh was ripped by four long scratches. Smoothing the bandage gently into place, she looked at her other breast. The skin was unbroken, but dark with bruises like a crescent of half a dozen dots. She lifted it and found a similar half-circle under the nipple.

Teeth marks?

But not from the teeth of a man.

Some kind of wild animal? A coyote, maybe?

Who are you trying to kid? she thought.

It was the beast.

Elizabeth Thorn's beast.

She couldn't remember any of it, but she knew it had to be so.

Oh God, the thing had raped her.

Quavering, she hugged her belly and leaned forward. She pressed her forehead against the door.

It had raped her. But it hadn't killed her. Someone had bandaged her wounds. And now she was a prisoner in the windowless house of Maggie Kutch.

It'll be back, she thought.

It wants me again.

15

Hardy, a distance up the sidewalk, paused near the fence and took a photo of Beast House. As he lowered the camera, Nora waved. He nodded a greeting, and came forward. In spite of the mild breeze, Tyler thought he must be stifling inside his sport jacket. She was too warm, herself, and wished she'd worn shorts or a skirt instead of her corduroys.

'You remember Tyler,' Nora said.

'Of course. How could I forget such a lovely creature?'

Reluctantly, she shook his offered hand. 'This is Abe Clanton,' she said.

'Pleased to meet you, Mr Hardy. I've read your books.'

Hardy looked surprised as he took Abe's hand. 'In the plural?'

'Sure. There were some thirty before *Horror at Black River Falls*?'

'Forty-eight, in fact. More than a few under pseudonyms. I'm delighted to find a man who knows I existed before *Horror*. Delighted and stunned.'

'I especially liked your *Death Defiers* series. Always kept an eye out for them in the PX.'

'Ah, you're a military man. I should've guessed. That straight-shouldered bearing. A Marine, no doubt.'

Abe looked amused. 'That's right.'

'The author of *Death Defiers* is Matt Scott. May I ask how you saw through my nom de plume?'

'They had your name on the copyright page.'

'A singularly literate fellow,' he said, and turned to Jack. 'Another leatherneck?'

'Used to be. Jack Wyatt.' They shook hands. 'I saw your movie.'

'Ah.'

'I'm a singularly illiterate fellow.'

Nora laughed. 'Hey, we met a guy last night you'll want to interview. Captain Frank. He lives in a bus over there.' She pointed toward the woods along the far side of Beach Road.

'Interview?' Hardy asked.

'He claims his father found the beast on some island and brought it here.'

'The beast?'

She nodded toward the old house.

'That beast?' Hardy asked.

'Yeah. He's full of all kinds of disgusting details.'

'Why should I be interested?'

'For your book.'

He stared at her, looking as if he might decide to smile. 'I believe I explained, last evening, that I have no intention of writing about Beast House.'

'That's right!' Nora snapped her fingers and looked very annoyed with herself for forgetting. 'You did say that. I remember.' Suddenly grinning, she shook a finger at him. 'You'd better interview Captain Frank for the book you're *not* going to write.'

Hardy chuckled.

'Now don't worry about us. We won't breathe a word to a living soul that you're not doing a book on Beast House. Mum's the word, right, everyone? Your secret is safe with us.'

Tyler looked around and saw that the line was moving toward the ticket booth. A tight, sick feeling seized her stomach. Calm down, she told herself. It's nothing to get crazy about. Maybe Dan won't be here, after all.

But if he is?

She could wait outside, avoid him.

That wouldn't be right.

She fumbled with the catch of her purse.

'I'll get it,' Abe said.

'No, you've already . . .'

But he stepped ahead of her and purchased two tickets from the smiling blonde girl at the window. They stepped aside to wait for the others.

'Thank you,' she said.

'Are you all right?'

'Not very.'

'I'm sure Dan'll be glad to see you.'

'It'll be easier if he's not.'

Abe's eyes looked solemn. He rubbed her shoulder lightly, and let his hand fall away as Nora and Jack approached.

Nora frowned with concern. 'Are you sure you want to go ahead with this?' she asked.

'No. But I will.'

'Is there a problem?' Hardy asked.

'Tyler's old boyfriend is supposed to be . . .'

'Nothing's wrong,' Tyler said, annoyed with Nora for broadcasting her private business to the man. She turned away quickly and stepped through the turnstile.

Abe joined her on the other side, and took hold of her hand. Tyler looked up at him. 'She's got a real mouth, sometimes.'

'I take it you don't care much for Gorman.'

'I think he's a sleaze.'

'I'd be inclined to agree with you.'

'I thought you were a big fan.'

'I've enjoyed some of his books. That's not the same as liking the guy who wrote them.'

They stopped behind the small group gathered in front of the porch. Nora and Jack came up next to them.

'What do we do, just walk in?' Nora asked.

'I'm sure there's a guide,' Abe said.

A guide. Dan? Tyler's heart gave a lurch. She squeezed Abe's hand more tightly, and stared at the shadowed door. She flinched as it swung open.

The person in the entryway wasn't Dan. She let out a deep, trembling breath as a gawky man stepped out. He looked about sixty, and walked with a stiffness as if he was in pain. Coming down the porch stairs, he held onto the railing. 'Tickets,' he said in a voice that sounded remarkably strong for a man of such frail appearance.

A couple of kids near the front backed out of his way.

Tyler heard a quiet click. She glanced sideways at Hardy, and was surprised not to find the camera at his eye. One hand was inside a pocket of his jacket. He gave her a quick smile, and took his hand out.

He's got a recorder in there, she thought. He's going to tape the tour.

Without asking permission? Of course, or he wouldn't be acting so sneaky. Illegal as hell, but that wouldn't bother Gorman Hardy.

It confirmed her opinion of the man.

Sleazy bastard, she thought.

Finished gathering the tickets, the bony man made his way up the porch stairs. He turned around and wiped his mouth with the back of a hand. 'Ladies and gents,' he proclaimed, 'it's now my honor to introduce you to the owner of Beast House, a gallant woman who passed through the purifyin' fire of tragedy and came out the stronger for it – Maggie Kutch, your personal guide for today's tour.' Like a tired ringmaster, he swept an arm toward the door and shuffled backwards to get out of the way.

An old woman waddled out of the house, bracing herself with an ebony cane. She looked old enough to be the man's mother but, in spite of the cane, she seemed to radiate strength. She was a big woman, broad-hipped, with a massive bosom swaying the entire front of her faded print dress as she limped to the edge of the porch. To Tyler, she looked like a rather stern grandmother. She wore tan support hose, and clunky black shoes with laces. As if to perk up her drab appearance, a bright red silken scarf wrapped her neck. Her face looked sour until she smiled. The smile wasn't particularly cheerful. It was almost a smirk.

'Welcome to Beast House,' she said. Her eyes roamed the group. Tyler felt a tingle of dread as the woman's gaze fell upon her. 'My name's Maggie Kutch, just like Wick told you, and it's my house.' She paused as if challenging someone to disagree with her. Not a sound came from the audience. Several people were scanning the house front or staring at their feet, apparently reluctant to look at her.

'I started showing my house to visitors all the way back in '31, not long after the beast took the lives of my husband and three children.

Yes, the beast. Not a knifetoting maniac like some folks'd want you to believe. If you don't think so, take a gander at this.' She plucked the scarf. As it slipped away from her neck, someone groaned. Maggie's fingers traced the puffy seams of scar tissue streaking her throat. 'No man did this to me. It was a beast with fangs and claws.' Her eyes gleamed as if she was proud of the marks. 'It was the same beast as killed ten people in this house, including my own husband and children.

'Now, you might be wondering why a gal'd want to take folks through her home that was a scene of such personal tragedy. It's an easy answer: M-O-N-E-Y.'

Tyler heard quiet laughter from Gorman.

The old woman swung up her cane and waved it toward a beam supporting the porch roof. 'Right here's where they lynched Gus Goucher. He was a lad of eighteen. He was passing through town, back in August of 1903, on his way to San Francisco where he aimed to work at the Sutro Baths, but he stopped here and asked to do some odd jobs in exchange for a meal. Lilly Thorn lived here back then with her two children. She was the widow of the famous bank robber, Lyle Thorn, and I always say she built this house with blood money. Blood comes of blood, I say. Anyway, Gus came along and she had him split up some firewood for her. He did his chore, took his meal for payment, and went on his way.

'That night, the beast came. It struck down Lilly's sister, who was visiting, and her children. Only just Lilly survived the attack, and they found her running down the road jabbering like a lunatic.

'Right off the bat, the house was searched from attic to cellar. They found no living creature inside, but only the torn, chewed bodies of the victims. A posse was got up. Over in the hills yonder, it came on Gus Goucher where he'd bedded down for the night. Him being a stranger, he was doomed from the start.

'He was given a proper trial. Some town folks had seen him at the Thorn place the day of the killings, and there weren't no witnesses to the slaughter with everyone dead but Lilly, and her raving. Quick as a flash, they judged him guilty. The night after the verdict came in, a mob busted him out of jail. They dragged the lad to this very spot, tossed the rope over this beam, and strung him up.

'Being amateurs, they done a poor job of it. Didn't think to tie him, but just hoisted him up. They say he hung here, flapping and kicking like a spastic for quite a good spell while he strangled.'

'Lovely,' Nora whispered.

'Poor Gus Goucher never killed nobody. It was the beast done it all.' She thumped her cane twice on the porch floor. 'Let's go in.'

As she turned away, Tyler looked up at Abe. He shook his head as if he found the situation grimly amusing.

'Barbie Doll was right,' Nora whispered. 'Tacky tacky.'

Climbing the porch stairs, Tyler released Abe's hand long enough to rub her sweaty palm on her corduroys. She had a leaden, sickish feeling in her stomach.

The group halted in the foyer. After the sunlight outside, the house seemed dark and cool. Tyler scanned the gloom, half expecting to spot Dan, in uniform, standing guard.

'Yuck,' said a girl near the front.

Smiling, Maggie pointed her cane at a stuffed monkey. It stood beside a wall, mouth frozen wide, teeth bared. 'Umbrella stand,' she said, and dropped her cane through the circle of its shaggy arms. 'Lilly was partial to monkeys.' She snatched up her cane and thumped the creature's head, bringing up a puff of dust.

'The first attack,' she said, 'came in the parlor. Right this way.'

Gorman jostled Tyler. 'Excuse me, dear,' he said, and made his way forward, pressing through the small group of people. He reached the door ahead of the rest, and followed Maggie through.

'A real go-getter,' Abe muttered.

'A creep,' Tyler said.

They entered the parlor. The group spread out along the length of a plush cordon. Just beyond the barrier bright red curtains hung from the ceiling to the floor, closed to conceal most of the room. Maggie, on the other side of the cordon, waited by a wall and caressed a fold of the velvety curtain. 'These are new,' she said. 'We just put 'em in. Gives a touch of class, don't you think?' She gripped a cord.

'Ethel Hughes, Lilly's sister, was in this room the night of August second, 1903. She'd come down for Lilly's wedding, which would've been the next week if tragedy hadn't struck and put an end to it all. The beast come in through there.' She nodded toward the door behind Tyler. 'It took Ethel unawares.'

She gave the cord a yank. The curtains skidded open. Tyler heard a few gasps. A girl in front of her backed up quickly, stepping on her toes. A red-haired woman turned her face away. A boy in a cowboy suit leaned over the cordon for a closer look. Gorman raised his camera. Maggie bounced her cane off the floor. 'No pictures,' she warned. 'Anybody wants a memento of the tour, he can pick up one of our souvenir guidebooks in the gift shop for six ninety-five.' Gorman lowered the camera and shook his head as if disgusted.

'Sure did a number on that babe,' whispered a man to Tyler's left.

Reluctantly, Tyler lowered her eyes to the form of Ethel Hughes.

The wax body was sprawled on the floor, one leg up and resting on the cushion of a couch. Its wide eyes gazed toward the ceiling. Its face was contorted with pain and horror. Its shredded gown, a white that had gone yellow like old paper, was blotched with rustcolored stains. The tatters covered little more than the breasts and pubic area. The exposed flesh, from neck to thighs, was punctured and striped with raw wounds. Bright crimson sheathed the body.

'The beast sprang over the back of the couch, taking Ethel by surprise while she was reading the *Saturday Evening Post*.' Maggie stepped past the body and pointed her cane at an open magazine spread out beyond the figure's outstretched right arm. 'This is the very issue she was reading when it got her.' She swept her cane around. 'Everything you see here is just the same as it was that night. Except for the body, of course.' She smiled. 'We couldn't have that, now could we? But we've got us the next best thing. I had this exact replica done up in wax by Monsieur Claude Dubois of Nice, France, way back in '36. Every detail is guaranteed, right down to each wound. Got my hands on the morgue photos.

'Like I say, it's all authentic. This is the very nightgown Ethel wore the night of the killing. Those brown spots are her actual blood.'

'Gross,' muttered the girl who'd stepped on Tyler's foot.

Maggie ignored her. 'When the beast finished with Ethel, it rampaged around the parlor. That bust of Caesar there on the mantel?' She indicated it with her cane. 'See how the nose is off? That's the work of the beast. It hurled that bust to the floor. It flung half a dozen porcelain figurines into the fireplace. It broke that chair. This beautiful rosewood table' – she tapped it with her cane – 'was thrown through this window. All the ruckus, of course, woke up everyone in the house. Lilly's room was right up there.' She poked her cane toward the ceiling. 'The beast must've heard her up and about. It went for the stairs.'

Maggie closed the curtains. She limped around the cordon, and led the group out of the parlor. Gorman stayed close to her. In a loud voice he said, 'May I ask how you can be certain of the order of events? As you mentioned earlier, there were no witnesses.'

'Police reports and photos,' she explained, starting up the stairway. 'Newspaper stories. It was pretty clear the way it all happened. The cops just followed the blood.'

'Had the beast been injured?'

She cast Gorman an amused glance. 'Ethel's blood,' she said. 'It dripped off the beast all the way up here to Lilly's room.' At the top of the stairs, she turned to the left.

Tyler, reaching the top, looked to the right. Red curtains surrounded an area in the center of the corridor near its far end, leaving only a narrow passageway on either side. Another exhibit. How many are there? she wondered. And how many could she stomach?

Abe gave her hand a reassuring squeeze, and they entered the bedroom of Lilly Thorn. Again, the group spread out facing a cordon and a wall of red curtains. Maggie, at the far end, tugged the pullcord. The curtains flew apart. A wax figure in a pink nightgown was sitting upright on the bed, a hand to its open mouth, frightened eyes gazing past the brass scrollwork at her feet.

'We're right above the parlor, now,' Maggie said. 'When all the commotion woke Lilly up, she dragged that dressing table over to the door for a barricade, and climbed out her window. She dropped to the roof of the bay window just a ways down, and jumped from there to the ground.'

Gorman made a disdainful snort.

Maggie glanced at him sharply. 'Something wrong with you?'

'No, no.' He shook his head. 'My mind just wandered there for . . .' His voice trailed off. 'Please continue.'

'I've always found it curious,' she said, 'that Lilly didn't try to save her children.'

'Panic,' suggested a man beside the redhead.

'Maybe that's it.' Maggie shut the curtains. The group followed her into the corridor. 'When the beast couldn't get into Lilly's room, he went down the hall.'

He, Tyler thought. Suddenly the beast had become a he instead of an it.

They passed the top of the stairway. As they neared the curtained enclosure, the group formed a single file line. Tyler let go of Abe's hand. He gestured her forward, and she walked ahead of him into the gap between the curtains and the wall. Her forearm brushed one of the folds. She flinched away from its touch, and felt goosebumps scurry up her skin. Then the corridor was clear, bright from a window at its end.

'The beast,' Maggie said, 'found this door open.' She entered a room on the left. They followed her inside, and Tyler was careful not to stand behind the girl who'd stepped on her. 'This is where the children slept, though I 'spect they were awake when the beast came – maybe hiding under their covers, froze up with fear. Earl was ten, his brother Sam just eight.'

The curtains slid open.

The two wax bodies lay facedown between the brass beds. Their bloody nightshirts were ripped to shreds, and so was their skin. Tyler looked away. A rocking horse with faded paint rested beside a washstand. In one corner was an Indian tom-tom. A baseball bat was propped against the wall behind it. Suddenly, the boys seemed real to Tyler. She imagined them at play, laughing and chasing each other. She gnawed her lower lip and turned her gaze to the window. She heard Maggie's voice, but didn't listen. On the lawn below, she saw a weathered, lattice-work gazebo. Beyond it, the fence. Then the hillside, golden brown in the sunlight, with a few patches of green bush, clumps of rock here and there, a scattering of trees. It looked so peaceful. As she watched, a seagull swooped down, perched on the fence between a couple of the spikes, and pecked at something, apparently finding a snack. She wished she was outside, not trapped inside this mausoleum. Maybe Gorman felt the same way, for she saw that he, too, was staring out of the window.

Maggie finished, and they followed her into the corridor. This time, passing the curtained area, Tyler walked closer to the wall and kept her arms tight against her sides. As they approached the top of the stairs, Maggie said, 'Sixteen nights we lived in this house before the beast came. My husband, Joseph, he couldn't abide sleeping in one of the murder rooms, so we settled ourselves in the guest room. Our daughters, Cynthia and Diana, they weren't so squeamish and took the boys' room we just left.'

She led them through a doorway on the right, directly across the corridor from the entrance to Lilly's room. A cordon was stretched from wall to wall, but the room beyond it was open. Except for one corner. There, a set of red curtains hung from a curved bar, enclosing a wedge of floor.

Maggie pointed her cane at a canopy bed. 'On May seventh, 1931, Joseph and I were sleeping here. It was close to fifty years back, but I remember it all like it was last night. There'd been a good bit of rain that day, and it was still coming down when we retired. We had the windows open, and I laid there listening to the rainfall. The girls were tucked in down the hall and my baby, Theodore, was snug in the nursery. I fell asleep, feeling peaceful and safe.

'Long about midnight, there come a sound of breaking glass from downstairs. Joseph got up quiet out of bed, and tiptoed over here.' She limped to a bureau, pulled open a drawer, and lifted out a pistol. 'He got this. It's an army model Colt .45 automatic.'

'Neat,' said the kid in the cowboy suit.

'Joseph cocked it, and I can still hear the noise of it.' Cane clamped under one arm, she clutched the black hood of the weapon and jerked it back and forward with a metallic snick-snack.

'Hope that's not loaded,' said the father of the girl.

'Couldn't hurt if it was,' Maggie told him. 'We plugged up the barrel with lead, this past year.' Aiming at the floor, she pulled the trigger. There was a clack. She returned the pistol to the drawer.

'Joseph took it with him,' she said, 'and left me alone in the room. I waited till I heard him on the stairs, then I crept out to the hall. I had to get to my children, you see.'

Leaving the curtains untouched, she stepped around the cordon. The group followed her into the corridor. She stopped at the head of the stairway. 'I was just here when I heard gunshots. Then come an awful scream from Joseph. I heard sounds of a scuffle, and I wanted to run, but I stood here frozen stiff, staring down through the darkness.'

She gazed down the stairs as if transfixed by the memory of it.

'Up the stairway come the beast,' she said in a low voice. 'I couldn't see too good, but his skin was white like a fish's belly, so white it seemed to almost glow. He walked upright like a man, only hunched over some. I knew I had to run and get to the children, but I couldn't stir a muscle. I could only just stare. Then he made a soft kind of laugh, and threw me to the floor. He tore at me with claws and teeth. I tried my best to fight him off but he was stronger than any ten men, and I was preparing to meet the Lord when Theodore started up crying way off in the nursery. Well, the beast heard it and climbed off me and went scampering down the hall.

'I was hurt bad, but I went chasing after him. I couldn't let him get my baby.'

She started hobbling down the corridor. Once again, Tyler pressed herself close to the wall to avoid contact with the curtains. There must be bodies inside, she thought. Mutilated corpses of wax.

Just across from the boys' room, Maggie stopped. She tapped her cane on a closed door to the right. 'This stood open,' she said. 'I peered inside. There, in the dark . . .'

'Aren't we going in?' asked the redhead.

Maggie glared at her. 'I never show the nursery.' Then she looked at the door as if she could see through it. 'There, in the dark, I saw the pale beast lift my infant from his cradle and tear him asunder. I was watching, numb with horror, when something gave my nightdress a yank. I found Cynthia and Diana behind me. Well, I took a hand of each, and we rushed off. We went this way.'

They followed Maggie through the gap on the other side of the curtains. She stopped at a closed door across the stairway. The group formed a half-circle around her.

'We got this far,' she said, 'before the beast leapt into the hall and came after us.' She pulled the door open. Peering into the dim recess, Tyler saw a staircase. The stairs led upward until the darkness consumed them. 'We ducked inside here, and I pulled the door shut. It was dark as a pit. I threw open the attic door at the top, and bolted it after us. Then we huddled in the musty blackness.

'We knew the beast was coming. We heard the creaking stairs, and he made quiet hissing sounds like he was laughing. Then he was sniffing at the door. We waited. The girls were sobbing. I can still feel how they both trembled in my arms. Suddenly, the door burst open and the beast fell upon us.'

Maggie eased the door shut. She leaned a shoulder against it, and let out a deep sigh.

'The screams,' she said. 'I'll never forget the screams, the snarls of the beast, the wet ripping sounds as he tore up my two little girls. I fought him until the screams stopped and he had me down. I don't know why he didn't kill me, and there's many a time I wished he had, but he just pinned me to the floor. I was too weak to fight him anymore, and I begged him to end it for me. After a minute, he scampered down the stairs leaving me alone up there with the bodies of my daughters. I never saw him again after that night. But others have.'

16

Janice lay motionless, staring at the mirrored celing. Sprawled on top of the pillows, she looked blue and dead like a corpse discarded on a rubbish pile. She was thinking about ways to commit suicide.

So far, she'd come up with a couple of possibilities. The light fixture in the center of the ceiling was about three feet beyond her reach. By stacking pillows, she could get to it. Unscrew the blue bulb. Stick in a finger. Electrocute herself. That would probably work. An easier method, the one she thought she might prefer, was to remove all her bandages and let herself bleed to death. Exploring her wounds, however, she'd found most of them to be superficial, little more than scratches and bites. They weren't bleeding much. She would have to work them open, or maybe take down that bulb and break it and use its glass like a knife to open her wrists or throat. She could do that.

There was one problem.

She didn't want to die.

They couldn't let her go, she was sure of that, but they had bandaged her wounds so they must want her to recover. Why? She could think of only one reason, and it sickened her: they wanted her alive as a plaything for the beast. Last time, she must have been unconscious. But if it came to her now, she would see it, feel its teeth and claws ripping her, its penis battering into her.

No, don't think about it. Maybe it won't happen.

It'll happen.

She pressed a hand tight against the pad between her legs.

I can't let it happen, she thought.

I've got to escape.

Sure. No sweat. Just break down the door and run like hell.

Little Joni, last summer, had escaped easily enough from that maniac who had them prisoners in the cabin. And Joni'd been tied to a bed. At least I'm not tied up, Janice thought. But the cabin door hadn't been locked from the outside, either.

They'll open the door, she realized. They'll have to. Someone, sooner or later, will come in to check on me, maybe to feed me, or – and the thought chilled her – to let in the beast.

When that door opened, she would get her chance.

But she had to be ready.

She rolled herself off the pillows, groaning as the movement awakened streaks and waves of pain. Crawling on her knees, she dragged several of the large pillows to the center of the room. She stacked them. As she pushed herself up to climb atop them, she realized that the bulb would be searing hot. She limped over to where she had been resting, and picked up another pillow. Its case felt like satin. She yanked, splitting one of the seams, and shook out the foam rubber stuffing. With her right hand wrapped in the slick fabric, she returned to the waist-high stack. She stepped onto the top. Her foot sank in, mashing deep. Arms out for balance, she leaned in, brought up her other foot, and straightened herself. The pillows wobbled under her. She teetered for a moment, then was steady.

With her covered hand, she reached up and gripped the blue bulb. She felt its warmth through the layers of satin. She twisted it. The bulb turned easily, and went out.

Not a shred of light entered the room to relieve the total blackness. Janice kept unscrewing the bulb, but the dark disoriented her. Though she tried to stand motionless, the pillows seemed to be shifting slowly under her feet. She swayed. Only her gentle hold on the bulb kept her from losing all sense of direction and falling.

It came loose in her hand.

Quickly, she took a blind leap forward. She seemed to drop for a very long time as if plunging into an abyss. Finally, the floor pounded her

feet. Windmilling, she fell backwards. The floor slammed her rump.
The back of her head and shoulders toppled the pillows. She writhed
against them as pain surged through her body.

Good one, she thought. You probably opened up everything with
that stunt.

But she felt proud. There was a ripple of excitement under the pain.
She'd done it! She pressed the bulb to her chest, and flinched at its fiery
touch.

Smart move.

Smart, all right. Now you've got a weapon.

She waited until the pain subsided a little, then crawled on her knees
through the dark. After a long while, she bumped a wall. The door, she
thought, should be over that way – somewhere to the left.

She didn't want broken glass where she would be waiting. Carefully,
she unwrapped the bulb. It was still warm, but not too hot to handle.
Gripping the base, she rapped its glass gently against the wall. Then
harder. It burst with a pop that sounded very loud in the silence. Sliding
her fingers up the neck, she felt a jagged rim.

She eased sideways. One hand on the wall, she made her way slowly
through the darkness until she found the door. She sat down beside it.
She leaned her back against the wall, drew up her knees, and waited.

From somewhere not far away came a sound like the cry of a baby.
Maybe a cat, she thought. What does the beast sound like? No, it
sounded too much like a human baby to be anything else. After a few
moments, it stopped. The house returned to silence.

Janice frowned. A baby? Maggie Kutch was far too old to be its
mother. Could it be, she wondered, that she was not the only prisoner
in the house?

17

'Twenty years went by,' Maggie said, 'before the beast struck again.'

They were back inside the bedroom Maggie had shared with her
husband. She was standing beside the red curtains that blocked one
corner, a hand on the pullcord.

'This was 1951. Tom Bagley and Larry Maywood, a couple of
youngsters twelve years old, broke into the house after dark. They
should've known better, both of them. They'd come on the tour plenty

of times, and heard me warn more than once that at night the beast prowls the house. I'spect curiosity got the best of them. Curiosity killed the cat.'

'Satisfaction brought it back,' mumbled the girl who'd stepped on Tyler's foot.

Maggie heard the comment, and smirked. 'Didn't bring back Tom Bagley,' she said. The curtains slid apart.

The girl gasped and took a quick step away. Jack, behind her, protected himself with a raised forearm, gently nudging her to a stop.

The cowboy said, 'Oh, wow.'

The wax body on the floor was mangled, its clothes torn open, a tatter of underpants draping its buttocks. The skin of its back was scored with scratches. Its neck was a pulpy stub. Its head lay nearby, eyes wide, mouth contorted in agony.

The other boy, about to raise the window, was peering over a shoulder at his dismembered friend. His face, oddly mashed and cracked, was somehow more unnerving to Tyler than the grisly remains on the floor.

'These two,' Maggie said, 'were in the house for a long spell, nosing around. They'd tried to pry open the nursery door. They'd gone up to the attic. But they were snooping here in this room when the beast found them. He struck down Tom, and Larry ran for the window. While the beast was tearing up his friend, Larry got away by jumping. 'Cept for me, Larry was the only soul ever to see the beast and live.'

Maggie smiled strangely. 'Now there's only just me. I hear Larry got himself killed in an accident last year.'

'What's wrong with his face?' Nora asked.

'Took a spill,' Maggie said. 'We tried as best we could to patch it up. Didn't do too well, did we? We got us a whole new head on order, but it ain't come in yet.'

She closed the curtains, and the group followed her out of the room. Hobbling past the top of the stairs, she stopped in front of the curtains that blocked the corridor. 'Here's our last exhibit of the tour,' she said. 'We just got it in this past spring. It's in a mighty inconvenient spot, but here's where it happened so here's where the display had to go or it just wouldn't be right.

'It happened just last year, back in the spring of '78. We had us a family name of Ziegler on the tour – husband, wife, and their boy about ten. Well, the boy, he got spooked on the tour. Started crying and carrying on, so his folks took him off before we finished up. From what the mother said later, the father was mighty annoyed with the boy. Thought he hadn't acted manly. The last thing he wanted was a sissy for a son, so he dragged the youngster back here after dark.' A corner of

Maggie's mouth curled up. 'Wanted to show him there weren't nothing to be afraid of. Only he was wrong and the boy was right. They broke in the back door, and they got just to here before the beast got them both.'

She yanked the pullcord. The front section of curtains flew open.

The boy was facedown, shirt torn from his back, his neck mauled.

The man sprawled beyond him was torn up, his severed arm lying across one thigh.

On the floor between them was a man in the shredded tan uniform of a police officer. His throat was torn out. Tyler stared at the grimacing face. She blinked as the corridor darkened. A stark blue aura flashed around the body. Through the ringing in her ears, she heard Maggie. 'A patrolman name of Dan Jenson, making his rounds . . .'

'Tyler? Tyler?' Abe's voice.

She opened her eyes. She was sitting on the floor, someone holding her from behind, her head down between her knees. She felt dizzy and nauseated. People were whispering. Raising her head, she saw Nora crouched at her side. Nora squeezed her hand. It was numb as if shot with Novocaine.

'You'll be okay,' Abe said from behind. That was him clutching her shoulders. 'Come on,' he said, 'let's get you out of here.' His hands slid under her armpits, and he lifted her. She glimpsed Dan's body again before Abe turned her away. No, not his body. A wax figure. But Dan.

Abe's firm hands guided her toward the stairs. 'I'm okay,' she muttered, shaking her head. He held her upright and loosened his grip, but stayed behind her as if prepared to stop another fall. 'I'm okay,' she said again. He came around to her side, and took hold of her upper arm.

'I'm sorry,' he said. His eyes looked sad and worried.

'I . . .' She looked back. Nora and Jack stood next to Abe. Down the corridor, several in the group were staring at her.

'We shouldn't have come,' Nora said. Her face was drawn with misery. 'Tyler, I'm sorry. I shouldn't have made you . . . Jesus, who would've thought . . .?' Her chin started trembling, and tears filled her eyes.

Tyler squeezed her hand. Then she rubbed her own forehead. The skin felt cool and damp. 'I want to get out of here,' she mumbled.

She thought, I'm going to throw up.

She started down the stairs, Abe hanging onto her arm. 'Hurry,' she said. Four steps from the bottom, she lunged free of his grip and raced down. She dashed across the foyer, past the rabid-looking stuffed monkey, and yanked open the door. Glaring sunlight blinded her. The porch reeked of decayed wood. She hurled herself against the railing, leaned far over it, and vomited onto the brown grass.

'Some folks can't take it,' Maggie said. 'We get them every so often. Most'll just drop out of the tour along the way, but I've had maybe a score faint on me, one time or another. They ain't always women, neither. I've seen big, burly fellows keel over like they'd been poleaxed.' She grinned. 'Just figure you got a little extra excitement for your money.'

She closed the curtains. 'That'll conclude our tour for this morning, folks.' Gorman stepped aside to let her pass. He followed close behind her. Over her shoulder, she said, 'Now don't forget to visit our gift shop downstairs, where you can purchase your illustrated booklet on the history of Beast House and choose from our assortment of souvenirs.'

At the bottom of the stairs, she swung her cane to the left. 'Just down the hall there.'

Glancing that way, German saw a wooden sign a short distance up the corridor. It read Souvenirs, and pointed to an open door. He hesitated while Maggie limped outside and several of the tourists stepped around him. He intended to visit the gift shop, but he didn't want to lose Tyler and the others.

An interview with Tyler would be marvelous. *Beast House is not for the squeamish. This young lady from our tour group actually passed out . . .*

He stepped to the threshold. Tyler, along with her three friends, was already out near the ticket booth, heading away. Maybe he could catch up with her at the motel.

He went to the gift shop, and was vaguely relieved to find others inside. Behind the counter stood the gawky, grim-looking fellow who'd taken the tickets and introduced Maggie. As the man rang up a sale, Gorman reached into his pocket and switched off the cassette recorder.

He certainly hoped it had picked up all of Maggie's spiel. It should've worked fine, he assured himself. After all, it was brand new and identical to the one he'd discarded.

He should check the tape, however, as soon as possible. If, for some reason, it hadn't operated properly, he would have to repeat the tour. He hoped to avoid that.

For the others, the displays must have seemed like grotesque curiosities – the work of a disturbed imagination, a sham to draw tourists. Gorman, however, knew better. For him, the mutilated mannequins seemed no less real than Brian's body impaled on the fence.

Brian.

Pausing by a shelf of ashtrays and plates, he glanced around at the cashier.

That old geezer, certainly, would be incapable of sticking Brian up there. The same went double for Maggie. Only someone with extraordinary strength could have accomplished that feat, or taken him down again. These two might very well, however, be accomplices. According to the diary, the beast had lived with Elizabeth Thorn for a period of time before she allowed it to slaughter her family. Perhaps Maggie, now, was its mistress. Something to think about.

Wandering among the display tables and shelves, Gorman loaded his arms with souvenir items: a strip of six color slides showing the front of the house and several of the murder scenes; half a dozen picture postcards; the glossy eight-by-ten-inch booklet rich with text and photos; a shotglass with a gilt sketch of the house; a coffee mug sporting a color rendition of the house and the legend BEAST HOUSE – MALCASA POINT, CALIF; a plastic back-scratcher with the same legend along its shaft and a white hand with claws for raking the itch; finally, two bumper stickers – BEWARE OF THE BEAST with a hand at each end, claws dripping red blood – and I LOVE BEAST HOUSE with an illustration of the building. Gorman had grinned when he picked up that one.

He browsed the shop for a while longer, but found no more items relating specifically to Beast House. He carried his load to the cashier. Without a word or smile, the man started ringing up the items. He looked frail and oddly prim with his gray workshirt buttoned to the throat, but he'd obviously neglected to shave that morning. His chin was spiky with gray stubble. Gorman cleared his throat to conceal the sound of switching on his recorder. 'Have you worked here long?' he asked.

'Long enough.'

'Have you ever seen the beast?'

'Nope.'

'Do you believe it actually exists?'

'You took the tour,' the man said without looking up.

'Yes.'

'Them folks didn't die of the whooping cough.'

You wouldn't know, of course, what became of the three bodies I happened to notice behind the house last night? What, he wondered, might the fellow say to that?

'Comes to twenty-nine dollars sixty-eight cents.'

Gorman paid cash. He watched for a receipt, but the tape was still curling out of the cash register when the man crinkled up the top of the loaded bag. 'May I have the receipt, please?'

'I got no use for it.' He tore it loose and slapped it down on the counter.

Gorman hurried out of the house. Squinting against the brightness, he looked for Tyler and her friends. They were nowhere in sight.

18

'Shall I take you back to the motel?' Abe asked.

Tyler, slumped in the passenger seat with her knees propped against the dash, shook her head and slowly unwrapped the stick of Doublemint Nora had given her. 'I don't think so,' she murmured. 'I don't think I want to be alone.'

Abe felt helpless, looking at her. He wished he could make her misery go away. He wanted to hold her gently and tell her it would be all right, but he knew that only time could blunt the shock and sorrow.

'Hey,' Nora said, 'why don't we head over to the beach? I always feel better at the beach when I'm low.'

Tyler folded the chewing gum and put it in her mouth. 'I'd like that.'

'My trunks are at the motel,' Jack said.

'We'll just walk on the sand.'

'I think I might like to swim,' Tyler said.

Her comment surprised Abe and pleased him. Many people in her place would want only to curl up alone with their loss. Her attitude seemed healthier than that. 'Swim we shall,' he said.

'We didn't even bring our suits,' Nora reminded her. 'I didn't, anyway, did you?'

'I want to buy a new one.'

'Sure. Okay. Me too.'

Abe pulled out and drove slowly up the road. 'Why don't we let you off at a store? You can buy your suits. Jack and I'll go on back to the motel for ours, and we'll pick you up in about fifteen minutes.'

'It may take longer,' Nora said.

On the next block, Abe spotted the sign for Will's Sporting Goods. White lettering on the display window announced guns, tackle, swimming and camping accessories. 'How about there?' he asked.

'We can give it a try,' Nora said.

He pulled to the curb. Tyler met his eyes. 'Hurry back,' she told him.

'I will. We'll meet you right here.'

She opened the door and climbed out. Nora pushed the seat-back forward. She looked at Abe as if about to say something, seemed to change her mind. She joined Tyler on the sidewalk. Abe waited for a car to pass, then swung onto the road.

'Christ,' Jack said. 'The poor kid.'

'She's holding up pretty well.'

'Gutsy.'

'Yeah.'

'Nora said she almost married the guy once. She finally figured she'd screwed up by turning him down, and came here to give him another shot.'

Abe nodded. He scanned the building fronts.

'Nora also said she was having second thoughts about it all. 'Cause of you.'

Abe said nothing, but he felt his heart speed up.

'She thinks Tyler's really fallen for you. No taste.'

Abe grinned. Then, down a sidestreet to the right, he spotted a pair of flag standards on the sidewalk. He turned. The gray stone building might be a post office, he realized, but it turned out to be the city hall.

'What are you doing?'

'You take the car. Get the trunks and some towels, and meet me back here. I want to do some checking.'

'On Jenson?'

'You got it.'

He eased in behind a pickup truck, left the keys in the ignition, and handed his room key to Jack. He left the car. He crossed the road at an angle away from the administrative offices' entrance, heading for a blue, five-pointed star suspended above a set of double glass doors. The doors read, Police Department Malcasa Point. Pushing one open, he entered a deserted waiting area. A partition of frosted glass ran the length of the counter top. He stepped up to one of its three windows.

'We'll want to impound it,' said the man. He was sitting on the corner of a nearby desk, his back to the window.

The female officer nodded. Her tan uniform was too tight across her broad chest and hips. She must be twenty-one, but she didn't look it. She wore her hair short, in a cut similar to Tyler. Her eyes were on the other cop, and she didn't notice Abe.

'Have Bix tow it in, but I want you supervising.'

'Oh, great. Bix is my favorite human.'

'Fortunes of war, Lucy. He's a jerk, that's why I want you out there. Give him half a chance, he'll screw up the works just to spite us. Soon as it's in the yard, let me know. I'll want to go over it myself.'

'Right.'

'Bix puts a grope on you, you have my permission to deck him.'

She had a nice smile. 'I'll run him in for nauseating a police officer.' She started to turn away, and spotted Abe. With a nod, she signaled that they had a visitor.

The man looked over his shoulder, smiled, and scooted off the desktop as Lucy headed for a side door. He was taller than Abe, with a lean, creased face. His gray hair was long at the sides as if to make up for what he lacked on top. His eyes were the same gray as his hair. Sniper eyes, Abe thought. But cop eyes, too – wary and somewhat bemused.

'Yessir,' he said. 'I'm Harry Purcell. What can I do for you?'

'I just finished a tour of Beast House.'

His smile slipped a bit. 'Yes?'

'They've got Dan Jenson on display over there.'

The smile vanished completely. 'I'm aware of that.'

'I was with a young lady who used to know him. Can you tell me what happened to him?'

Purcell's face pinched up as if he'd stubbed a toe. He said, 'Oooh. You mean she didn't know he was deceased?'

'That's what I mean. The first she knew was when she found his wax face staring up at her.'

'Oooh. That's raw, mighty raw. How's she bearing up?'

'She's managing.'

'The damn shit-house. Sometimes, I think I'd like to torch the place.'

'How was Jenson killed?'

'Went in without a backup. He was on routine patrol, noticed a light in one of the windows. Now, nobody goes in that place at night. Not even Kutch or Hapson. Claim they don't, anyway. So Jenson suspected prowlers. He radioed for backup, but we haven't got much personnel. Two-man shifts, and a watch commander on dispatch. Well, Sweeny'd picked that time to stop for a bite. Jenson said he'd wait for him, but then he went on in alone. And he didn't come out. When Sweeny got there, he found Jenson's radio car abandoned. He wouldn't go in the house alone, and I can't say I blame him. We rousted up the rest of the force, even got the volunteer fire department in on it, and went in. Found his body in the upstairs hallway. His, and the other two. Ziegler and his kid. Searched the place top to bottom, came up zilch.'

'What became of Jenson's body?'

'He had a sister come for it. Had it sent south. To Sacramento, I believe. It was a real shame. Dan was a fine young man.'

'There was a coroner's inquest?'

'Sure. Verdict was 'death at the hands of another' on all three of them. Trouble was, we couldn't come up with 'another.' We carried out a full investigation, but it ran out of steam. Just wasn't much to go on. Couldn't even say for sure it was a man that did it. Might've been a wild animal, but we couldn't think what. We've got some coyotes in the hills, but they're too small. We considered maybe a dog – it'd have to be the size of a mastiff or Dane. We even had some talk of bobcats and bears, though I don't know where one could've come from. But all that's pretty much ruled out. Those are furry creatures, and the only hairs we picked up in the vacuum were human.'

'Could the wounds have been made by a human?' Abe asked.

The cop shrugged. 'If he was mighty strong and had a good set of fingernails.'

'They looked like claw marks on the wax.'

'We had a theory he might've used some kind of device, like a spading-fork or maybe a glove fixed up with spikes of some sort. Sounds a bit farfetched, but the whole situation was pretty curious.'

'Think the beast did it?'

'That's sure what Maggie wants the whole world to think. Her business picked up a hundred percent after the killings. Which gives her something of a motive, in my opinion. If I was to hazard a guess – and I haven't got a speck of evidence to back it up – I'd say Maggie was in back of it. I think her boy, Axel, is physically capable of ripping a man's arm out of its socket. Maybe Wick or Maggie were with him. They took care of Ziegler and his kid, killed Dan when he came up, then used something to claw them up to make it look like the work of their beast and hightailed it before we got the house surrounded. That'd be my best guess, but like I say, you can't take a guess into court.'

'What about the other killings?'

He leaned forward, elbows on the counter. 'I'll tell you what I think, and I'm not the only one in town who suspects the same. I say Maggie Kutch, maybe with Wick Hapson's help, murdered her husband and kids back in '31, mutilated the bodies and started up this story about a mysterious creature to tie it in with the old Thorn killings and throw off suspicion. I was just a kid at the time, but I remember there was plenty of talk along those lines. Wick was in high school then and he used to do yard work at the Kutch place. There was talk about him and Maggie even before the killings. They came under plenty of suspicion, but it died down over the years. Started up again in the 'fifties, after the Bagley boy was murdered in there, but by then they'd been running the tour so long they half had people believing in that beast of theirs. And it didn't help any that the kid who survived – Maywood – claimed it was some kind of monster that did in his friend. Of course, he was hysterical. It was dark in there. He probably expected to see some kind of hellish creature and his eyes played tricks on him. Then again, maybe it was Wick in some kind of outfit. Who's to say?'

'You ever hear Captain Frank on the subject of the beast?'

'The old goat's got himself quite a yarn. What's he call it, Pogo?'

'Bobo.'

'If that guy told me I've got a nose on my face, I'd take a quick peek in the mirror before I'd believe him.'

Abe grinned. 'He's not too reliable?'

'Let's say he likes to be the center of attention, and he's figured out that just about everyone – but especially tourists – are as happy as pigs in shit to hear about the beast. He gives them what they want to hear, and he's center stage for half an hour or so.'

'He said the thing killed his sister.'

'I've checked it out. We've got files going back to 1853 when the town was founded. According to the reports, his sister was killed by a coyote. His father *had* been on a trade ship to Australia, but there's nothing to indicate he brought back an unusual animal. He could've, I suppose, but I think it's more likely Captain Frank just used his father's voyage to make the story sound good. If the old man had been a miner, he would've brought it up out of a shaft.'

'I see what you mean,' Abe said. 'I'd better get moving, I've got some people waiting for me.' He offered his hand, and the man shook it. 'I really appreciate your taking the time to tell me all this.'

'Sorry your friend had such a raw experience. You can tell her Dan died bravely in the line of duty, and we miss him around here.'

'I'll do that. Thanks again,' Abe said, and started to turn away.

'Say. One thing before you leave. You must've been in town last night, out at the Last Chance, or I don't suppose you would've heard the Bobo story.'

'That's right.'

'Stayed at the Welcome Inn?'

'From what I hear, it's the only motel in town.'

'Notice anything peculiar out there?'

'Peculiar? In what way?'

'Seems the Crogans, the family that runs the place, weren't anywhere around this morning. The cook phoned in around six to report it. The office was all locked up. We sent a man in, and it looks like nobody slept there last night. Just found their car abandoned down the road. No sign of them anywhere.'

'Odd.' Abe shook his head. 'No, I don't recall anything unusual.'

'We didn't think much of it till we found the car. That was about an hour ago. Seems like there might've been trouble.'

'I'll ask my friends if they noticed anything.'

'I'd appreciate it. We've got a man out at the Inn now to interview guests, but it seems most everyone's already taken off. Pay in advance, leave first thing in the morning. Folks on vacation, they always want an early start.'

'Well, I'll check.'

'Bring your friends around, if they saw or heard something. 'Course, all we've got now is a missing family. If it turns worse, we'll be in touch for sure.'

'Right. Well, I hope they show up.'

'You and me both.' He tipped a finger to his eyebrow. 'Have a good one.'

Outside, Abe scanned the roadside. The Mustang wasn't in sight so he walked to the corner. Looking down Front Street, he tried to spot Tyler and Nora. Apparently they were still shopping. After a car passed, he crossed and stood near the curb to wait for Jack.

Up the road a block, a blue and white patrol car swung out of the service station. That would be Lucy at the wheel, he thought, with Bix in the tow truck tailing her. As she drew near, she smiled at Abe and raised a hand. He returned her wave. Bix drove by with a finger deep in his mouth. The patrol car and tow truck moved slowly down the road, waited at a traffic light halfway through town, and moved on. They passed the ticket shack in front of Beast House, and soon disappeared where the road curved away into the wooded hills.

Abe turned his gaze to the sidewalk. A block down, a woman pushed a baby stroller into a shop. When they were out of the way, he could see down to the sporting goods store. Still no sign of Tyler or Nora.

The Mustang pulled up beside him. Its passenger seat was piled with towels, his blue swimming trunks on top. He lifted the stack and sat down.

'Took me a while,' Jack said. 'I got waylaid by a cop.'

'The disappearing family?'

'You know about that. I'll tell you something you don't know.' He checked the side mirror, and eased into the deserted lane. 'They aren't the only ones missing. I was talking to the cop when up comes that Hardy fellow and says his friend, that Blake character, hasn't turned up all morning. Hardy hasn't seen him since last night.'

'The plot thickens,' Abe said.

'Yep. The cop was so intrigued by that little development he lost his interest in me, or I'd still be there.'

'Well, I don't think the ladies are finished shopping yet, anyway.'

Jack parked in front of Will's Sporting Goods. 'We'll probably have a long wait,' he said. 'You get a couple of gals trying to make up their minds on swimwear, it could take all day. So, what did you find out about Jenson?'

19

'Turn here,' Nora said.

Tyler, in the back seat, kept her eyes down as Jack swung the car onto Beach Lane. She didn't want to see the road she'd driven yesterday, but her mind dwelled on it: the windowless brick house across the field to the left, the woods to the right, the row of mailboxes, Dan's mailbox. She saw herself and Nora walking Seaside's shadowy ruts, the strange man staring out at them through the screen. She remembered the desolate, abandoned look of Dan's cabin with its empty porch, and how she'd felt anxious to get away from it. Without knowing, she'd somehow known her search for Dan would end badly. Dead more than a year. God, it was hard to believe. He lives in Beast House? I wouldn't say that, not exactly. That crazy old man, Captain Frank, had known all along. He'd toyed with her. Even last night, he'd kept it to himself. Maybe he just didn't have the guts to come out with it. Maybe he'd wanted to, but couldn't force himself to be the bearer of such news. Probably holds himself responsible, figures it was his father's Bobo that did it.

She wished he had told her. Nothing could've dragged her into that awful place, if she'd known. Dan's body – no, not his body, just a wax dummy . . .

And she'd fainted. God, she'd fainted! Right in front of everyone. The memory made her skin go hot with embarrassment; just as it had every time she'd thought of it, even in the shop while trying to pick out a swimsuit.

Fainted. Barfed.

It would've been awful enough without all that, and she felt ashamed for letting the humiliation of it stand in the way of the grief she should feel over Dan's death. She should be mourning him, not blushing over the spectacle she'd made of herself.

But deep inside, where there should have been anguish, was only a hollow feeling that seemed distant from sorrow.

The car stopped.

'All out that's getting out,' Nora announced.

'You go on without me,' Abe said. 'I'll change in here.'

Tyler followed Nora out the driver's door.

'Too bad,' Nora said. 'I guess we won't have the beach to ourselves.'

Two other cars and a van were parked nearby, but Tyler saw no people about. They were probably already down at the ocean. 'I'll wait for Abe,' she said.

'No hurry,' Nora told her. 'We can all . . .'

Jack swatted her rump. 'Let's go,' he said.

The two of them started down a path along the low hillside, holding hands, Nora nodding as he spoke to her.

Tyler stepped to the front of the Mustang. She leaned against its hood, staring at the brown weeds and dusty path, very aware of Abe just behind her, probably watching her through the windshield as he changed into his trunks. She wondered why he hadn't put them on at the motel, as Jack must've done. She heard the quiet clink of his belt buckle. The car moved slightly against her rump, probably in response to Abe rising and settling in the seat as he took down his pants. Thinking about that, she felt a quick stir of excitement that made her guilt worse.

I'm not betraying Dan, she told herself. It was decided before I knew. I can't help how I feel. I can't. I'm sorry.

Her hands went quickly down the front of her blouse, flicking open its buttons. She slipped the sleeves down her arms, and draped the blouse across the hood. The sun's heat and the caressing breeze felt wonderful on her skin, and she could almost feel Abe gazing at her. She wondered if his trunks were on yet. Did the sight of her back, bare except for two thin cords, arouse him? She and Nora, after paying for their bikinis, had used the changing rooms to put them on. She almost wished, now, that she had left hers in its bag. She could've stripped naked here in the sunshine and the ocean breeze, with Abe watching in astonishment from the car. It seemed outlandish, but at the moment she felt capable of such actions. Giddy, maybe a little desperate. She could reach back, right now, and pluck the cords and let the top fall away and turn to face him.

He would think she'd gone mad.

Maybe I *have* gone mad.

Troubled by the urge to remove her top, she went ahead and opened her corduroys. She slid them down her legs, stepped out of them, placed them neatly on the hood without turning far enough to see Abe through the windshield. Then she leaned back again.

Abe was taking a very long time.

Maybe enjoying the show.

I ought to give him a *real* show.

My God, what's the matter with me?

Staring down at herself, she even wondered what had possessed her in the store. At home, she had a similar string bikini. She never wore it in public, only in the privacy of her enclosed sundeck. So why had she bought one just like it this morning? And why, even though it covered so little, did she have such a strong desire to pull it off and stand naked in front of Abe and . . .?

I *must* be crazy, she thought.

And it must have something to do with finding Dan that way. Something to do with fear and loneliness. Maybe more to do with the feel of the sun and the sea air and the slick fabric on her nipples and the taut press of it on her groin and knowing she was so very much alive like an insult to death.

The sound of the door opening interrupted her thoughts. She turned around and watched Abe step out of the car. He looked sleek and tanned. His boxer trunks were pale blue. He had a bundle of towels clamped under one arm. 'That's quite an outfit,' he said.

'Thanks. I like yours, too.'

He laughed. 'Want to leave your clothes here?' He held out a hand. She gave him the blouse and pants. He put them in the car and locked up. He approached without looking at her. A troubled frown had replaced his smile.

'What is it?' Tyler asked.

He shifted the bundle to his right arm, took hold of her hand, and led her toward the path. 'I didn't go back to the motel,' he said. 'I stopped in at the police department.'

'The police?'

'I wanted to get the story on Dan. I thought there were . . . things we should know.'

The tight sick feeling seemed to swell inside Tyler. 'And?' she murmured.

'I didn't find out much. He was murdered there in the house. They don't know who did it. A sister from Sacramento claimed his body.'

'Roberta. She's an accountant. She had dinner with us once at Ben Jenson's. A very nice person.'

Abe let go of her hand. He put an arm around her and eased her close to his side. 'I'm awfully sorry about all this.'

'At least . . . his parents aren't alive. It would've been terrible for them. He wasn't married?'

'I didn't ask. I assume he wasn't, since his sister . . .'

'Probably not. God, it's funny. Yesterday, my biggest worry was that he might be married. Then, today, I was so worried that he wouldn't be. And all the time, he was dead in that house for everyone to gawk at.'

'It's not him, Tyler.'

'Yeah, I know. I keep telling myself. God, you wouldn't think they'd be allowed to put someone on display like that.'

'Madame Tussaud's been doing it for two hundred years.'

'Doesn't make it right.'

'No,' Abe said, 'it doesn't.'

'It'd probably take a court order to get it out of there.'

The path curved around the slope, and Tyler saw Nora and Jack down at the water's edge. Combers were rolling in. Off to the side, a woman stood in the surf holding the hand of a toddler. A man was jogging along the shoreline, a black retriever prancing ahead of him. Stretched out on a blanket near the foot of the slope was a young couple embracing. Tyler felt Abe's hand caressing her side. She took a deep breath of the fresh, tangy air.

'When are you leaving?' she asked.

'There's no rush.'

'Today? Are you leaving today?'

'That depends.'

'On what?'

'On you.'

She stopped walking. Turning to her, Abe let the towels fall. He looked into her eyes as his hands slid up her arms, cupped her shoulders. 'I'll stay another night,' she said, 'if you will.'

He smiled slightly. 'Do you think Nora would object?'

'Surely you jest?'

He eased Tyler against him. Gently. One hand stroking her hair, the other light on her back. She hugged him tightly. He was warm and smooth and solid, and she remembered embracing him that morning and the way his hands had felt on her breasts. It seemed like a very long time ago. Dan had been there in the room with them like a chaperon. If I'm going to lose you to this guy, Abe had said, I'd rather not get in any deeper. I want you too much already. The memory of his words made Tyler's heart pound fast. Guilt swept through her, and she hugged Abe more tightly to ward it off. Though he stroked her hair and back gently, as if intent only upon consoling her, Tyler felt his rising hardness.

Abe stepped back. His smile trembled. 'I guess I can stay one more night.'

Tyler nodded. She was a little breathless. 'I would like that,' she said.

He looked toward the water, and Tyler's eyes strayed down to his trunks. The bulge slanted upward, forcing the elastic band slightly away from his waist. 'There might be a problem,' he said, and crouched to pick up the towels.

'A problem?'

They walked down the path.

'The owners of the motel seem to be missing. Their car was found abandoned this morning. Nobody seems to know what happened to them.'

'Do you think the motel might close?'

'Maybe there's someone to keep it running, I don't know.'

'Oh, great. It's the only place in town, isn't it?'

'Far as I know. Brian Blake also appears to be among the missing.'

'What the hell's going on?'

'I don't know.'

'Oh, man. This town. I knew when we got here it was a creepy place. I wanted to get out of here last night. And I might've, too, except for you.'

'Except for me?'

'It's all your fault,' Tyler said, and squeezed his hand.

'I'm sorry.'

'Don't be. Besides, I don't think I could've pried Nora away.'

In the sand at the bottom of the hill, Tyler kicked off her sandals. She picked them up and hooked her arm through Abe's. The sand felt hot, almost burning. Nora and Jack were a distance up the beach, wading through the wash, but they'd left their clothes behind in a heap. Tyler dropped her sandals next to the pile. Abe put down the towels.

'Shall we go in?' Tyler asked.

'We both need to cool off.'

With a laugh, she dashed across the sand. Abe ran along easily beside her. Cold water splashed up her legs. She kicked through a knee-high wave, charged into one that chilled her to the hips, then dived. She went rigid with the cold blast, but moments later it no longer felt so bad. She swam out, the swells lifting her, easing her down. When something seized her foot, she thought *shark*! And then she thought, Abe.

She tugged free, came up for air, and whirled around. A moment later, Abe's head popped to the surface, hair matted down, face shiny and dripping. She swatted water at him. He ducked under the surface. She watched him glide forward, saw his arms reach out, felt his hands on her hips. He pulled her down. His body slid against her as if it were oiled. He nuzzled the side of her neck, kissed her mouth. They rolled under the water, embracing. One of his thighs pressed between her spread legs and she quivered and scissored her legs shut, trapping it there. She shoved a hand down the back of his trunks, fingered the crease of his rump, clenched a firm buttock and writhed against him. But her lungs started to hurt. She pushed herself away from Abe, clawed to the surface, and gasped for air. Abe came up in front of her. Treading water, they panted for a while.

'Trying to drown me?' Tyler finally asked.

'*You* trying to drown *me*?'

'What a way to go,' she said. The words reminded her of Dan on the corridor floor, his throat torn out.

'What?' Abe asked.

'Nothing.'

'Nothing?'

'I keep . . . forgetting about Dan. Then I keep remembering.'

'Yeah.'

'Would you mind if we get out now?'

'Not if that's what you want.'

'We'd better.' She forced a smile. 'Before we lose our suits.'

'As good a reason as any.'

Side by side, they swam closer to shore. Then they waded out, the waves nudging their backs as if to hurry them along. 'Let's just walk,' Tyler said.

'Towel?'

'The sun will dry us.' She took Abe's hand, and they walked on the hard-packed sand, the wash of the ocean sometimes swirling over their feet. The sun felt hot and good. Gulls wheeled overhead, squealing. Jack and Nora, a distance up the beach, were strolling slowly toward them.

'There's something I want you to know,' Tyler said.

'Uh-oh.'

'Not really. It's just that . . . I don't want you to think . . . God, how can I say this? I felt the way I do about you before all this about Dan happened. You remember this morning in my room?'

'How could I forget?'

'That was before . . . the tour. I'd already made up my mind not to . . . get involved with him.'

Abe nodded as if he'd known that.

'I just don't want you to think the way I . . . I mean, I'm not on some kind of bizarre rebound. It has nothing to do with him. Hell, I wanted you last night. But he was in the way, even though . . . oh, God, doesn't that sound wonderful? He was in the way and now he's not.'

'I think I understand, Tyler.'

'You guys went in!' Nora said as she and Jack came near. 'Didn't you freeze your buns?'

'It wasn't too bad,' Tyler said. 'Give it a try.'

'No way. I'm gonna spread out one of those towels and catch some rays. We're gonna stay awhile, aren't we?'

'Sure,' Abe said. 'One thing, though. Is anyone opposed to staying over again tonight?'

'All *right!*' Nora wiggled her eyebrows at Jack. 'How about you, Tiger? Think you're up to it?'

'There might be a problem with the Inn,' he said to Abe.

'Weird, huh?' Nora asked. 'What do you suppose happened to those people?'

'I promised the cop I'd check about that,' Abe said. 'None of you noticed anything strange last night, did you?'

Nora said, 'Not a thing.' Jack shook his head.

'If the motel's going to close up,' Tyler said, 'we'd better find out.' Her heart started racing. 'Why don't Abe and I go on ahead and check it out? We can register, if everything's okay, and meet you back here.'

'Terrif.'

'That okay with you, Abe?' Tyler asked.

'Let's go.'

They left Nora and Jack spreading towels on the sand, and trudged up the slope. Tyler was eager and nervous. The parking area seemed very far away, as if the path had stretched itself simply to frustrate her. At last, they reached the car. Abe opened the passenger door. He rolled down its window, and tossed the towels into the back seat.

'Whoa,' Tyler said. 'I'd better put something on.'

'You look fine,' he said.

With a shrug, she climbed in. She jumped at the burning touch of the seat cover, then settled down and watched Abe wince as he sat behind the wheel. 'Hurt?' she asked.

'I can take it.'

'We should've put clothes on.'

'I like you this way.' Reaching over, he slid a hand up her leg. He patted her thigh, met her eyes for a moment, then started the car.

Tyler slumped down in her seat as they passed through the middle of town. Abe kept glancing at her, looking a bit amused. He drove in silence.

Nervous? she wondered.

'We'll check the office later,' he said finally.

Except for Gorman Hardy's Mercedes, the courtyard of the Welcome Inn was deserted.

'My room'll be fine,' Tyler whispered.

He parked in front of it. Tyler stepped out into the shade. A mild breeze chilled the sweat on her skin. Leaning over the back seat, she gathered her handbag and all her clothes.

Her hands were trembling. She dropped the room key on the stoop. Abe picked it up and unlocked the door.

The room was dusky, the curtains drifting out from the open windows. The bed Tyler had slept in last night was still unmade. She stepped over to the dressing table, and emptied her arms.

In the mirror, she saw Abe come up behind her. Parting her hair, he kissed the nape of her neck. He caressed her sides, her belly. She watched his hands glide upward, and moaned as they cupped her breasts through the filmy bikini.

'Tyler,' he whispered.

'Huh?'

'It's a nice name.'

'It's a weird name.'

'I like it. I like everything about you.'

'Flatterer.'

'Yeah.'

'Do you like my sweat?'

'I like how it makes you slippery,' he said, sliding his hands down her belly.

'Soap will do that, too.'

'Mmm.'

'Let's take a shower.'

He fingered the ties at her hip. She lifted his hand away. 'Patience. We've got to rinse the salt water off our suits.'

He laughed softly and followed her into the bathroom. Leaning over the tub, Tyler turned on the hot water faucet. She kept a hand under the spout. The water, cold at first, slowly became warm. She flinched with surprise when Abe touched her rump. His hand was big and warm. It moved slowly lower. She gasped and felt her legs go weak when it stole between them. She gripped the edge of the tub to hold herself steady. Steam rose from the splashing water, hot against her face. She looked around. Abe gave her an innocent smile, and his hand went away.

Tyler turned on the cold water. She adjusted the faucet and touched the water. Still too hot. She reached again to the faucet, and felt Abe's fingers on her hip. Looking back, she saw him pluck open the knotted cords. He let the ends fall. The white triangle at her groin swung away like a hinged flap. She twisted the faucet. Abe untied the other side. She turned the faucet slightly more and felt a tingling brush of fabric as Abe drew the garment away. He tossed it over her head. It dropped into the tub.

'You're very helpful,' Tyler said.

'I try to be.'

She touched the water. It felt right. 'What about your trunks?' she asked as she twisted the shower handle.

'That's your job.'

The spray came down. Straightening up quickly, Tyler yanked the shower curtain almost shut. She reached through the gap to test the temperature. Abe, standing beside her, moved a hand down her back and rump. 'It's ready,' she said.

'Ladies first.'

Tyler climbed into the tub. She passed through the spray and backed up against a tile wall. Abe stepped in. He closed the curtain and turned to face her, one eye squeezed shut against the pelting shower, a rather silly smile on his face.

Tyler eased into his arms. The water rained down on their faces as they kissed. His body was slick against her. His hands roamed down her back, caressed and plied her buttocks as if he was fascinated by the firm mounds. Then they slid up. They opened the ties behind her back, behind her neck. Holding onto the neck cords, he stepped away and peeled the bikini down. He let it fall to their feet. He gazed at her streaming breasts. He explored them with his hands, stroking and holding and squeezing, clasping the nipples between his thumb and forefingers, pinching them gently in a way that made Tyler catch her breath and squirm.

Crouching, he rubbed his face on them. She felt his nose, the tickle of an eyelash, the rasp of whiskers, kisses, the soft circling tip of his tongue, the firm pressure of his lips, the edges of his teeth. Tyler clenched his hair as he sucked. His mouth felt huge and powerful, drawing her in until it almost hurt, then going to her other breast and doing the same. As the mouth released her, she pulled his hair to make him stand. She latched her mouth against his, and writhed in his embrace.

Turning so the spray was on her back, she wiped the water from her eyes. She rubbed Abe's slippery shoulders and chest. She looked down at his bulging trunks. The narrow gap was there between the waist band and his belly, as she'd seen it on the path to the beach. Now she slipped her fingertips into the gap and drew the band toward her. Forehead resting on his chest, she stared down at him. His hands were motionless on her shoulders. She reached into the trunks, curled a hand around his thickness, and explored its hard length. Crouching, she pulled the trunks down his legs. He stepped out of them. Tyler's hands moved up his thighs. She gently squeezed the furry ṣac of his scrotum. She wrapped her fingers around his shaft, slid them lightly up and down, then kissed the slitted head. Her tongue swirled around the silken skin. Holding his buttocks, she licked down the underside, feeling the solid heat of him against her cheek. Then she took him in, lips stretching around his smooth flesh, tongue stroking. She drew him in deeply until her mouth could accept no more. He squirmed, clutching her hair, his rump flexed taut under her hands as she sucked.

'Better stop,' he warned in a husky voice.

She slid her mouth back, kissed the swollen knob, then sheathed him again.

'*Tyler.*' He pulled gently at her hair. She sucked hard as he eased her away. Then her mouth was empty and she rose and embraced him, feeling the hardness against her belly.

'I want you *now*,' she gasped into his mouth.

'Here?'

'Yes.' She lay down in the tub, pressing her knees to its walls, and Abe lowered himself onto her. The hot shower smacked her face. Then Abe's head blocked the spray. He was light on her, braced by his elbows and knees. As he kissed her, she felt a touch between her legs. He moved slowly, the head of his penis stroking her cleft. She flinched as it nudged her clitoris, squirmed and moaned as it stayed there, rubbing. Then it moved lower and very slowly slid in. She wanted it thrusting deep, but Abe held back as if to torture her. He withdrew completely, and she groaned. She dug her fingers into his rump. He pushed her opening. He entered. He suddenly shoved in fast and deep, spreading her, driving in farther and farther until she thought it impossible for there to be more – but there was more and it filled her.

They lay locked together, Abe deep in her body as if part of her. Neither of them moved. Tyler understood – and maybe so did Abe – how close they were to orgasms that would mean an ending, at least for now, to the terrible aching need for so deep a joining. She wanted to prolong the moment, to savor it.

The water was spraying down. It dripped off Abe's face onto Tyler's face as he kissed her lips, her nose, her eyes.

'Oh, Abe,' she whispered.

Behind the registration desk stood a portly, red-faced man in a white shirt and bow tie. Strands of hair crossed his head like streaks sketched on with a black pen. He made a lopsided smile. 'What can I do for you, folks?'

'We were guests last night,' Abe said. 'We'd like to extend our stay, if you'll be open.'

'Names?'

'Ours are under Branson,' Tyler said.

'Branson and Clanton,' Abe told him.

The man fingered through cards in a metal box. 'I'll be running the place for now,' he said as he searched.

'Have the police found out anything about the Crogans?' Abe asked.

'Looks bad. Blood in Marty's car. I'm his brother-in-law, you know. We've got a piece of this place, so I'll be seeing to matters. Hope my wife doesn't let the pharmacy go to hell.' He pulled out two cards. 'Here we go. How many nights will you be wanting to stay on?'

'One more,' Abe said. He tried to pay for all the rooms, but Tyler insisted on picking up the tab for hers and Nora's.

'Will the restaurant be open, too?' she asked.

The man nodded. 'We'll keep it running.'

'I hope everything turns out all right,' Abe said.

'I do, too, but I don't suppose it'll be that way. We've had folks disappear before in this town. It's not likely they'll show up again.'

'Take care, now,' Abe told him.

'I'll see your rooms are made up before long. I'll take care of it myself if I can't round up Lois. I think she knew I'd need her. That's why she hightailed it. Probably off at the beach with Haywood.'

'We're on our way to the beach,' Tyler said.

His eyebrows lifted. 'If you see Lois, you want to let her know her father needs her over here? I'd appreciate it. She's sixteen, long brown hair, wears this polka-dot bikini she ought to be ashamed of.'

'If we see her,' Tyler said, 'we'll tell her to come by.' He thanked her, and they left.

'She wasn't the one we saw,' Abe said as they stepped down the porch stairs.

'No, but she might be there now. It's been a couple of hours.'

'Doesn't seem that long.'

She grinned, and Abe patted her rump. He opened the passenger door. She climbed in. 'I hope Nora and Jack aren't burnt to a crisp,' she said.

'If they are, it was for a good cause.' Abe shut the door and walked around to his side of the car. As he sat down behind the wheel, Tyler leaned over. She kissed him.

She rode with her elbow out the window, the breeze tossing her hair and fluttering the front of her blouse. The two top buttons were open.

'Eyes on the road, buster.'

'It's not easy.'

She smiled and threw back her head. Abe glanced at her throat, the smooth tanned vee of skin below it, the pale slope of a breast as the breeze lifted a side of her blouse.

He turned away and watched the road. He felt very strange – pleasantly tired, happier than he could remember ever being before, yet troubled.

It couldn't be going better, he told himself

Maybe that's the problem.

Some problem

It's gone too well, too fast. It started less then twenty-four hours ago when he first saw her face – spattered by that lunatic's blood. When he first looked into her eyes, and felt as if he'd known her before. No, as if he *should* have known her before. As if she had always been out there, and he'd known it but not who she was or where to look. It was like finding a part of himself that had been lost.

From that time on, she'd been a constant presence in his mind. He'd wondered about her, worried and hoped. Yesterday afternoon had been very bad, especially when she went looking for Dan. During dinner and later, the threat from Dan had faded, but not completely, and he'd spent the night in a restless half-sleep, eager for the morning to come but dreading its arrival, afraid of losing her.

He nodded, realizing he'd discovered the source of his worry: he was *still* afraid of losing her.

The worry seemed unfounded. She'd apparently made up her mind in favor of Abe even before finding out about Dan's death. She wanted him – maybe as much as he wanted her. But their lovemaking had brought such a closeness, such a joining that he now had much more to lose than he'd ever thought possible.

It was amazing.

But frightening, too.

'You're looking mighty glum,' she said.

'Post-coital depression.'

She laughed. 'How long do you expect it to last?'

'Probably till we coit again.'

'Can it wait till after lunch?'

'If it must,' he said. He turned onto Beach Lane.

At the end of the dirt road, parked next to a pickup truck, was a long, gray Mercedes.

'That looks like Hardy's,' Tyler said. 'I wonder what Mr Wonderful's doing at the beach.'

20

'My father, he'd been living with the guilt more than thirty years, and he told me he couldn't abide it any longer.' Captain Frank raised the can of Bud to his mouth. He shut his eyes against the sun as he gulped.

Gorman took another can from the six-pack he'd brought along to lubricate the old man's tongue, and popped open its top. Captain Frank mashed his empty and tossed it. Gorman watched it drop a long way to the ground.

'It was then he told me, for the first time, all about Bobo and how Bobo must still be alive and murdering.'

'Have another,' Gorman said.

Captain Frank accepted the fresh can. 'Much obliged.' He settled back in his lawn chair and took a long drink. 'Well, I begged my father to let me go with him, but he'd have none of that. Wanted me to stay behind and look after Mother. It was as if he knew he'd never come back, and he didn't. He was a mighty fine shot with that Winchester of his. I 'spect Bobo must've snuck up on him, caught him from behind.' With his free hand, the old man savagely clawed the air. 'Just like that.'

'Was your father's body ever found?' Gorman asked.

'No, sir. I 'spect it's buried over yonder, more than likely in the cellar.'

'The cellar of Beast House?'

'That's what I figure.'

'If the beast actually killed him, as you believe, wouldn't the Kutch woman have put a replica of your father on display for the tour.'

'Could've, but she didn't. You ask me, the old bat's mighty careful who she exhibits. You look at who's in there. Take the Bagley kid, for instance. His friend, Maywood, got out alive and went running to the cops. Now how's she gonna deny the killing? She doesn't. She turned it to the good by having dummies made up. Same goes for the three last year. One's Danny Jenson, the cop. How's she gonna pretend it never happened? But let me tell you.' He squinted an eye at Gorman. 'There's plenty of folks just up and disappear. I figure Bobo got most of them. But old Maggie, she's not gonna put them on display when she's got a way to cover up. She'd have a whole house full, and how'd that look?' He took a long drink of beer.

'Four people disappeared last night,' Gorman said. 'The Crogans, who run the Welcome Inn . . .'

'Oh, dear Lord.'

'And a friend of mine.'

Captain Frank scowled at the top of his beer can.

'The Crogans' car was found abandoned this morning on the road to the highway.'

'Well, it got them. I was you, I wouldn't count on seeing my friend again. Or the Crogans, either. Their girl, she gone too?'

'Yes.'

He let out a long sigh. 'She was such a cute thing. Used to see her down at the beach. Always had a kind word. Goddamn, they should've known better. You just don't go near that house, not after dark, not unless you're looking to get yourself killed. They should've known that.'

'Does the beast actually leave the house?'

'Sure does. Unless Wick or Maggie are grabbing folks. One look at that pair, you know they'd be hard put to get away with it. Bobo's gotta be prowling around. In the hills back of the house. Down on the beach. Some twelve years back, we even had a gal disappear from the cabin next door.' He nodded to the right. 'Ry, that's her husband, he come home late from the Last Chance and she was gone. Folks all said she'd run off 'cause he was always whumping on her. But I knew different and told him so. He called me a screwy old fart and said to stay out of his business.'

He peered at Gorman and raised a thick white eyebrow. '*You* think I'm a screwy old fart?'

'Not at all,' Gorman assured him.

'Well, lots of folks do. They'll change their tune one of these days when I hand over Bobo's body.'

'You plan to kill it?'

'I'll get Bobo, or it'll get me.'

'Have you ever gone after it?'

'Why, sure. I've gone and laid ambush for it – oh, more times than I can count. But it's never showed up.'

'You've never seen it?'

'Not a once.'

'Have you ever gone into the house after it?'

'Now, that'd be trespassing.'

Gorman controlled his urge to smile. Obviously, the old man was afraid to enter Beast House. 'It seems,' he said, 'as if the house would be the best place to hunt it.'

Captain Frank squeezed his beer can and hurled it from the bus top. It hit a low-hanging tree branch and fell to the ground. 'Say, young man, how'd you like to take a look at my book?'

'What book?'

'I been keeping track. Yes, indeed. You'd be surprised.'

'I'd like very much to see it.'

The old man winked. 'Thought you might. You're a lot curiouser than most.' He pushed himself out of the lawn chair, and walked unsteadily along the top of the bus. 'Bring the beer along,' he said.

Gorman got to his knees and watched Captain Frank descend the wooden ladder. The moment the man was out of sight, he pulled out his pocket recorder. The tape was still running, but it must be near its end. The old geezer had talked for the better part of an hour – and what a story he'd told! Gorman couldn't have been more delighted. Everything was going his way. Everything! His fingers trembled with excitement as he ejected the tape's tiny cartridge, flipped it over, and slid it back into place. He returned the recorder to his jacket pocket. He grabbed an empty plastic ring of the six-pack. The two remaining cans clanked together at his side as he walked carefully toward the ladder.

He approached it with growing alarm. The ascent had been bad enough, but he suspected the descent would prove worse. The ladder was simply propped against the end of the bus, its highest rung level with his waist. What if it should tip over as he attempted to clamber on?

Gorman Hardy, noted author of *Horror at Black River Falls*, fell to his death . . .

Captain Frank was down below, gazing up at him.

'Would you mind holding the ladder for me?'

The old man shook his head as if he pitied Gorman, then stepped under the ladder and clutched its uprights.

If you're such a stalwart fellow, Gorman thought, why are you terrified of going after the beast? A screwy old fart, all right. And a coward. But his story was gold, and Gorman's fear subsided as he wondered about the man's book. Carefully, he mounted the ladder. It wobbled slightly. The rungs creaked under his weight. His legs felt weak and shaky, but finally he planted a foot on the solid ground.

'And you're still in one piece,' said Captain Frank.

Gorman forced a smile. He followed the man through a litter of beer cans alongside the painted bus. 'Did you paint this mural?'

'That I did.'

'I've never seen anything quite like it. Would you mind if I took a picture?'

'Help yourself. I'll just step inside and . . .'

'Stay here. I'd like you in the picture, too. The canvas and the artist.'

Captain Frank nodded. He moved to the open door of the bus as Gorman set down the beers and stepped away. In the viewfinder, the old man looked like a crazed tourist: Huckleberry Finn straw hat, red aloha shirt flapping in the breeze, plaid Bermuda shorts, spindly legs with drooping green socks and tattered blue tennis shoes. He held an arm out, a finger pointing at the mural.

Gorman took a few more backward steps to fit in the entire length of the bus, and triggered the shutter release. 'Marvelous! Now step over that way.' He waved the old man to the left. 'There. Right there. The ancient mariner and the albatross.'

'You know the poem?'

'Certainly. It's one of my favorites.' He moved in close and snapped the shot. 'Wonderful. Thank you.'

'Hope they turn out.'

'Shall we have a look at this book you mentioned?'

'Right this way.'

When the old man turned away to mount the steps, Gorman switched on his recorder. He retrieved the beers, and followed. He found Captain Frank in the driver's seat.

'Look here, matey.' With a sly wink, he whacked the sun visor. It flipped down. Secured to its back with duct tape was a sheathed knife. He tapped a fingernail against the staghorn handle. 'I'm ready for it, see? Just let old Bobo make a try for me.' He pushed up the visor, hunched over so his chin rested on the steering wheel, and reached under the seat. He came up with a western style revolver. 'My hogleg,' he announced. Thumbing back the hammer, he stared at the weapon as if it were a stunning woman. 'This darling's an Iver Johnson .44 magnum. She'll knock Bobo ass over tea kettle.'

'Is it loaded?' Gorman asked.

'Wouldn't do me much good empty.'

Gorman held his breath as Captain Frank lowered the hammer. When the revolver was safely stored away, the old man stood up. He stepped through the gap in the faded, split blanket draping the aisle. Gorman followed.

The rows of windows along both sides of the carriage had been painted over, tinting the dim light with hues of red, blue, green and yellow. A few, fortunately, were open to admit untarnished daylight and the fresh breeze. The original seats had been removed to make room for a strange assortment of furnishings: a cot with a rumpled quilt, a straight-backed wicker chair, a single lamp and several steamer trunks of various sizes, some standing on end, all cluttered with the odds and ends of Captain Frank's reclusive life. On the trunk nearest the cot, Gorman saw a copy of Peter Freuchen's *Book of the Seven Seas*, a Coleman lantern, a crushed beer can, and a revolver. He spotted three more weapons as the old man lowered himself onto the cot: a doublebarreled shotgun suspended from an overhead luggage rack by a pair of misshapen wire hangers, a saber propped against a metal partition near the side exit doors, and the butt of a pistol protruding from the open face port of a deep-sea diving helmet atop one of the trunks.

'You've got quite an arsenal,' he said.

'Yessir. Just let Bobo come. I don't care where I'm at. Here?' He snatched the revolver off the trunk and jabbed the air with its barrel as if taking hasty aim at a host of intruders. 'In my galley?' He swept the gun toward the rear of the bus, where a second blanket draped the aisle just beyond the side exit. 'I've got a .38 Smith and Wesson by my stove. I've got a Luger in the head. I don't care where I am, I'm ready. Just let Bobo make a try.'

He put down the revolver on the floor by his feet. 'Have a seat, here, matey,' he said, and patted the cot.

Gorman peeled the plastic rings off the remaining beers. He gave one of the cans to Captain Frank, and sat down beside him. He popped open his can while the captain cleared off the trunk. The beer had lost its chill. He took a few swallows and wished he'd had the foresight to bring along a bottle of gin for himself.

The old man opened the trunk and lifted out a battered, leatherbound volume that looked like a family photo album. He closed the trunk, and set the book on its lid midway between himself and Gorman. Leaning forward, he flipped open the cover.

'Fabulous,' Gorman said.

'My father, he did that. He wasn't the artist I am, but he done the best he could.'

The pencil sketch, creased and smudged as if it had spent a lot of time folded in someone's pocket, showed a snarling, snouted head.

'That's Bobo,' Captain Frank said. 'My father, he drew it aboard the *Mary Jane* on the return voyage.'

Gorman stared at the head. It was a frontal view, not much more than an oval with slanted eyes, a half circle to indicate the snout, and an open mouth revealing rows of pointed teeth.

'Not a hair on it,' the captain said. 'Not even an eyebrow or a lash. And skin as white as the belly of a fish. Like an albino. Just no color at all, except for its eyes. My father, he told me its eyes were as blue as the sky.'

He turned the page. The next sketch, a side view, showed the creature's blunt snout. Except for the snout, the head looked almost human. Where the ear should be, there was a circle the size of a dime. 'Where is its ear?' Gorman asked.

'That's it. Nothing to it but a hole with a little flap of skin over it.

That's to keep stuff from getting in. My father, he said Bobo could open up that flap like an eyelid and hear as good as a dog.'

'Incredible.'

Taped to the next page was a sketch of the beast standing upright. From waist to knees, its form had been obliterated by pencil marks as if someone had scratched over it in a fit of temper. The lead pencil point had even torn through the paper, rucking up an accordion wedge that had subsequently been smoothed down flat.

'What happened here?'

Captain Frank shook his head. He sighed. 'My mother did that. She was an awful prude, God rest her bones. I never got a chance, myself, to see the drawing before she ruined it.'

'That's a shame,' Gorman said. He studied what remained of the creature. Except for the claws on its fingers and toes, it appeared remarkably human. The shoulders and chest were broad, the limbs thick as if heavily muscled. One arm was longer than the other, but Gorman assumed that to be a fault of the artist. 'Do you know the size of it?'

Captain Frank took a drink of beer and rubbed his mouth. 'About three feet tall. That's what it was when my father got rid of it. 'Course, now, it wasn't much more than a year old, then. He said the full-grown ones they killed on the island were better than six feet.'

Gorman nodded, and Captain Frank turned the page. He expected another sketch, perhaps a rear view of the creature, but found instead a newspaper clipping. The handwritten scrawl at the top of the page read, '*Clarion*, July 21, 1902, Loreen'. The article's heading was printed in bold type.

MALCASA CHILD SLAIN
BY COYOTE

Loreen Newton, three-year-old daughter of Frank and Mary, was savagely attacked and slain in the yard of her parents' Front Street home. Alarmed by the child's screams . . .

Gorman shook his head as if dismayed, and turned to the next page without finishing the story. Taped to its center was the child's funeral notice. He didn't bother reading it. He flipped the leaf over, and unfolded the full front page of the *Clarion*'s August 3,1903 edition. He stared at the stark headline:

THREE MURDERED
AT THORN HOUSE!

'This is wonderful,' Gorman said.

'My father, he's the one saved these early articles. I'm the one added on, after he was gone, and put them all together here.'

After glancing at the four columns of small print, Gorman refolded the page. Subsequent articles described the capture, trial, and lynching of Gus Goucher. Then Gorman found another folded front page of the *Clarion*, this one recounting the slaughter, nearly thirty years later, of Maggie Kutch's husband and children. After a few follow-up stories, Gorman came upon a clipping about the disappearance of Captain Frank's father.

'Here's where I started keeping them,' the old man said.

Gorman scanned a story about the opening of Beast House for tours. Then he flipped through page after page of articles detailing the disappearances of townspeople and visitors, two or three for each year. 'That's a lot of missing people,' he said.

'It's just the ones that got reported. I figure there's plenty more, folks nobody missed.'

'And you suspect the beast was responsible for all this?'

'Maybe not all,' Captain Frank admitted. 'Some of those folks maybe just run off, or got themselves lost in the hills, or drowned. There's no telling how many, but I'll wager Bobo got his share of them.'

'Why was nothing done about it? This must be fifty or sixty missing persons over a twenty-year period.'

'Well, sir, the police, they didn't see anything so strange about it. Lord knows, I told them time after time it was the beast making off with those folks. Did they listen? No, indeed. They seemed to think it was normal, losing a couple folks a year.'

'Acceptable losses,' Gorman muttered.

'And they made up their minds, way back, that I'm just a loony. I can't even get them to listen to me anymore.'

'Have you showed this to them?' he asked, tapping the scrapbook.

'Sure. Like I say, they think I'm loony.'

Gorman came upon another full front page of the newspaper. This one dealt with the attack in 1951 on Tom Bagley and Larry Maywood. After follow-up stories came more pages with clippings about disappearances. Finally, near the back of the book, he found articles about last year's slayings of the Ziegler father and son, and patrolman Dan Jenson.

He reached a blank page.

Captain Frank took a swig of beer. 'That's all, till tomorrow's *Clarion*. I'll be adding whatever they print on this business you told me about – the Crogans and your friend. They'll go in, sure enough.'

'You're pretty confident Bobo got them?'

'I'd wager on it, matey.'

Gorman nodded. He gently closed the book, and stared at it. 'This is a very impressive document, Frank.'

'I always felt it's been my duty to keep a record of all these goings-on.'

'How would you feel about making it public?'

'Public?' The old man raised a bushy white eyebrow.

'I'd like to write up your story. Are you familiar with *People* magazine?'

'Aye.'

'I'm a staff writer for *People*. Maybe you saw my piece on Jerry Brown?' There must've been a piece on Brown recently, he thought.

'No, I . . .'

'Well, that's all right. The point is: I find myself shocked and amazed by what you've told me this afternoon, by the information in your scrapbook, by the very existence of a monstrosity such as Beast House, by the seeming indifference of the local authorities to what appears to be a seventy-five-year string of disappearances and grisly murders. With your cooperation, I'd be willing to do a feature article that exposes the truth of the situation. With enough public awareness, the authorities will be forced to take action. The story, of course, will focus on you.'

Captain Frank frowned as if thinking it over.

'What do you say?'

He sighed. 'I've always planned to take care of Bobo myself.'

'So much the better. If you can do that before the story's printed, we'll include your account of the hunt and photos of you with the body.'

'I don't know, Mr . . .'

'Wilcox. Harold Wilcox.'

'I don't know, Mr Wilcox. It does sound like a fine idea. Mighty fine. What'll I have to do?'

'Nothing, really. Just leave it to me. You've already given me sufficient information. Of course, I would need to borrow your scrapbook, at least long enough to have its contents photocopied. I'd be more than glad to give you a receipt for it. There must be a copying machine somewhere in town . . .'

'Over at Lincoln's Stationery.'

'Fine. I could have it done this afternoon and get it back to you . . .' He paused. 'Would tomorrow morning be convenient for you?'

'I do hate to let it out of my hands.'

'You're welcome to come along, if you don't trust me.'

'Oh, it's not that I don't trust you, Mr Wilcox.'

'I could probably get it back to you this evening, if that's preferable.'

Captain Frank chewed his lower lip.

'I tell you what. Suppose I leave a deposit with you? Say a hundred dollars. You keep my money until I return the book to you.'

'Well, that sounds fair enough.'

Gorman removed a pair of fifty-dollar bills from his wallet. 'Do you have some spare paper so we can write out the receipts?'

'I don't guess we need to,' Captain Frank said, and picked up the money. 'You just take good care of this book for me, and I'll take good care of your money.'

They shook hands.

With the scrapbook clamped under one arm, Gorman left the bus.

On his way through town, he spotted Lincoln's Stationery. He grinned, and kept on driving.

21

Tyler, sitting on the edge of the bed, rolled a stocking up her leg. As she clipped it to the straps of her black garter belt, someone knocked on the door. 'Who is it?' she called.

'Me,' came Abe's voice.

'Just a minute,' she said, and quickly started to put on the other stocking. 'Are you alone?'

'Very.'

'Poor man.'

'That's me.'

She finished with the stocking, and rushed to the door. Staying out of view behind it, she pulled it open. Abe stepped into the room. 'That was quick,' she said as she shut the door.

In the ten minutes since he left he had changed into navy slacks and a powder blue polo shirt. Tyler had managed to blow-dry her hair and begin dressing.

'I just couldn't stand being away from you,' he said.

She stepped into his arms and kissed him. His hands roamed down her back, curled over her bare buttocks, pulled her closer against him. 'Nice outfit,' he said after a while. He fingered a strap of her garter belt.

'Glad you like it,' Tyler said, and hugged him hard as Dan forced his way into her mind. Dan, who had given her the first one, gift-wrapped, during cocktails at the White Whale restaurant on Fisherman's Wharf. It was red and frilly with lace. He'd added a pair of nylons to the box. Without his asking, she'd excused herself and put them on in the restroom. And now he was dead, his savaged body on display – not his body, she reminded herself. Just a wax dummy.

'What's wrong?' Abe whispered.

She shrugged. 'I don't know.'

He took hold of her shoulders and eased her away. He stared into her eyes. 'I know what's bothering *me*,' he said.

'What?'

'Tomorrow.'

She moaned.

'I don't want to leave you.'

'We could stay another day.'

'I'd like to, but that would only be putting it off.'

'Let's keep putting it off,' Tyler said through a tight throat. Her eyes felt hot. Then they filled with tears. She lowered her head as the tears started sliding down her cheeks.

'When do you have to get back for your job?'

She shrugged.

'*Do* you have to get back for your job?'

She looked up at him. 'Do you want me to starve?'

'No. I want you to come with me.'

'You do?'

'Of course. I . . . I think you and I . . . I guess the thing of it is, I love you.'

'Oh, Abe.' Sobbing, she threw her arms around him. 'I love you so much.'

For a long time, they held each other. When Tyler finished crying, she wiped her eyes on the shoulder of his shirt and kissed him.

'Well, now that's settled . . .' he said.

'What'll we do?'

'Join Jack and Nora at the Happy Hour.'

'About tomorrow.'

'Whatever we decide, we'll do it together.'

'I do have to get back to LA. Some time.'

'Can you postpone it a few days?'

'Sure. I guess so.'

'Why don't we check with Nora, then? If everybody agrees, we'll head on over to my place.'

'Your place? What place?'

'The Pine Cone Lodge. It's a resort hotel up at Shasta.'

'It's *yours*?' Tyler couldn't keep the astonishment out of her voice.

'Dad's and mine. He's been after me to take over running the place so he can work in some more fishing. I won't start right away, though. Hell, he's waited this long. We can spend a while just fooling around. It's pretty nice up there. You can see how you like it, see if it's the sort of place where you might like to settle down, raise some kids . . .'

'Kids?'

'You know, those tiny little human things.'

'My God, Abe.'

'If all that fresh air is too much for you, or you want to hang onto your job, I've had an offer from an old buddy with the LA Sheriff's Department. He was pretty miffed when I turned him down. I'm sure he'd be more than happy, though, to . . .'

'No way,' Tyler said. 'I've never had anything against fresh air, and my job . . .' she shook her head, 'I can live without it. Besides.' She stared into his eyes. 'LA's no place to bring up kids.'

Grinning, he said, 'Well.'

'Well,' Tyler echoed. She kissed him again. 'I guess I'd better put some clothes on.'

'Don't do it on my account.'

Abe watched while she stepped into her pleated skirt and pulled her white cashmere sweater over her head. Sitting at the dressing table, she fastened a thin gold chain around her throat. Abe stood behind her, looking at her reflection as she brushed her hair and applied lipstick. Turning her head slightly, she studied a faint red blotch on the side of her neck. She wondered if she should try to cover it with makeup.

'How'd you get that?' Abe asked.

'You should know.'

He looked perplexed. 'Did *I* do that?'

'With your very own mouth, darling. I could show you five or six more, but since I'm already dressed . . .'

'It can wait till after dinner, I guess. It'll give me something to look forward to.'

She decided to leave it alone. After all, nobody would notice the blemish except perhaps Nora and Jack, and they were probably well aware that she and Abe had spent the afternoon making love. They had likely been busy with a similar pastime themselves.

She got up from the dressing table, slipped into her sandals, and picked up her purse.

'You've got your key?' Abe asked.

She nodded. He opened the door for her, and took her hand as they walked into the courtyard. In spite of the breeze, the late afternoon sun felt hot on Tyler's back. The air smelled sweet, an aroma of pine mixed with the fresh ocean scent. 'Is your Pine Cone Lodge like this?' she asked.

'It's a bit larger. You can see it for yourself tomorrow. Do you think Nora will mind the side trip?'

'I doubt that. She's always on the lookout for an adventure. Especially where there's a man involved. As long as Jack's going to be with us, I don't think she'll squawk.'

'We should change the driving arrangement so they can travel together.'

'So *they* can travel together?'

Abe squeezed her hand. 'Well, I wouldn't mind a new passenger. You're prettier than Jack.'

'Flatterer.'

They walked past the rear of Gorman Hardy's Mercedes, a reminder that Brian Blake had disappeared. Blake, the motel owners and their daughter. Though there'd been some speculation during lunch about the missing four, Tyler hadn't given them a thought all afternoon. She suddenly felt a little guilty about that, as if she'd selfishly ignored their plight, as if she'd neglected her duty to worry about them.

Whatever happened to them, she told herself, they won't be any better off with me worrying.

Besides, she didn't know the girl at all, had only spoken briefly with the father when they checked in, had seen the mother just for a few moments last evening at the restaurant, and disliked Brian Blake.

That shouldn't matter, she thought. If something awful happened to them, you should be concerned.

Okay, I'm concerned. Right now, I'm dwelling on them instead of thinking about myself and Abe. That's concern. I hope they're all right. There.

What could've happened to them?

Her mind suddenly filled with a picture of Maggie Kutch grinning, opening a red curtain to expose a display of Blake and the others, their mutilated bodies sprawled on the bloody floor of a room, Blake's head torn from his neck, his open eyes staring at her.

'God,' she muttered.

Abe looked at her.

'I got thinking about Blake and the others,' she explained. 'I hardly even know them.'

' "Every man's death diminishes me because I am a member of mankind",' Abe quoted.

'Do you think they're dead?'

'I have no idea, really. But I'd guess it's a strong possibility.'

'Do you think the beast . . .?'

'If you asked Captain Frank, I'm sure he'd say Bobo's behind it. I don't know about that. But it's pretty obvious that a lot of people get themselves murdered in this town.'

'I can't believe there's actually some kind of monster.'

'It's been my experience that most monsters are human.' He opened one of the double wooden doors of the Carriage House, and followed Tyler inside.

They stepped toward the deserted hostess station. The gooseneck lamp over its reservations book was dark.

'Dinner?' called a teenaged girl rushing toward them from the dining area. Her blonde hair was gathered into a ponytail. She wore a black skirt. Her white blouse was primly buttoned at the throat. 'I'm Lois,' she said before Abe could respond. 'I'll be your hostess for tonight.'

'The missing Lois,' Abe said.

'No, I'm not the one who's missing. It's my cousin, Janice, and . . .'

'Your father was looking for you earlier,' Abe told her. 'I see he found you.'

She rolled her eyes upward. 'Oh, that. He found me, all right. Boy. Now I know how the slaves felt. Too bad Lincoln didn't free me while he was at it. Anyway, you want a table for two?'

'We'll get back to you, Lois, after we've put away a couple of cocktails.'

'Oh, you're here for the Happy Hour.'

'Then dinner.'

'I could put you down now, if you'd like, and save you a nice table by a window.'

Tyler smiled. In spite of Lois's enslavement, she seemed eager to do the job well.

'Okay,' Abe said. 'How about two tables for two? We're with some friends.'

'I'd be glad to seat you together.'

Tyler said, 'Separate tables will be fine.'

Abe gave the girl his name, and she entered it in the reservations book. It was the only name on the page. 'Fine, Mr Clanton. Shall I call you in about an hour?'

'Perfect,' he said. 'You're very good at this. I thought your father planned to have you cleaning rooms?'

'He made me do some this afternoon. What a drag. This is much better. This is kind of fun, I guess.'

'Okay. Well, we'll see you later.'

They stepped around the partition and entered the cocktail lounge. Tyler looked immediately toward the corner booth they'd occupied yesterday. Nora and Jack were there.

So was Gorman Hardy.

'Damn,' she muttered.

'And you without panties.'

Tyler laughed. She felt herself blush, slightly embarrassed in spite of her pleasure that Abe was so aware of the fact. 'He'll never know,' she said. 'Besides, I don't think he'd be interested.'

Abe patted her rump. 'Any man would be interested.'

Nora spotted them and waved. Hardy, after a glance over his shoulder, slid his pair of drinks to the end of the table and scooted off the seat. He remained standing while they approached.

'Good evening, Tyler, Abe,' he said.

Tyler nodded but made no effort to smile. Abe shook the man's offered hand.

She sat down and pushed herself sideways. The leatherette upholstery felt cool through her skirt, then warm when she passed over the place, near the center, where Hardy had been sitting. She moved over until the seat was cool again. While Abe slid in beside her, Hardy took a chair from a nearby table and planted himself at the end.

'We were just talking about you,' Nora said.

Wonderful, Tyler thought.

'Yes,' Hardy told her. 'It must have been a terrible shock for you, coming upon your former lover that way.'

She narrowed her eyes at Nora, then turned to meet Hardy's eager gaze. 'It was not one of my better moments,' she said.

'Let me extend my sympathy to you.'

'Thanks.' With a feeling of relief, she saw the barmaid advancing toward their table.

'What would you like to drink?' Abe asked.

'A margarita, I think.'

Abe ordered margaritas for both of them.

'Be kind enough,' Hardy added, 'to refresh the drinks of my other friends. And my own, of course.'

A trifle premature, Tyler thought.

Nora was only halfway through her first Mai-Tai, with her free second drink untouched. Jack had just started working on his second stein of beer. Hardy, lifting a stemmed glass, polished off his first martini. He left the olive, and reached for the second glass. His eyes settled on Tyler.

'I am, as you've already surmised, writing a book about Beast House.

I realize it would be painful to you, but if you're willing to discuss your relationship with Mr Jenson and your reactions to viewing his mannequin . . .'

'I would not,' Tyler said.

'If we could get together later for an interview . . .'

His persistence made her seeth. 'How's your hearing, Mr Hardy?'

Nora drew back her head and stared at Tyler wide-eyed as if amazed by the retort. Jack looked at his beer and seemed to be struggling against a laugh. Abe studied his folded hands.

'I would be more than willing,' Hardy said, 'to pay you for the trouble.'

Abe spoke without looking up from his hands. 'The lady said no.'

'Would five hundred dollars change the lady's mind?'

'Five hundred dollars,' Tyler said, 'would not.' She turned sideways, an elbow on the table, and stared at him. 'In my opinion, any book you write about Beast House would be just as exploitive as Maggie Kutch and her goddamn dummies. I'll have no part of it. In fact, since I'm not a public figure, my right to privacy is protected by law and if my name appears in your miserable book I'll sue your ass.'

Hardy smiled at the outburst. 'All right, Tyler. You drive a hard bargain. I'm willing to go as high as eight hundred.'

'No, thank you.'

'A thousand.'

Nora, looking distressed, said, 'That's your rent for three months.'

'I don't need it that badly.'

'How about throwing some of that money my way,' Jack said.

'I was coming to that,' Hardy told him.

'Well, all right.'

He shook his head at Tyler as if she were a stubborn child more to be pitied than condemned. 'Are you certain I can't persuade you to change your mind?'

'Positive,' she said.

The barmaid arrived with the drinks. Hardy took a bill from his wallet.

'I'll take care of ours,' Abe told him.

'There's really no . . .' Hardy started.

'I'll take care of ours,' Abe repeated in the same even tone.

They each paid. The barmaid cleared off the empty glasses and left.

Tyler's hand trembled as she picked up her margarita. Abe turned to her. His face was solemn, but he winked and clinked his glass against hers. A few crumbs of grainy salt fell from the rim, sprinkling the backs of her fingers.

'As I was saying,' Hardy's voice intruded, 'I have indeed been considering a proposition for you.'

'Fire away.'

Looking into Abe's eyes, Tyler sipped her frothy drink.

'As you know, my associate, Brian Blake, seems to have disappeared.'

Frowning, Abe turned away. 'Along with three other people,' he said.

'That's correct. And the police seem to have no clue as to their whereabouts. In fact, I was speaking to an officer only a short time ago. They've been conducting a search of the woods in the vicinity of the abandoned car, but so far they've come up with nothing at all. They suspect foul play, though I prefer to think that Brian and the girl simply ran off together and the parents went in pursuit.'

'Your theory doesn't hold much water,' Abe said. 'You've written enough mysteries to see it's full of holes.'

Hardy shrugged elaborately. 'Very true. If this were a plot, however, I'm certain I could devise a sequence of events to explain the apparent inconsistencies, to plug the 'holes' as you put it. Let me put it before you, instead, that I've been a close acquaintance of Brian Blake for several years. To say that he is a womanizer would be a gross under-statement. I have no idea what might have befallen Janice's parents, but the girl herself is probably, at this very moment, in a motel somewhere along the highway with Brian betwixt her thighs.'

'Betwixt?' Jack mumbled.

'Let's hope so,' Abe said.

'I suspect they'll return eventually, but Brian once vanished for three weeks after meeting a young lady at the MGM in Vegas. I've told all this to the police, of course. They're checking with motels along the coast. Unfortunately, I'm in no position to wait. I have commitments that require me to leave here first thing in the morning.'

He nodded at Jack. 'This is where you come in. Or you, Abe. Either of you men, I'm sure, would be more than capable of doing this little assignment. Brian's responsibility, you see, was to photograph the interior of Beast House. He'd planned to do it tonight, but since he's not here . . .'

'You want one of us to do it,' Jack finished for him.

'I'm prepared to pay a thousand dollars.'

'Cash?' Jack asked,

'Two hundred cash, the balance by check.'

'Since you're offering that kind of money,' Abe said, 'I assume you don't have permission from the owner.'

'The Kutch woman won't allow photos of the displays.'

'So we're talking about an illegal entry,' Jack said.

'I shouldn't think that would present a problem to a man of your background.'

'A piece of cake.'

Abe looked at Hardy. 'This was supposed to be Blake's job. Was he trying to break in and get those photos last night.'

'No, no. In fact, he left the camera in his room. His disappearance, I'm sure, had nothing to do with our project.'

'If you want the pictures so badly,' Tyler said, 'why don't you break in and take them yourself?'

'I've considered that option, of course. The truth of the matter, quite simply, is that I would prefer not to. I admit the venture involves a certain amount of risk. I'm not as young as these men. For me, it would hardly be a "piece of cake". That's why I'm willing to pay such an exorbitant amount to have it done by one of them.'

In other words, Tyler thought, you're chicken.

He took a sip of his martini. Then, smiling as if quite pleased with himself, he reached into his back pocket and took out his wallet. He removed two bills. Tyler saw that they were hundreds. 'Do I have a volunteer?' he asked.

Jack and Abe looked at each other.

While they hesitated, Nora blurted, 'Shit, *I'll* do it.'

Hardy chuckled.

'You think I'm kidding? I can always use some extra . . .'

'I'll do it,' Jack said calmly. 'No sweat.' He reached out and Hardy placed the two hundred dollars in his hand.

'Are you sure you want to do that?' Abe asked him.

'Hey, a thousand bucks is a thousand bucks.' He grinned at Hardy. 'You've got the camera, film, flash equipment?'

'They're back in my room. I'll give you a check for the balance when you pick them up.'

'What is it you want, exactly? Just pictures of the dummies?'

'That's basically it. I'll require good coverage of each display, perhaps one long shot for the overview, and two or three from a closer range for details. I would also like the attic stairway and the attic itself, if possible. The nursery, if you're able to unlock its door. And the cellar. The cellar is extremely important. According to my sources, you should find a hole in its floor. A fairly large hole, perhaps two or three feet in diameter. I would like both a long shot and a close-up of that hole, if it exists.'

'Okay,' Jack said. 'You got it.'

'I'll go with you,' Nora said.

'No way, babe.'

'Oh, come on. You'll need a lookout, won't you?'

'I'll look out for myself,' he assured her.

'Please. I won't be in your way. I'd like to see what that place is like at night. Bet it's creepy as hell.'

'You just stay with Tyler and Abe.'

'Whether it's dangerous or not,' Abe told her, 'it is illegal. Better that you stay out of it.'

She frowned at her Mai-Tai, then at Jack. 'I don't think I like the idea of you going in there alone.'

'He won't be going in alone,' Abe said.

A chill crawled through the pit of Tyler's stomach. She stared at Abe. He put a hand on her thigh. 'Don't worry,' he said. 'We'll be back before you know it.'

'I can take care of it myself,' Jack told him.

'Sure you can. But you won't let your buddy miss out on the fun, will you?'

Tyler cut into her lamb chop. She forked a bite-sized piece and stared at it. Her mouth was dry. She didn't want to eat the lamb, or anything else.

'I'm sorry,' Abe said.

'I know. I'm sorry, too. That bastard.'

'Jack?'

'No, of course not. It's not his fault. It's that goddamn Gorman Hardy.'

'I can't let Jack go in alone.'

'I know you can't. I wouldn't ask you to. But don't you think there's any way you can talk him out of it?'

'A thousand dollars is a good piece of money. Besides, I've known Jack for a lot of years. He's a guy who likes to take chances. He gets a kick out of it. Don't let on to Hardy, but he could've got Jack to go in there for a six-pack of Dos Equiis.'

'What if I give him a thousand dollars not to? I'll let Hardy have his goddamn interview, and turn the money over to Jack.'

'You'd do that,' Abe asked, 'to stop him from going in?'

'To stop you.'

He looked down at his plate as if no longer able to bear her tormented eyes. 'I'll see if I can talk him out of it. I know he won't take your money, though, so forget about giving that interview.'

'Do you think he'll listen?'

'I could stop him, if I had to. But he's my friend. I know how eager he must be to get in there. Right now, he's probably hoping there *is* a beast just to make things more interesting.'

Tyler peered across the dimly lighted dining room at the corner table where Jack and Nora sat. Jack looked like an overgrown kid, grinning as he shoveled steak into his mouth.

'You think he really wants to do it that badly?'

'I know he does.'

'What about you?'

Abe raised his eyebrows. 'What do you mean?'

'Are you hoping there is a beast just to make things more interesting?'

He stared at her with solemn eyes. 'A lot of killing's gone on in that house. Whoever's behind it – or whatever – murdered Dan Jenson. I take that personally.'

'You didn't even know Dan.'

'You loved him once. If his killer's in that house and happens to come after me and Jack – well, it'll even things up a little. I don't expect that to happen, but if it does I'd be pretty damn happy about it.'

22

Janice's wait in the black room seemed endless. She regretted breaking the light bulb. She was glad to have a weapon, but the total darkness was bad. Some comfort came from the feel of the carpet under her rump and feet, the wall against her back. She even welcomed the pain of her wounds and the gurgling hunger growls of her stomach, for they helped confirm the reality of her body – a body she couldn't see and sometimes doubted.

Her hands roamed constantly over invisible, bare skin. Sometimes she stretched out flat to feel the carpet and the solid floor on the length of her. In that position the floating, disembodied sensations faded.

Her mind wandered restlessly.

What if nobody should come? What if they left her here to starve? She would die of thirst before starving. God, her mouth was dry. Her teeth felt like granite blocks.

She hadn't eaten since dinner last night. Breaded pork chops, white rice dripping with teriyaki sauce, iced tea. She wished she had a gallon of iced tea now. She would drink it straight from the pitcher, spilling some, letting it stream down her neck and chest.

They'll come, she told herself. Sooner or later. They wouldn't have brought me here and bandaged me just to let me die. They'll keep me alive for the beast.

Oh God, the beast.

But I'll fool them. They'll open that door and I'll be out like a flash and cut them up if I have to, they won't get me, they won't take me alive.

Or maybe the door will open and it'll be Dad or maybe the cops. They must be looking for me. But they wouldn't know where to look.

If only she had stayed home last night. It's a punishment. She'd had the hots for Brian and now she has to pay. What happened to Brian? He's probably dead. Maybe he's alive, though. Maybe in the house. A prisoner.

Somebody is. Somebody with a baby.

Maybe the house is full of prisoners.

That's why Kutch built it without windows. Not to keep out the beast, the way she sometimes claimed on the tours, but to keep her prisoners in.

Janice was sprawled flat on the floor, arms and legs stretched out, face pressing the carpet, her mind drifting from thought to thought when she suddenly heard footsteps. Her heart gave a lurch. She thrust herself up and crawled to the left, one hand raking the darkness in search of the wall. Her fingernails scraped against it. She slid her right hand sideways and felt the doorframe.

The footsteps sounded very close.

Patting the carpet, she tried to find the bulb. She'd left it near the door's edge, its jagged glass down so she wouldn't cut her fingers groping for it.

She heard the metallic scrape and snick of a key pushing into the lock.

Where is it?

Then the side of her right hand swept against the bulb. She clenched the grooved base, and started to rise as the door swung inward. The figure of a girl was silhouetted against the blue light from the corridor. She had a bag clamped under her chin, a can in one hand, a key in the other. Gasping, she took a quick step back as Janice lunged at her. The bag dropped to her feet.

Janice, surprised by the stranger's smaller size and apparent youth, couldn't bring herself to slash out. Instead, she grabbed a handful of the girl's T-shirt and yanked her forward. She hooked an arm around the girl's back, twisted, and slammed her against the doorframe. The girl grunted, but her left hand swung up, hammering the can against Janice's face. The blow stunned her. She staggered backwards, hanging onto the squirming body, and they both fell.

Janice was on the bottom. She rolled. She caught hold of the flailing arms, forced them to the carpet. As the girl bucked and writhed under her, she crawled up the body. She straddled the chest, used her knees to pin down the arms.

'Get *off* me,' the girl demanded. 'Get *off*!' Her legs flew up. A knee smashed against Janice's back. 'Bitch!'

Janice raised a fist. The girl's face, dim in the blue light from the corridor, looked fierce. But very young. She was probably thirteen or fourteen. She was part of this, though. She had to be taken care of. Janice shot her fist down. As it descended, the body jerked under her. The light swept away. A moment after her fist smashed the sneering face, the door banged shut.

She was in blackness again.

She punched blindly in a rage, each blow hurting her knuckles sending pain up her wrists and forearms.

The girl was sobbing. 'No. Stop. Please!'

'Shut up. Don't move or I'll kill you. I swear I'll kill you.' To prove her point, she clutched the girl's throat.

'I promise.'

'Okay.' She relaxed the pressure, but kept her fingers around the throat. 'How do I get out of here?'

'You can't.'

'Just watch me.'

'You can't,' the girl sobbed. 'The door's locked.'

'You unlocked it.'

'Just to . . . get in. When I kicked it shut, it locked again. Try it . . . if you don't believe me.'

'Where's the key?'

'In the hall. I dropped it in the hall.'

'You mean we're both locked in?'

'Yeah, and you'd better not hurt me or you'll be sorry.'

Janice slapped her face. 'Who else is in the house?'

'You'll find out.'

She slapped her again. 'No more wise answers, you little shit. Who's here?'

The girl sniffled. 'Maggie,' she muttered. 'And Wick. And Agnes. And my mom and brother.'

'I heard a baby.'

'That's my brother, Jud. He's six months.'

'And the beast?'

She hesitated.

'Do they keep it here?'

'They don't *keep* it. This is its home.'

'It just wanders around loose?'

'Sure.'

'Great.'

'They'll come looking for me. When I don't come back . . .'

'That's just fine. I'll be ready.'

'You can't get out of here. It's impossible. You think my mom'd still be around if there was a way out? She's tried over and over but we always catch her.'

'*We*? You mean your own mother's a prisoner and you help the others?'

'We can't let her get away. She'd ruin everything.'

'What kind of a kid are you?'

She didn't answer.

'What's your name?'

'Sandy. Sandy Hayes.'

'Well, Sandy Hayes, *I'm* going to get out of here and ruin everything and you can fucking well count on it.'

'Fat chance.'

Janice squeezed her throat. 'Okay, lie still. Don't even think about moving.' She climbed off Sandy's body. Kneeling beside her in the darkness, she felt along the T-shirt to the waist of the pants. She fingered a belt. She opened its buckle and tugged it free. Draping it around her neck so she wouldn't lose it, she patted the pants' pockets. They seemed to be empty. She unfastened the waist button, slid the zipper down, and yanked the pants down Sandy's legs. The girl wore shoes. She pulled them off, set them nearby, and finished removing the pants.

She tried to put them on. They were much too small. After a short struggle, she gave up.

She slid her hands up Sandy's legs and hooked her fingers under the elastic of her panties.

'Hey!'

'Shut up.' She drew the panties down. She tried them on. The filmy material had enough stretch to allow a snug fit. She clutched Sandy's thigh. 'Okay, sit up and take off your T-shirt.'

She waited for it.

'Here.'

She swept out a hand and took the garment. Spreading it against herself, she could feel that it was far too small. A tight fit would hurt her wounds. She stretched its neck, yanked until it tore, then split the fabric all the way down. She put the shirt on easily, like a smock, the opening at her back.

Using the belt, she bound Sandy's feet together.

The hands were still free. A bra might be useful for binding them. She moved her hand up the girl's belly and paused at the feel of tape. 'You're bandaged?'

'I hurt myself.'

Her fingers glided over Sandy's skin, touching two more bandages: one on the side, one on a breast. The girl wore no bra.

'How'd you get hurt?' Janice asked.

'The same as you.'

'What?'

'You know.'

'The beast?'

'Yeah, the beast. He gets rough sometimes when we're getting it on.'

'You *let* him?'

Janice's wrists were suddenly clenched in the dark.

'You'll let him, too. Just wait and see if you don't. You'll get so you can't wait for him to come to you.'

Janice jerked free of the girl's grip. 'You're nuts,' she said.

'You'll see. Even Mom loves it. She won't admit it but she loves it.'

'That's why she tries to escape.'

'She just does that 'cause of the baby. She's afraid they might kill it, but they won't. See, they think she'd try to kill herself if they hurt Jud, and they don't want that. They want her alive.'

'What for?'

'Same reason they want you alive. They want you. *He* wants you. To make babies.'

Janice felt a cold tightness inside, 'Babies?' she murmured. 'Whose babies? Wick's?'

'Don't be silly. Wick isn't allowed to touch us. He tried to screw me once, and Maggie beat the crap out of him. Nobody touches us but Seth or Jason.'

'Who are they?'

'Sons of Maggie and Xanadu.'

'Xanadu?' A chill scurried up Janice's back as she recognized the name from Lily Thorn's diary.

'He was murdered last year. Mom's boyfriend killed him and Zarth and Achilles, but he paid for it. Maggie nailed him.'

'My God,' Janice muttered. 'Those were all . . . beasts?'

'Zarth was Maggie's, and Achilles was Agnes's. Xanadu was the father of both. Rucker killed all three, but Maggie nailed him before he got Seth or Jason.'

'So . . . there are *two* beasts in the house? You said before there was just one.'

'*You* said there's one.'

'You didn't correct me.'

'Why should I?'

'You little shit.'

'Look, why don't you get off me? We can be friends. You're gonna be here a long time, and it'll be nicer for you if I like you. I can bring you up special stuff.'

'How do I get out of here?'

'I already told you, it's impossible.'

'Why?'

'They'll get you.'

'We're upstairs?'

'Yeah, but . . .'

'Which way's the staircase?'

'That's for me to know, you to find out.'

Janice straddled the girl again, and pinned her arms down. 'You said they'll be up here soon. They're gonna find you dead if you don't give me answers. Now which way are the stairs?'

'It doesn't matter. You can't get out anyway.'

'*Tell* me, damn it.'

'The door locks on the inside. Even if you . . .'

'Where's the key?'

'I'll never tell.'

Janice slapped her hard. The girl yelped with pain and twisted under her.

'Go ahead,' Sandy sobbed. 'Do whatever you want. I won't tell.'

Janice wondered where she'd lost the broken light bulb. Somewhere nearby probably. But she doubted she could force herself to cut up the girl anyway. She considered tearing off Sandy's bandages and digging into her wounds. The thought of it repulsed her.

'The key you used to get in here,' she said. 'Does it open the front door?'

'No,' Sandy murmured.

'Maggie must keep it with her.'

The girl sniffed, but didn't answer. Janice knew she must have guessed right. In that case, she would need to subdue Maggie to get the key – maybe take on the entire household. It seemed hopeless. 'The beasts,' she said.

'They're in the house?'

'Maybe.'

'If they're not here, where are they?'

'Sometimes . . .' she sobbed, 'sometimes they're in Beast House.'

'What do they do, wander back and forth?'

Sandy didn't answer.

'How do they get from here to there? They can't just go walking across the street?'

'Yes, they do.' She said it too quickly.

And Janice suddenly knew.

It seemed crazy, but so did the rest of this, and it appeared to be the only possibility. The original beast, Xanadu, had burrowed from the hillside and come up in Lilly Thorn's cellar. Why not another tunnel – one connecting the two houses? It would have to be a couple of hundred yards long, but why not? A tunnel leading from one cellar to the other. How else could the beasts move freely between the two houses? They certainly couldn't travel out in the open, walk across Front Street and through the gate without someone spotting them sooner or later. There had to be a tunnel.

And she would find it.

She didn't want Sandy to know what she had discovered.

'I guess I'll have to get that key from Maggie,' she said.

'You haven't got a chance.'

'We'll see.'

She climbed off Sandy, rolled her over, and sat on her rump. She slipped the T-shirt off, and fingered the three strips of tape used to hold the gauze pad to her left breast and shoulder. The ends on her breast had come unstuck, and dangled like small flaps. Gripping them, she peeled the bandage away from her torn flesh. She tugged the clinging strips off her back. When she tore away the pad, she had three strands of tape, each nearly a foot in length. She tugged on them. They seemed sturdy enough.

She pressed Sandy's wrists together and bound them tight with all three strips. She made sure the knots were secure. Then she rolled Sandy onto her back.

'Open your mouth.'

She felt the lips. They were pressed together. So she pinched Sandy's nostrils shut. The girl squirmed and moaned, but finally opened her mouth. Janice stuffed the bandage pad inside. She tore the center strip of tape off the bandage on her belly, stretched it across Sandy's open mouth, and pressed it firmly to her cheeks.

'No noise,' she warned. 'If I hear anything out of you, I'll come over and knock you senseless.'

The groaning stopped. The only sound was air hissing through Sandy's nose.

Janice put the T-shirt on again. She draped the girl's pants over her back, and crawled away slowly, one hand gliding over the carpet in search of the light bulb. She found it. Its jagged edge pricked her palm. Carefully, she picked it up. Near the door she came upon the can Sandy had dropped.

She left the pants and bulb and can against the wall where she could find them easily, then tried the door knob. It didn't move. The door had locked on shutting, just as Sandy had claimed. Though she was fairly sure the key had fallen in the corridor, she spent a long time searching for it.

Finally, she gave up. She sat beside the door, her back against the wall. She spread the pants across her lap and placed the bulb on them, base up. Then she picked up the can. It felt cold and heavy. It sloshed when she shook it.

Some kind of soda.

Her tongue rasped against the roof of her mouth, touched the dry blocks of her teeth.

Sandy had used the can as a weapon, bludgeoning her with it. Janice could use it that way, too, when the door opens.

But not if she drank its contents.

She licked the condensation off the can, and waited.

23

'Suppose we go along,' Nora said, 'and wait in the car?'

'Okay by me,' Jack said. He hitched up his sweatshirt and slid his Colt .45 semi-automatic under the waistband at the back of his jeans.

'I think it'd be better,' Abe said, 'if you and Tyler stayed behind. I don't know where we'll be leaving the car, but if a cop goes by and sees you two waiting, he might get suspicious.'

'Yeah,' Tyler agreed. 'That makes sense.'

'Why don't you wait at the Carriage House?' Jack suggested. 'Have a couple of drinks. We'll be back before you know it.'

Abe finished folding the thick blue blanket from his bed.

Jack slung the strap of Hardy's camera case over his shoulder.

'Go on out,' Abe told him. 'I'll be right with you.'

When they were alone, Tyler stepped into his arms. He held her gently against him. 'Just try not to think about it too much,' he said.

'Oh, sure.'

'Go over and have a couple of cocktails with Nora. Tell her about our plans for tomorrow. If you don't gulp your drinks, we'll be on our way back by the time you finish your second.'

'You'd better be.'

'Count on it.' He kissed Tyler, and she pressed herself fiercely against him. Slipping his hands under her sweater, he caressed the warm smoothness of her back. 'I love you so much,' he whispered.

'I love you, Abe.' She looked up at him. Her eyes were glossy with tears.

'Don't let some guy pick you up while you're waiting, or I'll be really ticked.'

She almost smiled.

With a last, brief kiss, he eased out of her arms. He picked up the blanket and opened the door. Jack was standing by the Mustang, his hands on Nora's hips.

'Let's get,' Abe said. He opened the driver's door, dropped the blanket onto the back seat and turned to Tyler. 'See you in a while,' he said.

She nodded. With the back of one hand, she rubbed her nose. Nora went over to her. They stood side by side, silhouetted by the porch light behind them.

'If you're not back in an hour,' Nora said, 'we'll call in the Marines.'

'Dipshit,' Jack called. 'We *are* the Marines.'

She gave them a thumbs-up and Tyler waved as Abe backed the car away. He waved out the window, then turned on the headlights and steered up the center of the courtyard.

'This is gonna be good,' Jack said.

'I just wish we could've done it without the girls knowing.'

'No chance of that with Gory-babes popping the question in front of everyone.'

'He's such an asshole.'

'Gutless, too. Shit, if I was gonna write a book about that joint, I'd want to get in there at night and see what it's like. Catch the ambience, you know?'

'He'll probably want to interview us about that,' Abe said, and turned left onto the road.

'If he does, let's charge him for it. He throws around money like confetti.' Jack rolled down a window and stuck his elbow out. 'His check better be good.'

'He wouldn't dare stiff you.'

'I oughta hang onto him till I can get to a bank tomorrow.'

'I wouldn't worry about it.'

'You'd better. It's half yours, you know.'

'I'm just along for the ride.'

'Bullshit. It's fifty-fifty.'

'Just buy me a drink when we get back to the inn, and we'll call it even.'

'You're an easy guy to please.'

He slowed down as they entered the business area. The coffee shop where they'd eaten lunch was still open. So was a liquor store across the road from it, and a bar on the next block. Otherwise, the town seemed closed up for the night. The road was deserted except for a few cars and pickup trucks parked along its curbs.

'By the way,' Abe said, 'how do you feel about the girls coming along with us tomorrow?'

'To the lodge, you mean?'

'That's what I mean.'

'Well, all right!'

'No objections?'

'You kidding me?'

'Tyler'll check with Nora about it tonight.'

'Nora will come. She's hot for my bod. Who can blame her? It's magnificent. So's hers, by the way.'

'I've noticed.'

He laughed. 'Yeah? How'd you manage that? You haven't taken your eyes off Tyler since we got here. You two are really in it deep. Man, I've seen the way you look at each other. When's the wedding?'

'We haven't quite gone that far yet.'

'Really? That's a surprise.'

'I want to spend a few more days with her before . . .'

'That's it. Let her stew. Don't wait too long, though, or *she*'ll propose to *you*.'

'I might enjoy that. What about you and Nora?'

'That gal's a real kick in the ass, but I'm not gonna even think about getting tied down. Shit, I been married to the Corps for twelve years. I need to hang loose, you know? But I sure don't mind hanging loose with her for a while. I've never had it so good, I'll tell you that right now.'

Abe slowed down and turned his head to the left as they passed Beast House. The ticket booth was shuttered, the lawn beyond the fence dark. No light came from any of the windows. 'Looks deserted,' he said.

'Wonder if Bobo's in there.'

'I wouldn't get my hopes up.'

The road curved and slanted upward into the wooded hills. Abe eased off the gas pedal. He searched the road-sides for a place to pull off, soon found a wide shoulder and swung over. He killed the headlights and engine.

In the silence, Jack said, 'Do you think there is such a thing?'

'As Bobo?'

'Yeah.'

'Doesn't seem likely. But you never know.' He reached in front of Jack, opened the glove compartment, and took out his .44 caliber Ruger Blackhawk. He removed a box of cartridges and stuffed it into a pocket of his nylon windbreaker. On the floor under his seat, he found his flashlight.

They climbed from the car.

Abe lifted the blanket off the back seat and clamped it under one arm. He pushed the barrel of his revolver down the back of his jeans. He held onto the flashlight, but didn't turn it on.

They walked straight across the road, stepped through undergrowth on the far side, and leaped over a ditch. They made their way up the slope until Abe could no longer see the road through the trees. Then they traversed the hillside, following it downward. The foliage and dead pine needles crunched loudly under their shoes.

In a hushed voice, Jack said. 'You know me, I'm not your superstitious type.'

'Except you carried a rabbit's foot through three tours in Nam.'

'Well, that's different. What I'm saying is, I'm the last guy who's gonna believe in shit like ghosts and monsters, right?'

'So you say.'

'But, you know, this Bobo's supposed to come from that island near Australia. Look at Australia. They've got animals there that look like jokes: kangaroos, wallabies, wombats, platypuses. Who's to say Captain Frank's old man couldn't have run into some weirdo species and brought one back with him?'

'He could've.'

'We oughta keep an eye out for it.'

'I intend to.'

'We oughta try and bag the fucker.'

'We oughta try and get in, take the pictures as fast as we can, and get back to the girls. I don't know about Nora, but Tyler's so worried she can hardly keep herself together.'

'Gory's paying a thousand for a few snapshots of the place, figure what he'd pay for that thing's carcass.' Jack laughed quietly. 'He'd probably get the damn thing stuffed and take it on *Johnny* with him.'

'Why don't *we* get it stuffed and stand it up in the lobby of the lodge?' Abe suggested.

'Yeah! We can say it's Bigfoot.'

'On second thought, Tyler wouldn't go for that.'

'See? She's already got you by the short hairs, and you're not even married yet.'

Abe elbowed him. Then, through the trees ahead, he saw the side fence of Beast House. He pointed to the right. They started across the hillside, well above the fence and parallel to it.

'We'll just sell the thing to Gory,' Jack whispered. 'For a bundle. We'll buy a beauty of a Chriscraft for the lodge.'

'A deal,' Abe said. 'If it exists and if it shows up.'

'Just our luck, it won't.'

They followed the hillside in silence. Abe studied the house and its grounds as he walked. The yard looked deserted. The windows at the house's side and rear were dark. He was certain that lights would be on if anyone was inside either cleaning the rooms or standing guard.

'If we find it occupied,' he said, 'we'll abort.'

'Right,' Jack agreed.

'As of last summer, at least, they apparently didn't have an alarm system or guard . . .'

'Just the beast.'

'So unless they've tightened up security since then, we shouldn't have any trouble along those lines.' The slope eased downward into a ravine. At its bottom, Abe trudged through the low brush to the rear corner of the fence. He followed the fence, watching the distant road until the house blocked it from his view. Glancing over his shoulder at Jack, he said, 'Any cops show up, we ditch our weapons. If we can't pull a disappearing act, let them take us for breaking and entering. That's a minor charge next to resisting arrest or firearms possession.'

'We can always pick them up later,' Jack said.

Abe stopped near the center of the fence. He tossed his blanket over the spikes. It dropped silently to the grass on the other side.

'Watch out for those points,' Jack said. 'You'll be singing soprano.'

They both hit the fence at once, grabbing the crossbar, leaping, bracing themselves with stiff arms, planting a foot on the bar between the sharp uprights and springing down. Abe snatched the blanket from the ground and dashed across the yard, past a ghostly white gazebo, into the dark moon-shadow cast by the house. With Jack close behind him, he climbed the porch stairs.

The floor creaked under his weight as he stepped to the back door. He peered through one of its glass panes. Except for murky light from the windows, the interior looked dark. He moved aside. 'This is your game,' he whispered. 'You want to do the honors?'

Jack rammed an elbow through the lower right pane. A burst of shattering glass broke the stillness. Shards rained down on the other side of the door, clattering and tinkling as they smashed against the floor.

'Such finesse,' Abe said.

'Got the job done,' Jack told him, and started to reach through the opening.

'Wait. Let's give it a couple of minutes, see if anyone shows up.'

Abe watched the door windows. He listened carefully. No lights appeared inside the house, and he heard only the night sounds of the breeze and crickets and a few distant birds. He also heard his own heartbeat. It was loud and fast. He licked his lips. His stomach felt knotted and there was a slight tremor in his leg muscles. He didn't like waiting.

'Okay,' he said finally.

Jack put an arm through the broken pane. He felt around for a few seconds. Then Abe heard the dry snap of a clacking bolt. Jack withdrew his arm, turned the knob, and opened the door. Its lower edge pushed through fallen glass as it swung wide. Jack twisted his hand on the knob to smear his fingerprints, and let go.

Abe followed him into the room. Turning on his flashlight, he swept its beam over cupboards, a long counter and sink, an old wood-burning stove.

Jack whispered, 'Should I get a shot of the kitchen?'

'Let's start upstairs and work our way down. Grab one of here on the way out, if you feel like it.' Abe shut off the flashlight and led the way down a corridor between the staircase and wall. Stopping in the foyer, he glanced at the parlor, at the hall leading to the gift shop. Both were dark and silent.

Fighting an urge to hold the banister, he started up the stairs. No matter how softly he put his feet down, every riser creaked and groaned in the silence. If nobody heard the window break, he told himself, nobody will hear this. The thought stole into his mind that perhaps the smashing glass *had* been heard. Instead of coming to investigate, it had decided to lie in wait.

It.

This place is getting to you.

At the top of the stairs, he looked to the left. Moonlight from a casement window cast a pale glow into the corridor. He saw no movement. To the right, the hall was black. He remembered a window at its far end, but the curtains of the Jenson display blocked out any light from that direction.

'Let's do the kids' room first,' he said. 'Work our way toward the front.'

With a nod, Jack walked quickly up the hall. Abe followed, watching his friend shove the curtains aside as he passed close to the wall. The motion of the fabric forced an image into Abe's mind of something alive hidden within the enclosure. His skin prickled when the velvety folds swung against him. He rushed through the gap.

On the other side, he looked over his shoulder. The curtains still swayed as if stirred by a wind. He switched the flashlight to his left hand, reached behind his back, and drew out his revolver. The walnut grips were slippery with his sweat, but the weight of the weapon felt good. He held it at his side as he entered the bedroom.

With an elbow, he nudged the door. It swung almost shut. He pressed his rump against it until the latch snapped into place.

Jack found the drawcords and pulled. The curtains skidded apart.

'Make it quick,' Abe whispered. He shoved the flashlight into a pocket of his windbreaker and stuffed the barrel of the revolver into the front pocket of his jeans.

The room had two windows, one on the wall facing town, the other facing the backyard and hills. Stepping over the wax bodies of Lilly Thorn's murdered sons, he hurried to the far window. He looked out at the rooftops of the businesses along Front Street, at the lighted road. A single car was heading north. He shook open the blanket and covered the window. 'Okay,' he said, and shut his eyes to save his night vision.

Through his lids, he saw a quick blink of brightness. He heard the buzz of the automatic film advance.

Jack whispered, 'Say cheese, fellas,' and snapped another picture. Then one more. 'Done,' he said.

Abe swung the blanket over one shoulder. He pulled out his revolver and returned to the door as Jack closed the curtains. Faced with the prospect of opening the door, he wished he hadn't shut it. His left hand hesitated on the knob.

Calm down, he warned himself.

He thumbed back the hammer of his .44 and yanked the door wide.

When nothing leapt at him, he let out a trembling breath. He kept his revolver cocked and stepped into the corridor.

'Fingerprints,' Jack said in a cheery voice that seemed too loud. 'I'll get 'em.'

Abe heard the knob rattle. Then Jack moved past him and crossed the hall to the nursery door. He tried the knob. 'How are you at picking locks?' he asked.

'Forget it,' Abe told him.

'I could kick it in.'

'Just grab a shot of the closed door. Hardy can run it with a mysterious caption. Hang on while I get the window.' He eased down the hammer and pushed the gun into his pocket as he rushed to the end of the corridor. Holding the blanket high to shield the window, he closed his eyes until Jack took the picture. Then he slung the blanket over his shoulder again, drew his revolver, and turned around.

Jack was gone.

The curtains surrounding the Jenson exhibit swayed a bit.

Abe's stomach tightened. 'Jack?' he asked.

No answer came.

He listened for sounds of a struggle, but heard only his own heartbeat.

He walked quickly toward the enclosure. Trying to keep the alarm out of his voice, he said, 'Jack, hold it in there.'

The bottom of the curtain flew up. He jerked back the hammer. A dim, bulky shape rose from a crouch. 'What's wrong?' Jack asked.

'You trying to spook me?'

Jack laughed. 'I didn't know you were spookable.' He held up the curtain while Abe ducked underneath.

'Let's just stay together, pal. I can't cover your ass if I can't see it.'

Jack let the curtain fall.

Abe took out his flashlight and turned it on. All around them, the red fabric hung from the ceiling to the floor. The air seemed heavy and warm, and he felt strangely vulnerable closed off from the rest of the corridor.

Jack stepped backwards, pushing out a side of the curtains, and raised the camera to his eye.

'Just a second.'

'What?'

Abe shone his beam on the wax figure of Dan Jenson. The body lay on its back near the forms of the Ziegler father and son, its throat torn open, its eyes glistening in the light. 'He's out of this,' Abe said.

Jack nodded. 'Yeah. I should've thought of that.'

Crouching, Abe grabbed its right ankle and dragged the mannequin through the split in the curtains. He switched off his light, stood up straight, and peered down the dark corridor. He breathed deeply. The cool air tasted fresh.

A thread of light flicked across the floor from behind him. He heard the camera hum. A shuffle of feet as Jack changed position for another shot.

In his mind, he heard Tyler gasp, saw the color drain from her face, her eyes roll upward, her knees fold. He felt her weight against his chest as he caught her. He remembered the vacant look in her eyes afterward, and how she'd rushed out the door ahead of him and vomited.

He raised his foot. He shot it down hard on the dummy's face, feeling the wax features mash and crumble under the sole of his shoe.

Jack came up behind him. 'Jesus! What're you . . .?'

'Taking care of business,' Abe said, and stomped the head again. 'Let the goddamn sightseers gawk at someone else.'

When he finished, he shone his light on the floor. Nothing remained of the head but a mat of smashed wax and hair, and two shattered eyes of glass.

He turned off his light.

'Let's get on with it,' he said. 'The girls are waiting.'

24

Janice had lost her battle of wills with the soda can. She had gulped down half the cola, then sipped the rest of it slowly, savoring its cold sweet taste. She felt guilty as she drank. The full can might've made a good weapon. But she'd found reasons to justify drinking: she was mad with thirst, she figured the soda would give her energy needed for her escape, and she only had two hands anyway. She wanted one hand for striking with the bulb, the other for thrusting Sandy's pants into the face of whoever might open the door. ·

Or *what*ever.

Of course, she could use the full can instead of the pants. With the can, she might be able to stun the intruder with a good shot to the head. The pants seemed like more of a sure thing, though. They would give her momentary advantage by blinding and confusing her opponent.

As the final drop fell into her mouth, she wondered whether she'd made the right choice. Too late now for worrying about it.

She squeezed the center of the can. It made noisy popping sounds as it collapsed. Something jagged scraped her palm. She explored the area with her fingertips, and found that the aluminum had split open at a corner where the can had buckled, leaving sharp edges. She gripped the top and bottom of the can, and wobbled them back and forth, cringing at the noise, until the two halves parted. She pressed their edges against her bare thighs. They felt very sharp.

As she wondered how the new weapons might be used, she heard a quiet creaking sound from the corridor. Her heart thumped wildly. She wished she had time to check on Sandy, make sure the girl was still bound and gagged, but she had to be ready.

She stuffed the base of the light bulb between her lips. It tasted bitter. Getting to her knees, she swung the pants over her back, the legs across her right shoulder. She gripped each of the can halves, their crimped edges outward.

From the corridor came the sounds of slow footsteps. Shoes on the hardwood floor. Shoes.

So it's a human. Thank God.

She pressed herself against the wall. Her heart was thudding a fierce cadence. She sidestepped twice to get farther from the door.

The footsteps stopped. She heard a quiet, 'Hmm?' Then a sound of crinkling paper.

The food bag Sandy had dropped.

A key snicked into the lock. The knob rattled. The door eased open. In the blue light from the hallway, Janice saw a hand on the knob. A forearm. Then a heavyset woman leaned into the gap and peered through the darkness. 'Sandy?' she asked. It sounded like Thandy. The husky voice was unfamiliar to Janice. Whoever the woman might be, she wasn't Maggie Kutch. Sandy had mentioned another woman, an Agnes.

'Thandy, why'th it dark?'

The door opened more. Agnes took a step into the room and bent over slightly as if to see better.

'Wha'th going on?' she asked. She sounded confused, but not alarmed. She bent over farther, and pressed one, hand on her knee. Her other hand dangled in front of her, holding the paper bag.

Sandy started to make grunting noises.

Agnes jerked upright.

Rushing up silently behind her, Janice rammed both sides of her face with the cans. A bellow of pain tore the silence. Agnes clutched her face and turned around. Janice raked out with one can, slashing the back of her hand. Whining, Agnes reached out. She knocked the can away. She wrapped her arms around Janice. Her stench was sour and putrid. She felt hot, and her clothes were damp.

Her breath exploded out as Janice slammed a knee into her belly. Her arms loosened. Janice drove her knee again into the soft belly. Agnes doubled. Her face hit the light bulb, jarring the metal base against Janice's teeth. Squealing, she fell to her knees.

Janice staggered away from her.

The door was still open.

She ran to it. Glancing down the corridor, she saw no one. She pulled the door shut and tugged the key from its lock. She clenched the key. Sandy had said it wouldn't open the front door, but maybe Sandy had lied.

Just past her door, the corridor stopped at a blank wall. In the other direction, it led past several doors. Most were shut. Near the far end was a banister. Janice took the bulb from her mouth and started toward the stairs, walking fast. She was fairly sure this level of the house must be deserted. Otherwise, someone probably would have responded to the commotion by now.

Deserted, maybe, except for Sandy's mother and the baby who must be locked in one of these rooms. As she hurried past the closed doors, she wondered about setting them free. Too dangerous. If she started opening doors, God only knew what she might run into. Once she was clear of the place, the cops could take care of the rest.

She came to the first open door. She glanced in as she stepped by it with two quick strides. The room was dark and silent.

One down, two to go.

She rushed by them both without incident. As she reached the banister, she flinched at a sudden knocking sound from behind. She had expected it, but it startled and unnerved her.

'He-e-elp!' Agnes yelled. Her voice was muffled. 'He-e-elp! Lemme out!'

Holding her breath, Janice started down the stairs. The area below was dim with blue light. She crouched to see under the ceiling. At the foot of the stairs was the foyer. And the front door!

The open area to the left was dark. To the right was the arched entryway to a room. That room was lighted blue. A dark curtain draped its wall. She saw a few scattered cushions covered with glossy fabric like satin, but no other furniture. She kept her eyes on its entry as she hurried to the bottom of the stairs.

The front door was no more than ten feet ahead. If she went to it, though, she would be in full view of anyone inside the room.

Sandy had claimed the key wouldn't fit.

Janice decided not to chance it. Eyes on the blue room, she eased around the newel post and tiptoed up a dark passage that ran between the staircase and wall. She followed it toward the back of the house and entered a room with a slick floor. This, she guessed, must be the kitchen. She closed the swinging door and felt along the wall for a switch. She found it. Blue light filled the room.

She stepped past the stove. Along the far wall was a sink, a long counter, cupboards above and below, but no door. Near the sink was a knife rack. She set down her bulb and key, her remaining half of the soda can. She selected a paring knife and a long knife with a serrated edge. She slid the paring knife into her panties. Its blade was cool against her hip. She clutched the long knife tightly in her right hand, and stepped to a closed door beside the refrigerator.

It wasn't locked. She pulled it open. Shadowy stairs led down to a blue lighted cellar. She pulled the door shut behind her. The air felt chilly. Shivering, she looked down at the blue carpet on the cellar floor. She saw a few scattered cushions.

Please, she thought, let it be empty.

Let there be a tunnel.

She took a deep shaky breath, and raced down.

The cellar was not empty.

With a gasp, Janice stopped abruptly. She squeezed the railing and stared through the dim light at the three figures.

They were against the wall. Two men and a woman. Naked and motionless. Their heads were drooped strangely. Janice took a step backwards up one stair before she noticed that their feet weren't touching the floor.

'My God,' she muttered.

She descended the rest of the stairs. Slowly, she approached the bodies.

Corpses, she thought. They're corpses.

One thigh of the woman was missing big chunks as if bites had been taken.

From the chest of each body protruded a steel point.

They're hung up on hooks.

Janice felt sick and numb. She moved closer. Her legs were trembling.

All three bodies were badly torn, sheathed with dry blood that looked purple in the blue light.

She raised her eyes to a face, and slapped a hand against her mouth to hold in a scream.

One eye was shut. The other stared down at her. The tongue was lolling out. In spite of its contorted features, she recognized the face. It belonged to Brian Blake.

She looked at the face of the man suspended beside Brian.

NO!

Then at the woman.

IMPOSSIBLE! NO!!

Backing away, shaking her head, she stared at the faces of her parents. She fell to her knees. She covered her face.

From behind Janice came the metallic clack of a door latch. She twisted around and looked at the top of the stairs. The door to the kitchen swung open.

Jack, standing in the doorway, snapped a photo of the stairs leading into the cellar of Beast House. 'Okay,' he whispered.

Abe turned on his flashlight. He stepped past Jack and started down. Halfway to the bottom, he stopped. He leaned over the railing and shone the beam into the space below the stairway. Nothing there. He leaned over the other side. A steamer trunk against the wall, but nothing else. Turning slowly, he raised his beam to the corner and swept it around the entire cellar. Along the walls, he saw a collection of old gardening tools: shovels, a rake and a hoe. Shelves, mostly empty but some lined with canning jars. Little else. The dirt floor was clear except for a few stacks of bushel baskets.

'Looks, okay,' Jack said.

With a nod, Abe stepped down the rest of the stairs. He turned around and aimed his beam at the steamer trunk. Its latches were in place. 'Get whatever you need,' he said, 'and let's go.'

Jack, at the foot of the stairs, took three shots. Abe kept his eyes shut against the quick bursts of light from the flash.

'Let's go.'

'Hang on. I want a look around.'

Abe gave him the flashlight. As Jack started to wander the cellar, he gazed up the stairway at the door. He imagined it swinging shut. If someone came from above and locked it . . .

'Over here,' Jack said.

'What?'

'That hole Gory talked about.'

Abe hurried across the dirt floor and joined Jack beside a crooked stack of bushel baskets. The hole at his feet was roughly circular and almost a yard in diameter. It didn't go straight down, but dropped away at a steep angle in the direction of the cellar's rear wall.

Abe covered his eyes. Jack took a photo.

'That's it,' Abe said. 'Let's go.'

'Take this a minute.' Jack handed the camera to him.

'What am I supposed to do with it?'

'Hang onto it.'

Crouching, Jack aimed the flashlight into the hole. He lowered his face close to the edge and peered in.

'The girls are waiting,' Abe said.

'I know.'

'We're already late.'

'A couple more minutes won't make that much difference.' Lying down flat, Jack started squirming head first into the hole.

'You've got to be kidding,' Abe muttered.

'I won't go far.' Jack's voice came up muffled.

'The fun part,' Abe said, 'will be backing out.'

In the last glow before the light faded out, Abe fell to his knees and clutched a cuff of Jack's jeans. Then he was in darkness. Looking over his shoulder, he watched the dim patch of gray at the cellar door.

They could be up there, right now. They could be on their way out of the house.

He yanked Jack's cuff. 'Come on.'

Jack was no longer moving.

'Are you okay?'

'Yeah.' His voice sounded thick as if he were speaking with a pillow over his mouth. 'Goes on and on,' he said.

'Come out of there.'

'Oh, shit.'

'What?'

'Something up ahead. Looking at me.'

Abe felt the hair rise on the back of his neck. 'What is it?'

'Let me get closer.'

'What *is* it? Is something *coming*?'

'It's not coming. Huh-uh. It's . . . an owl head. No owl, just its head. Man, there's all kind of bones and shit down here.'

'Great. Time to leave.' He grabbed Jack's ankles and started to drag him out.

Moments later, light appeared in the hole – a glowing rim around Jack's shoulder. His head appeared. Abe kept pulling. Jack worked his way backward, elbows shoving at the clay.

Then he was out.

'Infuckingcredible,' he said. 'I could only see about twenty feet, but you oughta see all that shit. Bones all over the place down there.'

'Human?'

'Nothing that big. Maybe dogs, cats, squirrels, raccoons. Smaller stuff, too, like from mice or rats. Why don't you take a quick look?'

'Thanks anyway.'

'I wonder if I could get a picture of that stuff. Worth a try, huh?'

The quick, soft sounds of footsteps rushing down the stairs sounded more animal than human.

Janice pressed herself against the moist clay wall of the tunnel and stared into the blue light. Her heart felt as if it might smash through her ribs. Her breath came in harsh sobs. She clutched the knife with both hands, blade toward the cellar, and held her breath.

She only glimpsed the beast as it passed the tunnel entrance. Her knees sagged. She braced herself against the wall to keep from falling. Her stomach lurched. She swallowed the hot, bitter fluid that rose in her throat.

This – or one like it – was the thing that had raped her. Its claws had ripped her flesh, its snouted mouth had sucked and gnawed her breasts, its penis had been deep inside her and she could still feel the hurt from it.

This – or its brother – was the thing that had murdered her parents and . . .

She heard a wet, tearing sound.

Pushing herself from the wall, she stepped across the tunnel. Shoulder against the cool clay on the other side, she eased her head past the corner.

The beast, hunched over slightly, had its back to Janice as its claws tore flesh and muscle from her mother's thigh. She watched, too stunned to move, as it raised the dripping load to its mouth.

A corner of her mind whispered for her to flee, to make good her escape while the creature was busy eating.

No, she thought. I can't.

The sound of its chewing made her gag. She covered her mouth and ducked out of sight, but she could still hear it.

Jesus. It's Mom. It's Mom the thing is . . .

And then she ran.

She wasn't quiet about it. She knew she should sneak but she couldn't, she rushed across the carpet and a savage growl rumbled from her throat and the thing heard her and looked around with scraps of flesh hanging from its mouth and it looked at her with blank pale eyes as if it didn't give a damn and kept on chewing as it turned and swung a clawed hand at her face. She ducked and rammed the blade into its belly. It roared, spewing the food onto her hair and back. Staggering, away, it smashed against her mother. The body's legs splayed out with the impact. The arms jumped. The head wobbled. The spike slipped out of sight as if sucked into the chest hole, and her mother dropped onto the beast, driving it to its knees.

Janice stepped back, staring at the tangled bodies, half convinced for a moment that her mother was somehow alive. Then the beast, down against the wall with the knife still embedded in its belly, grabbed her mother by the throat and groin and hurled her. The corpse flew at Janice, hit the carpet at her feet, and rolled toward her with flopping arms and legs.

Janice leaped out of its way, spun around, and raced back into the tunnel.

She should have kept on stabbing, damn it.

She cried out in agony as her shoulder slammed against the wall of the tunnel. She bounced off, collided with the other wall, and fell down sobbing. Quickly, she got to her feet. She stumbled onward, one arm out to feel her way, going slower now that she realized the tunnel had turns. Her right hip burned. She felt a warm trickle down her leg. The paring knife in her panties must have cut her during the fall. She pulled it out.

Except for her own sobbing and gasps for air and the slap of her feet on the hard earth of the tunnel floor, she heard nothing. If the beast was coming after her, it must be far back.

Maybe it was too badly hurt to follow.

It can see in the dark, that much she knew from the diary.

She wished she had burned the fucking diary.

None of this would've happened. She'd be safe in her bed at the inn and Mom and Dad would still be alive. How had it gotten to them, anyway? They must've come looking for her. God, she wished she'd stayed home. It was all her fault. She wished she'd never heard of Brian Blake or Gorman Hardy. They got her into this.

I got myself into this.

I got Mom and Dad killed.

But I can save myself. I can save that woman – Sandy's mother and the baby – if I can just get out of here. Get help.

Get to Beast House and out to the street. Get to the cops.

The wall went away from her knuckles. She felt blindly with both hands, discovered that the tunnel turned to the left, and hurried through the blackness.

What if there's a locked door at the other end?

There won't be. There can't be.

What if the other beast is waiting up ahead?

No.

What if Wick or Maggie or Agnes or Sandy or all of them reach Beast House first and cut me off?

I've still got a knife, she told herself. I'll rip them up.

And then her thoughts froze as she heard gasping, snarling noises from behind. She rushed on, driven by terror, heedless of the possible turns ahead. The sounds grew louder as she ran. She pumped her arms hard, stretched out her legs as far and fast as she could. Her lungs ached as she sucked breath. All her wounds burned as if their edges were splitting open from the strain. She winced as her right arm scraped a wall. Without slowing, she changed course toward the center.

Now the beast was very close. From the sound of its rattling growl, it could be no more than a yard or two back.

Her left side hit a wall. The blow twisted her. She slammed the moist surface, bounced off it, and fell. She landed on her back.

Staring up into the darkness, she couldn't see the beast. But she heard a dry hissing sound that was almost like laughter.

Something wet and slimy forced her legs apart. The T-shirt tugged at her, lifting her back from the ground for a moment before it came off her shoulders. She let its sleeves shoot down her limp arms. She felt the points of claws slide down her belly. Her panties were ripped away. Something warm splashed onto her belly, her chest. Its blood.

She felt its hot breath on her face.

'Bastard!' she shrieked, and drove the knife upward. It punched into the thing's flesh. She jerked it out and stabbed again as the beast wailed in pain. Then it batted her hand. The knife jumped from her numb fingers.

From just beyond her head came a scraping sound like wood sliding over dirt.

The beast clutched her shoulders, its claws digging in. Squirming, she rammed a knee into the thing. It kept its grip and knocked her leg aside. Its penis thrust against her thigh.

Its face, just above her own, was dead white and shiny like the flesh of a slug. Saliva spilled onto her from its wide mouth. She wondered why she could suddenly see its face and before she could figure it out the face jerked wildly upward.

The roar that blasted her ears sounded as if the world were exploding.

One of the creature's eyes was a shiny hole.

A side of its snout flew apart.

Its jaw disintegrated.

She turned her face away as what was left of the beast's head dropped onto her.

In the silence, Janice's ears rang.

A man's voice said, 'Holy shit.'

25

'How're you doing, ladies?' the barmaid asked.

'I could go for . . .' Nora started.

'I think we should leave,' Tyler interrupted.

'They said we should wait here.'

'I don't care.' She got up from the table.

Nora shrugged at the barmaid. 'Guess that's all,' she said. She joined Tyler, and they hurried through the dimly lighted cocktail lounge. 'What's the rush, kiddo?'

'I can't stand waiting any longer. They said they'd be back in an hour.'

'So they're twenty minutes late. Maybe it took them longer to get in than they planned.' In spite of the reassuring words, Tyler heard tension in her friend's voice.

She pushed through one of the heavy wooden doors and held it wide while Nora followed her out. She took a deep breath of the chilly night air. Stopping by the antique carriage near the entrance, she gazed toward the road. No cars passed.

Nora wrapped her arm across her breasts, apparently cold in her filmy orange blouse. 'Why don't we go back in and have another drink? They'll be along pretty soon. I'm sure they're all right.'

'Are you?'

'Sure. Come on, it's better than standing out here freezing our tails.'

'I'll go crazy if I sit still any longer.'

'What do you want to do?'

'I don't know. Why don't they come?'

'They're probably on the way, right now.'

Tyler caught her breath as headlights brightened the road. She stared through the trees, and sighed when the vehicle sped past. Just a pickup truck.

'Let's take the car,' she said.

'Okay. At least it'll be warm.'

They followed the walkway to the courtyard.

'Have you got your keys?' Nora asked.

'Yes.'

'Do you want to change first?'

'No.'

She rushed to keep up with Tyler's quick pace. 'What's the big hurry? We'll probably just pass them on the road, anyway, and have to turn around.'

'At least we'll know they're all right.'

'We could miss them, you know. If they parked on a side road . . .'

'We'll turn around and come back if we don't spot the car.' She unlocked her Omni, dropped behind the steering wheel, and reached over to flip up the lock button for Nora. She keyed the ignition as Nora climbed in. When the door thumped, she shot the car backwards.

'For Christsake, calm down.'

'I can't.' She sped toward the road.

'There's no reason to panic.'

'They should've been back by now.'

'I know, I know.'

'Goddamn it.'

'It's all right.'

'No, it's not.' She eased off the accelerator only long enough to glance both ways, then swung onto the road with a whine of skidding tires, and floored it.

Nora buckled her safety harness. 'Come on, do you want the cops to stop you?'

Shaking her head, she let up on the gas pedal. The lights of town appeared as she rounded a bend. She passed the closed service station. On the next block, she slowed almost to a stop as a Volkswagon backed into her lane from a parking space in front of a tavern. Then she had to stop for the town's blinking red traffic signal. The intersection was clear. She gunned through it.

'Keep an eye out for the Mustang,' Nora said. 'I'll take the right, you take the left.'

Few cars were parked along this end of the street. Just ahead, the curb in front of Beast House's long fence was vacant. So was the shoulder across the road. Passing Beach Lane, however, the corner of her eye picked up a bright beam.

'Hold it,' Nora said.

She hit the brake. As the car jerked to a stop, she looked past Nora at the single approaching light. 'That can't be them,' she said.

'Maybe they lost a headlight.'

She waited. The steering wheel was slick under her hands. She rubbed them dry on her skirt. The wool made whispery sounds against her stockings. Then she heard the sputtery grumble of an engine. Twisting around, she peered out the backseat window.

A motorcycle came scooting up the lane, followed by a plume of exhaust and dust swirling red in its taillight. Hunched over its bars was a hatless Captain Frank, his white hair and beard streaming in the wind. The cycle tipped away as it made a quick turn behind the Omni and sped north.

'Look at that sucker go,' Nora muttered.

Tyler stepped on the gas. She drove slowly past Beast House, staring at the grounds behind its fence, at its dark front porch, its windows. It looked bleak and deserted. She could hardly imagine anyone actually entering such a place at night.

Abe and Jack could be in there right now, she thought. Sneaking through pitch-black rooms and corridors, knowing they're late and trying to hurry . . .

Or maybe lying torn and dead, two more victims of . . .

No!

They're okay. They're all right. They're fine. They have guns. They're trained soldiers. Marines. Leather-necks.

Beast House fell out of sight as she followed the road's curve up the wooded hillside, but her mind stayed inside the house. She spread open curtains and stared at maimed bodies, wondering which were wax, which flesh, which Abe.

'There it is!' Nora blurted.

Tyler's eyes fixed on the Mustang. It was parked off the road just ahead. Its lights were out. She gazed through its rear window as she swung behind it. Nobody seemed to be inside.

'Shit,' Nora said. She reached over and patted Tyler's leg. 'Just sit back and try to relax. They'll be along any minute.'

Tyler killed the headlights and shut off the engine.

'I've got an idea,' Nora told her. She opened the glove compartment and pulled out the Automobile Club guidebook. 'This'll help pass the time. Turn on the overhead light.'

Tyler twisted the headlight knob. The ceiling light came on. Nora flipped through the pages. 'Let's see, now. Shasta. Here we go, Shasta Lake. It's here! The Pine Cone Lodge. My God, it's got five diamonds! The place must really be something, huh? Expensive, though. One person, fifty-five to sixty bucks a night. Two people, one bed, sixty-five bucks. Forty-five units. Twelve miles north of Redding, off Interstate-5. One and a half miles south of Bridge Bay Road turnoff. Overlooking Lake Shasta. Open all year. Spacious, beautifully decorated rooms with shower/baths, cable TV, fireplaces. Heated pool, whirlpools, free boats and motors. Fishing, water-skiing. It doesn't exactly sound like a dump.'

Tyler shook her head.

'You think you'll stay on there?'

'If he asks me to,' she muttered. 'Damn it, where *is* he?'

'Look, it probably took them ten or fifteen minutes just getting to the house from here.'

'Let's go over.'

'To the house? Are you nuts?'

'You can wait here if you want.'

'Christ, girl!'

Tyler turned off the light and opened her door. Before she could shut it, she saw Nora crawling across the bucket seats. She waited beside the car until her friend climbed out, then hurried across the road.

'We're hardly dressed to go traipsing through the woods.'

'I don't care.'

'You'll get runs in your stockings.'

Tyler stepped down the steep bank of a ditch, her sandals sliding on the dewy undergrowth, tendrils clutching at her ankles.

Nora skidded, landed on her rump, and picked herself up. 'Shit. Have you flipped or something?'

Without a word, Tyler leaned into the opposite slope and started to climb.

'If you've got it into your head to go inside the house, forget it. For starters, we'd never make it over the fence.'

Reaching the top of the embankment, Tyler clasped Nora's hand and pulled her up. She stepped through dark spaces between the trees.

'Besides, we haven't got guns. They've got guns. Not that I'd go in there if we did have . . .' Nora's voice faltered.

From down on the road to their left and far ahead came the quick, slapping sounds of feet racing over the pavement. Tyler's heart lurched. She stared through the pines at the moon-spotted road.

'It's them,' Nora whispered.

As hard as she listened, Tyler only heard one set of footfalls. Fighting an urge to cry out, she darted back to the edge of the ditch. Poised above the drop-off, she gazed down the road and saw a single runner dashing up the center line. She groaned as she recognized Jack's blocky figure.

'Oh Jesus,' Nora muttered.

Tyler threw herself down the embankment, stumbled through the growth at its bottom, scurried up the other side and lunged onto the road.

'Jack!'

The man kept running closer with short, choppy steps. He flapped an arm at her. 'Get in your car,' he called.

'Where's Abe?'

'At the house. He's all right. I've gotta meet him in front.'

'What happened?' Tyler asked.

'Later.' He hunched over the Mustang's door, shoved a key into its lock, opened it and climbed in.

'He said Abe's all right,' Nora gasped, coming up behind her. 'Told you . . . there was nothing to worry about.'

'Something happened,' Tyler said. Her near panic, she realized, had subsided into frustration.

They stood by the road while Jack swung the Mustang into a U-turn. As it shot off down the slope, Tyler raced to her car. 'Get in back,' she ordered. Jerking open her door, she flicked up the lock button for Nora.

The instant her friend was inside, she spun the steering wheel. The Omni made a tight circle, its headbeams sweeping the edge of the woods.

'Douse the lights,' Nora said.

She killed them, remembering that Jack had kept the Mustang dark as he sped down the slope.

'Geez, this is exciting.'

'Something must've gone wrong.'

'Stop worrying. Abe's all right.'

'I'll stop worrying when I see him.'

'You must really have it for that guy.'

'I do,' she said.

Hurtling around the curve at the bottom of the hill, she saw the Mustang's dark shape glide to the curb. It stopped in front of the ticket shack. She glanced at the grounds behind the fence, but saw no one.

Where's Abe? her mind screamed.

Jack leapt from the car. He left his door open, dashed around the front, and flung the passenger door wide.

Tyler steered in behind the Mustang. She hit the brakes. Her Omni skidded to a halt inches from the rear bumper. She jumped out, and took two quick steps before she saw, over the hood of her car, Abe come staggering from behind the ticket booth with a body slung over his shoulder in a fireman's carry.

Without room to step between the cars, Tyler crawled across the hood. She swung her legs down and rushed to Abe's side.

The girl he carried, wrapped in a blanket, was a blonde with hair hanging down over her face. Crouching, Abe lowered her feet to the sidewalk. Though she seemed conscious, her legs buckled. Jack grabbed her beneath the armpits, and the two men helped her into the Mustang's passenger-seat. Jack shut the door as Abe turned to Tyler.

'Are you okay?' she asked.

He nodded.

'What happened? Who's she?'

He shook his head. 'I'll go back in your car,' he said. 'Quick, let's get going.'

The sudden harsh knocking on Gorman's door sent a jolt through him, reminding him of last night when Marty and Claire had startled him from sleep. His calm returned when he realized it must be Jack and Abe. He checked his wristwatch. Eleven ten. They'd been gone for an hour and forty minutes, so they must've spent at least an hour inside Beast House shooting pictures.

'I'm coming,' he called. He closed Captain Frank's scrapbook, and slid it into a drawer of the lamp table. Before going to the door, he switched on his cassette recorder and pocketed it.

The man waiting under the porch light was neither Jack nor Abe.

'Captain Frank!' Gorman said, and forced a smile. 'I'm glad you're here. You must have come about your book.'

The old man looked angry.

'Come in, come in. I'm sorry I didn't manage to get it back to you this afternoon, but the copy machine at that shop was out of order. They told me they'd have it repaired before tomorrow morning, so . . .'

'Where is it?'

'Safe and sound,' Gorman said.

With a wary look in his eyes, Captain Frank followed him around the foot of the bed and watched as he removed the volume from the drawer. 'I'll take it now, Mr *Wilcox*,' he said.

'If you wish.'

'The fellow at the front desk, he says your name's Hardy.'

'It's true that's the name I registered under.'

'What's your real name?'

'Hardy. Wilcox, you see, is my pen name, my nom de plume. I use it for my by-line when I write for *People*.'

'Is that so?' He sounded skeptical. 'I think you aimed to steal my scrapbook off me.'

'Nonsense. I had every intention of returning it to you.'

'Aye. Maybe yes and maybe no.' Captain Frank pulled a scuffed leather wallet from a rear pocket of his Bermuda shorts, took out the pair of fifties, and held them toward Gorman.

Gorman stood motionless, the scrapbook in both hands. 'I take it, then, that you don't wish me to write the article.'

'Now I didn't say that, did I?'

'I can't write your story if you refuse to let me use this.' He shook the volume. 'It's a treasure, and I realize it must be priceless to you. I most certainly had no intention of purloining it. I would have returned it to you, this afternoon, if I'd had any inkling you might suspect me of such treachery. Is it my fault that the copy machine malfunctioned?'

'I don't 'spect so,' Captain Frank admitted. He looked almost contrite. 'All the same, I want you to take your money back and let me have the book. I just don't feel right, letting it out of my hands. I tell you what, I'll take it home with me and you come along tomorrow, if you're still of a mind to write this up. I'll drift on over with you, and we'll get us a copy made.'

Gorman made himself smile. 'That sounds perfectly reasonable,' he said. He handed the book to Captain Frank, took the money and stuffed it into his shirt pocket. 'I do apologize,' he said, 'for inconveniencing you in this way. If I'd had any idea . . .'

'No, no. That's just fine.'

'Would you care to join me for a drink? I'm afraid I haven't any beer on hand, but does a martini sound agreeable?'

The old man's eyes gleamed. 'Why thanks.'

'Have a seat,' Gorman told him.

As Captain Frank lowered himself onto one of the twin beds, Gorman turned to the dressing table. He uncapped a fresh bottle of gin, and watched its clear liquid splash into the beaker from his travel bar. His hand trembled.

The bus is an arsenal, he thought. I could get myself shot, sneaking in there. With enough martini in his system, however, the old bastard ought to sleep like the dead.

Gorman added a dash of vermouth. He slowly stirred the mixture.

Like the dead.

He knows my name. He'll make trouble if I rob him of his precious scrapbook. Assuming, of course, he doesn't wake up and shoot me.

A pillow over his face while he's sleeping in a drunken stupor . . .

It seemed too risky.

Gorman wanted the scrapbook. Photocopies, however, would serve almost as well.

If he goes into the store with me, he might find out I lied about the machine breaking down. He might rebel, at that point, and refuse to cooperate.

He's an old man. The authorities in this podunk town might simply assume he died of natural causes. A pillow over the face in the wee hours . . .

Or he might commit suicide.

Gorman saw himself in the dark bus, taking the revolver from under the driver's seat, pressing it against the sleeping man's temple and firing.

No, no, no. Neighbors might hear the gunshot.

It was worth considering, though. If he could get away unobserved . . .

He filled two of the motel tumblers nearly to their brims, and turned to Captain Frank. 'Here you go,' he said.

'Thank you, matey.'

Gorman sat on the edge of the other bed. He sipped his martini. The old man took a hefty swallow, and sighed. 'Ah, that does hit the spot.'

'Drink up. There's plenty more where that came from.'

'Did I tell you of the time I took the tour?'

'The Beast House tour? No. When was this?'

'The very day Maggie Kutch opened it up for folks. I was just a lad. I shined shoes over at Hub's barber shop for better than two weeks, saving every penny and just waiting for Maggie to start the tours. Nobody in town talked about anything else, once it got out what she was up to – with the dummies and all. My mother, she said it was an abomination against God.' He took another long drink. 'I knew she'd throw a fit if she found out I aimed to visit the place, so I kept it to myself and went over to go in with the first bunch. You've never seen such a crowd. Half the folks in town was there, lined up to buy tickets. I knew right then word'd get back to her. I just thing of it was, you see, I half expected to find my father inside.'

'He was dead by this time?' Gorman asked.

'Aye. But I knew it was Bobo done him in, and I figured Maggie might have him in wax. I just had to see for myself, you know.' He swallowed a mouthful of martini. 'Well, my father wasn't there. I 'spect I should've been glad, but I wasn't. *Damnation*, he belonged in there! He deserved it. Bobo was his in the first place. He found it and brought it to town and it killed him. If anybody was gonna be on display like that, it should've been him. When the tour got done, I stepped myself right up to Maggie Kutch and said, "Where's my father?" She gave me a smile that made me want to smash her face, and said, "Why, son, I hear he run off with that tart from Wanda's."'

'Wanda's?'

'That was a local house of ill repute. Well, everybody on the tour laughed fit to bust. I ran off. It was all I could do to keep from crying, having me and my father shamed that way in front of everyone.'

'That must have been awful for you.'

'Aye.' He drank all but a shallow puddle, stared into the glass, and finished it off. 'If that weren't bad enough, I got a whipping for my trouble. Reverend Thompson, he saw me go in with the others and wasn't he quick to tell on me? Mother, she laid into me with a switch so I couldn't sit down for a fortnight.'

Shaking his head as if in sympathy, Gorman stood up. 'Let me freshen your drink for you, Captain.' He took the man's glass to the pitcher and filled it. Sitting down again, he said, 'Tell me about your seafaring days. You must have seen a lot of the watery part of the world.'

'Not all that much. I run a fishing boat off the dock in Brandner Bay.

That's just up the coast about ten miles.' He took a drink. 'I always had a yearn to take a voyage. Fact is, I wanted to find me that island where my father come across Bobo. I figured I'd go in and see if there was more of them creatures. I had it in my head to wipe them out. But I never got around to it. Tell you the truth, I just couldn't force myself to leave. It was like I had to stay in Malcasa and keep an eye on Beast House. It's my destiny, you know, to stalk Bobo and lay it low.'

'Do you think there might be surviving . . .?' Gorman heard the sound of a car engine. 'Excuse me for a moment,' he said. Getting up, he stepped to the window. He pushed aside the curtain and peered out, cupping his hands beside his eyes to close off the reflection.

Two cars, a Mustang and a white Omni, drove through the courtyard. They turned toward the duplex of Abe and Jack. They stopped.

'Don't know whether there'd be survivors or not,' Captain Frank mumbled. 'I 'spect there might be.'

Gorman watched the car doors open. Tyler, Abe and Nora climbed out of the Omni.

'Curious thing,' Captain Frank went on, 'there being no wildlife on the island but those creatures, and them carnivorous. I given it a lot of thought.'

Abe opened the Mustang's passenger door. He and Jack helped someone out.

'I figure they polished off all the game, back somewhere along the line.'

In the light from Abe's porch, he saw that the passenger was a girl. Her hair was mussed. Her back was toward Gorman as they led her to the door. She wore a blanket that draped her body from shoulders to feet.

'So I 'spect, since they're meat-eaters, they must've kept going by eating each other.'

Though Gorman couldn't see the girl's face, he knew she must be Janice Crogan. He felt sick.

'You get that kind of thing happening a lot in your primitive cultures. Humans. They need their protein, you know. So they have wars with themselves, eat the ones killed in battle. Used to happen all the time.'

Gorman turned away from the window. Stunned, he dropped onto the edge of his bed.

Janice Crogan.

He'd sent those two bastards out to take photos, and they'd come back with Janice Crogan.

He lifted his glass off the floor and drank.

'So I figure,' Captain Frank said, 'that what my father and the crew of the *Mary Jane* ambushed was maybe just one tribe of the hellish beasts.'

Maybe it's not Janice, Gorman thought.

Who else *could* it be?

It certainly looked like her, but he couldn't be sure without seeing her face.

'If I'm not wrong, there's gonna be another tribe out there. Maybe two or three. Aye, who knows, the island might be . . .'

'I have to leave,' Gorman said. He stood up. 'I'd like to have you stay and talk, but some friends of mine just showed up.'

'Well, I want to thank you for . . .'

'Here.' Gorman capped the gin bottle. 'Why don't you take this along with you?'

'Oh, I couldn't take your bottle.'

'Please.' He thrust it toward the old man. 'Have yourself a nightcap when you get back to your bus. I'll be along in the morning and we'll have a copy made of your scrapbook.'

'A'right, matey. Thanks.'

Gorman picked up his room key and opened the door for Captain Frank. He stood beneath his porch light and stared across the courtyard at Abe's bungalow. His heart pounded furiously. In spite of the night's chill, sweat dripped down his face.

Captain Frank stowed the scrapbook and gin bottle in the saddlebags of his motorcycle. He mounted the bike. He stood on the starter, and the engine grumbled awake. With a wave he turned the bike, gunned it past the rear of Gorman's Mercedes, and sped toward the road.

26

Someone knocked on the door as Abe held the phone to his ear and listened to the faint ringing.

'Who is it?' Jack called.

'Gorman Hardy,' came the voice from outside.

Abe nodded. Jack pulled the door open and Gorman entered. The man, looking flushed and nervous, scanned the room. 'What happened?' he asked.

Jack put a finger to his lips.

'Where's everyone else?'

'The john.'

Gorman started for the bathroom, but Jack grabbed his arm. 'Just wait,' Jack told him.

'Malcasa Point Police Department,' said the voice on the phone. 'Officer Matthews speaking. May I help you?'

'I spoke to one of your people this morning.'

'Did you get the pictures?' Gorman asked Jack.

'Sure.'

'An Officer Purcell,' Abe went on. 'I realize he's probably off duty, but I'd like to speak with him. It's urgent.'

Gorman stared at Abe.

'I'll try to reach the chief at his home,' Matthews said. 'Give me your name and number, and I'll have him call you back right away.'

'Fine.' Abe gave his name. He read the Welcome Inn's number off the phone plate.

'Very good, Mr Clanton.'

'Tell him it's extremely important. If you can't get through to him, get back to me yourself.'

'I'll do that.'

Abe hung up.

'What's going on?' Gorman asked.

'We ran into your beast.'

'Wasted the sucker,' Jack added.

The man's mouth dropped open. 'You *killed* it?'

'Blew its fuckin' head off,' Jack told him, grinning.

'Who's the girl? I saw you come in with someone.'

'Janice Crogan,' Abe said. 'Apparently, she was out near Beast House last night with your friend Blake. She was pretty fuzzy about it all, but somehow she ended up a prisoner in the Kutch place. Blake's dead. So are the girl's parents.'

'Brian? Brian's dead? No!' He shook his head in disbelief. 'It can't be! He ... he's my best friend.'

'Janice says she found their bodies in the cellar of Kutch's house while she was getting away ...'

'With one of the beasts on her tail,' Jack added.

'*One* of the beasts?' Gorman asked.

'She said there's supposed to be a second one.'

'Incredible,' Gorman said.

'She's pretty beat up,' Abe told him. 'Mostly superficial scratches and bites apparently. Tyler and Nora are cleaning her up, checking her over.'

'Will she be all right?'

'Considering what she's been through, she seems to be in pretty good shape.'

The girl sat on the toilet seat, back resting against the tank, arms hanging at her sides, eyes staring ahead as if she were in a trance.

Tyler crouched in front of her, held her knees gently. 'It's all right, Janice. It's all right, now.'

Janice shook her head.

Nora turned on the shower.

'We'll help you get cleaned up now,' Tyler said. She spread the blanket open and moaned at the sight of Janice's torn, bruised skin – the blood and the filth.

'Jesus,' Nora muttered.

Tyler slipped the blanket off the girl's shoulders. 'Can you stand?'

Janice leaned forward. Nora and Tyler, on each side, helped her up. As Nora held the girl steady, Tyler stepped behind her. The girl's stringy hair was clotted with flecks of raw flesh. Bits of bloody matter clung to her back. Tyler gagged, eyes going wet. She took a deep breath and wiped her eyes. Both Janice's shoulders were raked and punctured. Lower down, her back was striped with claw marks. Her buttocks looked rubbed raw, as if she'd skinned them in a fall.

'The shower is going to hurt,' Tyler said.

'I've got it lukewarm.' Nora glanced at Janice's back and cringed. 'God Almighty.'

'One of us better get in with her.'

'Right.'

Nora quickly stripped while Tyler hung onto Janice's arm. When she was naked, she pushed aside the shower curtain and stepped into the tub. Together, they helped the girl climb over the side. Janice's mouth sprang open and she cried out as the spray struck her back. The water sliding toward the drain turned pink. Pieces of flesh floated in it. Tyler turned away. The toilet seat was smeared with blood. She shut her eyes and breathed deeply, trying not to vomit. Through the hiss of the shower, she heard the faint ring of a telephone.

'Abe Clanton.'

'Yes. This is Wallace Purcell from the police.'

'Thank you for calling. I'm the one who talked to you this morning about Beast House. My friend had been . . .'

'Oh yes. What seems to be the trouble?'

'We were out at the beach tonight,' Abe lied. 'On our way back, we spotted a young lady who looked like she'd been in some trouble. She was over near the front of Beast House, just outside the fence. She was naked and pretty beat up. We drove over to give her aid. It's Janice Crogan.'

'You *found* her?' Purcell sounded amazed.

'She had just escaped from the Kutch house. She said they took her there last night. Brian Blake and both her parents are dead. Their bodies are in Kutch's cellar.'

Purcell said nothing.

'The girl's with us. We're here at the Welcome Inn.'

'May I speak to her?'

'She's in the bathroom.'

'Did she describe her assailant?'

'Her assailant was the beast.'

'The *beast*?'

'It does exist. It apparently lives in the Kutch house. Maggie and the others keep it as a pet, or something.'

'And Janice claims this beast attacked her and killed her parents and Blake?'

'That's it. One more thing. Janice says she wasn't the only prisoner at the Kutch place. A woman is being kept there against her will, and she has an infant.'

Abe heard a sigh. 'Okay, Mr Clanton. Thank you for the information. We'll take care of the situation, and be in touch with you later.'

'Are you going out there?'

'You bet.'

'Okay. Very good. Be careful.'

'I always am. Later.' He hung up.

'What's the story?' Jack asked.

'The cavalry is going in.'

'Without us?' Jack asked.

'We weren't invited.'

'Let's invite ourselves.'

'I plan to.' Abe rushed past Gorman and knocked on the bathroom door.

Tyler opened it. Her face looked chalky.

'How's the girl?'

'A mess. But there doesn't seem to be much bleeding.' She glanced at Gorman. Looking back at Abe, she stepped out of the bathroom and shut the door. 'What's going on?'

'I just talked to the police. They're on the way to Kutch's. Jack and I are going to meet them there.'

Her mouth twisted. 'Don't go in.'

'We'll see if they need us.'

'Oh God, Abe.'

'I want you and Nora to stay here and look after the girl. Come out to the car with us. I've got a first-aid kit out there. Patch her up the best you can. When we get back, we'll see about getting her to a doctor or hospital.' He took Tyler's hand and led her to the door.

Jack and Gorman followed them out. 'Are you coming along?' Jack asked the man.

'Certainly. This may well be the climax of my story.' He slipped the camera strap over his head.

Abe opened the passenger door. Kneeling on the seat, he opened his glove compartment and took out a plastic box. He gave it to Tyler.

'Be careful,' she said.

'Don't worry.'

Jack, standing beside her, fed cartridges into the magazine of his .45.

'Do you have a gun for me?' Gorman asked.

'Sorry.'

Tyler wrapped her arms around Abe and held him tightly.

'I wonder if we might make a quick detour to Captain Frank's bus,' Gorman said. 'It's along the way. He has quite an arsenal, and I'm sure he wouldn't mind letting me use one of his guns.'

'No time,' Jack said.

Abe kissed Tyler hard on the lips. 'We'll be back before you know it.'

'That's what you said the last time.' Her voice sounded tight and shaky as if she might cry.

'And I did come back.'

'Took your time about it.'

'I'll be quick.' He patted her rump through the soft folds of her skirt. 'Get in there and take care of Janice.'

'Yes, sir.' Her chin trembled. She turned and rushed away.

'Let's haul ass,' Abe said.

Tyler shut the door and leaned back against it. Tears rolled down her face. Through her sobbing gasps, she heard the car speed off.

Damn it, how could he go and leave her again?

Because he's a man.

Because of his pride.

Because it's in his nature to help out even if it means putting himself on the line.

If he weren't that way, he wouldn't be Abe and maybe he would lack whatever it was that made her love him so desperately.

Damn it.

She wiped her face with a sleeve of her sweater. Then she pushed herself away from the door and walked across the deserted room.

From the bathroom came the steady rushing sound of the shower. She opened the door and stepped inside. Nora and Janice were dim shapes through the plastic curtain.

With a handful of toilet paper, she cleaned the blood off the seat. She flushed the paper.

'How's it going?' she asked, and skidded open the shower curtain enough to see inside.

Nora shook her head. Her lower lip was clamped between her teeth. She was sobbing as she gently slid a bar of soap over Janice's back.

Janice stood under the nozzle, her hands flat against the wall, her forehead resting on the tiles. With the blood and grime washed away, her tan lines were visible – a pale strip across her back, a pale triangle on her buttocks. The sight of them made the girl seem more real, more vulnerable than before – a teenager who sunbathes and likes the beach and somehow got caught up in the horror.

The bruises and scrapes would fade away, in time. Tyler hoped the bite marks and claw scratches would leave no permanent scars. A shame on a girl so beautiful. But they looked shallow, as if the beast had been struggling with her, maybe trying to hold her still, not kill her. If she was lucky, they might go away, too.

Crouching, Nora soaped Janice's legs.

'I've got a first-aid kit,' Tyler said. 'Abe thinks we might take you to a hospital when he gets back.'

Nora looked up. 'Where'd he go?'

'Back to the house. The Kutch place.'

Janice turned her head sharply and stared over her shoulder at Tyler.

'Jack and Hardy went with him. They're planning to meet the police there.'

'Oh shit,' Nora said.

Janice frowned. Her eyes looked alert. 'Police? They're going in?'

'I guess so.'

The girl pushed herself away from the wall. She squinted as the spray struck her face, and turned around. Dropping the soap, Nora stood up. 'What . . .?'

'I'm going.' She bent over and rubbed the backs of her legs to get the suds off.

'I think you'd better stay with us,' Nora told her. 'You're in no shape to . . .'

'I've gotta be there.'

Tyler grabbed a wet arm as Janice climbed over the side of the tub.

'I'm all right.'

The girl seemed steady on her feet. Tyler let go, pulled a towel off a nearby rack, and gave it to her. Janice started rubbing her hair furiously.

'The police will take care of it,' Nora said. 'You ought to lie down in bed and wait.'

She shook her head. 'It's my parents. It's *me*. I've gotta be there.'

Nora shut off the water. 'You haven't got any clothes.'

She dried her face. She winced, her face going tight with pain as she blotted water from a torn shoulder. 'I've got clothes. In my room.'

'Or a car,' Nora said, climbing from the tub. 'The cops impounded your parents' car.'

'I'll drive her,' Tyler said.

'Oh shit,' Nora said.

'You guys get dry. I'll get Janice some clothes.'

She rushed from the bathroom. She grabbed her handbag off Abe's bed and ran out the door. The cool breeze felt good as she raced across the courtyard.

This time, she thought, there won't be any waiting, any stewing as she wondered if Abe was all right. In ten minutes, she would be with him. If he'd already gone into the house, she would go in, too. She would be at his side and know.

She shoved her key into the lock, twisted it, opened the door and swept a hand along the wall until she found the light switch. The lamp between the beds came on.

Her bed was still unmade from her afternoon with Abe, its coverlet on the floor where they'd kicked it down, the sheets rumpled. On the other bed was her open suitcase. Bending over it, she snatched out a neatly folded pair of blue jeans, the yellow blouse she'd worn on the tour, a pair of fresh pink panties and her sneakers. A bra? The straps might hurt Janice.

She considered changing herself. Not enough time. Clutching the clothes to her chest, she dashed from the room. The door smashed shut as she leapt off the stoop.

Except for Hardy's Mercedes and her own Omni, the courtyard was vacant. She saw no one wandering about. The windows of the other bungalows were dark.

Stopping at her car, she pulled open the driver's door. A shoe fell as she reached inside to flip up the lock button. She opened the back door, flung the clothes onto the back seat, and tossed the shoe in after them.

Then she rushed to Abe's bungalow. She twisted the knob.

Locked. Of course.

She pounded the door.

Nora opened it. Her hair looked dark and matted as if she hadn't taken time to dry it enough, but she was dressed except for her blouse. 'I thought you were getting Janice some . . .'

'They're in the car. She can dress on the way. Let's go.'

Holding the blouse to her breats, Nora leaned out the doorway and glanced around.

'It's all right. Come on.'

Nora turned away. 'Come on,' she called into the room.

Janice didn't pause to question her. Nora stepped aside and let her pass. 'This car?' she asked, nodding toward the Omni. She fingered scratches at her side, but made no attempt to cover herself, as if unaware of her nakedness.

'I tossed some clothes in the back seat for you.'

With a nod, Janice started for the car. She moved stiffly, wincing as she climbed down the stairs, limping a bit as she stepped to the car. Nora, hurrying ahead of her, opened the rear door.

Tyler rushed to the driver's side and climbed in. The car wobbled as Nora dropped onto the passenger seat. Tyler twisted the ignition key.

'Let's take it easy,' Nora said. 'We've got an injured girl with us.'

'Hurry!' Janice blurted from the back seat.

Tyler rammed the shift into reverse and hit the gas pedal.

27

Abe eased off the accelerator as a pickup swung in from a sidestreet. It sped down Front ahead of them. It didn't stop for the blinking red traffic signal, and neither did Abe.

'Five'll get you ten that's the chief,' Jack said.

Just the other side of Beach Lane, it swerved onto the shoulder. Its tires kicked up dust as it lurched to a stop. Abe steered behind it.

'You lose,' Abe said as a stocky woman leapt from the pickup. Linda? No, Lucy, he recalled. She was out of uniform. She wore jeans and a flannel shirt. The shirt tail hung out, drawn in around her waist by her gunbelt. She glanced toward Abe's car, then turned and jogged past the front of her truck.

Abe, Jack, and Gorman climbed out. Gorman followed a few steps to the rear. Abe raised an open hand as their approach caught the attention of the others.

Four others. Lucy, Chief Purcell, and two officers in uniform. They stood near the open door of a police car. Another patrol car was parked just beyond them. The flashers were dark.

'Abe Clanton,' Abe said. 'This is Jack Wyatt, Gorman Hardy.'

Purcell nodded. 'You should've stayed at the Inn. But since you came, I want all of you to keep your distance. Stay here at the road unless we tell you otherwise. We don't want civilians getting mixed up with this.'

'Yes, sir,' Abe said. 'It's your ballgame. If you need a hand, though, give us a shout.'

'We'll take care of it,' Purcell said.

One of the patrolmen knelt on the car seat and came out, a moment later, with a shotgun. Abe recognized it as a .12 gauge Ithica semi-automatic.

'There's no rear exit to this place,' Purcell said.

'No windows, either,' Lucy added.

A quick flash of light made Lucy flinch. Purcell and the others frowned at Gorman.

Gorman snapped another photo. 'Thank you,' he said, and lowered the camera.

Purcell shook his head. 'Let's go.' He walked up the dirt driveway toward the house, Lucy at his side, the other two following.

'Are we simply going to stand here?' Gorman asked.

'We'll do as he said.'

Gorman took a step away, but Jack clamped a hand on the back of his neck. 'Stay,' he ordered. He looked at Abe. 'Do you think they amscrayed?'

'Their pickup's in front of the garage.'

'They must know the girl got away. They've got three stiffs in the basement, that woman and baby prisoners, and a beast in there. How're they gonna cover up all that?'

'I'd say they can't,' Abe said.

'Hope those cops know what they're doing.'

'They asked us to stay out of it. We'll stay out of it.'

Near the dark front porch, Purcell pointed to each side. The two uniformed patrolmen spread out. They positioned themselves to the left and right of the porch stairs. Purcell and Lucy mounted the stairs. Lucy drew her revolver and flattened her back against the wall. Purcell stepped in front of the door.

'I can't *see*,' Gorman complained in a whiny voice.

'Shut up,' Abe muttered.

He stared at the distant door. He saw the shape of Purcell raise a hand to knock. He couldn't hear the knock. Purcell lowered the hand to his side.

Abe realized he was holding his breath. He let it out.

Then a dim blue swath of light silhouetted Purcell and someone standing in the doorway. Abe heard his heartbeat. Seconds were passing. Purcell must, he thought, be talking to the person. Who was it, Maggie Kutch? Probably denying . . .

A man's voice, faint with the distance, cried out, 'No!' Purcell suddenly hunched. A gunshot popped in Abe's ears. Purcell doubled over and staggered backwards. As he tumbled down the porch stairs, a blast from somewhere to the side sent the cop with the shotgun spinning. The other cop whirled around and aimed toward the pickup. Before he could fire, a shot kicked his head back.

Lucy froze against the wall as if crucified.

Abe dashed between the parked cars. He jerked the revolver from the back of his jeans as he raced in a crouch up the driveway. 'Hit the deck!' he yelled at Lucy.

The front door slammed shut, cutting off the blue glow.

Lucy crouched. An instant later came the flat bang of a rifle. She dropped to one knee and swung her revolver toward the pickup. She fired four quick rounds. A man cried out, came stumbling into Abe's view from the cover of the pickup's hood, fell to one knee and aimed his rifle at Lucy. He jerked and flopped to the thunder as bullets from Lucy and Abe and Jack socked his body.

Abe straightened up. He heard nothing but the ringing in his ears.

The sprawled man didn't move.

Lucy was still on one knee. Through the ringing, Abe heard shell casings clatter and roll on the wooden floor of the porch. He realized she was reloading.

He and Jack hurried forward. He crouched over Purcell. The man was on his back, clutching his belly and squirming. 'Take it easy,' Abe told him. 'We'll get help for you.'

He heard quick footsteps behind him. As he stood, a blink of light illuminated the chief's contorted face and bloody shirt. 'For Christsake, Hardy!'

Gorman sidestepped and took another photo of Purcell, then rushed toward the officer who'd fallen to the left of the porch stairs.

Jack, kneeling by the one to the right, called, 'This one's dead.'

Lucy backed down the stairs, her revolver aimed at the closed door.

Light flashed as Gorman shot two photos of the cop at his feet. Abe shoved him roughly aside and dropped down next to the motionless body. This one had a chest wound. He searched the neck for a pulse. 'Dead,' he called. He straightened up. 'Lucy, get back to your car and radio for an ambulance.'

With a nod, she took off running for the road.

Jack was standing above the man who'd ambushed the two officers. Abe went over to him. 'It's the old shit that took our tickets,' Jack said.

'Guess we cancelled his,' Abe said.

Gorman, panting, ran up beside them. His flash lit the skinny, grizzled old man. In the instant of brightness, Abe saw half a dozen bullet holes in the front of his sodden shirt and trousers: small entry holes from Lucy's .38, large exits from the slugs that had caught him in the back. Gorman stepped to his feet, crouched, and took another picture.

'We going in?' Jack asked. His voice was hushed and eager.

'Right.'

'She's gonna be ready.'

'She'll expect us to break through the front door. We'll go in the back.'

'There is no back door,' Gorman pointed out.

'There's the tunnel.'

'Where you killed the beast?'

'Want to see it?' Jack said.

'I must.'

'Better grab a weapon,' Abe told him.

With a nod, Gorman rushed over to the head-shot policeman. Abe and Jack reloaded while he took two photos of the dead man, knelt down, and lifted the revolver out of the grass.

'Do you know how to use it?' Jack asked.

'I've had some experience.'

'Just don't point it at anyone you don't plan to shoot.'

'I'm not a fool,' Gorman said.

Abe stepped over to Purcell. The chief still held his belly, but he was no longer squirming. 'We're going in to take care of business,' Abe told him. 'Hang on here. An ambulance is on the way.'

As they started for the road, Abe saw Lucy running toward them. Clamped under one arm was a first-aid kit. Abe rushed up to her. 'We're going in through a tunnel under the house.'

'Maybe I'd better . . .'

'Take care of Purcell. Keep an eye on the front door, but don't try to go in.'

She nodded.

'Who shot Purcell?'

'The Kutch woman. Maggie. She was just talking calmly and all of a sudden . . .'

'If she comes out, blow her down.'

'You're fucking-A right I will.'

Abe slapped her back, and ran for the road. Jack and Gorman followed. Abe stopped at one of the police cars long enough to find a long-barreled flashlight. Racing across Front Street, he glimpsed headlights far to the left. From somewhere in the distance came the sound of a siren. He dashed past the Beast House ticket booth, vaulted the turnstile and ran up the walkway.

'Wait up!' Gorman called.

He took the porch stairs two at a time, stopped in front of the door, and rammed the heel of his shoe into it just below the handle. With a splintering crash, the door flew open.

He switched on the flashlight.

Jack came up behind him.

'Wait up,' Hardy called again. A moment later, he came huffing up the porch stairs.

The three men entered the house.

The beam of Abe's light caught the snarling face of a creature near the foyer wall. He turned his revolver on it, but held fire as he realized it was nothing but the old, stuffed monkey posed to hold umbrellas. He let out a deep breath.

'Let's take it cautious,' he whispered. 'There's one beast unaccounted for and three women.'

'Do you think they might be here?' Gorman asked.

'Anything's possible,' Jack told him.

'The tunnel's our way in,' Abe said, 'but it's their way out if they decide to retreat.'

'Do you think they had time to get here?'

'Yes,' Abe said. He started forward, the powerful beam of his flashlight pushing a stream of brightness into the dark.

Tyler swung off the road behind Abe's Mustang. The ambulance sped by. Near the porch of the Kutch house, a woman stood up and waved both arms. On the ground around her lay several motionless shapes. Tyler's throat constricted.

'My God,' Nora muttered.

The ambulance skidded onto the driveway, siren wailing, light flashing. It raced toward the woman.

'Follow it,' Janice said from the back seat.

Tyler stepped on the gas, swerved around Abe's car, and swung onto the driveway. The ambulance stopped. She slowed as she drew up behind it. Two attendants jumped down and ran to the back. As they opened the rear doors, she set the emergency brake.

'That guy down over there's a cop,' Nora said.

Tyler bolted from the car. She sprinted past the ambulance. In the glare of the whirling red lights, she saw a body to the left of the porch. It wore a uniform. A woman with a revolver in one hand was on her knees beside a man, gesturing to the attendants as they rushed forward with a stretcher. The man on the ground was a stranger.

'This is the guy from Beast House,' Nora called from the front of a pickup truck.

'Hey!' the woman shouted. 'Who are you people? Get out of here!'

'Were there three men here?' Tyler asked.

'Yes.'

'Where are they?'

She pointed. 'Said they're going through a tunnel.'

'Are they all right?'

'Yes! Get out of here!'

Tyler and Nora reached the Omni at the same moment. Janice was standing by the rear door. 'Get in,' Tyler snapped.

The three doors slammed shut.

'What're we doing?' Nora asked.

'Going after them.' Tyler rammed the shift into reverse and sped backwards toward the street.

'What good will that do?' Nora asked. 'We'll just be in their way.'

'We need guns,' Janice said.

Tyler mashed the brake. She shot the car forward, swung onto the grass beside the ambulance, and lurched to a stop. She and Nora leapt from the car.

'Hold it!' the woman cop yelled.

'We need their guns!' Tyler said. 'We want to help.'

'Help by getting out of here.'

The attendants lifted the fallen policeman onto the stretcher.

'Please!' Tyler said. 'We'll bring them back.'

The woman aimed her revolver at Tyler. 'Get!'

'For Christsake, lady!' Nora blurted.

She aimed at Nora.

'Stupid bitch!' Tyler cried. Whirling around, she climbed back into the car.

Nora dropped in and slammed her door.

'We're no good without guns,' Janice said.

Tyler steered the car around in a tight circle, then hit the brake. She stared past the tail of the pickup truck and across the treeless field at the woods beyond Beach Lane.

'Captain Frank,' she said.

'So what?'

'Hardy said he's got an arsenal.'

'Let's go!' Janice urged.

Tyler drove straight across the field, the car bouncing wildly over its bumpy earth, crunching through weeds and low bushes. Nora clung to the dashboard as jolts shook the car. Tyler struggled to keep her grip on the steering wheel. Soon, her headlights caught the row of mailboxes. She spotted the opening in the trees to the left as the car sprang over a small rise and dropped onto the dirt road.

'Oh shit!' Nora yelled.

Tyler yanked the wheel. She almost missed the tree. There was a jolt as she struck it. The right headlight smashed. But the car glanced off and kept moving, speeding down the narrow rutted lane of Seaside, its single beam thrusting into the dark.

'There it is,' Nora said.

Tyler shoved the brake pedal to the floor and steered for the bus. The car bounded off the road. Beer cans crunched under its tires. She blasted the horn.

Nora and Janice jumped out while she set the emergency brake. They were pounding the bus's door when she reached them.

'Wha's all this?'

Tyler spun around. Captain Frank's white-bearded face was at an open window halfway to the back of the bus. 'It's just us,' she said. 'Tyler and Nora. We talked at the bar last night, remember? We need your help.'

'Did I hear guns?' he asked. He sounded groggy.

'They're after the beast. Your Bobo. We want to help. Have you got guns?'

'Goin' after Bobo?'

'Hurry. You can come along if you want.'

'Uhhh.' His face left the window. A light came on inside the bus, illuminating its brightly colored panes. A few seconds later, the door wheezed open.

'My Lord, is that you, Janice Crogan?'

'It's me,' she said.

'Figured Bobo got you.'

'It did.'

'We've got to hurry,' Tyler said, stepping close to the door.

Captain Frank wore striped boxer shorts, and nothing else. His torso was matted with white hair. 'Grab some clothes,' Tyler said, 'and show us where you keep your guns.'

'Aye. Come on aboard, mateys.'

With the policeman's revolver clenched in his sweaty hand, Gorman followed Abe and Jack down the stairs to the cellar. He kept his other hand on the railing as he descended. Except for the bright path cast by the flashlight, all was black.

The risers creaked under their feet.

The dirt floor of the cellar below looked gray in the pale beam. Then the light swept from corner to corner. Shadows quivered and died as the light circled.

'There's your hole,' Abe whispered. He settled the beam on a patch of darkness near a pile of bushel baskets.

Gorman tried to speak. A choked sound came out. He cleared his throat and asked, 'Did you get pictures?'

'Sure,' Jack said. 'Then we heard Janice.'

In silence, Gorman followed them down to the cellar floor. They stood in a cluster at the foot of the stairs. Abe swung the light toward a wall beside the staircase. It stopped at a large steamer trunk. 'That's their door,' he said. Gorman noticed a short hank of rope nailed to a side of the trunk – apparently a handle for pulling it back against the wall.

The beam edged sideways. It lighted the tunnel entrance.

And the beast.

'Glad it didn't walk away,' Jack whispered.

They stepped closer.

The creature lay face down, just inside the tunnel, its shiny flesh so white it almost seemed to glow. Its back was splattered with gore. Gorman quickly looked away from the remains of its head.

'We didn't get any pictures of it,' Jack told him.

Gorman took a deep breath. 'Would you mind rolling it over?'

'We've got a job to do,' Abe said. 'You can stay here if you want.' He stepped over one of the outstretched arms and moved deeper into the tunnel.

'Wait. You can't leave me here.'

'Then come along,' Jack said, and went in after Abe.

The light faded to a dim glow as Abe disappeared around a bend. In another moment, Gorman would be left in darkness. Gritting his teeth, he started to edge past the beast. He stared at it, half expecting a clawed hand to dart for his ankle. Then the light was gone. He couldn't see the beast at all. Something nudged his shoe. With a yelp, he sprang away.

He rushed forward, bumped a moist wall, and felt his way along its turn until he spotted broken light ahead and the hurrying shapes of Jack and Abe.

'Wait for me!' he cried out.

Jack turned around. 'Quiet, damn it!'

Gorman quickly joined the two men. He stayed close to Jack. He couldn't free his mind from the beast at the tunnel's entrance. It must be dead. But had it stirred in the darkness, one of its sprawled legs knocking against his shoe? No, he must have simply kicked it in passing. It must be dead.

But what if it's not?

What if it's coming?

Ridiculous.

And yet, he could sense it creeping closer.

He stepped on the back of Jack's shoe.

'Damn it, watch where you're going.'

'Would you mind if I walk between you two?'

'Shit. Suit yourself. Step on Abe for a while.'

'Would you guys knock it off?' Abe whispered.

Jack pressed himself against a wall of the tunnel. Gorman moved past him. With the sound of Jack's footsteps behind him, he immediately felt better. But his heart continued to pound wildly. His mouth was dry and he felt vaguely nauseated. His legs trembled.

He wished he hadn't come along with these men. He wished he had stayed at the inn, out of harm's way.

Thinking of the inn reminded him of Janice.

So the girl wasn't dead. That was a blow. Apparently, at least, she had no suspicion that he'd murdered her parents. Thank God for that.

She would present a problem, however, even with the contracts destroyed. If she took the matter to court ... Of course, he might resolve the situation by giving her the agreed-upon amount.

Half of everything.

If *Black River* had been a blockbuster – a bunch of ghost nonsense with nothing but a single suicide (ah yes, suicide, Martha) to give it credibility and bolster sales – this one would skyrocket.

How many deaths? Four tonight. Three last night. Janice's imprisonment (I'll have to interview her about that), two captives in the Kutch house for God only knows how long. And the biggest bonus of all, the corpse of the beast.

National media coverage.

And me, Gorman Hardy, in the center of it all.

The potential was staggering.

Turning over half to Janice would be an outrage. If only the beast had killed her.

Without doubt, it had raped her.

And both her parents were killed.

Nobody would consider it unusual if a girl in such circumstances committed suicide.

He could hardly risk faking suicides for both Janice *and* Captain Frank.

There were other ways to handle Captain Frank.

Suicide was perfect for Janice. But what method? A girl would certainly be unlikely to blow out her brains. Slashing her wrists was out of the question: it would raise eyebrows if she died in the same manner as Brian's wife. An overdose? Perhaps. That might be difficult to arrange, but . . .

Following Abe around a bend in the tunnel, he saw a blue glow ahead. Abe switched off the flashlight. The glow, Gorman realized, must be coming from the cellar of the Kutch house. An icy tightness clutched his stomach. His heart thudded faster. His trembling legs felt leaden, as if they wanted to hold him back.

Jack nudged him from behind. 'Keep moving.'

He hadn't realized he'd stopped. He forced himself to take a step, another step.

Abe, a couple of yards ahead, crouched at the mouth of the tunnel. He inched his head forward and looked to both sides. Then he stood up and entered the cellar.

If there was any danger, Gorman told himself, Abe wouldn't walk in that way.

Clenching the revolver so hard his hand ached, he followed. His feet were silent on the blue carpet. As Abe strode toward the stairs, Gorman gazed to the right. On the far wall hung the bodies of two naked men – Marty Crogan and Brian. Their skin was blue in the strange light from the ceiling fixture. Their blood looked purple, almost black. Claire's body was sprawled on the carpet near one of the shiny cushions that littered the floor. He stared at the awful, gaping crater in her thigh. Panic choked him. He stood motionless, struggling for breath.

Jack, stepping in front of him, shook his shoulder. 'Hey,' the man whispered. 'Let's go.'

Gorman knocked the hand away, staggered backwards, twisted himself around and lurched for the tunnel. At its entrance, he glanced back. Abe and Jack, both standing at the foot of the stairs, watched him and said nothing. He flung himself into the darkness. He ran.

Let them think what they like.

Let them think I'm a coward.

With his left hand out, he felt the moist wall to keep his bearings and rushed away from the hideous blue light of the cellar.

Better the darkness. Better anything than to climb those stairs and enter that house. He dreaded coming to the end of the tunnel. The beast would be there. But it was dead (it *must* be dead), and a live beast was waiting for those two inside the Kutch house. Maggie with a gun, and maybe others, but most of all the beast – it *eats* people. Let it get those two fools.

It won't get me!

He ran until he collapsed. On hands and knees, he sucked in the dank air. He heard nothing except his noisy gasping and the pounding of his heart. He saw nothing but blackness.

How far had he come? Surely, he must be at least halfway. He wanted to rest, but he knew he wouldn't be safe until he was outside Beast House. He longed for the fresh night air, for the brightness of moonlight. He saw himself rushing across the lawn to Front Street, locking himself inside Abe's car . . . If only he were there *now*.

Pushing himself to his feet, he reached out to the wall. He looked over his shoulder. Then he started forward again. After a few shuffling steps, he managed a slow jog.

You're all right now, he told himself. You're almost out. You'll be there soon.

Try not to step on the beast.

I'll fall on it, and it'll . . .

If only he had a flashlight! Or even matches!

If only he knew how close it was!

It's dead. If you fall on it, you'll get messy but it's dead and can't hurt you and you'll know you made it to Beast House and you'll be outside in another minute.

Who says the living beast is in the Kutch house?

Who says it's not in Beast House?

That thought sent a shock of alarm through Gorman, but he kept on jogging. He shambled around a curve in the tunnel and saw dim light ahead.

There shouldn't be light.

It didn't make sense unless he'd somehow gotten turned around. But the light in the Kutch cellar was blue, not white like this.

He staggered around another bend, and stopped. He held his breath. He squinted against the glare.

A gasoline lantern. It hissed in the silence.

A bearded man – Captain Frank – was crouching over the sprawled body of the beast. He had rolled it onto its back. Just behind him stood a girl in a yellow blouse. Janice! Nora and Tyler were there, too. They all held guns. They were all staring at the beast.

Raising his revolver, Gorman took careful aim at Janice and fired.

28

A blast roared in Tyler's ears. Janice spun and smashed against her. The girl's pistol bounced off Tyler's foot. Falling back against the tunnel wall, she flung an arm around Janice to hold her up. She staggered sideways with the weight, and fell to the cellar floor just outside the tunnel.

'Don't shoot! It's me!' Hardy's voice.

'Stupid fuckhead!' Nora cried out.

'Oh my God, I didn't mean to . . . I thought . . . My God, is she all right?'

As Tyler pulled her arm out from under Janice, Nora dropped to her knees beside them. Captain Frank rushed over with the lantern.

'Oh my God,' Hardy muttered, staring down at the girl. 'I'm sorry. I'm sorry. I was so frightened I didn't know what I was . . .'

'Shut up!' Nora snapped.

Janice's eyes were open. Her face was contorted with agony. A bloom of red was quickly spreading over the front of her blouse. Nora ripped the blouse open. A button popped from it and flicked against Tyler's cheek. The blood was welling from a place just above the left breast, and close to the side. Nora slid fingers over the area, then pressed her palm tightly to the wound. Janice yelped and flinched.

Captain Frank, on his knees, slid the long blade of a knife up the girl's sleeve and sliced through the fabric. He rammed the knife into the dirt floor. 'Gotta turn her,' he muttered. 'See her back.'

'Yes,' Hardy said. 'There might be an exit wound.'

'Un . . .' Janice gasped. 'Under.' Her right arm lifted off the dirt and fell across her breasts. She pointed with a finger at her armpit.

Captain Frank eased her left arm away from her side. 'Here,' he said. 'Came out here. Nicked her arm, too.' He plucked a wadded red bandanna from a pocket of his Bermudas, pushed it against the wound, and drew her arm down to her side. 'That'll hold it.'

'We've gotta get her to a hospital,' Nora said. She looked over at

Tyler. 'That policewoman. She can use one of the car radios. Have her call in for an ambulance.'

'But Abe.'

'He can take care of himself, damn it.'

'I'm going on over, mateys,' Captain Frank mumbled. 'You can keep my Coleman.' He yanked his knife from the ground and stood up.

'I'll stay with Janice,' Hardy offered. 'I'll tend to her wounds. Nora, why don't you go out and see to an ambulance?'

She nodded. 'Okay.'

Hardy knelt beside Janice. Nora took his hand and placed it against the entry wound. 'Keep a firm pressure,' she told him. With her clean hand, she stroked the girl's forehead. 'You'll be fine, kiddo. I'll be back in a few minutes, and we'll get you out of here.'

As she rushed toward the cellar steps, Tyler entered the tunnel. In the dim light from the lantern, she stepped around the body of the beast. She followed Captain Frank into the darkness.

Jack, his back to the front door, curled a hand around the knob and tried to turn it. 'Locked,' he whispered.

Abe nodded. So they wouldn't be opening the door to let Lucy in. She was good with a gun. She might've been helpful. He considered shooting out the lock, but the noise would give away their presence.

So far, they had checked out the kitchen, the corridor and the dining room. All were lighted blue like the cellar. Though they'd been constantly alert for an attack, so far they'd seen no one. The house seemed deserted.

Maybe everyone had fled. Abe doubted that Kutch and her group could have escaped through the tunnel to Beast House. There may, of course, be another way out – a tunnel at the back, perhaps leading toward the beach. That was possible, though Abe hadn't noticed any other exit in the cellar.

More likely, they were still in the house.

He gazed up the stairs.

Then, from the left, came a quiet sound like a girl sobbing.

Crouching, Jack edged sideways toward the arched entryway. Abe stayed close to him, stepping silently backward, keeping the rear covered.

The walls of the room were draped, from ceiling to floor, with blue curtains. A chill crawled up Abe's back. His eyes raced along the heavy folds, searching for bulges, for feet protruding beneath the lower edges. He saw nothing to indicate another presence, but kept scanning the curtains as he followed Jack.

The room was bare of furniture. Its carpet was cluttered with pillows and cushions of shiny blue fabric – some alone, others piled up.

He heard the sobbing again.

It seemed to come from behind a waist-high heap of pillows near the end of the room. Abe aimed his revolver at the center of the mound and sidestepped closer as Jack headed around the far side.

'Over here,' Jack whispered, and knelt out of sight.

Abe sprang past the pile to regain his view of Jack, and saw a girl lying face down on the floor. She was naked. One arm was bent close to her head, the other out of sight beneath her body.

Jack, on one knee near her head, had his .45 aimed down at her. 'Don't move,' he whispered.

The girl sniffed.

Abe kicked into the mounded pillows, sending them flying until he could see the floor.

The girl lifted her face off the carpet. 'Help,' she said in a choked voice. 'Please. I'm hurt.'

'Get your other hand where I can see it,' Jack said. 'It better be empty.'

'Can't. I . . . my arm's broken.'

Abe pivoted for another quick scan of the room, then dropped a knee onto the girl's spine. Her back arched. Her head jerked back. He slammed the barrel of his revolver against her upper arm, jumped aside as she cried out, and used his left hand to tug the arm out from under her. She held a small caliber semi-automatic. He rapped her knuckles with his barrel. The pistol fell.

Now she was crying for real.

'Bastards!' she gasped. 'Stinking bastards!'

'Watch our tails,' Abe said.

Jack straightened up.

Abe shoved his revolver into his pocket. He twisted the girl's arm up behind her back.

'Let go! Asshole! You're gonna die!'

He yanked the belt from his trouser loops, forced her other arm up her back, and lashed them together.

'Where are the others?' he asked.

'You'll find out!'

'Upstairs?'

'Fuck you!'

He tugged the revolver from his pocket and picked up the girl's pistol.

'That belt won't hold her long,' Jack said.

'If she gives us any more grief, we'll kill her.' Abe stood up. He planted a foot on her back and shoved. 'Did you catch that, Tiger?'

'Fuck you!'

'Let's go,' Abe said.

'Upstairs?' Jack asked.

'You got it.'

Janice felt the hand go away from her chest. She pushed the palm of her right hand against the wound, and opened her eyes. Gorman Hardy was kneeling over her. 'Wha . . .'

'We've got to get out of here, Janice. We're in danger if we stay.'

'Huh?'

'The beast, I saw it move.'

She turned her head and looked toward the tunnel entrance. All she could see of the creature were its clawed feet. They looked motionless.

A cry leaped from her as German tugged her arms, raising her back off the dirt. She stiffened her neck to stop her head from swaying. The wound burned as if a white-hot poker had been driven through her body and was still there. The sodden rag dropped from under her arm. Warm blood trickled down her breast and side.

She slumped forward, head between her knees. Gorman let go and stepped behind her.

'Try to stand up,' he said.

She felt him against her back. His hands clutched her sides, and she writhed as one of them pressed against claw scratches. He moved his hands lower. 'Is this better?' he asked.

She nodded.

She drew her knees up and shoved her sneakers against the dirt as he lifted.

As she straightened, her balance shifted backwards and they both staggered. Gorman gasped behind her. One of his hands flew up and clenched her breast.

'Sorry,' he said, and moved the hand down.

He turned her toward the stairs.

Her legs felt warm and weak, but they held her up as Gorman guided her along. She looked up the steep stairway. 'Can't,' she murmured.

'It's all right. I'll hold you. We'll be up at the top in a jiffy and out of here.'

In a jiffy. He sounded almost cheerful.

With her right hand, she gripped the wooden banister. She placed a foot on the first riser. Gorman clutched her hips, and lifted. She struggled up the first stair, the second. Then a wave of dizziness hit her. Her legs folded. She fell against the railing and hugged it.

'Goddamn it,' Gorman muttered.

'I can't,' she gasped. 'I can't. Let me . . . wait for Nora.'

'Do you want me to leave you here alone with the beast? I tell you, it's not dead!'

'Don't leave me.'

She tried to push herself away from the banister. Gorman pulled at her shoulders, and she cried out. He eased her forward onto the stairs. Slowly, bracing herself with her good right arm, she crawled higher.

'That's good,' Gorman said. 'That's a lot better.' He stepped around Janice and climbed above her. 'Almost there,' he said.

Three stairs from the top, another dizzy spell hit her. Her stomach convulsed. She lunged forward, pressing her head between the planks, and vomited through the gap behind them. When she finished, she lay there gasping and sobbing.

'Quick!' Gorman said. 'My God, it's sitting up!'

She jerked her head free and looked down at the tunnel entrance. From this angle, she couldn't see the beast at all.

Neither, she realized, could Gorman.

She raised her face, blinking tears from her eyes. 'You can't . . .'

'Damn you!' he bellowed. 'Come *on*!'

She raised her arm toward a higher step. He grabbed its wrist with both hands and tugged, jerking her up and forward. Her cheek hit the edge of the landing. He dragged her. She scraped and bumped over the remaining stairs. With a final yank he threw her onto the landing.

'Okay,' he said. 'Up.'

She couldn't force herself to move.

Gorman stepped over her. He planted a foot beside each hip, and clutched her sides. A finger dug into the bullet hole under her arm, stunning her with a bolt of pain. He lifted her. First to her knees. Then to her feet. As she tried to lock her knees, he swung her around and pushed.

She plunged head first. She seemed to fall forever, a scream swelling in her chest as the stairs below drifted up at her. She flung an arm across her face. The arm went numb. The plank it hit burst apart. The top of her head skidded across the next one as her legs flew high and swung down. The edges of planks slammed her back and buttocks and legs. They scraped her back, bumped her head as she slid. Then she came to a stop, her rump on the cellar floor, her back against the stairs.

'My goodness,' said a voice above her. 'You fell.'

She brought her head forward, feeling a dim sense of relief that she could move it. Her legs were stretched out across the dirt. They seemed to belong to someone else. A sneaker had been lost in the fall. She wiggled her bare toes.

'But you're still alive.' She heard footfalls on the stairs. 'You must be part cat. Are you part cat, Janice? You're harder to kill than your mother was. A regular Rasputin.'

Across the cellar, near a stack of bushel baskets, a hand reached out of the ground.

Out of a hole in the cellar floor.

A dead-white hand, smudged with dirt but glistening in the lantern light. A hand with long, hooked claws.

Janice tumbled forward as something – Gorman's foot? – thrust against her back. Grunting, she sprawled face down.

Gorman rolled her over.

He straddled her, sat on her belly, smiled down at her. 'Unfortunately,' he said, 'you broke your head in the fall.' He gripped both sides of her head. 'I'm not sure I'm strong enough for this, but we'll give it the old college try.'

She drove a fist into his side. He grunted and his face twisted.

'Oh, you're a tough one.' He started to smile again, but then he looked up and his mouth sprang open. A shadow fell across Janice. The beast stood above her, reaching for Gorman. He sucked in a loud breath and flung out an arm to ward the thing off. His other hand went to his hip. Lifting her head, Janice saw him try to tug a revolver from his front pocket. He jerked the gun free as the beast's hands clamped the sides of his head. With strength she didn't know she possessed, Janice flung her right arm across her body, grabbed the rising barrel, and tore the gun from Gorman's hand.

The beast lifted him by the head. His feet swept past Janice's face. His shrieks hurt her ears.

She rolled over. Braced on her elbows, she turned the revolver around and cocked it.

The beast still had Gorman by his head. He waved his arms and kicked and screamed as it shook him. Then it flung him against a section of shelves. Wood splintered. He fell sprawling to the floor under an avalanche of jars. 'Shoot it!' he cried in a choked voice. He staggered to his feet. He stumbled backwards as the crouching beast lurched closer.

Janice fired.

The slug knocked a leg out from under Gorman.

He flopped onto his back. The beast sprang onto him. He let out a piercing scream as its snout thrust into his groin, snapping and ripping. Soon, he was only whimpering. The beast raised its head and seemed to stare at him for a few moments. Then it scurried up his body, opened its mouth wide, and bit into his face.

Janice watched.

She watched until Gorman no longer groaned and whimpered, until the convulsions stopped shaking him and he lay motionless.

The beast climbed off him. Its body was smeared with Gorman's blood. It turned toward Janice and stared at her.

Its penis thickened and grew and stood upright.

She fired.

The bullet whined off the stone wall beyond its head. Hunched over, the beast hesitated. Janice aimed at its chest. As she squeezed the trigger, the creature lurched aside. It sprang across the cellar floor toward the tunnel where the other beast lay dead. Janice swung the pistol, fired again and again. Then the hammer fell with a dry clack. The beast vanished into the tunnel.

29

Tyler stopped abruptly when she heard the sound – a single *pop* that surged down the tunnel from behind. 'A gunshot?' she whispered.

'Aye,' said Captain Frank.

She stood motionless in the dark, hanging onto the old man's hand, and wondered what it might mean. Nora had a pistol, but had left the house and probably wouldn't be back yet. That left Gorman. Who – or what – had he fired at?

'Trouble back there,' Captain Frank said.

'Yes.'

'Let's not poke.'

With a nod that he wouldn't see in the blackness, Tyler pulled his hand and led the way forward. Her shoulder bumped a wall. She stepped to the right, and kept going.

Another gunshot resounded through the tunnel, followed soon by a quick flurry that all ran together and might have been three shots or four.

What's going on back there?

'Lord,' muttered Captain Frank.

Tyler stood still. She listened for more gunfire, but heard only the thump of her heartbeat and the old man's quick breathing.

'Strange business,' she said.

His hand was hot and slippery in her grip. She kept hold of it, and started walking again. She swept the pistol from side to side ahead of her, feeling for walls. Her knuckles brushed moist clay. She turned slightly away.

She wished they hadn't left the Coleman lantern behind.

With light, they would be out of this tunnel by now, not staggering blindly along its twists and curves.

They must be nearing its end.

But the tunnel seemed to stretch on forever.

With Abe in the lead and Jack covering the rear, they had walked the length of the upstairs corridor. Every door was shut. At each of them, Abe pressed himself to the wall and tried the knob. Every door was locked.

At the end of the corridor, he whispered to Jack, 'Let's start by the stairs and smash them open.'

They were halfway back when a door swung open twenty feet ahead. They crouched and took aim.

'We're comin' out.' Abe recognized the husky voice of Maggie Kutch. 'Don't shoot us.'

'Come out slowly,' Abe said. 'Keep your hands in sight, and they'd better be empty.'

Through the doorway sidestepped a young woman. Maggie, behind her, had a hand around her neck and held a revolver to her head. The woman cradled a baby in her arms. It was silent, but awake and fingering a strap of her nightgown.

'Drop your guns,' Maggie said.

'You drop yours,' Abe said, 'and place your hands on top of your head.'

'I'll shoot her brains out.'

The possibility sickened Abe. Without their weapons, however, they would be at Kutch's mercy. He had little doubt that she would fire on them the instant they were disarmed.

'You'll be dead,' Jack said, 'before she hits the floor.'

'Let's not have any shooting,' Abe said. 'Leave the woman here with her baby, and you can walk out. We won't make any moves to stop you.'

'Think I'm a fool?' Kutch asked. 'You drop your guns before I count three, or else. One.'

'Don't do it,' Abe warned.

'No, please,' the woman begged. She clutched the baby to her chest.
'Two,' said Kutch. Her voice sounded calm, as if she knew they
would give up their guns to save the woman.

Tyler stepped into the dim blue light of the cellar. She stood motionless,
gazing at the two bodies that hung from the far wall, thinking for a
terrible moment that they were Abe and Jack.

Captain Frank bumped her side. 'Lord,' he whispered.

Her eyes lowered to the torn body of a woman sprawled on the floor.
She pulled her hand from Captain Frank's grip, covered her mouth and
turned to the stairway, and flinched as she heard gunshots from
somewhere above. She raced across the carpet. She grabbed the railing.
She started up, taking two stairs at a time.

With a look over her shoulder, she saw Captain Frank running in a
drunken weave to catch up. She couldn't wait for him. But as she started
to turn away, a pale shape sprang from the tunnel's darkness.

'Behind you!' she yelled.

The old man was too drunk or too slow. Even as he started to turn,
the lunging beast rammed clawed hands down on his shoulders. He
cried out. His legs folded. The beast batted the side of his head.
Growling, it bared its teeth. Its snout darted toward the back of his
neck.

Tyler fired. The blast stunned her ears. The revolver jumped.

She had aimed high, afraid of hitting Captain Frank. Her bullet
plowed up a tuft of carpet near the wall.

The beast stared up at her. Its slanted eyes didn't blink. Its snout was
smeared red, but not with Captain Frank's blood. Tyler remembered
the gunshots she'd heard in the tunnel. They had been fired at *this*
thing. Whose blood . . .?

It scurried off the back of Captain Frank and rushed forward in a low
crouch with its knuckles on the carpet like a gorilla. It was almost to the
foot of the stairs when Tyler squeezed off another shot. Splinters
exploded off the banister. The creature jerked its head aside as flying
needles of wood jabbed its face. Its right eye spat fluid. It slapped a
hand to its face. Screeching, it staggered backwards.

Tyler aimed at its head and fired and missed. She aimed at its chest
and fired. Her bullet slashed a red streak across the top of its shoulder.

She tried to think.

How many bullets had she fired?

The beast was standing upright with its head back, roaring with pain
or rage. It should be an easy target, but the angle was bad, shooting
down like this.

If she tried to finish it off, she would empty her gun. Then what good would she be to Abe?

Captain Frank's gun!

It lay on the carpet near his body.

Unfired. Full.

If she could get to it . . .

Holding her revolver with both hands, she aimed at the chest of the beast and squeezed the trigger.

The gun bucked. The creature grabbed its side, just above the hip. Spinning, it fell to one knee.

With the noise of the blast still ringing in her ears, she raced down the stairs. She rushed at the beast. She stabbed the muzzle against its head above an open hole where its ear should have been. Its elbow rammed into her thigh, knocking her leg back, twisting her. The front sight carved a gash across the side of its head as she started to fall. She jerked the trigger and wished she could call back the bullet because she knew, even as the gunshot crashed in her ears, that she had missed.

When Kutch said, 'Two,' the corridor roared.

Abe and Jack both fired at the same instant.

Abe had chosen, as his target, the area to the right of the young woman's ear. Maggie's gun was there. Half of her face was there, too, visible behind the woman's head.

Jack must have picked the same target.

Maggie's pistol leaped from her hand as if kicked, and bounced off her forehead. Her cheek blew open with a spray of blood. She flopped backwards. The woman with the baby hurled herself aside, hit the wall with her shoulder and sank to her knees. The baby cried wildly.

Maggie lay on her back. She didn't move.

Side by side, Abe and Jack ran forward. Abe stopped in front of the young woman. Jack went on ahead to check on Maggie.

'Are you all right?' Abe asked.

She nodded. She stroked the head of her baby, and looked up at Abe. 'Don't let . . .' She slipped a knuckle into the crying baby's mouth. Its wailing stopped. It sobbed and gummed her fingers. 'Don't let them get you,' she said. 'They're . . .' A muffled boom interrupted her. A gunshot from somewhere in the house.

'Jack, take these two outside.'

'Maggie's alive.'

'Leave her. Get these two . . .'

Jack's head jerked sideways. He swung his weapon. Abe pivoted, but before he could bring up his revolver a beast leaped onto him. It was half the size of the creature they had killed in the tunnel, but its weight caught him off balance. He fell onto the woman and baby, rolled off them, and let his gun fall so he could grab the throat of the beast as its mouth thrust toward his neck.

'Drop that knife!' Jack yelled.

Abe heard more far-off gunshots.

Then he glimpsed a fat woman in the doorway with a butcher knife. Her face was wrapped in bandages. He cried out in pain as claws raked his back. Then he was on top of the beast. It twisted and thrashed under him, and gurgled as his thumbs dug into its throat. Its claws tore at his sides and arms. Letting go with one hand, he smashed a fist against the side of its head. He struck it again. Then its teeth snapped shut on his fist. Pain shot up his arm. His left hand released its throat. He grabbed the top of its snout, forced his trapped hand down, and yanked the jaws wide. A gristly, cracking sound. The beast flinched rigid. Abe pulled his bloody hand from its mouth. The jaw hung slack, the tongue drooping out one side.

He ducked as it swung at him. Claws dug into his scalp, forcing his face down against the slick flesh of its chest. He drove fists into both its sides. The claws eased up. He shoved himself backwards, shaking his head free. Its penis rubbed his cheek. He jerked away from it, lunged farther back, and grabbed the beast's ankles.

It sat up, swatting at him, missing. On his knees, he dragged it. He lurched to his feet, pulling it along the carpet as it flailed the air and kicked its trapped legs.

'Hold still!' Jack yelled. 'I've got it.'

'Mine,' Abe grunted. He lifted the squirming beast. It flapped its arms. Its head slid across the carpet, then left the carpet. Abe swung the creature upward, turning, and slammed it against the corridor wall. Its head thudded on the wood. He released its ankles. It dropped to the floor.

As it tried to get up, Abe stomped on its head. He lost his balance, stumbled across the corridor and hit the wall. The fat woman in the doorway was staring at the beast, shaking her head and mumbling. Jack held his pistol on her. The butcher knife lay at her feet.

Breathless, Abe staggered over to her. He picked up the knife. He knelt over the writhing beast, flipped it onto its back, and slashed its throat. A hot splatter of blood blinded him, sprayed into his open mouth.

Tyler landed on her back in front of the kneeling beast. She started to bring up the gun. The beast knocked it from her hand. She flung up her other arm to block a blow to her face, but not in time. The impact dazed her. Her arm fell to the floor. She wanted to struggle, but her body seemed too weary. She felt as if she were outside herself, observing.

The beast straddled her.

Its claws hooked into the front of her sweater and ripped.

Its hands felt slimy on her breasts. Did they leave trails like a snail? Its claws scraped slightly, almost tickling. Its head moved down. Its tongue rasped over one of her nipples. Fluid from its punctured eye dribbled onto her chest. Its nose was cold like a dog's. Then she felt teeth on her breast, on the underside and top, and she knew it had her whole breast inside its mouth. Its tongue swirled and thrust.

The mouth went away. The cool air of the cellar chilled her wet flesh. The mouth took in her other breast. It was not so gentle, this time. Its teeth squeezed. She tried to lie still, but her muscles tensed. The jaws clamped tighter. The pain cleared her mind. She was no longer distant and observing, but she didn't dare to struggle. Not now. Not with her breast in its teeth. The creature squirmed, pulling on her. Then it let go.

Claws scratched her belly. They dug under the waistband of her skirt and pulled with such force that her rump lifted off the floor. Raising her head, she saw the beast on its knees between her legs, ripping away her skirt. It gave a final yank, and flung the garment aside.

She saw its huge, erect penis.

No!

Jerking her knees high, she rolled. Her foot brushed the creature. Then her legs were clear and she kept rolling, kept flipping herself over. She didn't look back.

Facedown, she shoved herself off the carpet. She staggered forward. The stairway was far to her left. She ran for it, and heard a rumbling growl behind her.

Claws pierced her shoulders. Weight pressed down, collapsing her legs. She fell. The floor hammered her knees and palms. With the beast on her back, she crawled closer to the stairs.

It reached under her. It gripped her breasts. Pulled. Her hands left the carpet. She was squeezed against its slick chest, lifted off her knees. Its teeth caught the side of her neck as if to hold her still. She felt its penis between her legs, shoving her higher as it carried her toward the stairs.

Kicking and squirming, Tyler clutched the creature's hands and tried to tear them away from her breasts. They squeezed more tightly. The claws dug in, piercing her skin.

The beast slammed her down against the stairs. The edges of the risers pounded her body. She felt the hands go away from her breasts. Claws scraped along her ribs and sides. They dug into her hips. The shaft began to slide backwards.

Tyler clamped her legs shut. She couldn't stop it, but the beast licked her neck and pushed forward again as if it liked the feel of her hugging thighs. Twisting, she darted a hand down between her body and the stairs. She gagged as she clutched the slimy flesh. Gripping it with all her strength, she snapped her hand sideways. It didn't break, or even bend. It moved forward and back, using her hand, while the panting beast lapped her neck.

She tugged. Her hand flew off the slick penis and struck one of the risers.

The beast clutched her thighs, pulled, lifted. Tyler's knees left the stairs. Clinging to the plank at her shoulders, she bucked and thrashed. 'No!' she shrieked.

Her right hand let go of the stair.

She slapped it down between her legs.

The beast thrust. Pounded the back of her hand with such force that her forehead bumped the edge of the higher step.

The penis didn't go away. It rubbed over her knuckles, moved down to her fingers, tried to nudge between them. Tyler shoved her hand lower.

The beast made a low, gurgling growl, its breath hot against her neck.

Then it bit.

Tyler whimpered as teeth sank into the back of her hand, tore the skin away, nibbled the raw wound, bit deeper. Her hand was on fire, but she kept it tight against her body.

Her mind was numb.

It can't have teeth. Not *there*!

But it did.

They burrowed into her hand and ripped like the teeth of a mad rat trying to eat its way through.

My God.

Oh my God.

The growls of the beast sounded almost like laughter as it chewed her hand.

It's enjoying this.

If it wanted, it could knock my hand out of the way. It doesn't have to do this.

Tyler heard blood pattering one of the steps.

She wished her hand would go numb. It seemed to grow more tender, instead. The teeth felt like white-hot needles as they nipped and tore. Her whole arm burned and trembled.

The teeth went away.

The growls of the beast no longer sounded amused. Suddenly, it roared. Claws stabbed her thighs as it jerked her backwards. It rammed. Tyler's hand exploded with pain. She shrieked as two of her fingers snapped.

A thunderous blast pounded her ears.

The claws jumped, raked her thighs, released her.

She fell sprawling onto the stairs.

Another explosion. She pushed herself up. Stared at her right hand. The back of it was bloody pulp. The two broken fingers had already begun to swell. Weeping, she turned herself over and saw Captain Frank standing above the beast.

It lay on its back, writhing. It had a hole through one side of its head, another through its chest. Tyler's eyes moved down to its huge penis. Sheathed with blood. Her blood. Shreds of skin clung to the blunt end. The teeth parted, snapped shut.

Captain Frank fired into its head until his gun was empty. He gave Tyler a crooked, slightly drunken smile. 'Didn't tell you?' he asked. He winked at her. He fiddled with his Luger. Its magazine dropped to the carpet. From the pocket of his baggy Bermuda shorts he took a full magazine. He slid it up the handle, and pulled at a mechanism on top of the pistol. 'Didn't I tell you I'd lay it low?' he asked, and started shooting again.

Tyler watched the dead beast jerk as bullets punched through it. Then she shut her eyes.

As the firing went on, she felt the stairway tremble under her.

'Ahoy there!' Captain Frank yelled.

The shooting stopped.

Tyler opened her eyes. Abe's face, upside down, was close above her. 'My God,' he said.

He stepped down the stairs and sat beside Tyler. She turned, and raised her arms to him.

30

Tyler held him fiercely. He stroked the back of her head. 'It's okay, it's all over,' he whispered. 'Are you hurt badly?'

'Just . . . my hand.'

Abe looked at it, pain in his eyes. 'Jesus,' he muttered. He started to take off his shirt.

'I blasted it to smithereens,' said Captain Frank. He sounded gleeful.

'Is Jack all right?' Tyler asked, as Abe began to wrap the shirt around her torn, broken hand.

'Jack's fine. We took care of business. Where's Nora?' he asked.

'I don't know. Outside, I guess.'

'That Hardy fella plugged Janice,' Captain Frank said. 'We left them back at the other house, and Nora ran off to get help.'

'Hardy *shot* her?'

'Took her for the beast.'

'Did he get her bad?'

'I guess she lived through that, but we heard some shots back there. This creature must've popped in on them before it come for us. Gave me a nasty wallop, but I'm okay. Come to my senses in time to blast it up.'

Abe finished wrapping Tyler's hand. 'Let's get out of this place. Get you to a hospital.' Gently, he pulled the tattered front of the sweater across her breasts.

She groaned as she sat up straight.

Captain Frank picked up the remains of her skirt. He looked away as he handed the garment to Abe.

Abe helped her stand. He wrapped the skirt around her. Captain Frank provided his belt to hold it up, then searched for her sandals. He found one half hidden under the first stair, the other near the head of the beast. Abe held her steady while she stepped into them.

The old man picked up the revolver he had let Tyler borrow, shoved it into a front pocket of his Bermudas, and slid his Luger into the other pocket. 'Guess we're all set,' he said.

He started up the stairs. Abe put an arm around Tyler's back, and together they climbed out of the cellar.

They entered the kitchen of the Kutch house. They walked down a narrow, blue-lighted corridor. A group of people was standing in the foyer. Jack had his gun aimed at a fat woman with a bandaged face who looked a lot like Maggie Kutch. A thin, pale woman in a nightgown stood with her back to the door. She held a baby to her chest.

Jack frowned. 'Holy shit,' he said. 'What are *you* doing here? Tyler? What happened?'

'They ran into another beast,' Abe said.

'Holy shit.'

'I laid it low,' said Captain Frank. 'Blew it to kingdom come, matey.'

'Where's Nora?'

'She's okay,' Tyler said. 'I think.'

'Where's that girl?' Abe asked. 'The one who tried to shoot us?'

'She's my daughter, Sandy,' said the woman with the baby.

'We looked for her.' Jack shrugged. 'Don't know where she went.'

'Okay. Well, let's get out of here.'

'The door's still locked,' Jack said.

'Let's shoot the lock.'

'I know where the key is,' said the woman with the baby. 'I'll get it. It'll only take a second.'

'Okay,' Abe said.

She held out the baby to Jack. 'Would you hold him? I'll be right back.'

'Sure.'

'He's Jud. Judgement Rucker Hayes.' Her voice trembled slightly as she spoke the name.

Jack took the baby and smiled down at it.

The woman started up the stairs.

'The key's up there?' Abe asked. He sounded worried.

'No sweat,' Jack said. 'Maggie's out cold. She'll be lucky if she makes it.'

'Okay. But don't go close to her.'

The woman hurried up the stairs. At the top, she turned left and disappeared down the corridor.

'We'll be out of here in a minute,' Abe said, and patted Tyler's back.

The baby in Jack's arms made gurgling sounds.

'He's a cute little fellow, isn't he?' Jack said. Smiling, the baby reached up and clenched his cheek. 'You're a toughie,' he said, and tickled Jud's belly.

The mother appeared at the head of the stairs.

'Get the key?' Abe asked.

She nodded. She started down.

The front of her nightgown was dark and matted to her breasts. Her face was spattered and dripping.

'My God,' Abe muttered. He rushed up the stairs. Her arm stretched down to him. From her fingers dangled a thin chain.

'The key,' she said.

'What happened? Are you hurt?'

'No. I'm just fine. Just fine. She . . . Maggie . . . she murdered Jud. Jud. My . . . the father of my child.'

Abe stepped onto the stair beside her. He put an arm around her back.

'I used the knife.'

He led her down.

'Maggie used a knife on Jud, and I used a knife on her.'

'It's all right,' Abe said.

'It felt right.'

'Maggie came to and attacked you when you went to get the key.'

'No. No, she . . .'

'That's the story.'

'Oh.'

Abe unlocked the front door and opened it slowly. 'We're coming out,' he called to the policewoman on the lawn. 'It's all over.'

The woman holstered her weapon.

Tyler followed Abe onto the porch, and took a deep breath of the night air. The ocean smelled good. The moon was high.

31

Sandy, huddled in the darkness of the storage area beneath the staircase, waited.

Hugging her knees to her breasts, she had listened to the gunshots and wanted to help. But she had already tried helping: the two men with the guns were too smart, too quick. And so she stayed hidden.

There were more gunshots.

Feet racing down the stairs, pounding down them so hard that dry flecks sprinkled her shoulder.

Then more footsteps making the planks squeak and groan over her head.

Then the voice of her mother calling out to her: Sandy, where are you? Please. Are you here? I still love you, honey. Everything will be all right, now.

She didn't move. She hardly dared to breath. Someone walked very close to the staircase panel but didn't open it – probably didn't realize it could be opened.

Soon afterwards, she heard other voices. She couldn't make out the words. Someone went upstairs. Someone else went part way up.

Then everyone was gone.

Still Sandy waited. She wondered what had happened: who had been shot and who survived? The thoughts made her feel sick.

Wick was probably dead. He was a creep, anyway. And Maggie and Agnes wouldn't be any great loss, either. But Seth and Jason and little Rune – if they'd been killed . . . She sniffled quietly in the darkness as tears trickled down her cheeks.

Later, more people came into the house. Sandy stretched out on her back, listening and waiting. The people stayed and stayed. She thought they might never go away. She was very tired, but her mind swirled, unsettling thoughts keeping her tense and awake.

What if they found her? No, they won't.

What had happened to Seth and Jason and Rune?

What would become of her? She was only fourteen. Wick was probably dead. Maggie had shot that cop and murdered Jud last year with Mom as a witness, so even if she had been taken alive she would never come back.

Agnes might come back. If they couldn't pin anything on her. If they didn't send her to the loony bin. Agnes was slow in the head, but not crazy so they might let her go. She would inherit the house – and Beast House.

Yes.

If Agnes came back, it wouldn't be so bad. Sandy could run things herself. She could start up the tours again.

And Agnes knew about babies. She'd helped in Mom's delivery.

She'll help me.

Sandy slid her hands over her belly. The turmoil in her mind subsided.

The voices outside her hiding place went on. Footsteps moved up and down the stairs.

She wondered, for a while, what name she should give the child? Seth? Jason? She didn't know which was the father. Besides, those were old-fashioned names. Nerdy. Maybe Rich or Clint or . . .

Then she fell asleep.

Epilogue

Tyler twisted her finger free of the baby's tight grip, and knocked on the cottage door.

'Who is it?'

'Me,' she said.

'Just a sec, hon. I ain't decent.'

'When has that ever stopped you?'

A moment later, Nora opened the door. She wore a yellow bikini that looked brand new and covered very little.

'You aren't losing any time,' Tyler said.

'I spotted Jack down at the dock. He didn't see me. I'm gonna surprise him. Hand over the kid.'

Laughing, Tyler held out the baby. He flung out his arms and legs as if afraid of being dropped, and grabbed a strap of Nora's bikini. Wrapping her arms around him, she held him close. 'I think I'd like to keep you, Scotty.'

'Get your own. I'm sure Jack would accommodate you.'

'I'm sure he would.' She sat on a side of the king-sized bed. 'So, how's life in the boondocks?'

'Couldn't be better. How's life in the urban sprawl?'

'It's getting to me. I spent the whole year thinking about this place. I guess it sort of grew on me. So did Jack.'

'He must've. You haven't unpacked yet.'

'I don't plan to stay.'

'But . . .'

'I'm gonna cajole Jack into letting me stay with him. Smart, huh? You can rent out this room to a paying customer. I saw the no vacancy sign out front.'

'He's got an A-frame just down the . . .'

'I know, I know. I haven't been exactly out of touch with him.' She flopped backwards across the bed and hoisted Scotty high. He gasped and started to cry. She lowered him quickly. 'Oh shit, now I did it.' Sitting up, she handed him back to Tyler.

He wrapped an arm around her neck and held on tight. 'Did big bad Nora scare you?'

'That's it, turn the kid against me. If it wasn't for me, he wouldn't be here. If I hadn't flipped the bird at that jerk on the highway . . .'

'That's right. Say thank you, Scotty.'

Scotty sobbed.

'Which reminds me,' Nora said. 'Guess where I spent last night? The Welcome Inn. They were full up, just like you guys, but Janice let me stay in her parents' room.'

'How is she doing?'

'You mean you don't know?'

'Well, I've seen her on television a few times and I know the book has been on the bestseller list for the past six weeks.'

'She got – good Christ – over a million for the paperback rights. The film's all set to go into production in about two weeks. They'll be shooting on location.'

'But how's she doing?'

The brightness left Nora's face. 'She woke me up last night, screaming. A nightmare. We stayed up till morning, talking. She has these nightmares but they used to be every night and now they're not so frequent. She said it helped, writing the book – got a lot of it out of her system. It also helped because she got involved with this guy, Steve Saunders. Hardy's agent sent him out to help her with the thing. He ghosted it for her, and then did the screenplay. I guess the two are thick as thieves, but he's back in LA till the shooting starts. I talked her into phoning him at about seven this morning, and that cheered her up. I guess she's doing okay.' Nora's smile returned. 'Hey, we went over to the Last Chance after dinner last night. Good old Captain Frank was in rare form. He's one hell of a local celebrity.'

'Bet he loves it.'

'The man's in his glory. You should've heard him. "Aye, I laid the beast low, mateys." Everybody in the place buying him drinks. He said to give you his regards, and I'm supposed to tell you that you're welcome to keep his belt.'

'I've been meaning to send it back.'

'You can save your postage.' She pushed herself off the bed. 'Well, kiddo, I'd love to stay here and chat all afternoon, but I have this pressing engagement. You know how it is.'

'I know.'

Nora stepped past her and opened the door.

'Wait,' Tyler said. 'Did you take the tour?'

'You've got to be kidding. For one thing, the line was about half a mile long. And they've raised the ticket price to twelve fifty. Must be making a mint.'

'Who?'

Nora shrugged. 'Kutch's daughter owns the place. I don't know who's guiding the tours. I caught a look at her. Some kid, can't be older than fourteen or fifteen.'

'The place should've been closed down.'

'Shit, it should've been burnt to the ground. But at least it hasn't got Dan anymore. I checked with somebody coming out, and he's not part of the Ziegler exhibit. I guess they haven't bothered to have him replaced.'

'I'm glad.'

'Hey, I almost forgot your book.' She stepped over to her open suitcase. From under the gown on top, she pulled out a book with the familiar dust jacket: *The Horror at Malcasa Point* by Janice Crogan. The cover showed a crude, childish sketch of a beast, pencil scratches obliterating its anatomy from hips to knees. 'Have you already got a copy?'

Tyler nodded.

'Well, I bet yours isn't autographed. Let me make sure this isn't Jack's.' She opened the book. 'Yep, this is the one.'

Tyler sat on the bed, rested Scotty on her lap, and accepted the book.

'See you later,' Nora said.

'The cocktail lounge at six,' Tyler reminded her.

'Right. We'll be there.'

Then Nora left.

Tyler turned to the title page. In blue ink just below the author's name was scrawled: To my good friend, Tyler and to Abe who saved my life – my thanks and best wishes. The things that go bump in the night are dead. Long live us. Love, Janice Crogan, August 3, 1980.

The Midnight Tour

This book is dedicated to
Ed Gorman
writer, publisher and friend

Ed, they don't make them
any better than you

Chapter One

Sandy's Story – August, 1980

'Ow!' Sandy said. 'Watch it with those teeth, buster. There. There, that's better. Little monkey. Are you my little monkey? Huh, are you?'

Through the open window behind her, she suddenly heard footfalls crunching the forest mat of pine needles and twigs near her trailer home.

Fear knocked her breath out.

Eric stopped sucking, as if he sensed her alarm. He let go of her nipple, tipped back his head and looked up at her face.

'It's all right,' she whispered.

Eric made a tiny whimper of concern.

'Shhhh.' Turning her head, Sandy looked over her shoulder. The curtains behind her were shut. She kept them that way most of the time, even though her trailer was hidden away in a clearing and strangers rarely stumbled upon it.

You just never knew.

Watching the curtains, she could see the gloom of dusk through the thin yellow fabric. But she saw no movement, no trace of the intruder.

At least he can't see us, either.

She wondered how she knew it was a man.

Maybe because of the heavy, sure sound of the footsteps.

He had already walked past the area directly behind her window. He kept going, and the crunching sounds faded a little.

Maybe he's leaving.

More likely, though, he was circling the trailer – heading for the side with the door.

Just go away! Whoever you are, get out of here!

For a few seconds, she couldn't hear him walking anymore.

Eric took her nipple into his mouth and resumed sucking.

Then the intruder climbed the stairs. The wood creaked and groaned.

Sandy turned her head and gazed at the door. It was directly across the narrow room from where she sat. It had no window.

Did I lock it?

I always lock it.

But did I?

She'd been awfully upset when she came in – hardly able to think straight.

I must've locked it.

No sound came from the other side of the door.

Sandy heard her heart pounding hard. And she heard the quiet suck and slurp of Eric at her breast.

The intruder knocked on the door.

Sandy flinched and Eric nipped her.

'Who is it?'

'Marlon Slade.' The voice was rich and deep like Darth Vader. 'We met this morning.'

'I know that.'

'I'd like to speak with you for a moment, Miss Blume.'

'What about?'

'May I please come in?'

'I don't think so. My dad'll be getting home from work any minute. He doesn't like me to have company when he isn't here.'

'Miss Blume, the mosquitoes are eating me alive. Please let me in.'

'Can't. I can hear you just fine through the door.'

The knob rattled. The sound sent a cold wash of panic through Sandy. 'Hey!' she shouted, springing to her feet. 'Don't do that!'

The door stayed shut.

She *had* locked it.

'I'd rather not discuss this through a door.'

'There's nothing to discuss.'

'If you don't think so, I'll wait out here and speak with your father. I'm sure he'll be interested in the offer, even if you're not.'

Standing in the middle of the room with Eric clutched in her arms, she shook her head and said, 'I *told* you I don't want to be in your movie.'

'Of *course* you want to be in it. Now, please be a dear and open the door.'

'No, thank you.'

Something thumped hard against it, making it jump.

Making Sandy jump.

Eric turned his head to look at the door.

'Stop that!' Sandy shouted.

Silence.

But no sound of retreat. Marlon Slade was still standing on the top stair in front of her door.

'We can talk about it tomorrow,' Sandy suggested. 'I'll come down to town, and . . .'

'No,' he said, just as if he knew she was lying. 'Let's talk about it now. I came all the way up from the road to this godforsaken . . . trailer. I will not go all the way *down* until we've spoken face to face about the situation.'

'There isn't any situation.'

'You're refusing to be in my film. I do not accept your refusal. That, young lady, is a *situation*. I'd like to discuss it with you face to face, like civilized people. Please! The mosquitoes are horrendous out here!'

'Then go away. It's simple.'

'I tell you what. I'll give you a hundred dollars if you let me in. Cash. You get it whether or not you agree to be in *The Horror*. How does that sound?'

'I don't need your money. I do all right.'

'I'm surprised Miss Kutch pays you anything.'

'I get generous tips.'

'I'm sure you do. You're a very beautiful young lady.'

Scowling at the door, she said, 'I'm a good guide.'

'Five hundred. I'll give you five hundred dollars in cash if you let me in.'

That was a lot of money, too much to turn down without a very good reason. If all she had to do was let him in and listen to his offer . . .

What've I got to lose?

'Okay. Just wait a minute. I'll be right back.'

She hurried up the hall to Eric's small bedroom. Leaning over the bars of his crib, she eased him onto the mattress. Then she lowered the lid, fastened the hasp and padlocked it.

'Now keep still, honey,' she whispered.

On her way out, she slid the door shut.

'I'll be right there,' she called. She rushed into her own room. The tan shorts and shirt of her guide uniform still lay rumpled on her bed where she'd thrown them. Her underwear and socks had already gone into the clothes hamper, but she hadn't figured out what to do about her uniform – there would be no more tours of Beast House for weeks, maybe not for a couple of months – so she'd left her uniform on the bed.

She grabbed the shorts, hopped into them, pulled them up, and fastened them. The moment her belt was buckled, she snatched her shirt off the bed and raced down the hall. As she hurried along, she worked her arms into the sleeves. When she reached the door, she turned her back to it and scanned the room while she fastened her shirt buttons.

Except for the rumpled old towel on the sofa, there was no evidence of the baby.

There was evidence of Sandy's father, though: an ashtray on the lamp table; an open pack of Camel cigarettes; copies of *Field and Stream* magazine, *The American Rifleman* and *Hustler* scattered about; and a nearly full bottle of Jim Beam bourbon on the kitchen counter. They were all positioned in plain sight.

Sandy fastened her last button, then tossed the towel behind the sofa.

She scanned the area once more.

That'll do it.

She went to the door, unlocked it, and swung it open. Marlon Slade started to enter. She blocked his way. 'That'll be five hundred bucks,' she said, putting out her hand.

'Ah, yes. It nearly slipped my mind.' Smiling but looking miffed, he dug into the back pocket of his slacks. They were the same tan color as Sandy's uniform, and their legs were tucked into the tops of black leather riding boots. Marlon's shirt was black silk. Around his neck, he wore a green ascot. Sandy supposed he was trying to look the way he thought a film director *ought* to look.

To her, he seemed like a pudgy kid playing dress-up.

He brought out his wallet and opened it. The bill compartment was fat with money.

'You're loaded,' Sandy said.

'I'll be considerably less loaded after I've paid the extortion.'

'It was your idea,' she reminded him.

He counted out hundreds and fifties into her waiting hand.

When she had the promised amount, she said, 'Thank you,' and stepped away from the door. Marlon entered. He shut the door.

Sandy folded the money. As she stuffed it into a pocket of her shorts, she saw that she'd buttoned her shirt crooked.

She met Marlon's eyes. He'd noticed, too.

'I had to put it on in a hurry,' she muttered, blushing.

He grinned. 'Sorry if I came at a bad time.'

'It's all right.' She almost told him that she'd just finished taking a shower. But she stopped herself in time. Better to leave him wondering than to get caught in a lie.

'Could I get you a drink?' she asked.

'That would be spiffy.'

Spiffy?

'My dad drinks bourbon,' she said, and nodded toward the bottle.

'Perfect. I'll have mine straight up.' He eased himself down on the sofa.

On her way to the counter, Sandy smiled over her shoulder and asked, 'Are you old enough to drink? I wouldn't want to corrupt you.'

He chortled. 'I'm older than I look.'

'That's good, because you look like you're ten.'

'Aren't we amusing?'

'Yep.' She took down a jelly glass and poured bourbon into it. Then she picked up the glass and started toward him.

'Won't you be joining me?' he asked.

'I'm a minor.'

'At the very least. How old *are* you?'

'A lady never tells her age.'

'Fourteen, fifteen?'

'I'm older than I look.'

'Is that so?'

'Sure is.'

'I'm twenty-four,' Marlon said.

'Congratulations.'

'And how old are you?'

'None of your business.' She handed the glass to him, then stepped back, crossed her arms and shifted her weight so she was standing mainly on her left leg with her hip shoved out.

Marlon took a sip of his drink, then sighed and said, 'Sit down. Please.' He patted the sofa cushion beside him.

'I'm okay right here.'

'Suit yourself.'

'How did you find my place?' she asked.

His eyes dipped, sneaking a look at her chest, then hurried up to her face. 'Agnes Kutch gave me directions,' he said.

'Is that so?'

'Of course.'

'She wouldn't do that. She doesn't tell *anyone*.'

'She told me.'

'No, she didn't. And nobody else *knows* where I live. What did you do, follow me?'

'Of course not. I was otherwise occupied at the time you ran off.'

She scowled at him. 'You had someone *else* follow me?'

He tried to look innocent, but the answer showed on his face.

'Well,' Sandy said, 'that stinks.'

'I needed to know where to find you.'

'Who did you sic on me?'

'One of my assistants.'

'Who?'

'It doesn't matter.'

'It sure does! He'll blab it around and pretty soon *everybody* will be coming up here.'

'She won't blab. I promise you that. You have my word of honor.'

'Oh, well . . . Your word of honor. Whoop-de-doo.'

'My word is gold.'

'Sure.' Keeping her arms crossed, she shifted her weight to her other foot. 'This is just dandy. Just peachy.'

'I want you in my film, Margaret.'

'I already turned you down. Didn't you believe me? You had to send a *spy* after me?'

'I want you as my Janice.'

'*What?*'

'I want you to play Janice Crogan.'

'That's ridiculous.'

'Not at all.'

'You're kidding, right?'

'I never kid about such things.'

'I thought you wanted me as a . . . an extra, or something.'

'I want you as my *lead*. I would've explained that to you this morning if you hadn't been so quick to run off.'

'But what about . . . whoever she is? The one you *hired* to play Janice.'

He took another sip of bourbon. 'Tricia Talbot. She threw in the towel.'

'What?'

'Quit. Last night.'

Sandy found herself smiling. 'You're kidding. Why'd she quit?'

'We had . . . creative differences.'

'What do you mean?'

'She wanted to do things her way, not mine. I refused to give in, so she walked.' He grinned. 'Not only did she walk, but she *drove*. She packed up and hightailed it back to San Francisco last night, leaving us *sans* a Janice. And we start filming tomorrow. I need *you* tomorrow, bright and early.'

'Can't you just make a phone call, or something, and get yourself a real actress?'

'Why would I want to do that, when *you're* here?'

'I'm not going to be in your movie, that's why.'

'You *must* be.'

'No, I mustn't.'

'You'll be perfect. You'll *be* Janice Crogan.'

'Why don't you get Janice? She's right here in town.'

'She won't be in the movie.'

'Well, that makes two of us.'

'Twenty-five thousand dollars.'

Sandy stared at him, shocked.

'*Twenty-five thousand?*' she asked, barely able to speak, her voice a whisper.

'For just ten or twelve weeks of work.'

She murmured, 'Can't.'

'And why can't you?'

'Just can't. I'm not an actress.'

'You don't *need* to be an actress. I'll make you a *star*.'

She smirked. 'Oh, yeah. A star. Every day and twice on Sundays.'

'You've got the *look*, Margaret.'

'I don't look much like Janice.'

'There's no reason why you should. We'll color your hair, of course. You'll be spectacular as a blonde.'

'Think so?'

'I know so.'

She grinned.

'And what's *that* about?' Marlon asked.

She imagined herself saying, 'I've got a little secret for you, buddy. Underneath this ugly brown dye job, I *am* a blonde.'

That'd sure open a can of worms.

'Is something amusing?' he asked.

'I wouldn't want to turn into a dumb blonde.'

'It would only be for the role.'

'I don't want the role.'

'I think you do, Margaret. I *know* you do. Everybody wants to be a star. And you have what it takes.'

'No, I don't.'

'The *look*.'

'Bull.'

Marlon took another sip of bourbon, then leaned sideways and set his glass on the lamp table. 'Let me show you something,' he said, getting to his feet. 'Do you have a mirror?'

'What kind of mirror?'

'The largest you have.'

'What do you want to do?'

'Come, come, come.' He swept toward Sandy, reaching for her.

She put out a hand to signal him back.

He took hold of it and drew her after him, striding toward the hallway.

'Hey, what're you doing?'

'We're off to see the mirror!'

'My dad'll be home!'

'I doubt it. I'm a director. I know stage props when I see them. A smoker doesn't live in this trailer.'

'He does, too.'

'My nose tells me otherwise. And it's a wise nose.'

He pulled her into the bathroom and halted in front of the medicine cabinet mirror. 'Surely we can do better than this!' He barged past her and towed her along.

'You live here alone,' he said. 'Admit it.'

'I do not.'

'Just like *The Little Girl Who Lived Down the Lane*. Jodie Foster. Did you see the movie?'

'No.'

'Bet you did.'

He stopped in front of Eric's room.

He reached for the door.

Sandy gave his hand a hard jerk, tugging him away from it. 'Not in there,' she gasped. 'It's my dad's room.'

'Ah, Dad.'

'I've got a big mirror in *my* room,' she blurted.

'*Splendid!*'

This time, Sandy led the way, rushing onward, pulling Marlon through the doorway of her bedroom. She stepped around the end of the bed and drew him to her side. They both faced her dresser.

And the mirror above it.

'*Fabulous*,' Marlon whispered. 'But we need light. It's *far* too dark in here. We must have *light* for the star to shine.' He let go of her hand and said, 'Stay. Observe the mirror. Observe *yourself* in the mirror.'

She went ahead and looked at herself.

'Big deal,' she muttered.

She could see Marlon in the mirror, too. He stood by the doorway, his hand on the light switch. 'Behold!' he proclaimed in a deep, resonant tone. Then he flicked the switch.

Crimson light filled the room.

'My lord,' Marlon said.

'It's just a red bulb,' Sandy explained.

'How remarkably gawdy.' In the mirror, she watched him glide toward her, his arms spread like wings, his shiny black shirt fluttering. The shirt looked purple in the red glow.

She felt a tingle creep up her back.

Why does he have to act so weird?

He swooped in behind Sandy and put his hands on her shoulders.

He stood *directly* behind her. She could only see the ends of his fingers. The rest of Marlon was hidden behind her body.

Then his head tilted sideways and she saw his chubby face in the mirror as if she were wearing it on her left shoulder.

'My glorious Margaret,' he intoned, his voice thick and low. 'My star.' He started rubbing her shoulders. 'You *shall* be my star.'

'Don't think so,' she muttered.

'Imagine yourself on the big screen,' he said. His hands gently, firmly massaged her shoulders and the sides of her neck. 'That's no mirror in front of us, that's a movie screen. And there you are, Margaret Blume, two stories high.'

'I just look like I've got a real bad sunburn,' she said, and yawned. Though she still felt a little jittery, the massage made her lazy, groggy. Her head began to wobble with the motions of the rubbing.

Then Marlon kissed the side of her neck.

'Hey, don't,' she murmured.

'Watch the mirror,' he said, his breath tickling her skin.

'Stop it.'

'It's all right. Nothing's wrong. Look at yourself. See how beautiful you are. See what your *audiences* will see.' His reflection smiled at her. Then his hands slid down over her shoulders, down her chest. 'You are so glorious,' he whispered, and closed his hands on her breasts. He rubbed them, gently squeezed them through the fabric of her shirt.

Sandy squirmed. 'Quit it,' she said.

'You don't mean that. It feels very good, doesn't it? I know that it does.'

In the mirror, she saw herself squirm and grab his hands and try to peel them off her breasts.

But he kept them on her.

'It's all right,' he said. 'Don't fight it. It feels good.'

'No!'

He suddenly released her breasts, ripped her shirt open and jerked it backward and down off her shoulders. She glimpsed herself bare to the waist, her skin bathed in scarlet light, her breasts lurching as she tried to twist away.

He grabbed her arms and pinned them against her sides.

'Look at yourself,' he said, still sounding very calm. 'That's no mirror.

You're on the big screen, thousands of people staring up at you in awe. You're a star. Everyone wants you. Everyone wants to look at you, to touch you, to fuck you.'

'*Leave me alone!*'

'You don't want that. You want to be up on the screen, huge and spectacular. Look at yourself.'

'*Let go of me right now, you bastard!*'

'You love it, you love it. You love *this*. See how you're watching yourself? You can't take your eyes away. You love how you look. Now, imagine yourself a hundred times larger. Stop that squirming!' He shook her roughly.

She watched her body jerk back and forth, her head bobbing, her breasts jumping.

He stopped shaking her. 'Now stand still,' he said, 'and I'll let go of you.'

'Let go,' she said. Her voice came out high and trembling. 'Please.'

Marlon released his tight grip on her arms. He slid the shirt down them. As it fell to the floor, he reached around and caressed her belly with both hands. Then his pudgy fingers went to her belt buckle.

Flinching rigid, she clutched his wrists and gasped, 'No!'

Marlon laughed softly and undid the buckle. Then he unfastened the button at her waist. As he started to pull her zipper down, Eric leaped out of the red glow, landed on the dresser, skidded to a halt and whirled to face them.

Marlon's laughter stopped. His fingers stopped.

Eric stood in a crouch on top of the dresser, his body glistening and ruddy. He snarled, baring his fangs, and raised his arms like a miniature boogeyman.

And sprang straight for Marlon's face.

As Eric flew at him, the director squeaked once in a high voice that sounded nothing at all like the rich resonance of Marlon Slade.

In the mirror, Sandy watched Marlon's horrified, pudgy face vanish – hidden behind the body of her son.

Marlon's fingers jerked away from the zipper of her shorts.

He stopped pressing against her back.

Her shorts fell to the floor.

They almost tripped Sandy as she whirled around and watched him stumble backward with Eric clinging to his face. He reached up to grab Eric. The bed knocked his legs out from under him. As he fell, he hurled the infant away.

'*No!*' Sandy cried out.

Her son crashed against the wall near the head of her bed. He bounced off and dropped to the floor, tumbling.

She kicked the shorts away from her feet, rushed over to him and crouched down.

He lay sprawled on his back, blinking up at her.

His teeth and muzzle were bloody. Sandy hoped the blood was all Marlon's.

She heard the director whimpering behind her. Looking over her shoulder, she saw him on his hands and knees. He raised his head and gaped at her, his mouth open, his face shredded. 'It's . . . it's one of *them!*' he gasped. 'Isn't it? Isn't it? My God! Did you see the little fucker attack me?' He pushed himself up, stood on his feet, and stared past Sandy at the baby sprawled on the floor. 'Look at that ugly fucker. Son-of-a-bitch! Where'd it come from? Good thing I was here, or it would've got *you.*'

Sandy glared at him and said, 'I don't think so. I'm his mom.'

'*What?*'

'He's my kid.'

Marlon staggered toward them, blood spilling from his tattered face.

Sandy stood up in front of him.

'Outa my way, bitch,' he gasped. When he said 'bitch,' blood blew off his lips and sprayed Sandy in the face. 'I've got some business to finish with your little monster, and then . . .'

She punched him in the nose.

His eyes bulged and he stumbled backward.

Sandy kicked one of his feet sideways. He tripped himself. With a gasp of alarm, he fell and landed on his rump. The trailer shook.

Sandy turned and lunged for the dresser.

Glimpsed a naked red woman rushing at the mirror.

Jerked open the middle drawer.

Snatched out her butcher knife.

'*You take this,*' *Agnes Kutch had said, holding out the big, old knife to her.* '*You gonna be moving outa the house and living in that trailer out there, you gotta have a weapon. Wish I had a gun to give you, but this here is a real good knife. Mama, she used it on a fella once.*'

'*I know,*' *Sandy'd told her.* '*I was there. I saw her do it.*'

She slammed the dresser drawer and turned to face Marlon.

He was already on his knees, struggling to stand up.

She raised the knife overhead.

Marlon screamed like a woman.

Afterward, Sandy took Eric into the shower with her. Standing under the hot spray, she held him to her chest.

Eric had a lump on his head. It must've been sore, because he winced when Sandy touched it – even when she kissed it. Otherwise, he seemed fine. Maybe a little more subdued than usual.

'My little guy,' she said, caressing him. 'You're such a brave little guy. You knew mommy was in trouble and you *dashed* to the rescue. My hero. Of course, I oughta spank your little ass for breaking the crib.'

She patted his little ass gently.

Then she started to cry.

Eric made quiet whimpery sounds against her neck.

After a while, Sandy sniffed and sighed. She said, 'How do you feel about blowing this town, honey? 'Cause I guess we can't stay. Not after this.'

Chapter Two

The Beast House Bus – June, 1997

As the bus started across the Golden Gate Bridge, the young woman in front stood up with her microphone and turned to face the riders. 'Good morning, everyone! Welcome aboard! I'll be your guide for the trip out to Malcasa Point this morning. My name is Patty – and yes, I'm Irish. My grandfather hails from Cork. His name is Bob.'

A few of the riders chuckled.

'I know, I know,' Patty said. 'Lame joke.'

'What a dip,' Monica muttered.

Owen nodded and gave her a slight smile. He thought it was a bit early in the game to be calling Patty a dip. Monica, obviously, had taken an instant dislike to her. Monica took instant dislikes to a great many things, but especially to other women . . . and *most* especially to attractive ones.

Patty was more attractive than most. Owen supposed she was about twenty-five years old. Her deeply tanned skin and short brown hair made her look athletic. Though you couldn't call her slender, she wasn't fat, either. Stout, maybe. Or *built*. Owen thought she looked very good in the tan shirt and shorts of her guide uniform.

'We're now crossing San Francisco's famous Golden Gate Bridge,' Patty said. 'If you look out the windows, you'll see that it is not golden, at all. It's red. It *used* to be golden, but the Bridge Authority changed its color to *blood red* in 1981 in honor of its gory neighbor to the north, Beast House.'

Several riders chuckled and a few even clapped.

'That's God's-own-truth,' Patty said, raising her right hand.

Monica leaned over and whispered to Owen, 'That isn't true, is it?'

'Sure, I think so,' he said.

'Can't be. They wouldn't paint it red because of some stupid *tourist trap*. Besides, that place is like ninety miles away.'

'You're probably right.'

'As you may already know,' Patty continued, 'the Golden Gate Bridge was given its name in honor of the famed *heavenly* Golden Gates belonging to Saint Peter. That's because so many people have entered Saint Peter's Golden Gates by jumping off this one.'

With that, Patty received general laughter and applause.

'Thank you, thank you. None of what I've just told you is true, of course. My grandfather Bob from Cork *did* kiss the Blarney Stone, and passed its gift of the gab down to me. It's in my genes, but we won't get into that. Anyhow, this is the *Beast House* Bus. If you want the facts about Golden Gate Bridge, take a Gray Line Tour – though I don't recommend it. I took the Gray Line city tour recently and found myself sitting in a rear seat, which was uncomfortably close to the bus's toilet. But you don't want to hear about that. I don't want to *think* about it. Let's get to the serious stuff. You must all be wondering what you're doing here . . .'

'She's sure got *that* right,' Monica whispered.

'. . . overview of what's ahead. We have a fairly long ride, to begin with. It's something more than a two-hour drive up the coast to Malcasa Point. And – guess what? – two or so hours *back* to San Francisco.'

'Two hours of *this?*' Monica whispered.

'We're scheduled to reach our destination at about ten-thirty. At that point, you'll be free to disembark and enjoy all the creepy delights of Beast House. Your price of admission will include a self-guided audio tour which usually takes people about an hour to complete. But feel free to spend as long as you wish in the house. Some people enjoy lingering around the murder sights and *immersing* themselves in the ambiance.'

Several riders chuckled about that. Monica rolled her eyes upward.

'In fact, you'll have plenty of time not only to tour Beast House, but to visit the gift shop and enjoy a leisurely lunch on the grounds. Beast House has a very good snack shop with *great* chili cheese dogs. I *love* them chili dogs!'

'And it shows,' Monica whispered.

'You should definitely check out the snack shop's menu. If nothing suits you, though, there are several good places to eat along the main street of town, easy to walk to. The bus doesn't leave Malcasa Point until one-thirty p.m., so you'll have three hours. That's a pretty fair amount of time. Make sure you don't miss Janice Crogan's Beast House museum on Front Street. If you still have time left over, you might take a stroll down to the beach. The beach is only a few hundred yards from Beast House. You might order a take-out lunch from the snack shop, and have yourselves a picnic. Just make sure to keep an eye on your watches. You'll be amazed at how fast those three hours fly by, and we don't want you missing the bus back to town. We like to pull out at one-thirty on the nose. That gets you back to your hotels by about four, so you'll have time to rest and clean up before you go out for your evening fun. I hope you all have big plans for tonight – maybe a nice dinner at Fisherman's Wharf. Now, I have some matters to take care of. I'll get back to you in a few minutes, and we'll talk a little about the history of Beast House.'

With a smile, Patty lowered her microphone and turned away.

'My God,' Monica said, 'it's the *whole day*.'

'We knew that,' Owen told her. 'The brochure . . .'

'I know we *knew* it. It's just now sinking in, that's all.'

'If you didn't want to do this, I wish you would've spoken up. I mean, it's a bit late to be changing our minds.'

'It's all right,' she said. 'It just seems like sort of a waste, when we've only got a week in San Francisco, to spend one entire day doing something like *this*. And our *first* day, too. We haven't even had a chance to see any of the city yet.'

Owen was tempted to remind her that, after checking into their hotel late yesterday afternoon, they'd spent several hours roaming Fisherman's Wharf. They'd eaten a fine dinner at Fisherman's Grotto, inspected souvenir shops, visited the Wax Museum, and hiked to Pier 39 where they'd gone on a couple of rides, watched a juggling show, and explored more souvenir shops. It seemed to him that they'd seen at least *something* of San Francisco. But pointing it out to Monica would be a big mistake. So he said, 'If I'd known you felt that way, we could've done something else. We didn't have to do this.'

'Well, that's all right.' She smiled gently and patted his leg. 'We'll get it over with today, and then we'll have the whole rest of the week for other things.'

Get it over with.

Oh, man.

'We didn't have to do it at all,' he told her. 'If you'd only let me know that you didn't *want* to . . .'

'Why *would* I want to? What's the big attraction of going to some crummy old house where a lot of people got murdered? In fact, I think the whole idea's a little sick. They shouldn't even *allow* tours of a place like that. And if they *do*, people ought to have the good sense not to go. It's perverted. *And* it's four hours on a damn bus.'

Owen stared at her. He felt as if he'd been bludgeoned.

'Are you calling *me* a pervert?' he asked.

She laughed and said, 'Don't be a dope,' and gave his leg a pat. 'I didn't mean *you*.' Mouth close to his ear, she whispered, 'I love you, silly. Do you think I'd love you if you were a pervert?'

'I am, you know.'

'Oh, ho ho. You're so funny. You're such a dope. But I love you anyway.' She kissed his ear, then eased away and treated him with her *wanton growl*.

God only knows where she'd picked it up. Probably from some movie.

Monica's wanton growl.

A soft grumble in the throat, accompanied by a slight baring of her teeth and a sultry gaze.

Owen hated it.

He'd hated it from the first time she tried it on him, six months ago.

Like Owen, Monica was a first-year teacher at Crawford Junior High School in Los Angeles. He'd met her at the start of the fall semester, back in September of the previous year. And he hadn't liked her one bit. His friend Henry, another teacher starting out at Crawford, hadn't liked her either. He'd said, 'She's such a fucking know-it-all,' and Owen had agreed. 'She acts like she thinks her shit smells like roses.' Owen had agreed with that, too. 'Too bad,' Henry had said, ''cause she's sort of a fox. I wouldn't mind playing a little hide-the-salami with her, if you know what I mean.' To that, Owen had responded, 'Not me. Hide the salami, it'll probably freeze and break off. And there you'd be, salamiless-in-Gaza.'

Though conceited, condescending, stiff and humorless and generally annoying, Monica was almost beautiful. She looked very similar to the way Elizabeth Taylor had looked in her early twenties. Similar, but different.

The differences were not to Monica's advantage.

But nobody ever mentioned them to her.

What they pointed out were the *similarities*.

It had probably been going on since Monica's early childhood – friends and relatives and teachers and kids in school and strangers stopping her on the street to tell her, 'Do you know, you're the spitting image of Elizabeth Taylor? It's absolutely uncanny. I can't believe my eyes.'

It must've been constant.

And, of course, she'd bought it.

In spite of the evidence of mirrors.

Owen figured it was little wonder that she'd grown up thinking she was the queen of the universe.

Henry had said, 'To know her is to loathe her.'

And Owen had agreed.

During the entire fall semester, he'd done his best to stay out of Monica's way. He'd wanted nothing to do with her. But they'd often been thrown together by circumstances. Since both were first-year English teachers at the same school, it was inevitable.

And Owen just *had* to be nice to her.

Whenever an encounter couldn't be avoided, he smiled and spoke to her in a friendly way as if he liked her. He was that way with everyone.

She seemed to react with her usual cold disdain.

Until that December morning when she asked him for a ride to the Christmas party. Cornering him in the teacher's lounge, she said, 'Could I ask you a big favor, Owen?'

'Sure, I guess so.'

'Are you planning to go to the faculty Christmas party?'

'Yeah, I guess so.'

'Will you be driving?'

Oh, no.

'Yes.'

'Are you taking a date?'

If only.

'No, probably not.'

'The reason I'm asking, Owen – I simply can't drive myself to the party. It's so dangerous for a woman to be out by herself, especially late at night.'

'It sure is. Dangerous for *anybody*.'

'But it's worse for a woman.'

'Sure. I'm sure it is. Worse.'

'And the party probably won't get over till sometime after midnight. I can't possibly drive home all by myself at an hour like that. So would you mind terribly taking me to the party? I don't think I'll be able to go, otherwise.'

Owen didn't want to do it. He didn't *like* her. But he'd already confessed his intention of going to the party without a date – blowing his best possible excuse. On the spur of the moment, he could think of no halfway decent reason to turn her down. So he smiled and said, 'Sure, I'd be glad to give you a ride.'

It turned out to be more than a ride: it turned out to be a date. After their arrival at the party, she wouldn't go away. She stayed by Owen's side. She held on to his arm. She led him here and there, keeping him while she chatted with an assortment of faculty members and their spouses – usually the very teachers Owen liked *least* and would've avoided, given the chance.

Finally, Owen managed to sneak away from her. He got himself a cupful of red, potent punch, then spent a few minutes with *his* friends, Henry and Jill and Maureen.

Three minutes, maybe four.

Then Henry, keeping lookout, said, 'Oops, here comes trouble. You're up Shit Creek now, buddy.'

Owen said, 'Delightful,' and gulped down his punch.

'If you can't stand her,' Maureen said, 'why not tell her to take a leap?'

'I can't do that.'

Monica, arriving, greeted everyone with a rigid smile. Then she grabbed Owen's arm and said to the others, 'Will you excuse us, please?'

'Can't,' Henry said. 'You're inexcusable.'

'Oh, ho ho. Very amusing.' With that, she led Owen away from his friends. As she hurried him along, she said with a pout, 'I thought you'd deserted me. You can't just bring a girl somewhere and leave her stranded, Owie.'

He hated to be called Owie.

He hated the tone of her voice, as if she were talking to a three-year-old.

He also hated to dance. But she squeezed his arm and said, 'How about tripping the light fantastic for a while?'

'I'm not much of a dancer,' he said.

'That's all right. I'm a *wonderful* dancer. *And* a wonderful teacher. I'll have you cutting the rug like Fred Astaire.'

'Fred Astaire's dead.'

She smiled, shook her head, and said, 'Don't be morbid, darling.'

Darling? Oh, my God.

'I'd really rather not dance,' he said.

He despised dancing in general, but was appalled by the idea of dancing with Monica – especially at the faculty Christmas party, surrounded by teachers, counselors, secretaries, vice principals . . . the principal himself. People he had to see every working day. People who *knew* him.

'You can't just bring me here and not dance with me. How would that look?'

You're not my date! he wanted to shout. *I gave you a ride! Say 'Thanks for the lift,' and leave me alone!*

He thought it, but didn't say it. Her feelings wouldn't just be hurt, they'd be trampled.

He finally said, 'I guess I can give it a try.'

She led him downstairs to the recreation room. It was decorated with red and green streamers, and dark except for the glow of Christmas tree lights strung across the ceiling. Owen noticed that there were no clear bulbs, no white bulbs. They were all deep, rich colors: blue and red and green and orange. They looked gawdy and wonderful, but didn't illuminate much.

Just as well, Owen thought.

The floor was crowded with dancing couples. Half of nearly every pair was somebody Owen knew from school. Many nodded, smiled, or spoke brief greetings as they made their way to the middle of the floor.

Stopping, Monica turned to him and gazed into his eyes.

She *is* pretty, Owen thought.

But he suspected that *anyone* would look good in the glow of all those Christmas tree lights. He could see the shine of them in Monica's hair, their sparkle in her eyes. They softened her face, blurring its harshness, hiding the arrogance and suspicion that could usually be seen in her eyes and lips.

She really did resemble Elizabeth Taylor. For the first time, the similarities seemed to surpass the differences.

And she looked great in her angora sweater. It hugged her body in such a way that each breast swelled out separately – they were twin, fuzzy white mounds with a glen between them.

She might've looked great in her pleated plaid skirt, too. It was very short and drifted softly against her thighs. But she'd ruined the skirt's appeal by wearing tights. The black tights encased her legs, showing off their slender curves but hiding every inch of skin.

'Just do what I do, darling,' she said.

With that, she stepped forward until their bodies met. She took hold of Owen's left hand, placed her own left hand on his shoulder, and said, 'Put your other hand in the middle of my back.'

He followed her instructions.

'That's right,' she whispered.

A new tune began to flow from the speakers. 'White Christmas,' sung by Bing Crosby.

They started to dance.

It was a slow dance, and they held each other close. Owen followed Monica's lead. It was easy; she hardly moved at all, just swayed back and forth and took small steps this way and that.

She smelled awfully good – some sort of perfume that filled Owen's mind with images of balmy nights and soft breezes in the tropics. He'd been smelling it all evening. But now it seemed to radiate off her skin in warm, rich waves.

A wonderful, exotic aroma.

But not nearly as wonderful or exotic as the *feel* of Monica as they danced: her face resting on his shoulder; her hair tickling the side of his face; her left hand caressing his back while her right clasped his hand; her breasts pushing firmly but softly against his chest; her belly pressed to his belly; her crotch rubbing him in a subtle way that seemed almost accidental; her thighs brushing against his with every step she took.

Before Bing was halfway through the song, Owen started getting hard.

Oh, terrific.

Just what I need.

Hoping Monica hadn't noticed it yet, he bent forward slightly to break contact down there.

'Don't be a silly,' she said.

Her left hand went down and pulled at his rump until he was tight against her again.

'Ooooh, Owen,' she said. Then she tilted back her head, looked him in the eyes, and let forth with her wanton growl.

Immediately, he hated it. Though it seemed to express approval and lust, its blatant phoniness made it seem like mockery.

She probably thinks it's a cute thing to do, he told himself. Maybe she even thinks it's sexy.

'A penny for your thoughts,' Monica said.

'Huh?'

'What're you daydreaming about?'

'I'm not daydreaming.'

'You're *always* off in your own little world.'

'I'm here,' he told her, and tried to smile.

'*Now* you are.'

'Sorry.'

'You're such a silly.' She gave his thigh a squeeze. 'What am I going to do with you?'

'Whatever you please,' he said. Then he leaned forward and looked past Monica to see out her window. Just a few feet beyond the edge of the road, there seemed to be a drop-off. He could see nothing down there except the ocean. 'Yikes,' he said.

'A thrill, isn't it?' She didn't sound thrilled, but she was smiling as if she were the only person in on a joke. 'If we die, guess whose fault it will be?'

'The bus driver's?'

'Think again.'

'Mine.'

'Ding! You win. You insisted on coming.'

'I didn't exactly insist. It was more like a suggestion.'

'We could be riding on a cable car right now.'

'We can ride on cable cars tomorrow.'

'If we're still alive.'

Chapter Three

Tuck and Dana

Lynn Tucker, sitting at the kitchen table, set down her cup of coffee and smiled when Dana came in. 'Hey, hey, look at you.'

Dana grinned and raised her arms. 'Just call me Ranger Rick.'

'You look great.'

'Thanks, Tuck. You, too.' Frowning, she said, 'I wish my uniform looked like that.' While Dana's tan shirt and shorts were stiff and creased and dark, Tuck's looked soft and faded. 'Want to trade?'

'Think mine'd fit you?' Tuck asked.

'Probably not.'

'Probably.' She laughed. 'What are you, now, about six-nine, seven feet?'

'Just six. But I'm dainty.'

Tuck pushed back her chair and said, 'Sit down, Miss Dainty. I'll get you a cup of coffee.'

'I can get it.'

'You're my guest.' Tuck stood up and headed for a cupboard. 'Besides, it's your first day. Tomorrow, I'll let you get your own coffee.'

'Okay,' Dana said. 'Thanks.' She pulled out a chair and sat at the table.

'As for your uniform,' Tuck said, 'it'll be a lot better after a few washings. What you need to do is wash both your uniforms every night whether they need it or not. That'll get the stiffness out. Before you know it, you'll look like an old hand.' She took down a cup and turned around. 'So, how did you sleep last night?'

'I zonked. I tell you, Tuck . . . I still can't believe I'm here. This is such a great place!'

'I thought you might like it.' She picked up the coffee pot and brought the clean cup over to the table. As she filled the cup for Dana, she said, 'One thing, okay? Try not to call me Tuck when we're over at the house. You know, in front of the others.'

'I'll try. Might be tough, though. I've been calling you Tuck since we were kids.'

'For which I've never properly repaid you.'

'Think nothing of it,' Dana said.

'Anyway, try to avoid it, okay? The thing is, I'm the boss of things over there. It's bad enough that I look like I'm only about fifteen years old.'

'A *mature* fifteen.'

'I'm also only twenty damn years old and have to go around giving orders to all these *older* people. All I'd need is to have them hear you calling me Tuck.'

'Don't they know your name's Tucker?'

'Maybe, maybe not. Nobody uses my last name over there, but they all know Janice is my stepmother. Maybe they think my name's Crogan.'

'She should've changed *her* name when she married your dad.'

'Would *you* change your name to Tucker?'

'If I married a guy named Tucker.'

'Anyway, she didn't. Just don't call me Tuck in front of the employees, okay?'

'You don't call me Moose, I won't call you Tuck.'

'I never called you Moose.'

'Right. You preferred Bullwinkle.'

'Okay, I won't call you Bullwinkle. I promise. Nothing but Dana. Or *Miss Lake*, if I have to berate you for doing something stupid.'

'Would I do something stupid?'

'Oh, not you.'

'So,' Dana said, 'what *should* I call you?'

'Boss lady.'

Dana cracked up, and Tuck grinned. She waited for Dana's laughter to subside, then said, 'Lynn would be fine.'

Nodding, Dana lifted her cup. Steam drifted off the dark surface of the coffee. She blew it gently away, then took a sip. 'Mm, good.'

'Do you want something to eat?'

'No, I'm fine.'

'Good. We don't have much time. We can grab a bite at the snack shop after we get there. Or we can stop for doughnuts on the way. Are you still a doughnut hound?'

'You bet,' Dana said. 'But I'm not that hungry right now. I don't usually eat much in the morning.'

'About ready to go?'

'Yep. You said to be ready by nine. I've been ready since I walked in.' She took another sip of coffee, then another.

'Take your time. We don't have to rush off right away. I'm the boss, after all.'

'Yeah, but you shouldn't be late.'

'Even if we don't get there till nine-thirty, I'll still be the first one to arrive. Nobody's all that gung-ho. It's just a job to them, you know?'

'What is it to you?'

'A *passion!*'

Dana laughed. 'Right.'

'Do you want the truth?'

'If you're up to it.'

'I *love* it all. I really do. I love being the boss . . .'

'You've always been great at giving orders.'

'It isn't just that, either. There's something about Beast House. It's got *history*, you know? An *awful* history, but . . . There's something sort of old and romantic and mysterious about the place. I just love it there. It's like a strange little piece of the past is still alive . . . I mean, you can *feel* it.'

'If you say so.'

'Did you feel it yesterday?'

'Mostly, I just felt a little spooked.'

Tuck grinned. 'Good. You're supposed to. But after you get used to the place, it probably won't seem so creepy anymore.'

'Probably?'

'Well, it actually seems to get *worse* instead of better for some people. That's pretty rare, though.'

'I hope that doesn't happen to me.'

'Don't worry. You'll be fine. Me, I like the place *more* all the time.'

'Someday, maybe it'll be *yours.*'

'I ain't gonna hold my breath,' Tuck said.

'You're Janice's only heir, aren't you?'

'Well, shit, I guess so. She doesn't have any brothers or sisters, and you *know* what happened to her parents.' Tuck frowned as if thinking about it for a few moments, then said, 'Other than Dad and me, she's got nobody else except an uncle and cousin. But Janice is just in her thirties, for godsake. I doubt if she'll be pitching forward on her nose in the near future. Besides which, she might even have a kid of her own someday.'

'She hasn't so far.'

'Yeah, but she's only been married for a couple of years.'

'She's how old?'

Tuck frowned for a moment, then said, 'Thirty-six.'

'Well, that's not *terribly* old to be starting a family.'

'For all I know, she might *already* be knocked up. And if she's not, she probably *will* be by the time they get back from the cruise. I mean, two months together in the South Pacific? I damn near get pregnant just *thinking* about it.'

'Have they been trying to have a baby?' Dana asked.

'Jeez! How would I know? She's a great gal and everything and we really like each other, but it's not like being with you. She my dad's *wife*. I mean, I can't just ask her about stuff like that.' Tuck raised her eyebrows. 'Do you want any more coffee?'

'Nope, I'm fine.'

'Maybe we'd better get going.' She reached across the table for Dana's cup. 'I'll rinse these out and batten down the hatches. You might want to grab your windbreaker. You never know when the fog'll come rolling in. It can get pretty nippy.'

Five minutes later, Dana followed Tuck into the three-car garage. They walked past the eighteen-foot cabin cruiser, then past a Mercedes, before climbing into the red Jeep Wrangler.

'I don't know how you can stand living in such squalor,' Dana said.

'It's tough.' As the automatic door rolled upward, Tuck started the Jeep's engine. 'I'll probably have to move out if I ever get married.'

'Don't get married. No guy would be worth it.'

'Nobody *I* know,' Tuck said. Laughing, she backed out of the garage.

As she turned the Jeep around, Dana gazed at the front of the house. With its many outside stairways, its passageways and balconies, the enormous stucco house looked more like a nice hotel than like a private home. 'It's *really* fabulous,' she said.

'Amazing what you can do with a few million bucks, isn't it?'

'I wouldn't mind living in a place like this.'

'You *are* living in a place like this,' Tuck said. 'All summer.' She aimed the remote over her shoulder. As the garage door started to close, she put the remote away and headed down the long, narrow driveway.

The morning air blew Dana's hair. She took deep breaths. She could smell the woods *and* the ocean.

Though the area immediately in front of the house was bright with sunlight, the driveway soon took them into thick woods. There, in shadows as heavy as dusk, the rays of the sun looked like golden pillars slanting down though the trees. Haze drifted like smoke in the gold.

Dana smiled at Tuck, and shook her head.

'Not exactly like Los Angeles, is it?' Tuck asked.

'Not exactly. I can't believe I'll be spending the whole summer here.'

'Neither can I. Man, am I ever glad you could come.'

'*You're* glad!'

'You bet I am.' Tuck picked up speed on the downhill. She took the curves awfully fast.

Too fast for Dana's taste.

Even with the seatbelt on, Dana felt her body being shoved from side to side as they raced around the bends.

It's okay, she told herself. Tuck knows what she's doing. She's probably driven in and out of this place thousands of times.

Tuck glanced at her and grinned, then faced the front again. Her long, blond hair was streaming behind her in the breeze. 'We're gonna have a great time,' she said.

'I hope so.'

If she doesn't slam us into a tree.

'And you know what?' Tuck asked. 'I couldn't have stayed home this summer if you hadn't agreed to come.'

'What? What do you mean?'

'They were all set to drag me along with them on their damn cruise.'

'Oh, that would've been a fate worse than death.'

'I *hate* cruises. Yuck!'

'Are you out of your mind?'

'Have you ever gone on one?'

'No.'

'Just wait.' Some hair blew across her face. She fingered it out of the way with one hand while she steered around a curve with the other. 'It's like being on a floating prison full of chipper weirdos. But Dad didn't want me staying here alone. So I'd be out somewhere on the briny sea, right now, if you hadn't come to stay. I owe you bigtime.'

Shrugging, Dana said, 'I'm sure you could've gotten somebody else.'

'I didn't want anyone else. You're my best friend. Besides, you're the only person Dad would've agreed to. It was you or nobody.'

'How come?'

'Hell, don't ask me. He likes you. He trusts you. He thinks you're a regular Girl Scout.'

'I've got *him* fooled.'

Tuck smiled at her. 'No you don't. He's right.'

'Aw, shucks.'

'Anyway, I thought you should know. It's not like I'm doing *you* all the big favors. You're doing a major one for *me* just by being here.'

'Why don't you do *me* a favor and slow down?'

'This is nothing. You wanta see me *really* go fast?'

'That's all right. Some other time. When I'm not in the car, for instance.'

'All right, all right.' Tuck eased her foot down on the brake pedal, and the Jeep slowed down.

'Thank you,' Dana said.

'You're always so cautious.'

'You're always so reckless. Maybe that's why your dad didn't want you to stay by yourself.'

'I don't think that's why.'

'Was he afraid you might throw wild parties?'

'Nah. It was the whole idea of me being alone in the house. You know, it's so enormous and there's nothing around it but the woods. No neighbors or anything. It *can* get a little creepy when you're there by yourself. Anyway, I think Dad had visions of the Manson family or Hannibal Lecter coming for me.'

'In which case, a lot of good *I'd* be.'

'It's just some sort of mental aberration on Dad's part. He seems to think I'll be fine if you're staying with me. It's not because you're such a big, strapping brute, either.'

'I hope not.'

'Not that you aren't.'

'I see that living in the lap of luxury hasn't robbed you of your native charm.'

'Nope. Thank God, huh?'

'Yeah. It would've been a major loss. Anyway, if they'd forced you to go on the cruise with them, what would they have done about Beast House?'

'Put Clyde in charge.'

'Who's Clyde?'

'Clyde Bennett. You met him yesterday. He's a charmer. He's gotta be thrilled to death about *me* being head honcho this summer.'

'Does he give you a hard time?' Dana asked.

'He used to.'

As they glided around a bend, the two-lane public road came into sight. Tuck slowed the Jeep and came to a complete stop. 'This is where you've gotta start being careful,' she explained. 'Some of the people around these parts drive like maniacs.' She eased forward, checking in both directions, then stepped on the gas. 'Beast House,' she yelled, 'here we come!'

Chapter Four

The Story According to Patty

'Hello again,' Patty said.

Owen, relieved by the interruption, settled back in his seat and leaned sideways a little to look up the aisle at the guide.

'Is everyone enjoying the scenery?' she asked. 'It's pretty terrific, isn't it?'

Looks good from here, Owen thought.

Patty was standing casually with the microphone close to her mouth. She held on to a support pole with her other hand. The hand was high, as if she'd raised her arm to ask a question.

'This section of Pacific Coast Highway can be a little frightening,' Patty said. 'But you folks probably enjoy a good scare, or you wouldn't be on your way to Beast House. Am I right?'

Some of the passengers responded, 'Right.' Others chuckled.

'To put your minds at ease, I can tell you that we haven't lost a bus over the cliffs in the past three weeks. That trip, I hear, was very exciting for a few seconds. But I miss the guide. She and I were pretty good friends. Her name was Bubbles.'

'Give me a break,' Monica muttered.

'Not Sandy?' asked a man in an aisle seat just in front of Patty.

'Good one,' she told him.

'How about Rocky?' suggested another passenger.

'Actually, all three perished. It was a terrible accident. But I'm sure we'll fare better. Won't we, Al?' The driver raised his arm and gave a thumbs-up. 'He doesn't let a little thing like cataracts get in his way.' After a short pause, Patty asked, 'How many of you have been to Beast House before?'

Looking around, Owen saw eight or ten of the passengers raise a hand.

'What's that, about one out of five? Pretty good. That's about typical. We get a lot of repeats. There's something about Beast House that just keeps drawing people back to it. Especially weirdos. No offense.'

A *lot* of riders laughed at that one.

'The house has had a long and colorful history. Mostly, the color has been red. I won't get into much of that, though. What I want to do, now, is tell you a few things that won't get covered to any extent on the tour.

'Beast House has been a popular tourist trap . . . attraction . . . since 1932. For those of you who aren't whizzes at math, that's a while ago. The Great Depression was going on. Herbert Hoover was President of the United States. Edward the Eighth sat on the throne of Great Britain. Germany's comeback kid, Adolph Hitler, was defeated that year in a run-off election for the presidency when a guy by the name of Hindenburg burst his balloon . . . so to speak.'

'Oh, the humanity,' someone threw in.

'Exactly,' Patty said. 'In 1932, the Japanese invaded Shanghai. Al Capone was sent to prison in Atlanta. The Lindberg baby got himself kidnapped and murdered. Amelia Earhart was still among the unvanished. Gary Cooper starred in *A Farewell to Arms* and Shirley Temple made her first movie. Not only that, but 1932 marked the birth of Senator Edward Kennedy and Elizabeth Taylor.'

'There you go,' Owen whispered to Monica. 'Liz.'

'But the *real* highlight of 1932 was the opening of Beast House. The Victorian-style house had already been standing for thirty years, but as a private home. It took Maggie Kutch to turn the place into one of America's most bizarre and infamous tourist attractions.

'Beast House had been built in 1902 by Lilly Thorn, widow of Lyle Thorn. Lyle, the leader of the Thorn Gang, was an outlaw known throughout the west during the latter years of the nineteenth century. You name it, he did it. He robbed banks, stage coaches, and trains. He rustled cattle and horses. It's said that he committed so many murders and rapes that nobody could keep track of them all. The brutal massacres of several entire families in the Arizona territory have been attributed to Lyle Thorn and his gang, but that's mostly speculation. Some people think the massacres were the work of Apaches. Nobody knows for sure. Nor does anyone know the fate of Lyle Thorn or his gang. Their depredations simply stopped in the early 1890s. We can only assume that he and his band of cutthroats came to a sudden, violent end.

'On their way to the end, however, they worked up a ton of bad karma. Lyle must've passed it on to his wife and children, and I think it all ended up in Beast House.

'As I mentioned, his wife's name was Lilly. They were Lyle and Lilly Thorn. But nobody around Malcasa Point ever saw Lyle. He had apparently "bought the ranch" before Lilly and the kids ever showed up in town. The boys were named Sam and Earl. It's believed that Lyle was their father, but nobody knows for sure.

'Anyway, Lilly and the two boys arrived in town in early 1902. And they were loaded. Apparently, Lyle's life of crime had been very lucrative. Before you know it, Lilly had a crew hard at work building her dream house.

'And they all lived happily ever after in the dream house until August 2, 1903, when the beast came up out of the cellar and ran amok, committing wholesale slaughter on her family. You'll hear all about that on the tour, though, so I won't get into it now.

'For now, we want to skip ahead about twenty-eight years. During most of that time, the Thorn house stood deserted. Nobody wanted to live there because of the killings. But in 1931, the Kutch family bought it and moved in. Maggie Kutch lived in the house with her husband, two little girls, and her baby son. For just about two weeks. Then one rainy night, her entire family was brutally slain by what she described as a "raving, white beast." Maggie was the only survivor.

'You might think that Maggie would've left town after such a tragedy. But she stayed and built a home for herself directly across the street from the old Victorian. Her new house was a fortress made of brick. And it didn't have a single window. You'll see it today. Unfortunately, the tour doesn't include the Kutch house. Maggie's daughter still lives there, so it's off limits.'

A blond kid a few rows ahead of Owen raised his hand.

'Question?' Patty asked.

'Yeah. If Maggie's whole family got slaughtered by the beast, how come she still has a daughter?'

'Good question. What's your name, friend?'

'Derek.'

'Well, Derek, here's the thing. Maggie gave birth to this daughter *after* the massacre. This one – her name's Agnes – was born several years later.'

'But you said her husband got killed by the beast.'

'He did. Later on, though, Maggie met someone else. This new man in her life became Agnes's father.'

'Oh, I get it. Okay. Thanks.'

'Thank you for asking, Derek. Now . . .' Patty frowned. 'Let's see, we'd just gotten Maggie moved into the brick house. Nobody quite knew what she was up to . . . why she would want to live there, right across the road from the house where the beast had murdered her family. That place was abandoned, boarded up. Some of the townfolk thought it should be torn down or burnt. At that time, they called it Massacre House. They said it was a blight on the good name of the town.

'But it remained standing, and pretty soon, large, mysterious crates began to arrive. The crates were carried up the porch stairs and into Massacre House. Can anyone tell me what was in them? Lab equipment for godless experiments? Or maybe . . .'

Derek raised his hand. Before Patty could call on him or anyone else, he blurted, 'I know what they had in them! Wax dummies of the dead guys!'

'That's right. Wax dummies of dead guys *and* gals. At the time, however, nobody had any idea what might be in the crates. They didn't get their answer until the summer of 1932. First, a ticket booth went up. Then a few signs. A sign at the top of the ticket book read, *BEAST HOUSE.* Another sign gave the times and prices of the tours. Back in those days, a tour cost only twenty-five cents. That's a far cry from what they'll be charging you people today. But a quarter meant something back in 1932. A lot of things did.

'Maggie put up one other sign before she opened Beast House to the public. My favorite. It was painted in red letters on an old wooden door. Unfortunately, it disappeared years and years ago. But you can see photos of it in Janice Crogan's Beast House Museum on Front Street. It goes like this. *"BEAST HOUSE! THE LEGENDARY, HISTORICAL SITE OF GHASTLY, MONSTROUS MURDERS! NOT ONE, BUT MANY! SEE WITH YOUR OWN EYES THE ACTUAL SCENES OF BRUTAL, BLOODY BUTCHERIES WHERE THEY HAPPENED! FEAST YOUR EYES ON AUTHENTIC REPRODUCTIONS OF THE BEAST'S RAVAGED VICTIMS – AS THEY WERE FOUND, IN THEIR ACTUAL DEATH GARMENTS. HEAR THE TRUE TALES OF THE BEAST AS TOLD BY ITS ONLY KNOWN SURVIVOR, MAGGIE KUTCH, PROPRIETOR OF BEAST HOUSE AND YOUR PERSONAL GUIDE."* '

Patty grinned and said, 'Love it. Plenty of the townfolks didn't, though. They tried to stop Maggie from opening the house, but she wasn't someone easily stopped and the first tour of Beast House took place, as scheduled, on July 1, 1932.

'Only a few people showed up for it. They were mostly locals. Some were the very people who'd protested against the place. Apparently, they were eager to see just how bad it really was. According to newspaper accounts, what they found was worse than they'd expected. The good folks were shocked and outraged. Several fainted. Others ran from the house, shrieking.

'Now that they'd seen the tour, they considered it an offense against human decency, God, motherhood, and good taste. One published report called it "An obscene display of vulgar savagery unfit for the eyes of civilized human beings." An editorial went this way: "Has our community now sunk into such a mire of depravity as to find entertainment in the lewd and gory depiction of scantily clad murder victims such as can be found in every corner of the blasphemy known as Beast House? For shame!" ' Grinning and shaking her head, Patty said, 'I like that, "For shame!" '

'Those people *hated* Beast House. They kept trying to shut it down. They couldn't manage that, but the town did pass an ordinance prohibiting children under the age of sixteen from going in.

'As the weeks went by, though, a funny thing happened. Local merchants began to notice they had more money in their cash registers at the end of the day. Pretty soon, it dawned on them that the extra cash had come from the pockets of strangers. There seemed to be a regular flow of visitors coming into town. They spent money at the gas station, the café, the ice-cream parlor, the pharmacy, the grocery store. You name the business, and out-of-towners were spending money there. And what was behind this influx of visitors?'

'BEAST HOUSE!' a girl shouted, beating Derek to the punch.

Derek frowned over his shoulder at her.

'That's right!' Patty said. 'Beast House! People were coming to Malcasa Point from nearby towns and farms, even all the way from Marin County, San Francisco and the East Bay, just to take the Beast House tour. But they didn't *only* take the tour; they were spending their money all over town. Suddenly, nobody had a bad word to say about Beast House and nobody wanted to shut it down anymore. Also, the restriction against kids was removed. Everyone was allowed to take the tour, regardless of age.

'Ever since then, Beast House has been drawing visitors to Malcasa Point. Not always in great numbers, though. For the first couple of decades, the numbers were pretty low, especially by today's standards. Some old records show that somewhere between thirty and fifty people per week were taking the tours.

'But Beast House's popularity grew during the 1950s, probably because a couple of kids broke in one night and ran into trouble.

According to the survivor, the trouble was a beast. He escaped, but his friend wasn't so lucky. You'll hear all about it during your audio tour of the house, so I won't go into the details. Because of the attack, however, interest in Beast House really surged in the fifties. Then it tapered off a little, but not very much. The House continued to pull in a steady stream of visitors until 1979.

'*Everyone* knows what happened in '79. If you didn't know about it, most of you wouldn't be riding on this bus today.'

'And wouldn't that be a shame,' Monica whispered.

'To make a long story short, in 1979 a lot of very nasty business hit the fan. And the fan was Beast House.'

Several passengers chuckled.

'It's all on the tour and in the books and movies, so I won't pile the details on. Suffice it to say that the summer of 1979 was a *festival* of disappearances, abductions, rapes, rescues, and brutal murders.

'To top it all off, the actual corpses of three beasts were discovered after the smoke cleared in '79. Two of them quickly disappeared under mysterious circumstances. The third body, though, was preserved by a taxidermist. It was displayed at Janice Crogan's Beast House Museum for several years until it was stolen in 1984. The museum still has photographs of it, and they can also be found in both of Janice's books.'

Someone near the back of the bus must've raised a hand, because Patty nodded and asked, 'Question?'

A man said, 'Is it true that the stolen beast turned up in some sort of a freak show?'

Patty grinned. 'And your name is?'

'Marv.'

'Well, Marv, you're probably speaking of the Hairless Orangutan of Borneo. It wasn't exactly in a freak show, but in an exhibit called Jasper's Oddities at the Funland amusement park.'

'Where's Funland?' Derek asked.

'It's in Boleta Bay,' Patty explained. 'On the coast just south of San Francisco.'

'And it's got the beast?'

'Well, it *had* a creature on exhibit that *might've* been a beast. I saw it a long time ago, myself.'

'So did I,' said a man sitting a few rows ahead of Owen. 'Name's Wayne. Do you think it was the actual beast, or some kind of fake? I heard it was a fake.'

'I can't say for sure. Nobody can. Like so many other things that have to do with Beast House, it's a mystery. And it'll have to stay a mystery, because a positive i.d. was never made and the so-called

Hairless Orangutan of Borneo disappeared in about 1988. *All* the Jasper's Oddities exhibits vanished one night, and the building was demolished shortly after that.'

'Did Janice Crogan ever get a look at the Hairless Orangutan?' Wayne asked.

'No, she never did.'

'She should've taken it back,' Derek said. 'If it was *her* monster and somebody stole it . . .'

'I talked to Janice about it, and she told me that she was glad to be rid of the thing. She didn't want it back. When she was keeping it in her museum, she had to face it every single day. It was an awfully vivid reminder of those terrible experiences she'd had in 1979. Also, she told me that it didn't smell terribly fresh.'

'Oh, yuck,' said the same girl who had cried out 'BEAST HOUSE!' a few minutes earlier.

'And what's your name, young lady?' Patty asked.

'None of your beeswax.'

'And what an unusual name that is,' Patty said. 'Do you have a nickname? Wax?'

'Try Bitch,' Owen whispered.

Monica rolled her eyeballs upward.

'Her name's Shareel,' said the man sitting beside her. Probably her father.

'Thank you,' Patty told him. 'And thank you for your comment about the odor, Shareel. According to Janice, the odor was faint but *very* yucky. She said it smelled like a dead rat.'

Shareel went, 'Ooooooo.'

'Apparently, that's what happens if taxidermy isn't done just right.'

'This is disgusting,' Monica whispered.

'Yeah,' Owen said, smiling.

'Don't tell me you *like* it.'

'Okay, I won't.'

Patty pointed to someone and said, 'Yes, Marv?'

'What can you tell us about its apparatus?'

She grinned and blushed. 'Its *apparatus?*'

'You know.'

'I certainly know, all right. But we don't talk about that.'

'It's in the books.'

'You're right. It's in the books. Not in the movies, though, and not on our tour. Not on *this* tour. If you're really curious about that sort of thing, we do offer a special, adults only tour of Beast House. Maybe some of you have heard of it. The Midnight Tour? It's quite an event.

Saturday nights only. A trip through Beast House starting at midnight, with our best guide leading the way. It's a hundred dollars per person, but the price includes a picnic dinner on the grounds of Beast House – with a no-host bar for the drinkers among you – followed by a special showing of *The Horror* at the town movie theater, and finally the special, unexpurgated tour in which you learn all the stuff that's too nasty for our regular tours. If any of you are interested, you can make reservations at the ticket office.'

'They only have it on Saturday nights?' Marv asked.

'That's right. One night a week.'

'Does the bus go out to it?'

'There isn't any special run for the Midnight Tour. What people sometimes do, though, is come in on the Saturday morning bus, spend the whole day, do the Midnight Tour, stay overnight at one of the motels in town, then catch the Sunday afternoon bus back to San Francisco. If you don't have your own car, that's about the only sensible way to do it. Imagine what it'd cost for a cab ride.'

'But kids aren't allowed?' Derek asked, sounding disappointed.

'No kids under the age of eighteen. Beast House rules.'

'That stinks.'

'I know. But, just figure, it'll give you something to look forward to doing when you're a little older.'

'It still stinks.'

'Well, there won't be much said on the Midnight Tour that isn't in Janice Crogan's books. So if you're really interested, Derek, read the books. Speaking of which, we've come back to where I was heading; one of the main participants in the Beast House mayhem of 1979 was an eighteen-year-old girl named Janice Crogan. You've all heard of her, right? She happens to be a very good friend of mine, and my employer.

'After surviving her ordeal, she wrote a nonfiction book called *The Horror at Malcasa Point*. It contains portions of Lilly Thorn's diary, a general history of Beast House, and a detailed account of the terrible experiences she had there in 1979. It also has quite a few photographs, including those photos I mentioned of the dead beast.' She smiled toward someone at the rear of the bus and said, 'Unfortunately, Marv, the photos don't show the area you're so interested in.'

'I'm not *that* interested,' he protested. 'Just wondering if what they say is true, you know?'

'Well, can you make the Midnight Tour?'

'Not likely. I've gotta get back to Chicago on Saturday.'

'In that case,' Patty said, 'I'll let you in on a little secret. I have it on good authority that the matter you're curious about is true. But you didn't hear it here. For those of you who don't know what we're talking about, you can satisfy your curiosity by going on the Midnight Tour or by reading either of Janice's books. One of which is *The Horror at Malcasa Point*, a nationwide bestseller published in 1980. How many of you have read it?'

Owen raised his hand. Looking around, he saw that only three other people had their hands up. One of them, a heavy bald guy near the back, he suspected of being Marv.

'Four out of about fifty. Not bad, considering it *is* a book. How many of you have seen any of the Beast House movies?'

Owen raised his hand. So did Monica. So did nearly everyone on the bus.

'Let's not get into the movies just yet. I need to finish plugging Janice's books. First came the big bestseller, *The Horror at Malcasa Point*. It only took her two months to write, which is a truly remarkable feat in itself, considering her injuries and all the horrors that she'd just gone through. I think it's amazing that she was able to write about those things at all. But she's such a strong person . . .' Patty stopped and looked away for a few seconds. Then she faced the passengers again and continued. 'Anyway, the book has been in print ever since 1980, and has been published in over fifteen different languages. If you're interested in purchasing a copy, they're available at the Beast House gift shop and at Janice's museum. You can buy the book in paperback, hardbound, or in a special limited edition with a white leather binding that simulates beast skin. Janice is usually around to sign the books, but she's off on an extended vacation with her husband. She did autograph a bunch of copies before she left, though, so nobody will have to be disappointed in that regard.' A grin spread across Patty's face. 'Though why anybody *cares* about autographs is beyond me.'

'It makes them more precious,' said an elderly woman sitting near the front. She had a soft, sing-song voice. 'I'm Matilda.'

'Nice to meet you, Matilda.'

'I have an autographed copy of *A Light in August* by Mr William Faulkner, and it just means the whole world to me.'

'Well, Janice Crogan ain't no Faulkner, as the saying goes. But she *is* a whole lot prettier. And she did sign a pile of books before she left on her trip. If you're interested, you'll be able to buy autographed copies at the same price as those that aren't. Of *both* books. Which brings me to Janice's second book, *Savage Times*, which is also available. It was published in 1990, and . . . How many of you are familiar with that one?'

Owen raised his hand. So did Marv. Nobody else.

'We have a couple of *real* fans here. *Savage Times* is an absolutely gorgeous book, but it's not cheap. It'll run you eighty-five bucks, plus tax. And as far as I'm concerned, it's worth more. We're talking about a very complete, detailed history of Malcasa Point and Beast House, and it even gets into the background of the beasts. Janice prepared the book in collaboration with an old-time native of the area, Captain Frank Sullivan. If you've read *Horror*, then you know about Captain Frank. The thing is, he had special knowledge of the beasts and kept an extensive scrapbook over the years. Janice and Captain Frank worked together on the book for almost ten years, collecting information, interviewing people, and gathering photographs and illustrations. Make sure and take a look at a copy of it sometime today. Even if you don't buy one, you shouldn't miss the opportunity to thumb through it.

'Now, let's talk about the movies. Everybody's seen the movies. At last count, there were seven of them. They're *all* available on video tape at the Beast House gift shop and at the museum. But of course, the 'must see' film is the original. *The Horror*. 1982. It was done by an independent film company that called itself Malcasa Pictures. Directed by Ray Cunningham. Screenplay by Steve Saunders based on Janice's nonfiction bestseller, *The Horror at Malcasa Point*. The film starred Melinda James in the role of Janice Crogan, and introduced Gunther Sligo as 'The Beast.' It almost didn't get made at all. I bet someone can tell us why.'

Owen raised his hand.

Patty smiled at him and nodded. 'You are?'

'Owen.'

'Hi, Owen.'

'Hi, Patty.'

A quiet grunting sound came from Monica.

'The reason it almost didn't get made?'

'Well, for one thing, they didn't know how to deal on film with the beast's "apparatus." '

Several passengers laughed. Monica groaned.

'But that's not what you're looking for.'

'It's something I try very hard to avoid,' Patty said.

More laughter.

'What I think you were getting at,' Owen continued, 'is that a couple of things happened just before they were supposed to start principle photography. For one, the guy who was originally going to direct it . . . I don't recall his name.'

'Marlon Slade.'

'Yeah, that's him. He apparently assaulted Tricia Talbot, who was supposed to be playing Janice Crogan. I guess he tried to, you know, *nail* her. But she got away from him and left town that night. And then *he* disappeared the next night.'

' "He" being Marlon Slade, the director.'

'Yeah. And I guess nobody ever found out what happened to him.'

'That's right,' Patty said. 'He vanished into thin air, went *kaput*, disappeared without a trace and has never been seen again. There is speculation that he ran off with a teenaged girl named Margaret Blume, who was the guide for the *real* Beast House tours before the arrival of the movie company. Slade's assistant told authorities that he'd gone looking for the girl's trailer home that evening. Evidently, he was planning to offer *her* the Janice Crogan role vacated by Tricia Talbot. But he never returned, and the beautiful young guide also disappeared, along with her trailer. Maybe she and Slade ran off together. Maybe there was foul play. Nobody knows. Another Beast House mystery.'

Chapter Five

Sandy's Story – August, 1980

After their shower, Sandy kissed Eric and lowered him into his crib. This time, she didn't bother trying to lock him in; he'd already broken out to save her from Slade, destroying two of the wooden slats at the front. The gate of his crib looked to Sandy like a smile with two missing teeth.

Besides, he seemed groggy and ready for sleep.

Sandy turned off his bedroom light, eased the door shut, then walked quietly into her own bedroom. Her tan shirt and shorts were still on the floor. She picked up the shirt, studied it in the red light, and found several drops of blood.

'Thanks a lot, Marlon,' she muttered.

She went ahead and put it on.

Her shorts had caught some blood, too.

As she stepped into them and pulled them up, she figured that her days as a Beast House guide were probably over, anyway. She *had* to leave town. Someone – if only Slade's assistant – knew that he'd intended to pay her a visit. He probably wouldn't be missed until morning. When they *did* miss him, though, suspicion would quickly turn toward Sandy. She and Eric had to be long gone before that happened.

Fastening her shorts, she scowled at Slade's body. The pudgy corpse lay sprawled on the floor, arms and legs in awkward positions that he never would've put them in on purpose. His shirt and trousers, ripped by Sandy's knife, looked as if they'd been twisted crooked and pasted to his body with gore. His face looked horrible: torn, purple and slimy. His blood-sotted hair was flat against his scalp.

Got what he had coming, the crud.

It had sure felt good, stabbing him. Maybe she shouldn't have done it so many times, though. She'd gotten a little bit carried away.

For a while there, he'd fought her. That accounted for plenty of his wounds. Sandy'd had to cut through his thrashing hands and arms to get at the vital areas. And he'd *kept on* struggling while she pounded the blade into his chest and neck and face. But she hadn't quit stabbing him even after he'd stopped fighting back.

Even after she knew he was dead.

Because he'd thrown Eric. He'd flung her *son* across the room and hurt him. That was Slade's worst offense. But he'd also *inflicted* himself on Sandy. If Eric hadn't come to the rescue, he would've raped her for sure.

'You're lucky I *ever* stopped stabbing you,' she muttered, then smiled as she realized what she'd said.

'Lucky,' she repeated. 'You're just brimming over with luck.'

But she'd made *such* a mess.

Too bad I didn't strangle him, she thought, and shook her head. It would've been impossible to strangle the man. Without Agnes Kutch's butcher knife, she wouldn't have stood a chance.

He would've raped her, beaten her, maybe even killed her.

And God only knows what he might've done to poor little Eric.

The knife had been her salvation.

The bloody mess was part of the price that had to be paid for survival.

Before getting into the shower with Eric, Sandy had decided to leave the cleanup for later. First things first. Get the hell out of town, *then* worry about disposing of Slade's body and trying to scrub the blood off the walls and floor.

She finished fastening her belt. Barefoot, she walked over to the body. The rug felt sodden and sticky under her feet.

Now I'll be tracking blood through the place!

Annoyed, she crouched beside Slade's right hip. She patted the outside of his front trouser pocket, felt a flat object and heard a slight rattle of keys.

She reached into the pocket. The wet lining clung to her hand. She wrinkled her nose, but dug deeper until she wrapped her fingers around the key case.

She pulled it out.

She wiped the black leather case against her shirt to clean it off, then dropped it into a front pocket of her shorts. Her hand felt tacky from Slade's pocket, so she rubbed it on her shirt.

She hoped the sticky wet stuff was only blood.

Standing up, she wondered how to avoid leaving a trail of bloody footprints on her way out.

Earlier, she hadn't been clear-headed enough to worry about such things. She'd carried Eric from the bedroom to the bathroom without giving a thought to the mess she was making. Those tracks would have to be cleaned up. But why double her work by making a *new* set all the way to the front door?

Her shirt was already ruined, anyway.

She took it off. Standing on her right foot, she used the shirt to wipe the blood off the bottom of her left foot. Then she took a giant step toward the bedroom doorway and set her clean foot down on a section of rug that didn't seem to have much blood on it. She shifted her weight to that foot. Standing on it, she crossed her right foot over her knee and wiped it clean.

When she started down the hall, her feet felt dry against the rug. She knew she wasn't leaving a trail, so she didn't bother looking back. There wasn't enough light to see much, anyway. Ahead of her, the bathroom light was still on. It filled the short hallway with a dim glow so she could see where she was going. She didn't want more.

She entered the bathroom, filled the sink with cold water, and stuffed her shirt into it. The water turned rosy. As she swirled the shirt around, hoping to rinse off the worst of the blood, she looked at herself in the mirror and found no blood on her face or chest or belly.

She didn't want to put the shirt back on. It would be cold and wet. Worse, it would still be stained with Slade's blood in spite of the washing. The idea of his blood touching her skin . . . She couldn't wear the shirt again. Wouldn't. But she didn't want to go for a clean one, either. She'd seen enough of Slade for a while. She'd *smelled* enough of him, too. And if she returned to her bedroom, her feet would get bloody again.

She let the water drain out of the sink, then held the shirt underneath the spigot and ran clean, cold water over it. She started to scrub the ruddy stains with a bar of soap.

And tried to think of something she might wear instead of the shirt.

She didn't have a great many clothes. All that she owned, she kept in her bedroom dresser and highboy.

Anything hanging outside on the line? No. And nothing but diapers and blankets in Eric's room. No clothes in the living room or kitchen.

I can't go wandering around in nothing but my shorts.

Who's going to see me, anyway? she suddenly thought.

Nobody'd *better* see me. It blows the whole plan if I get spotted taking his car.

But she didn't know where Slade's car might be. If she had to go traipsing halfway across town . . .

She shook her head.

The car wouldn't *be* halfway across town. The director was a tubby slob. A guy like that doesn't walk any farther than he has to. He might've been afraid to take his car very far up the hill – scared it might get stuck in a rut, or scratched by the trees and bushes – but he probably would've at least *started* driving up. Or maybe he'd left his car on the roadside at the foot of the hill. No big problem; the trees went nearly all the way to the edge of the pavement.

Regardless, Sandy didn't like the idea of going that far from home in nothing but her shorts.

She finished rinsing the suds out of her shirt, then shook it open. Just as she'd expected, plenty of stains remained.

I can't. I can't put this on.

She flopped the shirt over the shower curtain rod.

After drying her hands on a towel, she turned off the bathroom light and walked through the dark trailer until she found the switch by the front door. She flicked it. A lamp came on beside the sofa.

In the kitchen, she opened a drawer and took out an old dish drying towel. The flimsy white cloth had ragged edges and a couple of holes in it. Also, it was white. But she didn't have any dark ones.

This'll do, she thought.

She shook it open and tried to wrap it around her chest. It was too short for that. But it was long enough to hang from her shoulders to her waist, so she attempted to tie its corners together behind her neck. They wouldn't reach far enough. She took care of the problem with a six-inch bit of string she found in a drawer. In less than a minute, the dish towel draped her front like a large, flimsy bib. Her shoulders and back remained bare, but that was fine; the towel covered her front and it was clean and dry.

Now, all she needed was a weapon.

The weapon she wanted was Agnes's butcher knife.

After using it on Slade, she'd dropped it to the floor beside his body, hurried across the room and taken Eric into her arms.

If she wanted it, she would need to return to the bedroom.

No way.

'A knife's a knife,' she muttered. She didn't believe it, though. Not really.

Agnes's knife was special.

Now that she'd used it herself, it almost seemed to possess a protective magic. It had saved her from Slade. Maybe it would save her from *every* enemy.

'Bull,' she said.

Besides, she was pretty sure that she wouldn't really need a knife. This was a secret mission to retrieve Slade's car. The whole idea was to be sneaky and not have to fight anyone. A knife would just be a precaution.

In case.

There were several on a rack above the kitchen counter. She chose one that was just as large as Agnes's.

Knife in hand, she walked silently back to Eric's room. She stopped outside his door and listened. She heard the slow, easy hiss of his breathing. From the sound of it, she knew he was submerged in the depths of sleep.

She returned to the living room, opened the front door, and stepped outside. Though the day had been sunny and warm, the night was cool – chilly enough for a heavy shirt or windbreaker. She shivered a little as she shut the door and made her way carefully down the stairs.

The old, makeshift stairway wobbled. Its wooden planks felt damp and slippery from the moisture in the air. Sandy had fallen off it a couple of times in the month since moving into the trailer, but she didn't fall tonight.

The ground at the bottom of the stairs felt cool and wet. As she hurried along, pine needles clung to the bottoms of her feet.

She walked completely around the trailer, being careful not to trip over its hitch, bump into her barbecue grill, water tank, or propane tank, or collide with her clothes line. There was no sign of Slade's car, or anything unusual. Except for the patches of moonlight, the clearing that surrounded her trailer looked dark. The forest looked even darker; only flecks of moonlight made it down through the branches.

She found her way to the old tire tracks and started following them down the hillside. She'd been using the twin trails as footpaths ever since moving into the trailer, hiking downhill each morning on one side and hiking uphill every evening on the other. Weeds had grown high in the middle, but the paths were fairly clear and easy to see in the darkness.

She stayed in the one on the right.

Around every bend, she half expected to find Marlon Slade's car. But she rounded one bend after another without running into it.

Sandy didn't mind the hike. She was eager to find his car and get out of town, but she really enjoyed being out like this. She liked the free, exciting way it felt to be wandering the night in nothing except her shorts and the draping dish towel. She liked the feel of her moving body, and the fabric brushing softly against her skin. She liked the cool touch of the moving air. She liked the feel of the moist earth under her feet.

Her footfalls were almost silent. She could hear the wind sliding through the trees, the squeal of seagulls and the murmur of the distant surf.

Wherever we go, she thought, it has to be a place like this. We'll find a nice clearing in the hills overlooking the coast, and never leave.

Unless somebody makes us.

Another Marlon Slade.

'Rotten creep,' she muttered, and felt a tightness in her throat.

We shouldn't have to leave, she thought. It isn't fair.

They'd already been forced out of Agnes's house because of the damn movie people. She and Eric had been living there in secret, which had been a tricky business in the first place. But they couldn't possibly remain hidden once the filming began, so Agnes had made arrangements for them to move into the trailer.

She'd had mixed feelings about leaving Agnes's home.

She loved Agnes like a mother and sister and best friend all rolled into one, and had known she would miss her terribly. Not only that, but she'd been nervous about the idea of living alone.

While she'd sort of dreaded it, however, she'd also found herself thrilled by the prospect of having her own private place to live – even if it was nothing but a crummy old trailer.

She'd soon found that she *loved* living in the trailer.

As things turned out, she could've stayed at Agnes's house for another full month. The film had run into some kind of problem that had delayed the start of shooting.

But she was glad she'd had the month.

The way things looked now, it might be the *only* month she would ever spend in her trailer in the hills above Malcasa Point.

Maybe she would find another place just as good . . .

No. Impossible. Malcasa was her home. It was where she'd met Agnes and the others, where she'd fallen in love with the father of her child, where she'd given birth.

I don't want to leave!

Sandy began to weep as she walked down the trail.

She knew that she had to leave. There was no choice. She had to leave even though she'd killed Marlon Slade in self-defense and no jury would find her guilty of murder.

Because if she stayed, she would be found out. Eric would be found out. It would be the end of their lives together.

The towel came in handy. As she strode down the trail crying, she lifted it now and again to wipe the tears from her eyes and cheeks.

It just isn't fair, she thought. We never did anything wrong.

Well, not much, anyway.

Sandy tried to stop crying. It was noisy and messy and childish.

We'll be fine, she told herself. We'll just take the trailer someplace else and dump that dirty rotten son-of-bitch's body along the way and we'll live by ourselves in the hills and everything'll be fine.

Soon, she reached the bottom of the slope. Using a tree for cover, she glanced up and down the two-lane, paved road. No cars were coming.

Only one car was in sight.

Parked on the gravel by the side of the road, not far away, was a tiny MG convertible.

Sandy groaned.

No, she thought. Please. Don't let it be his.

She couldn't possibly tow the trailer behind *that*.

Taking the key case out of her pocket, she hurried over to the sports car. She jerked open its door, dropped into the bucket seat, chose a key and tried it in the ignition.

It fit.

With a moan, she slumped forward and rested her head against the steering wheel.

What now? she wondered.

We *have* to get away tonight.

Why not go ahead and try to drive it up to the trailer, hook it up and just see if . . . ?

Hook it up?

'Oh cripes,' she muttered. She flung open the door and rushed toward the rear of the car.

Even before she got there, she *knew* that she wouldn't find a trailer hitch.

And she was right.

Chapter Six

Tuck and Dana

Tuck rolled the wrought-iron gate open, then hurried back to the Jeep, hopped in and drove into the Beast House parking lot. She grinned at Dana. 'See? I told you we'd be the first ones here.'

'You almost have to be,' Dana pointed out. 'If anybody shows up before you, they've got no place to park.'

'Plenty of room on Front Street, long as you get here early.' She steered across the empty lot, heading for its far corner. 'Didn't used to have any parking lot at all. Back in the old days, this was all lawn over here and everybody had to park on the street.'

'Progress,' Dana said.

'Things just got out of hand after the first movie. They *had* to build a parking lot.' She eased her Jeep neatly into the space between the white lines, then shut off the engine.

'Do you always park all the way over here?' Dana asked as they climbed out.

'Yep.'

'You can't *get* any farther away from the gate.'

'I could've dropped you off back there.'

'That's all right,' Dana said. They met behind the Jeep and started walking toward the gate. 'It just seems like a funny place to park. You *are* the boss. You can park wherever you like.'

'I like my corner. For one thing, my car's tucked safely out of the way where nobody is likely to bang it up. The main thing, though – I don't want to be taking a good parking spot away from the paying customers.'

'That's very considerate.'

Tuck grinned. 'Just good business.'

'No wonder Janice has you running things.'

'It's probably just because I'm the daughter of her husband. When you have a family business, you try to have family running it. Nobody else cares as much, and a lot of employees will rip you off if they get half a chance.'

Side by side, they walked through the gate. Turning to the right, they followed the sidewalk toward the ticket booth and entrance.

A car coming toward them on Front Street slowed down. Its left-turn signal started to blink. Dana glimpsed a couple of adults in front, two or three kids in the back seat. Looking over her shoulder, she saw it turn through the gate of the parking lot.

'First customers of the day,' Tuck said.

'What time do you open the ticket booth?'

'Ten on the nose.'

Tuck turned aside before getting there, and started to unlock the entrance gate.

'Will I be selling tickets?' Dana asked.

'I thought I'd start you off today inside the house.'

'Fine.'

Tuck opened the gate. As soon as they were both inside, she shut it. Then they started up the walkway toward Beast House.

Dana tried not to look at the place. When Tuck had brought her here yesterday, she'd spent too long gazing at it, too long thinking about it. Ending up with a bad case of the creeps, she had almost refused to go in.

Can't let it get to me. It's just a house.

'We have regulars who handle the gift shop and snack bar,' Tuck explained, 'so you won't be involved in any of that. The guides basically have five different jobs: running the ticket booth, handing out and collecting the tape players, downstairs monitor, upstairs monitor, and supervisor.'

'That's you?'

'That's me. I'm basically in charge of the whole operation, and spend most of the day just wandering around, looking out for problems, trying to be friendly and helpful to our guests. I'm the person you'll come to if you have any trouble or questions. I thought you might start off as the upstairs monitor. Tomorrow, you'll have a different job. You'll be alternating on a daily basis with the other guides. It's very flexible, though. People do a lot of trading. The only thing you can't trade on is bus-tour guide. I suppose that's job number six, but I don't really count it. It's Patty's job. She lives in San Francisco, shows up here at about ten-thirty with a busload of tourists, wanders around being friendly and eating hot dogs, then takes off again at one-thirty and doesn't come back again till the next day. She's the only staff member you didn't get a chance to meet yesterday.'

They started to climb the porch stairs.

Dana suddenly felt a sinking sensation in her stomach, a weakness in her legs.

She turned her head to avoid looking at the hanged man.

It's all right, she told herself. Calm down. He's just a dummy. Nothing's going to happen.

She wiped her hands on the legs of her uniform shorts, and took a deep breath.

At the top of the six wooden stairs, Tuck smiled at her. 'Are you okay?'

'A little nervous, I guess.'

'Nobody's been killed here in years,' Tuck assured her. Then, grinning, she added, 'Nobody that we know about, anyhow.'

They stepped across the porch. As Tuck unlocked the front door, Dana noticed the brass knocker. A monkey's paw. It must've been there yesterday, but she didn't remember seeing it.

'You'll do fine,' Tuck told her.

'I hope so. The house *is* kind of creepy.'

'It's supposed to be.'

'I guess I'll get used to it.'

'I'm sure you will,' Tuck said, and swung the door open. As they walked in, she said, 'If you'd rather start with an outside job . . .'

'Upstairs monitor will be fine. The sooner I get used to working inside, the better.'

Tuck shut the front door, then leaned back against it. She slipped her hands casually into the front pockets of her shorts, crossed her ankles, and said, 'It's a pretty simple job, as work goes. Your main function will just be to wander around upstairs and keep an eye on things. There'll be a fairly steady stream of tourists all day. You need to make sure everyone behaves, nobody touches the exhibits. Commonsense stuff. It's mostly a security and public relations job.'

'What if there *is* trouble?'

'It's usually nothing more than kids acting up. Just tell them politely but firmly to behave themselves – same as you'd do if they were screwing around when you were on duty at the pool. But you'll have a walkie-talkie on your belt if anything serious happens. The rest of us'll drop everything and come running.'

'What sort of serious stuff might I expect?'

'Shootouts.'

'*What?*'

Tuck laughed. 'Naw. But any time you've got large numbers of people, things'll go wrong. A fight might break out. It's rare, but it happens. More often, we'll have somebody get indignant or outraged about the exhibits. I guess they didn't know what they were getting themselves into. They might need to be calmed down or escorted out. Also, we've had people sort of flip out once in a while.'

'Oh, great.'

'We call them flippers.'

'Cute.'

'I guess they're having what you might call panic attacks. It's an old place and smells a little musty. The hallways are sort of long and narrow. The exhibits are gory. The people are listening to some creepy, nasty stuff on their earphones. It apparently just overwhelms some of them, especially on a busy day when there might be some congestion in the rooms and hallways. You'll have flippers, fainters and barfers every so often.'

'It's sounding more fun all the time.'

'Not as much fun as the heart attacks.'

'You get heart attacks?'

'I don't, they do. Not often, though.'

'God almighty.'

'Where's the sweat, *life guard*?'

'I never thought I'd have to be giving CPR in a tourist attraction.'

'Think of Beast House as a big, dry swimming pool. Mostly, people just have fun. But we do have our emergencies from time to time. The trick is, get to the problem people before they go over the edge. They're easy to spot. Pale, sweaty faces, glassy eyes. Or instead of pale, they might be really flushed. Heavy breathing – that could mean trouble, too. When you spot somebody like that, lead him outside. They're usually fine as soon as they get into the fresh air. But don't be afraid to use the walkie-talkie. I'll be on the other end. If the problem is more than we can handle, I'll call for an ambulance or the cops or whatever we might need. They usually get here fast.'

Dana nodded.

'When there aren't problems,' Tuck went on, 'things can be a little dull for the floor monitors. The visitors will be getting the tour information through their headsets, so you don't have any sort of spiel. You'll just need to field questions.'

'Like "where's the bathroom?" '

'That's the most frequently asked question. You remember where they are?'

'Out behind the house in the snack shop area. Can't miss them.'

'Excellent!'

'You ain't dealing with a chimp.'

'Perhaps a moose . . .'

'Hey hey hey. Good thing I'm not sensitive about my size.'

'Hell, you love your size.'

'Allows me to intimidate shrimps like you.'

'Can't touch me, I'm the boss. Anyway, I'm sure you'll be fine answering questions. Big, smart college girl like you.'

'That's me.'

'You read both the books . . .'

'*Studied* them.'

'So you shouldn't have any trouble answering questions about the beast, and so forth. They *will* ask questions. If you don't know the answer to something, tell the person to see me. I'm the resident expert. If I don't know it, it ain't known.' She grinned.

'*And* you're modest.'

'I'm all things wonderful. Any questions?'

'About your wonderfulness, or . . .?'

'Oh, the job.'

'I guess I'll have plenty as things come up, but . . .'

'Hey, I'd better warn you about something before I forget. As guides, our official position on the beast's weenie is that we can't discuss it.'

'People *ask* about it?'

'All the time.'

'Oh, great.'

'Some are genuinely curious and figure we've got the inside scoop. But some of them just want to watch us squirm. A lot of guys think it's a real hoot.'

'But I'm not supposed to confirm or deny?'

'Right. Suggest they either sign up for the Midnight Tour, or read the books.'

'And push the Midnight Tour?' Dana asked, grinning.

'Yes! Please! My God! At every opportunity!'

'Is it any good?'

'*Is it any good?* It's great! *I'm* great! And I tell *all*! Besides which, people haven't experienced Beast House until they've been here at midnight.'

'Can't wait.'

'Oh, you'll love it.'

'Sure I will.'

Tuck laughed, then asked, 'Ready to go?'

'Go where?'

'This way.' She uncrossed her ankles, pushed off from the door with her rump, and headed across the foyer toward the parlor. 'I always do a quick walk-through first thing in the morning before we open her up . . . make sure everything's the way it ought to be. We don't want to have any surprises.'

Dana followed her into the parlor.

'Top of the morning to you, Ethel,' Tuck greeted the body on the floor. 'I hope you enjoyed a comfortable . . . *uh-oh*. What the hell?'

'Oh, man,' Dana muttered.

'See what I mean?' Tuck said, not sounding very upset. 'Surprises.'

Halfway across the parlor, behind a plush red cordon, the wax figure of Ethel Hughes lay sprawled on the floor. One bare leg was propped up on the cushion of the couch. Her eyes were wide open, her face contorted as if with agony or terror. Her white nightgown, drenched and splattered with bright red blood, was ripped open to reveal her bloody, torn skin.

Not just her arms and belly and thighs.

Her breasts.

Her groin.

Yesterday, those areas had been hidden beneath the tatters of Ethel's bloody gown.

'What happened?' Dana asked.

'I don't know,' Tuck said, her voice hushed. She glanced over her shoulder and out the doorway.

Dana looked, too. She saw only the empty foyer.

When Tuck walked toward the body, Dana stayed close to her side. They stopped at the red cordon a few feet away from the exhibit.

'Somebody must've wanted to check out her anatomy,' Tuck said.

'She sure looks real.'

Frowning, nodding, Tuck muttered, 'Maggie was a stickler for details. She started out with nothing but store dummies. But they weren't good enough. She ordered the realistic wax bodies as soon as she could afford it. They were supposed to be authentic in every detail.'

'Looks like they *are*.'

'You know why she wanted them anatomically correct?'

'No, why?'

' 'Cause she was nuts.' With a laugh, Tuck stepped over the rope. 'Actually, I think she wanted to make her exhibits match the crime scene photos.' Crouching beside the body, she lifted a torn flap of white fabric and draped it between Ethel's legs. 'That would've meant *showing* everything, so she ordered the wax figures with all their private parts in place. But then she must've changed her mind and decided to cover them up.' She carefully placed another strip of white linen over Ethel's groin. 'They sure wrecked the nightgown,' she said.

'Could've fooled me.'

'It's about *twice* as ripped up as it's supposed to be.' She started to rearrange the shreds to cover the dummy's breasts. 'Doesn't look like they damaged Ethel, though. She *seems* all right. We'll have to see about replacing the gown, though.'

'Is it the original?' Dana asked.

'No. A replica. Thank goodness for that. Janice moved all the original clothes over to her museum a long time ago. I thought it was a mistake, you know? And I told her so. I thought they should stay in their real death garments. Guess she was right and I was wrong.'

Tuck stood up, took a couple of steps backward, and peered down at the body. 'How does it look to you?' she asked.

'Lewd and indecent.'

'It's *supposed* to look lewd and indecent. But we wanta have the basics covered. You can't see them, can you?'

'The *basics*?'

'Nipples and vagina.'

'Ah. All right.' Dana sidestepped back and forth behind the cordon, even crouched a couple of times. 'I think you've got them pretty well covered.'

'Okay, great.' Tuck stepped over the cordon and headed for the door.

Dana hurried after her. 'How do you think it happened? You lock the place up at night . . .'

'Might've been a break-in. I'll have to check the windows and stuff. Or maybe somebody came in with a tour and didn't leave. You want to wait outside while I take a look around?'

'Why?'

'Might be somebody in here.'

Dana had already realized that. Hearing Tuck say the words, though, gave her a cold feeling. 'I'm supposed to go outside and let *you* handle him?' she asked.

Tuck shrugged and smiled.

'Not a chance,' Dana said.

The smile grew to a grin. 'You're a pal. True blue, gutsy, and *large*.'

Dana laughed.

'Let's do it,' Tuck said.

Together, they made their way quickly through the ground level of the house. As they searched each room, Tuck talked with barely a pause. 'Every once in a while, somebody gets the bright idea to spend the night. Which can be a real kick. I don't exactly blame them, but it's against the rules and we do a pretty good job of stopping them. The thing is, everyone gets a tape player and a set of headphones before they come in. Then they turn them in at the front gate when they leave. We count the players at the end of each day. If we don't get them all back, we figure somebody's unaccounted for and we go looking. Then we usually find the culprits trying to hide somewhere.'

Stopping in the kitchen, Tuck tried the knob of a shut door. 'Nobody got in this way,' she said. She took out her keys, unlocked the door, and swung it open.

Dana, close beside her, gazed down the stairway into the darkness of the cellar.

'Anybody down there?' Tuck called.

'Very amusing.'

'I know.' Leaving the door open, she resumed the search. 'It's really not all that difficult to pull an overnighter in here. You just have to be smart enough. You need someone else to turn in the player for you, or else you turn it in yourself and then find a way to sneak back into the house. It's not that tough if you use your head.'

'Is it usually teenagers?'

'Almost always. I've caught a lot of them trying, and they've all been teens. Sometimes, it's one guy doing it on a dare. But I've found three or four trying it together. And quite a few boy-girl couples. There are plenty of places to hide, if you're clever.'

'And I bet you know them all,' Dana said as they returned to the foyer.

'Most of them,' Tuck said.

They started up the stairs.

'No matter how careful we are, though, people still manage to slip through. We've had plenty of evidence of overnight visits. Since I've been here, we've found cigarette butts, graffiti, candy wrappers, condoms, tampons . . .'

'Oh, nice.'

At the top of the stairs, Tuck resumed her search but didn't stop talking.

'Assorted undergarments, mostly bras and panties. A pair of eye-glasses, a single shoe, keys and loose change that must've fallen out of somebody's pockets. And assorted examples of human fluids and excretions.'

'You're kidding.'

'Some people are pigs.'

'I'll say. But it sounds like they're getting in here all the time.'

'It really doesn't happen terribly often. But when it does . . . You know what they do sometimes? They hide out till after dark, then open a door and let in some of their friends. That way, you might get five or six people running around in here at night.'

After checking a couple of rooms, Tuck stopped at the closed door to the attic. She tried to twist its knob. 'Nobody got in here,' she said, then took out a key, unlocked the door and opened it. Inside, a cordon was stretched across the bottom of the stairs.

Dana glanced up the narrow stairwell. Darkness seemed to be seeping down into it from the attic at the top. She looked away quickly.

Tuck headed on down the corridor to resume the search. 'Oddly enough, they almost never wreck any of the exhibits when they're in here fooling around at night. We've hardly had any serious vandalism. I haven't quite figured out why. Maybe they're afraid it might be tempting fate – or the beast.'

'Have you had anything like this with Ethel's gown?'

'Not exactly. But I did come in one morning and find her wearing a pair of men's underwear.'

'Boxers or briefs?'

'White briefs. I thought it was pretty funny, actually. You could tell it was a prank. I don't like *this*, though. This looks like a guy wanting to check her out, maybe feel her up. You know? Makes me think he might be a little perverted. And hard up. If he's that hot for a dummy, just think what he might do to a couple of real-life gals like *us*.'

'He'd have to catch us first,' Dana said.

'You hold him, I'll run for help.'

'Thanks. But do you think he's still around?'

'It's possible. You never know. So far, I haven't bumped into anyone when I'm opening the place up. Most of them probably don't stick around till morning. If they do stay, they probably keep themselves hidden until the place is full of tourists – then they just blend in and leave.'

After checking the final room, Tuck and Dana returned to the corridor and headed for the stairs.

'Whoever did this,' Tuck said, 'it looks like he only bothered Ethel. Could've been a lot worse.'

They started down the stairs.

'Do you think somebody on the staff might've done it?' Dana asked. 'As a prank, or something?'

'Pretty heavy for a prank, ruining the gown like that. That sort of thing would get you fired. And maybe prosecuted. I'd probably bring charges against him for destruction of the property.'

'Him?'

'Had to be a guy, don't you think?'

Dana shook her head. 'Not necessarily. Might've been a gal wanting it to *look* like the work of a guy. There're all kinds of possibilities.'

'I suppose,' Tuck said.

As they walked from the foot of the stairs to the front door, she added, 'I still think it was probably a guy. No sign of a break-in, so I'd guess that he took the tour yesterday and liked the looks of Ethel.' She opened the door. Dana followed her onto the porch. 'He made sure to get his cassette player back to us, then he hid somewhere in the house until we'd locked up and gone home. After that, he had all the time in the world to fool around with her.'

Though they walked into sunlight as they descended the porch stairs, Dana didn't notice its brightness or feel its heat. Her mind was inside the Beast House parlor, gazing through the darkness at a figure hunched over the body of Ethel Hughes. In the dim moonlight from the window, she watched him rip at the mannequin's gown with both hands. He panted for air. He moaned as his hands latched on to her bare breasts. Then he was kissing them, licking them, then kissing his way down her body until his mouth found the crevice between her legs.

Tuck must've been thinking about him, too. 'If he got off,' she said, 'at least he didn't leave a mess on the floor.'

Dana felt heat rush to her face. 'Considerate of him.'

'Maybe he used a condom.'

'He couldn't have actually *penetrated* her.'

'Nah. Not very far, anyway.' Stopping, Tuck turned around and stared back at the house.

'What?' Dana asked.

'I wonder if I should go back in and check her mouth.'

'Good idea. I'll wait here.'

Shaking her head, Tuck glanced at her wristwatch. 'No time. We're already a couple of minutes late for the meeting. Come on.'

She led the way across the lawn, then up a walkway alongside the house. When they stepped past the rear corner, Dana saw three people waiting in front of the snack shop. Clyde and two young women – Rhonda and Sharon. They all wore the tan uniform with the red and white Beast House logo on the back of the shirt. Clyde wore long pants; the other two wore shorts. Clyde, standing, had a white Stryofoam cup in one hand and a cigarette in the other. The girls were seated at one of the small white tables. Rhonda, a husky brunette, drank from a cup while Sharon worked on a cigarette. Sharon, slim and deeply tanned, had a long tail of braided blond hair hanging down her back.

At the approach of Tuck and Dana, heads turned. Dana saw friendly smiles and nods from the girls, but Clyde looked somewhat annoyed.

'Hey, y'all,' Tuck said. 'Sorry we're late. How's everybody this morning?'

No complaints.

'You remember my friend, Dana Lake?'

More nods and smiles and soft-spoken greetings came from Rhonda and Sharon.

'She'll be the upstairs monitor today. Who's got downstairs?'

Squinting through pale smoke, Sharon said, 'That'll be me.'

'Good.' Tuck smiled at Dana. 'Sharon's our oldest hand.'

'Been here six years,' Sharon said to Dana. She looked as if she might be in her mid-twenties. Her voice was low and husky. With that voice, the sharp angles of her face and her excess of makeup, she seemed to Dana more like a barmaid than a tour guide. Not that Dana'd seen many barmaids, except in the movies. 'You have any questions,' Sharon said, 'just ask. I know damn near everything. What I don't know, I improvise.'

Dana smiled and nodded.

'Okay,' Tuck said. 'Who's out front?'

'I'm tickets,' Clyde said.

'I'm tape players,' said Rhonda. She had rosy cheeks and big, friendly eyes.

'Sharon, you were tape players yesterday?'

'Right,' Sharon said, raising two fingers and the cigarette between them.

'The count turned out okay?'

'Oh, yeah. You damn betcha. What's up? We have a hider last night?'

'Looks that way. Somebody ripped Ethel's nightgown. I fixed her up so she's decent enough for the public, and Dana and I did a quick search of the house. We didn't spot any other problems. No obvious signs of forced entry. It probably *was* a hider.'

'The count came out right on the button,' Sharon told her.

'Okay. Well, keep an eye out when you're inside today. Just because we couldn't find him doesn't mean he's gone.'

'You bet,' Sharon said.

'Everybody look sharp today,' Tuck said, her eyes roaming the others. 'The guy is probably some sort of pervert.'

'He fuck Ethel?' Sharon asked.

Clyde snorted out a laugh. Rhonda blushed.

'I don't think so,' Tuck said.

'Nobody'd do *that*,' Rhonda said, looking disturbed.

Sharon, grinning, shook her head. 'Well, don't let *me* burst your bubble.'

'I want everyone to be alert and careful,' Tuck said. 'Watch for anyone who seems to be lurking about or acting strange.'

'That'd be about half our customers,' Sharon said, then tipped a wink at Dana and took a puff on her cigarette. 'Poor Clyde, too. That boy's a lurker if I ever seen one.'

Clyde smirked at her, lit up another cigarette and said, 'You're just upset because I stopped lurking in your pants.'

'All right, folks, it's time we take our positions and open up. Any questions? No questions? Okay, let's do it.'

Chapter Seven

Sandy's Story – August, 1980

Sandy started Marlon Slade's MG, pushed the clutch pedal down with her foot, and shoved the shift around for a while until she found what was probably first gear. Then she let the clutch up. The car jolted forward and died.

'No problem,' she muttered.

In her whole life, she'd never tried to drive any vehicle except for Agnes Kutch's old pickup truck. And she'd only driven it a few times, off on back roads, because she was too young for a driver's license.

She'd done just fine with the steering side of things. It was the shifting that had always given her trouble. She'd killed the engine again and again, mostly when trying to start out.

'Yer poppin the clutch,' Agnes had explained from the passenger seat. 'Ease off her gentle and easy, and step on the gas as ya let her up.'

Following Agnes's advice now, Sandy twisted the ignition key, gave the engine some gas with her right foot, and raised her left foot very slowly to let the clutch pedal rise beneath it. The car started rolling forward.

'All right!'

She steered onto the road. Staying in first gear, she picked up speed. The engine revved, loud in her ears.

Gotta shift to second. Hope I don't kill the thing.

As she fingered the knob of the shift, she saw a pale, hazy glow of headbeams in the rearview mirror.

With a quick jerk of the wheel, she swerved off the pavement. The MG crunched over weeds and rocks, bouncing, jolting her. She floored the brake pedal. The car lurched to a stop. Its engine quit.

She glanced back and saw the car come around the bend. As its headlights swung toward her, she dropped sideways.

She lay across the passenger seat, gasping for breath, her heart slamming.

Had she been quick enough or had they already spotted her? What if the MG was so low that they would be able to see her lying across the seats as they drove by?

If they see me down like this, they'll stop for sure.

The car rushed closer with a sound like a strong wind bearing down.

Sandy fumbled with the dish towel and pressed it snugly against her breasts.

Light skimmed over the car. She saw it on the dashboard, saw it fill the rearview mirror. It reflected off the mirror and shined down as if trying to point her out.

Don't stop. Please, don't stop. Just keep going, whoever you are. This is none of your business.

She wondered if she would need the knife.

Before starting the car, she had bent over and tossed it underneath her seat.

Now, her legs were still in front of the knife. Her hip was on the seat above it. But her shoulder was planted in the passenger seat. She couldn't possibly reach the knife. Not without sitting up first.

The approaching car slowed down.

No, don't . . .

As its headlights moved on, the car itself crept up alongside the MG.

Sandy suddenly wondered if *it* had a trailer hitch.

Don't even think about it.

Just go away, whoever you are.

With a quiet whine of brakes, the car stopped.

'She's sure a peach,' a guy said.

He's seen me!

No, maybe he means the MG.

He had sounded as if he might be standing over the driver's door, peering in.

'What's it doing out here?' asked a different voice. The voice of someone farther away. Probably the driver.

A woman.

Sandy felt a sudden, vast relief.

'I reckon it broke down,' said the guy.

'Yeah. Or the dumb shit run outa gas.'

'Same thing.'

'No, it ain't,' the woman said.

'Sure is a peach.'

'Get on out and see what's in it, Bill. He might have some good stuff, a fancy-ass car like that.'

Don't do it, Bill! Stay in your car!

'What if the guy's just off in the trees takin' a whizz or something?' he asked.

'Ya gonna do it, or ya gonna sit here all night?'

'Wanta get me caught red-handed?'

'Yer as yella as peed-on snow.'

'Am not,' Bill said.

'Yella, yella, yella!'

'Shut up.'

'Fuck you.'

'Fuck *you!*'

'Don't you talk to me that way, ya yella bastard!'

Sandy heard skin hit skin. The woman blurted, '*Ow!*' Bill must've slapped her. 'Yella cocksucker!' she squealed.

Then came a flurry of blows and the woman yelping and cursing Bill and pleading for him to stop while he pounded her and grunted with the effort and gasped, 'Ya like that? How's this? Ya like this? Fucking bitch. Ya like *this?*'

'Stop it!' She was crying like a kid being spanked. 'Yer hurtin' me!'

'Yella, huh?'

'No! Please! I'm sorry. I didn't mean it!'

The blows kept falling.

The woman, sobbing wildly, grunted and cried out each time she was hit. 'I'm *sorry!*' she gasped. 'Ya ain't yella!'

'I'm fuckin' tired of yer mouth, bitch!'

'No! *OW!*'

'Ya like that? How 'bout *this?*'

Smack!

Shoving her elbow into the passenger seat, Sandy pushed herself up until she could see over the top of her driver's door. The other car was stopped on the road beside the MG, only four or five feet away.

Still too low for a view inside, Sandy grabbed the steering wheel with her left hand and pulled herself higher.

Bill seemed to be kneeling on the front seat, hunched over as he thrashed the woman behind the steering wheel. Sandy couldn't see her at all. But she could hear her crying and begging, could hear her clothes being torn, her skin being punched and slapped by Bill.

What's gonna happen when they stop?

One of them'll get out and find me, that's what.

She wished another car would show up. If it came from behind, Bill's car would be blocking the lane. Maybe he would quit beating the woman and make her drive away.

This was a back road, though. It didn't get used much, especially at night. Another car might come along seconds from now – or maybe not for hours.

I've gotta get out of here.

Sandy pulled herself up the rest of the way. Though she hunkered low behind the steering wheel, she knew that her shoulders and head were in plain sight. If Bill stopped beating on the woman and either of them looked . . .

Reaching down, Sandy fingered the floor underneath the seat and found the knife.

Just let him try any crap with me.

She set the knife down across her lap, then twisted the ignition key. The engine spluttered, roared to life.

Bill twisted and ducked his head to see out the passenger window. 'Hey!' he yelled.

Sandy stepped on the gas and let the clutch up. The MG jumped forward and died.

No!

In silence, it continued to roll forward.

Sandy tried to start the engine again. It sputtered, whinnied, didn't catch.

Looking back, she saw Bill's door fly open.

Her stomach knotted.

The engine caught.

Yes!

Easy does it! Easy does it!

She let up on the clutch and the tiny car surged forward, shoving her against the seatback. The leather was cool against her bare skin.

'Wait!' Bill shouted.

She looked back and saw him running toward her.

Gaining on her.

A big, heavy man with hair that was pale and curly in the moonlight. He wore a gray sweatshirt. The sleeves were cut off at the shoulders.

'Leave me alone!' Sandy yelled, swerving onto the pavement.

'Wait up! Where ya going? I ain't gonna hurt you!'

The engine seemed to shout in protest against going so fast in first gear.

Sandy glanced over her shoulder again.

And gasped.

Bill was almost on her.

She shoved in the clutch, jerked the stick backward hoping for second gear, and let the clutch up. The gears made a nasty grinding noise, so she shoved the pedal down again.

Though she hadn't killed the engine, she wasn't in gear.

She was coasting.

'No sweat,' she muttered, trying to calm herself. 'Just try it again, and . . .'

Bill grabbed her hair.

She couldn't turn her head, but she heard his hard breathing and his shoes smacking the pavement. 'Stop the car!' he yelled. He jerked her hair. It tugged at her scalp, turning her face to the right and pulling her head backward.

'Let *go* of me!' she cried out.

'Stop the fucking car!'

Suddenly not caring how much it might hurt or what damage it might do to her – wanting only to get away from this man – she stomped the gas pedal to the floor. The engine roared. The car, still out of gear, only coasted.

Shit!

'Stop the car or I'll rip your head off!'

She jerked the steering wheel.

The car cut sideways.

To the left.

Bill shouted, '*Watch out!*' Then he cried, '*Ah!*'

Sandy heard and felt only a slight bump, but the hand abruptly let go of her hair. She twisted her head and looked back.

Bill was down, tumbling on the pavement in the beams of his own car's headlights.

Giving up on second gear, Sandy tried third.

She let the clutch pedal up and the MG rushed forward as if given a quick, strong shove.

'All right!' she yelled.

In the rearview mirror, she saw Bill push himself to his knees. He seemed to be staring at her.

He was better lit than before.

Behind him, his car was on the move.

The woman must've recovered enough to drive. She was coming to pick him up.

Then they'll come after me!

As the car bore down on Bill, he raised an arm.

Then he tried to get up off his knees.

He shouted, '*Donnnnn't!*'

At the last instant, he tried to dive out of the way. But the car chopped his legs out from under him. He flew head first over the hood and crashed through the windshield.

Blasted through the glass all the way to his waist.

On the driver's side.

The car, still picking up speed, started to gain on Sandy. She stepped on the gas.

How can that woman see where she's driving?

Sandy raced around a curve and lost sight of the car.

A few seconds later, it showed in the rearview mirror.

It didn't make the curve.

Didn't even seem to try.

Just sped straight on and leaped off the road as if somebody'd decided on a scenic detour through the forest.

Sandy felt a chill prickle its way up her back.

She muttered, 'Holy crap.'

The headbeams pushed their brightness into the trees.

Sandy steered around another bend. After that, she could see nothing behind her except the dark road and the woods.

She listened for the sound of the car smashing into a tree.

Any second, now.

Would there be an explosion? She hoped not. If the car exploded, the forest might catch on fire.

She imagined a fire spreading over the wooded hills. And surrounding her trailer. She pictured Eric asleep in his crib as fire closed in.

No sound of a crash came to her.

I'm just too far away to hear it, that's all. There had to be a crash by now. How the hell far can you go speeding through the woods?

She imagined the car with its front crushed against a tree trunk, flames lapping up around the edges of its hood.

She picked up speed.

She should be at Agnes's house in a couple more minutes. But getting the woman to answer her door might take a while. Then Sandy would need to explain things, get the keys to the pickup truck, head back with it . . .

Maybe to find herself in the middle of a forest fire.

She stopped the MG, killing its engine. But she started the engine easily. In first gear, she made a U-turn.

She had no trouble finding the place where Bill's car had gone off the road and plunged into the woods. She pulled over to the side, stopped, picked up the butcher knife and climbed out.

Standing by the road, she stared into the trees.

Not much moonlight made it down through their heavy canopy of branches and leaves.

She couldn't see Bill's car.

She couldn't see flames, either.

That doesn't mean it isn't on fire.

Sandy put her back to the road and ran into the woods.

She knew it probably wasn't a good idea to run. Though she'd never put on the MG's headlights and her eyes were pretty well adjusted to the darkness, she could see almost nothing in front of her – just a few speckles and patches of moonlight, almost like bits of snow scattered here and there.

Running through the dark, she might trip and fall.

She had a knife in her hand. If she fell on that . . .

In her mind, she heard her mother warn, '*Be careful, you'll fall and put your eye out.*'

Mom.

Don't think about her. The hell with her. The traitor.

Sandy hated it when she happened to think of her mother.

Who needs her, anyway? I've got Eric.

She ran faster, pumping hard with her arms, flinging her legs out, her bare feet punching the mat of pine needles. Her breasts, swollen with milk for Eric, bounced and swung wildly. Her dish-towel bib flapped up and down, twisted, and soon ended up draping her right shoulder.

Where the hell's the car?

Though bushes sometimes whipped or scratched her legs, she realized that she wasn't dodging trees. The dark trunks flew by on both sides of her, but none was in the way.

Can't last long. Just a fluke.

Maybe there was a road here once.

But how could the gal steer through all this when she couldn't even see out her . . .

Something snagged Sandy's right foot. Though she jerked it free, she couldn't swing her leg forward fast enough. She fell headlong. On the way down, she stretched out her arms so the knife in her right hand would be safe overhead.

She landed on the damp carpet of the forest floor. Her breath knocked out, she skidded on her bare skin. Then she lay there, sprawled out, struggling for air.

The ground beneath her felt springy with layers of soft pine needles. They were wet with dew, and didn't feel too bad. Prickly, here and there. She also felt some twigs and pine cones pushing against her. She didn't like how they felt.

When she was able to breathe again, she stood up. Keeping the knife low in her right hand, she used her left hand to brush the clinging forest debris off her chest and breasts and belly. She bent down and rubbed it off the front of her shorts, her thighs and knees.

She still felt wet and dirty.

A lot of good my shower did.

At least I'm not bloody, she told herself.

Not that I know of.

As she started walking again, she took the towel from around her neck and used it to mop herself dry. Then she put it back on. It felt damp against her skin. She made a face.

I shouldn't even be out here, she thought. There isn't any fire. And if there is, what am I gonna do about it – beat it out with my wet dish rag?

She kept going, anyway.

She was pretty sure she wouldn't find a fire. But what *would* she find?

Nothing real cheerful, that's for sure.

As she hurried along, she realized that she *needed* to know what had become of the car, the woman and Bill. She had to know where they'd stopped – *if* they'd stopped.

Sure they did.

But she needed to see for herself. Otherwise, she might always be haunted by the idea of the car speeding through the night woods with Bill sticking out of its windshield. Going on and on . . .

She quickened her pace. Though tempted to run, she sure didn't want to fall again. She'd been lucky with the last fall. Next time, she might land on a sharp stick or something.

But I can't spend all night at this . . .

She started to trot. Slowly, at first. Then faster. Then even faster until she was racing along full speed.

Find that car and get out of here, get on over to Agnes's house . . .

The ground suddenly dropped out from under Sandy's feet.

Not again!

Plunging headlong down a slope, she stretched out her arms and saw lights off in the distance: the red ovals of a car's taillights and the white beam of a single headlight reaching into the woods.

Sandy hit the ground and sledded down on her chest until her shoulder hit a rock. She cried out. The blow turned her body sideways and she rolled, flipping from front to back to front to back, glimpsing the lights of the car with each rotation.

Instead of rolling straight for the bottom of the slope, she took a diagonal route. It ended when her left hip struck a tree. Still rolling fast, she grunted and rammed her belly against the trunk. And stopped hard.

When she could breathe again, she flopped onto her back and groaned.

At least I found the damn car, she told herself.

And she still had a grip on her knife. She was fairly sure she hadn't cut herself with it.

She turned over, pushed herself to her hands and knees, then stood up. Her body hurt in many places, but her right shoulder seemed to have the worst injury. It burned from its collision with the rock. It felt as if it had been pounded and scraped raw. She hoped it wasn't broken. It still seemed to work.

She'd lost her dish towel somewhere on the slope.

Have to look for it on the way back up.

In the meantime, she didn't much care about the loss of the towel. She was too hurt and filthy all over to bother cleaning herself with it. And she didn't need to worry, down here, about being half naked.

Bill certainly wouldn't be ogling her.

As for the woman, Sandy didn't care. She'd never had real trouble with any woman. It was only men who always wanted to stare at her and mess with her.

Dirty cruds, all of them.

Two down in one night, she thought. That's pretty good.

Limping slightly, she made her way toward the car.

It looked as if it had bounded down the slope, raced across the short clearing at the bottom, and finally met a tree. Though the taillights and one of the headlights still worked, the engine seemed to be dead. She saw no smoke or flames.

As she approached, she crouched slightly to look through the windows.

The woman was sitting up straight behind the steering wheel. She seemed to be gazing out through the hole in her windshield.

Bill no longer filled the hole.

He'd left his empty sweatshirt in the broken glass at the bottom of the hole, but he was gone.

With a quick, sick feeling, Sandy hurried forward.

She stared at the hood of the car.

Bill was gone from there, too.

But he hadn't gone far. Maybe fifteen or twenty feet.

The headlight pointed him out.

Sandy gasped. She almost ran away, but realized he didn't seem interested in her.

He couldn't even see her.

He was upright with his back toward Sandy, standing on his head – just on his head, not even supporting himself with his hands. Both his arms dangled, his hands limp against the ground.

It seemed a remarkable feat.

Until she noticed that he wasn't balancing himself on his head. Up above him, both his feet were wedged into the crotch of the tree trunk.

He was no acrobat, after all. Just a dead guy turned by accident into a freakish spectacle.

Sandy grimaced at him.

She could see how it might've happened: when the car struck the tree that demolished its right headlight, Bill had been shot backward, feet first, off the left side of the hood. He'd hit the ground and done a wild backward somersault toward a second tree. At the peak of the somersault, only his head touching the ground, he'd rammed both his feet into the V of the trunk and gotten stuck that way.

Staring at him, Sandy felt goosebumps prickle her skin.

Sure doesn't *look* accidental, she thought. Looks like somebody put him that way on purpose.

What if someone did, and he's still around?

Stupid, she thought. The guy just happened to end up like that.

Maybe.

Let's get.

But she couldn't. Not yet. First, she needed to check the woman.

She hurried around the rear of the car. In the red glow of the taillights, she saw that it had a trailer hitch.

Lot of good it'll do me.

She kept moving. Her right hand ached from clutching the knife so hard. She scanned the woods on all sides as she made her way toward the driver's door.

So dark.

Except where the headlight went, she could see almost nothing.

Somebody could sneak right up on me.

Take it easy. Nobody's around. It's just the three of us, and both of them are dead. Probably.

She crouched near the driver's door, saw the shape of the woman sitting behind the wheel, then opened the door.

The car filled with light from its ceiling bulb.

The woman wore a seatbelt. Her blouse was torn open and hung off one shoulder – probably the result of the beating, not the crash. From her face to her lap, she was coated with blood. It still dripped off her chin.

Dripped from her wide open mouth.

Her mouth was jammed full of bloody hair.

Not her hair.

Her own hair was all shaved off. The hair stuffing her mouth had to be Bill's.

It was easy to figure out how that had happened.

Sandy muttered, 'Jeez.'

The woman's head slowly turned toward her.

The eyes opened.

Chapter Eight

The Day Tour

'We'll be there in just a few minutes, now,' Patty announced. 'Any last questions before we arrive? Yes, Marv?'

'Are there plans to *ever* open the Kutch house for tours? I mean, it seems like the obvious thing. You could have people go over there through the underground tunnel, you know? It'd be incredible.'

'As a matter of fact, Janice purchased the Kutch house at the same time she bought Beast House. But a condition of the sale was that Agnes would be allowed to continue living there – and that it wouldn't be shown on tours – as long as she remains alive.'

'So if we wanta see it, we've gotta outlive Agnes?'

'That's right.'

'How old is she?'

Patty shook her head. 'I can't say for sure, but I suppose she must be about fifty-nine or sixty.'

'I won't hold my breath, then.'

A few of the passengers chuckled, but most didn't respond. Owen suspected that just about everyone on the bus had grown tired of Marv's incessant questions and comments. He was a little sick of Marv, himself.

The guy was like a hot-dog student, always popping his hand into the air, endlessly ready to answer questions or ask them, forever eager to show that he knew more than anyone else.

Every group seemed to have a Marv.

The Marvs often seemed interesting, at first. But they wore on you until you wished they would just shut up.

'Any more questions?' Patty asked. 'Yes, Marv?'

'How about giving me your phone number?'

A few passengers chuckled.

'Afraid not, Marv.'

Laughter and applause.

Owen looked over his shoulder. Marv was laughing, too, but his face was red.

Patty turned away. Ducking slightly, she peered out the windshield. She faced the group again, then held on to a pole while the bus made a right turn. 'Okay, folks, we're now on Front Street of Malcasa Point. You should be able to catch a few glimpses of the ocean off to the left of the bus.'

Leaning forward to see past Monica, Owen spotted a patch of pale blue water through a break in the trees. But he wasn't much interested in the Pacific. He swung his gaze northward, hoping to see the Kutch house.

'The Kutch house will shortly be coming up on the left side of the road,' Patty announced. 'Beast House itself will be on the right. If you can't see one or the other from your seat, don't worry about it; we'll be parking in just a few seconds and you'll have three hours to look them over.'

Owen spotted the Kutch house.

He'd seen it plenty of times before: in photographs and in movies.

But this is it. This is really it. Not a picture, the actual Kutch house. And I'm looking at it.

Except for the chainlink fence surrounding the property, it looked just as it did in the books and films. Brown-red bricks, almost like the color of old, dry blood. A weathered front door. Just the one door. No windows.

Not only were no other doors or windows in sight, but Owen knew that none existed.

The lack of any windows made the house seem more strange than he would've supposed.

He suddenly imagined Janice Crogan locked in one of its upstairs rooms, waking up naked on a mountain of pillows after being raped and abducted. This was one of his favorite scenes from her first book. He'd read it many times, daydreaming about being there, helping her, making love with her on the pillows.

He'd really hoped he might have a chance to meet her today.

Just my luck, she's out of town.

But she wouldn't be the Janice he knew from the books, anyway. Not really. That Janice had been eighteen years old. A teenager, not a thirty-six year-old woman.

And even if she hadn't grown older, she couldn't possibly have lived up to Owen's fantasies. No girl could be that beautiful, that sexy and tough and brave.

I'm probably lucky she *is* out of town, he told himself.

'Yoo-hoo,' Monica said. 'Anybody home? Planet Earth to Owen. Hello?'

He looked at her.

'Are we just going to sit here all day?' she asked.

He forced himself to smile at her before looking away.

The bus had already stopped. Passengers were making their way down the aisle to disembark.

'Get up, get up, get up,' Monica chanted, smiling slightly. The smile didn't match up very well with the smirk in her violet eyes.

'We don't have to barge right out,' he said.

'I thought you couldn't *wait* to get here.'

'There's no big hurry. We'll have three whole hours.'

'You're telling me.'

When the aisle was clear, Owen slipped his camera strap around his neck and stood up. He sidestepped into the aisle, then waited for Monica. Letting her go ahead of him, he realized that, right now, he didn't even like the way she looked from behind.

Her hair, with its pink bow and a flouncy ponytail, seemed like a phony attempt to make her look like a cute, perky kid.

Her back was too stiff, too arched.

Her white knit shirt was tight, but not as tight as her bra. Owen could see her bra through the fabric, its back strap squeezing her under the arms so that her flesh bulged over its top.

Her flesh also bulged over the tightly cinched waistband of her jeans.

The jeans themselves, brand-new and dark blue, swelled out to encase her hips and buttocks. They fit her so snugly that the denim seat looked solid.

If she falls on her ass, Owen thought, she'll bounce right up again.

Immediately, he felt guilty about the thought.

A moment later, he felt angry at himself for feeling guilty.

Would it kill her to wear stuff that fits?

He followed her down the bus stairs. Patty, waiting at the bottom, smiled at Monica and said, 'Watch your step, please.' Then she said, 'Have a good tour, Owen.'

'Thanks,' he told her.

And wondered if she had a boyfriend.

Probably.

Probably a strapping, handsome guy with a solid handshake and a ready smile.

Or maybe she's a lesbian.

Either way, I don't stand a chance.

Monica took hold of his hand, gave it a squeeze, and said, 'We might as well make the most of things. Maybe we can have a picnic on the beach or do something fun like that after we finish the tour.'

'Maybe so.'

Dragging him toward the end of the ticket line, she said, 'I just love beaches. They're so romantic.'

'Maybe we should've brought our suits.'

'Don't be a silly. We can't go swimming.'

'We probably *could*.'

'No swimming suits, no towels. And where would we change? Besides, I don't go in oceans. You never know what might be in the water. I don't relish the notion of catching hepititis *or* getting eaten alive by a shark.'

They stepped to the end of the line.

'Look at that,' Monica said. 'Fifteen dollars apiece. Isn't that ridiculous? How can they charge fifteen bucks for a thing like this?'

'Why not? It's the only place like this in the country – probably in the whole world.'

'It's robbery.'

'They're not forcing anyone to pay it.'

'Plus fifteen each for the bus ride. This is costing us *sixty dollars*.'

'It's costing *me* sixty dollars.' He grinned. 'Money well spent. Good thing we'll be gone before Saturday, or I'd be dragging you out here for the Midnight Tour. That'd *really* cost me an arm and a leg.'

'Would not.'

'No?'

She tilted back her head and showed her teeth. 'It'd cost zilch, because I wouldn't let you do it. You shouldn't be throwing away *this* kind of money, much less a couple of hundred dollars for some horrible *adults only* tour.'

'I bet it'd be great.'

'You would think so.'

'I mean, just to *be* inside Beast House late at night . . .'

His head swung sideways. And he saw Beast House.

It had been in full view ever since he'd stepped off the bus, but he'd paid no attention to it.

Until now.

Like the Kutch house across the street, it looked very much as he'd expected from seeing it in so many photographs and movies.

He'd already seen it hundreds of times.

Not the real thing, he told himself. This isn't a picture, this is *it*.

He stared at the house.

And felt a little disappointed.

It looked like just an ordinary old Victorian home, a little *more* ordinary than most of the restored Victorians he'd seen during his travels. Smaller. Not as ornate. A lot more dilapidated.

It's *supposed* to look dilapidated, he told himself. It's *Beast House*.

He wanted to feel a thrill of dread, but it didn't come.

Too much exposure to the place? he wondered. Had he spent too long staring at the photos in Janice Crogan's books? Had he seen *The Horror* and its sequels too many times?

On the other hand, maybe familiarity wasn't the problem. Maybe the problem was seeing it besieged by tourists – not a menacing old house, but a thriving attraction.

How can a place give you the willies when it has families parading in and out?

All these damn tourists, he thought.

And what am I, a native? I'm a tourist, the same as all the rest of them.

I'm the ULTIMATE tourist – I came on a bus. Gotta get back on it in three hours, so I can't even stay.

That's what I'd *like* to do, he thought. Stay. Stay till after closing time, till after dark. That'd be the only way to get the feel of the house. Stand out here by myself after everyone is gone and look at it through the fence – watch it in the darkness, in the moonlight.

He imagined himself saying to Monica, *Hey, how would you like to stay overnight here in town and catch the bus back to San Francisco tomorrow?*

What would her response be? *Are you nuts? Are you out of your mind? Three hours is three hours too long to be stuck in this miserable excuse for a town. There must be something seriously wrong with you to even consider spending a night here. Besides which, we've already paid for our room at the Holiday Inn. We certainly aren't going to pay for a room and then not spend the night in it. So get that out of your head right this very moment. I've never heard of anything so . . .*

Owen suddenly realized that the man in front of him was walking away. Nobody else remained between him and the ticket window.

Smiling at the large, broad-shouldered man behind the glass, he reached for his wallet and said, 'Hi. Two adults, please.' He paid with a Mastercard.

The man slipped a pair of tickets under the window to him, along with his receipt, a small brochure and a couple of coupons. 'Save your ticket stubs,' he said. 'If you show them at the Beast House Museum, you'll be able to get in for half price. These coupons are good for a ten per cent discount on any merchandise purchased at the gift shop or snack bar.'

'Thanks.'

'Take your tickets around to the side, and Rhonda will provide you with your audio equipment.'

'Thanks,' Owen said again.

'Enjoy the tour.'

'Thanks.' He stepped away from the window.

'Over this way,' Monica said.

He followed her around the corner of the ticket shack.

'Good morning,' Rhonda greeted them, smiling and somehow looking too young and too shy for the job. 'May I see your tickets, please?'

Owen gave them to her.

She tore them in half. 'Be sure to save your stubs,' she said, returning half of each ticket to Owen. 'You can get into the Beast House Museum on Front Street for half price.'

'We've already been told that,' Monica said.

Rhonda blushed. 'Oh. Anyway.' She shrugged, then turned around. The outer wall of the ticket shack looked like a huge, open cupboard. It was lined with shelves. About half the shelves were empty. The others held audio cassette players.

Rhonda pulled one down. It was slightly smaller than a paperback book, black plastic, with a bright orange strap. Earphones were attached. 'Here you are,' she said, and handed it to Monica. 'You just hang the player around your neck by the strap.'

'I can see that.'

Rhonda blushed again.

Owen felt like smacking Monica.

When Rhonda gave a player to him, he smiled, hung it around his neck, and said, 'Thank you very much.'

'You're welcome. It's a self-guided tour, and the players are all ready to go. You should wait until you reach the porch, which is Station Number One. You'll see a sign with the number one on it. Then stop there and push Play, which is the oblong button on top.' She pointed it out on Owen's machine. 'And this is the Stop button here. After the porch, you proceed from station to station. The tape will tell you what to do. But feel free to take as long as you wish with the tour. Okay? When you're done, just bring the players back to me. I'll be right here.'

'Okay, thank you,' Owen told her.

They started up the walkway toward Beast House.

'I love it already,' Monica said. By the snide tone of her voice, Owen figured that her remark was inspired by the sight of the mannequin hanging from the porch beam.

'That's poor Gus Goucher,' he explained.

'Yeah, I remember them lynching some guy. Which movie was that in, number two?'

'*The Horror 3 in 3-D*. But it happened in real life, Monica. Gus was a real person.'

'I know that.'

They halted behind a small group near the foot of the stairs. All wore headphones. Some turned this way and that as if surveying their general surroundings while they listened. Some looked down. A few whispered comments, nodded, chuckled. But most stood motionless and gazed up at the dangling body as they listened to their tapes.

'Lovely,' Monica muttered.

'He's not supposed to be pretty,' Owen whispered.

'He isn't.'

Gus's eyes bulged. His black, swollen tongue stuck out. His head was tilted sideways at a nasty angle so that his right ear almost touched his shoulder. But the worst part, for Owen, was the neck.

It was way too long.

That's why they call it 'stretching his neck.'

He'd seen photographs of such things.

But he didn't like how it looked.

The stretched neck made things seem a little too real.

From the shoulders down, Gus looked all right. He wore a plaid shirt, blue jeans and boots.

Monica lowered her head, inspected her cassette player for a moment, then thumbed one of the buttons on top of it. Owen heard the click. He started his own player, then gazed up at Gus.

After a brief, hissy sound, a woman began to speak.

'Good morning, and welcome to Beast House. My name is Janice Crogan.'

Janice!

Her voice was rich and exciting, but not the voice of a teenaged girl. This was Janice grown up.

'I'll be your guide today, with the help of old Maggie Kutch. Maggie created Beast House as an attaction after her family was murdered here, many years ago. If you had come here before her death in 1979, she would've been your guide. Old Maggie, fat and scarred, would've stood on the porch steps just in front of you, cane in hand as she introduced herself.

'Howdy, folks,' said a low, husky voice that clearly didn't belong to Janice. It sounded distant and a little scratchy like an old-time recording of a live concert or political speech. 'Welcome to Beast House. My name's Maggie Kutch, and I own it. I started off showing the place just after my husband and three children was butchered by the beast. Now, you might be asking yourselves how come I'd wanta show you my home after it was the scene of such awful grief to me. The answer's easy: m-o-n-e-y.'

'What you just heard was the actual voice of Maggie Kutch,' Janice explained. 'She conducted her tours for a great many years until her death in 1979. Even though she had rules against bringing recording devices into the house, quite a few people snuck them in anyway. We've been lucky enough to obtain several recordings of the tours, so you'll be able to hear Maggie tell the story in her own words, as if she herself were hobbling through the house as your own personal guide.

'You are now at Station One, which depicts the hanged body of Gus Goucher. Maggie never had a figure of Gus. He was added to the attraction in recent years, after my purchase of Beast House. If you'd been here in Maggie's day, she would've pointed her cane at the beam from which Gus now hangs, and told you . . .'

Maggie's voice returned. 'Right here's where they strung up poor Gus Goucher. He was only eighteen years old, and stopped by town on his way to San Francisco. He was going there to get a job at the Sutro Baths, where his brother worked. You know the Sutro Baths? They was like giant indoor swimming pools of hot water – salt water – right on the coast over near Cliff House. Cliff House, it's still there. Some of it is, anyhow. The Sutro Baths're long gone, but you can see the ruins down the bluff if you go to Cliff House.

'I reckon the Baths was quite a swell place, back then. Only Gus never made it there, because he showed up at this house on August 2, 1903.' Owen heard a couple of hard thumps and pictured Maggie pounding the tip of her cane against the porch floor. ' "Lilly Thorn, the outlaw's widow, lived here then, along with her two children and her visiting sister, Ethel. Gus split some firewood for Lilly, late that afternoon, and she paid him with a supper. Then he was on his way.

'That night, the beast struck. No one but Lilly lived through the attack. She ran into the street, screaming like a madwoman and waking up half the town. Well, the sheriff come along and searched the whole house from top to bottom. He didn't find no culprit. He found nothing but the torn up, chewed up bodies of Lilly's sister and two little boys. So then a posse was got up. They all went tromping around in the hills near the house, and who should they stumble on to but poor Gus Goucher, fast asleep by his campfire.

'Some of the posse recalled seeing him around Lilly's house. And there wasn't nobody to stand up for him, since he was just a stranger passing through. He might've sailed by, anyhow, if he'd only had them two strikes against him. But the third was the clencher. Gus had some blood on his clothes. So they dragged him back to town and had a trial for him over at the court house, which ain't around any longer as it burned to the ground back in 1916.

'At the trial, Gus said he was innocent. He claimed the blood came from a cut on his finger, and he had the cut, sure enough. Only the prosecutor said he might've cut himself on purpose so he'd have an excuse for the bloody clothes. And the jury, they believed him.'

'What about Lilly?' asked a young man. From the volume of his voice, Owen suspected he might've been the person secretly recording the tour. 'She saw what happened, didn't she? Why didn't she take the stand and clear Gus?'

'Why, son, she couldn't. Poor Lilly, she'd gone stark raving mad on account of the slaughter. She wasn't in shape to testify about *nothing*. At any rate, the jury took about two minutes flat to make up their minds. They found Gus guilty of triple murder, and the judge sentenced him to swing.

'Only thing is, the law never got a chance to carry out its sentence, because a mob beat it to the punch. The night after the trial, a bunch of townfolks dressed up in masks busted Gus out of jail. They dragged the poor lad to this very spot, whipped a rope over that beam right there, and strung him up.

'He was an innocent man, of course. Leastwise, as innocent as *any* man ever is. He didn't kill nobody at the Thorn house that night. Not unless he had claws. The beast done it. The beast done it all. Let's go on in, now.'

'You may climb the stairs, now,' Janice said. 'As you enter Beast House, you should note that this is not the original front door. The original was blasted open by a police shotgun in 1978, and is on permanent display at the Beast House Museum on Front Street.

'You should now proceed to Station Number Two, just inside the foyer and to your left. Stop the tape, and resume it when you're inside the parlor.'

Owen pressed the Stop button on his machine.

Monica smirked at him. 'Do you suppose it gets any better?'

'Let's go in and find out.'

Owen had been vaguely aware of people moving on, climbing the porch stairs and disappearing into the house while he'd been listening to the taped voices. Looking behind him as he followed Monica up the stairs, he saw a whole new bunch listening at Station One. Some gazed up at the hanged man with disgust, some looked fascinated, and others averted their eyes.

At the open door to Beast House, Monica stopped and turned to Owen. 'You first,' she said.

'If you'd rather not go in . . .'

'I'll go in.'

'You don't have to. You could wait out on the lawn, or go around to the snack shop or something.'

'And miss all the fun?'

'You don't seem to be having much fun.'

'Oh, you noticed?'

'Really. Why don't you just wander around for a while. I'll hurry.'

'I'll go in. Just remember I'm doing it for *you*, Owie. I'll hate it, but I'll do it – because I love you.'

Chapter Nine

Sandy's Story – August, 1980

The woman behind the steering wheel tried to say something, but the sounds she made were muffled and mushy.

With the thumb and forefinger of her left hand, Sandy dug into the woman's mouth and started pulling out Bill's hair. It dis-gusted her. It reminded her of cleaning out a bathtub drain, except that flesh and teeth came out along with the gobs of sticky hair.

When the mouth was just about clear, the woman gasped, 'Bless ya, girl. Bless ya.'

'Are you okay?' Sandy asked.

The woman choked out a rough, slurpy laugh, then said, 'Did I kill da cocksucker?'

'I guess so.'

'Go look. Gotta know.'

'I'm not going over there, lady. How bad are you hurt?'

'Don' know.'

'Can you move?'

'Don' know.'

'See if you can start the car.'

The woman slowly raised her right hand and turned the ignition key. The engine grumbled, caught, and rumbled on, staying alive. The woman turned her head toward Sandy. She grinned a bloody smile.

Though feeling a little sick, Sandy said, 'Scoot over and I'll drive.'

'Huh-uh. What about Bill?'

'Look at him. He's dead. You think he's not dead? My God, you probably swallowed some of his brains.'

The woman gurgled another laugh, then said, 'He sure pucked up my teet. But I gotta know.' She fumbled with the latch of her seatbelt.

'I tell you what,' Sandy said.

'Huh?'

'Go on and move over. Keep your eyes on me. I'll take care of things, and then we'll scoot.'

'Okay.'

Sandy trotted into the white beam of the headlight. She threw a huge shadow ahead of her. Her shadow darkened Bill's bare back.

When she got to him, she stepped aside so that neither her body nor her shadow would ruin the woman's view. Then she sank to her knees.

Bill looked as if his head had been buried in the ground to the tops of his ears.

Sandy clutched the hair on the back of his head. When she pulled, his head slid across the ground. It wasn't buried, after all – just smashed flat.

She tugged hard, pulling the body away from the tree, lifting its head as much as she could, wondering if the woman in the car could see that Bill's skull was caved in and half empty.

Then she reached around the front with her butcher knife and slit his throat.

She ran back to the car.

She threw herself into the driver's seat and slammed the door.

'Tanks,' the woman said.

Sandy smiled at her. 'Glad to help.'

'I'm Lib.'

'Lib?'

'Libby, Lib.'

'Good to meet you, Lib. I'm Charly. With a y. Let's get outa . . . Hey! All right!'

'Huh?' Lib asked.

'You've got automatic transmission!' She shoved the lever, then started to back up. For a moment, she was afraid that the right front of the car might remain stuck to the tree. But it came away all right with sounds like clinking glass and crunching tin.

'Where we goin'?' Lib asked.

'I don't know.'

She *didn't* know. The main thing, for now, was that the car worked. She carefully turned it around, then started driving slowly back through the woods and up the slope.

About halfway to the top, she spotted her dish towel on the ground. But she didn't dare stop for it.

She left the rag behind and kept her foot on the gas pedal.

They crept over the crest of the hill.

'There!' she gasped.

'Wha?'

'Made it.'

Not really, she thought, steering carefully through the woods. This is just the start. We'll probably get to the road okay, but then what?

'Where do you live, Lib?'

'Here.'

'Here in Malcasa?'

'Huh-uh. In my car.'

'You live in your car?'

'Yeah.'

'In *this* car?'

'Yeah.'

'You don't have a real home?'

'Hab you?'

'I've got a trailer,' Sandy said. 'It's not very far from here.'

'I got a trailer hitch.'

'I know. I saw it. But we've got one dead headlight and a smashed windshield. We'd be pulled over by the first cop that sees us. Then we'd both be busted.'

'Id was selp-depense. He beat me up.'

'Yeah, but he wasn't doing it when you ran him down. If they find out what happened, you'll end up in prison.'

'Puck dat.'

When the road came into sight through the trees, Sandy shut off the headlight. She drove to the edge of the pavement and stop-ped. The road looked dark and empty. She stared at the little MG.

'We take yers?' Lib asked.

'It isn't mine.'

'You was . . .'

'I know. The guy it belongs to is dead. I killed him.'

'Yer kiddin'.' She let out a wet, snorty laugh.

'He attacked me and my kid tonight.'

'Ya *killed* him?'

'Yeah.'

'Ain't dat a hoot? You'n me, we bote killers!'

'I don't know what to do about his car.'

'Can't pull no trailer wid it.'

'I know.'

'Leab it.'

'It's got my fingerprints on it.'

'Better wipe 'em opp.'

'Yeah. Okay. Wait here.'

Sandy left the engine running. When she opened the door, the overhead light came on. She looked over at Lib.

They looked at each other.

Lib had cleaned most of the blood off her face. She held a wadded, red bandana against her nose and mouth. A large, golden ring dangled from one of her ears. The lobe of her other ear was torn and bloody. She might be about thirty years old, but it was hard to tell because of her battered face. She was larger than Sandy, had broad shoulders, and looked strong. Her shaved head made her seem tough, even though her face was torn and puffy.

Lib took the rag away from her mouth and asked, 'Where's yer shirt?'

'Where's your hair?'

'Haw!'

'I'll be right back.'

Sandy climbed out of the car and shut its door. She hurried up the roadside to the MG, dropped into its driver's seat, and pulled out the ignition key.

She stuffed the key ring into a front pocket of her shorts. Then she leaned sideways and opened the glove compartment.

It held a small revolver.

Sandy pursed her lips, quickly pulled out the handgun and stuffed it into her pocket.

Then she reached into the glove compartment again. This time, she found a few maps and a small stack of paper napkins – Slade must've saved the napkins from visits to fast food joints.

Sandy took them out and snapped the compartment shut. There seemed to be six or eight napkins. She used them to wipe the front of the glove compartment, the dashboard, the gear shift knob and the steering wheel. She opened the driver's door, then wiped the inside handle.

The road was still dark and empty.

She climbed out, shut the door, and rubbed the outside handle. And the area around the handle. Then she made a quick swipe along the top of the door.

Shoving the napkins into a pocket, she hurried back to Lib's car.

'Whose car is this?' she asked Lib.

Lib sniffed loudly, then said, 'Mine.'

'Are you the real owner?'

'Sure.'

'The *registered* owner?'

'Y'kiddin' me?'

'Is that a yes or a no?'

'Puck no.'

'It's stolen?'

'Y'betcha.'

'Great.'

Sandy pulled onto the road, turned left, and headed for her trailer.

'How hot is it?' she asked, and put the headlight on.

'We'b had it a mont.'

'A month?'

'Stole it in Mexico. It's good 'n sape.'

'What are you, some kind of big-time criminal?'

Lib let out a laugh, then snorted. 'Dat's a good one. Bill 'n me, big time. Bonnie 'n Clyde. Dat's us. Know what? Bill was nuttin' but a chicken-shit bully wit da brain ob a worm.'

'Was he your husband?'

'Haw!'

'Guess not.'

'Wortless puck.'

Sandy slowed down as she approached her turn-off. The road ahead looked empty. In the rearview, she saw only darkness and bits of moonlight. She swung onto the dirt tracks and powered her way up the hillside. Bushes squeaked against the sides of the car, scraped against its undercarriage.

'Ya lib up here?'

'Yeah. Me and my kid.'

'How old's yer kid?'

'Six months.'

'A baby.'

'Yeah.'

'Boy 'r girl?'

'Boy.'

'Aw. Dat's nice, real nice. But ya don' gotta man?'

'Just him.'

'Bastard knock ya up 'n run off?'

'Knocked me up and got killed.'

'Aw.'

'Yeah.'

'Did ya lub him?'

'Yeah.'

'Shit.'

'Yeah.'

'Lipe's a bitch, den ya die.'

'That's what they say. Sort of.'

Lib laughed. Then she reached over and patted Sandy's leg. 'Yer a good kid, Charly.'

'Thanks.'

As she drove over the crest of the slope, the car's single headlight swept down from high in the trees and stretched across the clearing to her trailer.

'That's home,' Sandy said. 'Should we hitch it up to your car and get out of here?'

'We can try. Ya know how?'

'Sure. My friend Agnes and I pulled it up here with her pickup truck. I helped her do the whole thing.'

'Done it myselp a pew times,' Lib said. 'Use to hab me a peller wid a boat. Course now, there's dipprent kinds a hitches.'

'I hope these'll match,' Sandy said. 'If they don't, I guess we'll have to try Agnes.' She turned the car around, then backed it slowly toward the front of the trailer. 'After it's hooked up, we can go inside and get cleaned up and stuff before we take off.'

'Good deal.'

Sandy climbed out, leaving the engine running and the lights on. Lib met her behind the car.

'They look like they'll go together, don't they?'

'Reckon,' Lib said. 'Hey, ya got any beer? My mout's all busted up dis way. I could sure use me a cold beer. I tink it'd peel mighty good.'

'I don't have beer, but I've got a bottle of bourbon.'

'Dat'd do. Me, I'll get started hookin' up dis shit. You go 'n pine us dat bottle.'

'Okay, sure.'

Sandy hurried around to the side of her trailer, rushed up the wobbly stairs and opened the door. She stepped inside. She glanced around. Everything looked fine. The bottle of bourbon still stood open on the counter of the kitchen area. She grabbed it, started toward the door, then changed her mind and went on to Eric's room.

She rolled the bedroom door open a few inches.

Standing motionless, she heard the slow, steady hiss of his breathing. A tightness inside her seemed to loosen and a coldness seemed to grow warm.

He's all right. He's fine. Fast asleep.

She quietly rolled the door shut, then crept away.

Outside, she found Lib bending over the trailer hitch.

'Can I give you a hand with that?' she asked.

'Already got it. Just hang on hap a minute, an' we'll be all set. Ya got da booze?'

'I've got it.'

'Dare!' Lib stood up straight. Rubbing her hands on the front of her jeans, she came over to Sandy. She took the bottle, raised it to her lips, and filled her mouth with the bourbon. When her cheeks were bulging, she lowered the bottle. Sandy heard air hissing in and out her nostrils. Then came sloshing sounds. Lib's cheeks sank in, ballooned, fluttered. She seemed to be working the bourbon around her teeth and gums as if it were mouthwash. After a while, she stopped swishing and started to swallow. Finally, she opened her mouth and sighed.

'Ohhhh, Charly, dat's a mighty pine drink. Takes da pain right outa my teet.'

'You got some knocked out, I guess.'

'Bill's old head come bustin' right in. I reckon it took out a whole passel ob teet, top 'n bottom – eight or ten ob 'em. An' I got all dese bleedin' holes in my puckin' gums. But de booze sorta numbs 'em por me. Damn good stuff.'

She filled her mouth again until her cheeks were bloated, shut her eyes and sighed through her nose, then sloshed the bourbon all around for a while before swallowing.

'Yer a mighty pine girl, Charly.'

'Well, I'm glad the booze helps.'

'I'm gonna hap to buy me some new teet.'

'Yeah. There's a lot of stuff we'll need to do after we get out of here. Are we all hitched up, now?'

'Yep.'

'Why don't we go inside and get cleaned up? I'll have to unhook us from the tanks, but that oughta be the last thing before we take off. Do you have any clean clothes to wear? I've got some in the trailer, but they'd probably be a tight fit on you.'

'Da trunk,' Lib said, and filled her mouth again.

Sandy went to the driver's door of the car. Leaning in, she shut off the lights and engine, then pulled out the ignition key. She hurried to the trunk.

While she unlocked it, Lib sloshed bourbon.

Sandy raised the lid. Inside the trunk, she saw only darkness.

She heard Lib gulping.

Then Lib said, 'Just reach on in.'

She reached into the trunk. She wasn't sure what she expected to touch – suitcases, maybe. Instead of luggage, however, her hands met soft piles of fabric.

'Just grab me out sometin',' Lib said. 'Help yerself, too. Ya look like ya might be a little low in da duds department.'

'Thanks. I've got stuff to wear, but I'd have to track through a lot of blood to get to them.'

'Take whatcha want.'

Sandy lifted garments out of the trunk and held them high so she could see them in the moonlight. She put back a couple of dresses, a sport jacket, a pair of slacks, and an evening gown before settling on a two tops that appeared to be shirts or blouses.

'These okay?' she asked.

'Sure. Whatebber.'

Sandy shut the trunk. 'Let's go inside and clean up before we put them on.'

Lib nodded, then filled her mouth again.

Sandy led the way. As she climbed the stairs, she warned, 'Watch out you don't fall on the way up. This thing's kind of shaky.'

At the top, she entered the trailer.

And saw what she was carrying. The twin, short-sleeved blouses looked as if they were made of red silk. They gleamed in the lamplight. They looked enormous. Stitched in swirling gold letters on the back of each were the words, *Blazing Babes*.

Lib stepped into the trailer.

Sandy turned around to face her. 'Blazing Babes?'

Lib grinned. Though her puffy lips were shut, some bourbon dribbled out. She shrugged. She swallowed. After wiping off her lips and chin, she said, 'Me and Bill, we piggered it was maybe like a girl's soccer team or bowlin' team or sometin'.'

'They aren't yours?'

'Sure dey are. Didn't used to be, but dey are now.'

'They're stolen?'

'Hey, sugar, damn near everything I got's stolen. I'm a teep. Been a teep all my lipe. Dat okay?'

'I don't know. Are you going to steal from me?'

'No! What kinda lowlipe you tink I am? Yer my pard, aren't ya?'

'I guess so. But if we're going to travel together, you've gotta promise not to get us into trouble. I mean, we've both killed guys tonight. We need to disappear quietly. We can't go around stealing things.'

'Sure. I get it.'

'No more crimes.'

'Whatebber.' She raised her eyebrows. 'So, pretty nipty blouses, huh?'

Sandy smirked. 'Real nifty. Let's wash up and get them on. This way.' She led Lib to the bathroom and turned on its light. 'You can go ahead and use this. I'll get cleaned up in the kitchen.'

She draped one of the red blouses on a hook just inside the doorway for Lib, then stepped out into the hall.

'Be done in a jip,' Lib said. She raised the bottle toward Sandy. 'How 'bout a sip?'

'No thanks.'

'Last call.'

'You go ahead and finish it.'

'Know what you are? A princess, dat's what. A real puckin' princess.'

Sandy laughed and shook her head. 'That's me,' she said, then stepped away from the bathroom door. As she headed for her kitchen area, the shower started to run.

She tossed the other *Blazing Babes* blouse onto the kitchen counter, stepped to the sink and turned on the hot water. She took a clean dishwashing cloth out of the drawer.

Without a mirror, she couldn't see how her face looked. She assumed it must be a mess, though. Because, looking down, she *could* see her shoulders and arms and breasts and belly: they were filthy and scratched and even smeared with blood, here and there. Her shorts were dirty in front. Her legs had taken the same kind of punishment as her torso.

I probably need a shower worse than Lib does.

'What she needs,' Sandy whispered, 'is a puckin' dentist.'

Laughing softly, she soaked her cloth with hot water. Then she bent over the sink and started to wash her face.

She supposed she ought to use soap.

Soap seemed like too much bother.

This'll be fine.

The hot, sodden rag felt very good on her face. Water spilled down her neck and chest. She leaned against the edge of the sink, hoping to keep her shorts from getting wet. But when she started mopping her breasts, so much water sluiced down her belly that she knew it was hopeless. She tried to stop some of it with the rag. Too much got by, so she tucked the rag under her chin, took a step backward and reached for her belt, figuring to get out of the shorts before they became completely drenched.

Should've taken them off in the first . . .

Someone screamed.

Sandy's heart slammed. Her hands jumped away from her belt. She whirled around and ran for the bathroom, the dish cloth sliding down from under her chin, clinging to her chest, falling down between her breasts.

She shoved a hand into the right front pocket of her shorts.

She pulled out the small revolver from Slade's glove compartment.

And wondered if it was loaded.

Sure it is. Has to be.

And it had to be Lib screaming. Who else *could* it be?

But why?

Slade on the move, not really dead?

Nobody in the hallway.

Through the roaring in her own head, Sandy realized that the scream had stopped.

She lurched to a halt at the bathroom's open door.

The wet cloth unpeeled itself from her belly, tumbled, brushed her left thigh and fell to the floor.

The shower curtain was shut. She couldn't see through it. So she raced across the floor and threw it wide open.

Lib was standing in the shower stall, feet wide apart, knees bent, clutching Eric with both hands as if she'd braced herself and caught him in mid-leap.

She was breathing hard.

Water still sprayed from the shower nozzle.

Lib's naked body was smudged with bruises. Bruises the size of a fist. The size of an open hand. The size of a knee. Others the size of a bite, a pinch. Brown ones, purple ones, green ones, yellow ones.

She'd been beaten up plenty, over a long period of time.

Tonight must've been once too often.

Eyes fixed on Eric, she didn't look at Sandy.

After a while, she drew Eric in against her chest. As she cradled him, her eyes met Sandy's. 'What is he?' she asked, her voice soft.

'My kid.'

'Yer pet?'

'My baby. I'm his mother.'

'No poolin'?'

'No fooling.'

'Well, I'll be.' Shaking her head, Lib gently stroked Eric's back. 'Sorry I screamed like dat. Da little shit scampered in, ya know, and scared da hell outa me.'

Nodding, Sandy lowered the revolver. 'Don't call him a little shit,' she said.

'What's his name?'

'Eric.'

'Hiya, Eric. I'm Lib. Dat's short for Libby.' To Sandy, she said, 'Can he talk?'

'No.'

'He's sure an ugly little pucker. What'd his dad look like?'

'The same as him. And he isn't ugly.'

'*Cute*-ugly.'

'That's better.'

'Is he human?'

'Sort of.'

'Looks like he's part sometin' else. Like a bald monkey, or da creature prum da Black Lagoon or sometin'. But cute. Cute as a button.' To Eric, she said in baby talk, 'Yes, you are.' Then she kissed his forehead.

'You can't tell anyone about him,' Sandy said. 'He's my secret. And now he's *your* secret. He's the last of his kind – at least I think he is – and they'll kill him if they ever find him.'

'Who? Who'd wanta kill him?'

'Damn near everyone. To them, he's a monster. A beast.'

Lib's eyes widened. 'Is he one ob dem Beast House beasts?'

'His father was.'

'Holy smokin' Jesus. Ya tellin' me dey're *real*? I always piggered dey was made up. Like Martians, ya know? Or werewoops or sometin'.'

'They're real. You're holding one.'

Shaking her head slowly, Lib eased Eric away and lifted him in front of her face. 'Look at ya,' she said to him in a gentle, lilting voice. 'Just look at ya. Wowy, wowy. I sure wish *I'd* known yer old man.'

'Do you promise not to tell on us?' Sandy asked.

'Sure. Cross my heart an' hope to die.'

'If you tell, you *will* die. I'll see to it.'

'We'll be a pamily, da tree ob us.'

Pocketing the revolver, Sandy stepped over to the shower stall. She reached out for Eric. Lib passed the child gently into her hands. 'See ya later, baby,' she said.

Sandy saw tears in the woman's eyes.

'Are you all right?'

'Nebber had me no pamily bepore.'

Feeling a tightness in her throat, Sandy smiled at Lib and said, 'I don't know if we're quite a family yet, but I reckon we're partners.'

'Pards.' Lib sniffed, then reached out and squeezed Sandy's shoulder. 'Pards to da end.'

Chapter Ten

The Day Tour II

After the brilliant sunlight, the gloom inside Beast House made Owen feel as if he'd stepped into a dark closet. He took off his sunglasses. That helped.

'Good morning,' said a guide who was waiting inside the doorway. The nameplate on the front of her tan shirt read SHARON. Blonde, blue-eyed, slender and deeply tanned, she was the best-looking guide so far. 'Station Number Two is just inside the parlor there, but feel free to wander anywhere.'

'Thanks,' Owen said.

As they crossed the foyer, he noticed people starting up the stairway and others wandering into a narrow corridor beside the stairs. A couple came out of the parlor. He recognized them from the group in front of the porch. He thought they'd been on the bus, too, but wasn't sure. They didn't act as if they recognized him or Monica.

Which didn't surprise him.

Put a set of earphones on someone, he'd noticed, and the rest of the world pretty much disappears. Everything goes away except the sounds inside the person's head.

In the parlor, Owen found half a dozen people standing near a plush red cordon, gazing at the body on the floor. He couldn't find a sign to confirm that this was the second station of the tour; maybe someone was standing in front of it. But Janice on the tape *and* Sharon had directed them here. Also, some of the tourists looked like those who'd been gathered near the porch stairs.

Monica didn't seem to be in doubt. She thumbed her cassette player into action. Owen went ahead and turned his on.

'Welcome to Station Two,' said Janice's voice. 'You should be in the parlor, where Ethel Hughes was the first to die on the night of August 2, 1903. That's her body, stretched out on the floor beside the couch.'

Owen stared at the wax figure. It was sprawled on the floor, one leg up, its foot still resting on the seat cushion of the couch. There was terror on Ethel's face. She looked as if she'd died in the midst of a scream. Her white gown was bloodstained and shredded. Its tatters hung down her body, showing skin that had been savagely torn by claws and teeth.

Owen was surprised by the near nudity of the figure. The way the gown was ripped, Ethel's breasts were bare except for the nipples. Her hips and legs were exposed. Only a few dangling strips of white cloth saved her from being completely naked below her waist.

'Ethel was the sister of Lilly Thorn,' Owen heard Janice saying through his earphones. 'She actually lived in Portland, Oregon.

'Earlier that summer, Lilly had sent her children away to stay with Ethel, so that she could be alone in the house. She'd apparently wanted privacy in order to indulge in certain adult behaviors that are beyond the scope of our tour.'

After a brief pause, Janice's voice continued. 'On about June 29, Ethel returned to the Thorn house with Lilly's two children. She then stayed on, possibly planning to attend Lilly's wedding to the local doctor. Here's Maggie to tell you about it.

'Ethel Hughes, Lilly's sister, was in this very room on the night of August the second, 1903. She'd come down for Lilly's wedding, which would've been the next week if tragedy hadn't suddenly struck down their plans. Tragedy being the beast. Nobody knows how it got into the house, or where it come from. But it snuck up behind the couch and took Ethel unawares while she was busy reading her *Saturday Evening Post*. It jumped her and ripped her up till she looked just like you see her – all torn and dead.'

Janice's voice returned. 'The *Post* that Ethel was reading at the time of the attack was found on the floor near her body, exactly where you now see a later issue of the same magazine. The original *Post* stayed here in the parlor for many years while Maggie ran the tours. For the sake of preserving it, however, it has been moved to the Beast House Museum. The gown worn by Ethel is also on display at the museum. What you see here is an exact duplicate of the original, identical down to every rip and bloodstain.

'This *is* the original figure of Ethel Hughes, created in wax by M. Claude Dubois in 1936. The work was commissioned by Maggie Kutch. When placing the order for this and the figures of the two boys that you'll see upstairs, Maggie included photographs of the murder scenes, plus morgue photos of the corpses. She asked that the positions of the bodies, and all the injuries, be recreated with complete accuracy of detail.

'Generations of visitors from all over the world have stood where you are now standing and gazed down at this very replica of Ethel's ravaged body. This mannequin has also been seen in several popular films of *The Horror* series, which were based – sometimes very loosely – on my books about Beast House.

'Before we go on to the next station, I'd like to point out that the information we're presenting in this tour is based almost entirely on the tours given by Maggie Kutch from 1932 to 1979. Now, Maggie didn't always tell the truth – far from it. She knew much more than she ever told. When I bought this place, I made the decision to stay with Maggie's version for a couple of reasons. First, even though it's full of lies, it *is* the authentic Beast House tour. I wanted to give you, and all our visitors, a taste of how it might've been, many years ago, to be guided through the house by the woman who created the attraction in the first place. Second, the actual truth about Beast House isn't suitable for family entertainment. If you want to know the actual, true details of the history of Beast House, you'll find it in my books or on the Midnight Tour.

'And now, a few more words from Maggie. When she's finished, it'll be time to turn off your recorders and proceed to Station Three at the top of the stairway.

'After the beast got done murdering Ethel,' Maggie said, 'it went on a rampage around the room. It knocked over this bust of Caesar, breaking off his nose. See, there's his nose on the mantel.' Owen spotted the nose. Though it was out of reach beyond the cordon, it looked dirty, as if it had been handled too often by people with grimy fingers. He was surprised that nobody had stolen it.

'The beast just run amok for a while, dashing some figurines in the fireplace, turning over chairs. See this rosewood pedestal table? The beast threw it out the bay window over there. Must've made a mighty loud noise, all that glass getting smashed to smithereens.

'I reckon the racket likely woke up everybody in the house. Lilly's room was right above us. Maybe she got out of bed, and the beast heard her. It scooted out of here and went running for the stairs.'

Owen heard a click as Monica hit the Stop button of her player. His own player hissed quietly for a moment before he shut it off.

He and Monica had eased their way closer and closer to the cordon as those ahead of them finished listening and wandered off. Now, they stood at the rope.

Owen had been able to see Ethel all along, but this was as near to her as he could hope to get. Without stepping over the cordon.

He stared at her.

And tried to imagine her real. Tried, in his mind, to transform her like Pygmalion or Pinocchio into a human with soft, smooth skin.

But he couldn't make it happen.

Too many distractions. The other people in the room, especially Monica. And how Ethel's gown barely covered her. Owen wished a breeze would come along and blow some of those tatters aside.

Instead of making Ethel turn real in his mind, he pictured himself climbing over the cordon, kneeling over her, and peeking underneath the loose shreds of her gown.

Get off it, he told himself. She's a *dummy*.

Even so . . .

Monica nudged him with her elbow and whispered, 'Let's go, Owie.'

He followed her to the door. They stepped aside to make room for a couple of people trying to come in, then headed for the stairway.

Sharon, some distance away, was greeting new visitors. She had her back to Owen and Monica. Her blond hair hung down in a thick braid.

'That was certainly tacky,' Monica said.

'What was?'

'What do you think? Ethel. Good God. I didn't know this was going to be a peepshow. No wonder you were so eager to come here.'

They started to climb the stairs.

'Nothing you couldn't see on any beach,' Owen pointed out.

'In France, maybe.'

'Anyway, she's just a dummy.'

'It's pretty funny, they give all that lip service about keeping the dirty stuff out of the tour, then they show us something like that.'

'I didn't think it was that bad.'

'You wouldn't.'

At the top of the stairs, a sign on the wall read Station Three. 'Here we go again,' Monica muttered, starting her player.

Owen thumbed down the Play button on his machine, and heard Janice's voice.

'After finishing its brutal attack on Ethel, the beast ran out of the parlor and scurried up the stairs, leaving a trail of blood to mark his way. Ethel's blood. Look down, and you'll see stains on the floor. They've been copied from crime scene photos, and match the stains found on the hardwood floor the night of murder. Follow them to Lilly's bedroom and listen to what Maggie had to say.'

Monica, head down, followed the red stains. Owen walked behind her. His tape hissed, wordless for the few seconds that it took to reach the doorway of a bedroom.

'We're just above the parlor here,' Maggie explained. 'This is Lilly Thorn's bedroom. That's her on the bed.'

He entered the room behind Monica.

Only a few tourists were here. They were scattered along the length of the cordon, so Owen had a fine view of the bed.

Sitting upright on it was the figure of a young woman dressed in a pink nightgown. Eyes wide, mouth agape, hand to her mouth, she looked to Owen like a star of the silent screen demonstrating terror.

'All that commotion from downstairs woke Lilly up,' Maggie continued. 'She must've known something mighty awful was going on. Must've known she and her boys were in danger. But instead of running to save the kids, she climbed out of bed and shut her door. See that dressing table there? She dragged it over in front of the door so the intruder couldn't barge in. Then she climbed out her window. It wouldn't've been a long fall to the ground, but there's a bay window just below this one, and she dropped down on top of it. From there, it was an easy jump. She landed on her lawn and run away into the night.'

'Lilly made good her escape,' Janice said, her smooth voice replacing Maggie's gruffness. 'She escaped with her life, but not with her sanity. The wax figure that you see on the bed, done by Dubois, was based on a photograph that had been taken of Lilly at the time of her marriage to Lyle Thorn, the outlaw, several years earlier. This nightgown is an exact replica of the one she . . .'

'And the original can be found at the Beast House Museum,' Monica said in a sing-song, mocking voice that interferred with whatever Janice was saying on Owen's tape.

She pushed her Stop button.

Owen frowned at her.

He looked around. Though some people were entering the room, nobody stood nearby. Monica's mimickry had probably disturbed nobody but Owen.

'Cut it out,' he whispered.

She flashed her teeth at him.

Owen stopped his machine. He studied it, found the Rewind button, and pressed it.

'You're *not* going back?'

'Yeah, I am.'

'That was the end.'

'I *wasn't* to the end yet when you interrupted. You made me miss stuff.'

She rolled her eyes and muttered, 'You're kidding.'

Owen thumbed Play. Maggie said, 'from downstairs woke Lilly up. She must've known something mighty awful was going on.'

He'd rewound way too far.

As Maggie went on, he thought about hitting the Fast Forward.

Don't, he told himself. Just listen to it all again. So what if it takes a while? Monica can just wait. She should've kept her mouth shut.

He met her eyes.

She frowned.

'I rewound too far,' he explained.

'Good going.'

'This may take a minute.'

'Wonderful.'

'Shhhh. I'm trying to listen.'

'Cute move.'

'You don't have to wait for me.'

'You can really be a pain sometimes, do you know that?'

'You're going to make me miss stuff again. Then I'll have to rewind.'

She clamped her lips shut and glared at him.

Owen wished she *would* leave. He wanted to concentrate on the tour without any distractions – especially without the *negative* distractions provided by Monica. She was ruining it for him.

His tape reached the part that he'd missed.

As Monica had already told him, the original nightgown worn by Lilly on the night of the attack was on display at the Beast House Museum.

'You may now go down the hallway, and resume listening when you come to Station Four.'

He stopped the tape.

'All done?' Monica asked.

'Yep.'

'You're sure you didn't miss a single precious word?'

'I think that'll do it.'

This time, he led the way. Though he walked slowly toward the door, he didn't look back to make sure that Monica was staying with him. It made him feel rude, but he didn't care. If it offended her, good. For years, he'd been looking forward to Beast House. Now he was finally here, but Monica wouldn't let him enjoy it.

Big mistake.

And she thinks I'm actually going to marry her?

When hell freezes over.

He waited just inside the doorway while a family with three kids made their way into Lilly's bedroom. Everyone in the family wore earphones. Even their girl, who appeared to be about eight years old.

It didn't seem right, bringing a kid that age into a place like this.

People are so damn queer, he thought.

But what's really the harm? If the kid ever lays her eyes on the TV news, she'll see a lot worse than this.

When the door was clear, Owen moved into the hallway and stepped aside to avoid a man carrying an infant.

The baby didn't wear earphones. Owen smiled.

For just a moment, he pictured a kid of his own – but it was a girl and it looked like Monica.

No way, he thought.

My God, she could be pregnant right now for all I know! Who's to say she isn't? Condoms leak.

He wished he could simply close his eyes and make a wish and Monica would be gone . . .

'Oh, there's nothing much to see up there, anyway. But the attic isn't particularly safe. That's why we don't allow anyone up the stairs.'

Owen glanced at the person who was speaking.

A guide.

He started to look away.

She caught him looking and smiled.

He smiled back.

She turned her eyes away from him and resumed talking to a couple of teenagers who had stopped near the attic door. On the wall beside the doorway was a large number 7.

Owen kept moving.

He stared at her as he walked by.

Then he turned his head to look over his shoulder at her.

'Don't break your neck,' Monica said.

'Huh?'

'God almighty.'

'Huh?' Facing Monica, he raised his eyebrows. 'What're you talking about?'

'You know damn well.'

'What?'

'That dumb blonde in the guide suit back there.'

Was I that obvious?

'What makes you think she's dumb?' Owen asked, trying to sound amused.

'Just one look at her.'

'I wouldn't know. I didn't get that good of a look.'

'Sure you didn't.'

'I was trying to see up the attic stairs,' he said.

'Uh-huh, sure. She's not that hot, you know. If you ask me, she sort of looks like a horse.'

Yeah, a gorgeous thoroughbred.

'I don't know,' he said. 'I hardly saw her.'

He wished he'd had a better chance to see her.

She works here, he told himself. She'll still be around when we come back this way. Station Seven.

She'll probably be a big disappointment. Nobody can be that terrific. And even if she IS that terrific, I'd never stand a chance with her.

Guys like me don't even exist . . .

'Where you going, Bozo?' Monica asked. 'We just walked past Station Four.'

He stopped, looked over his shoulder, and saw the 4 painted on the wall of the hallway. 'Ah,' he said. Then, trying to smile at Monica, he said, 'Thanks.'

With a smug smile, she said, 'I think you'd lose your head if it wasn't attached.'

'Maybe.'

He pressed the Play button.

He expected Janice's voice, but Maggie's came on instead. 'When the beast couldn't get into Lilly's room, it turned around and came prowling down the hall this way, looking for someone to kill. It sniffed its way along like a bloodhound.'

Owen glanced toward the attic door, but too many people were in the way and he couldn't see the guide.

What if she's gone?

Never mind, he told himself. Just ignore her and enjoy the tour.

Sure.

'It *smelled* Lilly's kids,' Maggie was saying. 'It tracked their scent all the way down the hall, and found them in their bedroom. This is it, right here. Come on in.'

While Owen waited for a man to step out, Maggie's voice was silent. He imagined her leading a group of tourists into the room, making sure they were all inside before resuming her speech.

'Here we are,' she said.

Beyond the red cordon were twin, brass beds. The covers were thrown back and rumpled. The sheets were bright in the sunlight coming in through the windows, but spattered with dark stains.

The kids lay sprawled in the space between the beds. Their night-shirts had nearly been torn from their bodies. Sheds of the bloody fabric draped their buttocks.

'This is the bedroom where the children slept,' Maggie said. 'But I 'spect they were wide awake when the beast came after them. All the commotion was downstairs and way at the other end of the hall, but this ain't a real big house. And it's real quiet in the middle of the night. Noise carries. So they likely heard the beast slamming things around and pounding on their mama's door and roaring out its rage. If they heard it, they were too scared to move. All they could do was hide under their covers, the way kids do, froze up with fear and hoping it was just a bad dream and maybe it'd go away. Only it wasn't no dream, and it didn't go nowhere. It come for them.

'Earl was ten years old,' Maggie said. 'His brother, Sam, was only eight. They were both still in their beds when the beast got them. See the blood? They must've started off on their beds and ended up on the floor. Right there, that's where their bodies got found.'

Maggie stopped talking. Owen expected Janice to come on. But a couple of seconds later, Maggie's voice returned. She said, slowly and low, 'Imagine how scared they must've been, those little fellers. They likely reckoned it was the boogeyman. But I bet they figured every-thing'd turn out all right and they'd get saved at the last minute. Only they didn't get saved. The beast got them.

'It didn't kill them right away. That would've been a blessing. We can't really know what all went on here, but there's reports of townfolk hearing the screams of children in the night. Far-off screams that went on for good long time. Nobody could figure just where they were coming from, but afterwards, they knew. It was Lilly's boys crying out in horror and agony while the beast tormented them.

'It's said that Lilly heard their screams when she was running down Front Street, and that's what unhinged her mind.'

The tape went silent again for a few moments. Then Janice came on and said in a solemn voice, 'With the deaths of Lilly's two sons, the rampage ended. The beast vanished, and its crimes were placed on the head of poor Gus Goucher. Nobody knew that there *was* a beast. Only Lilly, perhaps – and she had been reduced to maniacal babbling.

'Which may or may not have been faked.

'If your curiosity has been aroused, I suggest that you read my books and take advantage of the Midnight Tour. You'll be surprised and maybe even shocked by what you learn.'

She paused for a moment or two, then started talking again. 'After the attack on Lilly Thorn's family on that horrible night in 1903, the house was abandoned. Nobody lived here again for twenty-eight years. Then, in 1931, it was purchased by Joseph Kutch. He moved in with his wife, Maggie, and their three children. But they were in the house for only two weeks before the beast struck.

'You may now move on to Station Five. Turn right just outside the door, and go down the corridor until you come to the top of the stairway.

There, you'll hear Maggie begin to tell you about the night that the beast attacked *her* family.'

He clicked the Stop button.

Monica looked at him and raised her eyebrows. 'Done?' she asked.

He nodded.

'Are you sure you don't want to rewind? Maybe you missed a word or two.'

'It's fine,' he said. He turned around and started across the room.

Already picturing the tall, beautiful guide.

Get a good look at her, this time.

When he reached the doorway, he stepped aside and gestured for Monica to precede him. 'Ladies first,' he said.

She gave him a look as if she knew exactly why he wanted her ahead of him. With a smirk, she halted and said, 'Age before beauty. *You* go first.'

He shrugged. He smiled. 'Okay. Just thought I should offer to protect your rear.'

'My rear's fine.'

'The beast likes to jump people from behind.'

'Sure.'

He stepped past Monica, turned right in the corridor, and walked slowly.

Slowly so she wouldn't sense his eagerness.

Slowly to give himself plenty of time for his inspection of the guide.

Already, his mouth was dry, his face hot, his heart pounding hard and fast.

He could see the attic door up ahead.

But so far, the guide was still out of sight. Too many people cluttered the hallway.

Why can't I spot her? She's taller than most of them.

No she isn't, he thought when he spied the pretty, young guide who was standing near the attic door. She isn't that tall *or* that beautiful.

How the hell did I . . .?

After a moment of shocked perplexity, he realized that this was not the same guide he'd seen earlier.

He felt a surge of relief.

Mixed with disappointment.

Where is she? Where'd she go? Maybe went on a break. Maybe she's gone for lunch.

What if I don't get to see her again?

As he approached the replacement, he heard her talking to a small group of people who were gathered near the open attic door. 'The attic's never been part of the regular tour.'

He stopped to listen.

'It's just not very safe. I do take people up there during the Midnight Tour every Saturday night. But that's a small, carefully supervised group. We can't leave it open for the general public. There aren't floorboards everywhere. Also, there's a lot of clutter. Too many places where the beast might be lurking.' She grinned.

According to the nametag on her chest, she was LYNN.

'We don't want to lose anybody,' she said.

Owen wanted to ask where the other guide had gone, but he didn't dare.

Monica would flip out.

'If we wait here long enough,' Monica whispered, 'maybe she'll turn into the beauty queen.'

'Very funny,' Owen told her.

He started walking again.

Where is she?

He stopped at Station Five, in the corridor a few feet beyond the top of the stairs.

Monica, stopping beside him, thumbed the Play button on her player. Owen started his tape.

What if she's gone for the day? What if I never see her again?

I can't let that happen, he told himself.

'We lived sixteen nights in this house,' Maggie said, 'before the beast struck.'

Chapter Eleven

Sandy's Story – August, 1980

Sandy carried Eric down the wobbly stairs in his travel basket – a wicker bassinet with a closed lid and handles at both ends. Worried about the slippery steps, she moved slowly and carefully. She sighed with relief when her feet met the ground.

She set down the basket.

Together, she and Lib lifted the stairway and shoved it inside her trailer. Lib stepped out of the way. Sandy swung the door shut.

Turning around, she found her new friend picking up Eric's basket by its two handles.

'We gonna keep him in dis?' Lib asked.

'We'd better. In case we get stopped.'

'Poor little pucker.'

'I don't think he minds. It seems pretty nice and cozy in there. And he's got his favorite dolls.'

'Can he breet okay?'

'Sure. All kinds of air gets in. He'll be fine. Let's just put him in the back seat.'

Sandy hurried ahead and opened the back door. Then she took the basket from Lib and lowered it onto the floor in front of the seat. It was a fairly tight squeeze. The wicker made dry, crackling sounds. Sandy figured that the tightness was good for Eric's safety in case of a crash.

She stepped back and shut the door.

'I guess I'll drive,' she said.

'How come?' asked Lib.

'You're drunk as a skunk.'

'Well, dat ain't nebber stopped me.'

'You polished off the whole bottle.'

'It weren't pull in da first place.'

'Anyway, you aren't in any shape to drive. Even if you weren't polluted, you just got the crap pounded out of you and half your teeth knocked out.'

'Hap ob 'em? Nah. Lots, dough.'

'Go on and get in. You can drive later if you feel like it.'

'Who says I wanta?'

Sandy shrugged, then opened the passenger door. When Lib was in, she shut the door and hurried around the front. She climbed into the driver's seat.

'Ya ebber towed sometin'?' Lib asked.

'No,' Sandy said, and started the engine.

'Here.' Reaching over, Lib pulled the shift lever backward from Park to Low. 'Try dis. And go slow.'

Sandy put on the headlight, then eased down on the gas pedal. Engine racing, the car began to move forward. She could feel the weight of the trailer and hear the rattling sounds it made as it bumped over the ground behind them.

She pictured Slade's body rolling and sliding around in the back bedroom, spreading his mess like a blood-soaked mop.

Maybe they should've done something with it.

At least, maybe, tied it down or thrown it into the shower stall. But they'd both been clean and wearing their *Blazing Babes* shirts by the time Lib had said, 'Ya gonna let me get a look at yer stip?'

'My what?' Sandy asked.

'Yer stip. Dat guy ya killed.'

'You want to see him?'

'Sure. Where's he at?'

'Why don't we just get going?'

Lib's puffy eyes narrowed. 'How I know ya really *got* a stip?'

Sandy suddenly understood: Lib needed to see the body, needed to know for certain that she hadn't lied about killing Slade.

We've both got to be killers. That's what makes us partners.

'Okay,' Sandy said. 'You wanta see him, you can see him. Come on.' She lowered Eric into his travel basket, then hurried down the hallway. Lib followed, bottle in hand.

Sandy slid open her bedroom door, flicked the light switch, then stepped back. 'Help yourself,' she said. 'But be careful not to step in any blood.'

Lib took a step into the room. A moment later, she spotted the body on the floor to her left. Sandy saw her back straighten. Then Lib crouched down. Her head shook slowly from side to side.

'Dis guy's massacerated.'

'Huh?'

'*What'd* he do to ya?'

'For one thing, he threw Eric across the room. And he tried to rape me.'

'Dis guy's deader 'n fried shit.'

'Yeah.'

She looked over her shoulder at Sandy, and smiled. 'Yer a mighty bad little dude, Charly.'

'He had it coming.'

'What're we gonna *do* wid him?'

'I figured to leave him in the room, here, and wait till we're someplace far away. I want to make his body disappear, you know? Someplace where it'll never be found. The thing is, there might be people who know he came looking for me tonight. Maybe if we both vanish off the face of the earth . . .'

'Suits me pine,' Lib said. 'Let's *all* banish.' Standing up, she put her hands on her hips and seemed to be studying the body. 'We get to moobin', he'll start to roll around. Wanta anchor him down or put him someplace?'

'Nah, that's all right. We'd get all messy. Let's just finish up and go.'

* * *

At least he's confined to the bedroom, Sandy thought as she drove slowly down the hillside, trying to stay in the ruts.

I shut the door, didn't I?

Sure I did.

In her imagination, though, she'd left the bedroom door wide open and she pictured Slade tumbling through it, rolling into the hallway, his bloody mutilated corpse somersaulting down the whole length of the trailer.

Probably didn't happen, she told herself. And if it *did*, the harm's already done.

Just try not to let the trailer flip over or you'll REALLY be in trouble.

In spite of the low gear, they were picking up speed on their way down the slope.

'Carepul,' Lib said.

Sandy eased down on the brake pedal for a few seconds and watched the speedometer needle sink. When she let up, it started to climb. So she put on the brakes again, squeezing the speed down, the needle dropping from 20 to 15 to 10. By the time she reached the edge of the paved road, she'd slowed almost to a stop.

The road looked empty, so she made a slow, right-hand turn. Then she shoved the shift lever to Drive and started to pick up speed. Cool air, smelling of the woods and ocean, blew straight into her face through the hole in the windshield.

'Made it,' Lib said, and patted her leg.

Sandy took a deep breath. She felt relief about coming down the hill without mishap, but now they were on a real road – where they were sure to be seen, sooner or later, by people in passing cars.

Maybe by cops.

A squirmy tightness came into her stomach.

'I don't know how far we'll be able to go,' she said. 'The way this car looks, we'll be stopped by the first cop who sees us.'

'Just tell him we hit a deer.'

That didn't seem like a bad idea. Vehicles crashed into deer fairly often in this area. That sort of accident might explain the damage to the car.

'But I don't have a driver's license,' Sandy explained.

'Huh?'

'I'm driving. No matter what we tell him, he'll want to see my license. And I don't have one.'

'I got one.'

'But you're smashed. And if he takes one look at you, he'll

know somebody pounded the crap out of you. If we get stopped, we're sunk.'

The single headlight caught a sign by the edge of the road:

WELCOME TO MALCASA POINT
POP. 2,600
HOME OF THE LEGENDARY 'BEAST HOUSE'
PLEASE DRIVE WITH CARE,
WE LOVE OUR CHILDREN.

Then the speed limit went down to 35.

Sandy took her foot off the gas pedal until the needle dropped to 30.

Turning her head slightly to the left, she stared out across the moonlit field at Agnes's house.

Home.

I'm going to miss it so much. And Agnes.

She ached to turn into the driveway.

One more look around. It might be my last chance forever. And give Agnes a last kiss before I go. I might never see her again. She might be dead by the time I ever . . .

'Place sure looks spooky at night,' Lib said.

It's not spooky, it's home.

She frowned at Lib, but saw that her friend's head was turned toward the right, toward Beast House.

So her frown became a smile. 'You oughta try being *inside* it in the middle of the night.'

'Tanks but no tanks.' She faced Sandy. 'So, is dat where you met Eric's padder?'

'He was known to hang around in there.' She turned her head for a final glimpse of Agnes's house. Her throat suddenly felt thick. Tears welled up in her eyes.

How can I just drive away like this and not even tell her goodbye or thanks or ANYTHING. She's the only person in the whole wide world who loves me.

Except Eric.

And a whisper came as if from a malicious twin caged in a corner of her mind, *What about Mom?*

No! Fuck her! She hates me! I hope she's dead.

The twin whispered, *No you don't. You miss the hell out of her.*

Bullshit!

'Uh-oh,' Lib said.

Sandy came out of her thoughts and spotted the trouble.

Several blocks ahead of them, a car with bright, twin headlights was making a left-hand turn onto Front Street. Squinting, Sandy tried to see if it had a light rack on top.

She couldn't tell.

But if it does . . .

'Hang on,' she said.

She hit the brakes and made a hard right. The force of the turn pushed her sideways against her door. Lib swayed toward her, but didn't fall. In the rearview mirror, she saw the trailer swing around behind them. It stayed up.

A growl came from Eric's basket.

'It's okay, honey,' Sandy said loudly, trying to sound confident and calm.

She raced toward the end of the block. At the corner, she turned left. She eased over to the curb, stopped, shut off the engine and killed the lights.

'If it comes,' she said, 'we'll duck out of sight.'

They waited.

Sandy's heart thudded and her mouth felt dry.

Lib made a quiet, throaty laugh.

'What's so funny?'

'Da pour ob us. Poor cop'd tink he popped in on a puckin' horror moobie, huh? Couple ob dames on da road widda butchered asshole in da trailer and a baby monster in da backseat.'

'Eric isn't a monster.'

'Tell dat to da cop.'

'I don't think we'll have to,' Sandy said. 'Not yet, anyway.'

Reaching forward, she twisted the ignition key and started the engine.

'Tink it's sape?' Lib asked.

'Yeah. It would've been here by now.'

She put on the headlight, then pulled forward, steered onto the road and picked up speed.

She wished she was back on Front Street. This might be her last time in Malcasa Point. It didn't seem right to miss all the old, familiar places along the main road if you wouldn't ever have a chance to see them again.

Better to be safe, though.

Anyway, who says I can't come back?

It'd be too dangerous, she told herself. Especially after tonight.

But I could come back. If I wanted to badly enough.

Ahead of her, the road dead-ended. She turned left and returned to Front Street. Waiting at a stop sign, she looked back at the town. There were no cars on the move. She saw no one. Some of the shops were lighted, but none seemed to be open.

The lone traffic signal, a flashing red light, blinked on and off and on again.

'Whatcha waitin' por?' Lib asked.

Sandy shrugged. 'Nothing,' she said. Then she turned right and put downtown behind her.

When she drove past the Welcome Inn, she tried not to look at it. But her eyes strayed over.

At the sight of the motel, memories rushed in.

Mom . . .

And that dirty rotten Jud. He'd seemed like such a good guy, at first . . .

And Larry. Poor, funny Larry.

She felt an emptiness inside. And a hurt.

They'd all betrayed her.

Well, not Larry. But he would've, probably. Just never got the chance.

It had all been so exciting, right at the start. A little scary, but fun, too. Taking off with Mom, so early in the morning. The all-day drive up the coast. Then the fog and the crash and Axel Kutch coming to the rescue. Their first night at the Welcome Inn. And the next day, going on the Beast House tour for the very first time.

Those had been such great times.

Only three years ago.

But it sure felt like longer. It felt like *eons*. She'd still been a kid. She'd still loved her mom . . .

She felt a tightness in her throat.

Screw it, she thought.

'Y'okay?' Lib asked.

'It's just . . . you know . . . I'm going to miss some stuff around here.'

'Yeah?'

'A *lot* of stuff.'

'Ya don't *gotta* leabe. Ain't nobody holdin' a gun to your head.'

'I *wouldn't* have to, except for that Slade. He wrecked everything.'

'Reckon he paid por it.'

Tears in her eyes, Sandy looked across at Lib. 'I just wanted to be left alone, you know? That's all I ever wanted. I had my job and my baby and Agnes and *every*thing till those damn movie people came along. They ruined it all.'

'It's the shits, honey.'

She took a very deep breath and exhaled slowly, letting the air puff out her cheeks and hiss through her pursed lips. When it was gone, she took a normal breath and said, 'Well. I guess we'll be fine, anyway. And maybe it's for the best, you know? Might be kind of fun, settling down someplace new. Maybe it'll turn out to be the best thing that ever happened to us.'

'Don't count on it.'

Sandy glanced at Lib and laughed.

Then Lib patted her on the thigh. 'Just gotta take stupp as it comes. Eben a bed ob roses got torns, and dare ain't a garden nowhere dat don't hab its share ob turds. You gotta watch your step, dat's all.'

'We'll both have to watch our steps.'

'But dat don't mean we can't hab pun.'

'Hab pun – will travel.'

'Puck you.'

Laughing, Sandy blurted, 'Puck *you*!'

'And da horse ya rode *in* on. How'd ya like it ip I busted out *yer* teet?'

'My *teeth*?'

'Yer *teet!*'

'My *what*?'

'Yer *choppers*, ya little shit.'

'Then I'd be talking like you, Lib, and neither one of us'd know what was going on.'

'Dat's real punny. Dat's hilarious.'

Sandy grinned at her and said, 'You know what?'

'What?'

'I'm already habbing pun.'

Lib gave her leg a gentle squeeze and said, 'Me, too.'

With that, they seemed to run out of things to say. Lib settled down in her seat and lowered her head. Sandy turned her attention to driving.

She wasn't exactly sure of her location.

Definitely on Pacific Coast Highway, somewhere north of town.

But not very far north.

Five or ten miles?

Though she'd traveled this section of road several times before, she couldn't remember being on it at night. In the darkness, nothing looked very familiar.

On the other hand, it *all* looked sort of familiar.

The right side of the road was bordered by densely wooded hills. On the left, across the narrow pavement, was a guard rail and a rocky shoreline and the ocean itself. The ocean looked black, but it didn't go far. Some distance out, maybe a mile or two, it vanished under fog.

The fog stretched across the ocean like a low range of soft, white hills. Under the light of the full moon, it looked whiter than fresh drifts of snow.

Beautiful, Sandy thought.

Not so beautiful when you're in it, though.

She sure hoped it would stay offshore.

Probably will, she told herself. It'd usually be in by now if it was coming.

She found herself remembering how it had come in during the afternoon that she and her mother were fleeing up the coast highway. The way it had reached up over the edges of the road like the tendrils of a ghostly sea creature testing the pavement, then silently crept all the way up, covering their car and the highway and the hills until all the world seemed gray. Until there was no longer a road to see, and they'd gone off into a ditch.

What if the fog had stayed offshore? Sandy wondered.

We wouldn't have crashed. Maybe Mom would've kept on driving all the way through Malcasa Point. We never would've spent the night at the Welcome Inn or gone to Beast House the next day.

And everything would've happened differently from then on.

A lot of people might still be alive, she thought. Mom and I might still be together.

Or maybe Dad would've caught up to us.

Screw it, she told herself. The fog *did* come in and we crashed and it all happened and there's no way to change it. And who'd *want* to change it, anyway, even if you had the chance?

Dad probably would've nailed us. *I'd* have spent the last three years dead.

There wouldn't be any Eric, either.

'It's funny how stuff goes,' she said.

Lib's only comment was a soft, rumbling snore.

Chapter Twelve

The Day Tour III

'Only sixteen nights,' Maggie said, her voice low and gruff through Owen's earphones. 'Then it came after us. It came right up these stairs.'

Several tourists were on their way up the stairs. Owen, Monica and the others at Station Five stepped back a little to let them by as Maggie continued to talk into Owen's ears.

'It was on the night of May seventh, 1931. Me and Joseph, we were in our bedroom just down the hall. We didn't use Lilly's room, as my husband figured it'd bring us bad luck. So we had the room across the hall from it. Our girls were way down at the other end of the hall, in the same room where Lilly's boys got themselves slaughtered. They didn't have no problems with it. Fact is, they claimed it was haunted by the little fellers, but liked 'em just fine. Now my little baby, Theodore, he was snug in the nursery. That's at the end of the hall, too, but over on the right. I keep the door locked and you can't go in. I don't let nobody in the nursery. It ain't part of the tour.

'Anyhow, it'd been a stormy, wet day – May seventh – but the rain slowed down after dark. We had our windows open. I recall how nice and peaceful the rain sounded when I was laying there in bed. I listened to it for a good long time. But it got hard to hear, 'cause of Joseph's snoring.

'By and by, I fell asleep, myself. I must've been sleeping light, though, 'cause long about midnight I heard a noise. It sounded like it came from downstairs. Sounded like breaking glass. It was loud enough to wake up Joseph, too. Well, he jumped out of bed real quick and quiet and hurried over here to the chest where he kept his pistol.'

'This portion of the tour,' Janice's voice broke in, 'used to take place in Maggie and Joseph's bedroom. She would walk over to their dresser, pull open a drawer and take out her husband's old Colt .45 automatic.'

'*This* pistol!' Maggie announced gleefully. 'Joseph kept the chamber empty, 'cause of the girls, but he had a clip in it, all right. So he had to work its top like this.' Owen heard a harsh metallic *chick-chack*, and pictured old Maggie grinning as she jacked a round into the chamber. 'It was awful loud, that noise. In the dark, like that. In the silence.

'With his pistol ready, Joseph snuck out into the hallway. I stayed in bed and listened. The rain had stopped by then, and the house was real quiet. I heard Joseph's footsteps out in the hall. But then he started to go downstairs. That's when I figured I'd best not just lay there. So I climbed out of bed and went out into the hall. I didn't much like the notion that me and the children were left alone, you see.'

'At this point,' Janice interrupted, 'Maggie put away the pistol and led her group of tourists out of the bedroom and into the hall. She brought them to the top of the stairway, where you are now standing.'

Maggie's voice returned.

'I was right here when gunshots came from downstairs. *BOOM! BOOM!* And then Joseph, he let out a scream fit to send shivers up a dead man. Lord, it turned my blood cold. But Joseph, he no sooner quit that awful scream than I heard feet thumping and scratching over the floor downstairs. They were bare feet. I could tell that from the sounds they made. And I could tell they had claws. It was the claws that made the scratching sounds.

'The sounds came from downstairs, but they were rushing closer. And I knew they didn't belong to Joseph. I thought maybe a bear had got into the house. But I've never been so wrong.

'I was scared solid. I stood here at the top of the stairs and I wanted to scream and run down the hall and get the kids out, only I couldn't move.

'Then the thing was on the stairs. I couldn't see much of how it looked, on account of the dark, but I saw how it stood upright like a man. It made snorty, laughing noises and hurried up the stairs. I still couldn't run off, much as I wanted to. And then it got to the top and leaped on me and threw me down on the floor.

'It ripped at me with its claws and teeth. I tried to fight it off, but I didn't stand a chance. It was so much bigger than me, and stronger than any man I ever seen. I pretty much counted myself a dead person, but all of a sudden my little baby, Theodore, started crying in his nursery. The beast heard him, climbed off me and went scurrying down the hall. It was going after Theodore.

'I was all scratched and bit and bloody, but I got to my feet and chased after it. *Had* to save my baby.'

Janice's voice returned. 'Maggie now led her tour group down the hall to the closed, locked door of the nursery. It is Station Six . . .'

Monica clicked off her player, looked Owen in the eyes, and raised her eyebrows.

Owen continued to listen.

' . . . the last door on the right, directly across from the boys' room. You may now turn off your tape players and resume listening when you reach the nursery's open door.'

He shut off his player.

'Beat you again,' Monica said.

'Yes, you did.' He decided to leave it at that.

'So now we have to walk all the way back to the *other* end of the hall again?'

'Looks that way,' Owen said.

'How stupid is that?' Monica said. 'We just came from there.'

'You don't *have* to go.'

'What am I supposed to do, wait here?'

'It's an option. Whatever you want.'

'This is all so incredibly lame. *And* perverted.'

'Well, I'm sorry. But you don't have to go through with the rest of it.'

Owen didn't want to start anything, so he tried to sound pleasant and sympathetic. 'You obviously aren't enjoying any of this. Why not just call it quits? You could stop listening and go on outside and wait for me. I'll be along pretty soon. We can meet out by the ticket booth, or something.'

'So then you can tell everyone what a party-pooper I am?'

'Huh? Tell who?'

'Oh, you know who. The usual suspects.'

'Huh?'

'Henry the Great, for instance. The fabulous Maureen. Jill, of course. And all the rest of your cronies.'

'My cronies? Jeez, Monica. They're just my friends. *Cronies*? And I'd hardly go around announcing to the world that you ducked out of the Beast House tour. I mean, why would anyone care?'

'Oh, they'd care all right. It'd just give them one more reason to laugh at me behind my back.'

'Nobody laughs at you.'

'Oh, sure.'

'Anyway, I won't tell a soul. Why don't you just go ahead and wait outside? I don't think there's much left. I'll be down in a few minutes and then we can go somewhere and have a nice lunch. How does that sound?'

Monica hoisted a single, thin eyebrow. 'Trying to get rid of me?'

'No. Of course not.'

'So you can go sniffing around for that blonde?'

'Huh?'

'You know who I mean.'

'I just want to do the rest of the tour, that's all.'

'Nobody's stopping you,' Monica said.

'Fine. So, are you coming, or do you want to wait for me outside?'

She fixed her eyes on him. Beautiful, violet eyes. But they looked as if they could see into Owen – knew him and found him pitiful and amusing and comtemptible. After a few moments of silence, Monica said, 'I believe I *will* wait outside, thank you. And I guess I know where *I* stand.'

Owen grimaced. 'What's *that* supposed to mean?'

'Isn't it obvious? *I'm* in the way. So I'll just go on outside, and you go on ahead and enjoy the tour.'

'Monica, for . . .'

'See you later. Maybe.' She cast him a mean twitch of a smile, then whirled away and trotted down the stairs.

Owen opened his mouth, then shut it. He felt sick inside as if he'd just caused an ugly accident.

It's not *my* fault, he told himself.

Other people were climbing the stairs, but he watched Monica on her way down. She descended the stairs with haughty stiffness. Her ponytail, mounted high on the back of her head by the girlish pink bow, bounced and flipped like the tail of an arrogant dog. She didn't look back at him.

If I don't go after her . . .

She wants me to miss Beast House!

Or maybe I'm just supposed to beg her to come back so we can finish the tour together.

Who the hell knows?

I'm not going after her.

He watched Monica walk out the front door. Then, still feeling sick, he turned away and started walking down the hallway toward the nursery.

How could she do this to me? We spent all that time coming here, and now she wants me to miss it.

A fucking power play.

Well, I'm not going to play along. The hell with her and her stupid games.

Owen joined a small group that was gathered just outside the nursery door. The door was open, but a cordon was stretched across the entrance to keep people out. Peering between a couple of heads, he glimpsed an old rocking horse on the floor, a wooden chest, and a cradle.

He adjusted his earphones, then thumbed the Play button.

Janice's voice said, 'Maggie never allowed tourists to see the nursery. She always kept the door closed and locked. When I purchased the house, however, I brought in a locksmith.'

She knew how much I wanted to see this stuff. Why couldn't she just go along with it?

'. . . in a jiffy, and we discovered that nothing had apparently been changed since the night when Theodore was killed.'

I don't go around and ruin things for her.

'. . . furniture was here, along with the baby's rattles and stuffed animals.'

It isn't fair.

'. . . cradle where he was sleeping . . . even his bloodstains on the floor.'

I've wanted to come here for years. Seen all the movies, read the books, and now finally I get a chance to come and she's gotta wreck it for me.

'. . . if the door had been locked and never opened again after that awful night.'

Thanks a hell of a lot, Monica.

'. . . nursery presents a gruesome and disturbing sight, I decided that everything should remain just as it was.'

She'll probably be pouting for the rest of the trip.

'. . . what Maggie . . .'

Like it's all my fault. Like I'm some sort of asshole. And I'm gonna be stuck with her pouting and giving me grief all week. Maybe she'll want to call the whole trip to a halt and fly on home tomorrow.

Maybe that'd wouldn't be such a bad thing.

'. . . I saw the awful, pale beast drag my little baby out of his cradle and fall upon him.'

It's Maggie. Shit, I've missed . . .

'. . . beyond my power to help him.'

Hand trembling, Owen shut off the player. He pushed the Rewind button.

As the tape hissed in his ears, a couple in front of him moved on, leaving the doorway clear. He stepped up to the cordon. Now he could see the entire nursery.

A rocking horse, its paint faded. Wooden blocks on the floor. A stuffed bunny, gray with dust and age.

Blood.

Dry blood, dark brown, all over the cradle and quilt.

A rag doll in the cradle, arms and legs spread, mouth a surprised O, cloth body stained all over. It looked like a mop-headed victim of a thrill killer.

The hardwood floor in front of the cradle was darkly stained.

On the flowered wallpaper six feet behind the cradle was a splatter pattern of blood that made Owen wonder if the beast had swung the baby around, maybe by its feet, after ripping it open.

There didn't seem to be a wax figure of the infant.

Good thing, Owen thought. The nursery was bad enough without that.

Good thing Monica isn't getting a look at this. She'd really flip out.

He could just hear her. *Oh, Owie, how can you stand to look at this? There must really be something wrong with you. Maybe you need therapy. Has that ever occurred to you? I think you should definitely see someone about your problems.*

The problem is you, honey.

Owen laughed softly.

A woman near his shoulder turned her head and frowned at him.

Blow it out your ass, lady.

'Sorry,' he muttered, trying to sound contrite.

She looked away.

And Owen suddenly realized that his tape player was still rewinding. *Shit!*

He pressed the Stop button, then the Play.

Maggie's voice.

'. . . got done murdering Ethel, it went on a rampage around the room. It knocked over this bust of Caesar, breaking off his nose. See, this . . .'

Owen shut it off.

He stared at the player.

How the hell far back . . .? That's in Ethel's room. Right at the start of the tour!

He sighed. He almost felt like crying.

Thanks a lot, Monica.

He pressed the Fast Forward button.

Now it's gonna take forever. And she'll be down there waiting for me, getting madder and madder . . .

He shut it off.

Then he stepped away from the nursery door and started making his way through the crowded hallway.

Heading for the stairs.

Because it was over.

He wouldn't be able to enjoy the tour, anyway. Not with Monica in his head.

Maybe someday I'll be able to come back again – without her – and get to go on the tour without having it ruined.

Owen walked out onto the porch of Beast House. The bright sunlight hurt his eyes and made him squint.

Monica, standing near the end of the porch, saw him and tilted her head sideways. Then she hurried over to him. 'That didn't take so long,' she said, sounding quite cheerful.

'Nope,' Owen said, and pulled off his earphones.

They stepped past the hanging body of Gus Goucher and walked down the stairs.

'So,' Monica said. 'Was it everything you expected?'

'It was fine.'

'Great! I'm glad at least *one* of us had a good time.'

'Yeah.'

She took hold of his hand as they walked toward the ticket booth. He didn't pull it away.

'Look at all these people,' she said. 'Don't they know what they're letting themselves in for?'

'Probably not,' Owen said.

As they neared the booth, he saw that the person handing out tape players to arriving visitors was the guide he'd seen by the attic stairs.

The tall, fabulous blonde.

The tight cold knot inside his chest suddenly seemed to start melting. *My God, look at her.*

'Oh, great,' Monica muttered. Apparently, she too had recognized the girl. 'King Kong.'

Owen felt no anger.

He stared at the guide. She was sure large, all right, but she had a very good figure. She looked great in the tan blouse and shorts that seemed to be the uniform for Beast House guides. Her bare arms and legs were softly tanned. Unfortunately, she wore sunglasses. He couldn't see her eyes, but he had no trouble remembering how they'd looked upstairs in the house – deep blue and intelligent and sensitive.

Though busy handing out tape players and giving instructions to a family of four, she flashed a smile of big white teeth at Owen and Monica. In a smooth, friendly voice, she said to them, 'I'll take those from you in just a moment, okay?'

'Fine,' Owen said. He felt weak.

He watched her until the family headed off toward Beast House. Then he and Monica stepped toward her. 'Sorry you had to wait,' she said, taking their players and headphones. 'I hope you enjoyed the tour.'

'It was very nice,' Owen said.

She wore a red plastic nameplate above her right breast. It read, DANA.

'Did you come from far away?' she asked.

'We took the bus over from San Francisco.'

'Really? How was the ride?'

'Long,' Monica said. 'Endless and . . .'

'It was fine,' Owen said, shooting a hard glance at Monica.

She gave him back a smug smile.

To Dana, he said, 'The guide on the bus – Patty – she was really good.'

'Glad to hear it. So, do you think Beast House was worth the trip?'

'I sure thought so,' Owen said.

In the corner of his eye, he saw Monica shaking her head.

'I thought it was really great,' he added.

'Terrific,' Dana said. 'Well, I hope you both enjoy the rest of your day.'

'Thank you. You, too.'

'So long, now.'

'Bye,' Owen said and hurried away from her, dragging Monica by the hand.

Chapter Thirteen

The Snack Stand

I wonder what *their* problem is, Dana thought as she watched the couple hurry away. The guy had seemed awfully embarrassed and uncomfortable about something. Girlfriend troubles, probably. The girl with him had looked smirky and mean.

She remembered seeing them upstairs, earlier.

The gal had seemed unpleasant even then. Maybe she was one of those people who hated the place.

Dana had spotted a few of those, already. You could tell just by looking that they found the tour disgusting and horrible. Hard to imagine they'd simply stumbled into the situation. How could they not know they were walking into a houseful of gruesome, nasty stories and exhibits?

Some of the visitors had probably gotten pushed into giving it a try. Maybe a friend or spouse or child had desperately wanted to do the Beast House tour, so they'd gone along, wanting to be good sports.

Lousy idea.

The tour was hard enough on people when they knew what to expect and wanted it – or *thought* they did.

Dana supposed that it turned out, for many, to be worse than they bargained for.

Sure was worse than I expected.

Even though Dana had pretty much known what she was in for, she hadn't lasted very long upstairs. She'd been fine for a while. But the hallway had become hot and stuffy later in the morning. And crowded. With every minute that passed, more and more people had packed themselves into the narrow spaces.

Some were arguing with each other. Little kids demanded this or that in whiny sharp voices. Mothers snapped at the kids. Fathers issued orders and threats. Babies squealed and bawled.

Along with the noisy mob and the heat came the odors. The air smelled heavy with them. In addition to the musty aroma natural to the old house, the air had grown thick with the pungency of sweet perfumes and aftershave lotions and sour sweat. You could smell food on the breaths of some people. Others reeked of stale cigarette smoke. Now and then, Dana even caught whiffs of farts.

Eventually, she'd found herself suffocating, dizzy and nauseous. Each time she blinked her eyes, everything in sight had flashed with rims of bright, electric blue. Slumping against a wall, she'd snatched the radio off her belt and called for Tuck.

Dana was pulled out of her thoughts by the approach of a couple of teenaged boys. Smiling, she said, 'Welcome to Beast House, guys.'

One smiled in a shy way, and the other said, 'Thanks.'

'May I see your tickets, please?' The boys handed them over, and she ripped them in half. Giving half a ticket back to each boy, she said, 'Be sure to keep your stubs, okay? They'll get you half-price admission to the Beast House Museum over on Front Street.'

'Is it any good?' asked the larger boy. He was tall and gawky, with stringy brown hair that fell past his shoulders. Dark blue sunglasses hid his eyes. He wore a T-shirt that read HOWARD STERN – KING OF ALL MEDIA.

'It's a must,' Dana told him. 'A lot of the actual stuff is over there. Like some of the real clothes the victims were wearing – all shredded and bloody.'

'Oh, cool,' said the Howard fan.

'*Way* cool,' said his buddy, a short and chubby fellow wearing a Beavis and Butthead T-shirt.

'You guys are gonna *love* this stuff,' Dana said, then turned away to take down a couple of tape players.

'I love it already,' the Howard fan said.

His friend cackled.

Dana turned around. 'Here you go, fellas.' She gave them the players. 'Hang these around your necks by the orange straps. It's a self-guided tour. The tapes are all rewound and ready to go. Just wait till you get to the front porch.'

'Where that stiff's hanging?'

The Beavis and Butthead fan cackled and blurted, '*Stiff!* He said *stiff!*'

Dana laughed and shook her head. 'Right. That's Station Number One, where the *stiff* is *hung*.'

'*Hung, hung, hung!*'

'When you get there,' Dana said, 'go ahead and press the Play button. That's this one right here.' With her forefinger extended, she touched the oblong button on top of the Howard fan's player. 'And this is the Stop button.' She pointed it out on his friend's player. 'After the porch, you go on inside and proceed from station to station. The tape will always tell you what to do.'

'I know what *I* want to do. Heh-heh.'

'Right,' Dana said. 'Maybe some other time. Anyway, feel free to take as long as you wish with the tour. When you're finished, just bring the tape players back to me.'

'Back to you! Back to you!'

'Please excuse my pal,' the Stern fan said. 'He's a retard.'

'Everything's cool, guys. Just have a good time in there. And don't let the beast get you.'

Side by side, the boys walked away from Dana, nodding, nudging each other with elbows, glancing back at her and grinning.

'You're a natural, babe.'

Surprised, Dana turned around and found Tuck smiling at her from the corner of the ticket booth.

'Hey, how's it going, boss?'

'Better and better. You were *great* with those guys.'

'Horny teenagers are my specialty.'

Tuck laughed. 'How are you feeling?'

'A lot better.'

'You look fine now. Looks like all you needed was some fresh air.'

'I'm really sorry I crapped out on you.'

'No problem. About ready to grab yourself some lunch?'

'Guess so.'

'I'll take over for you here.'

'Okay. Fine. Sure you can do without me?'

'No problem. The big rush is over. Anyway, this place can almost run itself – except for the ticket booth.' She glanced around. Then, leaning close to Dana, she said in a hushed voice, 'Clyde'll be going to lunch as soon as Sharon gets here. You might want to take off now and get a headstart.'

Dana laughed softly. 'Okay. Where does he usually eat lunch?'

'Up the street. Usually at Sarah's.'

'So if I go to the snack stand . . .?'

'Comes highly recommended.'

'See ya,' Dana said, and hurried off. But she slowed down when she found herself closing in on her two teenaged friends. They stood at Station One near the dangling feet of Gus Goucher, their heads tipped back.

Just my luck, Dana thought, they'll want to join me for lunch.

Nah. They're here for the tour, not to hit on me.

Yeah, sure.

Instead of staying on the walkway, which would lead her straight to the boys, she cut across the lawn. This was a more direct route, anyway.

The grass silenced her footfalls. Earlier, it had been wet with dew. Now, it was dry. It felt thick and soft under her shoes. She took a deep breath, savoring the warm smell. A smell of summer.

The scent reminded her of when she was a kid and school was out and she had the whole endless sweet summer ahead of her. For a moment, she felt that way again. But then it slipped away. Like the ghost of the girl Dana, long gone, sweeping through her and giving her an instant of childhood again, then rushing off, snatching it away and leaving an ache for what had been lost.

She sighed.

That's life, she thought.

Someone yelled, 'Hey, Dana!'

She looked over her shoulder.

Both the boys, still at the feet of Gus Goucher, were now turned toward her, smiling and waving.

She waved back and yelled, 'Have fun, guys. See you later.'

One of them said something to the other, who nodded eagerly. Then they started walking toward her.

'Go on back,' she called and waved them away. 'Enjoy the tour.'

'Can we come with you?'

'Sorry. Not where I'm going.'

They stopped and looked at each other.

One called, 'Going to the john?'

'We'll, like, supervise.'

'We'll guard the door.'

'I don't think so, guys. Thanks, anyway. Bye-bye, now.'

They waved, then turned around and started back. By the time Dana reached the walkway at the corner of the house, they were again staring up at Gus.

She smiled and rounded the corner. It was flattering that they'd been so interested in her, but she certainly didn't want to spend her lunch break with a couple of horny, awestruck teenagers.

Dana made her way to the rear of the house. Though the eating area was fairly crowded, she spotted a few vacant tables. There were short lines of waiting customers in front of the snack stand's two windows.

If I hit the john first, I might not get a table . . .

She needed to pee, but that could wait till after she'd eaten.

She started toward one of the lines.

If I don't *go to the john, it'll make me a liar.*

Besides, she really *had* to wash her hands before settling down for lunch.

God-only-knows what I've been touching.

So she turned away from the line and made a detour to the restroom. It was well-lighted, clean, and the air had a lemony scent. A few people were washing up at the sinks. Two of the four stalls were vacant, so she picked one and stepped in.

When she was done at the toilet, she went to the row of sinks and washed her hands with hot water and soap. She dried them with a paper towel, then kept the towel in her hand so she wouldn't have to touch the door handle.

Outside, she tossed the paper towel into a nearby trash basket.

As she walked toward the snack stand, she checked out the table situation. There seemed to be more vacant tables than a few minutes ago. And only three people were waiting at the snack shop windows.

Standing back a few feet, she studied the displays listing menu items.

There was the original Beastburger, the Cheese Beastburger, Bacon Beastburger, Chili Beastburger, and the Double-Decker Monsterburger Deluxe. If you weren't in the mood for ground beef patties, you could get the Red-Hot Beastie Weenie.

Dana grinned when she read that one.

She spent a couple more minutes enjoying the menu and trying to make up her mind. By the time she was ready to order, nobody was waiting at the window on her left. She stepped over to it.

Ducking down slightly to see inside, she smiled at the guy behind the window and said, 'Hi.'

'Oh, hello,' he said. 'You're Dana, right?'

'Yep.'

'I'm Warren.'

'Hi, Warren.'

Whoa! she thought. *Who's this? And how come Tuck didn't mention him?*

'How's your first day on the job?' he asked.

'Well . . . iffy. I almost upchucked upstairs . . .'

He smiled and shook his head and Dana couldn't believe she'd *said* that to him. She blushed fiercely.

'Other than that,' she added, 'it's been great.'

He laughed and said, 'Well, don't worry about it. Everyone feels squeamish their first day. You'll probably be fine.'

'Thanks. I hope so.'

'So, what can I get you?'

'I guess the hot dog.'

His smile grew. 'I'm afraid we don't serve hot dogs here.'

'Oh. Okay. So then, I guess I'll have one of those . . . uh . . . Red-Hot Beastie Weenies.'

'Excellent choice.'

'You make *everyone* say that?'

'Maybe not everyone.'

'Just the new kids?'

'Just the ladies.'

'That's cruel.'

He laughed softly. 'Maybe a little. Most people seem to have fun with it. Especially me.'

'They're pretty cute names. Who came up with them?'

'Ohhh . . . I don't know. Me, I guess.'

'You guess?'

'Pretty sure. Anyway, so far you'll be wanting one Red-Hot Beastie Weenie? Anything else?'

'I'll have some of those chili . . .' She checked the menu again. 'An order of Beastly Chili Fries with cheese. And medium Creature Cola.'

'Got it.' He hit a few keys on the register.

When the price came up, Dana reached deep into a front pocket of her shorts, pulled out a handful of bills, and gave Warren a ten.

He counted the change into her hand, then said, 'I'll bring it over to you when it's ready.'

'Where'll I be?' she asked.

'Don't worry, I'll find you. You can't go far.'

'Okay. Thanks.' Smiling, she turned away from the window and went in search of a table.

She found a small round table that was meant for two, but somebody had taken away one of its chairs.

Nearby, a larger table had a group of five seated around it. A man, a woman, and three kids.

That's where my extra chair went.

Doesn't matter, she told herself. It's only me.

Still, she felt a little irked about it.

She thought about finding a chair to replace it. But Warren might notice, might think she was getting a chair for him. That'd be pretty embarrassing.

So she went ahead and sat down and frowned at the empty place across the table where the second chair was supposed to be. Then she looked at the family.

She suddenly remembered them from inside the house.

And smiled about how the little girl, a cute blonde maybe five or six years old, had kept asking for her freedom. *Let go my hand, let go my hand. Pleeeease.* The mother, fairly patient, had explained, *We don't want to lose you in here, honey. There're so many people.* And the kid had insisted, *I'll be fine. I won't go 'way. Please, let go my hand.* Not whiny, but sounding quite calm about the situation. *I bet you're scared I'll break something, but I won't. Kimmy does not break things.*

Nifty kid, Dana thought.

Right now, the girl was frowning as if deep in thought as she nibbled on the tip of a French fry.

It seemed like a pretty nice family – even if the father *had* swiped Dana's chair. The kids hadn't been acting up very much in the house, and they were behaving fine, now. They appeared to be confident and happy, too.

It's because their parents treat them like humans, she thought.

She'd seen so many parents who didn't.

Everywhere she went, she saw horrible parents. At grocery stores, at malls, at public parks, this morning during her first hours in Beast House – but most especially at the swimming pool where she'd worked so many summers as a lifeguard. So many awful parents.

Some seemed to make it a point of honor to let their kids run wild. As if discipline might taint the self-esteem of the little charmers.

When Dana saw that, she wanted to kick their asses. The parents *and* the kids.

Other parents acted as if their children were criminals – snapping orders at them, berating them, jerking their arms, pinching them, swatting their little butts, smacking the backs of their heads. As if they thought life's greatest reward was a river of tears running down a child's face.

Dana always felt like crying when she saw that sort of thing.

She also felt like kicking the shit out of such parents, and hugging their kids.

It made her feel *wonderful* to see a family like this one.

I wouldn't mind having kids like those, she thought.

You get the kids you deserve.

Or maybe none at all, if you don't play your cards right or if you have bad luck.

'Found you,' Warren announced.

She turned and smiled at him.

He set a green plastic tray down on the table and slid it toward her. The Red-Hot Beastie Weenie and Beastly Chili Fries with cheese were in red plastic baskets lined with paper. There were two Creature Colas.

'Is one of those for you?' Dana asked.

'Yeah. Thought I'd take a little break. Windy's holding down the fort.'

'If you can find a chair . . .'

'No sweat.' He hurried to a nearby table where a heavy, bearded man was sitting with a husky woman. They both wore black T-shirts, black leather trousers, and grim tattoos. They looked like outlaw bikers.

The table was big enough for four people, but nobody else sat there. One of the extra chairs had already been taken. 'Mind if I borrow this?' Warren asked the man.

'It's a free country, Spike,' the fellow said, grinning and friendly. 'Help yerself.'

'Thank you,' Warren said. He lifted the chair and hurried back to Dana's table.

She grinned at him. 'Sit down and make yourself comfortable, Spike.'

Laughing softly, he sat down. 'I don't even know the guy.'

'Maybe you remind him of someone.'

'An old pal from the cell block?'

They both laughed.

'That's mean,' Dana told him. 'He seemed like a perfectly nice guy.'

'Yeah, he did. He probably *is* a nice guy.' Warren reached out and took his soda off the tray. He set it in front of him. As he tore the wrapper off his straw, he said, 'That's one thing about working here – you meet all kinds. Most of them turn out to be pretty friendly. Even the ones who look like Manson Family wannabes.'

'*You're* pretty friendly,' Dana said.

He stabbed the straw through the crossed slots in the plastic lid. 'No good reason not to be,' he said. He slid the straw down deeper. It rubbed the edges of the cross and made squawking noises. 'So, you're from Los Angeles?'

'Afraid so.'

'Why do you say that?' Keeping his eyes on Dana, he sucked some soda up his straw.

'You know,' she said. 'Los Angeles. Disaster City, USA. Riots, earth-quakes, shootouts, mudslides, fires. It's embarrassing to be from a place like that.'

Nodding, Warren gazed at her and sipped more cola.

She used both hands to pick up her Red-Hot Beastie Weenie. It was darkly grilled, at least two inches longer than its bun, and looked delicious. The aromas of the spicy hot dog, onion and tangy yellow mustard made her mouth fill with saliva.

Though she wanted to take a big bite out of it, she went on talking. 'Whenever I'm on a trip and tell people I'm from LA, I get these weird looks. Like there must be something wrong with me, living in a place like that.'

Warren took his mouth away from the straw. 'You won't get any weird looks from me.'

'Well, I'm glad to hear it.' She smiled at him and bit a crusty end off her wiener.

As she began to chew, Warren said, 'I'm from the People's Republic of Santa Monica.'

Her jaw dropped. But she shut it quickly, chewed and grinned. After swallowing some of the food, she blurted, 'That's even worse!' and was delighted that no bits of semi-masticated frankfurter flew from her mouth.

Warren laughed and shook his head. 'You're telling me. It's a *real* embarrassment.'

'I won't tell anyone.'

'Thanks,' he said. 'So where-abouts do you live?'

'Over near Rancho Park. How about you?'

'Well, I grew up in a house on Euclid.'

Dana grinned at him and said, 'I like to call it Thirteenth Street.'

He laughed. 'That's so stupid!' he blurted.

'Me?'

'*Them.* It used to drive me nuts. Changing a street's name so it *won't* be Thirteenth? I mean, it's smack dab between Twelfth and Fourteenth, what the hell do people *think* it is? Everybody *knows* it's Thirteenth Street!'

'Right! Isn't it nuts? Like skipping the thirteenth floor in a high-rise!'

'Exactly.'

'Not that I'm superstitious or anything,' Dana said.

'Yeah, me neither.'

'But let's get real.' *What's the matter with me? I'm running off at the mouth like a nincompoop!* 'It's not the *fourteenth* floor, it's the *thirteenth* floor. So, you're, what, avoiding all the bad-luck baggage of thirteen by not *calling* it that?'

'It's bull,' Warren said.

'Total bull. Thirteen, shmirteen.'

'People gotta get a life.'

Nodding briskly, Dana took another bite of her Red-Hot Beastie Weenie. Then she shrugged and tried to smile.

'Anyway,' Warren continued. 'Let's see.' He sucked some soda up his straw and swallowed. Then he raised his head, nodded slightly, and said, 'I got a little carried away.'

'Me, too.'

'Anyway, I grew up on Euclid . . .'

'Thirteenth Street,' Dana said through her mouthful.

A grin split his face. 'Cut it out, Dana.'

'So sorry.'

'Anyway, now I live here.'

'In *Beast House*?'

'Sure.'

'Where?' she asked, and finished swallowing.

'Over across the street. I've got a little cabin in the woods over there.'

'Neat!'

'It's not bad.'

'So you live in town permanently?'

'So far.'

'How did you end up here?'

'Oh, my Lord, I've *ended up*.'

'You know what I mean,' Dana said.

'Yeah. But you may think I'm a little nuts.'

'There are worse things.'

'I just . . . You've heard of *the call of the wild*, haven't you? Well, I suffer from *the call of the Beast*.'

Dana grinned and said, 'Sure.'

'No, it's the truth. We came here on vacation when I was a kid. I think I was probably about six years old.'

'Six? What year would that've been?'

He frowned. 'Eighty-one? Let's see. I'm twenty-two now, so if I was six then . . . that'd make it sixteen years ago and this is ninety-seven, so . . .'

'Yeah,' Dana said. 'That'd make it eighty-one. A year after *The Horror* was published.'

'You're right! Turns out, my mom was crazy about that book. That's why we came up here. She couldn't wait to take the tour. So it was summer vacation, and Dad had two weeks off and he drove us all the way up from Santa Monica . . .'

'Thirteenth Street.'

'Right. I'll never forget that trip. We came up the coast highway and stopped at some motel in Carmel. That made no impression at all, but then we stayed two nights in Boleta Bay and spent one whole day at Funland. I thought *that* was great.'

'Cool place,' Dana said.

'I *loved* it. I never wanted to leave. They had to drag me away in tears.

But the next day we drove straight through San Francisco without even stopping, and ended up *here*. The minute I saw Beast House . . . I didn't even know anything about the place. But I just . . . felt as if I'd been looking for it my whole life . . .'

'All six years.'

'Yeah. I know, it sounds weird. It *felt* weird. I felt as if I'd arrived home. Almost as if I'd lived here before and forgotten about it.'

'That *is* a bit odd,' Dana said.

'Maybe in a past life . . .'

'Do you believe in that stuff?'

'Not really,' Warren said. 'But I have *no* idea why I had such a strong affinity for the place.'

'Maybe it reminded you of some other house.'

'That's possible. I don't know. But it gets stranger. The next day, we went on the tour.'

'That's pretty heavy stuff for a six-year-old.'

'I *loved* it. But the odd part was, I felt like I'd been *in* the house before. I knew the layout.'

A chill crept up Dana's spine.

'The hallways and rooms . . . they were all familiar to me. I even knew which door led to the attic and where to find the entrance to the cellar.'

Dana muttered, 'Shit.'

'Yeah.'

'Are you kidding me?'

'Nope. Afraid not.'

'*That's* creepy.'

'It didn't seem creepy to me. Not at the time, anyway. Mind if I have a fry?'

'Help yourself, Spike.'

He smiled and reached over and took one of Dana's Beastly Chili Fries. Heavily laden with chili and melted cheese, it drooped on the way to his mouth. Some glop fell off, but he caught it with his other hand.

'Slob,' Dana said.

He poked the fry into his mouth, then ate the fallen chili and cheese out of his palm.

'What did your parents think?' she asked.

'I didn't make a big deal out of it.' Warren wiped his face with a napkin. 'I just asked if we'd ever been here before, and they said no, so I let it drop. But I do remember that I begged and begged to go on the tour again. Dad wanted no part of that, but Mom sort of wanted a second look, herself. So Dad and my brother took off. I think they went to the beach, and Mom and I went on the tour again. The details are kind of fuzzy. But I've always remembered it as one of the best days of my life. And I always wanted to come back.'

'Looks like you made it.'

'Yep. The year I turned eighteen, it was *adios* to the People's Republic, hello to Malcasa Point.'

'And you've been working here at the snack shop the whole time?'

'Well, I started as a guide.'

'And moved on to bigger and better things?'

He smiled. 'Something like that.' He glanced at his wristwatch. 'Uh-oh, break's over.' He sucked on his straw for a while, then got to his feet. 'It was really nice talking to you, Dana.'

'Same here.'

'See you around, okay?'

'Sure.'

Turning away, he tossed his cardboard container into a nearby trash barrel. Then he smiled over his shoulder and headed for the snack stand. He wore the tan shirt and shorts of a guide. They were faded like Tuck's. He seemed to be carrying his wallet in the left rear pocket of his shorts. It made a flat bulge. The pocket on the other side appeared to be empty. Its flap was buttoned down, and the fabric curved smoothly over his buttock. His legs looked strong and tanned. His socks were very white. His brown leather hiking boots looked dusty and scuffed as if they'd been on plenty of trails.

After he was gone, Dana took another bite out of her Red-Hot Beastie Weenie. It was no longer very hot, but it still tasted good.

It tasted just fine.

It was perhaps the best-tasting hot dog she'd ever sunk her teeth into.

I'm afraid we don't serve hot dogs here.

Oh, man.

Take it easy, she warned herself. You don't even know the guy. Maybe he's some kind of kook.

There's gotta be *something* wrong with him. You don't just run into a guy like him out of the blue and it turns out that he's as fine as he seems to be.

He didn't have any rings on his fingers.

But maybe he's going with someone.

Or gay.

Or dying of some horrible, incurable malady.

Or insane.

He *did* seem to have some rather odd and spooky notions about Beast House.

Won't hold that against him.

I'd like to hold *myself* against him.

She set down her wiener and started to work on the fries and smiled remembering how Warren's fry had bombed his hand.

Chapter Fourteen

Sandy's Story – August, 1980

Lib continued to sleep and snore while Sandy drove north on Pacific Coast Highway. Eric, in his basket behind the passenger seat, was probably snoring, too. Sandy couldn't hear him, though. Too much noise came from the night air rushing in through the broken windshield, from the heater blowing full blast, from the car's engine and from Lib.

Every once in a while, another vehicle came along. Some approached from the rear, others from the front.

The first time it happened, Sandy wanted to pull over but there were guard rails on both sides, trapping her on the pavement. So she clenched the steering wheel, held her breath, and drove on toward the glare of the headlights.

If it's the Highway Patrol . . .

I'll say a rock broke the windshield, she told herself. No, officer, I don't have a driver's license. I know I'm too young to drive, but Mom fell asleep at the wheel a while ago and we almost crashed. We couldn't just pull over . . . not out here in the middle of nowhere. We were afraid it wouldn't be safe. So we thought maybe it'd be all right for me to drive just for a few minutes while Mom took a little nap. I know it was terribly *wrong* officer, and I'm sorry, but . . .

It wasn't a Highway Patrol car.

A pickup truck shot past her, and kept going.

After that, approaching vehicles didn't bother Sandy nearly so much. She still grew somewhat tense, but she gave little thought to pulling over.

She had her story ready. It might work.

It wouldn't even be necessary, though, unless they got stopped by cops. And so far, there'd been none. Maybe the cops were all home asleep, or patrolling a *real* highway like the 101, over to the east. If you wanted to speed, that's the route you'd take, not this narrow, winding road along the shoreline.

Sooner or later, of course, they were *sure* to get stopped.

Their luck couldn't last forever.

She doubted it could last much past sunrise. In the light of day, there'd be a lot more traffic. *Everyone* would notice the head-sized hole in the windshield. Everyone would be able to see Sandy, too, and realize she looked too young to have a driver's license.

A cop was bound to drive by . . .

But dawn was still a few hours away when Sandy spotted an unmarked dirt road that looked promising. Small and dark, it led into the woods like the mouth of a secret mine. Glimpsing it as she drove by, she had doubts about its size. It looked awfully small, and the trailer was fairly large.

It'll be perfect, though, if we can just fit in.

There was no traffic in sight, so Sandy eased down on the brakes, brought the car to a halt, and started backing up. The trailer went crooked. She muttered, 'Damn,' and stopped. Then she pulled forward and tried reverse again. This time, the trailer cooperated. She backed her way well past the turn-off before starting forward. As she neared it again, she swung so wide that she entered the southbound lane. Then she steered for the dirt road.

Leaving the pavement behind, the car bounced and shook.

Lib snorted and woke up. 'Huh?' she asked. 'What's goin' on?'

'We had to get off the highway,' Sandy explained.

Entering the woods, she drove very slowly. She heard the leafy crunch of the tires, and scratchy, squeaky sounds that probably came from branches scraping against the sides of the trailer.

'I guess we fit,' she said.

'Huh? Yeah.'

'I wasn't sure the trailer'd make it.'

'*Where* we goin'?' Lib asked, still sounding groggy.

'I don't know. Just in here. This looks like it might be a good place to hide. I figure we shouldn't do any traveling in broad daylight.'

'Yeah,' Lib muttered. Then she moaned and said, 'Shit. I peel like I got myselp pounded to det widda baseball bat.'

'I bet you do.'

As Sandy drove deeper into the woods, Lib gently fingered her mouth, inside and out. Now and then, she winced. After a while, she started to weep quietly.

'You'll be okay,' Sandy told her.

'Shit. It hurts. Hurts like puckin' hell. And I'm gonna be so puckin' ugly, ain't no pella ebber gonna wanta look at me. . . . Not as I were much ob a prize *bepore*.' She let out an odd, honking snort.

Sandy reached over and squeezed her leg. 'Everything'll be fine, Libby. We'll get you some *new* teeth and you'll look better than ever.'

'Yeah? Well . . .' She sniffed. 'Ya got anudder bottle ob dat bourbon someplace?'

'Nope. Sorry.'

'Gotta get me some. I peel like shit.'

'There's plenty of aspirin and stuff in the trailer.'

'Dat'd help.'

Just ahead, there seemed to be a small open area. It would probably be a better place to stop than here, where the trees pressed in so tightly. Sandy said, 'Hang on just a minute,' and drove on into the clearing.

There, she eased the car to a stop. 'I guess we're probably far enough from the highway.'

'We gonna stay here?'

'For the time being.' She shut off the engine and headlight. The heater stopped blowing warm air against her legs. In the sudden silence, she heard a breeze sifting through the trees. The car's engine made quiet pinking sounds. 'Does it look all right to you?'

Lib turned her head slowly. 'Mighty damn puckin' dark out dare.'

'All the better. I want to get rid of the body. This looks like it'd be a good place for it.'

'We gettin' out?'

'I am,' Sandy said. She opened her door, stepped outside, then eased her door shut.

On the other side of the car, the passenger door opened and Lib climbed out.

'Take it easy when you shut the door,' Sandy told her in a hushed voice. 'We don't want to wake up Eric.'

'Tink he's asleep?'

'Pretty sure. He wouldn't be this quiet if he was awake.'

'Yeah?'

'Oh, yeah. He's a real little hellraiser.'

Lib shut her door gently. 'Gonna leab him in de car?'

'Yeah, I guess so.'

Sandy walked past the rear of the car and alongside the trailer. Reaching high, she opened the trailer door. The makeshift wooden stairway should've been right there, but she didn't see it. Leaning forward, she raised her arms and felt around in the darkness. Nothing.

'What's up?' Lib asked.

'I'm going in.' Sandy swung up a knee, planted it on the door sill, and climbed into the trailer.

'Where's da steps?' Lib asked.

'Don't know. Must've scooted off someplace. I'll find 'em for you.'

'Dat's all right. One ob us oughta stay out here and keep an eye on tings.'

'Chicken.'

'Dat's me.'

'They've gotta be here,' Sandy muttered.

'Don't go lookin' por dem steps on account ob me. Only ting I want's some aspirin.'

'You gonna make me do all the work? Climb on up.'

'You're in da way, honey.'

'That can be fixed.' Sandy started to crawl away from the door and put a hand down on something that felt like a face. Gasping, she jerked her hand back.

'Y'okay?'

'Guess I found Slade.'

'What's he doin'?'

'Not a hell of a lot.' Gritting her teeth, Sandy slowly lowered her open hand again. But not all the way. She stopped it slightly above where the face should be, then poked at the darkness below with her forefinger. The tip of her finger didn't touch anything, so she eased her hand downward ever so slowly. Her fingertip met a sticky surface. She shoved gently, wondering what it was. The surface felt solid, but yielded slightly. Exploring a bit more, she discovered a small curve. Something feathery brushed against her fingertip.

Lashes?

'Uck!' Her hand leaped high.

'What?'

'I touched his *eye!* Jeez! His bare eye!'

Lib laughed.

'Keep yuckin' it up, babe, 'cause here he comes.'

Having a very clear idea about where Slade's face should be, Sandy spread her hands and reached forward and down. She encountered damp, sticky fabric. Had to be his shirt. Patting her way to both his sides, she found his armpits. Then she grabbed hold and reared back. He scooted toward her just a little. She crawled backward and gave him another tug. He moved another inch or two.

Crawling farther, she felt the door sill beneath the toes of her shoes. On the other side of the sill, the floor went away. She kept pulling Slade until her knees felt the sill. Then she let go of him and climbed down.

'Can you give me a hand?'

'Sure.'

Side by side, Sandy and Lib reached into the trailer. Each grabbed one of Slade's armpits. When they pulled, he slid toward them. He came along fine until he was out just more than halfway down his back.

Suddenly, his torso tipped downward and his legs flew up.

Lib gasped.

Sandy blurted, 'Look out!'

As Slade's legs swung down, both women scurried for safety. But Lib didn't move fast enough. Before she could get clear, Slade's left shoe crashed against the top of her shoulder.

'*Ow!*' she cried out. Grabbing her shoulder, she stumbled backward.

Slade piled into the ground beside the trailer. He came to rest on his knees, rump up, face in the grass. Sandy didn't like him in that position, so she rammed him in the hip with her foot and he toppled over sideways.

'You okay?' she asked Lib.

'Shit,' Lib said, rubbing her shoulder. 'Dis ain't my night.'

'Your shoulder isn't broken or something, is it?'

'Naw.'

'Still works?'

'Reckon.'

'Wanta just help me drag him into the trees? Then you can go inside and take some aspirin and hit the sack, or something, if you want to.'

'Dat sounds good.' She came over and looked down at Slade. 'Which end you want?'

'Doesn't matter.'

'I'll grab his peet.'

'His *peter*?' Sandy asked, sounding shocked. 'Don't do that!'

'Hardy har har.'

'Why don't you grab his *feet*, instead? I'll take his arms.'

'Kick your ass prom here to next Sunday,' Lib muttered.

Laughing softly, Sandy crouched over Slade and took hold of his wrists. Then she waited while Lib bent down and clutched his ankles. 'Ready?' she asked.

'Heabe ho,' said Lib.

They both stood up straight, stretching Slade and raising him off the ground. Sandy sidestepped quickly, turning him. Then she started to trudge backward, lugging him away from the trailer. Lib followed, holding up his legs.

'Sure is a *hebby* son ob a bitch,' Lib muttered.

'Maybe you ladies should set him down.'

At the sound of the man's voice, Lib made a quick squeaky noise and dropped Slade's feet. Sandy, shocked, bent down slowly. When Slade's head rested on the ground, she lowered his arms and folded them across his chest. Then she stood up straight.

She and Lib, standing at opposite ends of the body, turned this way and that, trying to spot the source of the voice.

The man was not to be seen.

Sandy felt as if a vicious thug were kicking her in the heart.

'He's down,' Lib called, sounding almost breathless.

'Now,' the man said, 'stick your hands up.'

'Is that you, Marshal Dillon?' Sandy asked.

'Stick 'em up!'

She and Lib raised their arms overhead.

'Okay,' the man said. 'That's good. Now step back away from the body and keep backing up till you get to the trailer.'

Moments later, they were standing side by side, their backs against the side of the trailer, their arms still high.

A few yards straight in front of them, the trunk of a tree seemed to grow wider.

Someone was gliding out from behind it.

Someone as dark as the night.

When he stood separate from the tree, he switched on a flashlight. The stark white beam slanted down at Slade. It moved slowly up and down the mutilated body.

'Who killed this man?' he asked, swinging the beam over to Sandy.

Squinting, she turned her face away from the glare.

'Not me,' she said.

The light jerked away from her, then jabbed into Lib's eyes. 'Not me,' Lib said.

'What happened to your face?' he asked her.

'I got beat up wid an ugly stick.'

'How about some straight answers, ladies? You might think this is all funny as hell, but I don't see the humor. You've got a dead man here. So what's the story?'

'Are you a cop?' Sandy asked.

'No, but I've got a gun.' He turned the flashlight onto his own right hand. It was clutching a big, dark pistol. The barrel was aimed upward, not at Sandy or Lib. 'You're on my property. I want to know what you're doing here.'

'Isn't it pretty obvious?' Sandy asked.

'Cut out the wisecracks.'

Sandy shrugged.

'We just wanted to ditch da body,' Lib told him. 'Dat's all.'

'Suppose we just throw him back in the trailer and drive away?' Sandy suggested. 'How would that be? I mean, we weren't trying to unload him on you in particular. We don't even *know* you. We just wanted to get rid of him, that's all.'

'How'd he get killed?'

'He attacked me,' Sandy said.

'Uh-huh.'

'He was trying to rape me, all right? So I fought back. And I won. I had a knife handy, or maybe I'd be the one who ended up dead.'

He swung his light toward Lib. 'How do you fit in?'

'She . . .'

'I'm asking *her*, not you. What's your name?' he asked Lib.

'Bambi,' she said.

'Bambi? Like the deer?'

'Yeah. I got opp lucky. Day almost called me Tumper.'

'That's Thumper,' Sandy explained.

'What happened to your teeth, Bambi?'

'*He* knocked 'em clean out my head,' she explained, nodding in Slade's direction.

'Is that before or after he attacked this one?'

'Charly,' Sandy said. 'I'm Charly. Like in *Charlie's Angels*.'

'He beat me up pirst,' Lib explained. 'Den he went apter Charly.'

'He's my dad,' Sandy explained. 'Bambi, she's my stepmother. He was always beating the shit out of us and . . . you know, *messing* with me. So tonight I was ready for him and I got him with my knife.'

The beam of light swept down and returned to Slade's body.

Sounding appalled but calm, the man asked, 'This is your *father*?'

'Yeah. Dirty rotten son of a bitch.'

'You killed your own father?'

'Sure did. And I'm not sorry for it, either. He got what he had coming.'

The man slowly shook his head from side to side.

Keeping his light on Slade, he said, 'If what you're telling me is true, it sure sounds like self-defense. So why are you trying to hide the body? You should've just called the cops right after it happened and admitted everything. Nobody's going to blame you for trying to defend yourself like that.'

'Guess I was scared,' Sandy said. 'I've got a little baby, you know? I was scared they might take him away. I mean, I'm only fourteen, and . . .'

'You've got a *child*?'

'Yes sir. And *he's* the daddy.' She jabbed a finger toward Slade's body. 'He's my baby's daddy and *my* daddy, too.'

'Oh, my God.'

'Dey'll take away little Eric por sure,' Lib said. 'Dem polks at Child Welpare. Dat's how come we had to run opp and why we gotta hide da pucker's body.'

The man was silent for a while. Then he asked, 'Where are you from?'

'Noplace much,' Sandy told him. 'Last couple of months, we've just been on the road.'

'You live in this trailer?'

'Yes sir,' Sandy said.

'Where are you heading?'

'Noplace. Just figured we'd keep on going, and hope for the best.'

'What kind of money do you have?'

'A few bucks. You want it?'

He lowered the pistol. 'I'm not sure I believe everything you're telling me,' he said. 'But you two . . . It's pretty obvious you're in a jam. I'd be glad to help you, but I don't want to end up like this guy.'

'Are *you* fixin' to attack us?' Sandy asked.

'Not likely,' he said.

'Den it ain't likely we'll kill you,' Lib told him.

'Mom's right,' said Sandy.

'In that case . . . Maybe you'd like to be my guests. I've got a cabin just up the road a piece. You could probably use some food and a good night's sleep.'

'Got anything to drink at dat cabin ob yours?' Lib asked.

'Just about anything you might want.'

'Hot damn! Let's went, honey!'

The man said, 'My name's Harry. Harry Matthews.'

'I meant her,' Lib explained, swinging a thumb toward Sandy. 'I like to call my girl honey. But maybe I can call you honey, too, ip you treat us right.'

'Fine. So let's take care of this body, first. Then we'll go on up to my place.'

Chapter Fifteen

A Visit from Clyde

All afternoon, Dana's mind dwelled on Warren. She thought about the way he'd looked and the things he'd said. She wanted to know everything about him.

Tuck, no doubt, would be able to tell her plenty.

But Dana was afraid of hearing it. The guy just *couldn't* be as wonderful as he seemed. He must have some sort of awful flaw. After a talk with Tuck, she might want nothing more to do with him.

We can't talk about him here, anyway, she told herself. I'll wait till after work.

During a slow period in the middle of the afternoon, she was leaning against the side of the ticket booth, daydreaming about Warren, when Clyde stepped around the corner. He was carrying a stool with a padded seat.

'Interested?' he asked.

'I don't want to take *your* seat,' Dana told him.

'I've still got one.' He set down the stool for her.

'Well, thanks.'

As Dana climbed onto it, Clyde watched her closely. Though he wore sunglasses, their lenses weren't dark enough to hide the direction of his gaze. He mostly watched her breasts and crotch.

She was used to that sort of thing.

Sometimes she found it flattering, sometimes exciting. Often, though, it seemed like an embarrassing invasion of her privacy and annoyed or disgusted her.

Long ago, she'd discovered that her reaction depended on who was doing the staring.

Though Clyde was certainly handsome – well over six feet tall and built like a Mr Universe contestant – she didn't care much for him.

'So,' he said. He folded his arms across his massive chest and looked her in the eyes. 'How's it going?'

'Okay.'

'First day on the job.'

'Not bad,' she said.

'You have a little trouble upstairs?'

'No big deal.'

'Lynn pulled you out.'

'I just wasn't feeling very well. I needed some fresh air.'

'Where have I heard *that* before?'

'I wouldn't know.'

'Happens to everyone. Well, not *every*one. But just about. It's hard to last all day in there, especially for a beginner. I'll tell you your symptoms. Cold sweat, faintness, nausea, a sense of suffocation. Tell me I'm right.'

'You're right.'

'Of course I'm right. I've seen it a thousand times. Did you barf?'

'No.'

'Plenty do. You probably would've, except you got out in time.'

Dana tried to smile pleasantly. 'Well,' she said, 'I'm glad I didn't.'

'You know what it is?'

'What what is?'

'Purely psychological.'

'Ah.'

Nodding, he pulled a pack of Camels out of his shirt pocket. He held it toward Dana.

'No thanks,' she said.

He took one for himself and lit it up.

'See, you tell yourself it's just a house. You're just a tour guide in a house full of dummies . . . That *includes* the tourists. The dummies.'

She smiled and nodded.

'So, you *tell* yourself nothing is going on. But *plenty* is going on. It's *not* just a regular house with dummies inside. You *know* what really happened there, and you can't hide from it. The more you *try* to hide from the reality of the place, the more your subconscious works on you.' He nodded briskly. 'You know what that does to you?'

'What?'

'It screws up your entire system. Your whole internal organic structure *knows* where you are. So you don't breathe right. It's like you're afraid to take a deep breath when you're in there, like the air is full of *disease* because of all the death and decay. And you don't want to suck it into your own body. Do you see what I mean?'

'Sure,' she said.

A guy this handsome, she thought, shouldn't be cursed with such nutty ideas.

'So, see, what you're *doing* to yourself, you're giving your brain a case of air starvation. You know why you feel like you're suffocating in there?'

'Why?'

' 'Cause you *are*. You're trying subconsciously to hold your breath, see?'

'Uh-huh.'

'Does that make sense to you?'

'Sure.'

' 'Cause, subconsciously, you *don't* want to be breathing the fucked-up air inside that house.'

'Right.'

'You get it?' he asked, the cigarette bobbing between his lips.

'I get it.'

'See how it's all in your mind?'

'Yeah.'

'Now. Do you know how to fix it?'

'By breathing?'

'Absolutely. But it ain't that easy. See, your subconscious has a mind all its own.'

This time, Dana's smile was genuine.

Clyde smiled back at her, looking very pleased with himself. 'You can't just *order* your subconscious mind to let you breathe. Doesn't work that way. What you've gotta do is come to *terms* with Beast House.'

'Come to terms with it?'

'Absolutely. Denial ain't just a river in Egypt, you know.'

She managed a chuckle.

'Denial's behind all your problems.' He took a deep drag, then removed the cigarette from his mouth and pointed it at her. 'What you need to do is *accept* Beast House.'

What a load, she thought.

She said, 'Ah. Okay.'

'And it'll accept you,' he added.

She nodded.

'I can help you with that.'

'You can?'

'You want to get over it, don't you?'

'Sure.'

'You almost *have* to get over it. You're a Beast House guide. How can you be a guide if the place makes you sick?'

'Wouldn't be easy.'

'I just so happen to have a foolproof treatment. Are you interested?'

'I guess so.'

'Good. After work, we'll go and have dinner together and get started.'

'Started?'

'On your treatment.' He tossed the cigarette stub to the pavement and mashed it under his shoe.

'During dinner tonight?' Dana asked.

He flashed a smile. 'Everybody has to eat. How about the Carriage House restaurant? Have you ever eaten there?'

'No, but . . .'

'It's the best eatery in town. The *only* place in town where it's possible to get a decent dinner.'

'I'm afraid I can't,' she said, shaking her head and trying to look apologetic. 'Not tonight.'

'It'll be on me.'

'Well, thank you. That's very nice of you, Clyde, but I've already made plans for tonight.'

'So?'

'What do you mean?' Dana asked.

'Make *new* plans.'

'I can't do that.'

'Why not?'

'It wouldn't be right.'

Smirking, he shook his head and looked as if he pitied her. 'Well,' he said, 'it's your life.'

'I can't go back on my word. I'm sorry. Maybe some other night.'

'Maybe not,' he said. 'This might be your only chance.'

Lord, I hope so.

Dana shrugged, frowned slightly and said, 'Well, if it is, it is. That'd be up to you, I guess.'

'Once bitten, twice shy.'

'Nobody bit you.'

With a smile that didn't look very friendly, he said, 'You're making a very big mistake, you know.'

'I guess I'll just have to live with it.'

'You don't *have* to live with it. Just blow off this other guy while you've still got the chance.'

'Can't.'

'Who is he?'

'Nobody. None of your business.'

'It's Warren, right?'

'It's not Warren.'

Wish it was.

'Yeah, right.'

'It's not.'

'You don't want to go out with him.' Clyde lit up another Camel. 'He's a loser.'

'Thanks for the tip.'

'He's a fag.'

Heat rushed to her face. 'Shouldn't you be back in the ticket booth?'

'And sell tickets to who? You see any customers lining up?'

'Not at the moment.'

'And you won't. Nobody ever shows up this late.'

'Well, you don't have to stand here.'

Grinning, he said, 'You don't want to go out with a guy like Warren.'

'I already told you, I'm not.'

'So, then you'll come to dinner with me tonight?'

'No!'

Smiling languidly, he blew smoke into her face. 'Why not?'

'I – have – a – previous – engagement.'

'Still?'

She sighed. 'Yes.'

'With Warren?'

'No.'

'With who?'

'None of your business.'

'A mystery date.'

'Right. That's it. I have a mystery date.'

'Where's he taking you?'

'I don't know. He's going to surprise me. And if I did know, I wouldn't tell you. None of this is your business, Clyde. You really oughta learn how to take "no" for an answer. Now why don't you please drop it?'

Smiling with the cigarette pinched between his lips, he held up both hands as if surrendering. 'All right,' he said. 'I'm dropping it.'

'Thank you.'

'It's your loss.'

'I'm sure it is.'

'Going out with some pathetic loser when you could be going out with me.'

'I'll probably regret it.'

'You'll *definitely* regret it.' The smile still on his lips, his eyes went hard.

Dana felt a little cold and shaky inside.

That sure sounded like a threat. The creep just threatened me.

He turned away and stepped out of sight around the rear corner of the ticket booth. A moment later, the door banged shut.

Dana took an enormous breath, filling her lungs. She blew the air out through her pursed lips, then hopped up onto the stool.

She felt a little sick inside.

In her mind, she saw the sneer on Clyde's face as he said, *He's a fag.*

Warren's gay?

That figures. That just figures.

Unless maybe Clyde was lying. Wouldn't put it past him. What a prick. I wouldn't go out with him if . . .

The hell with him. What about Warren?

Warren hadn't *seemed* gay. You couldn't always tell, though. They didn't all prance around, flipping their hands in the air and rolling their eyes and talking like flamboyant broads. Many did, but certainly not all of them.

Tuck'll know, she told herself.

Might be nice if he is gay. Then we can just be friends, and not . . .

Damn it! Just when you think you've met . . .

Off in the distance, the front door of Beast House swung open. Five or six people stepped out onto the porch and started down the stairs. A couple of them were taking their earphones off.

About time, Dana thought. Customers.

She hopped off the stool and waited for them.

When they arrived, she chatted with them and took their players. After they left, she rewound all the tapes, then returned the players to the shelves behind her stool.

The shelves were nearly full. Only a dozen or so players were still out.

She glanced at her wristwatch.

4:35

In less than half an hour, ticket sales would stop for the day.

But the house would remain open until six, giving everyone time to complete the tour.

This could get boring.

She hopped up onto the stool.

Well, I'd rather be bored than have Clyde out here bothering me.

She supposed he was right about one thing, though: how could she spend the summer as a Beast House guide if the place made her feel ill?

I'll just have to get over it, she told herself.

Won't get over it by standing out here in the fresh air and sunlight. Why not go back in for the rest of the afternoon?

It seemed like a good idea.

She reached down for the walkie-talkie on her belt. But instead of pulling it free, she rested her hand on its warm plastic top.

I oughta stick this out. Tuck's already had to change stuff around because of me. Let's not cause any more trouble.

After this, she thought, I'll bring a book to read.

The time passed slowly.

At five o'clock, Clyde closed the ticket booth. He came around the rear corner. 'So, have you changed your mind about dinner?'

'Sorry,' Dana said.

'Your loss. I'll be taking off, now. One of the perks of working the ticket booth, you get to leave an hour early. Have fun.'

Nodding, she said, 'Bye.'

Clyde winked, stepped past her, then gracefully vaulted the turnstile and headed toward town. Not looking back, he waved.

Immediately, Dana felt a pleasant sense of lightness, of freedom.

Amazing, she thought, how one person can mess up your outlook.

He's gone, now. Enjoy it.

And enjoy it she did. It was one of those great afternoons when the sun is hot but a cool, moist breeze is blowing in from the Pacific. Seagulls squealed. She thought she could smell the ocean and the beach and the candy smell of suntan oil.

She pictured herself strolling barefoot along the beach, Warren by her side.

But if he's gay . . .

Doesn't mean we can't stroll on the beach together, she told herself.

Sure wouldn't be the same, though.

It made her feel cheated.

It gave her a tight, unpleasant feeling in the pit of her stomach.

Instead of being eager for six o'clock to arrive, she started to dread it. Because she might have to face Warren, and she would *definitely* be facing Tuck.

Tuck would know the truth about him.

And Dana wasn't so sure she wanted to find out.

I don't have to ask.

As closing time approached, however, she began to have new worries.

The shelves where she stored the tape players were nearly full. But not quite.

They had three empty spaces.

By six o'clock, the three players had still not been returned.

Chapter Sixteen

Sandy's Story – August, 1980

'I'll go and get a shovel,' Harry said. 'Why don't you ladies wait for me here?'

'Aren't you afraid we'll leave?' Sandy asked.

'Leave if you want. You're not my prisoners. But if you stay, I'll help you bury the guy. And you can spend the night at my place. I think you two could use a little rest.'

'Dat's for damn sure,' Lib said.

'While I'm gone, maybe you should strip him. We'll take his clothes and stuff back to the cabin with us and burn everything.'

'Done this sort of thing before?' Sandy asked.

'Just common sense. His body might get found someday. Better if it can't be identified.'

'Yeah, that's probably true,' Sandy said.

'Want the flashlight?' Harry asked.

'Don't you need it?'

'I can get by without it.' He handed the flashlight to Sandy, then said, 'I'll be back in about ten minutes.'

'Okay, see you.'

'Bring us someting to drink, huh?'

'I'll see what I can find.'

After he disappeared into the woods, Sandy could still hear his footsteps for a while. The crackling, crunching sounds finally faded out.

'What do you think?' she asked.

'About what?' Lib asked.

'Him. Harry.'

'Yum yum.'

'I'm serious.'

'Me, too.'

'He's seen Slade. And us.'

'Guess he aims to help us.'

'Do you really think so?' Sandy asked.

'He's goin' por a shovel.'

'Maybe he's going to call the cops.'

'Nah,' Lib said. 'Ip he was gonna do dat, he would ob made us go wit him.'

Sandy supposed she was right about that. The guy certainly hadn't acted as if he wanted to have them arrested. He'd actually seemed shocked by their story, and sympathetic. But maybe he'd been *too* sympathetic, too eager to take their side. Maybe he had something up his sleeve.

'I tink he's gonna help us bury da bastard.'

'Why would he want to do that?' Sandy asked.

'He's a guy. We're a couple ob babes. What da *you* tink? Probably wants to get in our pants.'

'If he tries anything with me,' Sandy said, 'I'll kill him.'

'Well, don't kill him till apter da hole's dug.'

'I'll try not to.'

'Shine dat light down here,' Lib said, and crouched over Slade's body.

Sandy lowered the pale beam.

'Dat's good. You just hold it dare, and I'll strip him.'

First, Lib removed Slade's wallet. Hardly giving it a glance, she tossed it to Sandy.

Sandy caught the wallet.

'Anything good in dat, we'll split it pipty-pipty, okay?'

'Sounds fair,' Sandy said. She stuffed the wallet into the back pocket of her shorts.

Lib searched the rest of Slade's pockets, but didn't take anything out. Then she removed his boots, his socks, and all the rest of his clothes. She stuffed his socks, underwear and ascot into his boots. After laying out his trousers on the ground, she spread his bloody, torn silk shirt along the legs and rolled them up together.

'Dare,' she said.

'Don't forget his wristwatch and rings.'

Lib took them. 'Dese oughta be wort a pew bucks,' she said.

'We'd better just get rid of them.'

Standing up, Lib asked, 'Gib 'em a toss?'

'Not here. Later.'

'Okie-doke.' Lib dropped them into the pocket of her *Blazing Babes* shirt. They made the silk bulge and sag over her left breast.

Sandy swept the flashlight down Slade's body for a final check.

'How da hell many times you stab dis guy?' Lib asked.

'A few.'

'Damn sight more dan a pew. Whoo! Hope you don't nebber get mad at *me*!'

'Just be good to Eric and you won't have to worry about it.' Sandy shut off the light.

'Hey, dat boy, he's aces wit me.'

Soon, Harry returned. Though he walked in darkness, he carried a lantern. It made quiet squeaking, clinking sounds as it swung by his left side. A shovel and pick ax, resting on his right shoulder, clanked together with each step he took.

'Hello, ladies,' he said.

He crouched and set down the lantern. Using both hands, he lifted the tools off his shoulder and lowered them to the ground.

'Brought you some refreshments,' he said. The front pockets of his trousers were bulging. He reached in and pulled out two cans. 'A beer for you, ma'am,' he said, stepping forward and handing a can to Lib. 'And a Pepsi for you, Charly.' He gave a cold can to Sandy.

'Thanks,' Sandy said.

Lib popped open her tab and took a long drink. Then she sighed. Then she said, 'You're a lipe-saber, Harry. Nuttin' beats a cold brew, and dat's a pact.'

'Glad to be of service,' he said. Then he turned away, squatted over his lantern and worked on it until it came alive, hissing like a bag of snakes and filling the clearing with brilliant light.

'Jeez, that's bright,' Sandy said.

'It's supposed to be,' Harry said.

'What if somebody sees it?'

'Not much chance of that.' Rising, he picked up the lantern by its wire handle and turned toward the body. His back stiffened. He muttered, 'Holy shit.'

Sandy couldn't blame him; Slade looked *awful*. She supposed he'd been no prize to begin with: soft and pudgy, his figure shaped like a bulb. In the glaring light, however, his dead skin was bluish-gray, his blood purple, his wounds raw, pulpy lips that looked wet and slippery.

'You must've really hated him,' Harry said.

'Yeah,' Sandy said. She sipped her soda, then added, 'He wasn't easy to kill, either.'

'Well, let's get him underground.'

Harry picked up the shovel. Carrying the lantern low by his side, he wandered the clearing with his head down. Every so often, he paused and jabbed the shovel against the ground. Then he stopped near a far edge of the clearing, set down the lantern, and stomped the shovel in with his foot. 'Somebody want to bring me the pick?'

Sandy hefted the pick off the ground. With Lib by her side, she carried it over to Harry.

'Don't need it quite yet,' he said.

Sandy let the pick fall to the ground.

Sipping their drinks, she and Lib watched Harry cut a shallow rectangle with the edge of his shovel. Then, slab by slab, he removed small sections of the surface soil along with the weeds and grass growing out of it. He set the slabs aside. When he was done, he had a three-by-six bed of bare earth. He started digging, piling the loose dirt at the opposite end from where he'd laid out the sod.

'Is there something we can do to help?' Sandy asked.

'Not at the moment,' he said. 'Thanks, though.'

A while later, he climbed out of the shallow hole. He took off his shirt, dropped it to the ground, and grabbed the pick ax. In the hole again, he swung the pick furiously, ripping into the earth. Sandy watched his muscles bulge and slide under his tanned skin. Soon, in spite of the night's chill, his back was shiny with sweat.

Switching to the shovel, he scooped out heaps of loose dirt and rocks.

When he paused to rest, the grave was knee deep. He was gasping for air. His hair was wet, matted down and clinging to his head. His dripping skin gleamed in the glare of the lantern.

'Hand me my shirt?' he asked.

Before Sandy could make a move for it, Lib snatched it off the ground. Instead of taking the shirt to him, she stepped backward. 'Whatcha want it por?'

'Just hand it over, okay?'

'Not ip you're gonna put it on.'

He smiled and shook his head. 'I just want to wipe off my sweat.'

'Reckon I'll let you hab it, den.' With that, she stepped forward and gave it to him.

'Thanks.'

Lib and Sandy both watched closely as he mopped the perspiration off his face, his broad shoulders, his chest, his belly.

'Dat's hot work, ain't it?' Lib said.

'I'll say.'

'Betcha'd feel better ip you took opp dem pants.'

He let out a short, breathless laugh. 'Well, thanks for the suggestion. Think I'll keep them on, though.'

'Chicken.'

'Cut it out, Lib,' Sandy said.

'Don't he look *hot*?'

'I'm sure he *is* hot.'

'I'm fine,' Harry insisted.

'You're *mighty* pine,' Lib told him.

'Well, thanks. You can hold this for me,' he added, and tossed his shirt to her. Then he hefted the pick and began swinging it again.

The next time he stopped to rest, Lib tossed the shirt to him without being asked. As he wiped his dripping body, Sandy said, 'Isn't that about deep enough?'

'Not even up to my waist, yet.'

'Pretty near,' Lib said.

'How deep are you planning to make it?' Sandy asked.

'Oh, I don't know. Deeper than this.'

'Maybe *we* should dig for a while,' she suggested.

'It'll go quicker if I do it.'

'*Bullshit!*' Lib blurted. 'I'm stronger dan *ten* men!' With that, she stepped to the edge of the grave. Stopping there, she waved a hand furiously at Harry. 'Outa my way! Make room por da best dang grabe-digger ebber walked da planet!'

Gazing up at her, Harry shook his head. 'Why don't you just wait up there, and I'll . . .'

She jerked open her *Blazing Babes* shirt and pulled it off. Twisting sideways, she flung the shirt to Sandy. Bare to the waist, she threw her arms high and leaped into the grave.

Harry scurried backward to get out of her way.

She landed on her feet, stumbled, bumped against the steep dirt wall of the grave, pushed herself away from it and stood up straight. Turning around, she gave Sandy a thumbs-up. Then she faced Harry.

'Howdy!' she blurted.

He shook his head. He glanced up at Sandy and shook his head some more. Then he said, 'Howdy, Bambi. Maybe you should climb out, now. We can't really get *any* digging done with both of us in here.'

'You get out and *I'll* dig,' she said.

'It'd be better if *you* got out.'

'Come on, Mom,' Sandy said.

'Tink I can't dig? I'm *strong!*' Stepping up close to Harry, she raised her right arm and brought her fist toward her face like a bodybuilder posing. 'See dat bicept?'

'Very nice,' Harry said.

'Peel it.'

'What?'

'*Peel* my muscle.'

'She wants you to *feel* it,' Sandy translated.

He made no move to feel it. 'I'm sure it's a fine muscle,' he said.

'You damn betcha. Gib it a peel.'

'Thanks, but . . .'

'Den how 'bout peelin' my tits?'

He glanced up at Sandy as if looking for another translation.

'She wants you to feel her tits.'

He grimaced. 'I know, I know. I figured that out.' To Lib, he said, 'You really shouldn't be doing this in front of Charly. I mean, come on. This is embarrassing. Why don't you just climb on out of here and let me finish digging . . .'

She threw herself forward, wrapping her arms around his back and squeezing herself against him.

'Mom!' Sandy cried out. 'Stop that!'

'Leabe us alone, dear.'

'Let go, Bambi,' Harry pleaded. 'Come on. Please. This isn't the time or the place.'

'Good as any,' she said, and slid down his body until Sandy could only see her head and hands. Her hands started unfastening Harry's belt.

'Quit it, Mom.'

'Go away. Less ya wanta come in and join us.'

'Hey,' Harry said. 'That's not . . .'

'Not enup room por tree ob us, anyhow.'

Harry grimaced up at Sandy. 'I'm sorry about this.'

'It's not your fault. It's . . .'

'*Mine!*' Lib cried out, and jerked his trousers down.

'Hey!' Harry gasped. 'Don't!' But he didn't try to stop her. He just stood there, naked down as far as the hole's edge allowed Sandy to see.

She saw plenty.

'*Niiiiice!*' Lib said.

Though Harry scowled and shook his head, he made no attempt to cover himself. To Sandy, he said, 'You really shouldn't be watching this.'

'Aren't you gonna stop her?'

Lib let out a laugh.

'I don't know how I can stop her without . . .'

He gasped and arched his back as Lib's fingers slid around him.

'. . . hurting her,' he finished.

'Hurt me wit dis, big boy.'

'What about the hole?' Sandy asked.

'Mine comes pirst!' Lib cried out, and laughed. Harry laughed, too.

'Great,' Sandy muttered. Then she turned her back on them.

Through the hiss of the lantern, Sandy heard Harry moan.

'How's dat peel?'

'Mmm.'

'Come on down here.' A short while later, Lib said, 'Get dese opp me, honey.'

'My pleasure,' said Harry.

Lib grunted a couple of times, then said, 'Yeah, dat's good. Mmmm. Nice and cool.'

Then came lots of moaning and sighing. Sandy stood there. She thought about walking away. But she stayed. She *wanted* to listen. It was embarrassing to hear such things. But the sounds excited her, too. She could so easily picture what was happening – easily feel Harry's body on top of her.

It could be me down there. I'm ten times better looking than Lib.

Shit, she's ugly as sin with her mouth all busted up that way.

How can he even stand to touch her?

So who'd wanta make it with that jerk, anyway? He's that damn eager to screw anything that moves . . . The hell with him.

The hell with Lib, too. What is she, some kind of nympho? She doesn't even know the guy.

Lib suddenly cried out, 'No. Stop! Yeeee! Dare's sometin' squirmy under me! Shit! Get opp! Get opp!'

'Sorry, sorry. What is it?'

'I don't know!'

'Probably just a worm or something,' Harry said.

'What do you expect?' Sandy called. 'Screwing in a grave?'

'Shut da puck up! Get down here, Harry. You get on da bottom, 'n I'll take da top. Okay?'

'Sure.'

'That way,' Sandy called, '*you* get the worms, Harry.'

'What are you, standing right there?'

'Sort of. But I'm not watching.'

'Why don't you take a little walk?'

'I'm fine right here.'

'Den just shut up,' Lib said.

'It's a free country.'

'You'd better go away, Charly.'

'Mom, don't you think you'd better warn him?'

'Warn me about what?' Harry asked.

'The *diseases*.'

'You're cruisin' por a bruisin', bitch.'

'What diseases?' Harry asked.

'She's lyin'. I ain't got nuttin'.'

'You name it, she's got it. If I had a whang, I wouldn't let her anywhere near it.'

'Don't listen to her,' Lib said. 'She don't know what she's talkin' about. She ain't my daughter, por one ting.'

'Mom!'

'She don't hardly eben *know* me. She's just sayin' dat shit 'cause she wants to stop you and me. She's jealous. *She* wants you. She's up dare all hot an boddered, creamin' her pants.'

'Like hell,' Sandy said.

'She's *not* your daughter?' Harry asked.

'Shut up, Mom!'

'I only just met her tonight.'

'So who's the dead guy?'

'Some puckin' movie director.'

'*Lib!*'

'He's *not* her father?'

'Nah.'

'You've both been handing me a pack of lies?'

'I'll tell you all 'bout da trute apter we . . .'

'Maybe you oughta get off me,' Harry said. 'I think we'd better . . .'

'You want *her*?' Lib asked. 'You want *Charly*?'

'I didn't say that.'

'Me pirst. You can hab her apter you get done wit me. I promise. She gibs you any shit, I'll eben hold her down por you.'

'But . . .'

'Less you don't *want* her.'

'I don't know. She's just a kid.'

'Dat don't matter.'

'I don't know what's going on, here. Let's just stop so I can try to figure . . .' He stopped talking and moaned.

'Yesssss,' Lib said.

'Uh. God. Oh.'

'All de waaaayyy.'

'Mmmmm.'

'You like?'

'Oh. Yeah. God.'

Sandy stepped to the edge of the grave with the lantern. All she could see of Harry were his legs. He seemed to be stretched out on the bottom of the grave, his trousers around his ankles. Lib's jeans and shoes were down there, too. She was naked and on her knees, hunched over him, gasping and groaning as she moved up and down. Her back and buttocks were dirty.

Sandy set down the lantern.

She raised the shovel high and swung it down hard.

Striking the back of Lib's head, it rang out like a bell.

Lib flopped down on Harry.

'Hey!' Harry gasped. 'What's going on? Bambi? Bambi? What the matter?'

'I think the shovel hit her,' Sandy said.

'*What*?'

'I hit her with your shovel.'

'Are you nuts?'

'Who, me?'

'My God, Charly!'

Harry's hands came out from under Lib. Grabbing her by the upper arms, he tried to push her up.

Sandy tossed aside the shovel and leaped off the edge of the grave. She landed with both feet in the middle of Lib's back.

Harry grunted.

'You all right?' Sandy asked.

'Uh!'

'You *won't* be!' Arms out for balance, she jumped up and down on Lib's back. Each time she landed, Harry let out a noise as if he'd been kicked in the stomach.

After five or six jumps, Sandy bent her knees and sat down on the edge of the grave, her shoes still planted in the middle of Lib's back.

'How are you doing, Harry?'

He moaned.

Leaning forward, Sandy stared down into the hole. She could see the back of Lib's head. She supposed that Harry's face must be directly under Lib's face, but the light didn't reach down that far.

'How was she, Harry? Was she to die for?'

He didn't answer.

Standing again, Sandy put her weight onto her right foot. With her left foot, she stomped the back of Lib's head. She felt the collision with Harry's face. She heard it, too.

'Did that hurt?' she asked.

Nothing.

She turned, stepped on Lib's buttocks, then on the backs of her legs. At the foot of the grave, she squatted over Harry's trousers. She found his pistol in one pocket, his wallet in another.

Sandy stuffed them into the pockets of her shorts, then climbed out.

Leaving the lantern, shovel and pick by the side of the grave, she hurried over to the body of Marlon Slade.

She bent over, grabbed his ankles, raised his legs, and dragged him across the clearing. It was tough work. By the time she reached the edge of the grave, she was sweaty and huffing for air.

She dropped his feet.

Then she picked up the lantern and crouched over the grave.

Harry's legs were still stretched out between Lib's legs. She was still on top of him, hiding most of his body. By lowering the lantern into the hole, however, Sandy could see more. Harry's right arm lay against the bottom of the hole at an angle away from his body. Lib's left breast drooped between his arm and his side just under his armpit. Her face was pressed against the side of his head.

Sandy could see a little of Harry's face.

His left eye, the profile of his nose, his lips and chin.

There was a lot of blood.

As she stared down at Harry, his eye blinked.

'Hello, Harry,' Sandy said.

He groaned.

'You still in her?'

His lips moved slightly, but he said nothing.

'Was she worth it?'

He said, 'Uhhh.'

'You two belong together.'

'Heh . . .'

'What?'

'Help,' he murmured.

'Maybe *Bambi'll* help you. She's very accommodating.'

With that, Sandy stood up. She stepped away from the grave, set down the lantern, then squatted beside the body of Marlon Slade.

'*Char . . .?*'

She tumbled Slade into the grave.

Then she filled it in.

Chapter Seventeen

No-Shows

When Dana saw Warren striding toward her across the front lawn of Beast House, she hopped off the stool and raised a hand in greeting. Her heart was pounding fast.

'You made it through your first day,' he called, still a distance away.

'Pretty much.'

'How'd it go?'

'Lunch went great.'

He grinned. 'Mine, too.' He stopped in front of her. Looking a little embarrassed, he pushed his hands into the front pockets of his shorts and tilted his head to one side. 'Anyway, it was sure nice to meet you.'

'Same here.'

'A fellow Southern Californian.'

'I'm no fellow,' Dana pointed out.

His grin widened and he blushed. 'No, you're sure not. Anyway, I'll probably be seeing you around.'

'Probably at the snack stand tomorrow.'

'Hope so.'

Looks like he's not gonna ask me out. Okay.

'Well,' he said, 'I guess I'd better get going.'

'Okay. You walking?'

'Yeah. My place is just over there.' He pointed across the street toward the wooded area just north of the old brick Kutch house.

'Your cabin's in the trees there?' Dana asked.

'Yep.'

'Do you have an ocean view?'

'Not much of one. You can see just a little water through the trees.'

'Sounds neat.'

'It's not bad.'

You're not much of a hint-taker, pal.

'Anyway,' he said, 'I guess I'd better get going.'

'Okay. See you tomorrow.'

'See you.' He turned away and opened the iron gate next to the turnstile. On the other side of it, he glanced back and smiled again. 'Take it easy, Dana.'

'Thanks.'

He started walking away.

'Hey, Warren?'

He stopped and turned toward her.

'You wouldn't want to stick around for a few minutes, would you? I might have to look through the house. We've got some no-shows.'

He stared at her, frowning slightly.

'Three players didn't get returned,' she explained.

'You're kidding.'

'I wish.'

He lifted an arm and checked his wristwatch. 'It's only ten after. They'll probably turn up. Some people don't pay much attention to what time it is.'

'Yeah, you're probably right.'

'Lynn's still here, isn't she?'

'She'd better be. She's my ride.'

'Anyone else?'

'I guess Rhonda's still around. Clyde took off at five, and Sharon left a few minutes ago.'

Nodding, Warren scowled toward the house. 'I guess I can wait a while . . . at least till . . . oh, here comes Lynn.'

Dana looked over her shoulder and saw Tuck trotting down the front porch stairs.

'So,' Warren said, 'I'll see you tomorrow.'

Dana swung her head around in time to see him smile, wave, and turn away. Trying not to let her surprise and disappointment show, she smiled back at him. 'Okay,' she called. 'See you tomorrow. Bye.'

'Bye.'

She watched him walk to the edge of Front Street. His head swung from side to side as he checked for traffic. Nothing seemed to be coming. He ran across the street, then turned to the right and walked quickly along the dirt shoulder. With each stride, pale puffs of dust drifted up behind his shoes.

'You met Warren,' Tuck said.

Dana turned around. 'Yeah.'

She felt herself tighten inside.

Don't ask.

'We've still got three tape players out,' she said.

'Three?' Tuck wrinkled her nose, pivoted and stepped closer to the shelves. Standing in front of them, she planted her hands on her hips. The breeze fluttered her shorts and blouse, and swept her long hair sideways. Streamers of hair blew across her face, but she made no attempt to brush them away.

What's taking her so long? Dana wondered.

The edges of the shelves were marked with red numbers spaced six or seven inches apart. Above each number, there was room for one cassette player and headphone set.

Returning the used ones, Dana had been careful to fill each place in order.

There were spaces for 150 of the listening machines.

All the shelves except one were completely loaded. But that final shelf was empty above 148, 149 and 150.

It shouldn't take a major study to figure out that three players were still out.

'Tuck?'

She turned around, frowning at Dana through her blowing blond hair. 'Looks like we've got a problem,' she said.

'You look worried,' Dana told her.

'I was just inside. I thought everybody'd cleared out. If three people are still in there, they must be hiding.'

'Doesn't this sort of thing happen all the time?'

'Not exactly *all* the time. And I'm particularly not thrilled that it's happening on top of the Ethel situation.'

For a moment, Dana didn't know what Tuck meant. Then she remembered how they'd found the Ethel that morning – the gown ripped where it wasn't supposed to be ripped, the mannequin's breasts and vagina exposed.

'You think there might be a connection?' she asked.

'Hope not.' She frowned. 'I suppose Clyde's long gone.'

'He took off at five.'

'Yeah, he does that. Times like this, I sort of wish we had a whole staff full of tough guys.'

'I shouldn't have let Warren leave.'

'That's okay. He wouldn't have been much help, anyway. Who *is* still here?'

'Just us and Rhonda, I guess. Maybe the girl who works with Warren at the snack counter . . .'

'Windy? She would've left by now. Same with Betty.'

'Who's Betty?'

'Runs the gift shop. You haven't met her yet?'

Dana shook her head.

'Sweet little white-haired gal.'

'Oh, her. I think I might've seen her leaving. She went through the side gate.'

'Probably with Windy. They ride together.'

'Oh, okay.'

'Guess it's just the three of us,' Tuck said. She pulled the walkie-talkie off her belt, raised it to her face and thumbed the talk button. 'Rhonda? Do you read me?' She released the button.

For a few seconds, her speaker buzzed and crackled. Then Rhonda's voice came out. 'I'm here.'

'What's your location?'

After a long pause, she said, 'The restroom.'

'Are you going to be long?'

'Well . . . Sort of. What's going on?'

'We've got three no-shows.'

'*Three?*'

'Yeah. Anyone there in the john with you?'

'Of *course* not! Cripes!'

'I didn't mean *that*.' Grinning, she added, 'You've got a dirty mind, Rhonda.'

'I do not!'

Tuck laughed. Then her grin faded and she said, 'When you're done, take a look around for our stragglers. Check both restrooms, the eating area, the gift shop. I'll come around and lock up later, but we need to find our missing customers. Okay?'

'I can't go into the men's restroom,' Rhonda said.

'Sure you can. Just knock first. Nobody's supposed to be in there, anyway. Dana and I will be going on into the house.'

'Do you want to wait for me?'

'Negative on that. Tell you what. When you get done there, come on out to the front of the house but don't go in. Just keep your eyes and ears open and get ready to call for help.'

Rhonda didn't respond.

'Did you get that?' Tuck asked.

'Maybe you oughta not go in,' Rhonda said. Even through the static, Dana could hear the tension in her voice.

'We'll be fine. Just do what I asked, okay?'

'Okay. Well, be very careful.'

'That's a big ten-four, darlin'.' Smiling, she gave Dana a nervous glance and returned the walkie-talkie to her belt. 'Probably nothing to worry about,' she said.

'If there's nothing to worry about, how come *you're* so damn worried?'

'Me? Ha ha! I *laugh* at danger!'

Dana laughed and shook her head.

'Let's go,' Tuck said. 'It is a good day to die.'

'Very amusing.'

Side by side, they started walking toward Beast House.

'Probably just some kids screwing around,' Tuck muttered.

'But they didn't return their players,' Dana said. 'So they must *know* we'll come in and look for them.'

'Maybe that's what they want. A little game of hide and seek.'

'You don't suppose . . .' Not wanting to go where the sentence was leading, she ended it.

'What?' Tuck asked.

She shrugged. 'Never mind.'

'Come on. Give.'

'Well . . . They won't, you know, try to *jump* us?'

'That's why I'm bringing you along, Bullwinkle.'

Dana lurched sideways, ramming Tuck off the walkway. Tuck stumbled through the grass, but didn't fall. 'Hey! Hey! Take it easy on the kid, huh?'

'I'll pound your butt for you.'

Laughing, Tuck returned to the walkway. 'You're such a hard-ass.'

'What do we do really?'

'If we get jumped?'

'Yeah?'

They started to climb the porch stairs. Dana glanced at the dangling body of Gus Goucher. Swaying and turning ever so slightly in the breeze, it made quiet, creaking sounds.

'Probably won't happen,' Tuck said.

'But what if it does?'

'You fight them off, and I'll run for it.'

'Seriously. I mean, what if it's three guys, and they're just waiting for us?'

'Are they *cute* guys?'

'Oh, very funny.'

Tuck hurried across the porch. As she pulled the door open, she said, 'It'll be fine. Probably. You go first.'

'Me?'

'Size before beauty.'

'Bitch,' Dana said, but she was smiling as she stepped over the threshold. She felt strange: amused, jittery, excited, but not terribly frightened.

Tuck came in. Instead of shutting the door, she swung it wide open and kicked a doorstop under its edge. 'In case we need to get out fast.'

'Great.'

Tuck grinned. Then she shouted, 'HELLO, EVERYONE! IT'S PAST CLOSING TIME! IT'S TIME FOR YOU TO LEAVE! PLEASE COME OUT NOW FROM WHEREVER YOU'RE HIDING, AND EXIT THROUGH THE FRONT DOOR.'

After her shouting, the house seemed very quiet.

Dana and Tuck stood in the foyer. They didn't move. They didn't talk. Dana barely breathed.

She wished she could *see*.

The sunlight coming through the doorway was so bright that she could hardly make out anything in the shadowy areas beyond its reach.

'Can *you* see?' she whispered.

'Not very well.'

'I feel like I'm half blind. Maybe we oughta shut the door.'

'And cut off our escape route?' Tuck asked.

'I'll protect you.'

'Oh. In that case . . .' Tuck turned around, kicked the block clear and eased the door shut, squeezing out the sunlight.

Murky gloom swallowed them.

'Fine,' Tuck whispered. 'Now we can *really* see.'

'It'll be okay. We just need to wait for our eyes to adjust.'

'In the meantime . . . WE KNOW YOU THREE ARE IN HERE. NOW, PLEASE COME OUT. WE'RE NOT GOING TO LEAVE UNTIL YOU COME OUT. OR UNTIL WE FIND YOU. WE *WILL* FIND YOU. WE'LL BE CONDUCTING A ROOM TO ROOM SEARCH – AND I KNOW *ALL* THE GOOD HIDING PLACES. SO MAKE IT EASY ON EVERYONE AND JUST COME OUT NOW.'

For a while, they listened.

'At what point do we call for the police?' Dana whispered.

'At no point, if we can help it. This is probably just a prank. But if it turns into something worse . . .'

'Hi!'

They both jumped.

Suddenly, laughter came pouring down from the same direction as the voice. A couple of vague, blurry figures were visible at the top of the stairs.

The laughing stopped.

'Very funny, fellows,' Tuck said. She sounded more cheerful than annoyed.

She's probably too relieved to be angry, Dana thought.

I sure am.

'Come on down, now,' Tuck said. 'It's time to leave.'

'Yes, ma'am,' one said.

'Are we, like, in trouble?' asked the other.

'Not so far,' Tuck told them.

They started down the stairs. They were about halfway to the bottom when Dana recognized them.

'My buddies,' she said.

'Yeah,' said the one in the Howard Stern T-shirt. 'Hi, Dana.'

'We're really sorry,' said the Beavis and Butthead fan. 'We didn't mean to, like, cause any trouble.'

'What *did* you mean to do?' Tuck asked.

'You're both such a couple of babes . . .'

'Yeah,' the other agreed. 'Real babes. We just thought, you know, like we'd sort of hang out in here.'

'We were hoping maybe you'd show up.'

'So we'd have a chance to, like, pop out and scare you half to death.'

'Maybe get you to scream.'

'Real nice,' Dana said.

'We weren't gonna *do* anything.'

'Nothing *bad*.'

'Figured it'd be cool to scare you, you know?'

'And, like, maybe you'd get a kick out of it?'

'It's fun to get scared.'

'Up to a point,' said the other.

'Yeah. Not *too* scared. Just *fun* scared.'

Dana shook her head.

'Like when you go in a spookhouse?'

'Only we thought it'd be better not to.'

'Sort of.'

'Yeah.'

'What you said about *three* people.'

'Freaked us out.'

''Cause there's only like *two* of us?'

'So that's when we figured we'd better come out, you know?'

'Like, who's Number Three?'

'Creeped us out.'

'Big time.'

'Freaky.'

'So that's how come we quit and came down.'

'We appreciate it,' Tuck said. 'Thanks for not making us hunt high and low for you.'

'Yeah, thanks,' Dana said.

'You're welcome. But it was like, shit, you know? Who *else* is in here?'

'And what if he's hiding where *we* are?'

'Like, same room, different corner.'

'Did you see or hear anything?' Tuck asked.

'Just you.'

'We didn't see Number Three.'

'Or hear him.'

'Or smell him.'

'Or her.'

'Or it.'

'But we, like, felt the *ambiance* of a third party.'

'Creeped us out.'

'But not, like, *that* much. I mean, we hereby volunteer to help you search for the missing party.'

'Right. We're scared, but we're not chicken.'

'We'll be your bodyguards.'

'Thanks,' Tuck said. 'If you want to be a real help, though, why don't you go on outside? Rhonda'll be coming along pretty soon and she might be worried about us. Just tell her everything's all right. Then you can either take off, or stick around for a while if you want to see who we turn up.'

'Rhonda?'

'She's another guide,' Tuck explained.

'She a babe?'

'A major babe,' Tuck said, grinning. 'She has a tendency to get nervous, though. So it'll be really nice if you keep her company till we come out.'

'We can do that.'

'Sure. Happy to.'

'Okay,' Tuck said. 'Thanks. One other thing.'

'Anything you say.'

'We're, like, at your service.'

'Stick close enough to the house so you can hear us if we call for help.'

'You gonna be calling for help?'

'Probably not. But you never know.'

'Sounds to me like you definitely need bodyguards.'

'We'd be happy to oblige.'

'We'd guard your bodies with our lives.'

'Or die trying.'

Dana laughed softly. 'You guys are okay.'

'Thanks.'

'Yeah.'

'What're your names?'

'I'm Arnold Anderson,' said the boy in the Howard Stern T-shirt.

'I'm Dennis Dexter?' said the Beavis and Butthead fan, lifting his voice at the end as if asking whether this was his name.

'A.A. 'n D.D.,' said Arnold. 'That's what we call ourselves.'

'And you're Dana and Lynn,' said Arnold.

'That's us,' Tuck said. 'Big D, Little L. Anyway, nice to meet you guys.'

'A pleasure to make your acquaintance,' said Dennis.

'A *great* pleasure,' said Arnold.

'You're, like, sure you want us to leave?'

'Yeah. Keep Rhonda company and stand watch outside.' Tuck stepped over to the door and opened it for them. Looking out, she said, 'I don't see Rhonda yet, but she'll probably be along any minute. See you later, guys.'

They headed for the doorway.

'Just shout if you need us,' Arnold said.

'We'll come and save you,' said Dennis. 'We'll, like, kick ass.'

'Sounds good,' Tuck said.

'Bye, guys,' Dana called after them.

Chapter Eighteen

The Search

As Arnold and Dennis trotted down the porch stairs, Tuck shut the door. 'Okay! That's two down, one to go. Now we've got the odds on *our* side.'

'I liked it better the other way,' Dana said. 'What sort of person would want to hide out alone in a place like this?'

'Maybe he isn't hiding,' Tuck suggested.

'What do you mean?'

'Maybe he dropped.'

'Oh, terrific.'

'Passed out, tossed a heart attack, popped an aneurism . . . Let's start upstairs and work our way down.'

Dana nodded and followed Tuck to the foot of the stairs. Staying close to each other, they started to climb. 'I won't shout any more,' Tuck said.

'Glad to hear it.'

'Unless we hit trouble. But if it's BIG trouble, let's just run like hell. Know what I mean?'

'Sure.'

'Like if a psycho starts coming down the stairs at us with a chain saw? We run. Got it?'

'Got it.'

'Or if a big white beast tries to nail us . . .'

'We run.'

'Right.'

'I get the picture. Thanks.'

When they reached the top of the stairs, they stopped and looked both ways. In each direction, the dim, shadowy hall looked deserted.

'You go that way,' Tuck said, 'I'll go this.'

'Bite me.'

'Don't you want to split up?'

'Sure. We'll split up and I'll wait for you outside.'

'Ah. Well. Never mind.'

Staying together, they turned to the left, walked in silence to the end of the corridor, and entered Lilly Thorn's bedroom. Dana waited just inside the doorway, keeping watch while Tuck hurried through the room, glanced here and there, checked inside the armoire and finally sprawled on the floor for a look under the bed.

Getting up, Tuck brushed her hands off against each other and shook her head.

They crossed the hall to the bedroom Maggie Kutch had shared with her husband. It contained Maggie's original furniture. But there were no wax figures of Maggie or any other member of her family. The exhibit showed a twelve-year-old boy, Larry Maywood, raising the window and looking over his shoulder in horror. His pal, Tom Bagley, lay mangled and bloody on the floor. Dana knew their story well. These two local boys had been avid fans of the tour. And they'd grown too curious. Late one night in 1951, they'd broken into the house to search for the beast. And they'd supposedly found it. Or it had found them.

Larry had escaped through the window, but poor Tom . . .

Dana glanced at Tom's severed head. It rested on the floor near his shoulder. Facing her. Staring up at her.

She looked away from it.

For a few seconds, she watched Tuck performing the search. Then she just *had* to look at Tom again.

He was still staring at her.

Of course he is. If he stops *staring at me, that's when I'd better start worrying.*

He gave her the creeps.

She kept trying to look away, but Tom's gaze kept pulling at her.

At last, Tuck finished the search. As she came toward the door, Dana quickly stepped out into the hallway.

Tuck frowned at her. 'You okay?'

'Yeah.'

'Not getting nauseous or anything?'

'So far, so good. I just didn't like the way Tom was staring at me.'

Tuck grinned. 'He loves the pretty girls.'

'Oh, thanks.'

'Has great eyes, doesn't he?'

'They're awful.'

'That's what I mean,' Tuck said. 'He upsets *lots* of people. They always get the idea he's staring at them. So, are you ready for the attic?'

'Ready as I'll ever be.'

Dana followed Tuck down the hallway.

Arriving at the entrance to the attic, Tuck unhooked one end of the plush red cordon and eased it down gently against the door frame.

'Chances are,' she whispered, 'we'll find our missing tourist up here.'

'Oh, good.'

'They love to hide in the attic.' Tuck reached up and clutched Dana's shoulder. Holding on, she raised a knee and pulled off her shoe. After taking off the other, she whispered, 'Lose your shoes. We want to take him by surprise.'

'How'll I kick his ass if I'm barefoot?'

'Toe his ass.'

Shaking her head, Dana grabbed Tuck's shoulder. As she pulled off her shoes, she noticed that she was trembling. And sweaty. Her blouse clung to her back. Her panties were sticking to her buttocks and groin. The feet of her socks were soaking wet.

'You all right?' Tuck whispered.

'A little scared.'

'I can take care of this if you wanta wait here for me.'

'No. We stay together.'

'You sure?'

'Sure I'm sure.'

'Well, I'll go up first.'

'Okay.'

Tuck started climbing the stairs. Dana followed close behind her. The stairway was narrow and steep. Dana had seen plenty of it, that morning.

It was Station Seven.

Every tourist had stopped in the corridor and gazed up the dim stairway while listening to the story of Maggie Kutch's flight for safety with her kids, the beast in hot pursuit.

Dana must've explained, at least twenty times, that the attic was off limits for reasons of safety.

But not off limits for us.

At the top of the stairs, Tuck reached out and turned the knob. Dana heard the latch click its release. The door creaked as Tuck pushed it open.

On the other side was darkness.

Instead of entering, Tuck reached around the corner. Her hand came back holding a flashlight. She showed it to Dana. With a smile, she gave it a twirl. Then she thumbed its switch. As a beam of bright light shot out, she stepped through the doorway.

Wait!

Dana rushed up the last few stairs and into the attic. She lurched to a stop behind Tuck, bumping her gently, then putting a hand on her shoulder.

Breathing hard, heart pounding, she watched the pale tube of light swing across the darkness. It lit galaxies of floating, swirling motes. It lit support beams, a sofa, chests of drawers, steamer trunks, chairs, lamps, tables . . .

A man.

Dana gasped.

'Just a dummy,' Tuck whispered.

With the flashlight, she quickly pointed out a couple of other mannequins. 'They used to be exhibits,' she explained. 'Stay here a minute.'

Dana nodded and stayed.

Tuck started roaming the attic, playing the beam of light this way and that, making shadows leap and spread. 'Doesn't look like our missing tourist is up here,' she said. 'Gotta make sure, though. When we leave, I'll lock the door. If he's in here, he'll be trapped. All night long.'

'That'd be pleasant,' Dana said.

'Yeah. Wouldn't it be? This place even gives *me* the creeps. I guess because the beast killed Maggie's little girls up here.'

'You come here with the Midnight Tour, don't you?'

'Sure do. It scares the crap out of everyone.' She laughed softly. 'I guess that about does it,' she said, and started wandering back toward the door.

Dana watched her approach.

And watched the attic behind her.

Half expecting a shape to come lurching suddenly out of the darkness.

Hurry up!

'I don't know which is scarier,' Tuck said, 'the attic or the cellar.'

'Let's just get out of here.'

Almost back to Dana, Tuck switched off the flashlight. Dana stepped sideways through the doorway and climbed down a couple of stairs. Head up, she watched her friend return the flashlight to its place just inside the attic.

Tuck stepped out and pulled the door shut.

Its latch clicked.

Dana watched her.

'Let's go,' Tuck said.

'Don't forget to lock it.'

'Oh, it doesn't lock.'

'You said . . .'

'That was just a fib in case our friend was listening.'

'You *aren't* going to lock it for the night?'

'Can't. The lock's broken. Has been for years.'

'Maybe you should get it fixed.'

'Maybe.' Tuck laughed softly, then started down the stairs.

Dana turned around and hurried to the bottom, glad to be putting distance between herself and the attic.

At the bottom, she picked up her shoes and stepped out of the way. Tuck hooked the cordon in place.

They both started putting on their shoes.

'Sorry I forgot to warn you about the dummies,' Tuck said.

'That's all right. What're they doing up there?'

'Just hanging out.' Finished putting on her shoes, Tuck stood up. 'Actually,' she said, 'they're former exhibits. One's the cop . . .'

'Dan Jenson?'

'Right. He was moved to the attic back in '79 after they busted him up. Then when Janice bought the place, she put the Zieglers up there with him. She needed to get them out of the middle of the hallway. Caused too much traffic conjestion. Ready to go?'

'All set.'

'Next stop,' Tuck said, 'the nursery.'

This time, Dana waited just outside the door while Tuck ducked under the cordon and hurried through the room.

Tuck found nobody.

They continued down the corridor to the room where Lilly's boys had been slain. Again, Dana waited while Tuck did a quick search.

'So that's it for up here?' Dana asked as they returned to the stairway.

'That's about it. The other doors are all kept shut and locked. Nobody can get into any of them without a key. So, I guess our boy must be downstairs.'

'Or girl.'

'It'll be a guy,' Tuck told her. 'Girls never pull this sort of crap. Not by themselves.'

'Never?'

'Hardly ever.'

'You saying girls are chicken?'

Tuck grinned. 'Maybe not chicken. Maybe just smarter.'

'I'll go along with that.'

Laughing, they started to descend the stairs.

'How often do you have to go through all this?' Dana asked.

'Pain in the ass, huh?'

'A major pain.'

'It gets easier the more often you do it.'

'I hope it's not *every* afternoon.'

'It varies. We'll sometimes go two or three weeks without a problem. Then again, sometimes it might be two or three days in a row.'

'I could do without it completely,' Dana said as they reached the bottom of the stairway.

'Rhonda's probably right outside. I can get her to finish up with me, if you'd rather . . .'

'Trying to get rid of me?'

'It's your first day. You've done plenty.'

'I'll stick with you,' Dana said.

'All right, good deal. Let's see how Ethel's doing.'

Dana followed Tuck into the parlor and watched her scurry about in search of the missing tourist.

'Are you sure we *started* with a hundred and fifty players?' Dana asked. 'Maybe we were one short . . .'

'Nope. I checked, myself. We started with a hundred and fifty players in full working order.'

'So one is *definitely* still out.'

'Yep.' Pausing, Tuck stared down at Ethel. 'She still decent?'

'Semi-decent.'

'Good enough. I'd sure like to get my hands on whoever was in here screwing around with her.'

'Better be careful what you wish for,' Dana said.

Tuck came out. Together, they crossed the foyer and entered the dining room. They both glanced under the table, then split up to walk around it. They met again before stepping into the kitchen.

As they searched the kitchen, Dana said, 'What if we can't find him?'

'If we can't, we can't.'

'Does it ever happen?'

'Now and then.'

'Somebody just *disappears?*'

Tuck grinned at her. 'Now and then.'

'Oh, terrific.'

Off to the side of the kitchen was a door marked EMPLOYEES ONLY. Dana opened it and leaned in. She glanced at the old-fashioned toilet, bath tub and sink. In one corner stood a water heater. On the floor was a modern electric space heater. There were plush purple rugs and matching towels.

But no tourist.

'Make sure nobody's in the tub,' Tuck said.

Dana groaned. Then she stepped through the doorway.

Tuck had pointed out the special 'employees only' restroom yesterday, but this was the first time Dana had entered it. The air smelled like fresh, scented soap. Murky light filtered in through the window curtains.

A breeze came in with the light, filling the curtains and lifting them gently.

Turning her back to the window, Dana stared at the bath tub. It looked very old and very large. It was nestled in shadows against the far wall.

From where she stood, she couldn't see all the way to its bottom.

If somebody's hiding down there . . .

How ironic to pee my pants a few steps away from a toilet.

Fear growing in her belly, she rushed toward the tub.

And saw its bottom.

Empty.

'All clear,' she called out. Then she added, 'I think I'll take advantage of the john while I'm here.'

'Help yourself.'

She returned to the door and shut it, then stepped over to the toilet.

This was really much nicer than the public restrooms out back.

Seated on the toilet, she found herself staring at the tub.

You hardly ever see them that big, she thought.

A green bath mat was draped over its side.

A bath mat?

'Hey, Tuck,' she called out, and realized she'd used the wrong name. 'Lynn? Does somebody actually take baths in here?'

No answer came.

Dana felt a tremor of dread.

'Lynn? Answer up.'

Silence.

'Very funny,' she called.

Nothing.

'Damn it, Lynn!'

Still nothing.

'You just gonna stand out there and pretend you've disappeared?'

Lynn didn't answer.

'Okay,' Dana said. 'Great.'

As fast as she could, she finished at the toilet. Holding her shorts up with one hand, she hurried to the door and pulled it open.

Tuck wasn't standing there, looking pleased by her prank.

Nor was she sprawled on the floor, bloody and dead.

Dana stepped out.

Tuck didn't seem to be in the kitchen at all.

Heart thudding, Dana buttoned the waist of her shorts. She pulled up the zipper. She buckled her belt.

In the room behind her, the toilet went silent.

Dana heard only her own quick heartbeat and breathing.

'*Tuck!*' she shouted.

'I'm in the cellar!' Tuck called. Her voice, sounding far away, came through the open pantry door at the other side of the kitchen. 'Be right up!'

Dana hurried to the pantry and looked in.

At the back of it, the cellar door stood wide open.

Dana walked slowly to the open door. Stopping, she peered down the steep wooden stairway. In the darkness near the bottom, the beam of a flashlight flitted this way and that. She couldn't see Tuck, though.

'Are you all right?' she called down the stairs.

'Fine. Just thought I'd check down here and save you the trouble.'

'Thanks a lot.'

'You're welcome.'

'I thought the beast had gotten you.'

'Not this time,' Tuck said.

'Anyone down there?'

'I don't think so.'

'Are you coming up?'

'In a second.'

'Come on up now, okay?'

'Do you wanta come down?'

'Not particularly,' Dana admitted.

'Didn't think so.'

'But I will if you don't come up.'

'Okay. Here I come, ready or not.'

At the bottom of the stairs, Tuck stepped into sight. She smiled up at Dana, then switched off her flashlight and started to climb.

'It's beginning to look like we've lost a tourist,' she said.

'What do we do about it?'

'Not much. We'll go ahead and lock the place up. And we'll check the parking lot before we leave, see if a car's been left behind.'

At the top of the stairs, she shut and locked the cellar door.

'Should we tell the police?' Dana asked.

'Tell them what? That one of our tape players is missing?'

'That a *person* is.'

'Somebody might've just absconded with one of our machines. It happens.'

'Have you had *people* disappear?'

'While taking the tours?'

'Yeah.'

'Not many,' Tuck said, and grinned.

Chapter Nineteen

In Hot Water

That night after supper, after reading, after watching some television, Tuck left the room and Dana flipped through channels. She was feeling groggy. She wondered whether to go to bed now or try to stay up for the eleven o'clock news.

Nothing much of interest seemed to be on the TV.

If she tried to read some more, she would undoubtedly nod off.

Tuck came back into the room. She had changed into a white terry-cloth robe.

'Going to bed?' Dana asked.

'Going for a dip. Want to join me?'

'Are you kidding? It's freezing out there.'

'It's not *freezing*. Anyway, I'm going in the hot tub, not the pool.'

'The hot tub?'

'It's great on chilly nights like this.'

'Sounds pretty nice,' Dana admitted.

'Nothing like it. I'll get us a bottle of wine and meet you out there. We'll celebrate your first day on the job.'

'Celebrate that I survived it.'

'Exactly.'

Dana shut off the TV.

'I'll grab a couple of towels, too,' Tuck said. 'But make sure you bring something warm to wear for afterwards. A robe, or something. Otherwise, you'll freeze your tail on the way back in.'

Tuck hurried away.

Dana trotted upstairs. In the guest bedroom, she turned on the light and pulled off her sweatshirt and shivered.

This is nuts, she thought.

Should be fun, though.

She took off the rest of her clothes, tossed her socks and underwear into the hamper, then opened a dresser drawer. She'd brought three swimsuits with her from home: a skimpy white bikini and two red tank suits left over from her days as a lifeguard. The bikini was meant for a special occasion – maybe an outing on the beach with just the right guy.

As if that's likely to happen.

Shivering, she pulled out one of the red suits, stepped into it, drew it up her body and slipped her arms through the shoulder straps. When she had it on, she looked at herself in the mirror. The suit was thin and tight. It showed *everything*. On lifeguard duty, she used to hide it under an official T-shirt and shorts so that she would only be seen in it during emergencies.

Not much for warmth, either.

In the mirror, she could see the goosebumps on her bare arms and legs. Her nipples were hard. They showed through the clinging suit as if she wore nothing but a layer of red paint.

At the closet, she put on a robe. She wrapped it snugly around her body and tied its belt as she left the room.

That's a lot better.

She hurried down the stairs, then turned around and walked over to the sliding glass door. On the other side of the glass, the pool area was well lighted. The water shimmered, clear pale blue with gentle ripples.

From the hot spa near the corner of the pool, steam drifted into the air. Dana couldn't see much of the spa itself – or Tuck. A patio table and chairs stood in the way. But a couple of large, folded towels were stacked on top of the table and a white robe was draped over one of the chairs. Dana figured that Tuck must've arrived.

She rolled open the door and stepped out. Her feet met cold concrete. Night air drifted up beneath her robe, chilling her legs. She slid the door shut, then hurried toward the spa.

Furniture no longer blocking her view, she saw Tuck shoulder-deep in the steaming, frothy water. A bottle of red wine and a couple of glasses stood on the concrete just behind her. She waved at Dana through the pale vapors.

'It's *cold* out here!' Dana called.

'Not in here. Hurry it up.'

Quickly, Dana pulled open her robe, slipped it off and swung it over the back of a patio chair.

'Suits are optional,' Tuck said.

'I opt to wear mine,' Dana said.

'Suit yourself.'

The spa was circular, about eight feet in diameter, and constructed of tiles that matched the nearby swimming pool.

Tuck was slouching against the opposite wall. Through the steam, Dana saw that Tuck's head, neck and shoulders were above the water's surface. The rest of her body was submerged but well lighted from below, quivering and trembling with the undulations of the water. Though the view was obscured by bubbles, she appeared to be wearing a bikini made of something that resembled doe skin.

'Suits optional, huh?' Dana asked. '*You're* wearing one.'

Tuck grinned up at her. 'Never said I wasn't. Just wanted to familiarize you with the house rules.'

'Any other rules I should know about?'

'Don't piss in the water.'

'Lovely.'

'Yep.'

Standing on one foot, Dana eased the other down into the water. And jerked it out. 'That's *hot!*'

'That's the idea.'

'You trying to boil us alive?'

'Moose soup.'

She tried again. This time, the water didn't hurt so much. She lowered her foot deeper. The swirling heat climbed her shin and calf and wrapped around her knee. Then her foot met the smooth tile of the seat. Standing on the seat, she committed her other leg to the water.

'See?' Tuck asked. 'It's not so bad. It seems a lot hotter than it really is.'

'By contrast with the frigid air?'

'Exactly.'

With a step forward, Dana dropped to the bottom of the spa. The hot water rushed all the way up to her waist. Flinching rigid, she gasped, '*Iiii-ee!*'

Tuck laughed. 'Pussy,' she said.

'Are you sure it's supposed to be this hot?'

'Just wait till you've been in it a few minutes, you'll be wanting it *hotter.*'

'I doubt that,' Dana said. Raising her arms, she eased herself down slowly, grimacing and hissing as the water climbed her belly and back and breasts. After her rump met the seat, she lowered her arms. Then she sighed with relief.

'Feels great, huh?' Tuck asked.

'I'm not so sure.'

Already, however, the heat was beginning to feel cozy rather than painful. And she began to feel the tickle of bubbles, the rub and caress of the water's currents.

'It's not so bad,' she said after a while.

'Ready for some wine?'

'Sure.'

Tuck stood up, turned partway around, and picked up the wine bottle.

'That's a neat swimming suit you've got on,' Dana said.

'Thanks.'

'Mug Tarzan?'

'Mugged Jane.'

When the glasses were full, Tuck picked them both up and turned around. Dana started to rise. But the air felt awfully cold where she was wet, so she stayed low and hobbled to the middle of the spa. Tuck handed a glass to her.

Instead of returning to her original seat, Dana made her way to the left and sat down closer to her friend.

'Here's to the start of a great summer,' Tuck said.

'I'll drink to that,' Dana said.

They clinked their glasses together.

Dana took a sip. The wine tasted heavy and fruity and tart. 'Good,' she said.

'This is the life, huh?'

'Not bad.'

'All we need is a couple of guys.'

'To ruin it,' Dana added.

'Ooooo.'

'You know what I mean. This is nice the way it is. Get a couple of guys in here, they'd start acting rowdy. They'd be yucking it up and grabbing at us. Trying to feel us up . . .'

'Get our suits off,' Tuck added.

'Exactly.'

'Doesn't sound *that* awful.'

'Maybe not.' Dana sipped some more wine. 'Depends on the guys, I guess. So, who would you *like* to have in here?'

'Nobody you know.'

'What's his name?'

'Ichabod Bibsdiddle.'

They stared at each other. Tuck nodded and frowned solemnly for a few seconds, then let go. When she finished laughing, she said, 'I don't *know*. I don't *have* a boyfriend. Not at the moment, anyway. I can't even think of any guy I'd really like to kiss, much less . . .'

'Didn't you just say you wanted a couple of fellas in here with us right now?'

'Yeah. So?'

'So, who would they be?'

'I don't know.' Tuck frowned for a moment, then answered, 'Guys who aren't dickheads.'

'And they are to be found . . . where?'

'Ah, they're somewhere. I don't know. I'll meet one someday. I have every confidence.'

'Guys must *always* be hitting on you.'

'Oh, sure. Not a day goes by. Hardly an *hour* goes by. But most of them are yucks. Weirdos, creeps and jerks.'

'But not *all* of them . . .'

'No, no. There are some really cool guys who come on to me now and then. And they always turn out to be visiting from Juno or Milbourne or some other place a zillion miles away.'

'Maybe you're just too picky.'

'Ha!'

'What about the locals?' Dana asked.

'Give me a break.'

'There's not one guy in all of Malcasa Point you don't consider a loser?'

'Nobody I'd want to *go* with.'

Heart pounding faster, Dana asked, 'So, what's the matter with Warren?'

'Ah-*ha! Warren!* I knew you'd be getting around to Warren. Surprised it took you this long.'

'So, what's wrong with him?'

'Did I say something was wrong with him?'

'Well, I guess you lumped him in with all the other losers and ne'er-do-wells in town. What's his problem?'

'You like him, don't you?'

'Sort of. All we really did was talk for a few minutes at lunch. And I saw him when he left work. I haven't gotten a chance to know him yet, but he seems like a nice enough guy.'

'Oh, he's *nice*, all right.'

'Is he gay?'

Tuck blurted out a laugh. 'Gay? Warren? Where'd you get *that* idea?'

'Clyde said he is.'

'Oh. Clyde. Clyde would. Clyde's a shit. He'll say anything. He probably told you that because *he* wants you.'

'Well, he ain't a-gonna get me.'

'Just never believe a word out of Clyde's mouth. And don't let him get you alone. He's not only a liar, he's a sneak. I wouldn't put anything past him. Especially where *you're* concerned. In case you haven't noticed, you're about ten times better looking than most gals. He'd probably do just about *anything* for a whack at you.'

'Terrific. Thanks for the warning.'

'He's already nailed every gal on the staff.'

'You're kidding.'

'Well, not Betty.'

'*You?*'

'Oh, yes. Even me.' Tuck grimaced, then tipped up her glass and gulped it empty. 'How about a refill?'

Dana finished her wine. She handed the glass to Tuck. 'How did he manage that?' she asked.

'Smooth talking, flattery, claims of undying love.' Tuck stood up, turned, and started pouring. 'Booze,' she said. 'A kiss here, a sneaky hand there. One thing leads to another. You know how it goes.'

'Afraid so.'

'My main problem was, I believed all his garbage. I trusted him. Make sure you don't.'

'Not a chance.'

'Don't believe a word out of his mouth.'

'Did he get *Rhonda*?'

'You bet.'

'My God. The poor kid. She seems so . . . innocent and vulnerable.'

'She never knew what hit her.' Tuck handed a full glass to Dana. 'I'd even warned her about Clyde, but she went for him anyway. He lured her, caught her, fucked her and dumped her. The same as he does to everyone.'

'He won't get me.'

'Just never let your guard down.'

'If he tries, he dies.'

Tuck laughed and shook her head.

'If Clyde's done all this stuff, how come he's still working here? Shouldn't you fire him?'

'I'd love to. But he pretty much behaves himself on the job. He saves his big seductions for *after hours*. And he hasn't broken any laws that I'm aware of. He just employs the standard, old-fashioned, tried and true methods of seduction. So far, at least. I've discussed the situation with Janice, but she won't fire him.'

'Has he nailed her?'

'Janice? Hey, bite your tongue. You're talking about my dad's wife, pal!' She stopped smiling. A moment later, she said, 'I can't imagine Clyde has gotten to Janice. For one thing, he's probably afraid to try. I mean, she *is* the owner. If he nailed her and dumped her like he does everyone else, she'd can his ass in a heartbeat. Besides, even if he had the guts to make the try, I bet he'd strike out. Janice really loves my dad. There's no way she'd let *any* other guy touch her. And she can be tough as nails. You know the stuff she's gone through. She takes shit from *no one*.'

'So why won't she fire him?'

'His job performance is excellent. If she fired him, she'd be setting herself up for a lawsuit. You can't just go around firing people unless their job performance sucks or they commit a crime or something. Even *then*, they'll sue you.'

'It's a wonderful world.'

'Well, Clyde's gonna screw up, one of these days. When he does, I'll be there and make sure he goes down for it.' She took a drink of wine, then lowered her glass until its base seemed to rest on the bubbly white water. Smiling, she said, 'Maybe you *should* go out with him. Maybe we'll get lucky and he'll assault you.'

'Oh, thanks for the suggestion. Real nice.'

'Then you can file criminal charges against him, and . . .'

'Give me a break,' Dana said. 'I don't care what kind of an asshole he is, I'm not going to set him up. I want nothing to *do* with him.'

'Yeah, well . . .' Tuck shrugged and grinned. 'I knew you wouldn't go for it. You're too much of a Girl Scout.'

'Darn right.'

'A goody-two-shoes.'

'Let's not push it, babe.'

'Anyway,' Tuck said, 'I wouldn't *let* you do something like that. I was just kidding around. The best thing you can do is stay out of his way. Don't even talk to him if you can help it.'

'I didn't want to talk to him *before* I knew all this. He just rubbed me the wrong way.'

'He'll rub you any way he can.'

'He won't get the opportunity.'

'Let's hope not.'

They both sat in silence for a while and sipped their wine. Though the water no longer seemed terribly hot, Dana felt awfully warm inside and out. With her free hand, she wiped sweat off her face.

When her glass was empty, she reached around and set it on the concrete.

'Refill?' Tuck asked.

'Maybe later,' she said. Then she stood up.

'You aren't leaving yet, are you?'

'Just need some fresh air.' She stepped onto the tile seat, then turned around and sat on the edge of the spa, her legs dangling into the hot water. The chill night air wrapped her wet body. It felt good after so much heat. Drops of water and sweat turned cold as they dribbled down her skin. She took a deep breath. 'That's better,' she said.

Tuck twisted sideways to look up at her. Then she spoke in a loud voice to be heard over the burbling and hissing sounds of the spa. 'If you really want to be a glutton for punishment, hop into the pool.'

From up here, Dana had a fine view of the swimming pool. Unlike the spa, it didn't steam. The sparkling water trembled under the mild breeze and looked frigid.

'This is fine,' Dana said. 'For now. So, tell me about Warren.'

'Ah. Okay.' Tuck climbed up and sat beside her. 'What do you want to know?'

'What *should* I know?'

'Well . . .' Tuck drank the last of the wine from her glass. 'I don't know about you,' she said, 'but *I'm* having a refill.'

'What is it, a long story?'

Tuck shrugged. 'We've got to polish off the bottle. Red's no good the next day.'

'If you say so.'

Their glasses full again, they each took a few sips. Then Tuck lowered her glass. Resting it on her thigh, she gazed out across the pool. 'Well,' she said. 'For starters, Warren . . .'

Her voice stopped.

'What?'

She whispered, '*Shit.*'

'What?' Dana asked.

Smiling at her, Tuck said, 'Just act natural. Pretend nothing's going on.'

'What *is* going on?'

'Someone's over there.'

'Huh?'

'Across the pool. In the bushes.'

Chapter Twenty

The Lurker

Trying not to show her alarm, Dana smiled and nodded. She kept her eyes on Tuck. 'Where exactly?' she asked.

Tuck took a drink of wine. Then she lifted her eyes, slid them to the right, and looked.

And looked.

'What's going on?'

'I don't see him now.'

Turning her head, Dana studied the area along the far side of the pool. All she saw was a broken wall of trees and bushes. The foliage crowding the edge of the concrete was brushed with light, but there were gaps here and there along the whole length of the pool. Deep, empty spaces filled with darkness.

Dana didn't see anyone.

But she suddenly realized how *alone* they were.

All by themselves in the spa. Tuck's house deserted. Wooded hills all around them.

Nowhere to run for help.

Nobody to hear them scream.

'I don't see him,' Dana said.

'Me neither. Not anymore.

'Maybe he left.'

'I don't know. He could be anywhere.'

'Well . . . not *anywhere*.'

'Damn near,' Tuck said.

'Where *was* he?'

'Okay. Look straight across at the corner of the pool, then go to the right about fifteen feet.'

Dana followed the instructions.

'See what looks like a Christmas tree?'

'Yeah.'

'He was in that dark place just to the right of it.'

Dana found the dark place. She nodded. 'Guess he isn't there now.'

'Why don't you go over and take a good look around?' Tuck suggested.

'Very funny. Maybe we'd better go inside.'

'Shit. Yeah. We'd better.'

'Let's just put down our glasses and leave everything right here.'
They both set down their glasses.
'Now what?' Tuck asked.
'Run like hell for the back door.'
'Think so? Maybe we should just act like nothing's wrong.'
'Why kid around?' Dana asked. 'Any second now, he might come after us. He might be sneaking closer even while we're discussing this.'
Tuck grimaced slightly. Her eyes flicked toward Dana.
Dana saw fear in them.
It *hurt* to find fear in Tuck's eyes, which usually showed wry humor and mischief and moxie. It made her want to hurt the person who had put it there.
'Don't worry,' she said, and gave Tuck's shoulder a gentle squeeze. 'I'll be right beside you. Nothing's going to happen.'
'Okay,' Tuck said. She nodded briskly. She still had the fear in her eyes.
'Ready?' Dana asked.
'You bet.'
'Let's hit it.'
They scurried to their feet, whirled around and ran, water flying off their legs, their bare feet smacking the concrete. Dana dashed around one side of the table, Tuck around the other. They converged beyond it and raced for the sliding door.
Realizing they might both reach it at the same moment, Dana slowed down. Tuck rushed ahead of her, jerked open the door and lunged out of the way to let Dana enter first.
Dana ran in.
Tuck lurched in behind her, pulling the door. It rolled shut with a heavy thud that seemed to shake the house. Tuck snapped down the locking lever.
Side by side, gasping for breath, they both stared out.
Except for the steam and the shifting, rippling surface of the pool, nothing moved.
'Well,' Tuck said. 'Guess he's not coming.'
'Doesn't look like it. Are you okay?'
'Sure. Fine.'
'Did you see who it was?'
'Nah.'
'What'd he look like?'
'Just . . . I don't know. I'm not sure what I saw. Part of an arm, maybe. I just caught a glimpse of it.'
'Are you sure it belonged to a *person*?'

Tuck turned her head and frowned at Dana. 'No, it was Bigfoot.'

'I didn't mean it like that.'

Suddenly tossing a smile at Dana, she said, 'Nah, couldn't have been Bigfoot. Wasn't hairy. Might've been a *beast*, though.'

'Sure.'

'The skin looked *awfully* white.'

'It was a *bare* arm?'

'Yeah,' Tuck said. 'Whoever he was, I don't think he had a shirt on. I think his shoulder was bare. Hmm. Maybe he was naked.' She reached for the door handle. 'I'll ask him in.'

'Sure you will.'

Tuck let go of the handle.

For a while, they didn't talk. They stood side by side, staring out.

Then Dana said, 'Do you have any idea who it might've been?'

'Not a clue.'

'I guess we can't go back out there.'

'You know what? Keep an eye on things. I'm calling the cops.'

Dana felt a sudden dropping sensation in her stomach.

Calling the cops.

Legs dripping, Tuck walked over to the lamp table at the far end of the couch.

She picked up the phone.

'You think it's *that* serious?' Dana asked.

'Don't you?'

'I guess so.'

Tuck tapped in three numbers.

'9–1–1?' Dana asked.

'You bet.'

'Jeez.'

This was like calling for an ambulance: an admission that the situation might be drastic.

Dana turned away to keep an eye on the pool area.

She saw nobody.

If he's out there, he's sure keeping out of sight.

'Hello?' Tuck said. After a brief pause, she said, 'Yes, I guess it's an emergency. We have a prowler behind the house. My friend and I were out by the pool, and I caught him spying on us from the bushes.' Pause. 'Tucker. Lynn Tucker . . . Oh, hi, George. Didn't recognize your voice . . . Yeah, we're fine. We ran into the house and locked the door, but we're afraid he might still be out there . . . No, he doesn't seem to be coming after us. Not yet, anyway.' She listened for a moment, then gave the house address. After another pause, she said, 'I don't have any idea who it is. I didn't see the face . . . White. And I think it's a male, but I really didn't get that good of a look . . . I don't know. I guess I'd say he's probably young. Not a kid, but not an old man . . . I only saw his *arm and shoulder*, George . . . Well, average size, I guess. No, cancel that. I don't know. I guess he seemed to be fairly large. But like I said, I couldn't see much. He might've *seemed* bigger than he really is . . . I don't know, maybe six feet something . . . How should I know? Based on a glimpse of his arm? . . . Well, how about a hundred and eighty, two hundred? Do you *have* to put something down? I really haven't got a clue. Can't you just send someone over? . . . Wearing? Nothing that I could see . . . Well, I can't say he was *naked*. All I saw was his *arm*, George. And it was bare, so I'm pretty sure he wasn't wearing any shirt . . . Nothing more I can think of . . . I don't know. At the moment, he isn't trying to kick the door in . . . *Isn't* . . . Okay, thanks. That's great . . . You, too, George. So long.'

She hung up.

Dana turned around. Tuck shook her head. 'That was my old pal, George. He's sending someone over.'

'Did he say how long it'd be?'

'Nope. He didn't say who he's sending, either. Wish I'd asked. I know everyone on the force. Their shifts change, though, so . . .' She shook her head. 'Hope it doesn't turn out to be Cochran. He's such an asshole. Anyway, I don't know about you, but *I'm* getting dressed. In case it *is* Cochran.'

'Why don't you go first?' Dana suggested. 'I'll keep watch on things down here.'

'Okay. Yell if anything happens.'

With that, Tuck whirled around and ran for the stairway. She rushed up the stairs, taking them two at a time.

Dana turned to the glass door.

The pool area still appeared to be deserted. But someone might easily be hiding in the bushes and trees.

Watching me.

Anyone spying from the other side of the pool would have a bright, clear view of Dana standing at the glass door.

She suddenly felt exposed, as if she were on display in her thin, clinging swimsuit. It was clammy against her skin. Chilly water trickled down her legs. She realized that she was shivering slightly. Without looking down at herself, she knew her skin was rumpled with goose-bumps, her nipples rigid and jutting out.

She was tempted to shut the drapes.

If I do that, I won't be able to see out. He might sneak up to the door.

Let him look at me all he wants. So what?

At the sound of Tuck thumping down the stairs, she turned around. Tuck now wore a bulky gray sweatshirt and white shorts that reached down almost to her knees. She was barefoot. In her right hand, swinging low by her side, was a very large revolver.

'A gun?' Dana asked.

'Not just *any* gun,' Tuck said. Striding toward her, she raised the weapon and pointed it toward the ceiling. 'This-here is your basic Smith & Wesson .44 magnum with an eight-inch barrel.' Squinting and snarling like Clint Eastwood, she said, '*Thee* most powerful handgun in the world.'

'Jesus,' Dana muttered.

'Nope. Dirty Harry. It's my dad's. And it's loaded with hollow points.' She twirled the barrel. 'Just in case our visitor makes a try for us before the cavalry arrives.'

'Don't let "the cavalry" see it. They might shoot *you*.'

'Yeah, I know. I'm not a dope. You can go on upstairs and get dressed now, if . . .'

The doorbell rang.

They both jumped.

'Too late,' Tuck said. 'Go get the door and I'll hide the cannon.'

Leaving Tuck behind, Dana hurried out of the room and down the short hallway to the foyer. At the door, she called, 'Who is it?'

'Police.'

She opened the main door. A few steps back from the screen door stood a woman in uniform. She held a long, black flashlight down by her side, but it wasn't turned on.

'Hello, officer,' Dana said.

The woman peered at her. 'Having some trouble here? A prowler?'

'Right.' Dana swung open the screen door. 'Come on in.'

The cop entered. She appeared to be older than Dana – maybe in her late twenties or early thirties. She was Dana's size, had a similar figure, and was extremely attractive. Though her eyes were a striking, pale blue color, they had a tough, ironic look. Her pale blond hair was cut very short.

A man-style haircut.

Dana suddenly felt self-conscious in her revealing swimsuit. She blushed as the cop looked her over.

A nameplate pinned above the uniform's right breast pocket read, CHANEY.

'You must be the lifeguard around here,' officer Chaney said. Coming up with a lopsided smile, she held out her hand.

'Right. I'm Dana Lake.' They shook hands.

'I'm Eve . . .'

'*Of Destruction!*' Tuck called, striding into the foyer without her revolver. 'How's it going, Eve?'

'Hey, Lynn.'

'You've met Dana?'

'Yep.'

'She's my old friend from LA,' Tuck explained. 'We're holding down the fort while Dad and Janice are off on their cruise.' To Dana, she said, 'This is Eve Chaney. We lucked out. She's the best damn cop in Malcasa Point, maybe in the country.'

Eve smiled. 'I'm not really the best,' she said. 'Just the most dangerous.'

'That's how come I call her Eve of Destruction,' Tuck explained. To Eve, she said, 'If I'd known it was you, I wouldn't have bothered hiding the forty-four. I was afraid it might be Cochran or some other jerk.'

'You lucked out. Cochran's on the day watch. So, what's going on? Trouble with a prowler?'

'Right. Out behind the pool.'

'Let's go,' Eve said. She stepped between them and led the way.

Dana hurried after her, eyes on the officer's back.

The pale blue blouse of Eve's uniform had short sleeves. It was wrinkled, probably from being pressed against the seatback of the patrol car. The way the blouse lay against her back, Dana could see that she wasn't wearing a protective vest.

Maybe cops don't get shot in this neck of the woods.

Just occasionally get torn up by a monster.

A Kevlar vest seemed to be about the *only* equipment Eve lacked. Her black leather belt was loaded. As she walked through the house, hips shifting with each stride, leather creaked and squeaked, metal rattled. She sounded as if she were wearing a horse saddle.

'How long since you saw him?' she asked.

Tuck shrugged. 'Ten minutes, maybe?'

'Something like that,' Dana agreed.

'And you don't have any idea who it might've been?'

'All I saw was an arm.'

Stopping a few paces from the glass door, Eve asked, 'Where was he?'

'Over there.' Tuck pointed. 'The other side of the pool. In the trees. But I don't think he's there anymore.'

At the sliding door, Eve stopped and switched off the lock. 'You two wait here. I'll take a look around.' She rolled the door open. With a glance back, she said, 'Go ahead and lock this after I'm out.'

'You're going out there alone?' Dana asked.

'Sure.'

'Be careful, okay?'

'You bet.'

Frowning, Tuck said, 'Maybe we oughta come with you. I can grab the forty-four, and . . .'

'No, that's all right. Thanks anyway. Just stay put.'

Chapter Twenty-One

Eve

Eve Chaney stepped outside, slid the door shut, then walked toward the pool.

'That takes guts,' Dana said.

'Eve's got 'em. I wasn't kidding when I said she's the best cop in town. Hell, she makes the others look like a bunch of sissies. She'll do *anything*. You wouldn't believe all the commendations she has. She's actually *shot* five or six bad guys.'

'Look at that,' Dana said, watching Eve through the glass door. 'She doesn't even have her gun out.'

A few strides away from the pool, Eve stopped walking. Her head moved slowly from side to side. Then she swung to the right, broke into a jog and hurried toward the end of the pool.

She runs like a guy, Dana thought.

Off to the right, beyond the pool's apron of well-lit concrete, Eve switched her flashlight on. With its strong beam slanting out ahead of her, she hunched over and ducked into the foliage.

'She isn't wearing any vest,' Dana said.

'Never does,' Tuck said. 'Which I think is stupid. I've told her so. I mean, plenty of other cops wear them *all* the time. She won't have anything to do with the things. She says they get in the way. And they're hot. And they hide her girlish figure.'

Dana chuckled. 'She said that?'

'She's sort of a wise-ass.'

'Like you. No wonder you think she's so great.'

'She worries me, though. I mean, she's *always* taking unnecessary risks. Like this thing about the Kevlar vests. Would it *kill* her to wear one?'

'Maybe she thinks she's invincible.'

'Maybe. I don't know what it is. She drives me up the wall. I mean, she's very smart and dedicated and everything, but . . . what the hell is *taking* her so long?'

'It hasn't been all that long,' Dana said.

'She thinks she's so tough.'

'Apparently, she *is* tough. From what you said . . .'

'But someone might get her from behind, you know?' Tuck grabbed the door handle.

'She told us to stay here.'

'She might be in trouble. What if she yells for help? We won't even be able to hear her.'

Tuck slid the door open. The night air came in, wrapping Dana with its chill.

Nobody was calling for help. Dana heard only the hissing, bubbling sounds of the spa and a few distant squeals that she supposed were coming from seagulls.

Tuck stepped out onto the patio.

'Get back in here!'

Not even glancing back, Tuck simply shook her head.

Dana stepped out and stood next to her. 'She *told* us to stay inside.'

'Yep. So what's she gonna do, arrest us?'

'Well, since we're out here anyway . . .' Dana stopped talking and walked away from Tuck's side.

'Where're you going? You'd better get back here.'

Ignoring Tuck, she strolled over to the table. She lifted her robe off the back of a chair and put it on. The soft fabric felt cozy. She was glad to be warm again, and glad to have her body covered, hidden away from anyone who might be out there watching. After tying her belt, she picked up Tuck's robe and both towels.

As she approached the door, Tuck gave her a peeved look.

'I was freezing,' Dana explained. 'Anyway, you're the one who wanted to come outside.'

'I didn't mean we should go *wandering around*.'

'I didn't wander far. Anyway, I'm back.'

After taking Tuck's robe and towels into the house, she came back out and stood beside her.

'I'm just a little rattled by all this,' Tuck said.

'I know. Me, too.'

'Isn't enough that somebody messes around with the Ethel exhibit. Isn't enough that we end up with *three* missing players and have to go on a search. And we've *still* got somebody missing. I mean, *that'd* be a bad day all by itself. That'd be a *shitty* day. But now we've gotta have some kind of *creep* lurking around the house with God-only-knows-*what* on his sick, perverted mind.'

'Maybe it's just a secret admirer,' Dana said.

'Like I just said, a sick, perverted creep. What the hell is taking Eve so long?'

'She's probably just doing a thorough search.'

'She shouldn't be taking *this* long.'

'I'm sure she's fine. Do you think it might all be connected?'

'Connected?' Tuck asked. 'What?'

'What you were just talking about. Maybe the guy who screwed around with Ethel had something to do with the missing tape player. And maybe he came over here.'

'I don't know,' Tuck said. 'I guess it's possible.'

'Maybe we should tell Eve about that stuff.'

In a half-joking voice, Tuck said, 'You mean, if she isn't dead?'

'She's not dead. Maybe she'll have some ideas about . . .'

'Let's just deal with one problem at a time, okay? Eve doesn't have to know about our troubles at Beast House. She might want to start an investigation. Next thing you know, *everybody'd* find out. It's nobody else's business.'

'If a customer disappeared . . .'

'Nobody disappeared. Not necessarily. We're just short one tape player, that's all.'

'But . . .'

'Nobody was looking for anyone and there weren't any leftover cars in the lot. That's pretty strong proof that we don't have a missing person. I know, maybe he went on the tour alone. Maybe he parked on the street somewhere, or walked over. For now, though, we don't have any good reason to start a major fuss about the situation. I don't want to go whining to the cops every time there's little glitch in things.'

'You called the cops tonight.'

'A prowler lurking by the pool is a *big* glitch. *For God's sake, where's Eve?*'

'She's probably . . .'

'*EVE!*' Tuck shouted.

No answer came.

'Oh, God,' Tuck muttered. 'Something's happened to her.'

'Maybe she's . . .'

'EVE! DAMN IT, WHERE ARE YOU?'

Over beyond the far, left-hand corner of the pool, Eve trudged out of the bushes. She was hunched over, her head down. When she stepped onto the concrete, she straightened up. 'What's the trouble?' she called.

'Are you okay?' Tuck asked.

'Fine. What's the trouble? Did you see him?'

'No.'

'What're you doing outside?'

'We got worried about you.'

Eve smirked and shook her head. Then she shut off her flashlight and came walking around the pool. As she neared Dana and Tuck, she said, 'Let's go back into the house.'

They went in without waiting for Eve to arrive. She entered after them, slid the door shut and locked it. Not saying a word, she turned her back to them and started to shut the curtains.

'Uh-oh,' Tuck said. 'I'm not sure I like the way this is going.'

Eve faced her and said, 'I know *I* don't.'

'Yuck,' Tuck said.

'Somebody was back there, all right.'

The words came as no surprise to Dana. After all, Tuck had *said* she'd seen someone. But Dana felt stunned, anyway, to hear a police officer confirm it. She felt a cold heaviness in the pit of her stomach.

'Did you see him?' Tuck asked.

Eve shook her head. 'Afraid not.'

'What *did* you find?'

'He'd tramped stuff down pretty well. In some places, the weeds were mashed flat against the ground. I think he must've spent quite a while back there.'

'Shit,' Tuck muttered.

'Anything else?' Dana asked.

'Not really. I can't even say with absolute certainty that it was a person. Might've been some kind of large animal.'

'I saw an arm,' Tuck reminded her. 'And shoulder.'

'I'm not doubting you,' Eve said. 'If you say it was a person, it probably was. I didn't see anything to suggest it *wasn't*. My guess is, you had a voyeur. He found himself a nice hiding place in the bushes to watch you two cavort in the swimming pool.'

'The spa,' Tuck said. 'We were in the hot spa.'

A smile broke out on Eve's face. 'Glad to hear that. I'd hate to think of anyone in the *swimming* pool on a night like this. Either way, though, it looks as if you had an audience.'

'Terrific,' Tuck said. 'At least we kept our suits on.'

'Even though it was optional,' Dana added.

'From the looks of things,' Eve said, 'I don't think he's a regular visitor. It's pretty thick and wild back there. Nothing was *worn down*. All the trampled places looked fresh. So this might've been his first night. That's the good news.'

'And the bad?' Dana asked.

Eve let out a gruff laugh. 'Where do I start?'

'Oh, that's comforting,' Tuck said.

'I gave the area a pretty good search, and he seems to be gone. But he might *not* be gone. Like I said, it's really *thick* back there. He might not've left, at all. He might be in there right now, hiding.'

'That *is* comforting.'

Eve shrugged a shoulder. 'I'm not here to comfort you, Lynn.'

'And why not?'

Eve laughed. 'Shut up and listen, okay?'

'Yes, Officer Chaney.'

'This is serious business.'

'I know.'

'Your prowler might *not* be gone. There's no way to be sure, one way or another. That's part of the bad news.'

'More to come,' Tuck said.

'Plenty. If he *has* left, he's very likely to return tomorrow night, or the night after tomorrow . . . Any time he gets the urge, he might just drop by in hopes of catching you in your swimsuits . . . or out of them.'

'Oh,' Tuck said, 'this is getting more wonderful every moment.'

'It gets better.'

'I was afraid of that.'

'There comes a time when most voyeurs get the urge to do more than watch.'

'I was afraid you might say that,' Tuck said.

Grimacing, Dana said, 'In other words, he might come for us?'

'No pun intended,' Tuck added.

Eve shook her head. 'Whoever this guy is,' she said, 'he probably has fantasies about raping you. One or the other of you, or both. The next step might be an attempt to *carry out* his fantasies.'

'Sounds reasonable,' Dana admitted. 'What should we do?'

'Be very careful. Make sure you always keep the doors and windows secured. Keep all the curtains shut so he can't see into the house. Don't go outside alone. Be especially careful at night, but keep your guard up all the time. Daylight's no guarantee of safety. I would certainly forget about using the pool or spa for a while. And Lynn, dig out your revolver and keep it handy.'

'So now we've got a Peeping Tom running our lives,' Tuck muttered.

'I'm just suggesting you take precautions.'

'Yeah. Hide indoors. Don't use the pool or spa. Man! This really sucks! What next, put bars on the windows?'

'I wouldn't recommend that,' Eve said. 'I'm just saying that you need to be especially careful for a while.'

'How *long* a while?' Tuck asked.

'We'll have to play it by ear.' Eve shrugged. 'The guy *might* not come back at all. I mean, he probably knows you're on to him, so maybe he'll move on to safer pastures. Or he might figure you're worth a little extra risk. Two gals for the price of one. And you're both a couple of babes.'

'Gee whiz, Eve . . .'

'You know it, I know it, *he* knows it. You're very good-looking gals, and he has the hots for you. He's already seen you in your swimsuits. That was probably a big treat, but what he *really* wants is to see you naked. So he'll most likely keep coming back for a period of time. Don't give him anything to see. Eventually, he'll figure it's useless. Then he'll probably go away and look elsewhere for his kicks.'

'Probably?' Tuck asked.

'I'm just giving you educated guesses,' Eve explained. 'The fact is, we don't even know for sure he is a Peeping Tom. Maybe he was out there for some other reason.'

'Such as?' Dana asked.

Eve shrugged. 'Could be just about anything.'

'Such as?'

'A thief. Maybe he was back there casing the house, and you just happened to come out so he stuck around for the show.'

'We converted him to voyeurism,' Tuck said.

They all smiled at that one.

'Now he'll keep coming back,' Tuck added.

Eve's smile slipped away. 'There's another possibility about the guy. You might not like to hear this, but . . .'

'You mean *this* one won't uplift our spirits?' Tuck asked.

'It's a little *more* on the scary side.'

'More scary than a thief or a Peeping Tom?'

'Chances are, he *is* a Peeping Tom. I'd bet on it. But you really have to consider the possibility that the guy . . . well, he might be *after* one or the other of you. He might be a stalker.'

'Yeah, that's what we want to hear.'

'You've both probably got guys falling for you all the time.'

'It happens,' Tuck said.

Dana nodded.

'Your prowler might be one of them,' Eve said. 'You get a guy who develops a mad crush on you. For one reason or another, he figures he doesn't stand a chance with you. So he goes nutty and forms an obsession.'

'Love it when that happens,' Tuck said.

'Pain in the butt,' Dana said.

'And it *can* be dangerous,' Eve explained. 'I mean, a lot of guys'll pester the hell out of you and make nuisances out of themselves, but if one actually goes to the extreme of following you around and *spying* on you, then you've got a major problem. He isn't just *longing* for you, he's *coming* for you. A guy like that can be *extremely* dangerous. He might even kill you.'

Nodding, Dana said, 'If he can't have us, nobody can.'

'Exactly.'

'Well, everyone,' Tuck said, 'I'm cheered up now.'

'The thing is,' Eve said, 'you might know who it is.' Glancing from Dana to Tuck, she asked, 'Can you think of anyone who might be obsessed with you? Anyone who seems to be watching you all the time or following you around? Maybe a fellow worker? Or somebody taking the tour?'

Dana thought of Clyde. She thought of Dennis and Arnold. Even Warren crossed her mind. But none of them seemed likely. She shook her head.

'I can't think of anyone,' Tuck said.

'Is there someone you've noticed taking the tour more than once?'

'That happens all the time,' Tuck said. 'People are always coming back for another visit. Hell, we've got regulars.'

'Might be one of those. You *think* he's coming back to see Beast House over and over again, but he's *actually* coming back so he can keep his eyes on *you*.'

'I guess that's possible,' Tuck admitted. 'But there're so many of them, I wouldn't know . . . Besides, you said this was probably the guy's first visit here.'

'Looked that way.'

'Chances are, then, he didn't come because of me. I mean, I'm *always* around. Why did he wait till tonight? He probably came because of Dana. This was *her* first day at Beast House.'

Eve looked at her. 'Your first day, huh?'

'Yep.'

'Anybody seem to be taking special interest in you?'

'Not really. Clyde, I suppose. He tried to ask me out for dinner tonight, and I turned him down. I don't want to get him into any trouble, though. I mean, this could've been *anyone*.'

'It doesn't seem like Clyde's style,' Tuck said.

'You never know,' Eve said. 'I wouldn't put much of anything past that guy.'

'You know him, huh?' Dana asked.

'You bet,' Eve said. 'A real prince.'

Tuck, suddenly grinning, said, 'Officer Chaney, here, is one of the precious few who *hasn't* gotten nailed by Clyde.'

'He's afraid of me,' Eve said. She showed her teeth. 'I can't imagine *why*. Anyway, aside from Clyde, was there anyone else today who seemed to be especially interested in you?'

'There was Warren. We talked for a while. He seemed really nice, but . . .'

'He is nice,' Eve said. 'I can't see him doing something like this.'

'Even if he had the urge,' Tuck said, 'he wouldn't have the guts.'

'He *is* pretty timid,' Eve agreed. 'Anybody else? Maybe a guy hanging around you while you were on duty?'

'Not really. A lot of people sort of . . . you know, gave me a second look. But I didn't notice anyone really *watching* me.'

'Well, keep an eye out for that sort of thing. Both of you. Tomorrow, pay close attention to anyone who seems too interested, maybe asks you a lot of questions, or just hangs around and stares at you. Anything at all suspicious. Okay? In the meantime, I'll write up a report on the situation. You take the precautions I told you about, and everything'll turn out fine.'

'Peachy,' Tuck said.

'I know it's a pain in the ass.'

'It's the way things go, nowadays,' Tuck said. 'The good guys have to lock themselves up, and the bad guys rule the night. The American way.'

'I hate to think that's how it works in this town,' Eve said. 'Believe me, I don't like it any better than you do. It's an *affront* to me. But I can't put down a bad guy till I know who he is. For now, you two should just be careful and lay low. I'll do what I can to end the situation.'

'We'll be careful,' Dana said.

'Sure,' Tuck said.

Eve unbuttoned a breast pocket, reached in and pulled out a business card. 'I'll give you my home phone number,' she said. She took out a pen. Holding the card in her open hand, she wrote her number on the back. 'You don't want someone like Cochran coming over. If anything develops when I'm not on duty, try me at home.'

'Will do,' Tuck said. 'Thanks.'

Eve handed the card to her. 'Okay. I'd better get going. You two be careful. Keep me informed. And keep your Smith handy, Lynn.' She faced Dana. 'Do you have a weapon?'

'Look at her size,' Tuck said.

Eve and Dana both gave her dirty looks.

Smiling at Dana, Eve said, 'A firearm. Do you have one?'

'No.'

'You should, you know.'

'Well . . . I guess I could go to the store tomorrow . . .'

'No good. There's a fifteen-day waiting period.' To Tuck, she said, 'You only have the one, don't you?'

'Afraid so.'

'Well . . .' Dropping to a crouch, Eve raised the cuff of her right trouser leg. A black, fabric holster was strapped around her ankle. She ripped open a velcro strap, pulled out a small pistol, then stood up and held it out to Dana. 'You can borrow this one for a while. It's a Sig Sauer .380 semi-automatic.'

'I can't take your gun,' Dana protested.

'It's just my backup piece,' Eve said. 'I've got plenty of others. A girl can never have too many guns. Now, do you know how to use a weapon like this?'

Chapter Twenty-Two

Ice

'Don't be such a gloomy gus, Owie,' Monica said, and squeezed his hand.

'I'm just tired,' he said. 'We've been on our feet for hours.'

'Aw, poor boy.'

'I think I've got blisters.'

'Well, we're almost home.'

Don't I wish, Owen thought. But it was nearly midnight and they weren't almost *home*; after spending hours at Pier 39, they were walking along the Embarcadaro on their way back to the hotel. The hotel was *not* home. Home, back in Los Angeles, was a one-room apartment where Owen lived *alone*.

Without Monica.

It still hurt him inside to realize that he'd allowed her to ruin the Beast House tour.

I should've gone ahead and finished it and the hell with her.

Some sort of damn female power game she was playing.

She'd won, too. And Beast House had lost.

I lost, he thought. I caved in, and she wrecked it for me.

After quitting the tour that morning, Owen had tried to remain pleasant in spite of his frustration and disappointment. He couldn't quite bring himself to be the life of the party, but at least he managed to smile and speak to Monica and pretend he still liked her.

At a restaurant on Front Street, he indulged himself in a Bloody Mary. Monica, between sips of white wine, tried to patch up the damage. 'I honestly didn't mean for *you* to leave,' she explained.

He knew she was lying. People *always* lied after such preliminaries as 'honestly,' or 'to tell you the absolute truth.'

She'd meant for him to quit the tour, all right. And she was no doubt secretly overjoyed that she'd wielded such power over him.

'I don't see *why* you didn't finish it,' she said. 'That was silly. I was perfectly willing to wait for you outside.'

'Yeah, well.'

'Why don't we go back after lunch?'

He shook his head.

'You definitely should. I mean it, Owie. It would be perfectly all right with me. I'll just wait outside for you.'

'I honestly don't care if I see the rest of it,' he said. 'I saw enough. It wasn't that great, anyway.'

'*I'll* say. What a ripoff! But I think you should go back, anyway. I don't want to be the one stopping you. I don't want you blaming *me* that you missed the rest of the tour.'

And who else would I blame?

'It's not your fault,' he said.

'I tell you what,' Monica said, widening her violet eyes. 'If you're sure you don't want to finish the house tour, we'll go to the museum after lunch. How about that? I mean, I'd sort of counted on going to the beach, but we can go to the museum instead. Would you like that?'

'Let's just go to the beach.'

'You really *should* see the museum. We came all the way out here.'

'No, that's okay.'

'Welllll . . . it's up to you.'

'The beach'll be fine.'

He meant it, too. He didn't *want* to visit the Beast House Museum. Not with Monica. She would be standing by his side, probably holding his hand, *ruining* it.

After lunch, they headed for the beach. On the way there, they followed a sandy, unpaved road that led them past the windowless Kutch house. Owen gave the house a few glances through the chainlink fence, but he didn't even try to appreciate it.

How could he appreciate *anything* with Monica at his side?

As it drew closer to departure time, they headed back to Front Street and boarded the bus. Monica took a window seat. Owen sat beside her.

He didn't try to look out the windows for a final glimpse of Beast House or the Kutch House. As the bus pulled away and drove slowly through town, he stared at the back of the seat in front of him. He didn't even turn his head for a look at the Welcome Inn, which had also been made famous by the *Horror* books and movies.

She ruined it for me. All of it.

Owen had a tightness in his throat.

When'll I ever make it back again?

Maybe the place won't even be here by the time I ever get back. Things happen. It might get shut down for some reason. It might burn to the ground.

I might keel over dead or get hit by a car.

You never know.

This might've been my one and only chance in my whole life to really experience this place.

Thanks a bunch, Monica.

Somewhere past the Welcome Inn, the bus turned around. 'We'll be making one more pass through town,' Patty announced into her microphone. 'It'll give you a final opportunity to see the sights and snap a quick photo or two before we head over to the Highway One.'

Final opportunity.

On the way back through town, Owen kept his eyes forward.

Monica kept her nose to the window.

As they left Malcasa Point behind, she smiled at him. Patting his thigh, she said, 'Maybe we'll have to come back again sometime and really do the place right.'

'Good idea,' Owen said.

Soon, Monica scooted down in her seat, folded her hands in her lap, and shut her eyes.

That's a very good idea, Owen thought. Take a nap. That's when you're at your best.

He leaned out into the aisle for a look at Patty. She was standing up

front, her back to Owen, bent over slightly and peering out the
windshield.

I bet she isn't a bitch like Monica, he thought. She seems so nice.

How about the other one?

Dana.

I wonder if Patty knows her. She must.

Why not go up and ask her?

Oh, sure.

He imagined himself saying, 'Hey, Patty? I was just wondering. I met
a guide named Dana today. Do you know her?' And Patty answers, 'Oh,
sure, she's my best friend.' And Owen says . . . what?

What do I say then? he wondered.

Doesn't matter, he thought. I'm not about to go up and talk to her.
And I'm never going to see Dana again. Even if I *do* get back to Malcasa
some day, she'll probably be long gone.

I'll never see her again.

He remembered how Dana had looked in the sunlight when he was
handing over his tape player. Her golden hair blowing softly in the
breeze, her skin tawny and smooth, her eyes deep and blue and full of
gentleness and understanding. He remembered her friendly voice.

*There are gals like Dana in this world, and I'm stuck with Monica. It isn't
fair.*

It hurt, thinking about the unfairness.

*Stop thinking about it. And don't think about Monica. Forget her. Just
think about Dana. Picture Dana. Forget everything else.*

Settling down in the seat, he closed his eyes and let his mind linger
on Dana. The images calmed him. She was so beautiful and sweet, and
she seemed to like him, too. Soon, he pictured himself unfastening a
button in the middle of her uniform blouse, slipping his hand inside
and discovering that she wasn't wearing a bra. He filled his hand with
the smooth bare skin of her breast.

When he woke up, the bus was nearing the toll booths of the Golden
Gate Bridge. He felt very fine – well rested and somewhat aroused – but
then he saw Monica slouched beside him and his good feelings ended.

Luckily, she was still asleep.

But she was wide awake and perky by the time the bus stopped at
their hotel.

Owen led the way up the aisle.

As they neared the front, Patty smiled and said, 'Hope you enjoyed
your visit to Beast House. Come and see it again sometime.'

'I will,' Owen said. 'Thank you.' Then he handed her a folded five-
dollar bill and added, 'I really enjoyed your part of the tour.'

'Well, thank you very much. Have a good evening, now, both of you.'

Monica, behind him, said nothing.

After the bus pulled away, Monica said, 'What did you give her?'

'A little tip.'

'How generous.'

'She was really good. You know, her talk on the way out.'

'That's what she gets paid for. You didn't have to *tip* her. My God, you'd think you were *made* of money.'

It's my money.

He thought it, but knew better than to say it.

To change the subject, he asked, 'Should we go up to the room for a while, or . . ?'

'And waste *more* time? We haven't done *anything* yet. Let's go look in some stores.'

For the next two hours, they roamed through shops along Fisherman's Wharf, in the Cannery and Ghiradelli Square.

Finally, Owen asked, 'Are you getting hungry yet?'

'Oh, I could eat any time.'

'Maybe we should start looking for a nice restaurant.'

She nodded. 'Anyplace would be fine with me.'

'Well . . .' He shrugged.

'How about Alioto's?' Monica asked.

'Okay, sure.'

They walked to the restaurant. After a brief wait, they were seated at a window table where they had a fine view of San Francisco Bay. Monica seemed delighted by it. Owen didn't care, but he agreed that it was beautiful.

He started with a Mai Tai. He munched on sour dough bread. Then he drank a second Mai Tai with his meal of crab legs. Monica sipped white wine and ate rare prime rib.

She chatted happily, apparently enjoying herself.

Good for her, Owen thought.

And he wondered what it might be like to have dinner at a place like this with someone like Dana. Or even Patty. Or even . . . damn near anyone but Monica.

What the hell am I doing with her?

'What would you like to do now?' he asked when they were done with dinner.

'What do *you* want to do?' Monica asked.

Go back to Malcasa Point, he thought.

But he said, 'Well, there's a *Ripley's Believe It or Not* place we walked by last night. How about paying it a visit?'

'Oh, it's probably full of gross stuff. I've had enough of that for one day, thank you very much. Let's go back to Pier 39.'

'Okay.'

'We missed a lot of things last night,' Monica pointed out.

'Well, we can go back. That'll be fine.'

So back they went to Pier 39.

There, Owen stayed by Monica's side while she explored every shop. In each place, she seemed to look at every item. At the Christmas store, she bought a golden ornament depicting the San Francisco skyline. At the magnet store, she bought a Golden Gate Bridge refrigerator magnet. At the shell store, she bought a little seashell man driving a little seashell car. 'Isn't it just adorable?' she asked.

'Very nice,' Owen said.

Later, they stood around and waited ten minutes for a stage show to start. The performer, however, turned out to be Wilma the Wonder Girl – the same juggler/comic they'd watched *last* night. 'Oh, God,' Owen said. 'I don't think I can watch her again.'

Monica cast him a pouty look. 'Aren't *we* in a fine mood?'

'Well, she was a smart-ass, abrasive, and not funny. And we've already *seen* her act. It'll probably be exactly the same, except for whatever poor stooge she drags out of the audience to humiliate *this* time.'

'If you don't want to stay for the show, just say so.'

'I'd rather not. I'm really getting tired. Can't we just go back to the hotel?'

'We can't go yet. You don't want to miss the seals, do you?'

'They're probably the same seals we saw last night.'

'Aren't they *darling*? Let's go watch them. Just for a little while, okay?'

'Sure. Okay.'

'They're just so cute.'

So Owen walked with Monica to the far end of the pier. There, they turned and followed the noise of barks and roars to the viewing area.

Out in the water a short distance away were hundreds of sea lions. Though they weren't directly illuminated, plenty of light reached them from the pier. Quite a few people stood at the wooden rail to watch them. Owen and Monica found an empty space at the rail.

'Aren't they just *wonderful*?' Monica said.

'Yeah, they're great.'

She squeezed his hand.

They stood there watching.

Owen's feet hurt, but he didn't complain. He just stood there and watched the sea lions.

And watched them.

And watched them.

This is what Monica wants to do, so we'll do it till she's done. I'm not going to ruin it for her the way she ruins everything for me.

Not many of the sea lions were swimming around. Most seemed to be piled on the numerous platforms, snuggling against each other – and on top of each other – resting or sleeping. Once in a while, one would slide off into the water. Sometimes, a sea lion would get tired of swimming, climb aboard a platform and nudge its way into the crowd. Every so often, a quarrel would seem to take place – two of the creatures darting their snouts at each other and barking. Mostly, though, nothing much happened.

This is such a thrill, Owen thought.

I can stand here with Monica for an hour and stare at a bunch of boring seals, but she won't even stick it out with me to the end of the Beast House tour. How is that fair?

'I guess I'm about ready to go,' Monica finally said. 'How about you?'

'I guess so.'

She squeezed his hand. As they started walking away, she said, 'We'll have to come back and see what they do in the daytime.'

'That's a good idea,' he said.

'I could watch them for hours, couldn't you?'

'I think we just did.'

Monica tossed back her head, barked out a laugh, then said, 'Oh, you're such a silly.'

Owen tried not to grimace as he trudged along the Embarcadaro with Monica. He probably wasn't the only person with sore feet. The walkway was crowded with other couples and families heading back toward the main area of Fisherman's Wharf – probably going to hotels or parked cars – now that most of Pier 39 had closed for the night.

The crowd walked a gauntlet of beggars/performers: a man who stood motionless on top of a box, apparently doing his impression of a statue; a lone saxophone player; a legless guy with a cardboard sign announcing he was a disabled Vietnam veteran; a trio of bongo players; the traditional blind man with dog; the crippled woman with baby; a fat woman in dirty white leotards who danced like a ballerina and appeared to be quite mad.

Owen glanced furtively at these people. He wished they would go away and leave everyone alone.

Hoping to escape from them, he and Monica crossed the road. They ran into a few beggars, anyway. And a stumbling drunk. And someone passed out in the entryway of a closed swimsuit boutique. But there didn't seem to be so many on this side of the road.

No matter where you go, Owen thought, you can't get away from them.

At last, he and Monica arrived at their hotel.

And finally they reached their room.

Owen pulled off his shoes and flopped onto the bed.

'Not so fast,' Monica said. 'We need ice.'

Ice. For their cream sodas. Monica absolutely *had* to drink a cream soda every night before bedtime.

Yesterday, after checking into the hotel, they'd immediately gone in search of a six-pack. The quest had taken them more than an hour.

She'll spend the whole afternoon hunting for cream soda, but can't hang on fifteen more minutes in Beast House . . .

And can't go after her own damn ice, even though my feet are killing me and she knows it.

Owen groaned, sat up, struggled into his shoes, and got to his feet. Then he limped over to the dresser and picked up the ice bucket.

'Do you want me to go with?' Monica asked.

'No, that's all right. You can just stay here and relax.'

'Do you have your key?'

He nodded and left the room. And limped down the hallway toward the distant ice machine.

Nobody else was around.

Owen felt as if somebody had spent hours whacking the bottoms of his feet. The carpet helped, but not much.

It certainly silenced his footsteps.

Voices came softly from behind some of the doors he passed.

He heard laughter, too.

Nice to know someone's having a good time.

At last, he staggered to a halt in front of the ice machine. He set the bucket onto the rack underneath the spout, then pressed a button. The machine groaned and rumbled. Gobs of ice started dropping into his bucket.

When the bucket was full, he released the button.

The machine went silent.

He heard the quiet *ding* announcing the arrival of an elevator.

Ice bucket in his hands, he started back toward the room.

And glanced to his left at the bank of elevators.

The doors of the nearest elevator stood wide open.

He saw no one.

He stepped toward the elevator.

Empty.

Why did it even stop here? he wondered.

For me.

Step right in, he thought. And leave. And never come back.

He smiled wistfully.

It'd sure fix Monica. She wouldn't know whether to shit or lay eggs.

But where would I go? he wondered. I've *gotta* get off my feet. Can't just go out and wander the streets. I'd need someplace to spend the night.

Check into a different room here?

Might be possible . . .

As if losing patience with Owen, the elevator shut its doors and descended without him.

Chapter Twenty-Three

Heat

Can't she even open the door for me?

The job required two hands, so Owen set the ice bucket on the floor in front of his feet. Then he pulled his wallet out of his left rear pocket. He fingered open its bill compartment and plucked out the plastic key card. After glancing at the diagram near the door handle, he turned the card around and ran it through the lock slot. A tiny green light came on. He quickly pushed down on the handle lever and shoved the door open.

Holding it open with a knee, he put away his card and wallet, then crouched and picked up the ice bucket. He shouldered the door wide and entered the room.

'I'm back,' he announced.

Monica didn't answer.

The bathroom door was shut. From the other side came the muffled hiss of spraying water.

She's taking a shower?

'Great,' Owen muttered.

I can't have half a minute off my feet without being sent for ice, and the moment I'm gone she heads for the shower. Very nice.

He carried the ice bucket over to the dresser and set it down. Then he sat on the end of the bed and pulled off his shoes.

And sighed.

It felt *so* good to have his shoes off.

He was tempted to massage his feet. That'd *really* feel good, but then his hands would smell like sweaty socks and he wouldn't be able to wash them until Monica got out of the bathroom.

Which might be half an hour.

Or longer.

The longer the better, he thought.

Stay in there forever, for all I care.

Feet dangling off the end of the bed, Owen eased down onto the mattress. The instant his head and back met the bed, his aches and soreness started to melt and flow away. He filled his lungs and sighed.

Don't get too comfortable, he warned himself. Still have to get up when Monica comes out.

Have a cream soda with her.

Change for bed, wash, brush my teeth . . .

He fell asleep, but not for long.

The clink of an ice clump dropping into a glass woke him up.

He raised his head off the mattress, then propped himself up on his elbows.

Monica, standing at the dresser, had her back to him as she popped open a can of cream soda. Her hair was wrapped in a tower of pink towel. She wore the black nightgown that she'd bought especially for this trip, that she'd modelled for him last night. It left most of her back bare. It draped her buttocks and surrounded her legs like a veil of smoke. She wore nothing underneath it.

Owen felt a squirm in his pants.

As cream soda gurgled into Monica's glass, he pushed himself up to his elbows.

'How was the shower?' he asked.

She swiveled toward him, smiling and giving him a side view of her right breast. Though covered by the nightie, it appeared to be cloaked in nothing but a shadow. 'It was grand,' she said. 'I feel *so* much better. *You* should try it.'

'I don't think I can stand up.'

She eyed his groin. '*Something* is.'

He blushed, then sat up so his bulge wouldn't show.

Smiling, Monica turned away long enough to set her can on the dresser. Glass in hand, she faced Owen. After a glance at his lap, she met his eyes. She raised her eyebrows high. Then she turned her face aside, raised her glass and tilted back her head. As she swallowed cream soda, she shifted her stance, thrusting her hips to the left and standing mostly on her left leg.

Posing.

Keeping her eyes away from Owen.

Keeping her arms out of the way so they wouldn't obstruct his view.

From where Owen sat near the edge of the mattress, she was almost close enough to touch. Her breasts swelled out at him, looking as if they might burst through the frail material holding them in.

The gown drifted in front of her groin, caressed her thighs, concealed nothing.

As Owen gazed at her, she glided her right foot forward and sideways. Then she lifted her right knee. Bare toes pressing against the carpet, she swayed her leg lazily from side to side. The motion drew Owen's eyes to where she obviously wanted them.

'What're you looking at, Owie?' she asked, her voice a teasy singsong.

Blushing again, he quickly raised his eyes. 'Nothing,' he said.

'Nothing, huh?' Monica lowered her glass. It was empty now except for some small clumps of ice. Reaching behind her, she set it next to the soda can. Then she eased backward against the edge of the dresser. She sat on it, put her arms down straight by her sides to hold on, and stretched out her legs. Then she smiled languidly at Owen.

'I bet I know what *you* want,' she said.

'What?'

'Nothing,' she said. She spread her knees, opening herself wide to his view, then swung them back together.

Owen smiled. 'What's going on?' he asked.

'Nothing.' She opened and shut her legs again. 'What makes you think something's going on?'

'I don't know.' He shrugged. 'You don't usually . . . act this way.'

'Don't I?' Instead of spreading her legs, she swiveled her shoulders. Her breasts, confined only by her flimsy nightgown, lurched heavily from side to side.

'What're you doing?' Owen asked.

'Nothing,' she said.

Her shoulders stopped, but her breasts didn't. The rough lurching came to an end, but they continued to swing from side to side, gradually slowing to a gentle sway before Monica stopped them with her hands. Holding them, she looked into Owen's eyes. 'How's that?' she asked.

'Fine.'

'And how's *this*?' she asked. Fingers hooked, she clawed the wispy fabric down, ripping it from her breasts, breaking both shoulder straps.

'*Jesus!*' Owen blurted.

As Monica's hands returned to the edge of the dresser, the gown drifted into a pile below her waist.

Owen gaped at her.

She's lost her mind!

'You gonna just sit there?' she asked.

Owen shook his head. He felt a little breathless. His mouth was dry, his heart pounding, his penis hard and achy. 'Are you okay?' he asked.

She smirked at him. 'Do I look okay?'

'You look great,' he said.

'Do I?'

'Yes.' And she *did* look great. Except for her eyes and smile. Something wrong there. Something mocking and haughty and a little frantic.

'Am I the fairest of them all?' she asked.

The question made something squirm in Owen's bowels.

'Sure you are,' he said.

Monica pushed at the edge of the dresser, lifting herself. No longer trapped under her buttocks, the nightie slid all the way down her legs and pooled around her feet.

'Are you *sure* about that?' she asked, sitting down again.

'Huh?'

'Who's the fairest?'

'You are.'

Her smile died. 'Fairer than Dana?' she asked.

The name slammed through Owen.

'Who?' he asked. He knew he must look shocked. He felt sick.

'Dana,' Monica said. 'Your precious Beast House guide.'

'Huh? I don't even . . .'

'Oh yes you do.'

'The guide on the bus?'

'*Dana!*'

'Huh? Do you mean the *big* one? The blonde?'

'Don't play stupid with me, Owie. I know you *way* too well. I see right through you.'

'I don't even know her.'

'But you lust for her, don't you?'

Shaking his head, he tried to smile. 'I lust only for you.'

'Sure. Like I believe that. I saw how you were looking at her.'

'This is ridiculous. She was just *there*. So what if I looked at her? If I hadn't *looked* at her, I might've bumped into her.'

'Ha ha. Not very funny.'

'You're making a big deal out of nothing. I don't know her. I don't care about her. I'll probably never even see her again.'

'Probably?'

'There's a pretty slim chance of it, don't you think?'

'Do you *want* to see her again?'

'No. Why should I?'

Monica smirked and made a snorting sound. Then she pushed herself away from the dresser. Standing straight, she reached up with both hands and unwrapped the towel from around her head. Eyes on Owen, she rubbed her hair with the towel. 'Why *would* you want to see Dana again?' she asked. Her breasts jiggled and hopped with the motions of her arms.

'I wouldn't,' Owen said. 'Can we stop talking about her now?'

Monica lowered the towel. Her hair was a dark, wild tangle. Tossing aside the towel, she stepped toward Owen. She bumped against his knees, so he moved them farther apart. She halted between his knees and started to unfasten the buttons of his shirt.

He reached up for her breasts.

She clutched his wrists. 'Not so fast, Owie.'

'Huh?'

'You can't touch me till I say you can.'

'Huh?'

'*Huh*?' she mimicked him. 'It's your punishment, dearie.'

'Punishment for what?'

'We don't want to talk about her anymore, remember?'

'For God's sake, Monica.'

'It's my way or the highway, sweetheart.'

The highway, he thought. Screw this. She's turned into some sort of raving, jealous lunatic. Over nothing. *Nothing!*

I've gotta get away from her.

But not now, not now.

He didn't know why, it made no sense at all, but he wanted Monica more right now than he'd ever wanted her before. He *ached* for her.

'Your way,' he gasped.

'Okay,' she said, and released her grip on his wrists. Owen lowered his hands. He rested them on his thighs and gazed at Monica's naked body. He wanted to lick the sweat off her skin. He wanted to suck on her breasts. But he forced himself to sit still while she finished unbuttoning his shirt.

She pulled the shirt off his shoulders and down his arms. As Owen freed his hands from the sleeves, she clutched his shoulders and pushed him backward. The mattress felt good under him.

Standing between his knees, Monica bent over him and unfastened his belt. She opened the waist button of his jeans, then slid the zipper down.

Owen sighed.

'You like?' Monica asked.

'It was feeling awfully tight in there.'

'Baby needs his freedom.'

'Yeah.'

The fingers of both her hands slipped beneath the elastic waistband of his underwear. They lifted, and he felt all the confinement go away.

'Ooo,' Monica said. 'Look at you.'

He couldn't look without lifting his head. And he didn't care to look. Not at himself. His gaze was latched on Monica as she struggled to tug his jeans and underwear out from under him. Rolling slightly from one side to the other, he helped her. No longer trapped under his buttocks, the pants raced down his legs as Monica scurried backward, pulling.

Then she lifted his feet, one at a time, and peeled off his socks.

Standing between his knees again, she bent over and glided her hands slowly up his thighs. Her thumbs rubbed against the sides of his groin.

Face looming over his penis, she said, 'Ooo, you are *so* big and hard.'

Owen felt her fingers encircle him.

They squeezed gently, and he groaned.

'Hard as a rock. Oh, Owie, I've never felt it so hard.'

Her fingers glided slowly upward.

'You must be *awfully* turned on.'

Her fingers went away.

'Bet you just can't wait to slip it into me,' she said. 'Can you?'

'Huh-uh.'

'Into my hot, wet pussy.'

Her fingers returned, curled lightly around him, and slid downward. Owen squirmed.

Monica let go, gently patted his thigh, and said, 'Afraid you'll just *have* to wait, honey.'

'Huh?' He lifted his head off the mattress.

Monica, smiling and shaking her head, backed away from the bed. 'No fucky-wucky for you tonight, Owie. You've been a bad boy.'

'*What?*'

'Too bad Dana can't be here for you.'

'*What?*'

Turning aside, she waved at him, said, '*Ciao*,' and walked out of sight.

A moment later, Owen heard the bathroom door bump shut. Next came the click of its lock.

When he woke up, the gray light of morning showed through a gap in the curtains. He was still naked, but he no longer lay at the end of the bed with his legs hanging over the edge. Sometime during the night, he must've gotten up and crawled under the covers. He had no memory of it, though.

The last thing he remembered, Monica had locked herself in the bathroom and he'd stayed on his back, feeling cheated and angry.

At first, he'd been tempted to jump up and run to the bathroom door, break it open and grab Monica and slam her against a wall and *shove it in.*

Fix her good. Fuck her till she can't see straight.

But he knew he could never do anything like that.

What he *could* do, he could walk over calmly to the door and talk to her. Apologize to her.

Apologize for what? She's the one who went nuts!

Just say whatever it takes, he told himself. Take all the blame for everything. Beg her if you have to. Just get her to come out.

She didn't take her nightie with her.

She's naked in there.

Get her to come out, and we can pick up where we left off.

Except that Owen felt as if he'd been bludgeoned.

She had no right to treat me that way.

He had a heavy ache in the pit of his stomach and he was limp and he wanted to slap her a good one across her smirking face.

Thinking back on it now, Owen couldn't recall getting up from the bed or moving his position at all. Nor could he remember Monica coming out of the bathroom.

She must've come out after he'd fallen asleep.

She was in the bed now, near him under the covers. From the sound of her slow, easy breaths, Owen supposed she was probably asleep.

Not so much as glancing in Monica's direction, he eased himself slowly, silently out of the bed. The room felt chilly. Starting to shiver, he glanced at the clock. Ten till six.

He crept past the foot of the bed. Her nightgown was still on the floor.

Seeing it, memories rammed through him. His throat went tight. A knot formed in his stomach.

He looked over at Monica.

She seemed to be lying on her side. Her hip made a high bulge in the covers. Her left shoulder protruded above the edge of the blanket, bare. He couldn't see her face at all, just her black hair spread over the pillow. The hair looked sleek and smooth. She must've brushed it while hiding in the bathroom last night.

Owen supposed she was probably naked under the covers.

He supposed he might pull them away and take a look. He might slip into the bed with her, wake her with gentle kisses and caresses.

You never know, I might get lucky.

Call that luck?

Even though he stood there naked, imagining how it could be, he felt no stir of arousal.

Instead, he felt slightly gleeful.

If I can get away with this . . .

Silently, he gathered clean clothes for himself. He took them into the bathroom, eased the door shut and locked it. He wanted to take a shower, but didn't dare. He *had* to pee, did so, but refrained from flushing. With water running slowly and quietly from the faucet, he washed his face and brushed his teeth. He didn't bother shaving. But he did comb his hair. Then he got dressed and silently eased open the bathroom door and stepped out.

Monica still lay on her side, her bare shoulder sticking out of the blanket.

Owen had never unpacked his suitcase. He'd simply left it open on a luggage rack inside the closet and removed items as he'd needed them.

It took him only a few minutes to gather his things and throw them in. He shut the suitcase. He carried it to the door, set it down, then silently made his way back through the room.

Monica remained on her side, apparently still asleep.

Owen picked up his overnight bag and his camera case, swung their straps over his shoulders, and walked silently back to the door. There, he hefted his suitcase. He slipped into the hallway and eased the door shut.

A smile tilted the corners of his mouth.

He walked away quickly.

Downstairs, the lobby was nearly deserted. Piped-in piano music played quietly. Owen recognized the melody as 'I Left My Heart In San Francisco.' A couple of guests were busy pouring themselves free cups of coffee. The young, uniformed woman behind the registration desk was looking through a magazine and paid no attention to Owen as he walked by.

Just outside the entryway, he found a cab waiting.
He took the cab to San Francisco International Airport.
Where he headed straight for a car rental agency.

Chapter Twenty-Four

Friday Morning

Dana woke up. She was lying on her side, snug in bed. Above her, a breeze lifted and swayed the curtains. The morning air felt chilly on her face.

Her alarm clock hadn't gone off yet.

What day is this? she wondered.

Friday.

Wondering how much time she had, she rolled over and looked at the clock on the nearby nightstand. Twenty till eight.

The alarm was set for eight-thirty.

Plenty of time. Go back to sleep for a while?

The pillow didn't feel quite right. She fluffed it, squeezed it, moved it this way and that under the side of her head until she found a more comfortable position. Then she shut her eyes and sighed.

This is nice, she thought.

Then she imagined how lunch might be today. Would Warren come over to her table?

Of course he will, she told herself.

She thought about how he would look in the sunlight. How he might smile. In her mind, he reached across the table and took hold of her hand.

So, how are things going today? she imagined him asking.

Just fine, thanks. Better all the time.

Same here, he told her. *Things just got terrific.*

Would that have anything to do with me?

It would have everything *to do with you.*

Dana felt herself smiling, blushing. She squirmed a little in the bed.

Still at the lunch table in her mind, she pictured herself saying to Warren, *Why, thank you. Maybe we should get together later and . . .*

Somewhere in the house, a sliding door squeaked on its runners and scattered Dana's fantasy. The faraway sound seemed to come from downstairs, where all the rear doors were sliders. But it might've come from somewhere else. Upstairs, the bedrooms all had sliding doors to their balconies.

Must be Tuck, Dana thought.

She heard another squeak. This time, it was followed by a quiet thump.

What's she doing? Going for an early morning swim?

Tuck hadn't gone for a swim yesterday morning – not that Dana knew about, anyway.

Doesn't mean she isn't doing it now.

It'd be nice down there, she thought. Nothing beats going for a swim first thing in the morning when you have the pool all to yourself and . . .

Did Tuck forget about our creepy visitor last night?

No, she couldn't have forgotten about him. She'd probably made up her mind to go for a swim, anyway.

Alone. Not such a great idea. Even if the jerk is long gone . . .

Maybe I should go down and keep her company.

Dana sighed again. She felt so cozy. But the pool would be great – clear and sparkling in the sunlight. She knew just how it would feel, too. After the cold shock of diving in, there'd be the sleek feel of the water rushing over her skin as she glided along beneath the surface.

Anyway, she thought, I shouldn't let Tuck swim alone. Not after last night.

She flung the covers aside and the chilly air swarmed her, soaking through her thin cotton nightshirt. Shivering, she scampered to the adjoining bathroom.

As she used the toilet, she saw her red swimsuit from last night. It was draped over the shower rod where she'd left it. Probably still damp. She could get a fresh, dry suit out of a drawer and . . .

What the heck, it'll get wet anyway in a couple of minutes.

After flushing the toilet, she pulled off her nightshirt. She hung it on the back of the door, then went to the tub and pulled down her swimsuit. She climbed into it. The clammy fabric clung to her skin, making her shudder and grimace.

Grabbing a towel, she rushed out of the bathroom. On her way through the bedroom, she draped the towel across her back and drew it around her chest like a cloak.

I'll be okay once I'm outside in the sunlight.

She hoped Tuck wouldn't mind having her solitude ruined.

But it's *never* safe to swim alone, she thought – even if you *don't* have some weirdo hanging around.

In the hall, striding past the open door of Tuck's room, she glanced in.

Tuck, braced up on her elbows, looked back at her.

She lurched to a stop.

'Mornin',' Tuck said, her voice husky as if she were barely awake. 'Goin' for a dip?'

Dana gaped at her.

Tuck's hair was a mess. She wore a blue pajama shirt that was twisted crooked and half unbuttoned. The covers were down around her waist.

'Whassa matter?' she asked.

'Were you just up?'

'Huh? No.'

'You didn't just come in from outside, or . . ?'

'Been right here.'

'You haven't gotten out of bed at all this morning?'

'No.'

'Promise?'

Her frown deepening, Tuck sat up. 'What's going on?'

'I heard a door. It slid open for a second, and then it slid shut.'

'When?'

'Just now. I don't know, four or five minutes ago.'

Tuck's lips twisted and curled. 'I've been right here,' she said.

'Did *you* hear anything?'

'A toilet flushed.'

'That was me.'

'Other than that . . .' Tuck shook her head slightly. 'I think I was asleep until the flush.'

'The sliding door was a couple of minutes before that. I figured you must've gone outside for a swim. I was just on my way to go down and join you.'

Tuck curled her upper lip. 'I wouldn't advise it,' she said.

They stared at each other.

'Are you *sure* what you heard was a sliding door?'

'What else makes a sound like that?'

Tuck was silent for a few seconds. Then she said, 'I don't know. Nothing. Not that I can think of.'

'You don't have a housekeeper, or . . . .?'

Tuck shook her head. 'Nobody is supposed to be here but us. Nobody else even has a key. Just Dad and Janice.'

'Maybe we'd better have a look around.'

'I'd say so.' Tuck kicked her legs free of the covers, scooted off the bed and got to her feet. She wore no pants. The loose pajama shirt draped her like a very short dress. She slipped her feet into a pair of flip-flops, then stepped over to the nightstand. There, she pulled open a drawer, reached inside, and hauled out her .44 magnum. 'Here we go again,' she said. 'Do you want to go back and get the gun Eve gave you, or. . .?'

'That's all right,' Dana said. 'I'll rely on you to blast the bad guys. If any.'

'I can't *imagine* what you heard.'

'If it wasn't a door,' Dana said, 'I don't know what it could've been.' She stepped out of the way to let Tuck pass, then walked beside her down the hall.

'The doors were all locked last night,' Tuck said.

'I know.'

'This is nuts.'

They started slowly down the stairs.

'Ever since you got here,' Tuck said, 'it's been one thing after another.'

'Maybe I brought it with me.'

Tuck grinned at her. 'Maybe you did.'

'Do you think we should call Eve?'

'Nah. At least not till we've had a good look around. We can't be bugging her with every little thing. Especially when we don't know what's happening.'

'I can tell you what happened,' Dana said as they stepped off the bottom stair. 'Somebody opened and shut a door. It wasn't me and you say it wasn't you.'

'Wasn't me.'

'So somebody else must've done it.'

Tuck made a face at her.

'He or she,' Dana said, 'was either leaving the house or coming in.'

'If he's in here now,' Tuck said, 'he'd better get ready to catch a bullet.'

Side by side, they searched the entire ground level of the house. Then they returned upstairs and searched every room. They found no one. They found nothing to suggest that a stranger had been present earlier. All the windows and doors were intact, shut and locked.

As they went downstairs again, Tuck grinned at Dana and said, 'At least nobody tampered with the dummies.'

Dana frowned at her, confused. 'The dummies? Oh!' Laughing, she said, 'Maybe, maybe not. Who knows what might've gone on while the dummies were sleeping?'

Tuck grimaced at her. 'That's a comforting thought.' At the bottom of the stairs, she said, 'Anyway, I'll brew up some coffee. It's still pretty early. You have time for that swim, if you want.'

'You going in?'

'Not me,' Tuck said. 'But help yourself.'

As they walked toward the kitchen, Dana said, 'We'd better stick together. He might still be in the house.'

'Not likely,' Tuck said. 'Nobody can hide from me. I would've found him.'

'You didn't exactly find the guy in Beast House yesterday.'

Grinning, Tuck nudged Dana with her elbow. 'We got two out of three. That ain't bad.' In the kitchen, she set her revolver on the table. She walked over to a cupboard, reached up and swung open its door. 'Besides,' she said, 'who knows? Maybe there *wasn't* anybody to find. Some jerk might've stolen that tape player.' As she reached high for the coffee filters, her pajama shirt glided up, baring the lower half of her buttocks. 'In which case, there is no missing customer.' She took down a filter and turned around. 'If there *is* someone missing, he isn't in Beast House. We would've found him.'

'If you say so,' Dana said.

'I say so. And there's nobody *here*, either. Not anymore.'

'You're probably right.'

'I know I'm right.' Tuck went to the refrigerator, opened it, and took out a can of ground coffee. Swinging the door shut, she stepped over to the coffee maker.

'I bet he was on his way out when I heard the door,' Dana said. 'He probably locked it, then slid it shut behind him.'

Tuck nodded and started scooping heaps of coffee into the filter. Glancing over her shoulder at Dana, she said, 'Or maybe nobody was here, at all.'

'I guess that's possible. I heard *something*, though. If it wasn't anybody coming or going . . . God knows. I didn't imagine it.'

'It might've been something else.'

'Such as?'

'I have no idea,' Tuck said. She shook her head. 'I sure hate to think it really *was* someone leaving the house. I mean, if it was . . . Who *was* it? How long was he inside with us? What the hell did he do while he was in here? How did he get in? And how do we keep him out from now on?'

'I have no idea,' Dana said. 'On all counts.'

As they drove up Front Street approaching Beast House, Dana pointed at an old blue Ford Granada parked at the curb. 'What about *that*?' she asked.

Tuck turned her head. The wind threw ribbons of blond hair across her face. 'What about it?'

'It was parked there when we drove home yesterday.'

'Was it?'

'Yep. Sure was. I used to have a boyfriend with a car like that.'

'Ah.' Tuck grinned at her. 'This boyfriend? Did he appear to have stalker tendencies?'

'No. Anyway, his car was green. But it's about the same, otherwise. That's why I noticed it so much yesterday.'

Slowing her Jeep, Tuck flicked the turn signal. 'So you think exactly what?'

'Maybe it belongs to the missing tourist.'

'Might belong to anyone,' Tuck said. She eased her car to the right and rolled to a stop in front of the parking lot's gate. 'Back in a minute.' She took the keys, hopped out and trotted up to the gate.

Dana looked around.

The parking lot was empty.

Off to the left of the gate, however, several people were milling about on the sidewalk, apparently waiting for the ticket booth to open.

They hadn't parked in the Beast House lot.

If they'd come by car, they'd parked elsewhere. Along Front Street, more than likely.

Maybe one of these people owned the Granada.

But it *had* been parked there yesterday – in exactly the same spot.

So what? Maybe it belongs to a repeat customer.

Eve Chaney, she remembered, had warned them to watch out for repeaters.

She scanned the group.

And caught a guy staring at her.

He began to turn his head away, then seemed to change his mind. Facing Dana, he smiled slightly and nodded. *Then* he turned away.

Do I know him?

He looked vaguely familiar – gawky and freckled, probably about her own age, with a shock of light brown hair that swept up from his scalp making him look like a human Woody Woodpecker.

His short-sleeved, Madras shirt was neatly tucked in. He wore tan trousers and brown leather hiking boots.

This isn't how he was dressed yesterday, Dana thought.

The boots and trousers might be the same, but he'd been wearing a different shirt. Cream-colored.

And he'd been with a snotty-looking brunette.

Dana scanned the group. The girl didn't seem to be there.

Tuck dropped into the driver's seat, pulled the door shut, and started the engine. 'I wouldn't get too excited about that Ford. You know? It might belong to anyone.' She drove into the parking lot.

'It might belong to the guy who vanished yesterday with the tape player.'

'But not necessarily.'

'You're in a state of denial,' Dana said.

Grinning, Tuck asked, 'Egypt?'

She steered diagonally across the lot and parked at the far corner. As she plucked out the ignition key, Dana took hold of her wrist and said, 'There's something else. It might be nothing, but you know how Eve told us to keep our eyes open for repeaters?'

'Yeah. We get a lot of them, though.'

'Two days in a row?' she asked, and released Tuck's wrist.

'It happens, but not very often. Unless you count people coming back for the Midnight Tour. They'll sometimes take the regular tour Saturday, then come back that night.'

'But this guy was here yesterday and he's back today. I just saw him out in front of the ticket booth.'

'Are you sure it's the same guy?'

'Positive. He was giving me the eye yesterday. In a furtive sort of way. And I was out front by the time he left. I took his tape player . . .'

'So he's not our vanishing mystery guest . . .'

'He might be our *other* mystery guest. That's what I'm getting at.'

'Just because he gave you the eye?'

'He wasn't alone yesterday. He had a gal with him. A girlfriend, maybe. The thing is, I don't think they were getting along very well. She was really pretty, in a way. But she had this horrible smirky look. Anyway, she doesn't seem to be with him this morning. It looks like maybe he came back without her.'

'That does seem slightly odd.'

'It just makes me wonder, you know? Maybe he's got a *thing* about me. *Or* about you. Maybe he got rid of the gal and followed us home after we left here yesterday.'

'I don't know. Sounds like you're making a lot out of not very much. All he did was *look* at you.'

'He seemed pretty intense. And now he's back without the girl. And I caught him *staring* at me.'

'Guys will stare. We don't want to go jumping to a lot of wild conclusions.'

'I'm *not*. I'm just saying he might be . . . a possible suspect.'

'He's over by the ticket booth?'

'He was. When we drove in. He's probably still there.'

Tuck swung open her door. 'Let's go,' she said, and climbed out.

Dana met her behind the Jeep. Side by side, they started walking toward the open gate. A couple of other cars were already coming in.

'Take a look at him as we go by,' Dana said. 'He'll be the skinny guy with the weird hair. He's in a Madras shirt.'

'I'll check him out. And why don't *you* stop and have a friendly little chat with him?'

'You're kidding.'

'Am not. Maybe you can find out what he's up to. I'll go ahead inside and start to open things up.'

'Alone?'

Tuck smiled and shook her head. 'Me?'

'Yes, you.'

'I do it all the time.'

'But there's been so much weird stuff,' Dana said. 'I'd better go in with you. I can talk to this guy later.'

'Nothing's going to happen.'

'But if it does, I'll be with you.'

Tuck, grinning, shook her head. 'My pal,' she said.

Chapter Twenty-Five

Sandy's Story – July 1992

When Sandy came out of the cabin, she found Eric waiting in the passenger seat of her pickup truck. Like a kid eager for the trip to begin, he grinned at her and bounced up and down.

Sandy felt a pang of regret.

Opening the driver's door, she said, 'I wish I *could* take you with me, honey.'

He tilted his head, gave her a sad look, and made a dog-like whimper. As if begging, *Please?*

Sandy climbed aboard. Leaning over, she put an arm around her son's shoulders, pulled him toward her and kissed his cheek. 'I'm sorry,' she said. 'Tell you what, we can make a night trip sometime soon. Maybe later this week. How does that sound?'

Chuffing, he nodded.

Ever since her son's infancy, Sandy had taken him on night trips into town once in a while as a special treat. He seemed to just love the adventure of it. But she had never taken him during the day. And never would. Risky enough, driving him into town in the middle of the night. She would have to be nuts to do it in daylight.

'Hop on out, now,' she told him.

He whined.

'Go on,' she said, gently easing him away.

He reached for the door handle, then looked back at Sandy. The ridges above his eyes lifted. They would've raised his eyebrows if he'd had any. But he had no brows, no hair anywhere on his body. Even puberty, which he'd apparently attained recently, hadn't resulted in any hair. He was bald all over, the same as his father and the others.

'Go on, now,' Sandy told him again. 'I'll be back in a few hours.'

He nodded, then swung open the door and jumped to the ground. He turned around and stared at Sandy.

'Could you shut the door for me?' she asked.

He reached out and whipped it shut. It slammed. Sandy cringed.

He didn't slam it that hard on purpose, she told herself. He's just too strong. And hasn't learned to control it yet. Smiling, she said, 'Next time, take it easy on the door, okay?'

He shrugged.

'Jerk,' she said.

He grinned.

Sandy started the engine, then called out the window, 'Try to stay out of trouble while I'm gone, okay? And don't talk to any strangers.'

An old joke between them.

Grinning, Eric bobbed his head.

Sandy backed up the truck, turned it around, then slowly drove away. In the side mirror, she saw Eric standing in front of the cabin.

He looked so damn lonely and forlorn.

Sandy felt her throat tighten up.

Poor kid, she thought.

It's not like we have any choice. We're doing the best we can.

Hell, we're doing pretty damn good, considering. At least we're alive and free and together. That's all that really counts.

She drove around a curve. No longer able to see Eric, she felt an ache of loss.

She *hated* leaving him alone for these drives into town.

Nothing's going to happen, she told herself. When I *am* home, he's off all day roaming around in the woods. So what does it really matter if I'm in town instead of the cabin?

It matters.

At a break in the trees, she turned her head and looked over at the burial place. She *always* had to look. Long ago, she'd given up fighting the urge.

She knew precisely where to look. But the grave was not to be seen. It lay hidden beneath a heavy cluster of bushes.

Glancing at the bushes, Sandy remembered when they hadn't been there. She remembered the look, the feel, and the strong dirt scent of the mound as it had been in the beginning. That first night, after piling in the dirt on Lib and Harry and Slade, she'd sat down on the mound because she was too worn out to go anywhere else and because she wasn't quite positive about Harry and Lib.

They were *probably* dead.

But maybe not.

One or the other of them might still be alive down there, badly hurt and short of air, but not quite dead. And maybe somehow strong enough to fight his or her way up through the dirt.

Not if I'm sitting on it.

Sitting on the grave, she'd thought about the three of them down there. A sandwich of naked bodies, Lib in the middle like a slab of meatloaf.

No, no, no, not meatloaf. It's a salami sandwich.

And Lib's in the middle, but she isn't the meat.

Hope she's happy. Should've kept her big mouth shut.

Driving on past the bushes where the grave lurked, Sandy remembered how angry she'd been, that night. Everything had seemed so fine between her and Lib until Harry had shown up. He'd ruined it.

We could've been a family.

But Lib had gone nuts for the guy and turned into a slut. A *talkative* slut, a *traitorous* slut. Didn't have an ounce of loyalty in her whole damn body. Couldn't *wait* to start spilling the beans.

She didn't even know the guy!

Sandy shook her head.

She felt like a different person from the girl sitting on top of the grave that night.

God, I was so young then. And so angry.

And jealous.

Ridiculous.

She wished she hadn't killed Harry and Lib. She *always* wished she hadn't done it.

Not that she felt very guilty about it. They both got what they deserved. They'd turned against her. Sooner or later, they would've turned against Eric, too. If she hadn't killed them, there would've been hell to pay.

But she'd liked them.

Both.

If things had worked out differently, Lib might've been like a big sister to her. Harry might've been like a brother.

Or lover.

Who knows?

Ever since that night twelve years ago, she couldn't drive past the grave without remembering it all.

Couldn't remember without wishing she hadn't killed them.

Wishing they hadn't made it necessary.

It all worked out for the best, she told herself.

Not for them.

Well, tough. They should have behaved.

Better that they *didn't* behave, she thought. Otherwise, I might've been lulled into trusting them. Then it would've been me and Eric getting the shaft.

This way, I got in the first strike.

What's that military term?

A *pre-emptive* strike.

Yeah.

I sure pre-empted the shit out of those two. Got them before they could get us.

Off through the trees, Pacific Coast Highway came into sight. Sandy drove ahead slowly, then stopped a few yards short of the heavy, iron gate barring her way. She hopped out and strode toward it. As she walked through shadows and brilliant sunlight, her boots crunched the fallen leaves, pine needles and twigs. Mixed in with the heavy scents of the woods was a fresh, strong smell of ocean. And a *feel* of the ocean's breeze, cooler and fresher than the sweet warm air of the woods.

It always got her just about now, on her way to open the gate.

My gate.

The dirt road hadn't been gated in Harry's days. Sandy, herself, had bought the barricade in town and hired a couple of guys to install it.

The gate did a fair job of keeping people out.

That, and the sign wired to its front:

PRIVATE PROPERTY
KEEP OUT
VIOLATORS SUBJECT TO PROSECUTION
AND TARGET PRACTICE

The sign was her own creation. She thought the 'target practice' bit, while threatening, showed a certain wit and style.

The sign and the gate itself seemed especially cool considering that the private property wasn't *hers*.

The land belonged to Harry Matthews.

He owned it. He was buried in it.

After removing the padlock, Sandy walked backward, pulling the gate. When it was wide open, she stepped back, read her sign and grinned. Then she hurried to the pickup. She rolled through, shut and locked the gate behind her, then drove slowly over the rough dirt tracks, bouncing and shaking until she reached the edge of the highway.

She waited until an enormous RV roared by. After that, the road was clear. She made a hard right turn onto the pavement and stepped on the gas.

The nearest town was Fort Platt, almost fifty miles up the coast. She turned on the radio. Reaching over in front of the passenger seat, she opened the glove compartment. Half a dozen cassette tapes were piled inside. She found her favorite Warren Zevon tape – the one with 'Roland the Headless Thompson Gunner.' Then she shut the compartment, slid the cassette into the slot in her radio, and pushed the start button.

'Now we're cookin',' she muttered.

As much as she regretted leaving Eric behind – and worried about his safety – she couldn't help but enjoy being alone on the road.

Free.

She settled back in the seat and smiled at the feel of the wind in her face.

Resting her left arm on the sill of the open window, she steered with one hand. She was wearing a sleeveless white blouse. Air rushed in through the arm hole, slid over her breasts, fluttered the front of the blouse. She unfastened a couple of buttons to let more air come in.

High above the ocean, she could see little more than the horizon when she looked straight to the left. Looking ahead, however, she could see down over the left side of the highway. A fabulous view stretched out ahead of her – miles of rough, rocky bluffs with patches of sandy beach down below, the ocean's frothy rows of combers rolling in. The water was pale blue and glinting sunlight. Far off to the west, a bank of fog lay across the water like a mat of snow.

To the right, she could see densely wooded hillsides and cloudless sky.

This is the life, she thought.

If you don't mind hiding your life away in the hills with a monster.

She felt a quick flush of guilt.

He's my *kid*, she told herself. He *is* my life.

He's a monster.

But he's mine and I love him. And what choice do I have, anyway?

She knew the choices.

She'd thought about them many times.

Alone during her long drives into town, she rarely *failed* to think about the choices.

There were only two, really. Either continue hiding out with Eric, or leave him.

It's not as if he really *needs* me anymore, she thought. He could get along just fine on his own.

Years ago, Eric had started chasing down and killing wild animals (and sometimes people) for his meals. He ate them where they fell, though he often brought back gifts of meat for Sandy to cook up for herself. Sure, he enjoyed special treats like pizza, popcorn, cake, chocolate-chip cookies – but he didn't *need* anything like that.

Didn't need Sandy at all, really.

Sure, he'd miss me. He'd miss his mom. But he could get along just fine without me.

And I'd be free. I could have my own life.

Without him.

She felt hot and sick with guilt . . . and with a vast, overwhelming loneliness.

I couldn't, she thought. I could never betray him like that. And God, I'd miss him. I just couldn't.

But the alternative seemed almost as terrible.

To spend her whole life in that little cabin, all alone except for Eric. No lovers, no *real* children.

Real?

Again, guilt surged through her.

You know what I mean, she thought. I know he's real. Do I *ever!* But, my God, is it so awful to wish for a normal life? A husband and *human* kids?

It's not that I don't love Eric, but . . .

'Shit,' she said.

She hated thinking about these things.

Just then, the song came on. The song she liked best. The weird and spooky ballad about Roland, the headless Thompson gunner.

She sang along with it and tried not to think about such matters as Eric and freedom.

It was after ten o'clock by the time she drove over the bridge and entered town. At a public phone inside the Sea Breeze Café, she dropped in a quarter and tapped in a number that she knew by heart.

After two rings, a familiar voice asked, 'May I help you?'

'Hi, Blaze, it's me.'

'Darrrling!'

'Could you use me today?'

'Could I? Of course! When could I *not* use you?'

'Just thought I'd check. Make sure you're not off on a cruise or something.'

'Oh, perish the thought! I may never go on a cruise again. I thought I'd die! Several people *did!* Ha!'

'Fun. Anyway, do you want me to come up to your place or should I meet you somewhere, or . . .?'

'Oh, come here first. If we decide on an outing, I'll drive.'

'Okay. Great. See you in a while.'

'Where are you calling from?'

'The Sea Breeze.'

'Ah. Then I'll see you in fifteen minutes.'

'So long, Blaze,' she said, and hung up.

She drove down the main street of Fort Platt. The town had a bay with a wharf and plenty of boats, but she knew of no military installation in the area. Maybe they should've called it *Port* Platt.

It always reminded her of Malcasa Point. Not that the two towns had much in common. Fort Platt sure didn't have any tacky attractions like Beast House. It wasn't very big on bait shops, liquor stores or cheap souvenir shops like Malcasa, either. No way. Fort Platt was a *class act*. Or so it seemed to fancy itself.

Like many other communities along the California coast, it had long ago acquired the reputation of being an 'artist's colony.' By the time Sandy had first ventured there, late in 1980, it had already mutated into a trendy vacation area.

The main road was lined with picturesque restaurants, boutiques selling candles and tea and handicrafts, bookstores that smelled of incense and carried books by environmentalists and obscure poets, and galleries featuring the works of local artists.

Such as Blaze O. Glory.

Just beyond the north end of town, Sandy turned right onto Buena Vista Parkway and headed inland. She followed the broad curvy road into the hills, turned onto Emerald Drive, then onto the narrow, twisty Crestline Lane. It led to the entrance of Blaze's driveway.

Stopping at the bottom of the steep driveway, she shifted to first gear. Then she started forward. The front of her pickup tilted toward the sky and she felt her weight shift against the seatback.

At the top, her hood lowered. She felt as if she were coming in for a landing – on a runway in front of a fabulous house made of glass and weathered wood.

She left her car in a parking area near the garage, then walked past the front of the house and climbed a dozen slate stairs to the porch.

She pressed the doorbell button.

Inside the house, chimes rang out a tune. The one about wanting a gal just like the gal who married dear old Dad.

She chuckled and shook her head.

Blaze opened the door. 'My *dear*!' he cried out and flung his arms wide.

Sandy stepped over the threshold.

He wrapped his arms around her and hugged her.

She gave his back a couple of pats. He was wearing a silk kimono. The fabric felt slick under her hands, and the heat of his skin radiated through it.

He eased her away and held her by the arms. 'Look at you. Oh, just *look* at you. Gorgeous! Absolutely gorgeous! As ever. Never change, darling! Whatever you do, never change!'

'You look pretty good yourself,' she said.

'Oh, dear, I know. I know! Ha! I look totally fabulous, don't I?'

'As ever.'

'Oh, I'm *so* glad you chose today to come by. You've absolutely *made* my day.' He swept her aside, then closed the front door and whirled around to face her. 'Oh, I do miss you when you're gone. You're such a *delight!* I do wish you'd move in. I have *oodles* of room.'

'I know. Maybe someday.'

'Oh, don't torment me with your empty promises. I know you'll never move in. But I do keep hoping, don't I? We could have such fine times, you and I.'

'I'm sure we would.'

'You are *so* gorgeous. And you're such a chameleon. So many moods and changes, so many shifts and nuances. If I had my way, you would be my *only* subject. I would spend every hour of my life painting no one but you.'

'Well, thanks.'

'We'd not only have a grand time, but we'd become *filthy rich*.'

'How *are* we doing?' Sandy asked.

'Modestly well.' Wiggling his eyebrows, Blaze slipped a hand into a pocket of his robe. He drew out a fat pack of bills that were folded in the middle and held together by two rubber bands. 'Your twenty per cent,' he said. He dropped it into Sandy's hand.

'Wow,' she said.

'Indeed. That's two thousand three hundred smackarooes.'

She grinned. 'Pretty good.'

Leaning toward her, Blaze narrowed one eye, lowered his voice and said, 'We are an unbeatable combination, Ashley. Your beauty and my genius in capturing you on canvas . . . But you need to *be* here. I require you *presence*.'

'Well, I just can't get out here very often, Blaze.'

'How far away *do* you live?'

'Far far.'

'You have no *desire* to be wealthy?'

'Two thousand bucks a month ain't hay.'

'But we could be doing so much better. We could make a *fortune*.'

'I thought you artistic types didn't care about money.'

'Am I not human? Do I not bleed? Do I not crave *goodies*?'

Laughing, Sandy stuffed the pack of money into a front pocket of her jeans. 'Well, Mr Greedy, we'd better get to it.'

'Yes! The sooner, the better!' Smiling, he raised both hands like a kid trying to feel raindrops. 'It's a lovely day. Shall we go down to the sea again?'

'Fine with me. You driving?'

'I've already packed the gear. All we need to do is change into more suitable attire, and we'll be off.'

Chapter Twenty-Six

Staff Encounters

In the parlor, Ethel looked as if she hadn't been tampered with overnight.

'So far, so good,' Dana said.

They searched more and more of the house.

Nobody jumped them.

Nothing seemed out of place.

All the mannequins appeared to be in their usual condition.

Done with the walk-through, Tuck and Dana headed for the front door. 'Maybe everything'll go a little more smoothly today,' Tuck said.

'We're getting off to a good start – if we don't include the intruder at *your* house.'

'Oh, thanks for reminding me.'

'You're welcome.'

'He's probably after *you*, you know.'

'Thank *you*,' Dana said.

'My pleasure.' She opened the door and Dana followed her onto the porch. 'Just be careful,' she said. 'Keep your eyes open, okay? Don't think you're necessarily safe just because it's broad daylight and there're lots of people around . . .' She shook her head. 'The house has a lot of little empty places. Places where things could happen. So don't let your guard down.'

Nodding, Dana said, 'You watch out, too.'

'You bet I will.'

Side by side, they trotted down the porch stairs. As they headed around the house, Dana felt her heartbeat quicken. 'Warren doesn't show up for the staff meetings, does he?' she asked.

'Not the guide meetings.' Tuck flashed a grin at her. 'So sorry.'

'Just asking.'

'*Sure* you are. Anyway, he's not actually staff. Not anymore. He owns the snack stand.'

'*Owns* it?'

'Oh, yeah. Makes a nice little profit off it, too. But he doesn't attend the guide meetings.'

'Ah.'

'Don't worry, you'll see him sooner or later.'

'I know. I wasn't . . .'

'*Sooner* if you buy yourself a cup of coffee before we get started.'

'He's here *now*?'

'Maybe.'

They stepped around the rear corner of the house.

'Yep,' Tuck said. 'He's here.'

Dana only saw the three other guides. Rhonda smiled and waved. Sharon lit up a cigarette. Clyde, off by himself with one foot up on a chair, held a cigarette in his lips and a white Styrofoam cup in one hand. Seeing Dana, he looked away.

'Warren's inside the snack stand,' Tuck explained.

Dana squinted at it. Though sunlight glared on the glass front, she could see that one of the serving windows was open. She smiled at Tuck. 'Can I get you anything?'

'I'm fine. But you'd better hurry.'

'Right back.' Quickening her pace, she angled away from Tuck and hurried over to the stand.

Warren stepped up to the window and smiled out at her. 'Morning, Dana.'

'Hi. Could I get a cup of coffee?'

'What size?'

'What sizes have you got?'

'Tom Thumb, Madame Blavatsky, and Cyclops.'

'You're kidding.'

'Yeah. Sorry about that.'

'I hope it doesn't get around.'

'I only try it out on special friends.'

Dana felt heat rush to her face. 'Well, thanks. So I guess your *medium*-sized coffee is the Madame Blavatsky?'

'You got it.'

'I'll have one.'

'Take anything in it?'

'Just coffee.'

'Coming right up.' Warren stepped away from the window.

Looking over her shoulder, Dana saw that the other guides were gathering around Tuck.

'Here you go.'

She reached into her pocket.

'This one's on me,' Warren said.

'Well . . . Thank you.'

'You're welcome. How did it go yesterday? Did those cassette players ever turn up?'

'Two out of three. One's still out.'

Warren grimaced slightly.

'What?'

He shook his head. 'It's been happening a lot lately, that's all. Maybe people stealing them. Anyway, I think Lynn's waiting for you.'

'I'd better get going. See you later, okay?'

'You bet,' he said.

'Thanks again for the coffee.' She picked up the stryofoam cup, turned away and started toward the group. She walked slowly, her eyes on the steaming, dark surface.

Is he still at the window? she wondered. Is he watching me? Is he interested?

He gave me free coffee, didn't he?

Yeah, but why was he in such a rush to scram, yesterday? Like he couldn't get away from me fast enough.

Scared I'd ask him to help me search the house.

'Okay,' Lynn said. 'We're all here.'

'Hi, Dana,' Rhonda said, smiling as her cheeks reddened.

'Hi, Rhonda. Sharon.'

Sharon, a cigarette jutting from a corner of her mouth, tipped her a wink. 'Day two.'

'Yep.'

Clyde stared at her through the drifting smoke of his Camel. She nodded a greeting to him, but refused to smile. He kept on staring at her.

Was that you at the pool last night, Clyde?

You in the house this morning?

What were you doing in there, spying on . . .?

'The good news,' Tuck said, 'is that nobody screwed around in Beast House last night.'

'Nobody you know about,' Sharon said.

Dana took a sip of coffee. It was very hot, and tasted like a French roast.

Warren makes good coffee, she thought.

'The bad news is, we came up short a cassette player yesterday. We started out *three* short, but Dana and I turned up two hiders. Just a couple of goofballs. They claimed not to know anything about another hider, and we couldn't turn anyone else up. So there's still one player outstanding.'

'Outstanding,' Clyde muttered.

Lynn said, 'We don't know of any missing tourists, though.'

'We never do, do we?'

'Probably because they *aren't* missing,' Lynn told him. 'If we had a customer vanish every time a player does, we would've gone out of business years ago.'

'So you say.'

'Get off it, Clyde,' Sharon said.

'I say the beast is back,' Clyde said. He tossed a quick smirk at Dana. 'Every so often, it puts the snatch on someone. Needs some fresh meat, you know what I mean?'

'He's just trying to scare you,' Rhonda said.

'I'm trembling,' Dana said.

'Maybe you *should* be. You might be next.'

'That's enough, Clyde,' Lynn said. 'Let's not make a big deal out of this. Far as we know, nobody's missing. The player's gone, that's all. People do steal the things. But we need to keep our eyes open. Maybe someone *did* get snatched, even though there's no reason to think so.

Another possibility is that we've got a hider. If it's a hider, he might still be in the house. No telling what he might be up to, so we need to be especially careful.'

'Do you suppose it's all connected?' Rhonda asked, frowning as if deep in thought.

'*What's* all connected?' Lynn asked.

Rhonda blushed. 'You know. The vandalism of Ethel, the missing tape player. They both happened on the same day, didn't they?'

'The vandalism might've been the night before,' Lynn said. 'But yeah, there could be a connection. I just don't think we know enough to draw any sort of conclusions yet.'

'*I've* got a couple of conclusions,' Sharon said, squinting through her cigarette smoke. 'I conclude something weird's going on. And I also conclude this might just be the start of it.'

Clyde widened his eyes. 'And it all began yesterday with the arrival of Dana.'

'Blow it out your ass,' Sharon told him.

'*Kiss* my ass.'

'Not with *these* lips.'

'That's enough,' Lynn said. 'For one thing, we had plenty of incidents *before* Dana came along. For another, Clyde, try not to be such a fuckwad.'

'Oooo,' he said. 'You'd better watch your language, little girl. I might have to get out a bar of soap.'

Ignoring his remark, Lynn glanced at her wristwatch. 'It's almost time to open. Any questions about your assignments?'

'I'd like to take the second floor,' Dana said. 'If that's all right. Since I screwed up yesterday.'

Sharon agreed to switch positions with her.

Smirking at Dana, Clyde said, 'Guess who has the first floor?'

'I don't see that as a problem,' Dana said. 'Do you?'

'Oh, no no. I see it as an *opportunity*.'

'*Are* we all set?' Lynn asked.

'Not quite,' said Clyde. He mashed the remains of his cigarette under his shoe.

'What is it now?'

'You called me a fuckwad,' he said.

'Right. So?'

'Did you mean it as a compliment?'

'Sure,' she said. 'Whatever you wanta think. Now let's get this show on the road.'

Clyde taking up the rear, they walked in a group around the side of the house. At the front, Lynn, Sharon and Rhonda cut across the lawn toward the ticket booth. Clyde stayed behind Dana. She resisted an urge to look back at him.

'Do you think I'm a fuckwad?' he asked.

Turning her head, she said, 'I wouldn't know.'

He hurried up to her. 'Lynn can't stand the fact that I broke up with her. She's hated me ever since.'

'No kidding?' Dana muttered.

'I'm afraid I broke her heart.'

'I guess you're a real heartbreaker.'

'So, how was your date last night?'

'Just fine.'

'Just fine? That's not much of a recommendation. If you'd been with me, your answer would have been "extraordinary." Or even "magnificent." '

'I'm sure.' She climbed the porch stairs.

Clyde hurried ahead of her and opened the front door of Beast House.

'Thanks.' She stepped over the threshold.

Rushing in behind her, Clyde jerked the door shut. It slammed the daylight out.

Dana could hardly see the stairway through the murky gloom.

'Sorry,' Clyde said. 'Do you need the light?'

'This is fine.'

'Could we talk for a minute?'

'I need to get upstairs.' She put a hand on the newel post and stepped onto the first stair.

'Nobody'll be in here for another five minutes, at least. So don't run off, all right?'

She climbed a few more stairs, anxious to get away from him.

Wait. Why not hear what he has to say?

Ask him a few questions.

Dana stopped and turned around. Clyde came toward her.

'Stay down there, okay? We can talk, but don't try to come up.'

He halted. 'Is this all right?'

'Fine. What do you want, Clyde?'

'I want us to be friends.'

'Friends. Right.'

Spreading his muscular arms, he said, 'There's still time.'

'Sure.'

'Do you already have another engagement planned for tonight?'

She realized that her heart was pounding fast.

'No, I don't,' she said. 'As a matter of fact, I didn't have one last night, either. I just didn't want to go out with you.'

'So you lied.'

'That's right.'

'Shame on you.'

'I know. I hate lies. That's why I'm leveling with you now. You and I are co-workers. I'd like for us to be friends, but I have no intention of going out with you.'

'Ah, the old "co-workers" ploy.'

'It's not a ploy.'

'Sure it is. It's just a handy excuse. Why don't you just come right out and say that you hate me.'

'I don't *hate* you.'

'Your *dear friend* Lynn has probably told you all sorts of terrible lies about me. She can't *stand* that I dumped her. Oh, she was absolutely nuts about me. She couldn't get enough of me. She was insatiable. We even did it right here inside Beast House. Countless times. In every room. Even in the attic. Even in the cellar.'

'Yeah, right.'

'She had to have me over and over again. I drove her crazy with lust. And with jealousy. She was *so* jealous, *so* possessive. I finally couldn't stand it any longer. The accusations. *Groundless* accusations. She thought I was fucking Sharon. She even accused me of seducing Rhonda. *Rhonda!* Can you believe it? Can you imagine, for one moment, that I would be interested in having sex with that childish, stupid *pig*?'

'Knock it off now.'

'God only knows what sort of lies Lynn's been telling you. And you probably *believe* her. Hell, why *wouldn't* you? She's your best friend. In your eyes, I'm sure she can do no wrong.'

'I wouldn't go that far.'

'I'm *not* a bad person. Even *she* didn't think so. She thought I was *great*. That's why she hates me so much now.'

'I think there's at least one more reason she hates you.'

'What's that?'

'You're a fuckwad.'

While standing on the stairs, Dana's eyes had adjusted to the dim light. She was able to see Clyde's lips tighten into a thin, angry line.

She turned her back to him and climbed the stairs.

'You'll change your tune,' he called.

She didn't answer, just kept climbing.

'You don't know what you're missing.'

She said nothing.

'You get a taste of me, *you* won't be able to get enough. None of them can. You'll be *begging for more*.'

At the top of the stairs, she turned to the right and started walking down the hallway.

'Don't let the beast get you!' Clyde yelled.

'Thanks for the warning,' Dana called. 'Have a nice day.'

She heard him mutter a word. It had only one syllable. Though she couldn't quite make it out, she was fairly sure that she knew what it was.

'What a charmer,' she whispered.

Then she smiled but couldn't stop trembling.

Chapter Twenty-Seven

Sandy's Story – July, 1992

'Looks like we'll have the beach to ourselves,' Sandy said, seeing no cars parked at the end of the dirt road.

'I certainly hope so,' Blaze said. 'I have my heart set.'

'I'm sure it'll be fine.'

He turned his Silverado around, then stopped it. They both climbed out and unloaded the gear.

'You carry the cooler and easel, if you will. I'll take the rest.'

'Right,' Sandy said. She *always* carried the cooler and easel. Blaze always carried his canvases, paint box, and a full backpack. And he always insisted that Sandy walk in front of him, even though he was the one choosing the destinations.

'It allows me time,' he had told her, 'to reacquaint myself with your form and flow.'

Sandy had left her own clothes back at his house, and now wore the blue silk dress that she'd found waiting for her in the guest room. Low cut in front and back, its top was held up by thin, wispy straps. The fabric of the dress, nearly weightless, felt like cool fluid against her skin.

Though she never let Blaze know when she might be coming to his house, he was always ready with a fabulous new costume for her. And she always gladly changed into it right away, even if they would be going no farther than his upstairs studio.

The garments never failed to be beautiful, clingy and revealing. Some were barely decent.

Like this one.

Not only was it semi-transparent, but its skirt was at the mercy of the wind.

The wind flipped it up as she bent over to lift the cooler.

'Oh, lovely,' Blaze commented.

'Dirty old man,' she said.

'Old? Bite your tongue!'

She stood up straight, the easel resting on her right shoulder. The cooler, down by her side, pulled at her left arm. She supposed it contained the usual picnic lunch of cheese, Italian salami, crackers, grapes, and two bottles of Champagne.

Grinning over her shoulder, she said, 'How old *are* you now, Blaze?'

'Twenty-nine.'

'Wow. That's truly amazing. You don't look a day over fifty.'

He arched an eyebrow. 'Fifty-eight, if you must know.'

'No kidding? You *do* look great.'

'Oh, I know, I know.' Grinning, he stroked the wavy silver hair above his right ear. 'I've been a raving beauty all my life and it's too late to quit now. Ha!'

'Ready to go?' Sandy asked.

'Lead on, MacQuiff.'

She frowned back at him. 'None of that, buster.'

He tilted his head sideways and gave her a look like a scolded, repentant kid. 'Forgive me, my dear.'

'Just try to restrain yourself,' she said, and started off.

A path led away from the road's end, curving along the side of a low, grassy hill before descending to the shore. It reminded Sandy of the way down to the beach at Malcasa Point.

How often had she taken the path down to *that* beach?

Dozens of times, at least. Maybe more than a hundred.

She found herself remembering the *first* time. With her mom and Jud and Larry.

Don't, she told herself.

She remembered riding Larry's back – playing 'horsey' as he twirled on the sand, squealing.

Poor old Larry.

Stop it! Don't think about any of that!

Blaze reminded her of Larry.

Good. Think about Blaze. Excellent idea.

Striding down the sandy path, she cast her memory back toward the time she'd met him. A long time ago. Twelve years.

I was hardly more than a kid . . .

The morning after the killings, Sandy had removed Eric from his cradle and gone exploring. About a hundred yards farther up the dirt road, they'd found Harry Matthews' log cabin. A large, blue pickup truck was parked beside it.

Leaving Eric on the ground for a few minutes, Sandy had crept around the outside of the cabin, pistol in hand.

Nobody seemed to be there.

She entered the front door and looked around.

Harry had apparently been living alone.

So she stepped outside and scooped up Eric and whispered, 'Looks like we've found us a home, honey.' She carried him in.

And there they stayed.

Right at the start, Sandy made up a story in case anyone should come along. She would claim that she was Harry's niece visiting him from Santa Monica. (She *had* lived in Santa Monica until she was twelve, so that'd be a good place to claim as her home.) If the story didn't work and real trouble started, or if somehow Eric got seen, she would simply kill the trouble-maker.

She never went anywhere without Harry's pistol in her pocket.

Day after day, however, nobody showed up.

They had no problems at all. The cabin and the surrounding woods seemed like a perfect hideaway, a sanctuary for herself and Eric.

He could grow up here . . .

But Sandy knew a problem was on its way.

As of the day they'd arrived, there had been only enough food in the cupboards, pantry and refrigerator to last for about two weeks.

Gradually, the supplies dwindled.

Dread stirred in her belly. Soon, she would need to leave the safety of the woods and venture into town for supplies.

On the bright side, she had some cash.

She'd been able to gather nearly four hundred dollars from her own purse, Lib's purse, and the wallets of Harry and Slade. She'd also found several credit cards and Harry's check book. The check book showed a balance of nearly nine thousand dollars.

The credit cards would do her no good at all.

The checks, on the other hand . . . She could use them to pay any bills that might come in the mail. Things like property tax, the electric bill (how nice that the cabin was wired for power!) or whatever else might turn up. Easy enough to forge Harry's signature. But she didn't see any safe way to use the checks for extra cash.

The cash wouldn't last forever.

Once it was gone . . .

Too soon, the time came to go into town for supplies.

Sandy didn't want to leave Eric alone, but what choice did she have? She *couldn't* take him with her; he'd be seen for sure. So after letting him suckle her that morning until he fell asleep, she carried him gently to his crib and put him down. Then she hurried out to Harry's pickup truck.

Lib's car and the trailer blocked the way out, but she managed to drive around them.

Fort Platt turned out to be a lot farther away than she'd thought.

It had taken her nearly an hour to get there.

The first thing she ran into, just on the other side of the bridge leading into town, was a place called the Sea Breeze Café. Though she felt an urgent need to buy supplies and rush back home to Eric, she *craved* a big, restaurant breakfast. Eggs over easy, bacon, hash browns, toast and coffee.

So she parked in its gravel lot, strolled in and . . .

No, she thought. That wasn't when I met Blaze. I didn't meet him until my *next* trip into town. That first time, I wanted to stop at the Sea Breeze, but didn't. I drove straight to the grocery store, bought two hundred dollars worth of food and stuff, and drove straight home.

And panicked.

Couldn't find Eric.

But then he turned up crawling around under the bed, happy as a clam.

It was two weeks later when . . .

That's the time I stopped for breakfast.

She'd hardly been able to enjoy it, though. For one thing, she felt guilty about spending the time away from Eric. For another, though the meal and tip would only cost about six dollars, it was money that would be gone forever.

I've gotta figure out a way to *make* money, she thought.

But how?

I can't go by my real name, don't have any fake i.d. or phoney Social Security number. Even if I had the right papers, I sure as hell couldn't get a job in town. Not unless it was just for a few hours one day a week or something. Wouldn't dare leave Eric alone any more than that.

I'm screwed, she thought.

There's a thought.

Make guys pay big bucks . . .

Yuck. No way.

There's gotta be something else I can do.

What am I good at? she wondered. I'm a hell of a Beast House tour guide. But that won't do me much good here and I can't exactly go back.

Besides, no matter what I *can* do, nobody'll hire me for any sort of legit job without an i.d. and a Social Security number.

Maybe there's something I can freelance at. Something I can do part time. Clean houses? Do yard work? Wash cars?

Beg on street corners?

Done with breakfast, depressed, Sandy parted with her money and went outside. She crossed the road and walked on the beach.

I'd better get to the store, she told herself.

Later. Just a little later.

She always felt better about life when she walked on the beach. Something about the fresh breeze, the sunlight, the steady roaring wash of the surf, the feel of the sand under her feet. They gave her a feeling of freedom, of wonderful possibilities.

She took off her shoes and socks, the better to feel the sand.

I'll think of something, she told herself as she strolled along.

This was obviously Fort Platt's main public beach. Though it wasn't exactly crowded, several people were sunbathing, stretched out on towels, napping or listening to radios or reading paperback books. Some kids played in the water. A gal was running with her Golden Retriever through the wet sand near the water's edge. A couple of young guys were tossing a Frisbee back and forth. Off in the distance, an artist was busy at a canvas. His subject appeared to be a tawny young man standing beside a surfboard.

That's it, Sandy thought. I'll be an artist.

A *stick-up* artist – the Jesse James of the Fort Platt beach.

She smirked at the notion.

But then she remembered Harry's pistol in her purse.

She *could* rob someone.

No way. I'd rather be a whore than a thief.

From another part of her mind, a voice chided, *What's a little armed robbery? You're too good to be a thief? You murdered three people, remember? Four if you count slitting the throat of Lib's husband.*

He shouldn't count, she told herself. He was probably dead already.

Anyway, she thought, I'm *not* going to rob anyone. I won't stoop to that. And even if I *wanted* to stoop that low, it'd be too damn stupid and dangerous. A stunt like that could get me thrown in jail. *Then* what would happen to Eric?

Nearing the artist and his model, Sandy realized that she would be walking between them if she didn't change course. The guy posing with his surfboard was right at the edge of the water. A wave would probably catch Sandy if she tried to walk behind him. Besides, she didn't really want to go anywhere near the guy. She supposed he was handsome enough to be a movie star, but he looked a little spooky to her. He was oily, muscle-bound, brown from the sun, and all he had on was the skimpiest, clingiest white bikini swimsuit she'd ever seen on a guy in real life.

Maybe she'd better circle around behind the painter. He looked like a decent fellow. About fifty years old, she supposed. Somewhat frail but also vibrant. Tidy and dapper in his Panama hat, white shirt and white trousers.

Either go around behind him, or just turn back. She really *should* be getting to the store.

But as she stood there trying to make up her mind, the painter cast her a cheery glance and said, 'Isn't he just the most *gorgeous* specimen?'

'Sure,' she said. 'If you say so.'

'Ha!'

The model, smirking at her, flexed a mound of bicep and made it hop.

'Oh, my,' the painter said. 'Now you have him showing off.'

'I know *I'm* bowled over,' Sandy said.

'Fuck off, little girl,' the model said.

'Tyrone!' snapped the artist. He seemed aghast. 'How *could* you!'

Tyrone answered with a snort.

'I'll not have you speaking to people that way! Especially not lovely young ladies. Not while you're in *my* employ! I won't *have* it!'

'You won't have it?' Tyrone asked, turning his smirk on the painter.

'No, I won't.'

'Then fuck you, you old queer.'

'How utterly charming. Go away.'

'You owe me a hundred bucks.'

'I believe the deal was for fifty.'

'You believe wrong, asshole.' Tyrone let the surfboard fall to the sand, then strode forward.

'Well, I suppose a hundred . . .' The artist reached into the back pocket of his white trousers and pulled out his wallet.

Tyrone stepped around the easel, glanced at the canvas, then faced the older man and held out a hand.

'A hundred bucks,' Tyrone said, and snapped his fingers.

'Don't *give* it to him,' Sandy said.

The painter gave her a defeated look. 'Oh, I believe I will.'

'You shouldn't.'

'I'd rather enjoy my health than . . .'

'I'm not even so sure you ought to give him fifty,' Sandy added. 'I mean, you had to fire him. You're not even done with the painting, are you?'

'No. I'd hardly gotten started on it.'

'Well, then . . .'

Tyrone turned on her. 'Look here, bitch. I already warned you once. Now get the fuck outa here. Or do you want to me to hurt you?'

'You're trying to rob this man,' Sandy pointed out.

'That's quite all right, dear. Please. I'll pay him the money, and . . .'

'Just the fifty, then.'

'Okay, that's it.' Tyrone trudged toward her, hunched over, arms out. 'You've had it.'

But he lurched to a stop when Sandy pulled the pistol out of her purse, jabbed it straight out toward the middle of his chest and said in a low, calm voice, 'Just try it, bub. I'll blow your ass to Kingdom Come.'

Tyrone gaped at her.

The painter, smiling gently, clapped his hands. 'Bravo, young lady! Bravo!'

After accepting his fifty dollars, Tyrone hefted his surfboard and trudged away, muttering.

'You are simply a marvel,' the painter told Sandy.

She put away the pistol, stepped up to him and offered her hand. 'My name's Ashley.'

'I'm Blaze.'

'Could you use a new model, Blaze?'

'Most certainly.'

'For fifty bucks, you can paint me.'

'I'd be most delighted.'

'Only thing is . . . What do you do with the paintings when you're done with them?'

'Sell them. They afford me a modest income.'

'So . . . like, other people might *see* them?'

'Is that a problem?'

'Sort of.'

'Well, considering your delicate age, I have no intention of asking you to disrobe.'

She blushed. 'It's not that.'

'What is it?'

'I don't want a bunch of strangers looking at me.'

He smiled gently. 'You want to be the subject of a painting, but you don't want people to look at it? I'm afraid that does present a bit of a difficulty.'

'Suppose the painting doesn't *look* like me?'

'And who *should* it look like?'

'Well, it can *sort of* look like me.'

'I should hope so. Otherwise, I fail to see the point in using you as a model.'

'I need the money.'

'I'd be happy to *give* you the fifty dollars. After all, you prevented Tyrone from stealing it.'

'I don't want a handout.'

'And *I* want you to pose for me. You have a special radiance, a strange and wonderful beauty. I *must* paint you. Suppose I raise the offer to a *hundred* dollars?'

'That's very nice of you, Blaze, but I'd still have the same problem even if you made it a thousand. The deal is, I'm sort of hiding from certain people. If you do a painting of me and they see it . . .' She shook her head. 'It'd be really bad.'

Blaze nodded, scowling. 'I see. You're on the lam. A desperado, of sorts. That explains the gat.'

'The truth is, there's a *guy* after me. This jerk named Steve from back home in Santa Monica. He's got the hots for me. He sort of . . . attacked me. He raped me, in point of fact. When I was still a little kid.'

'My God, how dreadful.'

'Well, they got him for it and sent him to prison. But now they've let him out.'

'They let him *out*? A man like that should *never* be allowed out of prison. Never! That's an outrage!'

'You're telling me. Anyway, I knew he'd be coming after me so I ran away from home. The way I see it, he can't rape me if he can't find me.'

'What about your parents?'

'Dead.'

'Oh, how awful.'

'I was living with an aunt. But she has a couple of kids of her own – little girls about the same age I was when Dad attacked *me*. So I figured I'd do us *all* a favor and hit the road.'

'*Dad?*'

'Huh?'

'*Dad* attacked you?'

'I didn't say that. Steve.' But she realized that she *had* said it. Her phoney story had veered too close to the truth – and they'd collided. She could feel herself blushing. The blush was probably a dead giveaway.

'Steve's your own father?' Blaze asked. 'You were molested by your father?'

'Yeah.'

'And you're running away from him?'

She nodded.

And she could see the belief in Blaze's eyes.

Why *shouldn't* he believe it? she thought. It's damn near the truth. Except that the name should be Roy, not Steve. And Roy's pursuit of her had come to a messy end in Beast House a couple of years ago.

Comes right down to it, Dad is *the reason I'm on the run.*

Dirty fucking bastard.

Blaze, staring into her eyes, put both his hands on her shoulders. He squeezed them gently. 'Do you need a place to stay?'

'No. Thanks, though. I have a place. It's a good hideout, but its sort of far away.'

'You have a place, but no money.'

'Not much.'

'I'll paint you. I'll pay you a hundred dollars today. And you needn't worry about being recognized. I'll capture your essence and beauty but conceal your identity.'

'Do you think you can do that?'

'Bite your tongue! You're speaking to Blaze O. Glory, the greatest artist of the age . . . whether anyone else knows it or not.'

Chapter Twenty-Eight

Owen Tries Again

Watching through the bars of the fence, Owen had seen Dana come around from behind Beast House with the other guides. Near the corner of the house, three of them, all females, had walked toward the ticket booth. Dana, followed by the male guide, had headed for the front porch.

She hadn't slowed down to walk with the guy.

Maybe she doesn't like him.

Good taste, Owen thought.

Owen hadn't seen much of him yesterday, but figured he knew the type. Handsome, big and muscular, arrogant, acts like he owns the world. Exactly the kind of jerk who always ended up with all the most beautiful women.

Like Dana.

The sort of women who couldn't be bothered with guys like Owen.

Maybe Dana's different, he told himself. She sure *seems* nice and friendly.

But I bet she wouldn't go out with me.

Not that I'd have the guts to ask.

He'd watched her climb the porch stairs, her calves smooth and dark, the tan seat of her uniform shorts pulling briefly smooth against one side of her rump, then the other. Her shorts had rear pockets with button-down flaps. The pockets didn't bulge. They seemed to be empty, the way they showed Dana's curves.

The male guide had chased her up the stairs, dodged the legs of Gus Goucher, and opened the door for Dana. Then he'd followed her into Beast House.

Earlier, Dana had gone inside with the small, cute guide. They'd come out about five minutes later. But Owen figured that she'd be staying inside, this time. She and the guy were probably taking their places to get ready for the tours.

Through the front window of the ticket booth, Owen saw a side door open. A guide entered and shut the door. It was the plump, friendly girl who'd taken their tickets yesterday.

Monica had gotten snippy with her.

Monica. Oh, my God.

Owen suddenly felt hot and squirmy.

What've I done?

He glanced at his wristwatch. Two minutes till ten. Though Monica was a late sleeper, she would certainly be awake by now. Awake and wondering where the hell Owen had disappeared to.

How could I do this to her?

She had it coming, he told himself.

But to just abandon her . . .

She'll be fine, he thought. Soon as she gets used to me being gone, she can relax and enjoy herself, explore all the wonders of San Francisco without the nuisance of *my* presence. The hotel's on my credit card. I left her airline ticket behind so she can fly home if she gets the urge. She has plenty of money, plus her own credit cards.

She'll get along just fine.

Never acted like she wanted me around in the first place.

Well, now she's got what she was asking for. Hope she's happy.

I did you a favor, bitch.

So why do I feel so guilty about it?

Owen had gone through these matters before.

Many times.

In the cab on his way to the airport, then during the long drive back through San Francisco, over the Golden Gate Bridge and up the coast to Malcasa Point, he'd studied his actions, struggled with guilt, tried to justify what he'd done, and wondered what the consequences might be.

He supposed he must've spent the better part of four hours going over it all.

For a while, he'd worried that Monica might call the police. She probably *would* have called them except for one thing: his luggage had disappeared with him. Which made it fairly clear that he'd gone away on purpose.

No crime in that, as far as he knew.

After all, it wasn't as if he'd run off and abandoned his spouse.

Owen had decided that he could stop worrying about the police.

But that still left him with plenty of other concerns.

Again and again, he'd concluded that he was definitely a jerk for ditching Monica. No question about that. A gentleman would never do such a thing. He should've stuck with her, no matter what.

But he was *delighted* that he hadn't.

She had it coming. What did she think, I'd hang around and take her crap forever?

Inside the ticket booth, the plump girl slid open the window.

A big, heavy guy with glasses was first in line. He stepped up to buy his ticket.

He was one of the eight or ten people who'd arrived before Owen. He wore a black cap backwards, its bill sticking out behind his head. Though it looked like a baseball cap, it bore a Beast House logo the same as the guides wore on their uniform shirts.

Earlier, Owen had been tempted to approach him.

Say hi, introduce himself, ask where he got the neat hat.

Why not? The guy seemed to be alone. He was about the same age as Owen, and he looked friendly enough.

But maybe he didn't want company.

Owen had decided not to bother him.

The guy stepped away from the window, clamped the ticket between his front teeth, and stuffed some bills into his wallet. Then he lifted the drooping tail of his shirt and shoved the wallet into a seat pocket of his plaid Bermuda shorts. His calves were round and pale. He wore moccasins and no socks.

Kind of a slob, Owen thought and watched him stroll around the corner of the ticket booth.

The others in line ahead of Owen seemed like ordinary tourist types. Three of them were gals, but they didn't interest him. They couldn't compare to Dana.

He pulled out his wallet and slipped a Visa card out of its slot in the leather.

Then he wondered if he should use cash, instead. His wallet was bulging. Here was a chance to slim it down by a hundred and fifteen dollars, especially if he paid with small bills.

But what if I get over to the Welcome Inn and find out they don't take credit cards?

I'd better hang on to my cash, he thought. Better safe than sorry.

What if they haven't got a vacancy?

Don't worry about it, he told himself. Just take things as they come.

He stepped up to the ticket window.

'Good morning,' the girl said. 'Welcome to Beast House.'

'Thanks.' He smiled in at her. The nametag on her chest read Rhonda. Though he remembered her from yesterday, he hadn't been able to recall her name.

Does she remember me?

'I'd like one general admission,' he told her. 'And can I also buy a ticket for tomorrow night's Midnight Tour?'

'The Midnight Tour? Let me check for you.' She turned aside and typed something into a computer. Nodding, she faced Owen. 'You're in luck. It hasn't sold out yet.'

'It sells out?'

'Oh, sure does. We like to keep it small and intimate, so we only allow thirteen guests.'

'Thirteen?'

'Don't worry, you'll just be number nine. Somebody else can be thirteen.'

'Lucky him. Or her.'

'We normally don't *tell* whoever it is.'

'Then how do I know *I'm* not thirteen.'

Rhonda blushed. 'You'll just have to take my word for it.'

'Happy to.'

A warm smile spread across her face. 'Will that be a single admission for you?'

'Right, just one.'

'That'll be a hundred dollars. Plus fifteen for today. How would you like to pay for that?'

'I guess I'll have you put it on this.' He pushed the Visa card across the counter.

After signing for the charge, he was given a receipt, his ticket for the daytime audio tour, and a large red ticket.

'Both tickets have coupons for discounts at the snack stand and museum.'

'Right.'

'The red one, that's your ticket for the Midnight Tour. It'll be your admission to the picnic which takes place here on the grounds tomorrow night at eight. After the picnic, there'll be a special ten o'clock showing of *The Horror* at the theater up the street. Then comes the tour itself.'

'At midnight?'

'On the dot. The guide will lead you over to Beast House after the movie ends. Anyway, all the details are written out for you on the back of the ticket. But if you have any questions, just ask. I'll be here all day today and tomorrow.'

'Okay. Thank you.'

'Enjoy yourself, Owen.'

'Thanks.'

He almost added 'Rhonda' to show that he'd noticed her name, too. But he stopped himself and stepped away from the window.

She'd seemed a little bit *too* friendly. Owen didn't want to encourage her.

If I get involved with anyone around here, it isn't going to be Rhonda.

Standing near the corner of the booth, he slipped the red ticket into his shirt pocket. It protruded a couple of inches.

What if it falls out and I lose it?

He considered folding the ticket in half.

Nah. It'll be all right. Long as I don't bend over too far, or something.

He put away his credit card, returned his wallet to the back pocket of his trousers, and stepped around the corner.

'Morning,' said another guide he recognized from yesterday. A blonde with a deep tan and pale blue eyes – a real beauty, but so athletic and tough-looking that Owen found her somewhat frightening. She looked like she ought to be a skiing instructor somewhere in the high Sierras. Or the Alps. According to the tag above her jutting right breast, her name was Sharon.

'Good morning,' Owen said, and gave her the ticket for today's tour. She tore it. 'You know about the discounts, right?'

'Yep.'

She handed the stub to him, then turned away and stepped over to the cupboard where the audio players were stored. She reached up and pulled one down. 'It's all rewound and ready to go,' she said, coming toward Owen. 'You wear it around your neck like this.'

She put it on him, leaning in close and raising her arms to lift the strap over his head. He smelled cigarette smoke and perfume and spearmint chewing gum.

He began to feel a little breathless and trembly.

'Thanks,' he said.

'I saw you here yesterday, didn't I?'

Heat rushed to his face. 'Yeah. But I didn't get to see everything. My girlfriend got sick and we had to leave.'

'Well, glad you could make it back. I guess you already know how the tour works.'

'Right.'

'Hope it goes better for you today.'

'Thanks. I'm sure it will.'

Turning toward the house, Owen put his headphones on.

Some of those who'd preceded him through the ticket line were gathered in front of the porch, eyes on the hanging body of Gus Goucher. The big guy with the Beast House cap was snapping photos of Gus.

As Owen approached, the others climbed the porch stairs and went into the house. The big guy stayed, ducking and bobbing with the big black camera at his eye.

One of the guides seemed to be watching him.

She was the small, cute blonde who'd given Dana a ride to work in her Jeep. The same one who'd briefly gone into Beast House with her. She stood at the top of the porch stairs, leaning back against a support post, one ankle resting across the other, arms folded across her chest.

She frowned slightly as she stared at the camera-happy fat guy.

She didn't even glance at Owen.

He felt like an intruder as he walked toward them.

He wondered if he should just keep moving. After all, he'd done Station One yesterday. He didn't really need to stop and listen to it all over again.

But if I don't stop, she'll think I goofed. She'll point out my mistake.

Besides, Owen really *wanted* to start from scratch. This time, with no Monica moaning and smirking by his side, he might be able to concentrate on the tour and really enjoy it.

He stopped a few paces away from the foot of the stairs, lifted the player to take a look at its control buttons, and was about to press Start when the big guy waved at him and called out, 'Hey, buddy?'

Owen raised his eyebrows and pointed to himself.

'Yeah, you. Wanta do me a big favor?'

Up on the porch, the guide uncrossed her arms and stood up straight.

'Could I get you to take my picture with poor old Gus here? Okay? You mind?'

'No, that'd be fine.'

The guy hurried toward him, smiling and nodding, reaching out with the camera.

Owen took it.

'It's all automatic. Just push this right here.'

'Got it.'

The big guy rushed up the porch stairs to Gus, stood close to the dangling legs, put an arm around them and smiled.

'Ready?' Owen asked.

'Just a sec.' He turned his head toward the guide. 'Why don't you come over and be in the picture, too?' he asked.

'Aaaa, you don't want me in it.'

'Sure, I do. Are you kidding?'

'You don't even know me.'

'I'm John,' he said. 'John Cromwell.'

'Nice to meet you, John.' She turned toward Owen. 'And you are?'

'Owen.'

'Hi, Owen.'

'Hi.'

'I'm Lynn,' she said, more to Owen than to John.

'Now we all know each other,' John said. 'Hop on over and join me in the picture.'

'Well, if you're sure . . .'

'Come on.'

Walking toward him, Lynn said, 'We'd better hurry, though. We don't want to be in the way of these people.'

Owen glanced back and saw a family of five strolling toward them. Earlier, they'd been directly behind him in the line. They'd seemed like nice people, the kids quiet and well-behaved.

When he returned his attention to the porch, he found John standing between Lynn and the lynched dummy – arms around both.

And Lynn seemed to have an arm around John.

Boy! How'd John manage that?

'Better take it,' Lynn said.

He snapped the photo.

John said, 'Take a second one, just in . . .' and squeezed Lynn in against his side.

She yelped and laughed as Owen took the second shot. Then she escaped and swatted John on his butt.

'Spank me again,' he told her. 'Please.'

Laughing, she shook her head. 'That's more than enough, Johnny boy.'

Owen climbed the porch stairs, ready to return John's camera.

'Thanks for the help,' John told him.

'No problem.'

Lynn glanced at Owen's chest. 'Ah, ha! I see you've bought a ticket for the Midnight Tour!'

He blushed and smiled. 'Yeah. I can't wait.'

'Doing it tomorrow night?' she asked.

'Yeah.'

'Me, too,' she said. 'I'll be your guide.'

'Really? Great!'

She turned to John. 'You coming on it, too?'

The big guy's mouth fell open. He blinked a few times. Then he said, '*You're* the guide?'

'I'm *always* the guide. It's my tour. I originated it.'

'Wow,' John said. He looked awestruck.

'So, are you gonna be there?'

'Uh . . . Gosh . . . I guess I'd sure *like* to. But it's like a hundred bucks, isn't it?'

'It *is* a hundred bucks.'

He grimaced. 'That's a lot of money.'

'Worth every nickle.'

'Bet it is,' he mumbled, shaking his head. 'But I don't know.'

'Well, I hope you decide to join us. I think there're still a few openings.'

'I just got number nine,' Owen said.

'That only leaves four,' Lynn said. Reaching out, she patted John's arm. 'Better make up your mind soon, pal.'

'I might just do it,' he said.

'I've gotta go.' Lynn started down the porch stairs. 'So long, Owen. So long, John. Hope I see you *both* tomorrow night.'

'Bye,' Owen called after her.

'See ya,' John called.

In front of the porch, Lynn made her way around the cluster of tourists at Station One and headed off to the side.

'What a bitchin' babe,' John said.

'Yeah,' said Owen, and gave him the camera.

'Wouldn't kick *her* outa bed. Know what I mean?'

'I know.'

'Man, I *gotta* go on that Midnight Tour.'

'It should be pretty cool.'

'I need me a hundred bucks.'

Uh-oh.

'They take credit cards,' Owen explained, starting to feel embarrassed and guilty.

'Who's got credit cards?'

Everybody I know, Owen thought.

This guy *hasn't* got credit cards?

'I maxed 'em all out,' John explained.

Brilliant, Owen thought.

John reached under the loose tail of his shirt and hauled out his wallet. He opened it. Owen caught a glimpse inside the bill compartment and looked away quickly.

He wanted nothing to do with any of this.

He wanted to be away from John and inside the house, alone, listening to the tape.

'Got only twenty-three bucks,' John announced. 'Shit.'

It's not my fault.

Owen wanted to say, 'Well, I'd better get on with the tour,' but he knew how awful that would sound. Why not just say, 'I don't give a rat's ass about your money troubles, fella. I don't even know you. Just leave me alone so I can enjoy the tour.'

'Did you bring your check book?' Owen asked.

'Nah, it's at home.'

'Where's home?'

'Mattoon.'

'*Where?*'

'Mattoon. Illinois.'

'My God, you're a long way from home.'

'You telling me?'

'And you left your check book all the way back in Illinois?'

'Sure. Closed the bank account before I took off.'

'Ah. So how did you get *here?*'

'Drove.'

'So you have a car?'

'Well, it's my brother's. I borrowed it off him.'

'And now all you've got to your name is twenty-three dollars?'

'That's about the size of it.'

Owen shook his head and laughed.

'What's so funny?'

'You're a couple of thousand miles from home and down to your last twenty bucks, but you managed to buy yourself a brand new Beast House hat *and* you blew fifteen bucks on today's tour.'

John grinned. His teeth were crooked and needed to be brushed. Owen looked away from them. 'That ain't all,' John said. 'I blew fifteen bucks on the tour *yesterday*, too.'

'Good God. You must be nuts.'

'Nuts about Beast House,' he said as if proud of himself. 'Thing is, I always aimed to get here with enough money left over for the Midnight Tour and the whole shebang, but I ran into some car trouble along the way and had to buy me a whole new radiator. Car's a piece of crap.'

'Well, I wish I could help you out. But . . .' He shrugged.

'Forget it,' John said. 'I ain't no freeloader. But you wanta do me a real big favor?'

Owen struggled not to groan. Trying to smile pleasantly, he asked, 'What sort of favor?'

'Take my camera with you on the Midnight Tour? Get me some pictures of the good stuff? And a couple pictures of Lynn, too. That way, at least I'll be able to see what I missed. How about it?'

'Well . . .'

John thrust the camera at him.

Owen held it away. 'No, no, wait. Just keep your camera, okay?'

'You won't . . .?' John looked ready to cry.

'The tour isn't till tomorrow night. I don't want to be . . . responsible for your camera. Look. Look. Tell you what. Are you hungry?'

'Starving.'

'Me, too. Why don't we go on over to the snack stand and have something to eat.'

John shook his head. 'Gotta save my money.'

'My treat. Come on. We can do the house tour later.'

'Well. Okay. Sure. Why not?'

Side by side, they trotted down the porch stairs.

How the hell did I get into this? Owen wondered.

Payback for dumping Monica?

Chapter Twenty-Nine

Sandy's Story – July, 1992

Reaching the beach ahead of Blaze, Sandy looked around. Nobody seemed to be out on the water. She studied the rocky bluffs on both sides of the beach and saw no one. Good thing. Because this was such a secluded patch of shoreline, Blaze probably intended her to pose in the nude.

She lowered the easel and cooler onto the sand, then sat on the cooler to wait for him. She could see him a distance up the trail, making his way carefully down its switchbacks, the wind fluttering his white shirt and trousers.

'Be careful!' she called.

'I'm quite all right,' he called down to her.

A few minutes later, huffing and red, he walked out onto the sand. 'Invigorating,' he said.

'Well, don't invigorate yourself into a heart attack.'

He flung back his head and filled his lungs. Then he said, 'Ahhhhh. Is this not delightful?'

She had to smile. 'It's pretty nice, all right.'

Blaze looked all around. 'I see we have our privacy.'

'Nobody else is nuts enough to come all the way down here.'

'Let's hope it remains that way. The sooner we start, the better.'

'I'm ready when you are.'

He laughed, then got to work setting up his equipment. Sandy remained seated on the cooler, but swiveled around to watch him. She knew better than to offer any help. Blaze, very particular about the positioning of his easel and canvas, wanted no interference.

He set up on the firm, damp sand just beyond the reach of the waves, his canvas at about a forty-five-degree angle to the shoreline.

'Where am *I* gonna be, in the ocean?'

He grinned at her. 'Precisely! It promises to be brilliant! You'll be trudging out of the sea, wet and bedraggled, half drowned – as if perhaps your ship went down a mile or two offshore. I'll call it, *Sole Survivor*.' He clapped his hands and blurted, 'Ha! I'll call it *Soul Survivor*, s-o-u-l. Or is that a bit too precious?'

'Maybe.'

'Well, I'll think of something. We should get started.'

Sandy stood up. Fingering the front of her gown, she said, 'You want this off?'

'I think not. You don't mind getting it wet?'

'Whatever you want.'

'I'm afraid if we're *sans* attire, we may lose the narrative. People will think you're returning from a frolic. We'd have all the drama of a skinny-dipping episode. No, no, we must have the gown! It will tell everyone that you've survived a mishap. You had no intention of taking a plunge. Perhaps your ship went down. Or you fell off a yacht, or leaped overboard to escape a madman. No one will quite know for sure *why* you were in the water. Do you see?'

'I see.'

'We attain *elusiveness*. Elusiveness, my dear, is what separates the artist from the mindless painter. We *hint* at mysterious vistas and depths.'

'So you want me to keep this on.'

'Precisely.'

'And wade into the water.'

'I need you to be drenched.'

'Including the hair?'

'Certainly!'

'My hair won't look too great if its all wet and stringy.'

'Be that as it may . . . You've been swimming for hours, struggling to reach land, so of course your hair *has* to be . . . No! No, no, no! Your hair shall be *dry*! Dry and windblown and fabulous, just as it is now. And the people will gaze in amazement and ask themselves *why*? *Why* is her hair dry? It will mystify everyone!'

'It'll give you some more of that elusiveness,' Sandy pointed out, grinning.

'Precisely! Look at her! She has barely escaped extinction in the briny deep, yet her hair is totally dry! *Why*? *Why* is the carcass of a leopard to be found near the summit of Kilimanjaro?'

'Huh?'

'Hemingway.'

'Muriel?'

'Bite your tongue.'

'Maybe we should keep the gown dry, too.'

'Don't be silly. Now, go on into the water. Drench yourself, but be careful of the hair.'

She slipped out of her sandals and walked over the warm, damp sand to the edge of the ocean. A wave was coming in. She waited for it, watched it curl and tumble and flatten out, sliding its frothy edge up the sand. The cold water washed over the tops of her feet, making her flinch.

As the wave receded, she hurried forward, splashing through the water until it reached her thighs. A wave washed against her, wetting her to the waist. After it had passed, she crouched down enough to let the next wave wash against her chest. Then she stood up straight and cupped water onto her shoulders.

Looking down, she saw that her shoulders and the tops of her breasts gleamed in the sunlight. The gown clung to her, blue and transparent. It revealed every detail of her body. But it didn't feel so great. No longer light and airy, it felt like a layer of someone else's wet skin.

She turned toward Blaze. He was gazing at her from behind his easel. 'How's this?' she called.

'Supurb! You look glorious! But be a dear and take a few steps forward. We don't want to have the water hiding those extraordinary legs.'

'Want me to stand on the beach?'

'No, no.'

As Sandy walked slowly closer to the shore, Blaze scurried over to her. He stepped into the water. Taking her gently by the shoulders, he moved backward. 'This way,' he said. 'A little more. Yes. Here. Right leg forward. Yes. Exactly. Lean into it. Now we turn you toward me.' He adusted her position. 'Yes. Now, hunch over. You're bone weary, barely able to stand on your feet.' He stepped back and studied her. 'Put your right hand on your knee. Yes, that's it. No. You're hunched over too much. We can't have your left arm dangling so much. It's in the way of your boobie. Stand a trifle straighter. More. Yes. Excellent.'

He hurried away. Once again standing behind his easel, he squinted at her. 'Now, look toward me, darling. Stare intently over my left shoulder as if perhaps you see something far down the beach. Yes. Exactly.' He squinted at her for a while, then frowned. 'No.'

'What?'

'It's simply not the way I . . . You need to look more . . . done in.'

'Want me to sprawl on the sand?'

'Not *that* done in. We need to maintain the illusion of movement.' He frowned at her for a few moments. Then he said, 'Don't move,' and scampered back to her. 'I'm afraid we may have to ruin your lovely dress.'

'Whatever works.'

He pulled out a Swiss Army knife, pried open one of its blades, and slit the left shoulder strap of Sandy's gown. The soaked fabric still adhered to her breast, so he peeled it down. 'Much better,' he said. '*Now*, you look distressed.'

'I *feel* a lot better,' she said, glad to have the clammy fabric off her breast. 'Maybe we should take it *all* off.'

'No no no. I already explained.'

'I know, I know.'

'This will be brilliant.' He started trotting back to his position behind the easel.

'Blaze?'

'Yes?' He glanced back.

'How about this?' Not waiting for a reply, she reached down and tore a slit up the front of her dress, baring her right leg all the way to her hip.

Blaze beamed at her. 'Perfect! You're a genius!'

'That's how come you give me twenty per cent.'

'No no no. I give you twenty per cent because you gave me no choice.'

'Feel free to dump me any time.'

'Don't tempt me.'

She knew he couldn't be tempted. The amount of money Blaze was making with his paintings of Sandy, he would probably be willing to part with *fifty* per cent if she gave him no other choice.

He seemed ready to begin, so she gazed intently into the distance beyond his left shoulder.

Not that there was much distance to gaze into.

About twenty feet behind Blaze was the side of a rocky outcropping. Sandy pretended it wasn't there, and gazed through it as if trying to identify something a few hundred yards away. An approaching stranger, maybe.

Then she began to wonder how much Blaze *would* be willing to pay her. Maybe even more than fifty per cent.

Without me . . .

At her first sight of Blaze's estate, Sandy had assumed that he was an enormously successful artist.

Not so.

He'd bought the estate with inherited money. His artwork sold only modestly well, earning him just enough income for a comfortable living.

Until Sandy showed up.

For the first couple of years, he'd paid her no more than the fifty dollars per session. And she'd been delighted to get it. After posing, she would hurry around to a few stores, buying food and supplies, picking up treats for Eric. Then she would hop into the pickup truck and rush home.

Near the end of the second year, however, Eric had started spending most of his days roaming the wooded hills. He was often nowhere to be found by the time Sandy returned from town. So she began to wonder why she bothered to hurry back.

One day, she *didn't* hurry back. Instead, she wandered the streets of Fort Platt, exploring the town, dropping into shops that she'd previously seen only from the outside.

Including the Beachside Gallery.

She entered the gallery feeling like an intruder. It was so *quiet*. Was she the only one here? Silently, hardly daring to breathe, she wandered among the paintings.

She half expected to be discovered and kicked out.

After all, at her age she could hardly be expected to have enough money to purchase much of anything.

She was well dressed, though. Blaze, that day, had outfitted her in tennis whites and she'd posed for him on a court behind the high school. She still wore the tennis skirt and pullover. She looked like a rich kid whose parents might belong to one of the nearby country clubs.

If they give me any crap, I'll threaten to sic my parents on them.

Sure, she thought.

Just act as if you belong here, she told herself. Act like you own the place.

Taking a deep, shaky breath, she wandered deeper into the gallery. She moved slowly and looked at every painting.

Many featured the surf crashing into rocky outcroppings. The surf crashed into them in daylight, at sunset, and in the moonlight. There were beautiful ocean vistas. Several underwater paintings depicted whales and dolphins. Sailboats glided into sunsets. She saw storm-tossed seas, a ghost ship with tattered sails, footprints in the sand along the shoreline, seagulls gliding through the pale sky.

And *Surfer Boy*, which showed a tawny, muscular young man wearing the skimpiest of swimsuits, posed on the beach with his surfboard. The sight of it gave Sandy a twist in the stomach.

Tyrone!

Stepping up close to the painting, she found Blaze's signature low in a corner.

The price tag showed $450 with a slash through it, replaced by $150.

Sandy smirked.

Having some trouble selling it?

'It's one of *my* favorites.'

She jumped, then whirled around.

A short, round woman gazed up at Sandy through huge round glasses with red plastic rims. Her gray hair was cut to an even dome of bristle. She wore huge, gold hoop earrings and a flowing muu-muu.

Offering a hand, she said, 'I'm Megan Willows, proprietor.'

'Hi.' Sandy shook her hand. 'I'm Ashley.'

'Ashley. A lovely name. I couldn't help noticing your interest in our *Surfer Boy*.'

She nodded. 'It sort of caught my eye.'

'You must have a very good eye, then. This is an earlier work by one of our fine local artists, Blaze O. Glory. His talent has absolutely *bloomed* in recent years.'

'Must've bloomed *after* he did this one,' Sandy said.

Megan chortled. 'You *do* have a good eye. This is certainly not one of his more mature works. But it does have a certain raw power, don't you think?'

'I guess so.'

'A lovely boy. Isn't he just scrumptious? Wouldn't you just like to *eat him up*?' Grinning, Megan clicked her teeth together.

'I don't know about *that*,' Sandy said.

'A figure of speech, Ashley. But wouldn't you just *adore* having him on your bedroom wall?'

'I don't know.'

'Or are you considering this as a gift?'

'No. I'm looking for myself. I got a ton of money for . . . my birthday.' She had almost said 'graduation,' but realized Megan might not believe it. Sandy looked mature for her age, but she might not pass for a high-school graduate. She shrugged and smiled. 'I thought I might want to spend it on some art.'

'That's a very wise decision, Ashley. A good piece of art is not only a pleasure to the soul, but often a sound investment. You certainly wouldn't go wrong, on either count, by purchasing *Surfer Boy*. And it *is* a wonderful bargain at a hundred and fifty dollars.'

'I don't think it's worth that much,' Sandy said. 'Not to me, anyway.'

'Well . . . I suppose I would be willing to mark it down to . . . shall we say, a hundred dollars?'

'I don't honestly think so,' Sandy said.

'It's a steal at that price. You wouldn't be able to *touch* one of his more recent pieces for . . .'

Sandy shook her head.

'Seventy-five dollars. I'm afraid that's as low as I'll be able to go. What do you think? That would include the frame, of course. The frame alone is worth fifty.' She blinked behind her goggles and grinned. 'So, do we have a sale?'

'I'm afraid not. You know what? I don't think my parents would approve of me buying a thing like that. I mean, it may be a just a little too *risqué*. You can darn near see his *unit*, if you know what I mean.'

'Well . . .' Megan chuckled. 'I suppose so. We wouldn't want to upset your parents, would we?'

'Not much.'

'Maybe I can interest you in something else?'

'Well, I *would* like to see some of the more recent work by this guy. Flame?'

'Blaze.'

'Right, him. Could I see something else of his?'

'I'm afraid we only have one in stock just now, and it's already sold. You're welcome to look at it, however.'

'I'd like to. Thanks.'

Leading her toward the other side of the gallery, Megan said, 'We do expect another one in, fairly soon. Perhaps in two or three weeks. We have a *terrible* time keeping his paintings in stock. Ah. Here we are.' Megan stepped aside, swept an arm toward the painting and said, '*Voila!*'

'Oh! That *is* nice.'

'Isn't it? Mmm.'

Sandy had posed for it only a month earlier. The setting *looked* great – a clearing in the deep woods, all rich green and shadows and golden pillars of sunlight slanting down through the trees. But there hadn't been a breath of a breeze. In the shadows and dampness of the sylvan scene, the mosquitos had been nearly overwhelming. Few had feasted on her, thanks to the repellent, but they'd mobbed her anyway. Some had gotten into her ears. One had even taken a detour into her eye.

The girl in the painting sure didn't *look* distressed, though. She seemed carefree and contented like a kid on the first day of summer vacation.

And a bit like a monkey.

She'd actually been standing on a stool, but the stool was nowhere to be seen.

She looked as if she'd been hiking through the woods, happened upon a likely limb, and leaped up to swing on it just for fun. She dangled crooked below the limb, hanging on with her right hand, her left arm waving, her left leg kicking out wildly to the side.

You're a tomboy frolicking in the forest, Blaze had told her.

A barefoot tomboy wearing cut-off blue jeans and a short-sleeved red shirt. The cut-offs were very short, faded almost to white, and torn at the sides. The red shirt, also faded, looked too small for her. The way she dangled, it was pulled up halfway to her ribcage, showing her midriff and navel and how her shorts hung so low they looked ready to fall down. Partly unbuttoned, the shirt showed the bare slope of her left breast.

Blaze had called the painting, *Huckleberry Fem*.

Below the sticker reading SOLD, Sandy saw the price tag.

$5,800.

'Holy smoke,' she muttered.

'If you ask me,' Megan said, 'it's a masterpiece. I absolutely *adore* it. Look at that girl. So . . . fresh and innocent. And yet so . . . *alluring*. It's as if Blaze has captured the magical blend of childhood innocence on the verge of blossoming sensuality.'

'Sure looks that way,' Sandy said.

'Wouldn't you just *love* to take her home with you?'

'Yeah. Sure would. Too bad it's already sold.'

'As I said, we'll probably be getting another one in fairly soon.'

'Are they all this good?'

'Oh, yes. The new ones most certainly are. Ever since he's been using Electra.'

'Huh?'

'Electra. That's the name of his model.'

'He uses the same model in all of them?'

'Oh, yes. Isn't she a *find*? She's simply *devastating*.'

Sandy almost slipped and said, *Thanks*. But she caught herself in time.

'She's Blaze's niece, you know. Such a beauty! She comes all the way up from San Francisco twice a month to pose for him. I've met her myself, and she is just the most *charming* creature.'

Liar, liar, pants on fire.

'Well,' Sandy said, 'I've got to be on my way. Maybe I'll come in for a look at the new one.'

'Try us early next week. Of course, we never know for sure when Blaze will come in, but we *are* the only gallery he deals with. If you want an Electra, this is the place to come. And, as I mentioned, they sell as fast as we're able to hang them on the wall. Your best bet would be to come in daily.'

'Well, we'll see. Thanks again.'

Sandy walked out of the gallery, amazed that Megan hadn't recognized her, determined never to return, delighted that paintings of *her* could be so highly prized, and looking foward to an increase in pay from Blaze.

A *big* increase.

And she'd gotten it.

She'd decided not to tell him about her visit to the art gallery, but just to . . .

'Be a good girl and wet yourself up again,' Blaze said, snapping Sandy out of the memories. 'You're losing your cling.'

'Wouldn't want to lose that,' she said. She stretched, then turned around and waded into deeper water. There, she dunked herself to the shoulders. The water felt cold and good. She came up with her dress clinging, her skin shiny wet.

'Fabulous,' Blaze said.

She returned to her former position and bent over with her right leg forward, her body turned slightly toward Blaze. She fixed her eyes on the rocks beyond him.

'Tilt your head up slightly. Good, good. Fabulous.'

Blaze resumed painting.

After a while, he said, 'This may be our masterpiece.'

'What's your asking price?' someone called.

The man's voice seemed to come from somewhere in the rocks beyond Blaze.

Chapter Thirty

Picture Perfect

At the snack stand, Owen asked for a Red-Hot Beastie Weenie, fries and a medium Creature Cola. John Cromwell ordered a Double-Decker Monsterburger Deluxe, Beastly Chili Fries with cheese, and a large Creature Cola. Owen paid for both meals.

'You're really a pal,' John said and patted him on the shoulder.

'Well, glad to help.'

'Most guys wouldn't do that, you know?'

'Well . . .'

'Good man. Hope I can do something for you some day.'

'Well, that's all right. Don't worry about it.'

Soon, the food was ready. They carried their trays over to a corner table and sat down.

John stripped off the paper and poked his straw through the split X on the lid of his drink. He sucked up some cola, then sighed. 'Know what I'll do for you? I'll take your picture.'

'Ah, that's . . .'

John shoved his chair back and stood up.

'You don't have to.'

'I want to. No, seriously.' Stepping away from the table, he raised the camera to his eye. 'Just act natural,' he said. 'None of this cheese shit.'

Owen laughed.

John snapped the shot, then sidestepped and took another. Then he returned to the table. 'I'll send 'em to you,' he said, sitting down.

Send them to me? He'll need my address.

What if he drops in for a visit?

'Ah,' Owen said, 'you don't have to . . .'

'Tell you what, pal. Know what I'll do? I saw you scoping out that guide. Lynn. A real babe-a-roo, huh? How about if I send you copies of the shots with her in 'em, too? Bet you'd like that, huh?'

'I guess so,' he admitted.

'You *guess* so.' John laughed.

'Yeah, that'd be fine.'

'It's done, man.' He stretched his mouth open wide and bit into his huge burger. Juices and melted cheese dribbled off and spattered the paper lining of the basket.

Mouth watering, Owen picked up his Red-Hot Beastie Weenie and took a bite. The buttery, grilled bun crunched. His teeth popped through the charbroiled skin of the hot dog. Warm, spicy juices flooded his mouth.

John said something, but his mouth was full so Owen couldn't understand a word that came out.

'Huh?'

John chewed for a while, swallowed a couple of times, and said with his mouth only half full, 'Weenie-eater.'

'That's me.'

For a while, they ate and didn't talk.

Owen thought about John's offer to send him photos of Lynn. He would be glad to get them, all right. But he wasn't eager to let John have his home address.

Even if I give it to him, he probably won't send the pictures. People are always making promises like that, but they hardly ever follow through.

Later, John paused in his eating and said, 'So, how about what we were talking about before?'

'What?'

'Will you take my camera with you on the Midnight Tour? Do that for me, I'll get doubles made and send you one of everything.'

Owen shook his head.

'Come on, man. Please. What's it gonna hurt?'

'I have my own camera.'

'No sweat. Take shots with both.'

'Do they even *allow* photography inside the house?'

'Can't use a flash. I already checked. But I got high-speed film. Four hundred. You don't gotta have a flash, not if there's any kind of decent light at all. So what kinda film *you* using?'

'Two hundred.'

'You're fucked. Won't get dick inside the house, night or day. Not without a flash.'

'I can buy a roll of four hundred before the tour.'

'Hey, come on, man.'

'Why don't I take tour pictures with *my* camera, have doubles made and send *you* a copy of everything?'

John grimaced. 'I haven't got anyplace you can *send* 'em to. I'm living in my *car*, man. I'd *never* get 'em. Jeez! Cut me a break, will you?' He suddenly smiled. The crevices between his teeth were calked with white pasty bun. 'Anyhow,' he said, 'I already got the pictures of Lynn on *my* camera. You want *them*, don't you?'

I'd want them a lot worse, Owen thought, if they were pictures of Dana.

Dana!

An idea struck him.

Stunned him.

He thought about it for a few seconds.

'What?' John asked.

'I tell you what,' Owen said. 'How would you like to go on the Midnight Tour, yourself?'

'You kidding?'

Owen leaned to the right and pulled out his wallet. He removed a fifty-dollar bill and reached across the table with it.

John frowned at the bill. 'What's that for?'

'A down payment on a job.'

'Who I gotta kill?'

'You don't have to *kill* anyone, but I want you to *shoot* one of the other guides.' Owen grinned, pleased by his pun, delighted by his plan. 'With your camera. Her name's Dana. She's probably working inside Beast House right now.'

'What's she look like?'

'Tall and blond. And extremely beautiful.'

'Right. The gorgeous one. Know just who you mean. Saw her yesterday, myself. A real honey. I got a stiffy just . . .'

'Hey.'

'Sure. Sorry. Didn't mean to offend you, pal. You want pictures of her, I'll take pictures. They have to be nudes or something?'

'Don't be a jerk. Just get me a few good snapshots of her. However you want to do it. Ask her permission, or do it on the sly, whatever. But don't involve me, okay? Just act like you're taking them for yourself.'

'No problemo.'

'I know, let's take the audio tour separately. I'll go first. Give me maybe a half hour headstart, then you come in and do the tour and take your pictures of Dana. When you're done, I'll meet you out front and we'll take a look around town. Maybe we can find some sort of one-hour film-developing place. Or maybe there's a place that'll do it overnight.'

'Might be,' John said, and sipped some cola. 'Wouldn't be surprised.'

'Soon as I have my pictures of Dana, I'll give you another fifty bucks and you can buy yourself a ticket for the Midnight Tour.'

John nodded, looking pleased for a few seconds. Then he frowned. 'What if they're all sold out by then?'

'Can you stick around and do the tour next week?'

John wrinkled his nose. 'I don't know, man. A week's a long time when you're flat busted. Can't we just go ahead and buy me the ticket now? Tell you what, we buy it now, then you keep it till I give you the pictures. How about that? Anything goes wrong, you can sell it to somebody else and make all your money back. Shit, you could maybe even *scalp* it and make yourself a profit. What do you say?'

Owen wanted photos of Dana.

'Sure,' he said. 'It's a deal.'

'You won't regret it, man. This is great! I'll get you some *great* pictures of that babe.'

They finished their meals. Then they hiked across the front lawn toward the ticket booth. Owen waited on the grass. John went up the walkway, spoke briefly with Sharon, then stepped out of sight. A few minutes later, he reappeared holding a red ticket. Sharon looked happy to see that he'd gotten it. They talked for a while, nodding and smiling. At last, Sharon had to hand out some tape players, so John strolled over to Owen.

'Good thing we didn't wait,' he said, waving the ticket. 'This was the last one they had for tomorrow night.'

Must be number thirteen.

'Lucky,' Owen said.

'Man, this is the luckiest day of my life. I'd give you a hug and kiss, only we don't want nobody thinking we're fags.'

Owen tried to smile. 'Wouldn't want that.' He held out his hand and John gave him the ticket.

'I get it back when you get the pictures of Dana, right?'

'Right,' Owen said, slipping it into the shirt pocket with his own ticket. 'Now, I'll go on in and do the tour. Why don't you spend a while over at the gift shop, or something?'

'Maybe I'll have me another burger. Can you spare a couple more bucks?'

'Sure.' Owen took out a ten-dollar bill. 'Take this and give me an *hour* headstart.'

'A whole hour?'

'Spend it eating,' Owen suggested, and handed him the ten.

'You're the boss.'

As John headed for the corner of the house, Owen returned to Station One. Standing at the foot of the stairs, he put on his headphones. He pressed the Play button. Then he gazed up at the lynched body of Gus as Janice Crogan began to tell the story.

Later, after listening about Ethel, Owen left the parlor and climbed the stairway. He looked up and down the corridor but didn't see Dana.

Never mind, he told himself. She's probably up here someplace.

He listened at Station Three, then shut off the player, stepped out of Lilly Thorn's bedroom and walked up the hallway toward Station Four.

Yesterday, he'd first seen Dana near the attic door.

Today, some tourists stood there, listening to their tapes and gazing up the stairway.

No Dana, though.

Where is she?

Up ahead, some people near the left side of the corridor wandered out of the way.

Owen saw her.

His heart seemed to lurch.

She was standing like a casual guard just outside the doorway of the boys' bedroom, nodding and smiling at the tourists who went by.

The bedroom, Station Four, was supposed to be Owen's next destination.

I'll have to walk right past her!

He had an urge to turn away.

Don't be such a damn chicken, he told himself. Just keep going, act natural. *She* doesn't know I have any feelings for her. I'm just another tourist.

He moved slowly, stepping around several people, trying not to look at her.

But as he neared the doorway, their eyes met.

'Morning,' Dana said.

'Hi.'

'Back again, huh?'

She remembers me!

Blushing fiercely, he nodded.

'Where's your friend?' she asked.

Owen pulled off his headphones. 'My friend?'

She must've seen me with John! Now what'll . . .

'The young lady who was with you yesterday,' Dana explained.

'Oh, her.'

I don't want to lie. Not to Dana.

'She didn't like this place,' he said. 'She kind of . . . kept complaining and ruining it. So today I came back without her.'

'Ditched her, huh?'

'Sort of.'

Dana glanced at her wristwatch. 'It's about time for my break. You want to come outside with me?'

'Outside? With you?'

'Yeah.'

'Right now?'

'If you'd rather not . . .'

'No. *No*. I'll come with you. Sure.'

Dana took a walkie-talkie from her belt. Holding it in front of her mouth, she thumbed a button and said, 'Lynn, it's Dana. I'm going for a break now. Okay? Over.'

A voice came back, 'Knock yourself out, hon.'

Dana smiled at Owen and said, 'Let's go.'

He followed her along the corridor and down the stairway. In the foyer, she said to the male guide, 'I'm taking off for a break, Clyde.'

Clyde cast a quick, distasteful glance at Owen, then nodded to Dana.

Owen hurried ahead to open the front door. Stepping out, Dana thanked him. He followed her to the bottom of the porch stairs.

'Let's go over here,' she said.

As he walked beside her, the grass was silent and soft under his shoes. His heart pounded hard. Sweat dribbled down his sides. His mouth was dry. The morning sun seemed to press a hot weight against the top of his head and shoulders. But a fine, cool breeze blew against him. It fluttered his shirt against his chest and belly. It smelled as if it had come from a long way off, traveling low over the ocean waves. He took a deep breath and sighed.

We're walking together. This is so incredible.

But what does she want?

Just past the corner of the house, Dana stopped and turned to him.

In the distance, people were strolling along the walkway between the ticket office and the front porch. Others, on their way to the eating area or gift shop or restroom, were walking toward the far corner of the house.

Dana and Owen had this section of lawn to themselves.

'Nice out here, isn't it?' Dana asked.

'Fantastic.'

He stared at her.

I can't believe we're standing out here.

I can't believe how incredible she looks.

Instead of revealing flaws, the bright sunlight seemed to highlight her beauty. Her hair glinted yellow and russet and gold. She had fine, pale down on her cheeks. Her eyes seemed a perfect match for the light blue color of the sky.

'What's her name?' Dana asked.

'Who?'

She frowned slightly. 'The girl from yesterday.'

'Oh. That was Monica.'

'Where is she today?'

He made a face. 'I left her at the hotel.'

'Here in town?'

'At Fisherman's Wharf.'

'You left her in *San Francisco*?'

'I know, I know. But she hated this place. She wouldn't let *me* enjoy the tour. I'd been looking forward to Beast House for *years*. And she spoiled it for me. She had snotty cracks about *everything*.'

'Including me, I suppose.'

Owen gaped at her. He nodded. 'How did *you* know?'

She grinned mysteriously. 'I know many things.'

'Did you overhear her, or . . .?'

'I couldn't help but notice the way you were looking at me yesterday.'

He felt as if his face might burst into flame.

Cringing, he said, 'Sorry.'

'Oh, that's all right. Fine with me. But it wasn't exactly fine with Monica, was it?'

'Not exactly.'

'I think she was really steamed. In the house. And then when I was taking your players at the front gate. She looked like she wanted to rip my face off.'

'She always blows everything out of proportion. I mean, I *have* to look at other women sometimes. You know? Or I'd bump into them.'

Dana laughed softly. 'So *that's* why you had your eyes glued to me – to avoid a collision.'

'Exactly.' Smiling, he added, 'Plus . . . uh . . . because I couldn't exactly *help* looking at you.'

'Why's that?'

'You know.'

'Right. I know. I'm *too big to miss*.'

Owen laughed. 'That's *not* why. It's because . . . I've never seen anyone so beautiful.'

Dana's face suddenly turned scarlet. 'Well, thanks. That's very nice of you to say so.'

'It's just the truth. You've seen mirrors, haven't you?'

'I don't look that great to me. Anyway, Owen.' She took a deep breath and said, 'Back to you and Monica.'

'If it's optional, could we maybe skip it?'

'It's mandatory. To me, it is – since you came back today without her and I might be part of the reason why.'

'Well . . .'

'Also, I see that you've got tickets in your pocket for the Midnight Tour.'

Nodding, he patted them.

What'll I say about the second ticket?

'Tomorrow night's tour?' Dana asked.

'Yeah.'

'Monica hates Beast House. She also hates me.'

'Oh, I wouldn't . . .'

'You're probably not bringing *her* on the Midnight Tour.'

'Nope.'

'And you're probably not planning a return trip to San Francisco *before* tomorrow night, are you?'

'No.'

'So you're just leaving Monica alone in a hotel in San Francisco for a few days?'

'I'm not really planning to go back at all.'

'*What?*'

'I *left* her. I snuck out of the room while she was asleep and . . .'

'Good God. Didn't say a word?'

'No way.'

'Did you leave a note or something?'

He shook his head.

'She might think you got *kidnapped* or *murdered* or something.'

'I doubt it. I took all my stuff with me. She'll probably figure I took an early flight home. And she'll know why, too.'

Grimacing, Dana shook her head. 'That's an awful thing to do to someone, Owen.'

'Yeah, I know. But she'll be fine.'

'She *won't* be fine. She'll be devastated.'

He smirked. 'You don't know Monica.'

'*Any* woman would be devastated if she's on a trip with a guy and he disappears on her.'

'Yeah, well. I know it wasn't a nice thing to do, but she had it coming. She was asking for it.'

'Where're you from?'

'We flew up from Los Angeles. And she has her return ticket. She also has plenty of money and everything. She can probably fly home today if she wants to. Or she can just go ahead and enjoy the rest of the vacation without me. I'm sure she'll enjoy it a lot *more* without me. All she ever did was whine about everything. I mean, you saw her. She's horrible. And she thought she *had* me. She actually believed I was going to *marry* her. I had to get out before it was too late.'

Dana kept grimacing and slowly shaking her head. 'Were you engaged?'

'Not yet.'

'How long had you been going together?'

'Since about Christmas.'

'And you dumped her because of yesterday?'

'Sort of.'

'Because she ruined your tour of Beast House? Or did it have to do with seeing me?'

Owen squirmed.

'I was ready to break up with her *before* yesterday,' he said. 'I just hadn't gotten around to it yet.'

'So what was it about yesterday that made up your mind?'

'She was just so bitchy about everything.'

'Did *I* have anything to do with your decision?'

Go for it, man!

He shrugged and said, 'Sort of. It was like a combination of things. I wanted to come back and do the tour without Monica screwing it up, and I really wanted to take the Midnight Tour – she *never* would've let me do that. And . . . I guess I was sort of hoping to see you again.'

'You didn't dump her *because* of me, did you?'

'Not really.'

'Oh, terrific, not really. Means maybe you did.'

Owen cringed and shrugged. Unable to look at her, he lowered his gaze to the grass in front of his shoes. Then he said, 'It's, uh . . . not like I expected to go *out* with you or anything. I mean, someone like you . . . you've probably already got guys all over the place. Last thing you need is someone like me. But the thing is, looking at you? And, you know, we talked a little when you were taking the players back? The thing is, you're like everything Monica isn't. Everything a guy could ever ask for. And there I was, stuck with this sneering, snotty bitch. How could I throw my life away with someone like her when there are people like *you* in the world? You know?'

'You've maybe got me overrated,' Dana said. Her voice sounded odd.

Owen lifted his gaze.

Dana's eyes were wet and shiny. Frowning, she turned away. 'I'd better get back to work.' She started walking.

Owen stayed by her side. 'I'm sorry if I upset you.'

'I'm fine.'

'And you don't have to worry, I won't hang around bothering you. I won't ask you out or anything.'

She glanced over at him.

He tried to smile. 'Not unless you want me to.'

'I don't know,' she said. 'I'll have to think about it.'

Oh, my God! She's going to think about it!

'Where'll you be staying tonight?' she asked.

Wow!

'I'm not sure. Probably the Welcome Inn, if they have a vacancy.'

'You haven't checked in yet?'

'No. I was planning to go over and register after lunch.'

'Where'd you stay *last* night?' she asked.

'Fisherman's Wharf.'

'Oh, that's right. You'd already told me that.'

'Yeah.'

'You sure you weren't *here* last night? I thought I saw you.'

Smiling, he shook his head. 'I *wish* I'd been here, that's for sure. But I was with good old Monica having one of the most miserable times of my life.'

Dana patted his back and said, 'Maybe tonight'll be better.'

She touched me!

Her hand had gone away, but Owen could still feel warmth where it had patted him.

Side by side, they climbed the porch stairs. Owen opened the door for Dana and they entered Beast House. Clyde was busy talking to someone. Several tourists were coming down the stairway, so Owen dropped back and let Dana go first.

He climbed the stairs behind her.

Staring at the backs of her legs, at the way her shorts slid against the curves of her buttocks.

She might go out with me.

She'll think about it.

My God!

Following Dana up the stairs, he suddenly knew for sure that leaving Monica was the best thing he'd ever done.

Chapter Thirty-One

Sandy's Story – July, 1992

Sandy couldn't see the intruder.

Then he stood up, rising into plain sight behind a boulder. The boulder, his hiding place, was only a couple of yards to the left of where Sandy had been gazing while she posed.

The moment she spotted him, she felt a hot flush of embarrassment. This wasn't the first time someone had interrupted a session. This time, at least, she wasn't entirely nude. Trying not to appear flustered, she simply lifted her left hand and cupped her bare breast.

'Sorry to bother you like this,' the young man called, and started working his way down toward the beach.

'No bother,' Blaze said, smiling and friendly.

And no wonder. After all, *Blaze* wasn't the one standing around half naked. And Blaze *was* gay and the intruder *was* incredibly handsome and bare-chested with a nice tan and sleek muscles and low, faded shorts.

He came leaping down from the rocks and landed on the sand.

'I didn't mean to intrude,' he explained, frowning and shaking his head. 'I didn't know you were down here. Not at first, anyway. I was just climbing around.' Twisting sideways, he gestured toward the high pile of rocks. 'No reason.' He smiled at Blaze, then met Sandy's eyes and said, 'Once I got a look at *you*, I couldn't leave.'

'Well, you've had your look, so . . .'

'My name's Terry.'

'Well, don't tarry on my account.'

He smiled slightly and shrugged. 'I take it you'd like me to leave.'

'We're sort of busy here.'

'I know. I'm sorry.' He glanced at the hand clasped to Sandy's breast, then met her eyes. 'You aren't going to tell me your name?'

'I only give it out on a "need to know" basis.'

He smiled. He had a great smile, full of white teeth and sincerity. 'That ought to include me. I *really* need to know.'

'Maybe some other time,' she told him.

'I'll look forward . . .'

'*I'm* Blaze,' Blaze proclaimed. 'Blaze O. Glory.'

'Pleased to meet you, Mr Glory.'

'Oh, do call me Blaze.'

'Blaze.' Terry smiled once more at Sandy, then turned away from her and walked toward Blaze. 'May I take a peek at the painting?'

'Certainly.' Blaze stepped back.

'Hey!' Sandy blurted. 'No! If he wants to see it, let him go to the gallery.'

'Oh, don't be a spoilsport,' Blaze told her.

Abruptly, Terry turned away, avoiding a look at the canvas. 'I'll wait till it's in the gallery,' he said.

'Oh, pay no attention to her.'

'That's fine. Sorry I interrupted.' Striding toward the bottom of the trail, he glanced back at Sandy and called out, 'So long. Maybe I'll see you around sometime.'

'Good-bye,' Sandy called to him.

She and Blaze both watched as he made his way up the trail.

'What a delightful fellow,' Blaze said.

'A real charmer,' Sandy said.

'And stunning.'

'He's all yours.'

'No, I'm afraid not. My dear, he's *yours* for the asking. He was absolutely smitten.'

'Aren't they all.'

'Well . . . I won't push. I know you've had several dreadful experiences. Men *can* be such thoughtless thugs. But some are wonderful. Some would never *dream* of attacking you or beating you or . . . or abandoning you.'

'I know that. I know it. The trouble is, you can't tell one from the other. Not till it's too late.'

*   *   *

'*Fini!*' Blaze proclaimed.

Sandy, stiff and hot, muttered, 'Finally.' She looked all around to make sure there were no intruders, then peeled off her dress and tossed it onto the beach. She turned around. After stretching, she waded farther out, dived into an oncoming wave, and swam for a while.

Ashore, she dried herself on a towel from Blaze's backpack. He'd also brought her a pair of shorts and a flower-print shirt to wear for the picnic and the ride back to his house.

Sitting on a beach towel, they sipped Champagne and nibbled on crackers, hard Italian salami and a tangy, sharp cheddar cheese.

'You're how old, now?' Blaze asked.

He *knew* her age. Though she'd given Blaze a lot of false information about herself, she'd never lied to him about her age. 'I can see where this is going,' she said.

'I'm not saying *Terry* is the one. But really, you need to give *someone* a try.'

'No, I don't.'

'Not *all* men are beasts.'

'*You're* okay.'

'And what about your son? Is *he* a beast?'

Sandy laughed and shook her head. 'No, of course not.'

'So, you see? That makes *two* of us who aren't horrors. Granted, I'm as queer as the day is long. Still, I *am* a man.'

'Sort of.'

'Bitch.'

'So, basically, you think I should start going out with guys?'

'Couldn't hurt.'

'*Could* hurt.'

'But it's worth the risk. Let me tell you, my dear. I'm one who knows. The greatest hurt of all is loneliness.'

'I'm not lonely.'

'Oh, you are. You're desperately lonely.'

'Am not.'

'You're just too tough to admit it.'

Back at Blaze's house, Sandy took a shower and got dressed in her old clothes.

She found Blaze waiting for her in the foyer. 'These're yours,' he said, and gave her the new shorts and shirt in a shopping bag. 'I'm sorry we were obliged to ruin that marvelous dress.'

Sandy smiled. 'Sorry, but not very. You *knew* what you'd be doing to it.'

'Nonsense.'

'Then why'd you bring the spare clothes?'

'Ah! True! Well.'

'It's all right. I expect you to ruin the outfits. You only do it about two-thirds of the time.'

Blaze laughed. 'Can't help myself.'

'I sometimes wonder if you're as gay as you pretend to be.'

'If I weren't, my dear, I would've ravished your gorgeous body eons ago. I'd be doing it on every possible occasion.'

Smiling, she gave him a hug and kiss. 'I might've liked that.'

'Oh, I would've driven you *mad* with ecstasy. But then we couldn't be great friends, could we? And we'd both be dirt poor, because I would never be able to finish any paintings. You'd no sooner strike a pose than I'd be overwhelmed with urges of the flesh and *leap* on you.'

'Lech.'

He gave her rump a swat. 'Now, leave if you must.' He opened the door for her.

'See you later.'

'Not nearly soon enough, I'm afraid.'

'Oh, don't pout,' she said, stepping outside.

'*Ciao*, babe!'

She gave him a wave, then trotted down the porch stairs and went to her pickup truck. As she opened the door, she looked back at Blaze. He still stood in the doorway. He waved at her, and she waved again. Then she climbed in, turned her truck around, and drove down the long, curving driveway.

As usual, she felt sad about leaving.

Blaze was her only friend. Driving away, she felt as if she were returning to solitary confinement.

It's hardly that, she told herself. I've got Eric.

I love Eric.

But he wasn't much of a companion. Sure, she could talk to him and he seemed to understand much of what she said. He couldn't talk back, though.

Maybe that's a blessing, she thought.

No, it's not.

Besides, Eric was hardly ever around the cabin anymore.

And *that* made her sad.

We've got to spend more time together, she told herself.

Doing what? Running through the woods?

She *used* to do that. When Eric had been younger, Sandy would often spend hours with him. They'd explore the wooded hills together, run side by side, chase down wildlife.

Correction, *he* would chase down the wildlife. Leaving me behind.

But she remembered how he always brought the fresh kill back to her. Far from home, she would cook her meat over a campfire while Eric, crouching at the other side of the fire, always devoured his portions raw.

Those had been great times.

But they'd pretty much gone away.

Kids grow up, she thought. Before you know it, they stop letting you be their best buddy. Even if *you* haven't changed, they suddenly see you as a nuisance.

But I *did* change, she reminded herself. I *made* myself into a nuisance.

Starting with the time Eric went chasing after a deer but brought back the boy instead.

Maybe I shouldn't have made such a big deal out of it.

Frowning, she drove slowly down the hillside road below Blaze's house.

I didn't make *that* big of a deal out of it, she told herself. It's not like I smacked him. Just calmly told him not to do it again. Hell, I even let him go ahead and *eat* the twerp. That was pretty damn understanding, if you ask me.

But I wouldn't eat any. That's what got to him. I already had the fire built and everything, and he brings back the prize for me – chased it down and killed it all by himself – and I won't touch it, won't cook it up, won't eat any.

She remembered how he'd crouched there, all bloody and silent, devouring a thigh and staring at her – a hurt look in his eyes as if he couldn't understand why Mom had turned against him.

She felt her throat tighten.

I should've just gone ahead and eaten the little shit.

Even now, she doubted that she would've been able to stomach such a meal. But she wished she'd given it a shot.

Nothing had been quite the same after that.

He damn sure never brought me any more dead people.

Sandy felt certain that Eric loved her no less than before, but she'd lost some of the closeness and trust.

Once that's gone, can you ever get it back?

Maybe. Who knows? Might be worth a try. Maybe if I go running with him again?

Hey, kid, how about letting the old mom tag along?

Nah. He wouldn't want me around. Afraid I might disapprove of something.

Which I might, too. God only knows what he does all day.

At the bottom of Buena Vista Parkway, Sandy eased her pickup to a halt and waited while a string of cars rushed by on Fort Platt Boulevard.

Maybe I *should* bring Eric into town with me one of these days, she thought. He's been wanting to do it for years. He would love it. If I did that, maybe we could be buddies again. I'd have to cover him up really good. Make some sort of outfit for him?

God, it'd be so risky.

Introduce him to Blaze.

What if Blaze freaks out?

What if Eric *eats* Blaze?

No, no, not a good . . .

A car bore down on her from behind, growing suddenly in the rearview mirror. A white sports car. A convertible.

In front of Sandy, a pickup truck sped by.

As she waited for it to pass, the sports car stopped behind her.

The driver raised a bare arm above the windshield, waved and smiled.

The guy from the beach!

Terry?

He followed me!

Sandy opened her door and leaned out. No cars were approaching from up the hill, so she shifted to Park, set her emergency brake and hopped down to the pavement.

Terry stayed in his driver's seat as she walked toward him. He still didn't have a shirt on.

'Hi,' Sandy said.

'We meet again,' said Terry.

'I noticed.' She thought that she ought to sound angry, but she couldn't quite pull it off. 'What do you think you're doing?'

'Making a nuisance of myself?' he suggested, and lifted his eyebrows.

'You followed us when we left the beach?'

'Did a pretty good job of it too, don't you think? Did you ever catch on?'

'Not till just now.'

'Well, just now is when you were *supposed* to catch on. I decided to spring out of nowhere and astonish you.'

'Really. So . . . now what?'

'I think we should spend some time together.'

'Why would I want to do that?'

'Why not?' he asked.

'For one thing, I have other things to do. For another, I don't even know you.'

'Terry Goodwin,' he said. He let go of the steering wheel and swung his left arm toward Sandy.

She shook his hand. 'I'm Ashley.'

Keeping her hand, he asked, 'Ashley what?'

'Maybe I don't *want* you knowing my last name. You seem to be some sort of stalker. You might look me up and arrive on my doorstep.'

'Pfff! Yeah! I'd be a fool *not* to.'

She laughed.

Still holding her hand, Terry said, 'I *had* to follow you. I know it makes me seem like a nut job, but . . . I couldn't just go home. Not without knowing who you are. What if I never got a chance to see you again? It would've been . . .' Scowling, he shook his head. 'I would've regretted it the rest of my life.'

She stared at him.

She felt strange inside. Warm and trembly.

'So what do you want?'

'I want you not to vanish.'

'I'm right here. Besides, you've got a pretty good hold on my hand. It'd be tough for me to vanish right now.'

'Where do you live?'

'Get real. Do I *look* like a moron?'

'Not in the least. Are you on your way home?'

'Not at the moment.'

He smiled gently and released her hand.

'I have to make a stop at the grocery store,' Sandy said. 'Do you want to come along?'

'You bet I do!'

'All right. See you there.'

Back in her pickup truck, Sandy drove to the grocery store. Terry followed her. In the parking lot, he swung his little car into the nearest space. He climbed out and came toward her, pulling a T-shirt down over his head.

'Ah, you're making yourself decent,' Sandy said.

'Not entirely.'

On the T-shirt, a cartoony wizard was pointing at Sandy as he intoned, 'Turn to shit.'

She burst out laughing. '*That's* nice.'

'I know. I really shouldn't wear it in public.'

'But you do.'

They walked side by side toward the store entrance.

'Afraid so. Want me to leave?'

'Just walk a few paces behind me.'

He started to drop back, so Sandy caught his hand and dragged him forward.

Inside the store, she grabbed a shopping cart. It had a wobbly front wheel that made the cart shimmy as she pushed it along.

'I'll push it for you,' Terry said.

'No, that's okay. I can push my own cart.'

'You sure?'

'Are you trying to annoy me?'

'I just want to be friends.'

'Oh ho ho.'

She made her way slowly up an aisle, sometimes pausing to snatch an item off its shelf and set it into her cart. Terry walked beside her – or behind her when the aisle became crowded. At the end of the aisle, she turned and started down the next.

'Do you live alone?' Terry asked.

'No, do you?'

'Me? All alone. I have a little beach cottage south of town. Which you're welcome to visit any time of the day or night.'

'You're a very hospitable guy.'

'You're not married, are you?' he asked.

'No, are you?'

'No.'

'*Have* you been married?' Sandy asked.

'You ask a lot of questions.'

'You started it.'

'I've never been married,' he said. 'What about you?'

'Nope. How old are you?'

'Twenty-eight.'

'And you've never been married? Why not?'

He grinned. 'Who knows? How old are you?'

'Not as old as you. You're *really* old. Amazing you've never been married. Something wrong with you?'

He laughed. 'Maybe I'm just picky. Who do you live with?'

Looking into his eyes, she said, 'My son.'

If Terry was put off by the news, he didn't let it show. 'Really? What's his name?'

'Eric.'

'That must be neat, having a kid. How old is he?'

'Twelve.'

At *that* news, he looked stunned. 'You're kidding. *Twelve?*'

'Sure.'

'So you were, what . . . *seven* when you had him?'

She grinned. 'A little older than that.'

'Amazing. So where's Eric while you're off modeling for Blaze?'

'He's usually in school.'

'Not during summer vacation, I hope.'

'No, no. He's home. My mother comes over to watch him when I have to go out.'

'That's got to be a major convenience. Great for both of you. It frees you up and she gets to spend time with her grandchild.'

'It's a pretty good deal,' Sandy said. She tried to hold on to her smile, but it fell. She turned to the shelves of groceries. She was facing a variety of mustards. She didn't need any mustard but she stared at the jars, anyway, as if trying to decide which to buy.

Shouldn't have said that stuff about Mom. That's what did it. Keep her out of it. How to ruin a fine day in one easy lesson.

'Are you okay?' Terry asked.

'Yeah. It's just . . . Eric wasn't feeling very well when I left this morning. I'm a little worried about him, that's all. I need to finish the shopping and get home.' She grabbed a sweet-hot mustard off the shelf, bent over her cart and put it in.

'How far away do you live?'

She opened her mouth to answer, then gave him a sharp look. 'Where I live is *my* business.'

'I just mean, if it's going to take you a while to get there, why don't you phone up your mother and make sure Eric's all right? Put your mind at ease.'

'That's a good idea,' she said. 'You want to watch the cart? I'll go find a phone. Be right back.' She hurried toward the front of the store. With a glance back, she saw that Terry was staying put.

Dumb. This is what comes of lying.

The public telephones were just outside the store's main exit. She glanced back to make sure Terry still wasn't coming, then stepped outside and pretended to call home. After talking into the mouthpiece for a couple of minutes, she hung up and went back into the store. Terry was exactly where she'd left him.

He minds well, she thought.

'Eric's fine,' she said.

'Glad to hear it. Feel better now?'

She nodded.

'The phone's a great invention,' Terry said.

'It can be.'

'So now you can relax and enjoy the shopping.'

'I guess so.'

'And since everything's fine on the home front, why don't you stop by at my place after we're done here?'

'And why would I want to do that?'

He grinned. 'It's a nice cottage. It has a nice view of the ocean. *I'm* nice. *You're* nice. We'll have a nice time.'

'Unless you get me inside the nice cottage and attack me.'

He suddenly looked at Sandy as if she'd turned into an odd specimen – an amusing, somewhat appalling, compelling creature unlike anything he'd ever seen before. In a solemn voice, he said, 'I wouldn't do that.'

'How do I know?'

He kept gazing at her. 'I guess you don't.'

'For all I know, you might be a very handsome, pleasant serial killer just looking for a chance to get me alone.'

'I'm not.'

'So you say. As if you'd *admit* it.'

He laughed and shook his head. 'If I wanted to jump you, I could've done it on the beach. I don't think Blaze would've been much of an obstacle.'

'Somebody might've come along,' Sandy pointed out. '*You* did. At your charming little beach cottage, though, you wouldn't have to worry about anyone walking in on us. There'd be complete privacy. You'd have me at your mercy.'

'That sounds like a pretty good deal.'

'And it might not even be *your* cottage. Maybe it's just an abandoned place you happen to know about.'

'Gotcha!' Grinning, he reached into a seat pocket of his shorts and pulled out his wallet. He flapped it open in front of her. On one side was an i.d. card. On the other side was a shiny silver badge.

Chapter Thirty-Two

Lunch Trouble

Just as Warren slid Dana's tray through the window, a crowd of Japanese tourists swarmed into the eating area. All of them seemed to be talking at once. Some went straight to tables. A few scattered and started snapping photos of each other. Several wandered about taping everything in sight with their camcorders. The line behind Dana tripled in length. The line at the other window doubled. Probably half the group headed directly for the gift shop.

Looking in at Warren, Dana said, 'Holy smoke.'

'We're very big with the Japanese,' Warren explained. 'We get busloads of them two or three times a week.'

'Must be great for business.'

'Can't complain,' Warren said. 'Only thing is, I was hoping I'd be able to have lunch with you.'

'Yeah, me too.' Trying not to let her disappointment show, she picked up her tray. 'Well, maybe I'll see you later.'

'How about after work?' he blurted.

'Today?'

'Yeah, if you want.'

'Sure!'

'We could go over to my place. I'll show you the beach and stuff. And I could throw something on the barbie . . .'

'Hey, that sounds great.'

'Meet you at the ticket office at closing time?'

'You bet,' she said. 'See you then.'

Dana found Tuck upstairs near the entrance to Lilly Thorn's room. 'That was quick,' Tuck said.

Dana nodded, grinning.

'What happened?'

'Well, a Japanese tour bus showed up and Warren couldn't have lunch with me.'

'Ah. And that makes you giddy – why?'

'He asked me over to his place! Right after work!'

'Today?'

'Yep. And we're gonna eat there.'

'So I shouldn't expect you for supper?'

'Nope.'

'Throwing me over for a guy, huh?'

'You better believe it.'

'How'll you get home?'

Dana shrugged.

'Maybe you should spend the night with him. Then you'd just have a convenient little hike to work in the morning.'

'I'm not going to spend the night with him.'

'How do you know?'

'I know.'

'Do you want me to pick you up at a certain time?'

'He'll probably drive me home.'

'What if he won't?'

'Why wouldn't he?'

Tuck shrugged. 'He might not want you to leave. Or you two might not be speaking to each other by the time you're ready to go. Or he might get drunk and pass out. Or . . .'

'Has he *done* anything like that?'

'Not that I know of. But guys will be guys.'

'I'm sure he'll be fine. But if he does give me trouble, I'll call you.'

'He doesn't have a phone.'

'Really?'

'You'll be trapped like a moose.'

'Up yours.'

'Tell you what. If you're not home by a certain time, I could drive over and pick you up.'

Dana grimaced. 'I don't know if *that's* such a great idea.'

'Couldn't hurt. If you're home by then, it's a moot point. If I get there and you want to *stay* with Warren, that'll be fine, too.'

'I guess that'd be okay.'

'What time? Two a.m.?'

'Very funny. How about midnight?'

'Fine.'

'But I'll be home long before then.'

'Let's hope not.' She gave Dana's arm a pat, then said, 'I'd better go downstairs and spell Clyde. 'See you . . .'

'Excuse me?'

Looking over her shoulder, Dana found a husky young man standing behind her.

'Oh, hi,' Tuck said to him. 'John?'

He beamed. 'John it is. That's right.'

'Hi, John,' Dana said, turning around. She'd noticed him earlier, herself. Hard *not* to notice a guy that size wearing black-rimmed glasses and a Beast House cap. She'd seen him up here *before* she went off to lunch.

The way he'd been wandering around, taking photos of everything in sight and fiddling with his tape player, she'd pegged him as a true aficionado of the house.

'John and I are old buddies,' Tuck said.

'I've got pictures of her with Gus,' John explained, patting his camera.

'Gus is the one that's hung,' Tuck said.

'Can I get a picture of you two together?' John asked. 'I'll send you a couple of copies.'

'Sounds good to me,' Tuck said. 'How about it, Dana?'

'Sure, why not?'

'That's great,' John said. 'That's really great.' As he took a few steps backward, Dana and Tuck stood side by side. 'I'm gonna have a great photo album of this place,' he said, and snapped a shot. 'Hang on. Let me get a couple more, just in case.'

He clicked more than a couple more.

Sidestepping, ducking, zooming in for closeups, he took shot after shot.

'I have to get going,' Tuck said.

'Ah. Fine. No problem. Okay if I get a couple with my flash, just in case?'

'Well . . .'

The flash blinked, hitting them with a flick of brightness.

'I've got [*flash*] high-speed film in here [*flash*] but you never can be too sure. It's awfully [*flash*] dark in this place [*flash*].'

'That's *enough*, John.' Tuck put a hand across her eyes. 'Knock it off.'

'Oh. Okay. Fine.' He lowered the camera. 'I *really* appreciate it. You'll never know how much I appreciate it.'

'Don't forget to send us copies,' Tuck said.

'Oh, I won't. But I guess I'll need your names and stuff.'

Tuck reached into a seat pocket of her shorts. She took out a wallet and removed a business card. 'Here you go. You can send them to me, and I'll see that Dana gets copies.'

He took the card, squinted at it, then smiled and slipped it into a pocket of his enormous, wrinkled shirt. 'Will do,' he said. 'And thanks again.'

He hurried away.

'I think he's in love with you,' Tuck said.

'Eat my shorts.'

'Bet *he'd* like to eat what's in 'em.'

'Hey, real nice. Aren't you supposed to be relieving Clyde, or something?'

'Oh, yeah. Thanks for reminding me.' She slugged Dana's arm. 'See ya later, alligator.'

'In a while, crock-a-shit.'

Laughing, Tuck headed for the stairs.

More than half an hour went by before the Japanese tour group entered the house. When Dana heard them flood in, she crouched and looked down the stairs. The foyer was packed.

A lot of flash photos were being taken.

But Tuck was down there, smiling and nodding and making no objections.

A slim young woman carrying a miniature flag seemed to be in charge of the group. She spoke loudly and clearly in Japanese. It made no sense at all to Dana, but every so often the guide spoke familiar names: Lilly Thorn, Ethel Hughes, Beast House, Maggie Kutch.

She couldn't spot a Beast House tape player around the neck of anyone in the bunch.

They probably all know English, she thought. But it *would* be better to get the tour in their own language.

She wondered how long they would be staying downstairs.

Five minutes, maybe?

Dana stood up, turned away and walked the entire floor, looking into rooms and counting heads from one end of the corridor to the other.

Twenty-eight already up here.

Gonna get crowded.

Should I warn them?

So they can do what? she wondered. Evacuate the building and come back later?

Most of those in the hallway were wandering around as if lost in trances, their eyes blank as they listened to the tapes.

Hell, they might not even notice.

Thinking it might be nice to greet such a large bunch of visitors from so far away, Dana returned to the top of the stairs. A few people were coming up, but they didn't belong to the group.

She nodded and stepped out of the way.

'A real traffic jam down there,' said the man in the lead. He was about the age of Dana's father, and had a nice smile.

The woman, trudging up behind him, said, 'The traffic jam'll be up here before you know it, Herbie.'

'I'm afraid you're right,' Dana said. 'If you'd like, you could leave for a while and come back after they're gone. We have a nice snack stand . . .'

'Oh, I don't think I could make it up these stairs again,' the woman said. 'We'll just have to make do the best . . .'

'*Lance?*'

'. . . we can.'

'*Lance!*'

Dana jerked her head to the left.

'*Lance! Where are you?*'

She spotted the woman in the middle of the corridor, a frantic look on her face. The headphones hung around her neck.

Did she lose her kid? Dana wondered.

She looked awfully young to have a wandering kid.

Hands out, palms up, she turned slowly as she looked around. '*Lance!*' she cried out. '*Where are you? Answer me this minute!*'

Dana ran toward her.

Every other tourist in the corridor seemed to be watching. Some were pulling off their headphones.

She stopped in front of the woman. 'Who's missing?' she asked.

'My boy. He was right beside me a minute ago, and suddenly he . . . he just *disappeared*.'

Dana snatched the walkie-talkie off her belt and thumbed the talk button. 'Tuck,' she said. 'We've got a missing boy. Over.'

'Nobody's getting past me. Describe the kid.'

'How old is he?' Dana asked the mother.

'Nine.'

'Hair color?'

'Blond.'

'He's nine years old,' she told Tuck. 'Blond hair.'

'How long has he been . . . oh, great. Here come the . . .' The walkie-talkie went silent, but Dana heard Tuck anyway. 'Hold it!' Tuck yelled. 'Yoshi, wait! Tell them to stop and stay away from the stairs. We have a problem.'

In a loud, clear voice, the Japanese tour guide started giving instructions to her group.

Dana turned her attention to Lance's mother. 'How long has he been gone?'

'Just a minute or two,' she said, her voice pitched high.

'You there, Tuck?'

'Yeah. Everything's under control down here. For now.'

'The kid's been gone a couple of minutes.'

'He has to still be up there. Look around. He probably wandered off by himself. Get back to me in about two minutes.'

'Will do.' Dana turned to the mother. 'He can't get out. Don't worry, we'll find him. Where were you when you noticed he was . . .'

'Is somebody looking for a kid?'

'Yes!' Dana called out.

A girl stepped forward. About ten years old, she looked like a tomboy in her short haircut and bib overalls. 'A little creep with yellow hair?'

The mother scowled. 'He's not a creep.'

'Matter of opinion, ma'am,' said the girl. 'Anyway, he ducked under the rope over there and ran up into the attic.'

'When was this?' Dana asked.

'Just before this lady started going all hysterical.'

'Was anybody with him?' Dana asked.

'Nope. He was all by himself. You should've seen the look on his face. He thought he was being oh-so-cute, but he wasn't. I don't happen to find it cute at all, breaking rules.'

Dana grinned at the girl. 'Neither do I. Thanks a lot for your help.'

'You're welcome.'

'What's your name?'

'Janey.'

'Stick around, Janey.' Raising the walkie-talkie, Dana hurried toward the attic. Tourists in the corridor stepped aside to let her by. 'Tuck? I just found a witness. Sounds like Lance took an excursion into the attic. I'm on my way.'

'Did he go up on his own?'

'That's what I hear.'

'Okay. Keep your speak button depressed. I wanta hear what's going on.'

'Right.'

At the attic doorway, Dana looked up the dark stairs. The entrance at the top looked like a black slab.

Unhooking one end of the cordon, she called, 'Lance, please come down from there. It's dangerous. We don't want you to hurt yourself.'

Lance didn't answer.

Dana swiveled around to face those who were clustered nearby. 'I don't want anyone coming up the stairs after me. The attic is off limits. Okay?'

'Want me to stand guard for you?' asked Janey.

'Sure. Thanks.'

Janey came over to the doorway. She turned toward the onlookers and folded her arms across her chest.

Dana started to climb the stairs. 'Lance,' she called. 'I'm coming up to find you. Why don't you . . .?'

Out of the darkness above her came a squeal.

Her skin rippled with goosebumps.

She raced up the stairs, taking them two at at time, her strong legs pumping.

Mixed in with the sound of her shoes striking the planks and the stairs creaking and groaning as she charged toward the top, she thought she heard other sounds.

Gaspy whimpers and quick footfalls.

Then something pale lurched into the black doorway and came down at her.

Is it him?

Dana had a quick urge to scream.

'Stop!' she yelled.

'*It's after me!*' the boy cried out.

He dodged to the other side of the stairway to get past Dana but she dropped the walkie-talkie and grabbed the banister with her right hand, flung out her left arm and hooked him across the chest. His whole weight suddenly tried to rip her backward and hurl her down the stairs, but she clung to the rail. The impact turned her sideways. Then the kid lost his momentum and she swung him in against her body.

'Let me go!' he gasped, thrashing. 'Let go! It's coming!'

'Calm down,' Dana said. She started carrying him down the stairs.

'Let me go! It's gonna get us!'

'Nothing's going to get us.'

'Hurry!'

Rushing down the stairs, she listened for sounds of footfalls behind her. She had an urge to look over her shoulder.

Only a few steps from the bottom, she thought, *Made it. No matter what, I'll make it to the hall before it gets me.*

Get real, she told herself. Nothing's up there.

She scampered down the final stairs and carried Lance out of the stairwell.

The onlookers applauded. She heard calls of 'Thata girl!' and 'Good going,' and 'Nicely done.'

She set Lance onto his feet and turned him around to face her. Holding him by the sides, she crouched and said, 'Everything's all right, Lance. Everything's fine.'

He gazed with wide eyes up the stairwell behind Dana. He was gasping and shaking.

'Nothing's up there,' she said.

'Oh yes, it is.'

Keeping hold of him, Dana checked him out from head to foot. His pale blue T-shirt was dark with sweat. It felt hot and damp under her hands.

Lance didn't seem to be injured.

She turned him around.

No damage that . . .

'*Don't you ever do that again! Do you hear me! Don't you EVER! You scared the daylights out of me!*'

'I was just . . .'

Smack!

He flinched in Dana's hands.

She stood up fast. 'Hey!'

He started crying.

'Don't you hit him,' Dana snapped.

'I'll hit him if I want.' As if to demonstrate, Lance's mother hauled back for another swing at his face.

'No!' Dana caught her wrist.

'Let go of me!'

'Don't hit the kid,' Dana said. 'It isn't nice to hit little kids.'

The mother spat at her.

The gob of saliva landed on Dana's uniform blouse just above her left breast.

'Lady,' Dana said.

Then Janey kicked the woman in the leg.

'Ow! You little *twat*!' Her left hand darted at Janey.

As the girl leaped away, Dana jerked the woman's right arm and swung her around and slammed her against the wall.

'That's *enough!*' Dana shouted in her face.

The woman blinked.

The spit had soaked through Dana's shirt. She felt its cool wetness against her skin.

With both hands, she clutched the front of the woman's white T-shirt. '*Calm down!*'

'Let go of me!'

'You cannot go around hitting people,' Dana said.

Or spitting on them, she thought.

And she *smelled* the woman's spit on her shirt. Felt it against her skin, and *smelled* it. It smelled like jasmine. It smelled like sneeze.

She suddenly gagged.

'Let go of me, or I'll . . .'

Dana felt it suddenly coming. She had time to turn away. But she chose not to. She kept her grip on the mother's T-shirt and lurched forward and threw up in her face.

For lunch, she'd had a Red-Hot Beastie Weenie, Beastly Chili Fries with cheese, and a strawberry flavored milkshake called a 'Bucket of Blood.'

Chapter Thirty-Three

Sandy's Story – July, 1992

The sight of Terry's badge seemed to freeze Sandy's mind. She gaped at it.

For God's sake, don't faint! Don't scream and run! Just act normal.

Sure thing.

Keeping her eyes on the badge, she tried to sound like Cagney as she said, 'So, you're a copper?'

'Right. Fort Platt Municipal Police Department.'

'I'm supposed to believe that?'

'If I'm not a cop, I've got a mighty fine shield and i.d. Look at that photo. That's me, right?'

She stared at the i.d. photo. 'Yep.'

'So I'm either a real cop or a *really* slick bad guy. But that isn't the point.' He flipped the police i.d. over. Underneath it was his driver's license. 'Look. See the address there? Fourteen Beach Drive? That's my cottage. If you follow me over, you can check the address before you even get out of your truck. If they don't match up, you can just drive on.'

'I guess I could do that,' Sandy said.

She felt numb.

'Sure,' she said. 'Why not?'

'Great!'

She smiled and nodded and resumed her grocery shopping.

Dazed.

Oh, my God. Oh, God. A cop. He's a cop. What'm I gonna do?

Go over to his place and kill him?

No, no, no. Can't do that. He's a nice guy. I like him. I can't kill him. Can't?

Okay. I could.

But even if I wanted to, all these people are seeing us together. I'd never get away with it.

Just play along. See what happens.

In the checkout line, a couple of customers greeted Terry and he responded as if they were his good friends. The cashier knew him, too. Her nametag read, MARGE. She said, 'Hey there, Ter. Whatcha up to?'

'No good, as usual.'

'Haw!'

As Marge slid the groceries across the scanner, Sandy said to her, 'Is this guy really a cop?'

'Oh, I'll say. He's a regular terror. Ain't you, Ter?'

'That's me.'

'You gonna handcuff her?' Marge asked him.

'Gonna try.'

A few minutes later, he beat Sandy to the shopping cart. She decided not to fight him for it. Outside, she walked beside him. 'You're a popular guy around here,' she said.

'For a serial killer.'

'Well, I guess you aren't one of those.'

'They *do* impersonate cops, sometimes. You can't be too careful.'

'Well, I'm convinced.'

When they reached her pickup truck, Terry unloaded the shopping cart for her. He even put the milk, butter, eggs and meat into the ice chest she'd brought along to keep them cold during the long trip home. After thanking him, she said, 'You lead the way.'

'You won't ditch me, will you?'

'If I do, I guess you can just run a make on my plates or something, huh?'

'I could. But I wouldn't. I *probably* wouldn't.'

'See you in a while,' she said. Then she climbed into her pickup, started the engine, and waited. After Terry's car went by, she backed out of her space and followed it.

A cop. He's a cop.

What if he does *run the license?*

He would find out that the vehicle was registered to Harry Matthews. And the computer would give him Harry's address – Sandy's address.

She had *that* covered, at least. During the past few years, she had managed to acquire the paperwork to back up four different false identities – including Ashley Matthews.

A girl named Ashley Matthews, born two years before Sandy, had died in an apartment fire at the age of nine.

Ralph had dug up her name – and the others. He did such things for a living, and he was good at it.

Thank God for private eyes, she thought as she turned left and followed Terry's car onto Fort Platt Boulevard.

And thank God for Blaze. If not for the large amounts of money coming in from the paintings, she never would've been able to afford Ralph's services.

So if Terry *does* check on me, she thought, I shouldn't have any trouble. No reason for him to think I'm *not* Harry's niece. If he asks about Harry, I'll say he's on a trip.

Everything'll be fine, she told herself.

Unless he comes over for a visit.

I can't let that happen.

How can I stop it?

Ahead of her, Terry's turn signal began to flash. He slowed down, then swung to the right.

I could just keep on going, Sandy thought.

But he'll know where to find me.

We'd have to get our stuff together and leave. Right away. Today. And find ourselves a new place to live.

Move in with Blaze?

Shaking her head, she made the turn and closed in on Terry's car. It had slowed down to wait for her. As she approached, it picked up speed and led her onto Beach Drive.

The quiet, one-lane road ran parallel to the ocean. Along both sides were wood-frame cottages and house-trailers. One of the trailers had a swing set on its side yard. A boy in a swimsuit was standing on the middle swing, making it sway from side to side. A German shepherd wearing a red bandana around its neck was roaming down the side of the road. A woman was squatting down, planting flowers in front of her cottage. An elderly couple sat on lawn chairs, one reading a newspaper, the other a paperback. A teenaged boy was busy with a hose and sponge, washing an old green Pontiac.

It looked like a nice place to live.

A lot nicer than a hideout in the woods.

Sandy felt a pull of regret.

Can't have everything, she told herself. Be happy with what you've got.

Just ahead of her, Terry slowed down and turned left onto a gravel driveway. It seemed plenty long enough for her car to fit in behind his. As she made the turn, she glanced at the mailbox: 14 Beach Drive.

It was Terry's place, all right.

She parked, climbed out of her pickup and walked toward him. 'I won't be able to stay long,' she said.

'Long enough to come in and have a drink?'

'Not sure I'd better come in.'

'That'll be fine. We can relax out back on the sundeck.'

Sandy followed him around the side of the car port. About a hundred yards ahead, the ocean rolled into shore. The beach stretched all the way to the rear of the cottage.

She pulled off her shoes and carried them. The dry, hot sand shifted under her feet.

At the bottom of the deck stairs, she stopped and watched Terry climb. He had fine, golden hair on the backs of his legs, and curly down just above his belt. His wallet made the left seat pocket of his shorts bulge. The other side of his shorts curved nicely against his buttock.

She felt a little funny about staring at his rear.

Normally, she wasn't much interested in such things.

She wondered what he was wearing under his shorts.

Get a grip, she told herself. The guy's a cop. I can't have anything to do with him.

Then what am I doing here?

'Coming up?' he asked.

'Sure.' She climbed the stairs. The sundeck had a redwood railing on three sides. On the fourth side, the deck joined the cottage. Which seemed to be made mostly of glass. Draperies were shut, however, so she couldn't see inside. The deck was furnished with a round glass table, a few folding chairs, two loungers with fabric pads, a couple of TV trays, and a barbecue grill.

'What can I get you?' Terry asked.

'I'll have to drive home pretty soon.'

'I have soft drinks. Or you might try a beer. One or two beers shouldn't impair you much.'

'A beer sounds good,' she said.

'I'll have to go in through the front.' He headed for the stairs.

Sandy glanced at the two sliding glass doors. 'You can't get in from here?'

'They only lock from the inside. This'll just take a minute, though. Make yourself at home.'

'I'll come with you,' Sandy told him.

'Fine.'

As they retraced their route to the front of the cottage, Terry smiled and said, 'I thought you didn't want to go in.'

'I was just being cautious.'

'And now you're not?'

'Maybe I was being *overly* cautious. I mean, you *are* a cop, right?'

'Right.'

When they reached the front door, he unlocked and opened it. Sandy followed him inside. The living room had a hardwood floor and several rugs. There were bookshelves, a stone fireplace, a television, an easy chair, and an old sofa with a coffee table in front and lamp tables at each end. On one wall was a seascape of the ocean at sunset. On another wall hung *The Sleeper*.

By Blaze O. Glory.

One of his more recent paintings.

It showed Sandy sprawled on a bed, eyes shut, her hair spread across the pillow, sunlight slanting down on her from a nearby window. She looked as if she'd tossed and turned during the night. By morning, the single sheet over her body was a twisted disarray. Her entire left leg had come out from under it. The sheet covered her right leg, then swept upward across her body at an angle, draping her belly and her left breast and shoulder, but leaving her right breast naked.

Sandy gaped at it. Then she turned to Terry.

His smile turned crooked and he blushed.

Sandy's heart thudded wildly. Her face felt hot. 'That's me,' she said, her voice coming out no louder than a whisper.

'I know,' he whispered back at her.

'My God.'

What's going *on*? she wondered. She felt very strange: confused, embarrassed, deceived and betrayed, frightened, flattered, vulnerable and excited. All at the same time.

'The painting's beautiful,' Terry said. '*You're* beautiful.'

'So . . . this morning wasn't an accident. You didn't just stumble onto us.'

'I had a spy in the camp.'

'Blaze?'

Terry nodded.

'That . . .'

'He meant well. He thought you and I might get along.'

'He set me up.'

'All he really did was tell me where you'd be.'

'Then he made sure I was half naked for the encounter.'

Smiling, Terry said, 'Well, he probably did *that* for artistic reasons.'

'Oh, sure.'

'He was just trying to help. He thinks you need someone . . . a friend. And he knew how much I wanted to meet you.'

'Because of *that*?' She nodded toward the painting.

'That. And others.'

'You have *more*?'

'No. Just the one. It's all I've been able to afford. But I've seen a few of the others. I wish I had them *all*.'

Staring into his eyes, she asked, 'Why?'

'Because they're of you.'

'They don't even *look* like me.'

'Sure they do. I mean, none of them looks *exactly* like you. Blaze doesn't get every feature just right. But all of them have . . . I don't know.' His blush deepened. 'Your beauty. Your magic. I wish he'd paint one that *really* looks like you.'

'He's not supposed to,' Sandy explained. 'I don't want everybody knowing it's *me* when they see these things.'

'Couldn't be anyone else,' Terry said. 'Not if they know you.'

'I'd better make Blaze give me a bigger nose or something.'

Laughing softly, Terry shook his head. 'Don't do that. He *should* make them look exactly like you. In the ways they're different, they lose.'

She gazed at him.

'Sorry,' he said. 'I didn't mean to upset you.'

'You didn't? Then how come you brought me in here? Did you think I wouldn't notice the painting?'

'I guess I wanted you to notice it.'

'So you *intended* to scare me away?'

'You're still here.'

'Hanging on by the fingernails.'

'How about that beer?'

'Maybe I'd better get the hell out of here. This is a little . . . strange.'

'How about if you get the hell out to the back deck?'

Staring into his eyes, she wasn't sure what she saw. A look of urgent hope?

Maybe that's lust.

What she didn't find in his eyes was any trace of malice.

'I guess the deck'll be okay,' she said.

He led her toward one of the sliding doors. 'How about the beer?' he asked.

'Make it a vodka, okay? If you have any. I'm beyond beer right now.'

'How about a vodka and tonic?'

'That'd be just right.'

He unlatched the door and rolled it open for her. Then he skidded the screen door out of the way.

'I'll be along in a minute,' he said.

Sandy stepped across the deck. Bending over slightly, she clutched the top of the redwood railing with both hands and gazed out over the beach. Not many people were in sight. Those that she could see were far away. There were a lot more seagulls than people. They swooped and flapped and squealed.

The sun felt hot, but a cool breeze blew into Sandy's face and ruffled her shirt.

This is so great, she thought.

And so horrible.

God, the guy is head-over-heels for me.

Not for me. For the gal in the paintings.

But she is me.

What am I gonna do?

Drink my drink and leave, she told herself. And avoid him from now on.

But what if he won't avoid me?

This sucks so bad.

But if it sucks so bad, she wondered, why do I feel so *great?*

I don't.

Don't lie. You do, too.

Okay. Great but miserable.

Hearing footsteps on the wood of the deck, she turned around. Terry set down a serving tray on top of the glass table. It had two vodka tonics on it. There was also a basket loaded with potato chips.

'Cocktails are served, ma'am,' he said, and pulled out a chair for Sandy.

'Thanks,' she said. She sat down.

'And thank *you* for sticking around. A lesser person might've fled the scene.'

'I *will* have to leave pretty soon. Mom and Eric . . .' She shrugged. 'I don't like to be away too long.'

'Any time you're ready to go, just holler.' Terry sat down and raised his glass. 'Here's how,' he said.

'Here's how.'

They clinked their glasses together, then drank.

'Ahhh,' Sandy said. 'This sure hits the spot.'

'Glad you like it. You know, you're really being a good sport about this.'

'Are we playing a game?'

'I just mean, I'm awfully glad you haven't flipped out and run away.'

'The urge exists. I'm holding it at bay.'

'I did think about hiding the picture. You know, this morning before I set out for the rendezvous. But that would've been like *assuming in advance* that I'd get you here, and I didn't want to do anything that might jinx the operation.' Laughing softly, he took another drink. 'Stupid, huh?'

'Not entirely.'

'Anyway, it seemed sort of stupid to me, but it's why I didn't hide the picture. Then I thought, well, if I *do* get you into the house, it'll be a good time for you to see it. I didn't much care for the subterfuge.'

Smiling, Sandy set down her glass. 'Why the subterfuge in the first place?'

'Well . . .'

'Well?'

'I never knew anything about you till about three months ago. There was an overnight break-in at the Beachside Gallery.'

'I never heard about that.'

'It was kept pretty quiet. Someone forced open the back door and trashed a few paintings. In fact, *all* the paintings in the place that seemed to be gay-oriented.'

'That must've included some by Blaze.'

'Right. A couple of them. Anyway, I was called over to the gallery in the morning when Megan opened up for business and discovered what had happened. She started showing me around. And that's when I saw *The Sleeper* for the first time. It just . . . knocked my socks off. I mean . . . I had to have it. I'd never *seen* a painting that hit me that way.'

'Blaze is pretty good,' Sandy said.

'And his model is *spectacular*.'

'I'm just a dame.'

Terry laughed. 'Yeah. So anyway, I bought *The Sleeper* right then and there – right in the middle of my investigation. Had to max out my Visa card, but . . .' He shrugged. 'A small price to pay.'

'A *hefty* price.'

'I *had* to have that painting. And I had to . . . meet you. Megan couldn't tell me much. And I guess her information wasn't exactly accurate, either. She told me your name was Electra, for one thing.'

'It's my *nom de nudie*.'

Terry laughed. 'She also said you're Blaze's niece and you live in San Francisco. You're not his niece, are you?'

'Nope.'

'What about San Francisco? *Is* that where you live?'

'I'll never tell.'

'Why not?'

'If I tell you all my secrets, I'll lose my membership in the Mysterious Dames Society.' She poked a potato chip into her mouth and crunched it. 'Then where would I be?'

'Will you at least tell me your real name?'

'What'd Blaze say it is?'

'Just Ashley. He wouldn't tell me your last name.'

'Good for him!'

'He said I should ask you.'

'What else did he say about me?'

'He claimed not to know where you live. He said you just show up at his place every couple of weeks, then take off again after you're done posing. He mentioned that you have a son. That's about it. Well . . . and that he thought we'd make a nice couple.'

'Good ol' Blaze.'

'So I suggested that maybe he should introduce me to you, but he didn't want to do it that way. He thought you wouldn't like him trying to "fix you up" with a friend. That you'd resent it, and I'd stand a better chance if I just happened to run into you by accident. He thought I should put in an appearance while you were out posing for him. And I went along with it. I knew it was kind of a screwy idea, but Blaze completely refused to just *introduce* me to you.'

'He enjoys his melodramas,' Sandy said.

'Guess so. Anyway, I figured "whatever it takes." This morning, he gave me the call, said you were coming in and told me where he'd be taking you.'

Sandy shook her head.

'I *am* sorry about tricking you. But I just *had* to meet you. I would've done anything.'

'*Anything?*'

'Pretty near.'

'A desperate man. That's flattering *and* scary.'

'Well, I'll be perfectly straightforward and honest from now on. I promise.'

'From now on, huh? That's assuming we'll be seeing more of each other.'

'I wouldn't mind,' he said.

'What do you *have* in mind?'

'This sort of thing, I guess. Seeing each other. Talking. You know.'

'That might be nice.'

He looked relieved and glad.

'There is a problem, though. I've got Eric. And we *do* live pretty far away. I usually don't make it into town more than a couple of times a month.'

'I guess I could live with that.'

'You wouldn't have any choice. It's that or nothing. Twice a month is all I can get away.'

'You don't have any other guys, do you?'

'Just Eric.' She met Terry's eyes. 'I've had some bad luck with the men in my life. I'll probably have bad luck with you.'

'But you're willing to give me a try? Give *us* a try?'

'On one condition.'

'Anything.'

'You have to promise you'll never come to *my* place,' she said.

'I don't even know where it is.'

'But you're a cop. You could probably find out easily enough. If you haven't already.'

'I haven't.'

'The thing is, whatever we do, I don't want Eric involved. He and I . . . we're very close. I think he'd see you as an interloper who's trying to take his mom away from him. He's insecure enough as it is. So you have to promise *never under any circumstances* to come out to the house.'

'I promise.'

'Cross your heart and hope to die?'

'Cross my heart and hope to die.' With his forefinger, he marked an X over his heart. Then he leaned forward and reached across the table. Sandy reached out, too. He took hold of her hand and gently squeezed it.

A few minutes later, done with her drink, she said, 'I'd better get going.'

'How about staying for one more round?'

'Afraid not. And you should know better.'

'I do. But I hate to see you go so soon.'

'I'll be back in town before you know it.'

'How *will* I know it?' he asked.

'Oh, Blaze will probably tip you off.'

He laughed. 'Come on.'

'I'll call and let you know. Or I'll drop by.'

'What if I'm not here?'

She grinned. 'Then you might miss me.'

'I'm *usually* home during the day. I work the graveyard shift. Wednesdays and Thursdays off. And I've got an answering machine, so if you call in advance . . .'

'I'll try not to miss you,' Sandy said. Then she scooted back her chair and stood up.

Terry got to his feet and pulled out his wallet. He searched it, frowning, then came up with a business card. 'Need a pen. I'll write my home phone number on the back.' He returned the wallet to his pocket, then turned around and reached for the sliding door. 'This'll just take me a second. Want to come in?'

'I'll wait for you here.'

He rolled open the door and stepped inside. While he was away,

Sandy ate a few more potato chips. Then she drank the melted ice water at the bottom of her glass.

Terry came out and handed the card to her. 'My home number's on the back.'

'Thanks.' She slipped it into a rear pocket of her jeans. 'I'd better get going.'

Terry stepped toward the open door.

'I think I'll go around the side.'

'This way's shorter,' he pointed out.

'But it might *take* longer. You might decide to show me your bedroom and you might talk me into testing the bed.' Smiling, she shook her head. 'No telling what might happen after that. And whatever does, it might take hours.'

'Whoa! Jeez!'

'And I've already been gone too long. So I'll go *this* way.'

She picked up her shoes and walked toward the porch stairs.

'I'll come with you.' He hurried down the stairs after Sandy. At the bottom, he caught up to her and took her hand. As they walked past the rear of the car port, he said, 'Maybe we can get together longer next time. Maybe have a picnic on the beach or something. Maybe go in for a swim.'

'We'll do something,' she said.

'It's a pretty nice beach.'

'You're a pretty nice guy.' She freed her hand, then slipped her arm across his back, low against the warm bare skin above of his shorts. As she curled her hand against his side, he put his arm on her back. She felt his hand against her shoulder-blade.

When they came around the front of the car port, she stopped to put on her shoes. Terry held her steady. Then she turned to him.

She was tall enough to look him straight in the eyes.

He gazed into her eyes for a long time as if he couldn't get enough of them. And she gazed into his, wondering and hoping.

Finally, Sandy said, 'I've gotta get going. Thanks for the drink and everything.'

'Any time. Day or night. Feel free to . . .'

She darted forward, kissed him fast on the lips, then whirled around and hurried to her pickup truck. She was inside it with the door shut by the time Terry got to her.

He looked at her through the open window. 'I'm going to miss you,' he said.

'You can't miss me. We don't know each other.'

'Oh. Okay. That's good to know.'

'Anyway, you have *The Sleeper* to keep you company.' She twisted in her seat and leaned toward the open window and Terry's face was there, sad as if she were already gone, but his mouth found her lips and kissed them with gentleness and longing and silent need.

When it was over, she backed her truck down his driveway to the road. She waved good-bye and he returned the wave and stayed there by the driveway, watching while she drove away.

Oh, God, she thought, I miss him already.

I can't miss him. We don't even know each other.

She had a strong urge to turn the truck around and go back.

Why not? Why the hell not? Eric's probably romping around the woods, doesn't even know or care that I'm not back yet.

But she kept on driving, heading for home.

Like a good little mommy.

Leaving behind the one and only man she'd ever felt this way about.

Felt what way?

What is it, love?

'I can't be in love with him,' Sandy whispered. 'I don't even know him.'

I could remedy that.

She imagined herself making a U-turn and speeding back to his cottage.

She didn't do it, though.

I'll see him again soon enough, she told herself. Shouldn't go rushing into anything. God knows, I've waited *this* long for a guy, I can wait two more weeks.

Chapter Thirty-Four

Big John

'Man, you really missed out,' John said as Owen walked toward him. The big guy was standing on the sidewalk not far from the ticket booth, grinning and shaking his head. 'Where were you, anyhow?'

'Taking a look around town. I checked out the museum.'

'Did that yesterday. Cool stuff in there, huh?'

'Yeah. But I'd always wanted to meet Janice Crogan. She owns it, you know.'

'Hey, what *doesn't* she own in this town?'

'Anyway, I found a photography place that develops film in an hour. It's just up the road a couple of blocks.' He glanced toward the ticket booth. Rhonda was behind the window, and Sharon was busy outfitting a family of five with tape players. 'Let's walk,' Owen said.

They headed north on Front Street.

'Did you get the pictures?' he asked.

'Ohhhh, yeah.'

'Dana, right?'

John grinned. 'Got a whole bunch of Dana and some more of Lynn, too. But then you wouldn't believe what happened. Really too bad you missed it, man. Wow.'

'You gonna tell me?'

'Sure. Why not? What are buddies for, huh?'

Buddies?

Oh, great, he thinks I'm his buddy.

'Okay. Here's the thing. So I'm upstairs. I get our luscious sweethearts to pose for me, you know, and then I'm still hanging around and all hell breaks loose. Some little asshole gets away from his mom and she's like *"Oh my God, he's been kidnapped! I'll never see him alive again!"* Lynn, she's gone by then. So it's all up to Dana, you know? She goes running up the hall to see what's wrong. You oughta see her run, man. She's got these tits on her, and . . .'

'Hey.'

'Yeah, yeah. Sorry. But she does. You oughta see 'em when she runs.'

'Cut it out!'

John laughed. 'Anyway . . . So then there's this girl, she saw the missing brat hightail it up the attic stairs.'

'He wasn't kidnapped after all, huh?'

'Nope, just thought he'd visit the attic. Which is off limits, you know.'

'I know.'

'So Dana, she goes up to get him and all of a sudden the kid lets out this scream like he just bumped into Freddie Krueger or something. I can't see too much on account of all these rubber-neckers around the door, but I hear the kid yelling that something's after him. Next thing you know, out Dana comes carrying him.'

'*Carrying* him?'

'Yeah! Like she'd snatched him off his feet. Had him hugged like this.' John demonstrated with his arms. 'There's an idea for you, pal. Run up into the attic, maybe she'll carry *you* down.'

'I'll be sure to do that. Was the kid okay?'

'Sure. He was fine. Just scared shitless. But then, get this. Dana, she's looking the kid over and all of a sudden the mom hauls off and whacks him across the face. Which *really* pisses off Dana. Next thing you know, she's yelling at Mom for hitting the kid, and the gal hocks one on her.'

'She *spat* on Dana?'

'Yeah! Man, you should've seen it. A big old gob. Lands on her shirt. Right here.' He pointed at his own shirt, just above the pocket. 'Note how I'm not saying word one about it being on her tit.'

'Very decent of you.'

'Anyway, so Dana grabs her and pins her to a wall and *pukes* on her.'

'*What?*'

'She *up*chucked all over the gal.'

Owen grimaced.

'Man, it was awesome! God only knows what Dana'd been eating, but . . .'

'That's okay,' Owen said. 'You don't have to go into it.'

'Whatever it was . . .'

'Hey!'

'All right, all right. Sorry.'

'So what happened *after* she threw up on the mother?'

'That's when the reinforcements showed up. Lynn, Sharon and some guy . . .'

'Must've been Clyde.'

'Yeah. So Sharon and Clyde, they escort Mom and the kid out of the house. I heard 'em say something about cleaning her up. Man, you should've seen her. She was dripping puke all down the hall.'

'What happened to Dana?'

'Well, Lynn shut the attic door and kept people away from the mess. While she was doing that, Dana went off and came back with a mop and stuff. Then Lynn sort of directed traffic while Dana took care of the mess.'

'Don't they have a janitor?'

'Nah. Lynn takes care of everything. She's Janice Crogan's daughter, you know that?'

'Huh? Really?'

'Her step-daughter,' John explained. 'She's married to Lynn's dad.'

'I had no idea.'

'And Janice is away on a trip . . .'

'I knew that.'

'So Lynn's in charge of the whole works till she gets back.'

'How do you *know* all this stuff?'

John shrugged. 'Been around a couple of days. And I pay attention. I keep my eyes open. I listen. People say stuff. You put two and two together.'

'What do you know about Dana?'

'Has a weak stomach.'

'Very funny.'

'Doesn't like it if you hit kids.'

'I'll try to restrain myself around her.'

'Great set of hooters.'

'Stop that.'

'She's living with Lynn.'

'How do you know?' Owen asked.

'Saw them drive in together this morning.'

'I saw that, too. Doesn't mean they live together. Maybe they car pool, or . . .'

'Well, I also heard some things.'

'Like what?'

'Like Dana has some kind of hot date tonight.'

The news gave Owen a sick feeling.

'They were talking about Lynn picking her up later and bringing her home. Home being *Lynn's* place. So obviously they're living together.'

'She has a *date*?'

'Buck up, little buckeroo.' John slapped his shoulder. 'At least she's not a lesbo.'

'Who's she seeing?'

'Didn't catch that part. All I know is, he's a guy. And it sounds like Dana hasn't gone out with him before.'

Is it *me*? Owen suddenly wondered. Did John overhear them talking about a date with *me*?

No way!

But we *did* have that nice talk this morning, Owen reminded himself. And Dana *did* seem to like me. A little, at least. Maybe. Thought I was a jerk for ditching Monica, but her eyes got wet when I said that stuff about how she was everything a guy could ever want.

I touched her. I moved her.

And I promised not to bother her . . . unless she wanted me to. Joking like. But she didn't take it like a joke. She said she would think about it.

And she asked where I'm staying tonight!

My God, Owen thought. Maybe she *does* plan to see me.

I *might* be the hot date!

But I told her I'd be at the Welcome Inn. I've gotta get over there. What if they don't have any vacancies?

He checked his wristwatch.

Almost two o'clock.

'What's up?' John asked. 'Wishing you were the lucky guy?'

'Sort of.'

'Don't waste your time, pal. Guys like you and me, we're *never* the lucky guy. Not when it comes to babes like Dana or Lynn. They got a word for guys like us.'

'What's that?'

'Losers.'

'Speak for yourself.'

John laughed. 'Only one way you'd ever stand a chance with a gal like Dana – knock her out and tie her up.'

'You're disgusting.'

He laughed again and said, 'Truth hurts.'

'Fuck you.'

'Wanta?'

Owen snarled at him.

Laughing, John reached over suddenly and pinched his nipple. Owen yelped 'Ouch!' and swatted his hand away.

'Not much up top,' John said.

'Leave me alone!'

'Aw, that didn't hurt you.'

'Did, too.' Owen stopped at the curb. On the other side of the street was the photo shop. 'Just keep your hands to yourself, okay?'

'If you say so. Is that the place?' John asked.

'Yeah. Is your roll finished?'

'Yep.' He reached into his shirt pocket and pulled out a black plastic canister. 'I'm all reloaded and everything.'

They crossed the street and entered the shop.

A man behind the counter looked up at them. He had no hair or eyebrows. He was too tall, too thin. He looked as if he'd been grabbed at each end and stretched by someone playful and malicious. 'Help you?' he asked.

'We'd like to get some film developed,' Owen said.

John set the container on top of the glass counter. The man picked it up, opened it, and dumped the roll of film into his hand. His fingers were nearly twice as long as Owen's. 'Uh-huh,' he said. 'Twenty-four color prints. I can take care of that for you.'

'We'd like two copies of each,' Owen said.

'Better make it four,' John said.

'Four?' Owen asked.

'Two for us, two for the girls.' Grinning, he said, 'I promised 'em.'

'That's okay.'

'Four copies each?' the man asked. 'That'll run you.'

'That's okay,' Owen said. 'When can we pick them up?'

'When do you need them?'

'The sooner the better, I guess.'

The man glanced over his shoulder at the wall clock. Though mounted above a door, it was nearly level with his head. 'I'd say I can likely have them done for you before closing time.'

'When's that?' Owen asked.

'Six o'clock.'

'That's *four* hours,' John pointed out, glowering at the man. 'Your sign says *one*-hour developing.'

'You want four copies?'

'You telling me it takes four times as long?'

The man's thin lips pressed together tightly and curled up at each end. 'Might,' he said. 'Might take longer. But I close at six, either way.'

'Six'll be fine,' Owen told him, trying to sound especially friendly and sincere. 'Really. We've got no problem with that. My friend's a trouble-maker.'

'I 'spect he is,' the man said.

Owen hauled out his wallet and removed a fifty-dollar bill. 'I'd be glad to pay in advance.'

The man eyed the bill. He nodded as if agreeing with himself about a matter of little importance. 'No need for that,' he said. 'Come in here around five, maybe I'll have 'em done for you by then.'

'Thanks. Thank you.'

Outside, John patted Owen on the back and said, 'Well done, young fella.'

'Yeah, right.'

'Looks like *we* have some time on our hands. So, what'll we do for the next three hours?'

'I don't know,' Owen said. He crossed the street, John by his side, and headed south.

'Wanta go back to Beast House and scope out the babes for a while?'

'Not really.'

'What do *you* wanta do?'

'Actually, we don't really need to . . . We could, like, each do our own thing and meet back at the photo shop at five.'

John laughed. 'Trying to get rid of me?'

'No, but . . . I could use some time by myself.'

'What for?'

'Maybe I'd just like to be alone for a while.'

'So you can go to your room and freshen up?'

'I don't *have* a room.'

'Ah! Okay. I get it. You need to find yourself a place to stay tonight, am I right?'

'I thought I'd drive around and see what's available.'

'Good deal. Might I suggest the Welcome Inn? Best place in town. *Plus* it has all that history. I fully intended to stay there myself before my fucking radiator exploded. Get a room with two beds, and I'll keep you company.'

Owen grimaced. 'I really don't want a room-mate, John.'

'Sure you do.'

'No. I don't. Really.'

'Come on. I've been sleeping in my *car*, man. It's been a week since I took a shower. Anyway, it won't cost you hardly anything. These motels, they charge you pretty much the same for two people as one.'

Owen shook his head.

'Come on, man. Do a guy a favor.'

'I'd like to have some time by myself.'

'You can have *that* any old time. I'm not asking you to *marry* me. Besides. You and me, we make a good team. You can use me. Look how I took those pictures for you.'

'I'm giving you a *hundred-dollar ticket* for them.'

'But you'd never have the guts to take 'em like that yourself. You need a guy like me around. I can do stuff for you. I'll do *anything*, man. Please.'

I'm never gonna get rid of this guy!

'I tell you what,' Owen said. 'I want some time by myself.'

'Hey, but . . .'

'Listen! I don't like all this pressure. If you want to use my room tonight, give me a little space. Right now, I want to get in my car and drive over to the motel – by myself. They might not even have any vacancies. And the more time I waste arguing with you . . .'

'Okay, okay. Go. I'll find something to do without you.'

'Good. We'll meet at the photo shop at five. After we get the pictures, I'll let you know about tonight.'

John raised his hand. 'See you there.' He stopped walking.

They were still a half a block from the entrance to the Beast House parking lot.

'Fine,' Owen said.

'Fine. Go.'

'Okay.' Owen turned away from him and resumed walking.

He had an urge to look back, but he resisted it.

'Hey, Owen?' John called.

He looked around.

'Don't forget it's a *midnight* tour. You'd better get reservations for tomorrow night, too.' He held up two fingers and smiled rather sadly.

He was still standing in the same place on the sidewalk a few minutes later when Owen pulled out of the parking lot in his rental car and swung right onto Front Street.

John looked like a big, abandoned kid.

Owen slowed down and pulled over. He pushed a button to lower the passenger window. 'Okay,' he called. 'Come on.'

Crouching to see inside, John shook his head. 'Thanks. But a deal's a deal. You go on ahead and make your reservations. I'll find something else to do till five.'

'Are you sure?'

'Yeah. You don't need me hanging around all the time.'

'Okay. See you later, then.'

'See you, pal.'

Owen drove on. In the side mirror, he saw John standing on the sidewalk, watching him.

Not such a bad guy.

The beeping alarm on his wristwatch woke Owen up. He was lying on top of a bed. The room was almost dark, but a strip of sunlight came in through a gap where the curtains didn't quite meet.

Still on his back, he raised his arm.

The luminous numbers on his wristwatch showed 4:30.

He shut off the alarm.

But he didn't get up.

No big hurry, he thought. It'll only take five or ten minutes to drive over to the photo shop.

I could even skip it.

No law says I have to go and pick up the pictures. I can just stay here. That'd be the end of my troubles with John, at least for today. Deal with him tomorrow.

Besides, what if Dana calls while I'm gone?

Turning his head, Owen looked at the telephone.

She might call any second.

She probably won't call at all, he thought. She wouldn't go out with a guy like me. Her date's with somebody else. A strong, handsome, sun-tanned jock.

Anyway, if she *does* call, the front desk will take a message.

Maybe she'll just drop in.

He imagined her stepping up to the door of his motel room and knocking on it. In his mind, she was wearing her guide uniform. A couple of the top buttons were unfastened. 'Just thought I'd drop by and see how you're doing, Owen.'

'Would you like to come in?'

'Thought you'd never ask.' She stepped into his room and wrapped her arms around him and pulled him against her body. 'I know we just met,' she said, 'but I haven't been able to stop thinking about . . .'

Someone knocked on the door of Owen's room.

He bolted upright, his heart suddenly thudding.

It can't be Dana, he thought as he scurried off the bed. No way. That sort of thing just doesn't happen. Not to me.

Maybe this once . . .

He jerked open the door.

'Hey, pal, how's our room?'

'What're *you* doing here?'

'Look what *I've* got.' John held up a bag. 'Mr Cucumber got done with the pictures early, so I saved us both some time and picked 'em up.' He stepped into the room. 'They cost me down to my last nickle, pretty near. But I figure you'll reimburse me. Too bad you couldn't get a room in the old wing.'

'They were all full.'

'Yeah, bet they go fast. Everybody wants to be in the section where stuff really happened. Guess we were lucky to get anything.'

'This was the last room available,' Owen said.

'I know, I know. I saw 'em turn on the No Vacancy sign right after you went in the office.'

'What the hell did you do, *follow* me?'

'Shit, no. You *told* me you were coming here. I just hopped into my buggy and sailed on over. Wanted to see if you'd get us a room.' A grin suddenly spread across John's face. 'And which one,' he added.

'Real nice.'

'But please note, I did *not* disturb you. I allowed you your space.'

'Yeah. Thanks a lot.'

John spread the curtains wide, and afternoon sunlight flooded the room.

'Not bad, not bad. A queen and a single, huh? Who gets the queen?' He sat down on the queen-sized mattress and bounced.

'I do.'

'I'm bigger than you. Don't you think *I* should get the bigger bed?'

'No. I'm paying. And what makes you think I'm going to let you stay?'

'What're you gonna do, throw me out? If you throw me out, I take *these* with me.' He reached into the bag and pulled out an envelope thick with photographs. 'I've already taken a peek. They're *hot*. That Dana, she's a babe and a half.'

'Let me see.'

'Who gets the queen?'

'Oh, for the . . .'

'I can always leave.'

'You really are a jerk.'

'I'm the jerk with guts enough to take photos of your secret honey.'

'Okay. Fine. You win. Take the queen.'

'Thank you.'

Chapter Thirty-Five

Warren's Place

'You're out of uniform,' Warren said as he met Dana in front of the ticket booth.

'Had a little mishap.'

'So I heard.' He smiled at her. For a moment, she thought he might reach out and take her hand. But he didn't. 'Sounds like the gal deserved what she got,' he said.

'Well, I didn't exactly premeditate the attack. Talk about *embarrassing*. I wanted to crawl in a hole. And then the gift shop was out of my size. They were out of *most* sizes, for that matter.' She looked down at her huge, flapping T-shirt. It drooped over her shoulders. It hung down low enough to cover her shorts when the wind wasn't flinging and lifting it. 'I know I'm big, but this thing would fit Jabba the Hutt.'

'Looks good,' Warren said.

'Well, thanks.'

'Ready to go?'

'Sure.'

Staying by Warren's side, she stepped to the edge of Front Street. Traffic was coming from both directions. Warren's head turned from side to side as if he were watching a tennis match. Glancing Dana's way, he caught her looking at him. He smiled.

Then came a break in the traffic and they hurried across.

They stopped just short of the high, chainlink fence in front of the Kutch property.

Dana stared at the house.

'Have you ever been in there?' she asked.

'Not in the house itself. I've trespassed on the grounds, though. I was hoping to get a look inside.'

'No windows.'

'I knocked on the door.'

'You *knocked*?'

'Oh, yeah. I thought maybe I'd introduce myself to Agnes. I brought her a bouquet of flowers.'

'That was nice.'

'Well, you know. All women are supposed to love flowers. Agnes Kutch is apparently nuts, but she's still a woman. Thought I'd try to win her over and maybe she'd give me a tour of her house. But she wouldn't open the door. She doesn't open it for anyone.'

'I've heard she's sort of a recluse.'

'*Sort* of. It's like she's hiding in there. She has a remote system for opening the gate of her driveway. Whatever she needs, she orders it by phone and has it delivered. See how the porch is all enclosed? They leave the stuff inside and she gets it after they've gone.'

Warren turned away. Dana stayed with him. Together, they walked along the sandy patch between Front Street and the fence.

'She can't stay in the house *all* the time, can she?'

'Looks like she does.'

'She must pay her bills somehow.'

'Janice pays them. Everything is billed to Janice.'

'So, does *Janice* ever see her?'

Warren shook his head. 'Not in the past four or five years. Nobody has.'

'How creepy.'

'Well, you can't really expect someone like Agnes to be normal. When you think about what she's been through.'

'You're probably right about that,' Dana said.

'Amazing she survived,' Warren said. 'Here. Up this way.'

They headed to the left up a narrow lane of asphalt. The road was cracked and pitted. Grass and dandelions grew in some of the fissures.

'Going nuts was probably her way of coping with it,' Dana said.

'I guess you either go nuts or kill yourself.'

As they walked along, Dana looked over at the Kutch house. She imagined a withered, hunched old crone lurching through its blue-lit rooms. 'What kind of life could she have in there? What does she do all day?'

'God knows,' Warren said.

'Glad *I* don't.'

'An advantage of not being God.'

'I wonder if she's got a TV.'

'Last time Janice was inside, she didn't.'

'And all the lights are blue?'

'Red.'

'I thought . . .'

'They *were* blue. Back when everything happened. But Agnes switched over to red lights a year or so later.'

'I hadn't heard about that. Do you think she was trying to cheer the place up?'

Laughing softly, Warren shook his head. 'If that was the idea, I guess it didn't work. Janice said it was like looking at the world through blood-colored glasses.'

'You'd think *she* would've appreciated the change.'

'Janice? You'd think so, but she didn't.'

'I can't even imagine her going *into* the Kutch house. After what happened to her in there?'

Warren met Dana's eyes, then quickly looked away and said, 'Neither can I.'

For a while, they walked up the lane in silence. Dana heard the squeals of seagulls. The wind hissed through the nearby trees.

It seemed to be blowing much stronger as they neared the ocean. It flung Dana's hair. It pricked her legs with flying sand. It flapped her T-shirt, sometimes pressed the thin fabric against her body, other times blew underneath it and billowed it out. Once, the wind flung her T-shirt up as if to show Warren her bra. While the shirt was up, sharp bits of sand blasted against Dana's belly. She pulled her T-shirt down, then switched the purse strap to her other shoulder so it crossed her chest like a bandolier. The wind was no match for the leather strap.

'Would you like to go to the beach for a while?' Warren asked. 'Or straight to my cabin?'

'How about your cabin?'

'Good idea. Awfully windy today.'

'I noticed.'

When they came to a long row of rural mailboxes, Warren opened one and pulled out a handful of envelopes and catalogs. He shut it, then nodded to the right at a side road. Narrow and unpaved, the lane stretched off into a shadowy, wooded area. 'This way,' he said.

The trees kept most of the wind out. Dana could feel the heat again. The road, dim with shadows, was littered with bright dabs of sunlight. Pine needles crunched softly under her shoes. The air smelled of Christmas trees.

'I like it in here,' she said.

'It's not LA, is it?'

'Makes me wonder why I live there.'

'Why *do* you?'

'I don't know. I grew up in LA. My parents live there. Most of my friends, too. I've thought about moving away, but . . . there's so much I'd *miss*. Earthquakes, riots, fires, floods, the late-night crackle of gunfire.'

Warren laughed.

'I really do like the restaurants and movie theaters. And the beach.'

'I hear you're a lifeguard.'

'I've *been* a lifeguard.'

'Just like *Bay Watch*, huh?'

Grinning, she said, 'Oh, yeah. It's me and Mitch. Actually, my life-guarding has mostly been confined to swimming pools.'

'You didn't feel like doing it this summer?'

'I liked the idea of coming up here. And I hadn't seen Lynn in a while.'

'Well, she has a pool. You can lifeguard her.'

'Right! She needs it.'

She really *might* need it, Dana suddenly thought. She'll probably go out there tonight with or without me, no matter *who* might be lurking around.

What if something happens to her?

'You really do need to keep an eye on her,' Warren said. 'She's . . . maybe a little too daring for her own good.'

'Oh, yeah, I know. More guts than sense.'

'Here's my place.' He nodded toward a log cabin off to the left. It had a screened-in porch along the entire front, and a large stone chimney at one end. Sunlight coming down through the trees dappled the cabin and yard with gold. The yard was forest floor: pine needles and cones, twigs, rocks, saplings and scattered trees.

'It's like a vacation cottage,' Dana said.

'If you're having a really *cheap* vacation.'

'I think it's nice,' Dana said, following Warren toward the porch.

'I like it. But wait till you meet my neighbors. The Seven Dwarfs live over that way.' He nodded to the right. 'And over there . . .' He pointed at a bleak-looking cabin some distance to the left. 'That's where my buddy Ed lives. Ed Gein.'

'Oh. Charming. You'll have to introduce us.'

'I don't know. Ed's sort of a loner.'

'Ah, but I bet he'd like *me*.'

'He'd *love* you.'

'With mustard and relish?'

Warren's head swung around. He looked surprised and delighted. 'You're *bad*,' he said.

'*You're* the one who brought up Ed Gein.'

'He doesn't really live there.'

'Glad to hear it.'

Warren trotted up the porch stairs. He pulled open the screen door and held it for Dana.

Before entering, she paused and said, 'I'm not on the menu *here*, am I?'

'You're safe with me.'

'Okay, then.' She stepped through the doorway, then moved out of the way to let Warren by. He fumbled with a load of keys, chose one, and unlocked the cabin's main door.

'You mean to tell me that you keep your door locked? In a bucolic place like this?'

'When you've got Ed Gein on one side and the Three Stooges on the other . . .'

'The Seven Dwarfs.'

'Oh. Right.' He opened the door. 'Come on in.'

Dana followed him into the cabin. Straight ahead, on the other side of the living room, was a picture window bright with sunlight. A couch was facing it. She stepped around the couch and walked up to the window.

Behind the house, the woods continued for twenty-five or thirty feet. But there were few trees. Through the spaces between them, Dana could see down to the beach. The surf was rolling in. A man, looking very haggard, was jogging near the water.

Warren came over and stood beside her.

'Great view,' she said.

'Look at the fog out there.'

It lay spread across the ocean, far out, thick and pure white in the sunlight.

'Think it'll come in?' Dana asked.

'Hard to say. Sometimes, it just stays offshore all night.'

'Must look great in the moonlight.'

'Oh, it does. Stick around long enough and you'll get to see it. Either out there, or up close and personal.'

'That'd be nice,' Dana said. 'I'm not sure how long I can stay, though. I'm a little nervous about leaving Lynn by herself.'

Warren looked concerned. 'Is something wrong with her?'

Should I tell him? Dana wondered. What if *he's* the prowler.

Not likely.

'Somebody was hanging around outside the house last night.'

And inside it this morning?

'Like a prowler?' Warren asked.

'I guess. We were in the hot spa and Lynn saw him. He was apparently hiding in the bushes on the other side of the swimming pool.'

'Did she recognize him?'

'All she saw was his arm, I guess. A bare arm.'

Warren grimaced. 'What'd you do?' he asked.

'Ran into the house and locked the door. Lynn phoned the police. Then we kept an eye on things till a cop showed up.'

Why didn't I tell him about the gun?

He doesn't need to know everything, she thought. He sure *seems* like a nice guy, but . . .

'Which cop?' Warren asked.

'Eve Chaney.'

'Ah-ha! Eve of Destruction! What'd you think of her?'

'Very impressive.'

'Yeah. I'll say. I'd sure hate to get on her bad side.'

'Having seen her,' Dana said, 'I don't think she *has* a bad side.'

'That isn't exactly what . . .'

'I know. But she sure is a good-looking woman, isn't she?'

'She's not bad.' Warren hesitated, then said, 'But you're better looking than she is.'

'I don't know about *that*.'

'I do.'

'Well . . . Thanks.'

He gazed into her eyes.

Her heart thumped hard and fast.

'Anyway,' Warren whispered, 'that's my opinion. For what it's worth.'

'It's worth plenty. To me.'

He glanced at her lips, then met her eyes again.

Come on, do it. Don't just look.

'I bet you could use a drink,' he said.

Damn!

'Sure. Sounds good.'

'Do you like margaritas?'

She nodded.

'Why don't you relax in here and enjoy the view? I'll get changed real fast. Then I'll make the drinks and bring 'em in.'

She watched Warren hurry off to a bedroom. After he shut the door, she set down her purse and sank onto the couch. She sighed deeply.

Take it easy, she told herself.

But he didn't even make a try! He should've kissed me right then. What's wrong with him?

He's a gentleman, she thought.

Or maybe he *is* gay.

Maybe it's something wrong with me.

When the door opened, Dana looked over her shoulder. Warren came out of his bedroom. His tan uniform was gone. He now wore sandals, white trousers and a bright, flower-patterned shirt. Loose and untucked, the shirt floated around him like silk.

'Drinks coming up,' he said, hurrying toward the kitchen.

'Mind if I join you?'

'Help yourself.'

Dana followed him into the kitchen. 'You got all dressed up,' she pointed out.

'I hate to stay in my work clothes. By the end of the day, they always smell like burgers and fries.'

'I'd think that would be nice.'

'It gets old.' He removed some bottles from a cupboard. 'Anyway, you were telling me about your prowler?'

'Oh, yeah. Well, Eve went hunting for him around the other side of the pool, but he got away. She found where he'd been, though. He'd trampled the area pretty good. She figured he must've been spying on us.'

'I don't like the sound of that.'

'Neither did we.'

Warren set the bottles on the counter, then turned around to face her. 'Some kind of Peeping Tom?'

'That's one of the possibilities.'

'No wonder you're worried. Any ideas at all about who it might be?'

She shook her head. 'Clyde?'

Laughter burst out of Warren. He looked surprised by it, himself.

Dana started laughing with him. When she stopped, she said, 'You don't think Clyde is a likely suspect?'

'It isn't that. I wouldn't put *anything* past him. It's just that he's *such* a jerk. And he's the first name out of your mouth.'

'Anyway,' Dana said, 'we don't have any reason to suspect him except for the fact that he *is* such a jerk. And he's shown some interest in me at work.'

'I bet he'd love to get his hands on you.'

'He'd better not hold his breath.'

Warren turned away and continued preparing the drinks.

'He isn't my type,' she said.

'Then you're the exception. Most women find him irresistible.'

'So I've heard. Personally, I find him creepy.'

'Glad to hear it.'

'We don't really think he's our prowler, though. He doesn't seem like the type to sneak around and spy on people.'

'You have to be careful of him, though.'

'Oh, I am. But it's this *prowler* who has me worried. I mean, there's no telling what he might try. And I just *know* Tuck's going to . . .'

'Tuck?' Warren turned around.

Oh, no!

'Lynn.'

'You called her Tuck?'

'She's gonna kill me.'

A smile spread across Warren's face. 'As in *Friar Tuck*? Robin Hood and his merry men?'

'As in a lot of stuff. It's short for Tucker. I've always called her Tuck, but she didn't want me to say it around any of you guys.'

'Why not? I think it's cute.'

'She used to have trouble with people making fun of it. A *lot* of trouble. It rhymes with a certain something.'

'That might cause problems.'

'Maybe you could pretend I never said it.'

'I suppose that's possible. What'll you give me to keep my mouth shut?'

'What do you want?' Dana asked.

He glanced at her lips.

Here we go again, she thought as her heart quickened its pounding.

'Could I try on your lipstick?' he asked.

NO!!!

She supposed her shock must've showed.

Smiling, Warren said, 'Plant it on me with your mouth.'

Chapter Thirty-Six

Sandy's Story – July, 1992

She *couldn't* wait two weeks.

She couldn't wait two days.

She could barely last overnight, tossing and turning in her bed, her mind in a turmoil, her body feverish as she wondered and hoped and worried.

In the morning, she woke up naked under her twisted sheet. She was surprised to realize that she must've been asleep. Raising her head and looking down at herself, she had to smile. Just like *The Sleeper*. But sweaty and messy, skin flushed, creased here and there from wrinkles in the sheets.

Not a pretty sight, she thought. Good thing Terry can't see me now.

But she suddenly wished that he *could*. Wished he were here in the room with her right this minute.

I could be at his place in a couple of hours.

The notion shocked her with its urgency.

Why not!

She squirmed and stretched on the bed, then climbed off. Her nightgown was on the floor. She vaguely remembered sitting up in the middle of the night, breathless and soaked with sweat, pulling the nightgown up over her head and throwing it aside.

She picked it up. It still felt damp.

At the sound of a grunt, she turned her head and saw Eric standing in the bedroom doorway. He smiled and raised a hand. 'Morning there, hotshot,' she said. 'I picked up something special for breakfast yesterday. You want to hang around for it? I'll just be a few minutes. I have to take a shower.'

He nodded. But he stayed in the doorway, staring at her.

'What?' she asked.

With a shrug, he turned around and wandered away.

She tossed her nightgown into the hamper, then headed for the bathroom.

Why did he look at me that way? she wondered.

She glanced down at herself.

Sure, she was naked. But that was nothing new. She often went around without anything on, and Eric himself *never* wore clothes. It had always been that way. It seemed perfectly natural.

So why did he stare at me like that?

Maybe I *do* look different, she thought. She entered the bathroom and studied herself in the mirror. Her smoothly tanned skin had a more rosy look than usual. She must've picked up a little too much sun yesterday in spite of her sun block. That happened fairly often, but . . .

Was Eric suspicious?

Maybe he noticed the extra color and didn't understand how she managed to get it while buying groceries.

Or was it something else?

Could he tell, by looking, that she'd met Terry yesterday and . . .?

She swept the shower curtain aside and found bloodstains in the tub.

'Eric!' she yelled. 'Get in here!'

He showed up quickly and offered a nervous smile.

'What's this?' Sandy pointed into the tub.

Eric groaned.

'How many times have I asked you to clean out the tub after you're done? *Especially* after you've slaughtered some damn thing?'

Looking miserable, he shrugged.

'I mean, *man!* Don't you think it's high time for you to start cleaning up your *own* messes? You're *thirteen!* I've got better things to do than waste my whole life cleaning *up* after you!'

Eric whimpered and lowered his head.

Something seemed to crumble inside Sandy. 'Oh,' she said. 'Hey.' She hurried over to him, wrapped her arms around him and drew him against her. 'I'm sorry,' she said. She gently stroked his back. 'I'm sorry, honey. Mommy shouldn't have yelled at you. Okay?'

He pressed his face against the side of her neck.

'Better?' she asked.

He sighed.

'I don't like it when I have to yell at you, honey. But you need to learn to start cleaning up after yourself. You're getting to be a big boy, you know? I don't want people saying my big fellow's a slob.'

The way he started to jiggle, Sandy knew he must be laughing. He *did* seem to understand so much. If only he could talk . . .

'You all better now?' she asked.

He sniffed and nodded.

'I'll take care of the mess this time,' she told him. 'But from now on, I want to you make a little more effort to clean up after yourself. Is it a deal?'

He grunted and nodded some more.

'Okay, then,' Sandy said.

She let go of him, but he still clung to her. 'Okay if I take my shower now?'

He shook his head.

'What do you want?'

His hands began moving in big circles over her back, the way he did when he soaped her.

'Okay,' Sandy said. 'You can come in with me. It's been a while, hasn't it?'

In the shower, they stood together under the hot spray. Eric soaped her first, rubbing the slippery bar all over her body. Then she did the same for him.

After they'd rinsed all the soap off their bodies, Sandy shut off the water and Eric slid open the shower curtain. They climbed out. Eric handed a towel to her.

As she dried herself, Sandy said, 'I need to go back into town this morning.'

Eric furrowed his brow.

'I know. I hate to leave you again so soon. I really should've taken care of this yesterday, but I sort of ran out of time.'

Not exactly a lie, she told herself.

Eric didn't look pleased.

'Oh, don't give me the sourpuss routine. Why does it even *matter* if I leave? You're never around, anyway. And it's not as if you'll let me come with you. What am I supposed to do, just hang around the house all day and *be here* in case you happen to drop in?'

He scowled at her.

'Real nice,' she said. 'Anyway, I *have* to go. I'm sure you'll get along just fine without me.'

He growled.

'Hey!' she snapped.

Eric flinched at the sharpness of her voice. Glaring at her, he threw his towel to the floor. Then he whirled around and stomped out of the bathroom.

'Wait,' Sandy said. 'Eric!'

He hurried down the hallway, feet thumping, claws clicking against the hardwood floor.

'I bought us some chocolate doughnuts yesterday!' she called.

Seconds later, she heard the front door slam.

'*Shit!*'

She suddenly felt like crying.

She almost didn't leave. But she wanted worse than ever to see Terry. And what was the point in staying? Eric was nowhere to be seen. Though he might be hanging around to spy on her, he had probably run off sulking into the woods.

Ready to go, she went out to the pickup truck.

Yesterday, she'd found Eric waiting in the passenger seat as if eager for a ride.

Seeing the seat empty today made her throat feel tight. 'Eric?' she called toward the woods. 'I'm sorry! Okay? Look, I'll stay home if you really want me to. We'll have the chocolate doughnuts. What do you say?'

She waited, listening, turning slowly and looking for him in the bushes and trees. He remained silent and hidden.

'If you don't want me to go, you'd better come out.'

He didn't come out.

Stepping up to the side of the pickup, Sandy tossed her beach blanket into the bed. Then she reached over the panel and set down the canvas bag in which she had packed her swimsuit, sun block, a couple of towels and a paperback novel.

'Last call, Eric!' she yelled. 'I'll stay if you want me to, but you've got to come out! I'm not staying home for you if you're not going to be here!'

She waited, listened.

'No? Okay. See you later.'

She climbed into the truck, swung her purse onto the passenger seat, and started the engine. As she drove down the rough, unpaved road through the woods, she kept looking for him. But he didn't show.

She glanced at the place where Slade, Harry Matthews and Lib were buried.

I'm on my way to visit a cop?

Real smart.

If I had a lick of sense, I wouldn't get involved with anyone, *much less a cop. I must be out of my mind.*

I oughta turn around right now and go back to the cabin.

Instead of turning around, she drove to the gate.

I'll go back to the house, all right. After I've seen Terry. Maybe not till after dark, if I get lucky.

As she unlocked the gate and swung it open, she thought about calling out one more time for Eric.

Why bother? He had his chances.

But she couldn't help it. 'Eric?' she shouted.

No answer.

Good!

In the pickup again, she drove through the open gate. Then she hopped out, shut the gate and locked it.

He made his choice, she told herself.

Back inside the truck, she drove slowly forward, bouncing and shaking her way down the shadowy tracks until she came to the edge of Pacific Coast Highway.

It was a little after nine o'clock when she turned onto Beach Drive. Nobody was stirring. Copies of the morning newspaper still lay on several lawns and driveways. She supposed that some of the residents had already gone to work for the day, while others weren't yet up and around.

What if Terry isn't up?

No big deal, she told herself. If he isn't, he *should* be.

Just so he's home.

His car was in his driveway. His newspaper lay on the grass in front of his porch.

Sandy stopped and shut off her engine.

What if he just got to bed? she wondered. What's the graveyard shift, midnight to eight?

Ah, but this is Friday. He has Wednesdays and Thursdays off, so he wouldn't have worked last night.

She put the keys in her purse and climbed out. Then she eased the door shut so that it hardly made any noise. She walked slowly around the front of her truck – and realized she was *sneaking*.

If I'm this afraid of waking him up, she thought, maybe I'd better just leave.

She could drive to the café, have a nice breakfast and come back in an hour or so.

Bending over, she picked up Terry's newspaper. She carried it up his porch stairs and stopped in front of his door and stood there. She stared at the doorbell button, but didn't reach for it.

What if I wake him up?

What if he's not alone?

What if he's actually married? She might've been at work yesterday when I was here.

Don't be ridiculous, Sandy told herself. He's not married. For one thing, no wife is going to let a guy keep a painting like *The Sleeper* in his living room. And he wouldn't want a steady girlfriend to see something like that, either.

He's single and unattached, just like he said.

Trembling, heart thudding, Sandy raised her hand toward the doorbell button.

And stopped with her finger an inch away from it.

I can't do this. He's not expecting me. He'll think I'm a nutcake. I'll just go away and come back a little later.

She took a step backward, crouched, and gently placed his newspaper on the welcome mat. Then she turned around and started down the stairs.

This is the guy who ambushed me, she suddenly thought. Blew five thousand bucks on a painting of me. Tracked me to Blaze. Set me up. Climbed around on those rocks to meet me 'by accident.'

And he's gonna mind a surprise visit?

She turned around and climbed the porch stairs. Not pausing for an instant, she jabbed the doorbell button. Then she swooped down and snatched up his newspaper.

Though her confidence had returned, her calm hadn't.

As she waited, she felt weak and trembly. Her heart pounded fast and hard. Underneath her loose shirt, drops of sweat dribbled down her sides. They ran all the way down from her armpits to her waist, cool and tickling.

From behind the door came a quiet sound of footsteps.

Oh, my God. He's coming.

She took a deep, deep breath.

Calm down, calm down.

He opened the door.

'Your paper, sir,' Sandy said.

He looked stunned. He gaped at her.

'Ashley?' he whispered.

'At your service, sir.'

Grinning and shaking his head, he stepped backward. 'Come on in.'

'Thanks.' She entered, and he shut the door.

'I can't believe you're here,' he said.

'I just happened to be dropping by.'

He laughed.

'I know it's early,' she said. 'I was afraid I might wake you up. Guess I did, huh?'

Grinning, he said, 'I must look a fright.'

Sandy laughed. 'You look perfect.'

His hair was mussed and he wore an old, faded blue bathrobe. He looked as if he'd outgrown it. The sleeves were too short and the front wouldn't shut all the way across his chest. The edges didn't meet until just above his waist, where the robe was held shut by his cloth belt.

'I *did* wake you up, didn't I?' Sandy asked.

'Ask me if I mind.'

'Do you mind?'

'Oh, man, you've got to be kidding.' He grinned and shook his head. 'So, would you like a cup of coffee, or something?'

'I'd like a kiss.'

'I thought you were going to make me wait two weeks.'

'I couldn't wait.'

'What about your son?'

'He's all right. He's with my mother. All day.'

'*All* day?'

'Overnight, even.' She slipped the strap off her shoulder and lowered her purse to the floor.

'You can stay with me all day?' Terry asked.

'If you want me to.'

'Oh. Man.' Stepping forward, he put his arms around her. 'Yes,' he said, and drew her in gently.

She tilted her head so their noses wouldn't bump.

His mouth pressed against her parted lips.

His chest pushed against her breasts.

Still holding the newspaper, Sandy let it drop behind him. It hit the floor with a soft *whop*. She squeezed herself against him.

And suddenly she felt as if she were being drawn into a strange and wonderful place where she'd never been before. Getting lost in it.

Oh my God, she thought.

Too soon, his mouth went away. He whispered, 'Wow.'

'Wow yourself,' she told him.

'*Now* do you want some coffee?' he asked.

'No. But you go ahead and have some. If you'd rather have coffee than me.'

He seemed to groan and laugh at the same time. His body still jerking with the laughter, he planted his mouth on hers. Then he stopped laughing. His hands glided down her back, rubbing her through the slippery fabric of her silk blouse and skirt. He moaned as he caressed her buttocks. Then he eased his hands up beneath the tail of her blouse. They drifted slowly up her back, lightly touching her skin. As they roamed, she felt a hardness push against her through the front of her skirt.

His hands tried to come around.

She was pressed too tightly against him for that.

Though she didn't want to move, wanted only to stay this way, Terry's body warm and strong and hard, his mouth open and wet, she wanted too to feel his hands on her breasts and on her belly and everywhere else they wanted to go. So she released him and took a small step backward.

His hands, still under her blouse, came around beneath her arms and curled over her breasts. He sighed. He had a delirious look in his eyes. His mouth hung open. His lips and chin were shiny with spit.

His robe seemed to be wider open than before, but Sandy couldn't see down very far. Her view was blocked by the bulging top of her blouse.

She watched the shapes of his hands under the silk as they explored her breasts.

Reaching up, she unbuttoned her blouse. She spread it open, slipped it off her shoulders, and shook it down her arms until it fell to the floor behind her.

Terry let go and stepped back and stared at her.

And she stared at him.

His cloth belt had come loose. The front of his robe hung open a few inches all the way down. He seemed unaware of it, though. He appeared to be transfixed by the view of Sandy. But then he must've noticed where her gaze was aimed. He glanced down at himself, made a quiet 'Uh' sound, and started to shut the robe.

'Don't,' Sandy said. 'Don't do that. Take it off.'

He closed his mouth. He wiped his lips with the back of one hand. Then, gazing into her eyes, he took off the robe and dropped it to the floor.

Just below his waist, his tan stopped. It started again partway down his thighs.

'Turn around,' Sandy said.

He raised his eyebrows.

'I want to look at you.'

'I'm just a regular guy,' he said, his voice shaking slightly.

'I haven't seen that many.'

'Oh? Okay.' He turned around slowly. Though the curtains were shut across the glass wall behind him, plenty of light filtered in. Sandy stared at his profile, then at his back, and then at his other side as he continued to turn.

When he was facing her again, he said, 'Want to take your skirt off?'

Smiling, she unfastened the button and zipper at the side of her skirt. The skirt fell, clinging to her legs until it came to rest around her ankles. She stepped out of it. Then she bent over. Standing on one leg at a time, she pulled off her sneakers and tossed them out of the way.

'Now you turn around,' Terry said. 'I want to look at you.'

'I'm just a regular gal.'

'Not even close.'

She began to turn around very slowly.

Terry murmured, 'God.'

Facing him again, Sandy whispered, 'Come here.'

He stepped close to her. When he was a stride away, she motioned for him to halt. He stood there, arms at his sides.

Without looking down, she reached out and curled her fingers around him. He gasped and arched his back.

'You want to put this exactly where?' she whispered.

He sort of smiled.

'Here?' Sandy asked.

She took a step closer to him, pushing down gently at the stiffness with her hand. As her breasts touched his chest, she felt the rub between her legs. She let go and moved in more, feeling him press up against her. Kissing him, she squeezed her thighs together. He felt hot and thick between them.

His hands rushed feverishly up and down her back. He writhed against her.

Huffing for air, he pulled his mouth away and gasped, 'Bedroom?'

'Here.'

'Couch?'

'Here.'

His hands slid all the way down Sandy's back and under her buttocks. Clutching her there, he pulled upward, spreading her cheeks so she felt cool air between them as he lifted. She went to her tiptoes. A moment later, her feet came off the floor and she opened her legs wide.

As he raised her, she felt her sweaty breasts slide against his sweaty chest, felt her slick belly slide upward against his slick belly, felt the thickness between her thighs follow her upward, pressing at her.

Then she could see over the top of Terry's head.

She gazed at the bright curtains but didn't really see them, didn't really see anything because her world had become the feel of Terry's penis down there touching her, nudging her open, delving.

She clutched the sweaty hair on the sides of his head.

Gasping and whimpering, she threw her own head back and stared at the ceiling.

Then he eased her downward.

He was all wet and slippery outside Sandy, stout and thick inside. Lowering her slowly, not thrusting himself but only lowering her very slowly as if to torment her by holding back, he pushed in, spreading her, climbing snugly higher and deeper. On her way down, she whimpered and kissed his eyes and his nose. And then he stopped lowering her.

'What?' she gasped.

'You . . . okay?'

'Huh?'

'Am I . . . hurting you?'

'No.'

'Should I stop?'

'*No!*' She cried the word out in such a loud, urgent voice that she shocked even herself.

Terry flinched. He grunted, 'Ah.' Then his hands seemed to drop out from under her buttocks.

She plunged, letting out a yell of shocked delight as she rammed down and felt the full solid length of him shove its way up her. Then her groin bumped his. He was all the way in, all the way home.

'Yes!' Sandy whispered.

She locked her mouth against his.

Arms and legs wrapped around Terry as if she were climbing a tree, she pushed her tongue into his mouth, squirmed and moaned.

Terry, though no bigger than Sandy, held her and stayed in her and sank to a crouch. Then a hand moved to the center of her spine. Holding her, staying in her, he tipped her backward and lowered her onto the rug.

Sandy planted her feet on both sides of him.

He pulled nearly out of her and thrust back in.

Sandy arched her back, crying out.

Terry took his mouth away from hers. He raised his face. It was dripping with sweat. 'Did I . . . hurt you that time?' he gasped.

'No! God, no!'

'Are you sure?'

She saw a gleam of mischief in his eyes.

'Bastard,' she said.

He smiled. 'Want me to stop?'

'*No!*' She laughed and sobbed. Then, as she blurted, '*Stop fooling around* . . .'

Terry started to thrust.

'*and fuck* . . .'

The noise of exploding plate glass roared through the room.

'. . . *me!*'

Jammed in to the hilt, suddenly throbbing and squirting, Terry jerked his head toward the noise.

Sandy, head turning at the same instant, saw the curtain rush forward, bulging away from whatever was left of the glass wall behind it. Through the curtain, she could see a dark shape lurching in from the deck.

Almost the shape of a man.

But not a man.

'*No!*' she shrieked through the clamor of raining shards.

Terry shoved himself up and popped out of her, shooting semen onto her thigh. As he struggled to stand, Eric found his way out from under the curtain and flung it down.

He seemed to be bleeding all over. Pieces of glass jutted out of his skin.

Spreading his arms, he roared at Terry.

And charged him.

'*No!*' Sandy shouted. '*Don't!*'

Terry hurled himself at Eric.

'*No!*' Sandy shouted. '*Stop it!*' She lunged toward them, hoping to throw herself between them.

But it was happening so fast.

Everything was so fast except Sandy.

She felt as if she were running underwater or through a nightmare where she was only allowed to move in slow motion as she raced the distance of no more than six feet toward the gap between the man she loved and the son she loved. She reached out with both arms. She cried '*No!*' as she raced, but could hardly hear it through Eric's roar of fury.

An image flashed through her mind of three kids racing toward each other hoping to catch the same high-hit baseball, all of them yelling, 'It's mine! It's mine!'

Terry glanced at her and yelled, '*Get back!*' His arm darted out to hold her off.

Eric took a swipe, ripping off half his face.

Screaming, Sandy launched herself at Eric.

He clubbed her aside with a forearm. She staggered backward, flapping her arms.

Still on her feet, she saw Terry trying to run away.

Going to get his gun?

Eric bounded after him.

Then the front of the coffee table knocked Sandy's feet out from under her. She flew backward. Her rump smacked the top of the table. Teetering, she slid on what felt like magazines. Then she tumbled off the other side and dropped into the gap between the table and couch, her head shoving at the couch, her legs kicking toward the ceiling, the edge of the table scraping a hot path down her back.

She stopped when the floor caught her behind the shoulders. Her head was jammed forward, her back curled, her rump off the floor, the side of the table propping up her legs, her feet in the air.

As she wheezed for breath, she heard Eric snarling and grunting.

'*Eric!*' she yelled. '*Leave him alone!*'

She bucked and thrashed. The coffee table scooted. The couch scooted. In a frenzy, she twisted and kicked and squirmed, turning herself until at last she fell lengthwise into the gap, landing on her side with a floor-level view under the table to the middle of the room where Eric was hunkered down, his bloody snout buried in Terry's groin.

A roar seemed to fill Sandy's head.

She didn't know where it came from, but obviously not from Eric: his mouth was full.

The roar went on as she stumbled to her feet and rushed out from behind the table and ran at him.

Sandy knew what she was doing.

But it seemed very much like someone else running toward the beast and the dead man.

Can't be me. This can't be happening.

Someone else throwing herself onto Eric, wrestling him away from Terry's carcass.

Someone else under him, pinned to the floor, staring up at his bloody snout and fierce blue eyes.

Then someone else getting squeezed and sucked and gnawed on.

Then someone else sprawled under his powerful body, whimpering and trying to fight him off, her skin being cut by the glass shards embedded in his flesh as he squirmed and grunted and plunged.

Not me.

This can't be happening.

Please.

Chapter Thirty-Seven

Secrets

Laughter exploded out of Dana when Warren said to plant the lipstick with her lips. But her laughing stopped as he came up close to her and put his arms around her and kissed her on the mouth.

He kissed her as if he'd been wanting to do it for a long time.

But he didn't explore her with his hands, didn't squeeze her tightly against his body. Dana leaned forward until her breasts touched his chest.

Then Warren stopped kissing her. He stared into her eyes. She watched the way his eyes flicked back and forth.

'Where were we?' he whispered.

'Kissing.'

A smile spread over his face. 'Yeah,' he said.

'You wanted to try on my lipstick.'

'I don't think you're wearing any.'

'I'm not.'

'I just wanted to kiss you.'

'That's nice,' Dana said.

'It *was* nice.'

So let's do it again, she thought.

Let's not push him.

'It was *very* nice,' she said.

'We'll have to try it again sometime.'

No time like the present.

'Anyway,' he said, 'your secret is now safe with me.'

'What secret?'

'That you blurted out "Tuck." '

'Oh. That's right.'

'Never happened.'

'And if it happens again,' she said, 'we'll know how to handle it.'

'That's right.'

'Tuck,' she said.

Warren put his arms around Dana and kissed her again. This time, his hands moved gently up and down her back. She could feel his body against her.

When the kiss ended, she whispered 'Tuck' against his lips.

He kissed her harder, deeper. He pressed himself against her. His hands rubbed up and down her back.

But they wouldn't come around to her front. They wouldn't stray lower than the waist of her shorts. They wouldn't slip under the back of her T-shirt.

So Dana put her hands under the hanging tail of Warren's shirt and lightly caressed his buttocks and eased her hands higher until they found the smooth, bare skin of his back.

His mouth broke away from her.

'Tuck,' she whispered.

He stared into her eyes. His mouth was wet and shiny around the lips.

'Tuck,' Dana said again.

His head shook.

'Tuck?' she asked.

'Uhh . . . Maybe we oughta slow down.'

'That's supposed to be *my* line,' Dana said.

'Sorry.'

'That's okay. I wasn't planning to use it, anyway.'

'Didn't think so.' He smiled. Stepping back, he ran the back of his hand across his mouth.

'Is everything all right?' Dana asked.

'Better than all right.'

'Are you sure?'

'Oh, yeah. But . . . I didn't really expect to . . . you know . . . have things happen so fast.'

'I didn't expect to like you so much,' Dana said.

'I've got an idea. Why don't I go ahead and make the margaritas? Then we can sit around and have a few drinks and get to know each other a little better. How does that sound?'

'Sounds fine.'

Maybe he'll tell me what's wrong. Something has to be wrong.

Maybe it's my breath.

Maybe he's secretly married.

Has a terminal illness.

Oh, God, don't let it be anything terrible. Please. I really, really like this guy.

When Warren was done blending the margaritas, he filled two glasses and asked Dana to carry them.

'Where to?' she asked.

'How about the porch? I've got a table out there.'

'Sounds good.'

'I'll be along in a minute,' he said.

Dana carried the drinks to the porch. She found a small, wooden table at the far end. It looked clean, and had a red candle in the center. She set down the drinks.

Warren came in with a bowl of corn tortilla chips and a bowl of salsa. They sat down on wicker chairs.

A mild breeze drifted in through the screens. Looking to her right, Dana could see through the trees to the ocean. The fog was still far out. She turned to Warren as he lifted his glass.

'To the prettiest girl I know,' he said.

'Thanks. To my favorite guy.'

They clinked the rims of their glasses together, then drank.

'Oh, this is really good,' Dana said.

'I made 'em Mexican style.'

'As opposed to?'

'US restaurant style. Be careful, though. They're very strong.'

'I'll drink slowly.'

Warren set down his glass. Smile fading, he looked Dana in the eyes. 'You *will* stay for dinner, won't you?'

'I'm invited, aren't I?'

'I not only invited you, I ran home right afterwards to thaw out a steak and put it in marinade.'

'Can't miss that. Unless you *throw* me out.'

'What about Lynn and the prowler?'

'Tuck?'

His smile returned. 'Let's not start that again.'

Dana smiled innocently and shrugged her shoulders. Then she said, 'I think as long as I get back before very late.'

'Before dark?'

'Maybe not *that* early.'

'I tell you what. Just let me know.'

'When it is time to go, will you drive me?'

'That can probably be arranged.'

After pouring refills and adding a handful of chips to the bowl, Warren said, 'I'd better get the fire started.'

'Can I come?'

'Sure. You want to bring my drink with you?'

'I'll bring 'em both.' Dana stuffed a crisp, salty chip into her mouth, then got to her feet and picked up her glass and Warren's.

Ever so slightly, the porch seemed to tilt.

'These babies *are* strong,' she said. 'But deee-licious.'

Warren smiled back at her. At the far corner of the porch, he picked up a bag of charcoal briquettes and a tin of lighter fluid. He carried them to the screen door, bumped it open with his shoulder, and trotted down the stairs.

Dana followed him, moving slowly, being careful not to spill the drinks.

Just past the end of the porch, they stopped at a red brick fireplace. Warren removed the grill. Then he up-ended the sack of briquettes, sending black chunks tumbling out.

'This is like what they call a *bus*man's holiday,' Dana said.

'I guess so.'

'Here you've been slaving over a hot grill all day, and now you're at it again.'

'Oh, I don't mind. I enjoy it.' He set down the bag, arranged some of the briquettes by hand, then set the black iron grill into place.

'I hear you *own* the snack stand,' Dana said.

'That's right.' He started squirting fluid onto the pile of briquettes.

'How did you go from Beast House guide to snack-stand owner?'

He squirted out more and more fluid. It made the briquettes look wet and shiny, but only for a moment. No sooner did they get soaked than they appeared to be dry again. Dry, but a slightly darker shade of black.

'Well,' Warren said, 'I had to get out of the guide business.'

'How come?'

Shaking his head, he set down the can. 'The house. It finally got to me.' He reached into a pocket of his white trousers and pulled out a book of matches. 'I just couldn't go in anymore.' Crouching, he struck a match. Its head flared. He touched the flame to a briquette. Blue and yellow fire began to spread over the surface. He moved his match to another lump. Then another. Soon, the entire pile was bathed in a low, fluttering fire. 'That should do it,' he said.

He stepped over to Dana and accepted his glass.

Standing side by side, they sipped their margaritas.

Dana took deep breaths. She smelled the ocean, the pine trees, and the warm scents of the barbeque. The odor from the barbecue was mostly burning fuel, she supposed. But it was a good, familiar aroma. It reminded her of fine times when she was a kid and her father cooked steaks on their backyard grill.

'If it doesn't go out,' Warren said, 'I should be able to throw on the meat in about half an hour.'

'Sounds good.'

'Want to go back into the porch?'

'I'd rather stay here. This is nice.'

'It *is* nice.'

'So,' Dana said. She sipped her drink. 'Let's see. Yesterday, you were telling me how you had this huge *attraction* to Beast House. Like you *belonged* there.'

'I did.'

'So what happened? All of a sudden, you just couldn't *go in*?'

He nodded.

'How come?'

He shrugged, then took a drink. 'The place suddenly *got* to me.'

'Got to you how?'

'Just . . . realizing that all those people had *really* died in there. That it wasn't make-believe. I'd always thought of the place as . . . like a carnival funhouse. But then it all turned real in my head and I couldn't stand to be inside it anymore.'

'What made that happen?'

He shrugged again. 'Just happened,' he muttered. After another sip of margarita, he said, 'Anyway, Janice didn't want to lose me, so she offered me the snack stand.'

'She *gave* it to you?'

'It pretty much amounts to that. She gets a small percentage of the profits.'

'But you actually *own* it?'

'Right.'

'That's pretty cool.' Dana sipped her margarita. Then she reached over and put a hand on his back. She moved it lightly, sliding the silk fabric against his skin. 'So,' she said. 'Now that I know you're a big, successful business man, tell me your deepest, darkest secret.'

She couldn't believe she'd asked.

'Do I *have* a deep, dark secret?' he asked.

'Oh, I bet you do.'

And maybe it'll tell me why you stopped things in the kitchen.

Any normal guy . . .

'What makes you think so?'

'Everybody has at least one deep, dark secret,' she said. 'I want to know yours.' Her hand continued to roam his back.

'What's yours?' he asked.

'I asked you first.'

'I wonder if the fire's still going.'

Dana saw no flames, but that was normal. Warren stepped away from her and lowered an open hand close to the grill. 'Yeah, it's fine.'

'I'll tell you mine,' she said.

He turned to face her, but stayed near the fireplace. 'You don't have to.'

'I want to. I want you to know me. Do you want to know me?'

'Yes.'

'Then I have to tell you my deepest, darkest secret.' Her heart was pounding fast. Her voice sounded as if it were coming from someone else.

'You don't have to. You're not completely sober.'

'I know what I'm doing.'

'Tomorrow, you might wish you hadn't said anything.'

'No. I'll tell you mine and you tell me yours.'

'I'm not sure this is such a great idea, Dana.'

'Hey,' she said. 'After I tell you the worst, it'll all be downhill. Everything about me'll be *better*. Know what I mean?'

'I think you should wait till some other time.'

'No. Now's . . .'

'I don't even know your favorite color yet, and you wanta tell me . . .'

'Blue. Royal blue.'

'What's your favorite song?'

'When I was fifteen, I had this terrible crush on my English teacher. Mr Johnson. I guess he was about thirty, and . . .'

'Don't tell me this now. You're half drunk, and . . .'

'Mr Johnson had a wife.'

'I got attacked in Beast House,' Warren said.

'*What?*'

'About two years ago.'

'Oh, my God!'

She hadn't expected *this*.

'How?' she asked. 'What happened?'

He drank his glass empty and set it down on the fireplace. 'If I tell you, you've got to keep it a secret. You can't tell anyone. Not even Lynn. Do you promise?'

This is serious.

'I promise,' Dana said. 'But you don't have to tell me.'

'*Now* you tell me.'

She smiled and almost sobbed. 'I'm sorry. I didn't want to force you into . . .'

'It's all right. I'd have to tell you sooner or later. Might as well get it over with.'

'Are you sure?'

Nodding, he said, 'What happened, we came up a couple of tape players short at closing time. Janice and I did a search of the house, but we couldn't find anyone. She was pretty upset about it. We'd been having a lot of trouble with that sort of thing. Players missing. People staying overnight. Vandalism. I figured, this time, they wouldn't get away with it. So I went in by myself at around midnight. Didn't tell anyone. I just snuck in, figuring I'd probably catch a couple of teenagers, scare the hell out of them, then make them clean up whatever mess they'd made and throw them out.

'But I couldn't find anyone. What I *did* find . . . You know the iron door down in the cellar?'

'Yeah.' Dana lifted her glass and noticed it was empty.

'Can I get you a refill?'

'No. Thanks. What about the door?'

'You know how it's always padlocked from the Kutch side?'

'Yeah.'

'Well, the padlock was off. It was down on the tunnel floor, and the door was ajar.'

'Jeez.'

'What I thought was, maybe these jokers had reached through the bars and picked the lock so they could go through the tunnel.'

'Pay a visit to old lady Kutch?'

'You bet. *Everybody* wants to see what it's like inside her house.'

'Including you.'

'I *used* to,' Warren said. 'And that night was my big chance. It was perfect. The lock was already off. I had a responsibility to find the intruders. They'd given me a great excuse in case I ran into Agnes at the other end.'

'And you *did* it? You went through the tunnel?'

'I never got the chance. I opened the door a little wider and bent down to pick up the lock, and . . . I guess I hadn't been exactly *alone* down there. I got jumped.'

He unbuttoned his bright silk shirt and took it off.

Dana stared at the scars on his shoulders.

He turned around.

'My God,' Dana murmured.

The nape of his neck, his shoulders, his upper back . . . a tangle of scars as if he'd been mauled by a pack of raging cats.

He turned to face her again. Looking miserable, he said, 'That's why I . . . stopped things in the kitchen. You don't want to just stumble onto a mess like this.'

Dana felt tears stinging her eyes, running down her face.

She went to Warren and set her glass on the fireplace beside his glass. She put her arms around him. 'Tuck,' she said.

Before he had a chance to respond, she kissed him. Her hands glided up his bare back. She wanted to touch his scars, caress them, let him know they didn't repel her.

Holding her by the sides, he pushed her gently away. He shook his head.

'What's wrong?'

'Everything.'

'So you've got a few scars. I don't . . .'

'These aren't the worst of them.'

'I don't care.'

'I do.'

'Show me?'

He stared into her eyes. His head jerked very slightly from side to side. 'Nobody's ever . . . I've never shown them to anyone. Just Janice. She . . . bandaged me afterward.'

'Can I see?'

He studied her eyes, but didn't answer.

'I'll have to see, sooner or later.'

'Why's that?'

'Why do you think?'

'You tell me.'

'It's customary to remove one's clothes before making love.' As she spoke those words, her face burned.

'We don't have to,' Warren said.

'Which? Make love or remove our clothes?'

'Either. Both.'

'Don't you *wanta*?'

'Of course I want to. Are you kidding? I haven't . . . you know . . . I haven't let anyone get *near* me, much less . . . I want you so badly . . . You're all I've been able to think about since we met yesterday. But I just can't . . .'

Reaching down with both hands, Dana started to unfasten his belt.

He clutched her wrists.

'No,' he said.

'It's all right.'

'No, it's not. If you knew . . .'

'I want to know. I want to know everything.'

'You just *think* you do.'

'Warren . . .'

'Trust me.'

'I never trust *anyone* who says "trust me." '

'Okay. Okay.' He shoved Dana's hands away, then turned around.

'Don't be angry,' she said.

'I'm not. It's just . . .' He shook his head. His arms moved, and Dana heard the jingle of his belt buckle.

'If you don't want to do this . . .'

'I don't,' he said. He bent over, pulling down his white trousers and his shorts in the same quick movement.

Dana gritted her teeth, but didn't make a sound.

Warren straightened up and stood there.

His buttocks and the backs of his thighs looked as if they'd once been shredded by claws, gnawed on.

The sight made Dana feel squirmy.

'That isn't so bad,' she said.

'It's hideous.'

'What *did* it to you?'

'The thing that jumped me in the cellar.'

'But *what*?'

'What do you think?'

'I don't know.'

Warren pulled up his pants, fastened them, and turned around. His face looked grim.

'Do you think it was a bear?' he asked. 'Maybe a bobcat? An escaped gorilla?'

'I don't know. Tell me.'

'I'm not going to say it,' he told her.

'Why not?'

'I don't want you thinking I'm crazy. Or a liar.'

'A *beast* did it?'

'Is that your best guess?'

'I guess so.'

'You don't really believe in the beasts, do you?'

She shrugged. 'I don't know. Yeah. Maybe. There've been eyewitnesses.'

'Maybe they were nuts or drunk or lying about what they saw.'

'There were beast bodies.'

'I've never seen one, have you?'

'No, but . . .'

'Anyway, who's to say they weren't fakes?'

'I don't think they were,' Dana said, staring into Warren's eyes. 'I think the beasts might've really existed. Lynn certainly believes in them. So does her father. And if they aren't real, Janice is a liar.'

'Or crazy.'

'I don't think she is. I don't think you are, either. But the beasts . . . they're all supposed to be dead.'

'I know.'

'They were all killed off in '79.'

A corner of Warren's mouth tilted upward. 'Were they?' he asked.

'It *was* a beast?'

'Maybe it was someone wearing a beast *costume*.'

'*Was* it?'

'Why do you think I haven't stepped foot inside Beast House since the night it happened?'

'Oh, my God.'

'And there's one other thing,' Warren said. 'Whatever it was that ripped me up that night . . . it . . . it molested me.' He met Dana's eyes. 'It pinned me down on the floor of the cellar and . . .'

Dana hurried over to him and took him into her arms.

He hugged her tightly.

He began to cry.

'It's all right,' she whispered, stroking his back. 'It's all right, honey. It's all right. Everything's fine.'

Chapter Thirty-Eight

Sandy's Story – July, 1992

Sandy knew something was wrong.

She hurt everywhere. She was lying on her back, but not on a bed. The hardness underneath her felt like a floor. A floor with a rug.

She felt as if someone had worked her over, inside and out. With a club. With teeth. With knives, maybe.

Then she remembered.

She opened her eyes and turned her head.

On the floor beside her were remains.

Terry. Oh, my God!

Grimacing and groaning as pains swarmed her from everywhere, Sandy sat up.

Parts of Terry were scattered around the room.

She started to sob.

It hurt very badly to cry.

Later, she forced herself to stand up.

Trying not to step on broken glass or pieces of Terry, she walked out of the room. She searched the cottage.

Eric seemed to be gone.

Of course he's gone, Sandy thought. After what he did . . .

He must've run away.

She needed to go after him.

Find him fast.

Take him home.

Or kill him.

Look what he did to my Terry!

Look what he did to me!

Fucking monster!

But she couldn't go searching for Eric like this.

She hurried into Terry's bathroom and started the shower and stood under it. The hot spray burnt her wounds. Blood streamed down her body.

She realized this was her second shower of the day. The earlier one, she'd taken with Eric. He'd been so sweet, so gentle . . .

How could he do this!

Maybe he thought he was saving me. The same as he saved me from Slade. Thought he was doing a good thing.

She did have a vague memory of crying out 'No!' once or twice. Listening from out on the deck, maybe he'd misunderstood and charged in to rescue her.

How did he get here in the first place?

In the bed of the pickup, she thought. No other way seemed possible. She was certain he hadn't been there when she'd left the cabin or when she'd opened the gate. But maybe after she'd shut it. Maybe he'd been hiding in the trees, waiting for her to climb back into the driver's seat and get the truck moving. Then he'd rushed over and leapt into the back. That section of road was so bumpy that she wouldn't have felt anything unusual.

He wanted a ride into town.

Or maybe he just had to find out what I was doing. How come I was leaving him two days in a row? I'd never done it before. What was so special that I couldn't wait?

Terry was so special.

DAMN IT!

If only she'd stayed home.

Or never met Terry at all, so he would still be alive.

Or never given birth to Eric.

No, don't wish that.

I do! I do! I wish he'd never been born!

He was just trying to . . .

It had nothing to do with rescuing me, she suddenly realized. It was spite. It was jealousy.

He needs me all to himself.

After the shower, Sandy got blood on the towel.

She had so many wounds from the broken glass and Eric's claws and teeth that it seemed pointless to worry about bandages. None seemed to be bleeding seriously, anyway. Just leaking a little.

Besides, some of the injuries were where she wouldn't be able reach them. On her back. Or inside.

In Terry's bedroom, she put on a pair of his briefs and a T-shirt. They clung to the moisture of her skin and the seepage from her injuries.

In the living room, she picked up the skirt and blouse that she'd worn from home. No blood showed on them, so she put them on over the T-shirt and briefs. Then she stepped into her sneakers. She found her purse near the door and slipped its strap over her shoulder.

It was heavy with the weight of her pistol.

Turning around, she gazed at the ruin of Terry's living room. And the dismembered remains of his body.

She had already made up her mind to leave everything in place.

No point in trying to clean the mess or destroy evidence. Sure, the cops would realize Terry had been with a woman. But there was no crime in that.

No woman had done this to him.

No man had done this to him, either.

Terry hadn't been murdered, he'd been torn to shreds and partly devoured by a wild animal. You could tell that just by looking.

And if you did more than look – if you ran laboratory tests – the teeth and claw marks and saliva and semen would confirm what you already knew: Terry Goodwin had suffered his fatal injuries as the result of a vicious animal attack.

They couldn't tell you what *sort* of animal, though.

Over the years, whenever the remains of Eric's human victims had been found, the blame had always been placed on mountain lions, bears or coyotes.

Such an animal would probably catch the blame for this, too. Not that there'd be many facts to support such a theory. Just that the evidence pointed to *some* sort of wild carnivore with sharp teeth and claws. Something *like* a mountain lion, a bear or a coyote.

Some folks, of course, were bound to suspect that Terry had fallen victim to one of those *beasts*. After all, Malcasa Point was only about a hundred miles to the south. *Everybody* knew about the beasts. Most of the people in Fort Platt had probably gone on the Beast House tour at one time or another. Most had certainly seen the movies, too, and some had undoubtedly read the books.

People would *wonder*.

But nobody was likely to believe – or suggest – that a beast had killed Terry.

The beasts were like UFOs. Only kids, drunks, and morons believed in them.

And me, Sandy thought. And me.

She opened Terry's front door and stepped out onto the porch. Without even glancing around to see if there might be a witness, she turned to the doorway and raised a hand in farewell. 'See you later, Terry,' she said in a cheerful voice. 'And thanks again. I really had a great time.'

When she said that, she had a sudden urge to scream. But she kept smiling.

Nodding and smiling, she said, 'Okay. Sure. Tomorrow would be great. See you then.'

Leaning inside, she pulled the door shut. Still smiling, she trotted down the porch stairs and walked toward her pickup truck.

She glimpsed a few neighbors here and there. But nobody was nearby. And nobody seemed to be watching her.

On her way to the pickup truck, she took the keys out of her purse.

Instead of walking around the front of the truck, she went behind it. Along the way, she glanced over the side panel. Her beach blanket was spread out on top of something lumpy the size of a man.

None of Eric stuck out.

From the contours, though, he seemed to be curled on his side in a fetal position.

I'll take care of you when we get home, Sandy thought. But she kept her mouth shut, kept walking, opened the driver's door and climbed in behind the wheel.

On the long drive home, she couldn't force her mind away from what had happened back at Terry's place.

She had never felt so sick and horrible before.

Never.

So wracked by guilt and shame and loss.

I didn't just lose Terry, I lost Eric. He's not my son anymore. Not after this.

How could he do that to Terry?

How could he do that to ME?

Oh, my God! What if I get pregnant?

It could happen.

She heard herself let out a moan of despair.

I'd rather die . . .

Driving south on Pacific Coast Highway, she often had a cliff just a few feet to her right. There was sometimes a low barrier, but frequently nothing . . .

Just a strip of gravel, then a few feet of dirt or rocks or weeds, then an edge.

And air.

A slight jerk of her arms, and she could put an end to it all.

A long fall.

A hard landing on boulders or beach.

An end for herself and Eric and the baby that might soon begin to grow inside her.

Eric's brother, Eric's son.

Another monster.

Another killer.

I've done enough damage, she thought. The *beasts* have done enough damage, too.

Kill Eric, kill myself and whatever chance he has for an offspring, and that'll be the end of it.

No more beasts.

It can all end here and now.

As she watched the side of the highway, waiting for an opening in the guard rails, she felt a trickle inside her. She wasn't sure what it might be. Blood or semen, she supposed. Whatever it was, it dribbled slowly downward.

Terry's semen?

If I do get pregnant, she thought, maybe it'll be from him. *It'd be a fifty-fifty chance.*

Clenching the steering wheel, she groaned.

Just like Mom, she thought.

Her mother had gone through an entire pregnancy not knowing whether she was carrying the child of her dead lover or the child of a beast.

I probably won't even *get* pregnant, Sandy told herself.

But if I do, it'll be the same.

Way too much the same.

Too damn weird.

It would just be a coincidence, she told herself. But it *felt* like much more than a coincidence. It felt almost like an inescapable destiny. As if she were trapped in a sequence of events planned out well in advance by unseen forces. This is all meant to be, she thought.

I'm meant to do a replay of what happened to Mom.

Maybe it hadn't gone according to plan with her, and Somebody needs to try again.

'Ridiculous,' she muttered.

What Somebody is doing is playing games with me.

'I'm not playing,' she said.

Even as she spoke the words, however, she knew that she had no choice. If her life was being manipulated by God or the Fates or some other prankster, the game was out of her control. She could do nothing to change anything.

Am I meant to fly off the next cliff? she wondered.

Who the hell knows?

'Who the hell cares?' she asked. 'I'll do what I want.'

Which is what They want.

Is it?

What *do* I want? she wondered.

For starters, how about staying alive long enough to find out whether I'm pregnant? And then to find out if it's Terry's child. For starters.

So I won't be driving off any cliff today, she thought. So what'll I do about Eric?

Shoot him.

The pickup bounced and lurched as Sandy drove over the bumpy dirt road. The rough ride punished her body, but she was hardly aware of the many pains. She seemed to be far away from them, watching from a distance.

She stopped at the gate.

And stared at it.

I can't do this, she thought.

She seemed to be far away from the thought.

The woman in the driver's seat twisted off the ignition and pulled out the key. Turning sideways, she reached into her purse. She pulled out the revolver.

I bet I'm not meant to do *this*, she thought.

I can't.

Watch.

She watched.

She seemed to be two places at once.

One place was outside her body, standing maybe a few feet away, observing the behavior of this grim and battered and heartbroken woman and wondering what she might do next.

The other place was inside herself, where she was full of pain but numb and dazed and determined.

Revolver heavy in her right hand, she swung open the driver's door and jumped to the ground.

Do it fast while he's still under the blanket, she told herself. Before he knows what's happening.

Before he looks at me.

If he looks at me, I won't be able . . .

She sidestepped, keeping her back to the pickup truck. Then she thumbed back the hammer and whirled around, raising the weapon, taking quick aim over the side panel and down at the beach blanket.

It was rumpled and bloody.

It no longer covered Eric.

He was gone.

Chapter Thirty-Nine

Flying Fists

'A fabulous dinner,' John said. 'I thank you from the bottom of my stomach.'

'You're welcome,' Owen muttered. He added a twenty per cent tip to the credit card slip, wrote down the total, and signed his name. 'Ready to go?'

'I believe so.'

They scooted over the soft leather cushions of the booth and made their way through the dimly lit restaurant. Along the way, they were thanked by their waitress and by the host. Owen returned a 'You're welcome' that was far more enthusiastic than the one he had bestowed on John Cromwell.

Outside, the sunlight looked dusty and golden. The shadows of the trees were long.

They walked through the parking lot toward their room.

'Okay,' Owen said. 'You got your dinner at the Carriage House. Now what's your big plan for a night I'll supposedly remember the rest of my life?'

'How would you like to pay a little visit to your honey?'

'Dana?'

'Who else? I know where she lives.'

'Sure you do.'

'Oh, I do.'

Owen took out his room key and unlocked the door. As he stepped inside, he turned his eyes to the telephone.

No blinking red light.

No messages.

He was disappointed, but not surprised. He and John hadn't left the room until 6:30. Dana almost certainly would've called by then if she'd had any intention of seeing him tonight.

Her 'date' was obviously with someone else.

Assuming she had a date at all.

John might've made up the whole business.

Dropping onto the end of his bed, Owen asked, 'Even if you *do* know where she lives, she's out with some guy tonight. Remember?'

'Dates don't last forever.' John leaned backward, his rump sinking into the front edge of the dresser in front of Owen. He folded his arms.

He raised his eyebrows. 'When she gets back, my boy, we can be waiting for her.'

'Oh, that sounds like a really fine idea. Then what, we *jump* her?'

'Wanta?'

'Go fuck yourself.'

John chuckled. 'How would you like to fuck *her*?'

'Shut up.'

'Just pulling your chain.'

'Well, stop it.'

'Wouldn't you like to *see* her, though?'

'Not with you around.'

'I *have* to be around. I know where she lives. And I'm the guy with the good camera. How would you like some *more* photos of her?'

Owen stared at him.

'You were drooling all over those pictures of her and Lynn.'

'Was not.'

'Were, too. And you think she looks hot in *those*, just imagine how she must look when she goes on a date. Bet she doesn't wear that uniform. She probably puts on a nice dress, you know? Maybe a low-cut little number that shows off her cleavage. Know what I mean? Maybe a nice, tiny little skirt that's hardly big enough to hide her snatch.'

'You're a pig.'

'You love it.'

'I do not.'

'Bet you've got a big ol' stiffy right now just from thinking about her.'

'Do not.'

'Prove it. Let's see?'

'Go to hell.'

'Stand up, man.'

'If I do stand up,' Owen said, 'I'm gonna punch your face in for you.'

'Oooo, I'm trembling.'

Owen got to his feet.

John pointed at the front of his trousers. 'See? What'd I tell you?'

'What'd I tell *you*?' Owen asked, and slammed him in the side of the face. John made a quick, hurt sound. The blow knocked his head sideways. Spit flew out of his mouth. The glasses leaped off his face, clattered against the wall and fell to the dresser top.

Uncrossing his arms, he put up one hand to fend off Owen. With his other hand, he tried to push himself off the dresser. Owen planted a punch deep in his big, soft belly.

John squealed. He started to fold over, but Owen blocked his way, shoved him up, pounded him in the chest and stomach with a left and a right and a left. Each time he was hit, he made a quick whimper.

Owen backed off.

John slumped forward and fell to the floor. Wheezing and sobbing, he pushed himself up. He hobbled to the queen-sized bed and eased himself down on it. Kneeling, he pulled the pillow out from under the bedspread. Then he flopped on his belly and buried his face in the pillow.

'I warned you,' Owen said. He felt sick.

John just kept crying.

'You shouldn't have said that stuff.'

Voice muffled by the pillow, John said, 'You . . . didn't have to . . . hurt me.'

Owen had never done anything like that before . . . not *pounded* someone.

He'd thought it would feel great to punch the crap out of a fat, obnoxious slob like John.

Maybe if the guy had fought back.

This is how you must feel if you stomp on a parakeet, he thought. Or kick a cat across a room.

He had a tightness inside his throat and chest. A heaviness inside his stomach. He felt as if he might throw up or begin to cry.

'Are you okay?' he asked. His voice sounded high-pitched.

'No. You *hurt* me.'

'I'm sorry.'

'All I wanted was . . . just to be . . . your friend.'

'I'm really sorry.'

John, sobbing, rolled onto his side. He looked odd and vulnerable without his glasses, as if his face had been stripped naked. His arms were hugging his belly.

'I'll get your glasses,' Owen said.

John snuffled.

Owen went over to the dresser. He found John's glasses on a plastic tray beside the ice bucket. When he picked them up, the right lens dropped out and struck the dresser top and broke into three pieces.

'Shit,' Owen muttered.

'What?'

'They're broken.'

John sighed loudly. He sobbed a couple of times, then said, 'Lemme see?'

Owen picked up the pieces of the lens. 'I'm sorry,' he said. 'I didn't mean to wreck your glasses.'

Sitting up, John swung his legs over the edge of the bed. He cupped his hands above his lap, and Owen gave him the broken remains of the glasses.

'Some friend you are,' he said.

Owen sat on the edge of the other bed and leaned toward him. 'How do you feel?'

John shook his head.

'Do you need a doctor?'

'How would I know? I've never gotten beat up before.'

'That's surprising.'

'Hardy-har,' John said.

'Do you want to hit me?'

'No. Why would I want to hit you?'

'I hit you.'

'Two wrongs don't make a right.'

'Come on, why don't you take a swing at me?'

'No thanks.'

'Come on.'

'I'm a lover, not a fighter.'

Owen laughed. John looked up at him, a slight smile on his face.

His left cheek was swollen and red.

Owen felt bad again.

'Maybe we can get your glasses repaired in the morning,' he said.

'Gonna need a new lens. And frame. See how the frame's busted?'

Owen saw.

'You did that,' John said.

'I know. I'm sorry. I'll get you a nice, new pair.'

'You think that'll make everything okay?' John asked.

'No. But I do wish I hadn't hit you.'

'Not as much as I do.'

'I know. I'm sorry. Look, should we go out and get some ice cream or something? Would that make you feel better?'

'Nice, big dessert for the fat boy.'

'I could go for some, myself. There's an ice-cream shop across from the photo place.'

'Yeah.'

'Wanta drive over there? I'll treat you to a cone.'

'Wonder if they've got waffle cones,' John said.

'Probably.'

'I love waffle cones.'

'Let's go see.'

'Promise you won't hit me anymore?' John asked.

'I promise.'

'Cross your heart and hope to die?'

'Yeah. Cross my heart.

' 'Cause it doesn't feel good, you know?'

'I know.'

'That's how they killed Houdini.'

'I know. I'm sorry.'

John wiped his eyes, then got to his feet. As he straightened up, he winced. 'Feel like my stomach's all fucked up.'

'Maybe you *do* need a doctor.'

'Ice cream oughta fix me up.'

'Okay. Let me hit the john first.'

'You already did.'

'Oh. Sorry about that.' Owen hurried into the bathroom, used the toilet, then washed his hands.

When he came out, a telephone directory lay open on one of the beds. John, bending over it, flashed a smile at Owen and ripped out a page.

'Hey! What'd you do that for?'

'Just in case.'

'In case of what?'

'Case you change your mind about paying a visit to Dana.' His eyes, red and watery, looked strange without glasses. 'This has her address on it.' He fluttered the page. '*Lynn*'s address.' He started to fold it.

'You know her last name?'

'I know many things.'

'What is it?'

'Tucker.'

'What's Dana's last name?'

'*That* I don't know. I know *many* things, not *every*thing. But if we go over there tonight, maybe we can find out.'

'We're going for ice cream,' Owen said. 'Nothing else. And you shouldn't tear pages out of telephone books. Other people might want to use them, you know.'

John smirked. 'My bad.'

'You really are an asshole.'

'Least I don't go around *punching* people.'

Outside, Owen pulled the door shut and tried the knob to make sure it was locked.

'Since you're buying,' John said, 'I'll drive.'

'Without your glasses? That'd be fun.'

John smiled and blinked at him. 'Contacts, man. Ever hear of contacts?'

'You've got contacts on?'

'Sure.'

'How come you were wearing *glasses*?'

'I look good in 'em.'

'Sure.'

'So, I'll do the driving.'

'No, you won't. It's a rent-a-car. Nobody's allowed to drive it but . . .'

'Not *your* car, mine. Come on.' He nodded toward an ancient Ford Granada parked in a far corner of the lot. It looked as if it had seen better decades.

'Does it work okay?' Owen asked as they walked toward it.

'It runs. Has a brand-new radiator, too. Might blow up, but it won't overheat.'

'Maybe we should take my car.'

'No, no. I insist.'

When they reached John's car, he opened the passenger door. The seat and floor were hidden underneath candy wrappers, maps, magazines and books. Owen glimpsed a *Hustler*, a *Scream Factory*, and a paperback copy of *The Horror at Malcasa Point*. Then John got in the way, bent over, and started tossing the material over the seatback.

'Nice,' Owen muttered.

'Huh?'

'Nice way to treat books and stuff.'

'You're really some kind of tight-ass, Owen. You oughta loosen up, man.'

'So I can be more like you?'

'Couldn't hurt.' A moment later, John scuttled backward. '*Voilà*,' he said, and swept a hand toward the passenger seat.

Owen could see it, now.

The floor in front of the seat was still cluttered, but nothing remained on the seat cushion except a few scattered puffs of grimy popcorn, a chewing gum wrapper, and crumbs from assorted chips and cookies. Owen was tempted to brush them off with his hand. But that would've required touching the seat's upholstery. Touching the *stains*. Some were pale, some dark. Some looked as if they might be sticky. Owen suspected catsup, mustard, blood, 'secret sauce,' salsa, honey, coffee, maybe chili. He *hoped* that snot, feces and semen weren't among the substances.

Don't bet on it.

'It's not very clean,' he said.

John dropped into the driver's seat, shaking his car. Then he looked across at Owen and said, 'Don't be a wimp.'

'I don't want to get my pants dirty.'

'Awww. Well, sit on a map or something.'

Among the debris on the floor was a copy of *Fangoria* magazine. Owen held it up. 'This okay?'

'Whatever.'

Owen flopped the magazine onto the seat, opened it to the middle, and sat down on it.

John started the car. As he backed it toward the middle of the lot, he grinned and said, 'What do you think *Dana's* doing right now?'

'I wouldn't know. And I don't want to talk about her. And I especially don't want *you* to talk about her. Don't even *think* about her.'

John laughed. 'Man, you've got it bad. Know what? I can take her or leave her.'

'Then leave her.'

John pulled out of the parking lot, swinging left onto Front Street. He stepped on the gas. The car leaped ahead. '*Lynn's* the one I like. She is *so* fucking cute. I'd like to rip her clothes off and . . .'

'Would you *please* shut up?'

'You take Dana, I'll take Lynn.'

'We're not *taking* anyone. We're just gonna get a couple of ice-cream cones, then go back to the Welcome Inn.'

'We oughta at *least* drive by their house.'

Chapter Forty

The Ride Home

Warren stopped his car at Front Street, waited for a van to pass, then swung to the left and picked up speed. Ahead, the town was brightly lit. There wasn't much traffic, though.

'You know how to get there?' Dana asked.

'Oh, I've been to the house a few times. Janice has parties fairly often. Staff parties. Barbecues out by the pool. I guess Lynn's planning to throw a party in a couple of weeks, keep up the tradition in Janice's absence.'

'That should be fun. You planning to come?'

'If I'm invited.'

'Oh, I bet you will be.'

He turned his head and smiled at Dana through the darkness. 'Just don't count on me swimming,' he said.

'You could wear a wetsuit.'

'I don't think so.'

'Do you *ever* go swimming?'

'Sometimes in the ocean. Late at night.'

'I'd like to do that with you.'

'Might be arranged. It's a trifle cold, though.'

'Maybe we can go in Lynn's pool sometime.'

'I don't think so.'

'I could send her away for a couple of hours.'

Warren shook his head. 'I wouldn't want to take the chance.'

'Your scars aren't *that* bad. It's not like you're hideously deformed or anything . . . or repulsive.'

'They apparently didn't repulse *you*.'

Dana reached over and put a hand on his thigh. She felt the heat of his leg through his trousers. 'You know what?' she said. 'Maybe Lynn *should* see them.'

'No way.'

'They're not that . . .'

'Give her a glimpse of my scars and she'll know right away what happened to me.'

'What does Lynn *think* happened to you?'

'We told her the truth, up to a point. I went into Beast House at night because of the missing tape players. Down in the cellar, I was jumped by a couple of teenagers. They beat the crap out of me and I got cut on some broken glass. That's what we told Lynn.'

'What about the cops?' Dana asked.

'We didn't tell them a thing. We didn't tell *anyone* a thing except Lynn. And her father, of course. Janice was taking care of my injuries, so we had to tell them something.'

'But not the truth?'

He shook his head. 'I can live without being famous for a thing like that.'

'Janice went along with keeping it a secret?'

'Yeah. She didn't want me humiliated.'

'It might've have been good for business.'

'I'm sure it would've been. We kidded around about that. Doing an ad campaign. "The beast is back and it wants *you!*" But she never really tried to make me go public.'

'Maybe the public *should* be told . . . warned.'

'Maybe,' Warren said, and stopped at a blinking red traffic light. Except for his car, the intersection was empty. He drove on. 'Thing is, who would really believe a warning like that? Most people really *don't* believe in the beasts. Evidence or no evidence. They're like Bigfoot. Like vampires or werewolves. We'd sound like lunatics. We'd get accused of being frauds . . . And there's no telling how a thing like that might play out. We might have even *more* people trying to sneak into the house at night. A warning might cause *more* attacks.'

Dana frowned through the darkness at him. 'The Midnight Tour goes in at night.'

'It's never been attacked.'

'At least not so far?'

'For all we know,' Warren said, 'the beast hasn't been in the house since the night it got me.'

'But it might be there *every* night.'

'No. Janice made sure things were safe. She cancelled the Midnight Tour and spent every night for more than two weeks in Beast House.'

'By herself?'

'Yeah. With Jerry's .44 magnum. Most of the time, she stayed in the cellar. In the dark. Just waiting for the beast to come along.'

'My God. Is she nuts or something?'

'Brave,' Warren said.

'At least. I can't *imagine* doing something like that. Actually, I *can*. If I were out of my mind.'

'Well, she felt that she had to do it.'

'What did she tell *Mister* Tucker about her nightly disappearing act?'

'Just that she wanted to guard the house from overnight intruders. And that she was hoping to catch the guys who'd assaulted me. Jerry and Lynn both volunteered for the job, but Janice wouldn't let them. She insisted on handling it herself. Anyway, nothing happened. The beast never showed up. So then she had a lock installed on *our* side of the tunnel door.'

'Is that how it got in? Through the Kutch tunnel?'

'Could be. Seems likely, since the lock was off.'

'Did anyone talk to Agnes about it? Or search her house?'

'Nope. Couldn't do it without involving the police and getting a search warrant.'

'Why couldn't Janice just drop in on her?'

'She tried, but Agnes wouldn't come to the door. And Janice didn't want to force the issue because part of her original deal was that Agnes's house would be out of bounds.'

'So Agnes might've been *harboring* whatever attacked you?'

'Possible,' Warren said. 'Or maybe she didn't have anything to do with it. The thing could've gotten in from *our* side. Maybe it was out in the hills behind the house and found an entrance to the burrow.'

'But the locked cover . . .?'

'. . . was put in *after* I got attacked.'

'Ah.'

'Before that, we had an open hole in the cellar floor – with cordons around it so the tourists wouldn't fall in. No telling what might've come crawling out of it at night.'

Dana realized she had goosebumps. Rubbing one of her forearms, she said, 'But nothing can get in *now*?'

'Wouldn't be easy. And if it *did*, we'd find out first thing in the morning. You know how Lynn checks through the whole house . . .'

'I've been with her.'

'She always makes a trip down into the cellar, doesn't she?'

'Yeah.'

'That's to make sure nothing's *open* down there.' Warren flicked on his turn signal, then slowed down. 'If she finds a lock off, anything like that, she's supposed to run like hell, clear the house if someone else is inside, then lock the front door and notify Janice.'

'Who will then come over with the Smith & Wesson?'

'That's the plan,' Warren said. He turned right and started up the road. On both sides, trees loomed over them. No moonlight reached the pavement. The only light came from his car's bright headbeams. 'So far,' he said, 'everything's been fine. Nothing's gotten in and nobody else has been attacked.'

'Nobody you know about.'

'Yeah. Well . . . I know what you mean. The tape players that don't come back. But there are so many possible explanations for that. And nobody *seems* to be missing.'

'People must go missing all the time,' Dana said.

'Oh, I suppose so. Not out of Beast House, though. Not as far as we know. And we'd probably hear about it if a wife or daughter or someone disappeared during a tour.' He grinned at Dana. 'As you found out the hard way.'

'Thanks for reminding me.'

'Wish I could've been there.'

'So you could watch me hurl? If I'd had another margarita or two, I could've put on a demonstration for you tonight.'

'Maybe some other time.'

'Hope not,' Dana said. 'By the way, you know . . . speaking of the little tyke who ran up the attic stairs . . . Lance? You obviously heard about my trouble with his mother, but did you also know that he screamed when he was up in the attic and he came running down the stairs in a panic, yelling his head off about being chased?'

'Oh, yeah. I heard about that, too.'

'He said something was *after* him. But then all the trouble started with his mother and I never got to ask him about it.'

'Nobody did,' Warren said. 'He and his mom took off the minute they got out of the house. But Lynn went up into the attic to investigate.'

'Right. She told me.'

'Nobody there. Which is pretty much what she expected. That sort of thing happens every so often – people get a case of *beast on the brain* and think they see one. Especially kids. They scream loud enough to wake the dead, run like hell, and scare the bejezus out of everyone. But it's just their imaginations going wild.'

He turned onto the narrow, sloping driveway.

We're almost back!

Dana suddenly felt a hollow ache.

Reaching over to Warren, she squeezed his thigh. 'Will you come in with me?'

'If you want.'

'Sure I want.'

'I guess I could at least come in long enough to make sure everything's okay . . . and say hi to *Tuck*.'

'Don't you *dare!*'

Warren laughed.

'I already paid you off. Remember?'

'Maybe you need to pay me off again.'

'Bastard,' Dana said, grinning.

'That's me.'

'What do I have to give you this time?'

'Surprise me.'

'Okay. Maybe. But not while you're driving.'

Soon, the house came into sight at the top of the driveway. Its porch was lighted, and so were some of the windows. Spotlights brightened the broad area of pavement in front of the three-car garage. A blue Range Rover was parked there, off to the left.

Warren stopped behind it, killed his headlights and shut off his engine.

'Looks like Tuck has a visitor,' he said.

'*Lynn* has a visitor.'

'Tuck,' Warren corrected her. 'You haven't given me that extra payment yet.'

'Maybe you'll get it now,' Dana said. 'But you have to close your eyes first.'

He shut them.

'Don't open them till I say so.'

'Okay.'

'This is terrible, you know,' Dana said. 'Making me pay and pay and pay. All for a little slip of the tongue.'

'And I intend to make you *keep* paying,' Warren said.

'Maybe *this* will satisfy you.'

'Hmmm?'

'Put out your hands.'

'Okay.'

'You may now open your eyes.'

He opened them, glanced at the bra in his hands, then quickly looked at Dana.

She'd already put her T-shirt back on.

'Will *that* keep your mouth shut?'

He laughed. 'Sure. Do I get to keep it?'

'Of course.'

He draped the bra over the white leg of his trousers and turned toward her. She twisted in her seat, leaned in and kissed him. As they kissed, she felt his hand on her right breast. There was only the thin fabric of her T-shirt in the way. She felt the heat of his moving hand. He rubbed her, gently squeezed her, fingered her nipple.

Squirming and moaning, she lowered a hand onto the lap of his trousers. Soon, Warren was also moaning and squirming.

Later, he lifted the T-shirt up over her breasts.

Later, she pulled his zipper down.

Still later, as they held each other and tried to catch their breaths, Warren murmured, ''Fraid I can't . . . go in with you now.'

'We'll wait till we've . . . calmed down.'

'Won't help. My pants.'

'What's wrong with 'em?'

'Mess.'

'Huh?'

'Feel.'

'Where?'

He guided her hand.

'Oh,' she said. 'Sorry about that.'

He laughed.

'Why don't you come in the house . . . too?'

He laughed harder.

'We can throw them in the washer,' Dana said.

'Oh, sure. With Lynn and her friend there?'

'We could be sneaky.'

'No, no. I'd better just get going.'

'I hope it *is* a friend.'

'Was she expecting anyone?'

Dana shook her head. 'Not that I know of.'

'I doubt if anything's wrong.'

'But you don't know who might own a thing like that?'

'Hell, I don't know anyone who could *afford* one. Except for Janice, of course. It looks brand-new, too. Doesn't even have its license plate.'

'Maybe you *should* come in with me.'

'I could walk you to the door, anyway – stick with you till we find out who's there.'

Smiling, Dana said, 'You could hold my bra in front so nobody'll see your wet places.'

'Maybe you should put it *on*.' He lifted her bra by a shoulder strap.

'It's for you. You've got to keep it so you'll always remember tonight.'

'I'll never forget tonight.'

'A souvenir couldn't hurt.'

Smiling, he shook his head. 'If you insist.'

'I insist.'

'Thanks,' he said.

'Now, fork over your shorts.'

'Huh?'

'I want a souvenir, too.'

'You're kidding.'

'Nope.'

'But they're . . . wet.'

'All the better.'

Shaking his head and chuckling softly, Warren unbuckled his belt. 'This won't be easy,' he said. 'The steering wheel . . .'

'Nothing really worth doing is ever easy.'

'Tell me if you see anyone coming.'

Dana laughed. 'I'll alert you immediately.'

Trousers and shorts around his ankles, he said, 'Sure hope I don't get in an accident on the way home.'

'If you're in an accident bad enough for anyone to find out you haven't got underwear on, that'll be the least of your worries.'

'You may be right.'

'Of course I am.'

When the shorts were off, he handed them to Dana. 'Thank you, sir,' she said, folding them. She waited until he had his trousers on again, then leaned over and gave him a quick kiss. 'Thanks for the dinner, too. The steak was fabulous . . . once we finally got to it.'

He gazed into her eyes. 'I wish you didn't have to go in.'

'Me, too. But I have to. It's already later than I planned. Tuck's going to start worrying.'

'You might be the farthest thing from her mind right about now.'

'That's another thing – I need to get in there and meet the mysterious visitor.' She reached for the door handle.

'Wait,' Warren said. 'When'll we get together again?'

'Tomorrow, I guess.'

'Want to come over to my place after work?' he asked. 'Maybe we can go down to the beach if the weather's nice.'

'I don't know. We'll see. The thing is, I'll have to be back at Beast House before eight.'

'What for?'

'The picnic and stuff. I'm doing the whole bit tomorrow night.'

'The Midnight Tour?'

She nodded.

'Do you have to?'

'I want to. And I've already told Tuck that I would. She's sort of counting on me to be there. Anyway, it'll probably take me a day or two to recover from tonight.'

Warren huffed out a breath. It sounded almost like a laugh. 'You think *you* had it tough?'

'Aw, poor boy.' Smiling, she patted his cheek.

'I sure wish you'd spend tomorrow night with me,' he said.

Dana's hand remained on his cheek. It drifted, caressing him. 'Me, too,' she said. 'But I gave my word about the tour.'

'If you explain to Lynn . . .'

'Nah. Anyway, maybe we can get together Sunday night. And Beast House is closed on Monday. Maybe we could spend the day together.'

He nodded. 'That'd be great.'

'Yeah.'

'But I still wish you wouldn't go on the tour.'

Dana lowered her hand. 'It *is* safe, isn't it?'

He didn't answer.

'*Is* it?'

'*I* wouldn't go in there at night.'

'*You* won't go in there in daylight.'

'What I meant was, I wouldn't if I were *you*.'

'So it's *not* safe?'

'It probably is,' he said, his voice at a higher pitch than usual. He grimaced as if in pain. 'The beast hasn't shown up since the night it came after me. And there've been plenty of Midnight Tours since then. I guess you could say it's safe. But you never know. You just never know. If I ran things, there wouldn't *be* any more Midnight Tours. I'd make sure nobody *ever* got into Beast House after dark. I think it's tempting fate. One of these times, the shit's going to hit the fan.' For a few moments, he stared into Dana's eyes and didn't speak. Then he said, 'I don't want you in there when it does.'

'Tuck goes in every Saturday night,' Dana said. 'She doesn't even *know* that a beast attacked you. She thinks they're all dead. The way you and Janice kept her in the dark, she isn't even aware of the *risk* she's running.'

'I doubt if it would stop her.'

'Maybe not. But she oughta be *told*.'

'You won't tell her, will you?'

I should, she thought. I really should.

'I *can't* have people knowing what happened to me in there,' Warren said.

'You told *me*.'

'Because I . . . I *had* to. I couldn't let there be any lies between us.' He tried to smile. 'Besides, you wanted to know my deepest, darkest secret, right?'

'Yeah.'

'So I told you. But it has to *stay* a secret. If it ever gets out . . . that'd be it for me. You know? I'd have to leave.'

'Leave?'

'I couldn't stay in a town where people knew that about me. I'd probably just drive away and nobody would ever see me again.'

'Can't have you doing that,' Dana said.

'Then don't tell on me.'

'I won't tell,' Dana said, 'but I'll be on the Midnight Tour tomorrow night.'

Warren shook his head.

Trembling, Dana leaned close to him. 'If the place isn't safe for me, it isn't safe for Tuck, either. Or for the thirteen guests. So I *have* to go in with them.'

'You wouldn't be much help . . .'

'I'd have to *try*. I'm a lifeguard, remember?' She kissed him lightly, quickly, then leaned away and swung open her door. 'Tell you what,' she said. 'You don't have to walk me to the door. Just wait here. I'll take a peek inside and let you know if everything's okay.'

She grabbed her purse and climbed out. On her way around the front of Warren's car, she slipped the strap onto her shoulder. She stuffed his underwear into a front pocket of her shorts.

'I'll be right back,' she called over her shoulder. 'If I'm not, you'd better come running and rescue me.'

Chapter Forty-One

Spies

Earlier, Owen and John had been sitting in the car behind the ice-cream stand, still working on the stumps of their cones, when John said, 'How about going for a little drive in the hills?'

'Are you kidding? I know where you want to go.'

'What do *you* wanta do, go back to the motel and sit in our *room* till bedtime?'

'I don't . . .'

'Watch *television*?'

'I just don't think we should . . .'

'Play *footsie* with me?'

'No.'

'Suck my dick?'

'Shut up!'

'Beat me up some more?'

'Don't tempt me.'

'Hey, man, you owe me. You really hurt me *and* you busted my glasses.'

'You've got your contacts.'

'I like my *glasses*, man. They make me look smart.'

'Sure they do.'

'Anyway, *I'm* going for a drive. You're too chicken to come with me, that's your prerogative.' He stuffed the dripping end of the cone into his mouth, wiped his hand on the leg of his Bermuda shorts, then started the car. Headlights on, he drove onto Front Street. 'What's it gonna be?' he asked, his mouth full, his words mushy. 'Just say the word, I'll drop you off at the motel and go without you.'

'You're never gonna find their house, anyway. Just because you've got the address . . .'

'Good point.'

A block later, John swung his old car onto the lot of a gas station, parked beside the mini-mart, and hurried inside. He came out carrying a map. Grinning, he dropped onto the driver's seat, rocking the car. 'Malcasa Point and vicinity,' he said. '*Still* think I'll never find their house?'

'Even if you can, you *shouldn't*.'

'That's okay, I'll drop you off. God knows, I don't wanta make you do anything against your *principles*. No sweat off my nuts if you wanta miss out on the chance of a lifetime.'

'If you go, I go.'

A big grin blossomed on John's face. 'Why am I not surprised?'

'But it's not so I can spy on anyone. It's to keep an eye on you.'

Laughing, John said, 'We know.'

We know.

Sure that's why.

He *ached* to spy on Dana.

But he didn't do such things.

Ever.

We'll never find the house anyway, he told himself as they drove past the Welcome Inn and headed up Pacific Coast Highway.

'That's it!' John blurted, stopping his car at the foot of a driveway. The rural mailbox beside the driveway not only showed the address they wanted, but bore the names Tucker and Crogan.

The sight of the names gave Owen a sudden sickish feeling down low inside.

Dusk had already deepened into night. The driveway curved uphill into dark, heavy woods. There was no sign of a house, or any light.

'Let's just get out of here,' Owen said.

'Good idea.'

John sped forward, leaving the driveway behind. But just up the road, just around a curve, he stopped his car and shut off its headlights. 'We'll walk from here.'

'Let's just leave,' Owen said. 'Let's go back to town. Come on. We'll think of something else to do.'

'I know what *I'm* gonna do. Gonna find the fuckin' house and see what the babes are up to. You don't wanta come, stay here.'

'We're gonna get in trouble.'

'Not if we don't get caught.' John opened his door. 'You coming?'

'I don't know.'

'*Live* a little, man. Don't be a loser all your life.'

'I'm not a loser.'

'*I'm* going. With or without you.' John climbed out, eased his door shut, then hurried around to the trunk.

Owen followed and found him twisting a telephoto lens onto his camera.

'No.'

'Yes.'

'Don't.'

'We'll get doubles made. That's if we get lucky and find anyone worth shooting.'

'You can't do this.'

'Sure I can. That's the difference between me and you, buddy. You *wanta* do shit, I *do* it.' Laughing, John slammed the trunk shut. 'Come if you're coming.'

'You asshole.'

'I'm the best thing that's ever happened to you.'

'Bullshit.'

Together, they left the road and started climbing the dark, wooded hillside.

John gasped and huffed for breath.

Owen smiled. He said, 'Hope you don't have a heart attack, you fat piece of shit.'

'Eat me,' John said.

It took some hard work and searching, but at last they found the house.

Then they crept around its perimeter, staying in the shadows of the forest, and came upon a swimming pool behind the house. Though the pool was deserted, its lights were on. It shimmered, clear and blue. Steam was drifting off the surface of the hot spa over at the pool's far corner.

'Let's . . . stick around,' John whispered, out of breath. 'See what happens.'

'We oughta just *go*.'

'Not me, man. This is perfect.' He panted for air, then continued. 'You wanta chicken out, go ahead. I'm staying. I'm not gonna miss *this*.'

'We're *tresspassing*.'

'Big fucking deal.'

'If we get thrown in jail, we could miss the Midnight Tour.'

'Hey, man, that's a chance I'll take . . . You know what we got here? Lynn's gonna come outa the house . . . any minute . . . and take herself a swim. Maybe go in the Jacuzzi.' After pausing for air, he went on. 'And who knows what the fuck she'll be wearing? Maybe nothing! . . . No neighbors, man . . . She might go skinny-dipping . . . Dana, too.'

'Dana's on a date.'

'Maybe she is, maybe she isn't. You wanta . . . miss a chance to see her skinny-dipping?'

Owen didn't need to think about that one. 'I guess not,' he whispered.

'You *guess*.'

Not that it'll happen. Great stuff like that never happens. Not to me.

They found a good place to hide in the bushes near the end of the pool, directly across from the hot spa. Kneeling down, they began to wait.

Though lights were on inside the house, all the curtains were shut. Owen couldn't see through them. Nor could he hear any sounds from the house. The wind was loud in the trees and bushes.

Maybe nobody's home.

Somebody must be, he told himself. You don't go off and leave your pool lights on. For that matter, you don't crank up your hot spa unless you're planning to use it.

Somebody *has* to be home . . . and has to come out.

But nobody did.

Ten minutes passed. Fifteen.

Watching the steam rise, Owen wished *he* could jump into the spa. He wished he'd worn his windbreaker. Or even a long-sleeved shirt. He thought about how badly he would like to be back in the warmth of his room at the Welcome Inn.

After half an hour of waiting, Owen swayed sideways, bumped his shoulder against John and whispered, '*Now* can we go?'

'Go whenever you want to. *I'm* staying.'

'How long?'

'Long as it takes.'

'Aren't you freezing?'

'Ask me if I care.'

'This is insane.'

'Think so? What if I wimp out and take off – and two minutes later, out come the babes . . . bare-ass naked?'

'Like *that's* gonna happen.'

'You'll never find out if you go running away like a . . .'

At the back of the house, a curtain was sliding aside. Owen saw someone behind the glass door. As he tried to figure out who it might be, the door glided open and Lynn stepped out.

John nudged him. 'Here we go!'

Hardly able to believe this was really happening, Owen watched Lynn stride toward the hot spa at the corner of the pool. She wasn't much compared to Dana, but she was cute, all right. Really cute. And *what* was she wearing?

White tennis shoes and no socks.

Hugged against her belly was a folded blue towel.

At the edge of the spa, she crouched and set down the towel.

Owen heard a click. It came from beside him. He knew what it was, but he didn't look.

Couldn't take his eyes off Lynn as she stood up.

Didn't care that she wasn't naked.

Her swimsuit looked like small, buttery patches of doe skin tied to her body with leather strings.

John clicked more photos. His automatic film advance made a quiet buzzing sound after each shot.

Lynn didn't seem to hear the camera.

Instead of climbing into the spa, she turned away from it and walked toward a corner of the house.

There were no buttery patches of doe skin behind Lynn. Owen could hardly even see the strings.

Beside him, John moaned. The camera clicked and buzzed.

'Save some film for Dana,' Owen whispered. His voice came out raspy and trembling.

'Don't worry, man. I've got plenty. Look at her, will you?'

'Yeah.'

'How'd you like to lick the sweat off an ass like that?'

'Shut up.'

'You'd love it.'

Lynn vanished around the corner of the house. Then came an engine noise, followed by burbly sounds from the hot spa. Through the steam, Owen saw the water in the small enclosure turn frothy white. Its surface began to shift and roll.

Lynn came back around the corner. Though her breasts were no larger than oranges, they jiggled nicely inside the loose patches of doe skin as she walked. Twin thongs slanted down from her hips to her crotch, where they met two corners of a tiny leather triangle.

John took more snapshots.

Owen moaned softly. He ached. He couldn't believe he was actually here, crouching in bushes, seeing *this*.

At the edge of the spa, Lynn kicked off her shoes. Then she climbed down. When she was seated, the water covered her to the neck.

'Wanta leave *now*?' John whispered.

'Go to hell.'

John chuckled.

After that, it was a matter of waiting. With Lynn's fine body submerged, there wasn't much to see.

Maybe Dana would show up.

She might, Owen told himself. She really might. After all, she lives here. Even if she *is* on a date, she's bound to come home sooner or later.

Doesn't mean she'll come out to the pool.

But she might.

And even if she *doesn't* show up, Owen thought, it'll be worth sticking around. Lynn can't stay in there all night. We'll get at least one more good look at her.

John put an arm around Owen's back, pulled him closer, and whispered in his ear, 'Wanta drop in on her?'

'Are you nuts?'

'Hey, man, maybe she'd like some company.' The warm breath tickled the inside of Owen's ear. 'A couple of studs like us . . .'

'No.'

'I'm so fuckin' horny . . .'

'Try anything and I'll rip up your Midnight Tour ticket *and* kick your ass.'

'How do you know she doesn't *want* it?'

'From you and me? I'd bet a million bucks.'

'I don't know, man. She's gotta be feeling *awfully* horny.' He squeezed Owen's arm. 'That hot water rubbing her all over, and she's got damn near nothing on. Bet she'd *love* to have a couple of guys jump in with her right about now.'

Owen shook his head. His heart was thumping fast and hard. 'Knock it off.'

'Let's do it. Come on, buddy. It's the chance of a lifetime.'

Voice shaking, Owen said, 'Yeah, to end up in prison.'

'We're not gonna *rape* her. We'll just go over and say hi and see what happens. You know?'

'No.'

'You *wanta* do it, man. I *know* you wanta.'

'I do not.'

'You're just chicken.'

'Are you completely out of your mind?'

'Wouldn't you just love to jump in the water and rip that little bikini thing off her and . . .'

'No. Now, cut it out. Shut up.'

'I'm gonna do it,' John said. He gave Owen's arm another squeeze, then let go. 'Stay here and miss the fun if you wanta, but *I'm* goin' for the gold.'

Owen clutched his shoulder.

Someone called, 'Hey!'

Owen's heart lurched.

Across the pool, Lynn turned her head.

Over near the corner of the house, a woman walked into the light, a hand raised in greeting.

Dana!

She's here! She's HERE! Oh, my God!

Owen gazed at her, shocked with surprise and delight. This was way too good to be true.

But what happened to her hair?

The last time he'd seen Dana, just this afternoon, her blond hair had been flowing down past her shoulders. Now, it was short and mannish.

Why'd she wanta get it all cut off?

It *does* look good this way, he realized. *Real* good.

Focused so much on Lynn for the past few minutes, Owen had almost forgotten how incredibly beautiful *Dana* was.

God, look at her!

She wore faded jeans and a blue chambray shirt. The shirt loomed out with the push of her breasts. It wasn't tucked in. Its long sleeves were rolled halfway up her slender forearms.

As she walked toward Lynn, she was smiling and shaking her head. She was talking, too, but Owen couldn't hear a word she said. He couldn't hear Lynn, either.

Just as well, he thought. If we can't hear them, they can't hear us.

'Who the hell's the gorgeous *babe*?' John whispered.

'It's Dana.'

'My ass. That ain't Dana.'

'She must've gotten a haircut, that's . . .'

It isn't!

'You're right,' Owen said.

The stranger seemed to be Dana's size. She had about the same height and build and complexion. Her hair, though cut so short, was Dana's shade of gold. At this distance, illuminated by the pool lights, even her face resembled Dana's face.

Resembled Dana's, but didn't quite match it.

She might've been a sister. A slightly older sister, more athletic, a little tougher, sharper, more intense.

More beautiful.

She *can't* be more beautiful than Dana, Owen told himself.

'You believe it, man?' John asked.

Owen shook his head.

'Looks like some kinda Australian super-model.'

'Yeah.'

Lynn suddenly leaned to the right, reached out fast and snatched something out of her folded towel.

A revolver.

A *huge* revolver that gleamed like silver.

'Holy shit,' John said.

Waving the handgun, Lynn smiled up at the new arrival and said something.

The new gal grinned and nodded. Her lips moved. She nodded some more.

Lynn slipped the revolver back inside the folds of her towel. Then she stood up, turned around and climbed out of the spa.

Owen stared at her back and buttocks and legs. They were ruddy from the heat of the water, shiny in the lights.

After Lynn disappeared inside the house, the newcomer turned toward the pool. She seemed to be gazing across it, studying the long, thick row of shrubbery and small trees.

Almost as if *inspecting* it.

Does she know we're here?

No. She couldn't.

For a few moments, she seemed to be gazing straight at the place where Owen and John were kneeling.

Owen didn't move. He held his breath.

Then the woman's eyes moved on.

John made a 'Whew' sound.

Owen resumed breathing.

On the other side of the pool, the gorgeous stranger started to unbutton her shirt.

'Oh, man,' John murmured.

As the buttons came undone, Owen saw that she was wearing something red underneath her blue shirt. She pulled off the outer shirt. The red belonged to a T-shirt. It hugged her body, and so did the straps of a brown leather harness.

The harness supported a shoulder holster.

She pulled a dark pistol out of the holster, bent down and set it on top of Lynn's towel. Then she stepped over to the patio table. She draped her blue shirt over the back of a chair, removed her holster rig and put it on the table. Next, she pulled out a chair and sat down and took off her boots.

John nudged him. 'She's going *in*, man.'

'Looks that way.'

'Shit! Is this our lucky night, or what?'

'You're lucky you didn't get shot.'

'Fuck you.'

Done removing her socks, the woman stood up. She unfastened her jeans, pulled them down and stepped out of them. Her red T-shirt reached down like a very short, tight skirt to the tops of her thighs. Owen wished he could see under its edge, but he couldn't – not even when she crouched to pick up her jeans.

Turning around, she bent over to drape her jeans on the chair.

Owen saw her bare buttocks.

His breath caught.

With her back to the pool, she pulled up the T-shirt and drew it over her head.

She was naked.

She tossed her T-shirt onto the chair, then turned away from the table.

Turned toward the spa.

Toward the pool and Owen and John.

Owen heard the click and buzz of John's camera.

The camera! Yes! He's getting pictures of her!

Take a million!

Bless you, John Cromwell. And thank God for your telephoto lens.

If only we had a camcorder!

Owen gaped at the woman, astounded by his good luck, hardly able to believe that he was actually here, spying from the bushes on someone who was not only absolutely naked but more beautiful and exciting than anyone he'd ever seen or imagined.

She had a soft, mellow tan all the way down her body. Every muscle looked sleek and strong. Her breasts, firm and round and heavy, were tipped with large, stiff nipples. Below her ribcage, her belly sloped in, flat and smooth. Twin hollows slanted downward from her hips, leading to a tuft of golden curls.

As she walked toward the spa, Owen glimpsed a fleshy cleft below the curls. Flushed and aching, he quickly lifted his gaze to her breasts. He saw how they bounced and swayed.

At the edge of the spa, she balanced on her left leg and dipped in her right foot. She took it out, dipped it in again, then shrugged and stepped all the way down, bending her left leg and holding out her arms like wings to steady herself. Owen again saw the split between her legs.

John clicked photos.

On the edge of losing control, Owen shut his eyes.

Are you nuts! Look at her! Don't miss this!

If I look, I'll come in my pants.

So what?

He opened his eyes and saw that she was already shoulder deep in the spa.

Okay, he told himself. Fine. I'll be all right, now.

Maybe.

Out of the house's back door stepped Lynn. She was carrying a bottle of red wine, two glasses, and a big blue towel.

'How you doing, man?' John whispered.

'Great.'

'Is this the best, or what?'

'It's the best, all right.'

Grinning, John gave his shoulder a squeeze. 'Looks like they're gonna have a party.'

'Yeah.'

'I gotta reload.'

'Hurry,' Owen said. He watched Lynn fill the glasses with wine, climb down into the spa and hand a glass to the beautiful stranger.

After Lynn sat down, they touched their glasses together.

Owen imagined the musical tone of their rims clinking. He couldn't hear it, though.

He could hear the thumping of the heart inside him.

He could hear the buzz of John's film rewinding close to his right side.

He could hear the wind in the trees behind him.

He could hear the burble of the spa in front of him and the noise of the heater off around the corner of the house.

As the wine glasses clinked together in silence, he also heard a single, phlegmy cough.

It came from somewhere in the bushes to his left.

'What was that?' Owen whispered.

'What was what?'

'Didn't you hear it? Like a cough? From over there?'

'Nah.'

Chapter Forty-Two

Pool Party

Dana hurried back to Warren's car. 'It's okay,' she said. 'I think the visitor's a friend.'

'You don't sound so sure.'

'Didn't see his face.' At the driver's window, Dana bent over and put her hands on the sill. 'Who do you know with short blond hair?'

'Clyde?'

Dana laughed. 'Can't be him. Whoever he is, Tuck's drinking wine with him in the Jacuzzi.'

'If they're drinking in the Jacuzzi, he *must* be a friend.'

'Yep. So I guess there's nothing to worry about.'

'Guess not.'

Dana leaned in and kissed him softly on the mouth. 'See ya,' she whispered. Then she backed away, smiling and waving. 'Don't get in any accidents,' she warned.

Laughing, Warren started the car.

As he turned it around, Dana thought about going to him, hopping in, saying, 'Never mind. Tuck's fine. Let's go back to your place.'

While she was still thinking about it, Warren drove away.

She sighed, then went into the house.

Feeling almost naked without her bra, she wasn't especially eager to meet Tuck's friend.

Besides, maybe Tuck wouldn't want any extra company.

Maybe I'll just go on upstairs . . .

But who's the guy? she wondered.

I really *should* at least go out and say hello. Be rude not to. Anyway, Tuck needs to know I got home all right.

She walked to the back door, eased it open, and stepped outside.

The two in the spa were sitting side by side, holding wine glasses above the bubbly surface of the water. Though they had their backs to Dana, she could see a side of Tuck's face. Tuck was laughing and talking. From where Dana stood, she could only see the back of the stranger's head.

On the patio table was a leather rig that looked like a shoulder holster.

A blue shirt, a red T-shirt, and jeans were draped over a nearby chair.

What'd this guy do, undress out here?

The back of his head suddenly looked familiar.

Eve!

Dana laughed. 'Hiya, guys!' she called.

They both looked around at her.

'Hey there,' Eve said, a warm smile spreading over her face.

'Back already?' Tuck asked. 'How'd it go?'

'Not bad.'

'Eve just got here. Why don't you join the party? Go get yourself a glass if you want. Or you can drink straight out of the bottle.'

'I think I'll pass on the wine,' Dana said, stepping around to the side of the spa. 'I've had some margaritas.' At her feet were two folded towels. One had a pistol on top. 'That must be yours,' she said to Eve.

'Yep.' Eve took a sip of wine. Her shoulders, though out of the water, were shiny wet. Seeing no straps, Dana lowered her gaze. The spa was brightly lighted from the bottom. Through the shimmering water, she saw that Eve wore nothing at all. Her naked body seemed to ripple and sway with the currents.

Giving Tuck a quick check, Dana glimpsed a skimpy leather outfit. She returned her attention to Eve, who was setting her glass on the ledge.

'It's my night off,' Eve told her. 'I just thought I'd stop by to see how you two were getting along. After last night, I was a little worried.'

'She scared me shitless,' Tuck said, grinning. 'She just came walking around the corner and *yelled* at me.'

'I had to yell or you wouldn't have heard me.'

'I must've jumped a mile.'

'I couldn't believe she was actually *out* here.'

'Doesn't surprise me,' Dana said.

'I was perfectly safe,' Tuck said. 'Brought the cannon.'

'It's inside the other towel,' Eve explained. 'She brandished it for my benefit.'

'So you're out here with *two* guns.'

'We're a regular NRA convention,' Tuck said. 'Go get yours and we'll *all* be armed.'

'I have it.'

'Huh?'

Smiling, Dana patted the side of her purse.

'You've been *carrying* it?' Tuck asked.

'Won't do me any good if I don't have it.'

'Bust her ass, Eve.'

Eve laughed, shook her head, and took a drink of wine. 'Arrest her for carrying *my* pistol? I don't think so. Anyway, she *should* keep it with her.'

'Some cop you are,' Tuck said. Smiling up at Dana, she asked, 'Are you gonna come in, or just stand there?'

'You'd better come in,' Eve said.

'You look cold,' Tuck said.

'It is a little chilly out here.'

'Nice and toasty in here,' Tuck said. 'Just strip and jump in. That's what Eve did.'

'Maybe I'd better go get my suit on.'

'Don't bother.'

'Feels a lot better without,' Eve told her.

'I thought we weren't supposed to give our prowler anything to see,' Dana said. 'We probably shouldn't even be *out* here, much less stripping.'

'You're right about that,' Eve said. 'It isn't exactly the smart thing to do. But since Lynn was already out here . . .'

'It's okay,' Tuck interrupted. 'Eve's a cop and you're a life-guard. And now that you mention it . . . I guess *I'll* avail myself of the optional clothing rule. Why not? If the Peeping Tom *is* here, he might as well get a good show.' She set down her glass and reached behind her neck.

'What the heck?' Dana said. She moved away from the spa, kicked off her shoes, peeled off her socks, then pulled down her shorts and panties and stepped out of them. Her enormous white T-shirt hung down halfway to her knees.

'That'll make a good nightshirt,' Tuck called.

If I take it off, Dana thought, she'll wonder what happened to my bra.

Hell, she's already noticed it's gone. They both must've noticed the minute I showed up. They're not blind.

Tuck swung the bottom of her swimsuit out of the water and dropped it next to the wine bottle. 'Yesss,' she said. 'Oh, that *does* feel good.'

A cold breeze fluttered Dana's T-shirt, slipped underneath it and raced up her body, making her shiver.

Get this over with . . .

She pulled the T-shirt off, let it fall, then stepped quickly over to the spa. She sat down on its ledge, lowered her feet into the churning hot water, then stood on the submerged tile of the bench and stepped down. The liquid heat raced up her legs and between them and wrapped her to the waist.

'*Uh!*' she grunted.

'Great, huh?' Tuck asked.

'I'm . . . scorched.'

'Pussy,' Tuck said.

Eve laughed.

Dana waded over to the side and eased herself down onto the bench. She gasped when the hot water clutched her breasts. Then she sighed and slouched backward until it lapped her chin.

'Nice?' Eve asked.

'Give me three minutes, I'll be soft-boiled.'

'I guess your date went well,' Tuck said.

'Pretty good.'

'I'd say better than *pretty* good.' From the grin on her face, Dana knew she was referring to the vanished bra.

But Dana didn't want to talk about it. Especially not in front of Eve. She liked Eve, but hardly knew her and didn't want to speak about her feelings for Warren in front of her. For that matter, she wasn't sure how much she wanted to tell Tuck. Better to hold it all inside, private and safe and special. Keep it her own, at least for a while.

'I'd still be at *his* place,' she said, 'except I was afraid *you'd* decide to risk life and limb by doing something monumentally stupid. Which you, of course, did.'

'Of course,' said Tuck.

'Pretty damn reckless,' Eve agreed, shaking her head but smiling.

'You're *both* a couple of pussies,' Tuck said. 'Anyway, I was ready for any eventuality.'

'Don't go looking for trouble,' Eve said, 'just because you have a gun.'

'*You* do.'

'Trouble's my job.'

'You're off duty tonight. But you came over looking for trouble, anyway.'

'Just wanted to make sure you two didn't get yourselves reamed by some bad-ass pervert, that's all.' She poured more wine into her glass, then into Tuck's. 'Didn't expect any of *this*, though. This is very nice.'

'Come over any time,' Tuck said.

'Thanks,' Eve said, then offered the bottle to Dana. 'Have some?'

Dana shook her head. 'No thanks.'

Eve set the bottle aside, then took a sip from her glass. 'I was *planning* to scout around the grounds, make sure your friend wasn't lurking around.' Lowering the glass slightly, she scanned the dense row of bushes and small trees beyond the far side of the pool. 'Never exactly got around to doing that.'

'Shame on you,' Tuck said.

'You distracted me with this stuff about the wine and Jacuzzi.'

Dana suddenly found herself staring at the bushes.

Especially at the dark space where Tuck had seen the prowler last night.

'You're not *worrying*, are you?' Tuck asked her.

'If nobody checked over there . . .'

'So what if somebody *is* there?' Tuck said. 'We're armed to the *teeth*. Anyone tries any shit with us, we'll blow 'im to kingdom come.'

'I should've checked,' Eve said.

'Don't worry about it. Forget it.'

'It's the main reason I came over in the first place.'

Eve stood up. She turned around and set her glass on the ledge.

'Hey, don't bother,' Tuck said.

'It'll just take me a few minutes. Then we'll know for sure that everything's safe.'

'We're safe *here*. I don't want you going over there. What if somebody *is* there?'

'Then he'll be in big trouble, won't he?' Eve stepped onto the submerged bench, then onto the ledge. Water spilling off her body and spattering the concrete, she hurried over to the towels. She squatted and snatched up her pistol.

'Wait,' Dana said. 'Tuck's right. You really shouldn't go over there.'

'Don't worry about it. I'll be right back.'

'Maybe you *won't*!' Tuck said. 'Come on, you're gonna ruin the party.'

Still squatting, Eve shifted the pistol to her left hand. She pushed her right hand into the folds of Tuck's towel and pulled out the .44 magnum. 'Mind if I borrow this?'

'Yeah, I mind. Just stay here.'

'If somebody *is* hiding over there,' Eve said, 'I think we should find out about it.'

'Doesn't mean *you* have to risk your ass.'

The huge revolver in one hand, the black automatic in the other, Eve stood up. 'This better be loaded.'

'Damn it, Eve!'

Eve smiled, said, 'Take it easy,' then started striding toward the end of the pool.

Dana leaped up. 'Wait!' she called. 'I'm coming, too.'

'Me, too!' Tuck shouted.

Eve stopped and faced them. 'No. Just . . .'

They both sprang out of the spa.

'All for one and one for all!' Tuck yelled.

'Jesus H. Christ,' Eve said.

Water dribbling off her body, Dana crouched over her purse,

fumbled inside and pulled out the pistol that Eve had loaned her last night.

As she rushed toward her two friends, she saw Eve hand the Smith & Wesson to Tuck.

'Be careful with it,' Eve said.

'Don't you want to deputize us?' Tuck asked.

'Where would I pin the badges?'

'We don't need no steenking badges.'

Eve in the lead, Dana and Tuck side by side a few paces behind her, they walked the length of the swimming pool, turned the corner, and headed for the dark row of bushes.

'If there *is* a Peeping Tom,' Tuck said, 'he'll think he's having a wet dream.'

'Oh fuck,' John muttered, 'I'd love to get a shot of *this*.'

'Don't try it. We've gotta get out of here.'

In Owen's mind, John ignored him and lurched out of the bushes, onto the pool's apron straight in front of the spectacular trio and raised the big-lensed camera for what might've been the greatest photo of his entire life – and they opened up on him, their guns roaring, fire flashing from their muzzles. Owen could see how the flashes threw stark light across their wet, naked bodies. And he could see how the slugs struck John, smacking holes in him, making him twirl and dance in slow motion until he fell on his back.

Grabbing John's arm, squeezing it, Owen blurted, 'Come on!'

And John didn't try for the shot. 'Yeah,' he said. 'Let's book.'

Side by side, they scurried backward.

We'll be okay, Owen told himself. They'll never see us in here. Not without a flashlight.

He was nearly certain they had no flashlight.

As he crawled backward, he kept his eyes forward and watched for them. He ought to be able to see their legs through the bushes when they got to this end of the pool. Probably a few seconds from now.

Rustly sounds came from the bushes to his left.

Oh jeez, somebody IS over there!

The cough, a few minutes before Dana's arrival, had frightened him badly.

But he'd heard nothing more from over there.

With Dana's arrival, he'd been able to push his worries aside. Awestruck, he'd watched her remove her clothes. He'd been stunned to discover, when she pulled off her T-shirt, that she wasn't wearing a bra.

'Ah, look at them titties,' John had said, inspecting her through his telephoto lens.

Owen had resisted an urge to hit him. He'd learned his lesson about that sort of thing. Besides, a blow might've jiggled the camera and ruined a shot.

The camera had clicked and buzzed again and again as Dana drew the T-shirt over her head, dropped it, and stepped down into the spa.

Then John had said, 'Show's over. Ready to go?'

'No way.'

'What, you don't want to *leave*? I thought you couldn't *wait*.'

'Blow it out your ass, Cromwell.'

'Think maybe they'll have an orgy?'

'Shhh.'

'A three-way babe orgy.'

'Shut up.'

'How'd you like to get in the middle of *that*?'

The mere thought of it excited Owen. 'Just shut up, okay? You want them to hear you?'

'They can't hear shit . . . those bubbles and everything.'

'Maybe. But I'm not so sure we're the only ones over here.'

'What, your phantom cougher?'

'It sure *sounded* like a cough.'

'Why don't you go investigate, offer him a lozenge?'

'I haven't *got* a lozenge.'

'What're they gonna do, just sit in there and drink all night? Come on, babes, let's have some action.'

'Would you please be quiet?'

Not long after that, the beautiful stranger had climbed out of the spa.

'Oh man, oh man,' John had murmured, his camera clicking and buzzing.

'Oh shit,' Owen had said. 'She's getting the guns! She *heard* you, you asshole!'

'Take it easy.'

Then Dana had stood up and climbed out, followed by Lynn.

'Oh man,' John had said, snapping shots rapid-fire, 'look at Lynn, look at Lynn. Oh man, she shaves it!'

I see, I see!

'We've died and gone to heaven, man!'

Except that Dana, down on one knee, had just pulled a pistol out of her purse. And Eve had just handed the giant silver revolver to Lynn.

And then they were all together, coming around the pool

like a bizarre version of the Earps on their way to the O.K. Corral.

Side by side, Owen and John kept crawling backward. Owen watched for the legs of the women.

'I meant to bring a flashlight,' he heard one of them say. Her voice came from the left and sounded as if she was still down by the deep end.

'Want me to run in the house and get one?' He recognized Lynn's voice.

'No, don't bother. Let's get this over with.'

'What was that?' Dana asked.

Bowels going cold, Owen stopped crawling. John stopped, too.

'Did you hear something?' the stranger asked.

'I thought I did. In there.'

'What?' Lynn asked.

'Like leaves.'

'Probably just the wind,' Lynn said.

'Maybe.'

'*I'm a police officer,*' the stranger said suddenly in a loud, hard voice that made Owen flinch. '*Come out of the bushes. We know you're in there. Come out slowly with your hands over your head.*'

Owen turned his head. John, on hands and knees, seemed to be looking at him.

Softly, Owen went, 'Shhh.'

'*I'll give you five seconds. Then I'm in coming after you. If you make me do that, I'm gonna be pissed.*'

Owen counted slowly to five, then to ten.

'*Here I come,*' she announced.

'You're not really . . . ?' Lynn's voice.

'You two wait here. Keep your weapons ready, but try not to shoot *me.*'

'If you go in, I go in,' Dana said.

'Me, too,' said Lynn. 'All for one . . .'

John suddenly whispered, 'Let's get the fuck outa here.'

They resumed crawling backward.

Fast.

For a few seconds, Owen heard talk about getting scratched by the bushes.

Then the stranger announced in a loud voice, '*Here we come, ready or not.*'

Chapter Forty-Three

Here They Come

Scurrying backward, Owen heard something shaking the bushes to his left.

The gals?

No. They were tromping through the foliage in the same direction, but farther away.

It's that other guy.

No longer trapped in the thick shrubbery, Owen turned himself around, scrambled to his feet and dashed into the woods. John ran close behind him. They were both gasping for air. Their shoes pounded the ground, crunching the undergrowth and snapping twigs.

The woods were awfully dark. Owen could see nothing except dim shapes of gray and black and a few pale speckles of moonlight.

He was risking a bad fall. Or a collision with a tree.

But at least he was putting distance between himself and the heavily armed women.

As the ground began to slope downward, he slowed his pace slightly.

They won't follow us this far, he thought.

Still running, he glanced over his shoulder.

Nothing back there except a dark, wooded hillside.

We left 'em in the dust.

Hell, they probably never did more than take a little stroll through the shrubs.

If we give them a few more minutes, he thought, they'll be back in the water.

How about going back for a return visit?

Not a good idea. That'd *really* be pushing our luck.

Better not mention it to John. He'll have us going back there for sure.

John?

Slowing down to an easy jog, Owen again looked behind him.

He saw the dark, wooded slope, but he didn't see John.

Or hear him.

No thudding of shoes, no huffing of breath.

Where'd he go?

Probably couldn't keep up with me, Owen thought. The fat slob. Must've stopped to rest. Or maybe he tripped or something.

Owen walked over to a tree, turned around, then leaned back against its trunk to wait for John. He was out of breath, himself. His clothes were clinging to him, and sweat trickled down his face. He wiped his face with a sleeve of his shirt.

Okay, Cromwell, where are you?

What'd you do, decide to take a nap?

Owen gazed at the hillside rising above him and expected to see his obnoxious friend come chugging down it at any second, shirt flapping, camera swinging by its strap.

Tuck, holding her .44 magnum high, climbed down into the steaming water. 'I got pricked so many times,' she said, 'I feel like a two-dollar whore.'

'Don't say I didn't warn you.' Eve crouched and placed her pistol on top of the towel.

She's not taking it in with her, Dana noted. Even though the weapon would still be within easy reach, it seemed like a good sign that Eve was willing to let go of it.

So Dana squatted down over her purse and slipped her pistol inside. Then she followed Eve into the spa. The water, she supposed, was every bit as hot as before. But it didn't seem to burn her this time.

Its heat took away her shivers and seemed to soften the tightness of her muscles. It even made her scratches feel better.

'Think he'll be back?' Tuck asked.

'You never know,' Eve said. 'I bet we gave him a hell of a scare.'

'Also gave him a hell of a show,' Dana pointed out.

'He probably won't be back tonight, anyway,' Eve said.

'Took off like a scalded monkey.' Tuck set her revolver on the ledge and picked up her wine glass. It was nearly empty.

'Too bad he waited so long,' Eve said. 'Could've saved us from getting scratched all to hell in those bushes.'

'You would've gone in anyway,' Tuck said, then drained her glass. 'You'll go in *any*where.'

'Maybe not anywhere.'

'I was afraid you might take off after him.'

'I gave it some thought,' Eve admitted.

'He sounded big,' Dana said.

Eve shrugged her bare shoulders. Dana noticed a few red scratches on them, and some faint scars as if she'd done this sort of thing before. 'I wasn't worried about that. But I didn't want to go chasing him through the woods and leave you two behind. He might've circled back . . .'

'If you'd *tried* to chase him,' Tuck said, 'I would've tackled you.'

'Fat chance.'

'Okay, maybe not. So I would've told my big buddy Bullwinkle to do it.'

Eve looked at Dana. 'Bullwinkle?'

'That's me.'

'Well, you're about my size. I'm sure you *could* tackle me if you set your mind to it.'

'That's why I keep her around,' Tuck explained. 'Now, everybody stay put. The night's still young. I'll get us a new bottle.' She set her glass out of the way, then hurled herself out of the spa. Dripping, not even bothering to grab a towel, she ran naked into the house.

Eve said to Dana, 'You actually broke your evening short so you could come back and watch out for Lynn?'

'Afraid so.'

'That takes some real loyalty.'

'I *knew* she'd come out here.'

'I had my suspicions, too.'

'Glad you came by,' Dana told her.

'I messed up, though. I should've scouted around first thing . . . *with* my flashlight.'

'Oh, well, no harm done.'

'I'm not so sure of that. We really did give the guy an eyeful. He'll be back for sure, sooner or later.'

'You'll have to keep coming back to protect us.'

'You mind?'

'Not at all.'

'Maybe I'll use some of my comp time, take a few nights off and keep coming over till I manage to nail him.'

'Really?'

'Sure.'

'That's a lot of trouble.'

'No big deal. Hey, I don't have enough friends to let stuff *happen* to them.'

Staring into Eve's eyes, Dana nodded.

'I look out for my friends,' Eve said. 'And I destroy my enemies.'

'Glad you're on *our* side.'

'I'll get this guy. Maybe tomorrow night . . .'

'Tomorrow night, we won't be here.'

Eve looked puzzled. Then her face seemed to light up. 'Oh! Of course not. The Midnight Tour. You're going, too?'

'I thought I'd give it a try.'

'That'll be fun.'

'Have you ever done it?'

'A few times. It's terrific.'

'Here comes the *vino*,' Tuck announced, hurrying toward them. She held a bottle of red wine in one hand, a corkscrew in the other. A few strides from the edge of the spa, she stopped, bent over slightly and clamped the bottle between her thighs. 'Ah! That's cold!'

'Don't do anything obscene with it,' Eve said.

Laughing, Tuck wrapped her left hand around the neck of the bottle. 'I'm not that kinda girl,' she said. With her right hand, she started twisting the screw into the cork. 'So what did I miss?' she asked.

'I was just telling Dana that I'll take a few nights off work and try to catch this guy.'

'Good deal!'

'And I mentioned about tomorrow night,' Dana added.

'Ah. Yeah.' Tuck twisted the screw deeper. 'Dana's gonna try the tour.'

'So she tells me.'

'How about you, Eve? Wanta come along, too?'

'Wouldn't mind. You sure there's room?'

'For you, there's always room. Just make sure you wear your uniform.' She grunted and tugged, legs squeezing the bottle hard, tremors shaking her body. 'The guests . . . love it.' With a sucking *pomp!* the cork sprang out. Tuck's arm leaped high. 'Got it!'

'Bravo!' Eve said.

Dana clapped.

Climbing down into the spa, Tuck asked, 'So you'll come?'

'If you really want me to.'

'Sure. It'll be great.' To Dana, she said, 'The guests love it when Eve's on the tour. You've seen her in uniform.' She started to fill a glass. 'We make like she *has* to come . . . You know, for safety reasons. In case the beast shows up.'

'But so far it hasn't?' Dana asked.

'So far.' Tuck handed the glass to Eve, then filled her own. 'But who knows? Maybe one of these nights . . .'

'That's what Warren's afraid of,' Dana said.

They both looked at her.

Oh, no! What'd I say?

'Maybe I'll have a little wine, after all.'

'Glass?' Tuck asked.

Dana shook her head. 'That's all right.' She accepted the bottle and took a swig from it. The wine was cold and not too sweet. 'He just thinks the Midnight Tour is dangerous. He's afraid somebody'll get hurt one of these times.'

Tuck sat down, the bubbly water rising to her shoulders. 'He's been spooked,' she said, 'ever since he got jumped that time.'

'What's that?' Eve asked. 'Warren got jumped? When?'

'A couple of years ago.' Eve shrugged, then sipped wine from her glass. 'He got beaten up one night by some teenagers.'

'Inside Beast House?'

'Yeah.'

'Did you report it?'

'To the police? Nah. It was no big deal. He got some bruises and cuts, that's all. He didn't even need a doctor.'

'What *else* has happened in the house?'

'Nothing much,' Tuck said.

'Such as?'

'Just little stuff.'

'Such as?' Eve repeated.

'You know. The usual. Cassette players not getting returned. Kids trying to stay overnight.'

'Assaults? Murders?'

'Nah, nothing like that.'

'Disappearances?'

'Not really,' Tuck said. 'They just turn out to be false alarms. Like that kid today.' She nodded at Dana.

'Some mother flew off the handle this afternoon,' Dana explained. 'She thought her kid had vanished.'

'Turned out to be a false alarm,' Tuck said.

'He'd gone sneaking up into the attic.'

'You got him back all right?' Eve asked.

'Oh, yeah.' Dana chuckled, then took a sip from the wine bottle. 'I wasn't halfway up the stairs before he let out a scream and came running down in a panic. He claimed something was up there . . . and *chasing* him.'

'*Was* anything up there?'

Dana shrugged. 'I never got to . . .'

'I went up and checked it out,' Tuck interrupted.

'You obviously didn't run into a beast,' Eve said.

'Nope. But I did find something interesting.' Leaning forward, she looked at Dana. 'Remember Thursday morning? How Ethel's gown was all torn up?'

'Yeah.'

'What's *that* about?' Eve asked.

'Somebody'd gotten into the parlor overnight and messed around with the Ethel dummy. Her gown was torn. More so than usual. I mean, *everything* was showing. I think the guy must've been a pervert or something. Fooled around with her, you know? Anyway, when I was searching the attic this afternoon because of the kid, I found a piece of Ethel's gown.'

Dana stared at her. 'You're kidding.'

'Nope.'

'What was it doing in the attic?'

'Not much. Just lying on the floor.'

'Are you sure it was fabric from Ethel's gown?' Eve asked.

'Oh, yeah, pretty sure.'

'When you found the tampering with Ethel, did you look for signs of forced entry?'

Tuck grinned. 'Into Ethel?'

'Into the house.'

'Weren't any,' she said. 'But you know how it goes. Somebody hides while we're open for the tours.'

'And this kid today claimed someone else was in the attic with him?'

'Yeah, but nobody *was*.'

'Are you sure?'

'I looked.'

'Everywhere?' Eve asked.

Tuck shrugged. 'You've been in the attic. It's a huge mess. Would've taken me an *hour* to look everywhere.'

'Has anything else happened in the past few days?'

'A couple of disappearing cassette players.'

'And there was that car on Front Street,' Dana pointed out. 'It's been there since Thursday.'

'What sort of car?' Eve asked.

'An old blue Ford Granada.'

'Is it still there?' Tuck asked.

'I think so,' Dana said. 'I'm not sure. It was still there this morning, but . . .'

'I'll stop by and take a look tonight. Where exactly was it parked?'

Dana thought for a moment, then said, 'On the east side of Front Street, just about half a block north of Beast House.'

'If it's still there, I'll run a check on the plates and see what I can find out about the owner.'

'If you find out he vanished without a trace,' Tuck said, 'make sure and let us know.'

'You can bet on it.'

*   *   *

Standing on the wooded slope with his back against the tree, Owen didn't think he could wait much longer.

He was getting too scared.

He wished he had the courage to call out John's name. But he was afraid of who might hear him – who might come looking for him in the darkness.

Anyway, calling out for John wouldn't do any good.

Owen had already figured out the possibilities.

John might be playing a trick on him – ditching him or hiding nearby to enjoy Owen's torment.

Or maybe he'd returned to the pool to spy on the gals for a while longer.

Or somehow, he'd gotten lost and wandered out of earshot.

Or maybe he'd had a bad accident, rendering him unconscious or dead.

Or he'd gotten attacked – abducted or killed.

Owen hadn't been able to think of any other alternatives. One of them, he figured, almost *had* to be the truth. And no matter which it might be, he couldn't see any benefit to calling out for John.

I can't just stand here all night!

What'll I do?

He knew one thing he could not do: ascend the hillside.

But what if John crashed into a tree and he's out cold up there?

I would've heard it happen, he told himself. The guy was right on my tail.

And I didn't hear anything.

How could that be? he wondered.

Wondering about it gave him goosebumps.

The bastard probably just stopped on his own, turned around and sneaked away.

He's probably waiting for me down at the car.

Goosebumps still prickling his skin, Owen pushed himself away from the tree, turned around and started rushing downhill through the darkness.

He ran with his hands out in front of him in case of a collision.

As he ran, he thought he heard someone huffing behind him. But he looked back and nobody was there.

He thought he heard *other* quick, pounding feet.

Looking back, he saw no one.

Nobody's after me!

But he looked back again.

And again.

He heard himself make whimpery noises as he panted for breath.

And thought he heard someone *else* whimpering in the night behind him.

Cut it out! Nobody's after me!

I'm gonna get down to the road and find John's lousy heap of a car and he'll be waiting in it, laughing at me.

At last, Owen found a road.

And finally, he found John's car.

Wheezing, whimpering, hardly able to stay on his feet, he staggered down the narrow road toward the rear of the old Ford Granada. He stumbled to the passenger door. Crouching, he looked through the open window.

Where the hell ARE you?

He opened the door. The overhead bulb cast a dim, yellowish light through the car's interior.

No John in the front seat.

No John in the back seat.

No key in the ignition.

Where is he? What'll I do?

Feeling confused, worn out and helpless, Owen climbed into the car. He sat down on the crunched copy of *Fangoria* and pulled his door shut.

The overhead light went out.

He waited in darkness for John's return.

Chapter Forty-Four

Sandy's Story – June, 1997

She drove down Front Street, looking for the blue Ford Granada. There were only a couple of cars parked on the street near Beast House, and neither fit Dana's description.

So maybe its owner hadn't vanished, after all.

But a *lot* of funny stuff had gone on recently inside Beast House.

Worth checking out, Sandy thought.

She turned her Range Rover around and drove back into town. A block past Beast House, she made a right turn and headed up a sidestreet. She parked at the curb. On both sides of the street, all the places of business were closed for the night.

This time, she didn't leave her flashlight behind.

Though she carried it, she didn't turn it on.

Staying a block east of Front Street, she made her way back toward Beast House.

She was shivering, but doubted that it had much to do with the chilly breeze or her damp hair or the fact that she'd just spent more than an hour in the steaming hot water of a spa. The shivers, she was sure, had mostly to do with Eric.

What if he's in there?

Ever since the day he ran off, five years ago, she'd looked forward with terrible hope and dread to the time when they might meet again.

If he hadn't fled, she would have shot him. She was pretty sure of that.

But now?

I'll still shoot him, she told herself. For what he did to Terry. For what he did to me. To stop him from hurting anyone else.

I'll kill him, all right.

If I find him.

At the rear of the Beast House grounds, Sandy came to the old iron fence with the spikes along the top. A lot had been changed over the years, but this section of fence remained the same.

Standing close to the bars, she scanned the area ahead.

She remembered a time when there'd been no paved patio area behind the house. No snack stand. No tables and chairs. No gift shop. No restrooms. None of this. Just the old gazebo – now on display in Janice Crogan's museum – and a big, grassy lawn that Wick used to mow once a week. She remembered times when she would sit in the gazebo in the evenings, all alone. And times when she made love on the dewy grass late at night. With Seth. With Jason.

Eric might very well have been conceived on such a night, his father gleaming white as snow in the moonlight.

Sandy liked to think that Seth was Eric's father. Seth was such a sweetheart. And gentle. Not like Jason. Seth probably was the father, but she couldn't be sure.

Doesn't matter, she told herself, suddenly feeling a pain of loss. They're both dead, anyway. And Eric'll be dead, too, if I find him.

Crouching, she slipped the flashlight between the iron bars of the fence. She set it on the grass, then climbed the iron bars. At the top, she imagined falling onto the spikes, feeling one or two of them drive up through her jeans and into . . .

Stop it!

She leaped, dropped to the grass, and rolled. Then she retrieved her flashlight. Its ribbed casing was wet with dew. She wiped it with the tail of her outer shirt, then ran across the moonlit grass. She entered the paved patio through a gap between the gift shop and snack stand.

Warren's snack stand.

If it was really teenagers that jumped him, she thought, why the big secret?

Because it wasn't teenagers. It was a beast. It was Eric. And Warren was afraid somebody might find out Eric did more than just beat him up – so he concocted a lie.

That explains a lot, Sandy thought.

Explains why Warren quit being a Beast House guide *and* how he suddenly became the owner of the snack stand.

Janice must've bribed him with it.

Which would mean she knew the truth.

Which would mean she's been letting the tours continue – even the Midnight Tour – knowing a beast was back.

How could she *do* a thing like that? Sandy wondered.

The answer came to her mind in the old, familiar voice of Maggie Kutch – 'Easy: m-o-n-e-y.'

No, Sandy thought. Janice isn't like that. She wouldn't risk the lives of innocent people that way. So maybe she *doesn't* know what really happened to Warren.

Or maybe it *was* teenagers.

Eric would've killed him.

Sandy climbed the wooden stairs to the back porch of Beast House.

Warren would be dead, she told herself, if Eric had attacked him. Dead like Terry and all the others. So obviously, Eric wasn't responsible for . . .

He didn't kill me.

That's different, she thought. I'm his mother. He hardly hurt me at all – a few scratches, a few bites, nothing major.

Everybody else, he rips apart.

He would've shredded Warren, killed him.

So maybe it was teenagers, after all.

The porch door was locked. Clamping the flashlight between her thighs, Sandy dug into a front pocket of her jeans and pulled out a folding Buck knife. She opened the four-inch blade and slipped it into the crack between the screen door and its frame.

A simple hook and eye secured the door.

She couldn't see them, but she knew they were there. They'd been there in the old days when she was a guide. And they'd still been there the last time she'd secretly entered Beast House to search for Eric.

After first returning to Malcasa Point in early 1993, she'd gone into the house two or three nights a week. But that hadn't lasted long. Soon, she'd tapered off to once or twice a month as she began to give up her theory that Eric would return to the town of his birth, the home of his ancestors.

He's not a homing pigeon, she used to tell herself.

But then she would think of all the stories she'd heard about cats and dogs finding their way home from enormous distances . . .

Their cabin to Malcasa Point wouldn't be any great trick. A person could walk the distance in less than a week, no trouble at all.

Eric, apparently, hadn't.

Maybe he just wasn't interested in returning to Malcasa Point. Or maybe he didn't know how. Or he *couldn't* return because he'd been injured or killed.

Maybe I'm the reason he hasn't come. He might've figured that I'd be here, waiting to kill him.

Though Sandy could only guess at the reason, the fact was that she never found Eric – or any trace of his presence – during her clandestine visits to Beast House.

She'd made her last illegal entry near the end of 1994.

Here we go again, she thought.

With a flick of the knife, she tapped the unseen hook out of its unseen eye. She folded the knife, slipped it into her pocket, then took the flashlight from between her thighs and opened the screen door. Inside the porch, she eased the door shut. She fastened its hook.

Turning around slowly, flashlight off, she scanned the dark porch. During the day, it served as a makeshift lounge area for Beast House staff members. She knew there was a sofa, a card table, a couple of old lounge chairs and a small refrigerator. Now, they made a jumble of motionless shadows. She smelled a faint, stale odor of cigarette butts.

Facing the back door of the house, Sandy listened. She heard the quick thumping of her own heart. Off in the hills, an owl hooted. She also noticed a quiet *shhhhh* that might be the breeze or might be a car rushing down Front Street.

Nobody here but me.

She stepped to the wooden door. Again, she clamped the flashlight between her legs. Hands free, she removed a slim leather case from a breast pocket of her outer shirt. She opened it and drew out her pick and tension bar.

She felt for the door knob, found the lock hole, then slipped her tools into it.

She needed no light for picking the lock.

Inside the kitchen of Beast House – the door shut and locked behind her back – Sandy put away the tools. Then she took slow, deep breaths, trying to calm down.

This was *another* reason she'd given up the break-ins.

Too damn rough on the nerves.

Her heart was trying to smash its way out of her chest. Sweat trickled down her face and neck. The flashlight felt slippery in her hand.

With the tail of her outer shirt, she wiped her face.

Then she made her way slowly through the kitchen.

Nothing to be afraid of, she told herself.

I'm the baddest son-of-a-bitch in the Valley.

She smiled, but her smile trembled.

She knew that she wasn't afraid of physical harm to herself . . . and she certainly didn't fear 'the beast.' She had no reason to fear being caught trespassing, either; not only was she a police officer, but she was one of Lynn Tucker's best friends. If taken for a prowler, she could simply explain that she'd entered to investigate something. Maybe she'd noticed a flicker of light in one of the windows . . .

She feared none of that. What terrified her was the possibility of confronting her son.

Her baby.

Eric.

She had always loved him. Even before his birth, when he was an unseen force slumbering in her womb, she'd loved him. After his birth, she'd cherished him even more. She would've done anything for him. She would've died for him. She *did* kill for him, and he had killed for her.

But Eric had also murdered Terry.

And he had taken Sandy by force and made her pregnant, and *caused all that.*

She had to kill him. For what he'd done to Terry. For what he'd done to her and what she'd *had* to do because of it. But she still loved him. She would never be able to stop loving him, no matter what he might do, but she had to kill him nonetheless.

He probably isn't here, anyway, she told herself.

But maybe he is.

Something had scared the kid in the attic.

While still in the spa, Sandy had decided to try the attic first.

She left the kitchen and walked slowly along the narrow passage to the foot of the stairway. Then she stepped around the newel post and began to climb the stairs. She made no attempt for silence. Her western boots clumped against the wood. The old planks creaked and moaned under her weight.

The noises seemed very loud in the silence. Sandy figured they could probably be heard throughout the house – except perhaps in the attic and cellar.

They might warn Eric of her approach.

Good.

Be smart and run for your life, honey. Momma's here to gun you down.

At the top of the stairs, she turned to the right and walked heavily down the hallway. She stopped at the attic door. It was shut. With her left hand, she unhooked one end of the cordon and let it fall. Then she gave the knob a twist. The door wasn't locked. She swung it open.

The stairway to the attic was as black as a mine shaft.

Sandy switched her flashlight on. Its beam drilled through the darkness, slanting upward all the way to the shut door at the top of the stairs.

She changed the flashlight to her left hand.

With her right hand, she unholstered her 9mm Sig Sauer semi-automatic. A hollow-point in the chamber and the hammer down, the double-action pistol was ready to fire. A pull of the trigger would do it.

The bright beam trembling on the attic door, Sandy began to climb the stairs. The stairwell was hot and stuffy. She panted for breath. She blinked sweat out of her eyes. She could feel her T-shirt clinging to her back. Sweat dribbled down her inner thighs. The moist seat of her jeans pressed against her buttocks as she climbed.

Don't let him be up here, she thought.

Please, God, I don't want to kill him. But I will. You know I will. If you don't want me to, don't let me find him.

At the top, she clamped the flashlight between her thighs. Then she used her empty hand to turn the knob and shove the door. It swung open, hinges squealing, and the beam of her light tunneled into the attic.

Reaching down, she pulled the flashlight free. She held it low and off to the side as she stepped over the threshold. Just inside the doorway, she began to move the flashlight slowly. The pale beam, aswirl with specks like miniature snowflakes, drifted at hip level from one side of the attic toward the other.

It lit the steeply slanted roof, thick support beams, the broken-faced mannequin of Officer Dan Jenson . . .

The kid didn't run into any beast, just caught a glimpse of poor Dan! Mystery solved.

Though Sandy felt her tension start melting away, she continued to move her light across the attic. It revealed old steamer trunks and suitcases, cardboard boxes, dummies of the two Zieglers, framed paintings stacked against a wall, a few rolled rugs, an ancient wheelchair, a tattered sofa, a rocking chair, a pedestal table and other odds and ends of old furniture.

Then her flashlight illuminated a hunched, furry creature with wild eyes and teeth bared in a mad snarl.

Vincent, the stuffed monkey. A nineteenth-century umbrella stand, it used to reside in the foyer.

Sandy smiled, recalling how it often freaked the kids out.

Maybe that's why Janice stored it away.

Though Sandy had been in the attic several times, on her own and with the Midnight Tour, she hadn't seen Vincent in years. Not since her old days as a guide.

She smiled at the hideous monkey. 'How you doing, Vincent old pal?' She stepped closer to him and squatted down – grimacing as her buttocks and crotch pushed against the sweaty denim of her jeans. 'You're looking a bit the worse for wear,' she said.

His short brown fur looked a lot more ratty and filthy than she remembered. If she dared to pat him on top of the head, a cloud of dust would probably rise.

He seemed to be glaring into her eyes.

In the old days, to test her courage, Sandy used to dare herself to insert her forefinger into his open mouth. She'd always been sure that Vincent, though dead and stuffed, wouldn't miss the opportunity to bite her finger off. She'd also known that he *couldn't*. He was dead and stuffed. If he *tried* to bite her finger, his jaw would probably break off.

Still, she'd never been able to do it.

Sandy hadn't feared the fangs of living beasts, but the teeth of poor old Vincent always terrified her.

'You don't scare me now,' she whispered.

She set her pistol on the floor.

'You wouldn't bite your old friend, would you?'

Vincent glared at her.

'You better not,' she warned him.

Then she eased her forefinger into his mouth.

And gasped out a yelp of fright as she was clutched from behind by her crotch and neck and jerked high. The flashlight flew from her hand. Her head pounded against a roof beam. As the light blinked out, she felt herself slam against the attic floor.

Chapter Forty-Five

Rude Awakening

Dana woke up feeling chilly. She was curled on her side, covered only by the top sheet. She supposed she must've thrown off the blanket.

The bedroom was gray with early morning light.

She glanced at the clock.

6:20

Mmm. Great. I can go back to sleep. If I can just get warm.

Straightening her left leg, she tried to feel the blanket. There seemed to be nothing down there except the lightweight sheet.

Her blanket must've fallen off the end of the bed.

Only one way to retrieve it – by getting up.

Dana groaned.

She didn't want to move. Even though the sheet that covered her to the shoulders felt unpleasantly cool, the mattress underneath her body was cozy and warm.

She imagined Warren being in the bed, too. Asleep on the other side of it.

If only, she thought.

His side of the bed would be nice and warm. She would roll toward him and squirm closer until she could feel his heat. Then she would rest her face on his shoulder, curl an arm across chest, swing a leg over his thighs. She would stay on him like that, and fall asleep.

What's he wearing? she wondered.

Soft, flannel pajamas.

In the morning, she would wake up first. And watch him sleep for a while. Then she would sneak her hand into the open fly of his pajama bottoms . . .

Moaning, Dana rolled toward the other side of the bed. It was empty. Of course.

Warren's probably fast asleep in his own bed right now.

Maybe he's lying awake, the same as me. Wishing he could turn over and take me in his arms.

If I don't go on the tour, she thought, we can be together tonight.

The tour'll be fun.

Anyway, I promised Tuck.

Would she really mind if I missed it? Dana wondered. She'll still have Eve with her. It's not like she has to have an *entourage*. Why don't

I just tell her that I'd like to see Warren tonight, but I'll go on the tour with her *next* Saturday?

Not a bad idea, she thought.

She imagined herself stepping up to the window of the snack stand, Warren smiling out at her. He would say, 'You look wonderful this morning, Dana.'

And she would say, 'Guess what! I can see you tonight, after all. I decided to bag the Midnight Tour.'

'Great!'

Excited by her plan, she no longer felt drowsy *or* chilly.

But this was too early for starting the day.

I'll take a pee, she thought. Then I'll get nice and cozy and try to grab a couple more hours of sleep.

Flopping onto her back, she swept the top sheet away and sat up.

Then gazed down at herself.

She'd gone to bed last night wearing a white cotton nightshirt.

She still wore it.

But now it hung from her shoulders, ripped wide open down the front.

'Uh-oh,' she muttered.

What the hell's going on?

She stared at her nightshirt's ragged edges.

I didn't do it, did I?

If I didn't, who did?

She recalled the strange sound she'd heard yesterday just after waking up – a door sliding shut as if an overnight intruder were sneaking out of the house.

She suddenly felt crawly.

Goosebumps prickled her skin.

Take it easy, she told herself. Maybe I did it in my sleep.

Not likely, but possible.

And maybe not quite as far-fetched as the idea that a *prowler* was in here and ripped it open.

If he ripped it open, what else did he do?

What if he *messed* with me?

Climbing off the bed, Dana felt her soreness.

That's from Warren, she told herself.

Is it?

She wanted to turn on a light. She wanted to take off the split nightshirt and study herself in a mirror.

But two strides away from the bed, her bare left foot kicked something heavy and hard.

She cried out in pain.

The kicked object spun across the floor and vanished behind a corner of the dresser.

Hurt foot up, Dana hopped backward on her good foot and dropped onto the edge of the bed. She sat there, face contorted, throat tight, toes throbbing. Very quickly, however, the pain subsided.

Then she scooted sideways on the mattress, reached out and turned on the lamp. Three of her toes looked red. So did a dozen or so scratches on her legs and belly and breasts. And several mouth-shaped blotches.

The toes got that way from smashing against that *thing* on the floor.

The scratches all came from roaming the bushes behind Tuck's pool last night. Probably.

The blotches all came from Warren's mouth. Probably.

Warren really wracked me up, she thought. I won't be the same for a week.

Neither will he.

Smiling slightly, she decided nobody else had been tampering with her body.

Probably.

Maybe she *had* torn the nightshirt herself. Maybe got carried away, dreaming.

As a kid, she'd sleepwalked a few times.

Maybe it was something like that.

But what the hell did I kick? she wondered. A shoe?

I don't think it was a shoe.

She stood up. Her injured toes ached, but not too badly. Trying to keep the pressure off them, she limped over to the dresser.

And stepped past it.

On the floor in front of her feet was an expensive-looking camera with a telephoto lens.

She crouched over it.

A Minolta.

She reached for it.

She grabbed the thick lens, but it felt moist and sticky.

She jerked her hand away.

And stared at the red stain across her palm and fingers.

'Oh, shit,' she muttered. Then she yelled, '*Tuck!*'

Seconds later, Dana heard racing footsteps.

Thank God she's all right.

If that IS Tuck.

Better be.

Suddenly, Tuck lurched through the doorway. She wore a blue pajama shirt. Though only two of its buttons were fastened, it apparently hadn't been torn open. Her hair was mussed. She was breathing hard. She held the huge, stainless-steel magnum in her hand. 'What happened?' she gasped.

'Somebody . . . look.' Dana brushed her fingertips against the torn edges of her nightshirt.

'Huh? How'd that happen?'

'I don't know. I woke up and . . .' She shook her head. 'Somebody must've done it while I was asleep.'

'You think so?'

'I don't think *I* did it. Did *you* do it?'

'Not hardly.'

'And look at this.' She stepped over to the camera and nudged it with her right foot.

'A nice one.'

'But whose *is* it? It's not mine.'

Tuck's mouth tilted crooked. 'Is now, huh?'

A laugh escaped from Dana. 'Yeah, sure.'

'It's a beauty.' Crouching, Tuck reached for the camera.

'Better not touch it. You'll get blood on you.'

'Huh?'

Dana held out her stained hand.

'Oh, yuck. That's from the camera?'

'Yeah.'

'Shit.' Tuck stood up and took a step backward. Frowning, she looked from the camera to Dana's exposed body. 'Whose blood?'

'Not mine.'

'Then it must be his.' She looked down at the carpet, her gaze roaming. 'I don't see any more.' She held out her revolver toward Dana. 'Why don't you hold on to this and I'll call Eve.'

Dana took the weapon.

Tuck stepped over to the telephone extension on the nightstand. She tapped in three numbers. Then she said, 'Malcasa Point . . . The number for Eve Chaney. C-h-a-n-e-y . . . Right.'

Seconds later, her fingers scurried over the keys, entering Eve's telephone number.

Then she stared at Dana and listened.

She made a face. 'Answering machine.'

'Maybe she screens her calls.'

Tuck nodded, waited, then said, 'Eve? This is Lynn Tucker. Pick up if you're there, okay? Eve? Yo, Eve! Pick up! I'm sorry to be calling at this hour, but we've had another problem over here. Somebody was in

Dana's room. He cut open her nightshirt, maybe took some pictures of her. We don't know if he's still in the house. His *camera* is. And it has blood on it. He might've cut himself with whatever he used on Dana's nightshirt. I don't know. Where the hell *are* you? Anyway, give me a call when you can.' She hung up and said, 'Shit.'

'Heavy sleeper,' Dana suggested.

'Who knows.'

'I hope she got home all right.'

'Like we don't have enough to worry about.'

'Should we call 911?'

'About us or Eve?'

'Us. I think it'd be a little premature to call the cops about Eve.'

'I don't want to call them period – have one of those assholes like Cochran show up in half an hour or so. You start telling *him* what happened, he'll get himself a fuckin' boner.' She held out her hand, and Dana gave the revolver to her. 'You get your gun and we'll take a look around. The bastard's probably long gone, but you never know.'

Dana's purse was hanging by its strap from the closet door. She walked over to it, reached in, and pulled out the pistol Eve had loaned to her.

'How do you suppose he keeps getting in?' she asked.

Tuck shook her head. 'No idea. But I know he'll never get in *again*. Not if we find him. I'll blow his ass off.'

Chapter Forty-Six

Owen's Bad Night

They were chasing Owen over a sunny, deserted stretch of beach. He was terrified, but he didn't know why. They were Dana and Lynn and the beautiful stranger from the Jacuzzi. They looked great. They were golden in the sunlight. Except for their cowboy hats and western boots, they were naked.

They'll never catch me, not in those shit-kicker boots.

But they were *gaining* on him!

If they get me . . .

He wasn't sure what would happen if they caught him, but he knew it would be horrible.

They'll do me like they did Cromwell.

He wasn't sure what they'd done to John. All he knew was that his friend had been running just behind him down the beach and then he was gone.

What'd they do to him?

Something monstrous.

And they'll do it to me if they catch me.

He glanced back.

They were so much closer than before!

He felt a scream rising in his chest.

And suddenly he heard the *vroom!* of a car engine. Speeding straight toward him, sand blooming behind it, was John's old blue dune buggy.

He's coming to the rescue!

'*Hurry!*' Owen yelled.

It raced closer, closer.

Glancing back, he saw the women stop running.

They're giving up!

Laughing with relief, he ran toward the dune buggy.

As it bore down on him, he saw that the driver wasn't John.

Of course not. They got John, remember?

The driver was Monica, teeth bared, glee in her violet eyes, her raven hair blowing wild. Her arms and shoulders were bare. Tied around her neck was a silk scarf. It matched her eyes, and flowed behind her in the wind.

She's gonna run me over!

'*No!*' he yelled, and woke up.

Morning. At last.

But the engine sound was real.

Heart pounding, Owen scurried off the bed and ran to the window. He pulled its heavy curtains apart. Sunlight flooded his room.

Over to the right, a white Porsche was backing out of a parking space. It stopped for a moment, its engine rumbling. Then it swung away and thundered toward the exit.

Owen let his hands fall. The curtains stayed open.

He scanned the entire courtyard, looking for John's old Ford.

Most of the parking spaces were empty.

They'd been packed last night when he finally got back. By then, the Welcome Inn's neon 'No Vacancy' sign had been glowing by the side of the road.

He'd sure been glad to see that sign.

* * *

Up in the wooded hills last night, waiting for John, Owen feared that he would never get back.

He sat in the car all alone, surrounded by darkness.

Afraid a hand might reach in and grab him, he soon rolled up the windows and locked the doors. But with all fresh air cut off, strange, disgusting odors seemed to rise around him and envelop him.

He tried to put up with the stink.

Then he thought, What's a window going to keep out? I'm no safer in here than I'd be outside.

He didn't exactly believe that, so it took a lot of courage to open the door and climb out.

It was good to get away from the nasty odors.

But he felt exposed.

After standing in front of the car for a while, he climbed up and sat on its hood.

And sat there.

Surrounded by darkness.

Shivering with cold and fear.

They could get me from any side!

He stuck with it, though.

He frequently checked his wristwatch. Each minute seemed to last for ten. When his watch showed 11:30, he told himself that he would wait till midnight.

If John isn't back by then, I'll walk to the motel.

Or try to, anyway.

On the way up, he hadn't paid close attention to the route. A downhill course, however, should take him to Front Street somewhere north of town. Make a left, and he'd get to the Welcome Inn sooner or later.

It's probably no more than four or five miles, he thought.

If I have to walk back, that'll be it for John. He doesn't get into the room tonight and he doesn't go on the Midnight Tour. Not on the ticket I paid for. I'll rip it to shreds.

Don't rip it up, he told himself. Turn it in at the ticket office and get a refund.

Or scalp it tomorrow night. I can probably sell it for a lot more than I paid for it. Maybe a hundred and fifty, two hundred bucks. I should shoot for two hundred . . .

Right. Sure thing. John has the pictures, so I'll give him whatever he wants.

If he ever shows up.

At 11:41, Owen heard crunching noises in the woods to his right.

They sounded like footsteps.

He felt his scrotum shrivel.

Maybe it's John, he told himself.

Staring into the trees beside the road, he saw nothing except motionless shadows and bits of moonlight.

The noises stopped.

He opened his mouth, but couldn't force himself to call out.

If it's John, why doesn't he come out? Why's he doing this to me?

What if it ISN'T John?

Owen glanced at his wristwatch.

11:43

'Well,' he muttered. 'Guess it's about time to get going.'

He jumped down from the hood and walked slowly away from the front of John's car.

Slowly for a few strides, then faster.

Then faster.

The moment he rounded the curve in the road, he broke into a run. Shoes smacking the pavement, arms pumping, he sprinted for all his worth. He ran on and on.

At last, worn out, he slowed to a walk. Aching, panting, drenched in sweat, he turned around.

Nobody was chasing him.

Got away just in the nick of time.

With frequent glances over his shoulder, Owen walked the rest of the way back to the Welcome Inn.

Nobody gave chase.

No cars passed him, not even while he walked along Front Street.

He saw nobody at all.

When he finally spotted the neon 'No Vacancy' sign of the Welcome Inn, he felt saved.

I'm all right now.

Though the courtyard was crowded with parked cars, nobody was roaming about. The room windows were dark. He heard no voices, no laughter.

Am I the only one up at this hour?

Trying to be quiet, he let himself into his room. It felt hot and stuffy. He turned on a light and looked around. There were John's broken glasses on top of the nightstand. And there was the telephone directory where he'd found Lynn's address.

No John.

What did you think, he'd beat you back? He's still up there, having the time of his life.

Or else dead.

He'll be back, Owen told himself. Any minute now, he'll come pounding on the door, wanting in. And then he'll brag about all the great stuff I missed.

In the bathroom, Owen shut and locked the door. Then he took off his clothes. They were filthy and sodden with sweat. He piled them in a corner of the floor, bent over the tub and turned the water on. It thundered out of the spigot.

He hoped the noise of the plumbing wouldn't disturb anyone.

But he *had* to take a shower.

He made it quick.

As he stood beneath the hot spray, he thought he heard voices, people knocking on the door of his room, even the ringing of his telephone.

But nobody was there when he got out.

The red light on the phone wasn't blinking, so nobody had called and left a message.

He stepped back into the bathroom, but left the door wide open while he dried himself, brushed his teeth, then urinated and flushed the toilet.

Done in the bathroom, he searched his suitcase and pulled out his pajamas. They were white and neatly folded. He hadn't worn them at all since leaving Los Angeles, but tonight he might need to haul himself out of bed to let John in. So he put them on.

I guess I'll *have* to let him in, Owen thought.

Then he gave the bed a quick inspection. Satisfied that there was nothing disturbing between its sheets, he turned off the light and climbed in.

It felt great.

He sighed with pleasure, shut his eyes, and fell asleep.

And lurched awake in the dark room, sweaty and gasping, his heart slamming with fright.

He sat up and turned on the nightstand lamp. He checked his wristwatch.

3:20

He looked at the other bed.

Where the hell is he!

Owen switched the lamp off. He flopped back down on the bed and shoved aside the blanket. Even the sheet seemed too hot, so he flipped it away. He shut his eyes and tried to sleep.

His mind was a turmoil, swirling with a seemingly endless string of feverish scenerios about John, about Dana and Lynn and the beautiful but dangerous stranger, about whoever or whatever had been lurking nearby in the bushes, even about Monica. Some of the images terrified him. Others wracked him with guilt. One moved him with hopes of love. A few made him grow hard with lust. He writhed on the bed, his damp pajamas twisted around his body. He lost track of when he was awake, when asleep. The scenerios wouldn't stop. They seemed too vivid to be dreams. More like hallucinations.

Every so often, cars drove up. There were knocks on the door and he climbed out of bed, thinking John had finally returned. The first time, John stood there headless. Another time, he seemed all right but out of breath and frantic. '*Let me in! Let me in! It's after me!*'

'*What's after you?*'

'*The great white ape! Let me in!*'

Still another time, Owen had opened the door and found John naked and torn and bloody all over, his stiff severed penis protruding from his mouth like a cigar.

'*Need a light?*' Owen asked.

In answer, John jerked his mouth open wide and the penis fell out and he screamed like a terrified lunatic.

Longest damn night of my life, Owen thought as he stared out the window at the sunny courtyard.

John's car wasn't there.

I wonder if I should call the police.

And tell them what? he asked himself. That we were up in the hills last night spying on some naked gals in a Jacuzzi and John disappeared?

Real cute.

Besides, who's to say he isn't perfectly all right? He might've even ended up in the sack with one of those gals.

Fat chance.

The hell with him anyway. He's a jerk.

Owen turned away from the window.

Might as well get dressed and . . .

I'd better take another shower first, he thought. He certainly needed one. And maybe a long, hot shower would loosen up his tense muscles, help him to calm down.

Inside the bathroom, he shut and locked the door and peeled off his damp pajamas.

As he stood under the hot spray, he decided that he would have a nice breakfast, then go over to Beast House and try to get a refund on John's ticket for the Midnight Tour.

'*Your ticket? Well, you disappeared, old pal. I really didn't think you'd have any use for it, so I sold it.*'

'YOU SOLD MY TICKET???'
'Sorry.'
A weary smile lifted the corners of Owen's mouth.

Chapter Forty-Seven

Saturday Gets Under Way

'Wake up! Yo! Time to rise and shine, your highness. It's me. Lynn. You there? You gonna pick up? Where the hell are you? Anyway, we had a visitor last night – as you already know if you listened to the previous message. We subsequently searched the house but didn't have any luck finding him. Don't know how he got in, either. But then, you're the trained investigator, not us. And you're making yourself conveniently scarce. Bitch. Hey, we *are* starting to worry about you. Not that you can't take care of yourself, but . . . Never mind. We're leaving for work in a couple of minutes. You can call me there or drop by. And don't forget about tonight. We're expecting you for the tour – in full battle regalia. Plan to get there in time for the picnic if you can. But don't make us wait all day to hear from you, okay? It'd be nice to know you didn't have an accident and shoot off your toe or something. Not that we care. Anyway, take it easy. Bye.'

On the way to Beast House in the passenger seat of the Jeep, Dana pictured herself asleep in the bedroom while someone hunched over her in the darkness, sliced her nightshirt all the way down, spread it open and snapped photographs of her body.
Did he use a flash?
Why didn't I wake up?
And why did he leave his camera behind?
She realized that Tuck had spoken to her. 'Huh?' she asked.
'The blue Granada. It's gone.'
Dana looked at the area of curb where the car used to be. 'You're right. Maybe its owner finally showed up.'
'Or Eve had it towed away last night.'
'But where is *she?*' Dana asked.
Tuck shook her head. 'Who knows? Maybe she spent the night some-where with a secret boyfriend. Or maybe she was at home and just

couldn't hear the phone from her bedroom. Or heard it, but didn't feel like answering.'

'Do you think she's all right?'

Tuck shrugged. 'I don't know. But I think it's way too early to start worrying.'

'When *should* we start worrying?'

Tuck swung off Front Street. She stopped at the closed gate to the Beast House parking lot, then met Dana's eyes. 'If she doesn't show up for the Midnight Tour.'

Tuck and Dana entered Beast House together for the walk-through.

In the attic, Tuck pointed out where she'd found the patch of fabric from Ethel's gown – at the feet of a scraggly, stuffed brown monkey.

Dana had never seen the monkey before. 'Where'd *that* thing come from?' she asked.

'Oh, that's Vincent the umbrella stand. Maybe *he's* the one who monkeyed with Ethel.'

Dana smiled and shook her head.

'You know what?' Tuck said. 'This is a little strange. Should've mentioned it to Eve last night. Vincent isn't supposed to be here.'

'Where *is* he supposed to be?'

'He *used* to be down in the foyer where everybody'd see him when they started the tour. He freaked people out. Kids used to *cry*. Even adults thought he was awful. So I'm told. Janice had him removed before my time. She actually couldn't stand the cute little guy.'

'Nothing cute about him.'

'Oh, I don't know.' Reaching down, Tuck patted the top of his head. Pale dust rose. He wobbled slightly.

'Real nice. Touch him.'

'The thing is, Janice hid him. She put him way over there in a back corner and covered him with a sheet so nobody would see him.'

'You saw him.'

'What can I say? I'm a snoop. Anyway, he was tucked out of sight until yesterday. Obviously, somebody moved him.'

'Great,' Dana muttered.

'Maybe whoever messed with Ethel. Or maybe it was the kid.'

'Lance?'

'Yeah.'

'I doubt if he was up here long enough. But you know what? This monkey might be what scared the crap out of him.'

'A cute little fellow like Vincent?' Tuck asked, and again patted the monkey's head.

* * *

Unwilling to wait alone in the kitchen, Dana followed Tuck down the cellar stairs. They creaked under her footfalls. As she decended, she smelled dank earth and felt the air grow cool. 'Charming place,' she muttered.

'You should see it at night.'

'Can't wait.'

'I get people sometimes, they won't even come down here. Or they'll start down, then run back up. You believe it? They fork out a hundred bucks for the tour, then can't even work up the nerve to visit the cellar.'

'I'm on their side,' Dana said.

At the bottom of the stairs, she quickly scanned the cellar. She'd only been down here once before, during Tuck's 'orientation' tour on Wednesday. She hadn't liked it then. Now, she liked it even less. It seemed more cluttered than the attic. Lit by one dim, bare bulb dangling by a wire, it had too many shadows, too many dark places where someone might crouch and lurk.

'I think I'll just wait right here,' she said.

'Pussy.'

'Meow.'

'Oh, that's pathetic.' Footsteps silent on the dirt floor, Tuck walked toward the tunnel hatch.

The area in front of it had been cleared of junk.

The floor hatch was Station Twelve of the audio tour.

From where Dana stood, she couldn't see much of the round steel cover because Tuck stood in the way.

Glancing over her shoulder, Tuck asked, 'Ever see *The House on Haunted Hill*? William Castle? Had Vincent Price in it? I caught it on cable a few months ago. There's this *awful* scene in the cellar. The candles blow out . . .' She grinned. 'Scared the bejeezus out of me.'

'I'm glad. Can we get out of here?'

Laughing, Tuck crouched over the hatch and tested the padlock. 'Well, this one's okay,' she said.

'Do you always check the locks?'

'Every morning,' she said on her way back. 'We don't want any surprises, do we?'

'Seems like we get them whether we want them or not.'

'Some surprises are worse than others.'

As Dana watched, Tuck made her way over to the 'old jailhouse door.' Never intended for jail use, however, it had been special-ordered by Janice to seal off the Beast House end of the tunnel leading westward to the Kutch house.

Through the bars of the door, Dana could see the opening of the tunnel. Light spilled in from the cellar, then faded to blackness.

Tuck stepped up to the door.

That's where Warren got jumped.

Dana slipped a hand into the baggy front pocket of her uniform shorts and wrapped her fingers around the grips of her pistol.

How could they not tell Tuck about what happened to Warren? My God, she comes in at night. Week in, week out.

Doesn't know any better.

It's all a lark for her.

I oughta tell her, myself.

'Locked up tight as a frog's asshole,' Tuck said.

'Good. Let's get out of here.'

Dana waved to the others, then veered off and headed for the snack stand.

Warren smiled at her through the order window. 'Morning,' he said.

'Hi.'

She had a sudden urge to embrace him.

'Can I come in for a minute?' she asked.

'If you don't mind everybody knowing.'

'I don't mind. Do you?'

'Go to the back.'

Dana hurried around to the rear of the snack stand. There, Warren opened a door for her. She rushed up a couple of stairs and into the small enclosure. Warren shut the door and turned to her.

'Missed you,' he said, taking her into his arms.

'Me, too.'

They kissed gently. Dana pulled him hard against her. She could feel the moist heat of his mouth. She could feel his chest and belly. She could feel his breathing. She moaned with the feel of him.

After a few seconds, they ended the kiss and loosened their embrace.

'Have a good time after I dropped you off?' Warren asked.

'Oh, I've had better – like back at your place. How about you?'

'Well, I got lonely and tried on your bra.'

Laughing softly, Dana said, 'I tried on your underwear.'

'Oh, gross. Did you?'

'Maybe I'm wearing 'em now.'

While one of his hands stayed in the middle of her back, the other glided down and felt her through the seat of her uniform shorts. 'You're not really, are you?'

'That's for me to know . . .'

'And for *me* to find out?'

'But not now,' Dana said. 'I've gotta go out and get to work.' She kissed him on the mouth, then eased away. 'See you later.'

Opening the door for her, Warren asked, 'Are you still planning to go on the tour tonight?'

'Afraid so.'

'I wish you'd change your mind about that.'

'Me, too,' Dana said, and hurried out.

Chapter Forty-Eight

A Ticket to Die for

After breakfast, Owen walked to Beast House. The morning was fresh and sunny. He couldn't really enjoy it, though. Nor could he look forward with much enthusiasm to the Midnight Tour.

John hung over his head.

He'll kill me if I sell his ticket.

Probably won't *kill* me, Owen thought, but he'll sure as hell never forgive me. It'll crush him. I can forget about ever seeing those pictures he took last night.

Oh, God, I've *gotta* see those! I've gotta have *copies!*

Do I? he asked himself. Even if the pictures turn out fine, they'll never be as good as what I saw.

Walking along Front Street, he called an image into his mind of Dana standing by the Jacuzzi and pulling off her huge white T-shirt. He saw her so clearly that he started to get hard.

The hell with John's pictures, he thought. The hell with John. If he shows up, I'll just smile and say, 'Sorry, but you disappeared. I didn't think you'd be back, so I took in your ticket for a refund.'

'*YOU WHAT!!!*'

Anyway, Owen told himself, maybe John *won't* be back. Maybe something actually did happen to him.

He's probably fine.

Sure.

'He won't be so fine,' Owen muttered, 'when he drags his fat, sorry ass back from wherever he's been all night and finds out his little prank cheated him out of the Midnight Tour.'

Though feeling sick with tension – and probably lack of sleep – Owen grinned.

By the time John shows up, he thought, it'll be a done deal.

If he shows up.

As Owen walked closer to the ticket booth, he saw that only eight or ten people were standing in line.

Won't be much of a wait.

After I get my refund, he thought, maybe I should go back to the room and take a nap. A long nap. Maybe I can sleep all afternoon. Then I'll be good and fresh for tonight.

As he walked closer to the ticket booth, he looked through its glass.

And saw Dana at work inside.

Oh, no!

Heat flashed through his body. He felt as if his skin might burst into flame. Sweat seemed to spill out of every pore.

He didn't think Dana had seen him yet; she was talking to a customer.

Afraid that stopping might draw attention to himself, he slowed down, turned his head as if looking back for someone, then made a casual U-turn and started walking away.

At the first intersection, he turned to the right and stepped past the corner of a bakery.

Can't see me now.

He stopped and took deep breaths, trying to calm down.

Now what? he wondered. I can't ask for a refund, not with Dana working the booth. She knows all about me and Monica and how I feel about her and . . . Oh, man, I saw her *naked* last night. How can I face her?

She doesn't *know* I watched her.

Unless John told.

They caught him and made him talk?

Don't be ridiculous, Owen thought. The only way she could know is if John went back and joined the party and shot off his mouth.

Wouldn't put it past him.

But if that's what he did, where is he?

In jail?

That's possible, Owen thought. If he went back, maybe they had him arrested. That would certainly explain why he hasn't turned up yet.

Turned up where?

Owen had been away from the motel room for more than an hour and a half.

Maybe he's back by now.

As Owen hiked toward the motel, he thought, I have all day to return the ticket. Maybe if I time things to show up during Dana's lunch break . . .

But he didn't know when that might be.

I'd have to go back and hang around . . .

It seemed too risky. And too much trouble.

Besides, he could always sell the ticket to a tourist at the last minute.

What if John turns up before then?

I'll say I already sold it. That'll fix him. See the look on his face. Then, if he's good, I can surprise him with it.

The best of both worlds, Owen thought.

When Owen entered his room at the Welcome Inn, John still wasn't there.

Both beds had already been made, their blankets smooth and flat, pillows neatly arranged at the heads. There were fresh glasses on the tray with the ice bucket, clean towels and washcloths in the bathroom.

Owen shut the curtains, closing out most of the light. Then he changed into his pajamas, pulled back the blanket of the bed he'd used last night, and climbed between the sheets.

Lying on his back, he raised his left arm and stared at his wristwatch.

Maybe set the alarm for five or six, he thought. Just to make sure I don't oversleep and miss the tour.

I probably won't even fall asleep at all, but I'd better play it safe.

He decided to set the alarm for 4:00 p.m. That would give him time to try the ticket booth once more before closing time.

What if Dana's still there?

Cross that bridge when I come to it.

He saw himself step up to the ticket window. Dana smiled at him. A soft, warm smile that made him long for her. 'Hi, Owen,' she said.

'Hi, Dana.'

'You just keep coming back for more, don't you? What are you, a glutton for punishment?'

'I can't get enough of Beast House,' he told her, thinking *I can't get enough of you, either.*

'Where were you last night?' she asked.

The question knocked his breath out.

As he tried to think of a lie, Dana said, 'I thought we had a date.'

'We did?'

A look of disappointment on her face, she nodded and said, 'I stopped by the motel, but you weren't there.'

Oh, no. Oh, no. It can't be true.

'I *really* wanted to see you,' she said.

'I really wanted to see *you*, too.'

'I missed you so much, Owen.' Reaching out through the ticket window, she gently took hold of his hands.

In his right hand, he was holding John's ticket for the Midnight Tour. Dana saw it. 'Oh, you're going on the tour tonight?'

'Yes.'

'Me, too.'

'That's great.'

'Will you be alone?'

His heart pounded hard. 'Yes.'

'Me, too. Do you think we could . . . do it together?'

Somewhere, a car door slammed. Owen woke up, realized he'd only been dreaming, and almost cried.

He hoped to fall asleep again quickly and return to the dream.

But you never get the great ones back. Just the nightmares.

Owen was rushing through the halls of a huge old school building, jerking open doors and glancing into classrooms. At any second, the tardy bell would ring. *Where's my room? Gotta find it! Oh, my God, where is it? I'll never find it in time. If only I knew the room number!*

Suddenly, the bell rang.

No! I'm late!

He woke up.

The noise wasn't the tardy bell, after all. It came from the telephone on his nightstand. Each time the phone rang, the little red message light flickered.

He squirmed toward the edge of the bed.

Who could it be? Nobody knows I'm here.

Just John.

Maybe wants me to bail him out.

Bracing himself up with an elbow, he reached out and picked up the phone. 'Hello?'

Through the earpiece came an empty sound, a quiet hiss.

'Hello?' he asked again.

At the other end of the line, the caller hung up.

Owen hung up, too. Then he flopped onto his back and shut his eyes and sighed.

No big deal, he told himself. Probably a wrong number.

But it must've come through the motel switchboard.

So what? Who cares?

He looked at his wristwatch.

3:50

His alarm would be going off in ten minutes. But he felt awfully groggy. He didn't *want* to get up in ten minutes and go over to the ticket booth.

Besides, it's probably still Dana. I'll just sell the damn thing when I go over for the picnic. Somebody's bound to want it.

He reset his wristwatch alarm for 6:30 p.m. That would give him an hour to get ready for the night's big events, plus half an hour to rid himself of John's ticket.

Owen woke up sweaty and hungry.

He checked his wristwatch. It showed 6:10.

Sitting up, he looked around the room. He saw John's glasses on the dresser and felt his stomach squirm.

Still not back.

It's all gonna start in a couple of hours, man. Where are you?

Owen climbed out of bed. He took still another shower, then sprayed his armpits with Right Guard, shaved, combed his hair and brushed his teeth.

By 6:45, he was dressed and almost ready to leave.

He grabbed his camera and hung its strap over one shoulder.

Then he slipped the two Midnight Tour tickets into the left breast pocket of his sport shirt.

He had already decided to walk.

He made sure he had the room key, then opened the door.

He'd expected golden sunlight, warmth, and a mild breeze. But sometime during the afternoon, while he'd been shut away in his room with the curtains closed, a fog had crept in.

It drifted like a gray mist around the cars in the parking lot. Owen could barely see to the other side of the motel courtyard. The cabins over there were fuzzy blurs.

A chill had arrived with the fog.

Owen hurried inside the room for his windbreaker. On the back, CRAWFORD JUNIOR HIGH SCHOOL was emblazoned in big gold letters. He tossed his camera onto the bed, slipped his arms into the sleeves of the windbreaker, fastened a couple of the front snaps, then rushed outside.

The jacket helped, but its sleeves felt cool against his bare arms.

He paused for a moment, wondering if he should go back inside and put on a long-sleeved shirt.

Gonna be indoors most of the time, anyway.

Then he wondered if he should give up the idea of walking, and take his rental car instead.

Probably crash and kill myself.

Besides, he thought, it'll be neat to walk through the fog.

He set off for Beast House.

Halfway there, he realized he had left his camera in the room.

The hell with it. Wrong film, anyway.

He kept on, but he felt its loss – and wondered what else would go wrong.

Stopping at the corner of the high, iron fence, Owen looked through its bars. He was half an hour early. Though he saw no tourists on the grounds, most of the regular guides were busy getting ready for the picnic. He spotted Dana right away, helping a guy carry a picnic table across the front lawn.

Two other picnic tables had already been brought out, along with a couple of smaller tables and three barbecue grills. Near the picnic tables, a bar was being set up by the only person not wearing a Beast House uniform. This man sported a red jacket, a white shirt, and a red bow-tie.

Owen found Dana again.

She put down her end of the table. Then the guy from the other end walked toward her, smiling and talking.

Who the hell is he?

He looked a little familiar . . .

The lunch-counter guy?

He joined up with Dana. As they headed away, Dana slipped an open hand inside a seat pocket of his shorts.

Owen suddenly felt as if he'd been slugged in the guts.

What did you expect? Of course *she's got a boyfriend.*

Sure, he thought. But that doesn't mean I have to like it.

Dana and her friend disappeared around a corner of the house.

Since she's busy, Owen thought, who's minding the ticket booth?

Probably no one. The self-guided tours were over for the day and the Midnight Tour had been sold out since yesterday, so the ticket booth would probably be closed.

Closed or not, a number of people were milling about the area in front of it. Waiting for the festivities to start, he supposed.

Maybe one of them could use a ticket.

Owen started walking toward the gathered tourists.

John wasn't among them.

A couple of the gals were real babes, even though one of them looked like a weirdo.

Pity you're gonna miss this, buddy.

Owen wandered through the group. He nodded greetings to those who seemed to notice him, and kept on moving. Leaving them all behind, he stepped over to the gate of the parking lot. It was still open. The lot was empty except for seven or eight cars.

John's blue Ford Granada wasn't among them.

Still up in the hills? Or maybe it got towed off and impounded by the cops.

Owen turned his back to the parking lot.

Nobody seemed to be watching him.

Scanning the group, he found the best-looking gal. Maybe thirty, she had light brown hair, a deep tan, and lively eyes. She was slender, but not skinny. She had a firm, athletic look. For whatever reason, she was dressed in a white tennis outfit: a knit pullover shirt, a sweater tied around her neck, a very short pleated skirt, ankle socks with puffy little balls at the back, and sneakers.

She was with a man who wore a red knit pullover and plaid Bermuda shorts. He looked husky and powerful and cheerful.

No wonder he's cheerful, Owen thought. Has a gal looks like that.

Owen turned his attention to the weirdo. Probably no older than twenty, she had done herself up in *vampire chic*. She was at least six feet tall and as sleek as a cover girl. Her skin looked smooth and oddly white. Her raven hair was cut short, slicked down. Her pierced left eyebrow sported a ring. Her eyelids were blue. She wore a gold stud in her nose, a ring in her upper lip. Her lipstick was black. She had about six rings along the rim of each ear. A tattoo of barbed wire surrounded her neck. She wore a black bra that looked like satin, no shirt at all, a belly-button ring, and an open jacket of black leather. Low and tight around her hips was a pair of black leather short-shorts. Below them, her long legs were bare and very white. She wore black boots that reached almost to her knees.

She wasn't alone.

Her handsome young friend had a delicate, rather feminine face. Compared to her, he looked almost clean-cut. He showed no signs of makeup, piercings or tattoos. His shaggy blond hair blew softly in the breeze. He wore a loose, long-sleeved shirt that appeared to be black silk. Unbuttoned, it exposed pale, hairless skin almost down to his waist, where the shirt was tucked into black leather trousers. His belt buckle was a white, snouted beast, possibly carved from ivory.

There's a real fan, Owen thought.

These two are really into it. If the tour gets boring, I can just watch them.

Owen noticed that he wasn't the only one checking out the weirdos: so were two guys standing near the road. One was a beanpole with stringy brown hair. The other was short and pudgy and had a crew cut.

They both wore gray sweatshirts, plaid Bermuda shorts, white socks and sneakers.

They hardly looked old enough for an 'adults only' tour. The cut-off age was supposed to be eighteen. These two might've been sixteen. Had they used fake i.d.'s to buy their tickets?

Maybe they don't *have* tickets.

Maybe they aren't even here for the tour.

Owen supposed that they could've simply stopped by to enjoy the spectacle of the vampire queen and her eunuch. They kept glancing at the pair, whispering, chuckling and elbowing each other.

Couple of dorks.

Owen *hoped* they wouldn't be going on the tour; they'd probably interrupt Lynn, laugh when they shouldn't, make wisecracks . . .

Jungle Jim, eyeing those two, seemed to share Owen's opinion. Maybe fifty years old, with a lean and rugged face, he studied them with a haughty look. One of his eyebrows was cocked as he surveyed the guys through his gold-rimmed glasses. He wore a safari jacket replete with epaulets, pocket flaps and a cloth belt. His tan trousers, matching the jacket, were tucked into the high tops of his paratrooper boots. His outfit seemed incomplete without a hunting knife and a high-powered rifle. He did, however, carry a weathered black camera around his neck.

Maybe he's a photo journalist, Owen thought – just back from covering tribal warfare in Rwanda.

The only remaining early-arrivals were a man and woman who appeared to be married. Thirty-five to forty years old, they were both slender, attractive and nicely dressed.

The man, going bald on top, made up for the loss with thick eyebrows and a heavy mustache. He had lively, almost impish eyes that seemed to be scanning the area in search of oddities or mischief. His clothing looked new and expensive: a crew-neck, camel sweater with long sleeves; trim gray slacks; and black leather wingtip shoes.

His wife had thick brown hair, a lovely face, a creamy complexion and fabulous eyes.

Make that *three* babes, Owen thought. Then he felt a little guilty. This woman was beautiful, but it seemed wrong to consider her a babe. She seemed too . . . dignified. A woman, not a babe.

Her eyes somehow looked calm and excited and amused and intelligent all at the same time. She wore a fuzzy, forest green sweater over a white blouse with an open collar. Her bare neck looked long and sleek. The sweater, rising over the push of her breasts, reached down past the waist of her skirt – a kilt of Stuart plaid. Below the hem of her kilt, her legs looked bare. She wore no socks. On her feet were brown, penny loafers.

What a great-looking couple, Owen thought. Doctors, maybe. Or professors. What the hell are they doing at a place like this?

Nobody else seemed to be standing around.

Owen counted.

Ten, including himself.

He had one extra ticket in his pocket. So only two people (other than John) were missing.

He glanced at his wristwatch.

7:52

In eight minutes, the picnic would start.

I'd better stop screwing around and do something about the ticket.

Reaching inside his windbreaker, Owen fingered the tickets in his shirt pocket and pulled one out. He raised it overhead. 'Excuse me, everyone!' he announced. 'Do all of you have tickets for tonight? I have an extra one I'd be glad to sell.'

The vampire queen gave him a narrow glance. Her eunuch ignored him. The tennis lady and her husband politely looked at Owen and shook their heads.

'Sorry, man,' said the beanpole.

His chubby friend said, 'Can't help you, dude – we got ours.'

Not such bad guys.

Jungle Jim took the pipe out of his mouth, scowled at Owen and proclaimed in an excessively loud, high-pitched voice, 'Sorry, old chap. It seems we all had the foresight to purchase our tickets in advance.'

'That's what I did,' Owen explained. 'I bought two, but then my friend got sick. I was hoping maybe I could unload his ticket.'

The well-dressed, mustached man said, 'You might be able to turn it in for a refund.'

His wife nodded in agreement. Large eyes fixed on Owen, she looked concerned. 'I should think you might be able to sell it without too much trouble. This is an *awfully* popular attraction.'

'From what we hear,' said her husband, 'it's *always* a sellout.'

'That's right. So there may very well be people trying to get tickets at the last moment.'

'*I'll* take the ticket off your hands!' piped a familiar voice from behind Owen.

His stomach knotted.

The woman smiled as if delighted by Owen's quick success.

'There you go,' said her husband.

'Dude!' proclaimed the chubby teenager.

The skinny sidekick gave Owen a thumb's up.

Jungle Jim planted the pipe between his teeth and nodded briskly at Owen, looking pleased with himself as if he'd caused the customer to materialize.

Trying to keep a smile on his face, Owen turned around.

'Surprise!' Monica greeted him, strutting out of the parking lot. 'I'm feeling so much better suddenly,' she announced. 'Now you won't need to sell my ticket!'

He gaped at her.

Smirking, she plucked the ticket out of his hand. Then she swung an arm around his back, pulled herself against him, stood on her tiptoes and kissed him on the mouth.

A moment later, she whirled away. 'Hello, everyone! I'm Monica! I was suffering from a terrible migraine, but I'm feeling *so* much better now. I think we're going to have a *super* time tonight, don't you?'

Chapter Forty-Nine

Tickets and Badges

'Anything I can do to help?' Dana asked as Warren slapped a hamburger patty onto the barbecue. The meat hissed as it hit the grill.

'You can just stand there looking beautiful,' Warren said.

She laughed.

Tuck, suddenly behind her, said, 'I'm gonna puke.'

Dana turned and smiled at her. 'The hamburgers smell great to me.'

'It ain't the burgers, it's *him*.' She nodded at Warren.

'You weren't supposed to hear it,' he said.

'Well, lordy, don't say repulsive stuff like that in *public*. And especially not at a *picnic*. You'll spoil appetites.'

'*I* thought it was fine,' Dana said.

'You would.' Tuck rapped Dana lightly on the upper arm. She had a small paper bag in her hand. As it bumped against Dana, whatever was inside clacked and clicked together. 'Anyway, why don't you come along – if you can tear yourself away from Golden Lips. I'm about to greet our esteemed guests. You want to experience the full treatment, don't you?'

'Well . . .' She looked at Warren.

'Go ahead. I can get along without you for a few minutes.'

'Okay. See you.'

They walked away, Tuck swinging the bag by her side. 'Ah,' she said. 'Summer romances.'

'Feels like a *winter* romance.'

'Yeah. A bit of a nip in the air, huh? But it's great atmosphere.' She looked over her shoulder at Beast House. 'This is how it oughta be *all* the time. I mean, talk about bleak and spooky. Our friends are gonna eat it up.'

'Speaking of friends, what about Eve?'

Tuck grimaced. 'I don't know. But it's still early. She has plenty of time to get here before the tour.'

'I'm really starting to worry about her.'

'Yeah. Me, too. She's probably all right, though. I mean, I pity anyone who'd try to mess with her. We don't call her Eve of Destruction for nothing.' Suddenly raising a hand and waving, Tuck called out, 'Hello, everyone!' to the people waiting on the other side of the fence.

Some of them ignored her. Others nodded or waved or returned tentative greetings. One guy, costumed either for Halloween or a safari into darkest Africa, raised the stem of his pipe and called out in a harsh voice, 'Those who are about to die salute you!'

'Aw, nobody's gonna die,' Tuck said. 'Not tonight, anyway – if we're lucky.'

As she unlocked the gate, the tourists migrated toward it.

Dana recognized two of them . . . no, *four* of them.

There were her two goofy teenaged friends from Thursday – Arnold and someone? They'd caused some trouble by hiding in the house after closing time, but they'd been pretty nice about it. They seemed a bit young to be doing the Midnight Tour.

Doesn't matter to me.

She was glad to see them.

The other two familiar faces belonged to Owen and his snotty girlfriend. Mona? No, Monica.

The girl he'd dumped in San Francisco.

What's *she* doing here? Dana wondered.

Owen didn't seem very happy. His face was flushed. He met Dana's eyes for an instant and quickly looked away. Monica cast a smirk in her direction.

Dana smiled at her, then turned away and saw a couple who looked as if they'd come here to audition for roles in remakes of *The Rocky Horror Picture Show*.

Charming, she thought.

At least a *few* of the bunch looked fairly normal. Though why a gal would come to the Midnight Tour in her tennis outfit . . . didn't she have time to go home and change?

Done with the lock, Tuck swung open the gate and asked, 'Everbody hungry?'

'I'm beastly starved!' said the safari man.

Dana's two friends from Thursday smirked and nudged each other.

'Before we start,' Tuck said, 'I have a few words to say. I'm Lynn Tucker, and I'm the official guide for the Beast House Midnight Tour. This is my old friend and new assistant, Dana Lake. We'll be with you till the bitter end. In case you're wondering, that'll be at about two a.m. Here's how the schedule goes.

'You'll have two hours for the picnic. There's a no-host bar . . . meaning you'll have to shell out cash if you want to get liquored up – but soft drinks and your picnic dinners are included in the price of your tickets. Feel free to roam the grounds. Beast House will be closed until the tour starts, but we're keeping the gift shop open until nine. As a Midnight Tourist, you'll get a special ten per cent discount on any purchases you make.

'Feel free to leave the grounds at any time. We'll be handing out souvenir badges that'll get you back in.

'Our special screening of *The Horror* will take place at the Haunted Palace movie theater on Front Street.' She pointed to the right. 'You can't miss it. Just be at the main entrance by ten o'clock. After the film, Dana and I will lead you back here for the Midnight Tour.

'Any questions about the schedule?' Tuck asked. Not waiting more than half a second, she said, 'Okay! Let's get this show on the road. Welcome to the Midnight Tour picnic. I'll take your tickets as you come in, and Dana will give each of you a badge.'

'We getta keep 'em?' asked the chubby kid.

'You're Dennis, right?'

He beamed as if proud that Tuck had remembered his name. 'That's right, ma'am. Dennis Dexter. D.D.'

'Call me Lynn, okay? And yes, the badges will be yours to keep. Okay, let's get started.'

She passed the bag to Dana, then stepped forward to start taking tickets.

Dana reached into the bag. When she tried to scoop up a handful of badges, points pricked her. She winced and jerked her hand out. It looked okay except for a single, bright red drop of blood on the tip of her middle finger.

Just lick it off and . . .

As she raised the finger toward her mouth, someone caught her wrist and said, 'Mine.'

Dana looked up into blue-shadowed, leering eyes.

'No,' she said. Though she spoke softly, everyone nearby suddenly went silent. Heads turned. People were staring, frowning, gathering closer so they wouldn't miss whatever might be happening. 'Please let go,' Dana said. 'I don't . . .'

Her fingertip vanished into the mouth of the creepy vampire gal. She felt the suck of warm, quick lips.

Onlookers gasped, flinched and muttered.

'Hey!' Dana jerked her hand back.

Tuck, watching, had a strange smile on her face as if she couldn't believe what had just happened.

'Mmmm, delicious,' the creep said. She licked her black lips. 'Now we're sisters. My name is Vein. V-e-i-n as in bloooood vessel.'

'Right,' Dana muttered. Being more careful this time, she reached into the bag and took out a badge. It was round with a pin on the back, like a political campaign button. Larger than a silver dollar, it showed a small black rendition of Beast House on a scarlet background. Around the rim, in black letters, it read MIDNIGHT TOURIST.

'Pin it on me.' Vein spread open her black leather jacket and thrust her bra-clad breasts toward Dana.

'Thanks anyway,' Dana said. 'Here. Just take it.'

'No no no. Pin it on me, dahhhling.'

'What's the problem here?' Tuck asked.

'Dana's shy,' Vein said.

'*I'm* not,' Tuck said, and snatched the badge out of Dana's hand. Grinning up at Vein, she asked, 'Where do you want it?'

Vein patted the front of her left bra cup, sending a tremor through her breast.

'I wouldn't want to poke you,' Tuck said.

'Oh, feel free.'

'How about here?' Not waiting for an answer, Tuck slipped a finger under the left shoulder strap, pulled it away from Vein's skin, and pinned the badge to it.

'Thank you so much, my dear.'

Tuck patted the badge. 'I'm here to serve,' she said. Then she dipped a hand into Dana's bag, came up with another badge, and turned to Vein's blond friend. 'Would you like me to pin yours on, too?'

Looking at Tuck with sultry eyes, the blonde said, 'I'm Darke.'

'Could've fooled me,' Tuck said.

Darke's tongue darted out and wiggled at her.

'Trying to upstage the beast?' Tuck asked.

Several of the others laughed.

'Way cool,' said Arnold.

Safari man blurted, 'Bravo!'

Vein and Darke strolled away holding hands.

Everyone seemed to be watching them.

After they were out of earshot – probably – the woman in the tennis outfit said, 'To think they're someone's children.'

'I don't envy their parents,' said the fellow beside her. Probably her husband.

'Did you see what she did?' Dennis asked. 'She sucked Dana's blood.'

'Cool,' Arnold said.

'Nothing cool about it, young chap! Assault and battery, plain and simple. She ought to be incarcerated!'

'They *do* seem a bit eccentric,' said a mustached man who looked as if he'd stepped out of *Gentleman's Quarterly*. 'Personally, though, I feel as if I've already gotten at least *half* my money's worth. I can hardly wait to see what Vein does next.'

'Maybe she'll suck *me*,' Dennis said, and blushed as his comment raised some laughter.

'You *already* suck, dipshit.'

Dana started to laugh.

Raising a hand, Tuck announced, 'I'm still open to the idea of taking your tickets and letting you in. Anybody interested?'

First to come through was the safari man. As Dana offered the badge to him, he said, 'I'd be pleased to inspect your wound. I'm a doctor, you know.'

'Are you?'

'Dr Clive Bixby, Ph.D., professor of literature, U.C. Santa Cruz.'

'Ah. You're not a medical doctor?'

'Hasn't stopped me yet! I'm a master of many arts, including but not limited to the art of healing.'

Dana raised her finger.

He took the pipe out of his mouth, removed his glasses, and peered at her fingertip. 'Antiseptic! Bandage! Take two aspirin. Call me in the morning.' He hiked up an eyebrow, jabbed the pipe into his teeth, and put his glasses back on. 'In case of infection,' he said, 'we'll *remove* it.'

'Oh, great.'

'Cheers,' he said, and hurried on.

Next to come through was the stocky man, followed by his wife in the tennis outfit. They smiled and took their badges, thanked Dana and moved on.

Normal people, Dana thought.

Then came Owen and Monica.

I'd better watch my mouth.

'Welcome aboard,' she said to Owen.

'Hi,' he said. He looked as if he wanted to scream or run away.

'Glad to see you both made it,' she said. She handed one badge to Owen, another to Monica. Speaking directly to Monica, she said, 'I hope you have a really good time tonight.'

Bobbing her head and showing her teeth, Monica said, 'Thank you so very much. I'm sure it will be memorable. For all of us.'

Owen cringed.

Poor guy. What'd she do, track him down?

Monica pulled his hand, dragging him away.

When Arnold stepped up to Dana, he said, 'Weird chick, huh?'

'Pretty weird.'

'Did it hurt?'

'What?'

'How she got your finger. Did she, like, *bite* it?'

'Oh, *her*. No, she didn't bite. I'm fine.'

'That's good. I mean, it was cool and all, but it wouldn't be so cool if she hurt you.'

'Sure hope she hasn't got rabies,' Dennis threw in.

'Shut up, shithead.'

'*I* wanta pin a badge on her. I'd stick it in her tittie. Prick her tittie.'

'Okay, Dennis,' Dana said.

'I'd, like, prick her *anywhere*.'

Arnold slugged him on the arm.

'Ow!'

'Don't be such an ass-wipe.'

'That *hurt*, dude.'

Dana quickly gave them badges. 'Go on in and have a good time, okay? Try to be nice.'

Next in line was the mustached man. 'Is it always this zany?' he asked.

'This is my first time,' Dana explained, and handed a badge to him.

'I won't even ask you to pin it on me.'

'I'd be happy to pin one on *you*.'

He blushed slightly and glanced at the woman beside him. 'I'm not sure Alison would appreciate that. But thank you for the offer. I'm Andy Lawrence, by the way. This is my wife, Alison.'

'Nice to meet you,' Dana said. 'I hope you enjoy yourselves tonight.'

'It's off to a pretty good start,' Andy said. 'They were ringers, weren't they?'

'Huh?'

'Vein and Darke. Ringers. It was staged?'

'I wish.'

Looking amused, Alison said, 'We thought it might be part of the show. It seemed slightly too bizarre to be real.'

'You should've been at *this* end.'

'Are you all right?' Alison asked.

'Fine.'

'You really *ought* to put some antiseptic on it.'

'I should say so,' Andy agreed. 'You never know where a mouth like that might've been.'

'Thanks. I'll take care of it.'

As they walked away, Tuck stepped over. 'We're still short two customers. I'll stick around and watch for them. Why don't you go on over and enjoy the picnic? You shouldn't leave Warren alone for very long – he'll suffer withdrawal pangs. Might start weeping, or something.'

Dana gave her the finger.

Laughing, Tuck asked, 'Too bad about that. Now you'll turn *in*to one.'

'A finger?'

'A Vein.'

'If that happens, put me out of my misery.'

'Cheerfully. With a nipple-ring-extractor.'

Dana cringed. 'Don't say stuff like that. Jeez! I hurt just thinking about it. Besides, what makes you think she *has* nipple rings?'

'What makes you think she *doesn't?*'

'I'm getting out of here.' She gave Tuck the bag of badges. 'See you later,' she said. 'Try not to poke yourself.'

Chapter Fifty

Picnic

'Buy me a glass of white wine, Owie.'

'Sure,' he said, and hurried over the grass to the bar.

Darke, in front of him, was paying for two glasses of red wine.

'I thought you folks only drank blood,' Owen said.

Darke picked up the glasses and looked at him with lazy, half-shut eyes. 'Is that an observation or an offer?'

Wishing he'd kept his mouth shut, Owen shrugged. 'Just asking. My name's Owen.' He thought about putting out his hand for a shake, but Darke was holding two drinks.

Just as well.

Owen didn't really want to *touch* a freaky, effeminate guy like this.

'I'm Darke.'

'I know. I heard.'

'What's your blood type, Owen?'

The question made him feel nervous. 'I don't know.'

'Vein prefers O negative.'

'Ah.'

'I simply like mine *warm*.'

'I like mine on the rocks,' Owen said, and tried to smile.

Darke looked unamused. 'We'll see you later.'

As Darke glided away, Owen turned to the bar and took a deep breath.

'Don't let her rattle you,' the bartender said.

'Huh?'

'She's just trying to shake your cage.'

'*She?*'

'Her.'

Owen glanced over his shoulder at Darke. 'Her? That's not woman. Is it?'

'You better believe it, sonny.'

He found the idea strangely exciting. 'How do you know?'

The bartender winked and said, 'Oh, nothing much gets past *me*. So, what'll you have?'

'A white wine and a vodka tonic.'

'Comin' right up.' As he prepared the drinks, he asked, 'A squeeze of lime in the vodka tonic?'

'Sure. Thanks. Are you absolutely *sure* that was a woman?'

'Not only was, still is.'

Owen chuckled nervously and shook his head. He paid for the drinks, leaving the bartender a large tip. Then he picked up the glasses and turned around.

He saw Darke standing with Vein.

Is it possible?

The bartender was probably just pulling my chain, he told himself, and looked for Dana. He spotted her striding toward the barbecue grills . . . toward the one in particular where her loverboy was busy turning hamburgers.

She wasn't wearing a jacket.

Isn't she cold? Owen wondered.

He thought about offering his windbreaker to her.

Oh, Monica would love that.

He stared at the way Dana's rump moved inside the seat of her shorts as she walked.

Catching loverboy's eye, she raised an arm in greeting.

Owen looked away.

And found Monica staring at him. He forced himself to smile.

Approaching her, he kept the smile on his face.

Why the hell did she come back? Doesn't she know when she's not wanted? Ha! That's a good one.

He stopped in front of Monica and gave her the glass of wine.

'Thank you, kind sir,' she said, her voice lilting.

'You're welcome.'

'You don't seem very happy that I'm here.'

'Why *are* you here?'

She sipped some wine, then smiled. 'Did you really think I'd let you get away?'

'Monica . . .'

'You never had me fooled,' she said. 'I knew *exactly* where you'd gone. Back here to Beast House and your precious slut.'

'Don't talk about her that way.'

'I'll talk about her any way I like.' Monica looked toward Dana and glared at her. 'The overgrown bitch. I can't imagine what you see in her.'

'I didn't leave because of her. I left because of *you*.'

'As if.'

'It's true.'

'You *loved* me till she came along.'

Let's change the subject fast, he thought. And said, 'So how did you get here? Take the bus, or . . .?'

'You've got to be kidding. Do you think I'd put myself through *that* again?'

'What did you do?'

'Rented a car.'

'When was that?' Owen asked. Suddenly, he was afraid to hear the answer.

What if she's been here all along? Watching me. Following me. Maybe

SHE was the one in the bushes last night . . . did something to John so she could get his ticket.

No, that's ridiculous.

'Oh, I've been here for a while,' she said. With a benign smile, she added, 'As a matter of fact, honey, you and I have adjoining rooms.'

'*What?*'

'At the Welcome Inn.'

Monica made the mystery call!

Though still shocked and disoriented, Owen felt a small measure of relief. The ringing phone had shaken him awake at about a quarter till four this afternoon. If Monica had come into town earlier, she would've called sooner.

'You're the one who phoned?' he asked.

'That's right.'

'Ahhh.'

Owen took a few swallows of his drink, enjoying its taste.

She got into town this afternoon – had nothing to do with John or the creep in the bushes or anything else that happened yesterday.

Probably.

'You were in your room all by yourself,' Monica told him, looking very pleased with herself. 'I knew you must be missing me, so I phoned to invite you over for a little lovey-dovey.' Taking a drink of wine, she stared at him over the rim of her glass. 'I was sprawled on the bed, all decked out in my birthday suit. I'd already opened my side of the connecting door. When you picked up the phone, I planned to say, "Come and get it, big fella." But then I heard your voice and realized that you didn't deserve me. Not after what you'd done. I don't put out for naughty little boys who run away from me. So I hung up.'

'What a shame,' Owen said.

'You'll have to *earn* your way back.'

'I'm not interested.'

'Oh yes, you are. Can't fool Monica. I know you want me. You *always* want me. You're so predicatable.' Stepping closer to him, she pressed her open hand against the front of his trousers.

Owen took a quick step backward.

Raising her upper lip, Monica growled softly.

'Stop that.'

She smiled. 'You want me right now.'

'Right now, I want a hamburger.'

He turned and walked away, but Monica stayed by his side like a perky, vengeful shadow.

How am I *ever* going to get rid of her? he wondered.

He felt trapped, crushed.

No matter what, tonight's ruined. She'll make sure of that.

Owen sipped his drink, nodded and smiled at some of the other Midnight Tourists as he made his way toward the barbecue grills. There were three grills. On one, hamburgers sizzled. Dana was manning it with her loverboy. Sirloin steaks were being prepared on the second grill by the chubby, shy guide named Rhonda. The third grill held a combination of hot dogs and Polish sausages. Behind it, turning the food with tongs, was a young brunette who didn't look familiar to Owen.

'Over here,' Monica said, and headed for the third grill.

'I thought I'd have a hamburger.'

'Don't be ridiculous. You know how much you love Polish sausage.'

'I like hamburgers, too.'

'You just want to flirt with your slut. Besides, look at her. She already *has* a boyfriend, and he's a lot more handsome than you. She won't give you the time of day. Now, come on. You *know* you'd rather eat Polish sausage.'

I'll get a burger later, Owen told himself.

He followed Monica to the third grill.

'May I help you please?' the worker asked. Like the others, she wore the tan uniform of a Beast House guide. Owen guessed she was no older than twenty. She had short brown hair and large, nervous eyes. Her nameplate read, WINDY.

'We'll have two Polish sausages with the works,' Monica told her.

'Are you a guide?' Owen asked. 'I don't think I've seen you before.'

'I work at the snack stand,' she said, smiling a little.

'I thought *he* did,' Owen said, and nodded toward loverboy.

'Warren? He owns it. I help out part time at the windows. I served your lunch yesterday.'

'Really?'

'You and your friend.'

Holy shit!

'Ah,' Owen said. He smiled and nodded as if nothing had gone wrong. 'That's right. I remember you now.'

Windy turned away to finish preparing the sandwiches.

'What friend?' Monica asked.

'Just some guy I met.'

'Guy. I'm sure.'

Windy came back with two paper plates. On each was a Polish sausage in a long roll. They were gloppy with yellow mustard, onions and peppers. Steam rose off the grilled sausages as she handed the plates to Monica and Owen.

'Enjoy them,' she said, smiling pleasantly.

'Thank you, Windy,' Owen said.

'You're an absolute treasure,' Monica said.

Windy's smile slipped crooked.

Owen cringed.

As he hurried away, Monica kept pace beside him and said, 'So, Owie, tell me more about your mysterious friend.'

'It was a guy.'

'Mmm. I'm sure.'

'If you don't believe me, go back and ask Windy.'

'Oh, that won't be necessary. I believe you. If you say your friend was a guy, your friend was a guy.'

He hurried to the nearest picnic table. A few people were already there, but one of the side benches had room for two. 'Mind if we join you?' he asked.

'Sit, dude,'

'You, too, dudette.'

They climbed over the bench, placed their plates and glasses on the table cloth, and sat down.

'Hi,' Owen said. 'I'm Owen and this is Monica.'

'Dude. I'm Dennis.'

'I'm Arnold.'

'We're A.A. and D.D.'

'Nice to meet you, guys.'

Monica, ignoring them, took a drink of wine.

'Dr Clive Bixby, here!' proclaimed Jungle Jim. He waved from the other end of the table, then bit into a hamburger.

Ignoring it all, Monica set down her glass. She turned her head toward Owen, smiled with mocking sweetness, and said, 'So, what was your friend's name?'

'John.'

'What an unusual name.'

'It is?'

'For a girl. And how was she in bed?'

'John was a guy.'

'So you say.'

He stared into Monica's eyes. In them, he saw cold, amused contempt.

He picked up his icy glass in one hand, his Polish sausage sandwich in the other, stood up and climbed off the bench. 'Excuse me,' he said.

'Where're you going now?'

'Just stay here.'

He rushed away. After a few seconds, he glanced back. Monica was twisted around on the bench, watching him but still seated.

Fucking bitch, ruins everything!

She was still on the bench when he reached the corner of Beast House.

He hurried to the rear patio area and entered the men's restroom.

It was well lighted, clean-smelling, and it seemed to be deserted. It had five stalls. He entered the one in the middle. The toilet seat looked clean. He locked the stall door, then sat down.

And drank his drink.

And ate his Polish sausage sandwich.

And struggled to keep from crying.

After a while, Owen began to feel better. The vodka tonic had warmed him up inside, calmed him down – and the sausage had tasted awfully good.

He looked at his wristwatch.

8:40

The movie wouldn't be starting for another hour and twenty minutes.

I oughta just wait here, he thought. Let Monica enjoy her *own* company till ten, see how she likes it.

But I'll miss the whole picnic.

I want another drink. I want a cheeseburger. I want to be where I can at least look at Dana every once in a while.

He suddenly imagined John Cromwell chuckling, shaking his head and saying, *'What's the matter with you, buddy? Hiding in the john 'cause you're scared of that smirky twat? Fuck it, man. Go out and have a good time. She gives you any trouble, stomp her ass.'*

Owen smiled. Right on, he thought.

Then he heard the restroom door swing open.

Shit!

He heard footfalls on the tile floor. Someone took two or three steps, then stopped. The door bumped shut.

Silence.

More silence.

Is it Monica? Would she really dare come into a men's john?

It didn't seem likely . . . but she might.

Why is she just *standing* there? he wondered.

He didn't like that.

'Helllowwww, Owennnn!' Not Monica's voice.

'Youuu-whoooo.' A second voice. Also, not Monica's.

One sounded like a female voice, but the other . . . sounded like Darke.

It's them.

Vein and Darke.

Oh my God!

'We know you're here,' Vein said.

'Are you trying to hide from us?' asked Darke.

'I'm not hiding,' Owen said. 'I'm having . . . a little stomach trouble.'

'Liar, liar, pants on fire,' sang Darke.

'We know why you're here,' said Vein.

'She isn't coming,' Darke said.

'Nobody is.'

'We're all alone.'

'Just the three of us.'

Trying to keep the worry out of his voice, Owen said, 'Uhhh . . . This is a *men's* restroom, you know.'

'Woops,' said Vein. 'Are you going to report us?'

'No, but . . .'

Footsteps.

Here they come!

'I'll be done in just a minute,' Owen said. 'Why don't we meet outside, or something?'

'This is such a nice, private place,' Vein said.

The door of the stall to Owen's left squeaked open. Footsteps strolled past his bolted door. A second later, the stall door to his right swung open.

What're they doing?

They won't try anything . . .

He tipped back his head.

Vein on the left and Darke on the right grinned down at Owen from the top of the stall partitions. He supposed they must be standing on the toilets.

'There you are,' said Darke.

'Such a modest boy,' said Vein. 'Takes a crap with his pants up.'

Blushing fiercely, he said, 'I just came in here for some peace and quiet.' He stood up. He shifted his empty glass to his left hand. With his right, he snapped the bolt clear. 'You can have the place to yourselves, now.' He pulled the stall door open. Stepping out, he said, 'I'd better be getting back to the picnic.'

Vein and Darke leaped from their stalls, Vein in front of him, Darke behind him.

Vein blocked his way to the exit. Leering, she stretched her arms to each side. The motion spread the front of her black leather jacket. He glanced at her canyon of cleavage, at the snowy white breasts bulging from the cups of her bra. 'You don't want to leave,' she said.

'I'd really better be going.' He looked over his shoulder.

Darke gazed at him with languid, half-shut eyes and whispered, 'Stay.'

He turned toward Vein. She still held her arms out.

What would happen if I plow through her? She's bigger than I am, but . . .

Her left leg swung up. Swiftly and gracefully, she bent slightly at the waist and swept her right arm down and withdrew a knife from inside her boot.

Owen felt himself shrivel.

'Hey,' he said.

Vein grinned.

Owen looked at Darke, then at Vein. Then he turned slowly sideways. As he backed toward the wall, he found that he could keep his eyes on both of them at the same time. They made it easier by closing in.

'What do you want?' he asked, his voice shaking.

'Some of your blood,' said Vein.

'You're . . . kidding.' His back met the wall.

'Do you see us smiling?' Darke asked.

They were *both* smiling, but not as if much was funny.

Darke came in from the left, Vein from the right. They didn't stop until they were close enough to touch him.

'You *can't*,' Owen said.

'Certainly we can,' Vein said.

'And certainly we will,' said Darke. Reaching out, she took the glass from his hand.

'Somebody might come in,' he told them.

'Somebody might not.'

'It'll only take a few minutes,' Darke said, setting his glass on the floor.

'You can't *do* this.'

'Yesss,' said Darke. 'We can.'

Vein took hold of his hair and pressed his head against the wall.

'I'll yell! Somebody'll come and . . .'

His words stopped as his hand was lifted and slipped inside Darke's open black shirt and guided to a breast.

The bartender had been right.

The breast was a small, smooth mound under Owen's hand, tipped with a turgid nipple.

Vein's black lips pressed against his mouth. As her tongue thrust in, Owen felt fingers quickly unbuttoning his shirt. As he fondled Darke's breast, someone unfastened his trousers.

Pinned to the wall, he felt hands and mouths, tongues and teeth, quick hot flicks of the knife.

They sucked him, both at once.

What if somone comes in?

Nobody came in.

Not as they sucked and caressed him.

Not as he fondled and sucked and delved into them.

Not as all three of them sank onto the cold tile floor.

Not as Vein smothered him between her pillowy breasts and Darke straddled him, impaling herself.

Finally, drained, Owen lay sprawled on his back while Vein and Darke climbed off him and glided away.

'Why me?' he asked.

Vein, naked except for her boots, licked blood from her knife blade. 'Don't ask me, dahhling. It was Darke's idea.' She raised her left leg and slipped the knife down into the top of her boot.

Bending over, Darke stepped into her black leather pants. 'You're a nice guy,' she said, pulling them up.

'I am?'

'Sweet,' added Darke, fastening her belt. It had the white beast-head buckle, but Owen found that it didn't interest him nearly so much as Darke's breasts. They were so small and pale and had such large, dark nipples. He remembered their springy feel, their heat, their taste. He started getting hard again.

Darke glanced at his rising penis, smiled and met his eyes. 'Nice guys shouldn't always have to finish last,' she said. Digging a hand into a front pocket of her pants, she walked over to him. She pulled out a few bandages, then crouched beside him and tore one open.

Chapter Fifty-One

Final Warning

With only half an hour left before showtime at the movie theater, there wasn't much activity on the front lawn of Beast House. All the tourists seemed to be done with their main courses. Some sat at a table, chatting as they nibbled cake or sipped drinks. Others stood around in a small cluster, each holding a cocktail or a glass of wine. Several had drifted away.

Monica sat at one of the picnic tables, sipping red wine, talking and laughing with Dr Clive Bixby and the two late arrivals, a young, married couple named Phil and Connie.

Phil and Connie seemed like nice folks. Real Beast House fans. While Warren had prepared their burgers, they'd told Dana about ordering their Midnight Tour tickets six months in advance, then driving all the way up from San Diego (with a stopover in Boleta Bay) for tonight's festivities. They'd almost made it without incident, but a radiator hose had popped on Pacific Coast Highway only five miles south of town. So they'd walked the rest of the way and arrived an hour late.

Though Phil and Connie hadn't missed out on any of the food or drinks, they'd gotten ambushed by Monica and the professor.

Must be loads of laughs, Dana thought.

Maybe I should go to their rescue.

She put a hand on Warren's back. 'I think I'll join our friends over there.'

'Sure. Go ahead.'

'You could come, too. Doesn't look like we're being overrun by customers.'

Rhonda and Windy had already abandoned their grills. They were sitting across from each other at a picnic table, eating steaks and talking.

'I think I'm about ready for some food.' Warren said. 'How about you?'

'I'm starving.'

'You could've gone ahead and eaten.'

'Without you?'

'What'll you have?'

'How about a cheeseburger with the works?'

'My specialty.' He glanced at the three dark, dried-up patties already on the grill. 'Guess I'll throw on some fresh ones. You can go ahead and sit down. I'll be along when the burgers are done.'

'I'll get the drinks,' Dana said. 'What would you like?'

'Maybe a beer.'

'Coming up.' She patted his back, then walked over to the bar.

Biff was there, getting more refills for himself and his wife, Eleanor. Though Dana hadn't been trying to keep track, she'd seen Biff over here a number of times.

They're really gonna be juiced, she thought as she watched the bartender pour Scotch into two glasses half full of ice.

'After that,' Biff told him, 'it was hit the ball, drag Bob, hit the ball, drag Bob.'

Dana recognized the old joke. She wondered how many times the bartender had heard it.

He laughed, though.

Biff paid him, tucked a bill into the tip glass, then picked up his drinks and turned around. Dana sidestepped out of his way. He didn't seem to notice her. He walked carefully toward the place where his wife was standing with Tuck and the Lawrences. In spite of the chill, Eleanor hadn't put on her sweater. It was still tied around her neck and hanging down her back.

'*They're* feeling no pain,' the bartender said.

'The way his wife is dressed,' Dana said, 'she needs all the anti-freeze she can get.'

'And what'll *you* have?'

'A couple of beers.'

'Bud, Bud Lite, Corona . . .?'

'A couple of Buds would be great.'

He turned away from the counter and bent over an ice chest.

'My name's Dana, by the way.'

'I'm Hank.'

'Nice to meet you, Hank,' Dana said as he came back to the counter with a can of beer in each hand.

'Haven't seen you around before,' he said, snapping open the cans.

'This'll be my first Midnight Tour.' She opened her purse, took out her wallet, and found a ten-dollar bill.

'You're going *inside* tonight?' Hank asked, taking the bill.

'Yep.'

'Couldn't pay me enough to do that. Not at night. Hell, no.' He counted change into her hand. 'Not that I'm chicken. Just got more sense than that. Not that I'm saying *you* haven't got sense.'

Laughing, Dana slipped a bill into his tip glass.

'Thanks.'

'Have things *happened* on the Midnight Tour?' Dana asked.

'Folks go in, they don't come out.'

'Really?'

'That's what I hear.'

'Do you *know* of anyone not coming out?'

'I've heard plenty. I was in your shoes, I wouldn't go in there.'

'Sounds like traitor talk.'

Hank laughed.

'Do you say this stuff to the guests?'

'Sure. Why not? They already paid, right? Who's gonna get scared off after they've already forked out a hundred bucks? Anyhow, Lynn and Janice, they say I oughta keep it up. Folks come here to get scared, ain't that so? I give 'em what they're here for.'

'Ah, I see. It's just an act.'

'Nope, it ain't no act. I wouldn't step foot in that place for a million bucks. Not after dark. Not in broad daylight, either, for that matter, if you wanta know the truth. You couldn't *drag* me in there, night *or* day.'

'The last of the beasts were killed in seventy-nine,' Dana told him.

'So they say. But I ain't gonna stake my life on it. You shouldn't either. You're a mighty damn attractive lady, and it'd be a rotten shame if one of those critters laid its claws on you.'

Smiling, Dana said, 'I wouldn't care for that, myself.'

'Well, you may find it amusing now, but it ain't funny at all – what one of them monsters'd do to a honey like you. It'd rip the clothes off your back and have it's *way* with you, for starters. Know what I mean?'

Nodding, she said, 'I'd better get going. Nice meeting you, Hank.'

'It's got a tool on it the size of a belly club – with *teeth like a rat!*'

'See you later, Hank.' She hurried away from him. Instead of heading for the table to rescue Phil and Connie, she returned to Warren. She handed him a can of beer. 'Hank the bartender just warned me off the Midnight Tour.'

'Good for him,' Warren said.

'He's a pretty creepy guy.'

'What'd he have to say?'

Aware of Warren's own experiences in Beast House, she hesitated and felt herself blush. 'The usual. But he got pretty graphic about the thing's anatomy.'

Warren slipped a spatula under one of the patties. He flipped the burger. It hit the grill sizzling. 'I can't actually vouch for the business about the mouth and teeth down there. That part of it might be a myth. Or it might not be.' He flipped the other burger. 'Either way, you wouldn't want to get nailed by one.'

'I know *I* wouldn't.'

'Even if you survive, you'll never be the same.'

'Maybe we can have matching scars,' Dana said.

'It's nothing to joke about.'

'I'm sorry.' She lifted her can of Bud and took a drink.

'Well now,' Warren said.

'What.'

'Look.' He nodded to the left.

Off in the distance, three figures came striding across the lawn. Even though they were fuzzy through the fog, Dana instantly recognized Vein by her size and outfit. And that had to be Darke on the left. But who was the guy in the middle?

Owen?

'What's he doing with *them*?' Dana asked.

'Found a couple of new friends?' Warren suggested.

'Ohhh boy.'

Hand in hand, the trio walked diagonally across the front lawn. If they didn't change direction, they would end up at the front gate.

Probably on their way to the movie theater.

Is Owen planning to sit with *them*? Dana wondered.

Can't blame the guy. *I'd* sit with them, too, she thought, if it'd keep Monica away from me.

She glanced at the abandoned girlfriend.

Monica had been seated in the same place during the entire picnic, not once leaving her bench. Dr Bixby, sitting across from her, had sometimes strutted away to bring her refills of wine.

At the moment, the professor was holding forth with great conviction and volume about Bigfoot. Monica, Phil and Connie seemed to be paying close attention to his lecture.

The angle taken by Owen, Vein and Darke would lead them straight into Monica's line of vision.

Maybe Bixby's head'll block her view . . .

Tuck suddenly seemed to be aware of possible trouble. She ended whatever discussion she'd been having with Biff, Eleanor, Andy and Alison, stepped away from their group and watched Owen hurry by with Vein and Darke. Then she checked on Monica. After that, head rising slightly, she seemed to look at Dana.

Dana nodded to her.

Tuck nodded back.

Any second, now . . .

Monica flinched, her back jerking rigid.

'Saw 'em,' Warren muttered.

'Yep,' said Dana.

Monica started to rise from her bench. She stood halfway up, possibly to eliminate Dr Bixby's head from the picture.

'She might not recognize Owen,' Warren said. 'All this fog, that could be just about anyone.'

'Process of elimination might give her a clue,' Dana said. 'He's only been missing for the whole picnic.'

Monica sank back down in her seat.

Bixby said something to her. Dana caught only the word, 'wrong.'

Monica shook her head, her ponytail jerking from side to side. Then, leaning forward, she reached across the table and patted the professor's hand.

'Crisis averted,' Warren said.

Tuck seemed to agree. She stopped watching, glanced at her wrist-watch, then turned around and rejoined her small group.

'Guess the burgers are done,' Warren said.

'I'll get the buns. You want mayo or mustard?'

'Mayo.'

'Excellent choice.'

Warren tossed slabs of cheese onto the dark patties while Dana slathered the buns with mayonaise.

Just as Warren was slipping the patties onto their buns, Tuck announced, 'It's ten till ten, everyone. If you're interested in the special Midnight Tour screening of *The Horror*, better start heading over to the Haunted Palace theater. The film will begin at ten. I'm on my way over right now, so you can follow me if you like.'

Tuck stepped closer to her group. A few seconds later, they began heading for the gate, Tuck leading the way.

By the time Dana and Warren were ready to find seats, nobody remained at any of the tables except Windy and Rhonda. Hank was busy cleaning up his bar.

Dana saw Monica leave the grounds, walking with Dr Bixby.

'Maybe she's found true love,' Warren said.

Dana let out a laugh. 'I hope so. But somehow I doubt it.'

'Shall we sit with Rhonda and Windy?' Warren asked.

'I think we probably should.'

'Mind if we join you?' Warren called to them.

'Come on over, boss,' Windy called, and Rhonda smiled at them.

On the way over, Warren said to Dana, 'If you're not careful, you'll miss the start of the movie.'

'I've seen it before.'

'But never the special, exclusive screening for the Midnight Tour.'

'I can catch it next week.'

'You really *should* see it tonight, or you won't get the full experience.' Sounding hopeful, he added, 'Unless you've changed your mind about the tour.'

'No, I still want to do that.'

'You shouldn't miss the movie, then.'

'But I want to eat with you.'

'Well . . . the show never starts on time, anyway. You probably have fifteen or twenty minutes.'

'Then I'll eat with you *and* catch the movie.'

They sat down beside each other, across the table from Rhonda and Windy.

Dana took a long drink of beer. 'What about Hank?' she asked. 'Do you think he'd like to join us?'

'He's awful,' Rhonda said. 'Have you ever *talked* to him? Yug!'

'He's a real sicko,' Windy said.

'Besides which,' said Warren, 'he never eats with us. We've asked him before. He likes to get out of here as early as he can. Which reminds me – do you want another beer?'

'Sounds good,' Dana said.

'Ladies?'

'No thanks,' Rhonda said. 'I'm about ready to get started with the cleanup.'

'Me, too,' said Windy. 'The sooner we start, the sooner we'll be done.'

Warren excused himself and hurried toward the bar.

Smiling, Windy leaned foward and said to Dana, 'Whatever you've been doing to him, don't stop. Okay? He's been like a new man ever since you first showed up.'

Dana grinned. 'Glad to hear it.'

'But he's worried about you. He has a real problem with anyone going in the house after dark. Do you know what happened to him in there?'

'He told me,' Dana said, and wondered what he'd told Windy. A lot, probably. After all, they worked together inside the snack stand day after day. 'He got beaten up by some thugs?' Dana asked.

To Dana's relief, Windy nodded.

Then Windy said, 'He's really scared something might happen to you if you go on the tour.'

'I guess it shows he cares.'

'Cares a *lot*,' Windy said. 'You ask me, he's in love with you.' She glanced to the side. 'Here he comes. Don't tell him I said that, okay?'

Feeling a tightness in her throat, Dana smiled at the girl.

Warren placed an open can of beer in front of Dana, then climbed over the bench and sat down beside her.

'Thanks for the brew,' she said, and put a hand on his back.

He leaned sideways, bumping her gently. Then he said, 'You're going to be late for the movie if you don't start eating.'

'I had to wait for you.'

'I'm here. Eat.'

She took a large bite out of her cheeseburger, moaning with pleasure as the flavors flooded her mouth.

'Tell you what,' Windy said. 'Why don't you *both* go to the movie?'

'That's a *great* idea,' Rhonda agreed.

Warren shook his head. 'I can't leave you two with all this mess.'

'We insist,' Windy said. 'Besides, Lynn'll be along in a little while and give us a hand.'

'That's awfully nice of you, but . . .'

'It's no big deal,' Windy said.

'We insist,' said Rhonda.

'If it'll make you feel better, you can do *our* share of the cleanup next week.'

'Well, in that case . . .'

'We accept your offer,' Dana said. 'And thank you. That's *very* nice.'

'You'd better get going,' Windy said.

'Take your food with you,' Rhonda suggested. 'You can eat and drink as you walk.'

'Wanta?' Warren asked Dana.

'Fine with me.'

Leaving their plates on the table, they picked up their burgers and beers. Then they climbed clear of the bench. On their way around the table, they both thanked Windy and Rhonda again.

As they hurried toward the gate, Rhonda called, 'See you later.'

'See you,' Dana called back.

'Be good,' Rhonda advised.

Windy elbowed her. 'Don't tell them *that*.'

The two girls laughed.

'*Don't* be good,' Rhonda called.

'Be *great!*' shouted Windy.

Chapter Fifty-Two

The Haunted Palace

When Owen arrived at the theater with Vein and Darke, the marquee was dark, the ticket booth empty. But the lobby lights were on. Through the glass door, Owen saw a Beast House guide standing alone on the red carpet, staring out at them.

The big, smirky-looking guy.

The muscle-bound jerk.

God's gift to women.

Clyde.

He strolled over to the door and opened it. 'Midnight Tourists?' he asked, a cigarette jerking between his lips.

Owen tapped a finger against the badge pinned to his chest.

Clyde nodded at it, then glanced at Darke. She dipped fingers into a breast pocket of her black silk shirt, drew out her red badge and showed it to him.

'And how about you?' he asked Vein.

After leaving the men's restroom at Beast House, she had zipped up her leather jacket. Now, she skidded the zipper down and pulled her jacket wide open.

Clyde grinned around his cigarette. 'Ah,' he said. '*There* it is. Please come in.'

They entered the lobby.

Though Clyde couldn't seem to take his eyes off Vein's chest, he made no lewd or suggestive comments.

Probably afraid of us, Owen thought.

Clyde seemed large and strong enough to handle all three of them at once, but Owen figured he must be creeped out – at least a little – by Vein and Darke.

'The show'll be starting in just a few minutes,' he said. 'Feel free to wait out here in the lobby, if you like. Or you can go in and choose your seats.' As if addressing only Vein, he said, 'My name's Clyde. I'm one of the Beast House tour guides.'

'Will you be our guide tonight?' Vein asked.

'Not tonight. That'll be Lynn Tucker.'

'Pity,' Vein said.

'I'm only the projectionist for tonight.' He tapped some ash from his cigarette. 'But I work Wednesday through Sunday at Beast House.'

'Maybe we'll see each other again,' Vein said.

Clyde grinned and nodded.

'That wasn't a come-on,' Darke told him. 'That was a threat.'

Clyde stood taller and his eyes narrowed. 'Maybe you three had better go in and take your seats.'

Vein pursed her black lips and kissed the air. 'It's been a slice, dahhhling.' To Owen and Darke, she said, 'Come along, dears.'

They followed her into the theater auditorium. Overhead lights were on, illuminating two aisles, row upon row of empty red seats, a slim edge of stage and an enormous white movie screen.

Sitting near the middle of the second row were Dennis and Arnold. They looked over their shoulders and waved.

'Dudes!' called Dennis.

'Greetings!' called Arnold.

'Children of the night!'

'Vampires rule!'

Vein bared her teeth at them.

'Whoa!'

'Awesome!'

'How you doing, guys?' Owen called.

'Flyin' high, dude!'

'Top notch!'

Darke stuck out her tongue and wiggled it at them.

Dennis hooted.

Arnold squealed.

Then Vein pulled her jacket off, swung it over one shoulder, and started striding down the aisle.

Dennis and Arnold stared at her, struck silent.

Vein stopped a few rows back from the guys. 'In here,' she said to Owen and Darke. She sidestepped toward the middle of the row. Owen went in next, followed by Darke. Arriving at the seat she wanted, Vein spread her leather jacket across its back. Then she turned toward the watching boys. 'It promises to be a most interesting night,' she said to them. Writhing, she slid her tongue across her lips and gave her left breast a slow massage through her bra. 'See you later, dahhhlings,' she said, and sank down into her seat.

Dennis and Arnold turned toward the screen.

Vein grinned. Darke laughed softly. Owen sat between them, feeling a little nervous but also, strangely, very safe. As if he'd found himself a couple of spectacular bodyguards – weird, maybe, but *his*.

It seemed more like some sort of wild dream.

A great dream.

After so many things going so badly, to be followed into the men's room by these two bizarre, incredible strangers . . .

Did we really do all that?

Damn straight, he thought, and smiled. He could feel the reality of it all over his body.

They aren't exactly strangers anymore.

Turning his head, he looked at Darke. She was staring forward, her eyes half shut.

How could I ever think she was a guy?

She looked at him. A corner of her mouth tilted slightly. Then she leaned toward him, reached over the chair arm that separated them, and gently took hold of his hand.

His heart raced. His mouth went dry.

This is crazy, he thought.

She's holding my hand like a normal girl.

But the feel of a girl's hand hadn't made Owen feel like *this* in a very long time. Not since he was thirteen, he supposed. Thirteen and holding Nancy Farrow's hand . . .

'Is this row all right with you, professor?'

Monica's voice.

It gave Owen a sudden sick feeling.

Darke's hand tightened its grip.

'Lady's choice,' Bixby said, his voice booming at its usual volume.

Owen swung his head, peered over his right shoulder and saw Monica coming down the aisle with the professor.

'What do you want to do?' Darke whispered.

The sound of her voice sent a thrilling warmth through Owen. He looked into her eyes. 'I don't know.'

'I don't want to get you in trouble,' she said.

'Speak for yourself,' Vein said.

'I mean it.' Darke released her hold on Owen's hand, but he kept his grip on hers. Her eyes widened a little. She pressed her lips together.

'This'll be fine,' Monica said.

Owen kept his eyes on Darke's eyes. But he noticed that Monica's voice had come from nearby.

'If you want her back,' Darke whispered, 'I can help.'

'I don't.'

'Are you sure?'

'I can't stand her.'

Nodding slightly, Darke squeezed his hand. Her eyes shifted sideways, then returned to Owen. 'Looks like she's going to sit behind us.'

'Owie, is that you?'

He twisted in his seat and forced himself to smile. 'Hello, Monica.'

She sat down directly behind Darke. 'You've met Professor Bixby, haven't you?'

'Hi, Clive.'

'Owie,' Clive boomed, and dropped into the seat behind him. 'Too bad you missed the picnic. We had a ripping good time!'

'Glad to hear it,' Owen said.

'Had a spot of digestive trouble, did you?'

'Right.'

'A shame. Likely the Polish sausage. But of course, your sister *also* ate the Polish, and had no trouble at all.'

'Owie has *such* sensitive bowels,' Monica explained, smiling at Darke. *Sister?*

Twisting around farther, Owen said to Bixby, 'If my bowels are sensitive, it's because Monica is such a pain in the ass. I didn't have digestive troubles. I escaped from the picnic to get away from *her*. And she's *not* my sister. She's my *former* girl friend. Presently, she's my *stalker*.'

Clive looked astonished. 'I say,' he said.

Monica, sitting rigid and motionless, smiled sweetly at Owen and said, 'I'm the best thing that ever happened to you, buster.'

'What a laugh. You're an obnoxious bitch and I'm sick of you.'

'That's no way to talk to the lady, young chap,' Bixby said.

Darke turned her head. 'What's with you and your fake accent, professor?'

'Ah! Now we have the *castrato* weighing in.'

'Get bit,' Darke said.

Vein twisted around. 'Can't we all just get along?' she said, glancing from Bixby to Monica. 'Otherwise, I may pay you a visit during the show. You might not care for that.'

They both stared at her.

The lights went off.

Owen turned forward.

In the total darkness, Monica said, 'I've had enough of this foolishness. Come back here and sit with me, Owen. Right now. I'm not kidding.'

He didn't answer.

Suddenly, a spotlight came on. Its beam slanted down through the darkness and lit the center of the stage. There stood Lynn Tucker, a microphone in one hand.

'I guess everyone's here,' she said. 'Welcome to the Haunted Palace. Before we start the film, let me give you some background. In 1982, the year of *The Horror's* original release, Malcasa Point didn't have a functioning movie theater. The old theater had burnt down a few years earlier. But Janice Crogan really wanted *The Horror* to be shown *somewhere* in town. After all, she'd written the book it was based on, and the film was about Malcasa Point. It'd be a shame, she thought, if none of her friends or neighbors would get a chance to see it. So she asked for permission to show the film at the high-school auditorium. No dice. The Legion hall. No dice. The Elks. Nope. The K. of C. Huh-uh. She even asked permission at a couple of local churches. Everybody refused. When *The Horror* came out, Janice could find only one suitable place to show it – the dining room of the Welcome Inn. She *owned* the Welcome Inn, and she couldn't very well refuse her own request.'

A few quiet chuckles came from audience members scattered around the auditorium.

Monica said, 'Lame.'

'The very first local screening took place at ten o'clock on a Saturday night in the dining room of the Welcome Inn – projected onto a bed sheet that Janice hung on the wall. There was standing room only. Soon after that, Janice purchased a parcel of property and began the construction of her own movie theater. She modelled it after a place called The Haunted Palace that she'd read about . . .'

'Poe,' proclaimed Dr Bixby. ' "A hideous throng rush out forever, and laugh – but smile no more." '

Lynn smiled. 'Nifty poem.'

'It's called, "The Haunted Palace." It can be found in "The Fall of the House of Usher." '

'That was *not* Janice Crogan's source,' Darke said in a firm, clear voice.

'I beg to differ,' Bixby said.

'Actually,' Lynn said, 'that's correct. Was that you, Darke?'

'That was me.'

'You know your stuff.'

'Thanks.'

'Janice's inspiration for The Haunted Palace didn't come from Edgar Allan Poe, it came from a relatively unknown horror novel published in 1982. The book told about a movie theater that exclusively showed horror films . . .'

'And snuff films,' Darke whispered to Owen.

He nodded.

'. . . what Janice wanted to do with *her* theater.'

'I read it,' Owen said. As Darke smiled and nodded, he whispered the title of the book, the name of the author.

'. . . under construction, she continued to show *The Horror* every Saturday night at . . .'

'I love his stuff,' Darke whispered.

'. . . Welcome Inn's dining room.'

'Me, too,' whispered Owen.

Darke squeezed his hand.

'. . . until she opened The Haunted Palace in 1984. From that time on, this theater has been running a full schedule of classic and contemporary horror films. But every Saturday night, it closes its doors to the general public at about nine o'clock and opens again at ten for the exclusive, Midnight Tour screening of *The Horror*.

'Before I go on to talk to you about the film itself, are there any questions about the theater?'

'Does it, like, show the *good* stuff?'

Lynn smiled and shook her head. 'Such as?'

'*I Spit on Your Grave*, man. It's the best.'

'How about *Cannibal*? That's *way* cool.'

'*The Hills Have Eyes?*'

'What about *Chain Saw?*'

'*Last House on the Left?*'

Lynn held up a hand. 'Those have all been shown here, guys, but . . .'

'What's *your* fave?'

'Hard to say. But we do need to start *The Horror* fairly soon. If you'll leave your names and addresses, we'll put you on The Haunted Palace mailing list. There's a sign-up sheet in the theater lobby. Any more questions?'

'Do you show *Cabin Boy*?'

'I'm not sure it's a horror film,' Lynn said.

'Sure it is. It's got, like, a *giant*.'

'It's got, like, *Dave*.'

'Young men!' Bixby bellowed. 'Some of us are not *interested* in your drivel.'

'Like, chill, dude,' Dennis said.

'Take a Prozac, ass-wipe,' said Arnold.

Lynn frowned at them. 'That's enough, guys. I'd like to get in a few words about the movie.'

Behind Owen, Bixby muttered, 'Did one of those little shits call me an ass-wipe?'

'Okay,' Lynn said into the microphone. 'Most of you are probably already familiar with the background of *The Horror*, or you wouldn't be here. So I'll make it brief. The film was based on Janice Crogan's 1980 bestseller, *The Horror at Malcasa Point*, and made by an independent film company that called itself Malcasa Pictures. The screenplay was written by Steve Saunders, and the director was Ray Cunningham. The entire picture was filmed on location here in town in the summer of 1980.

'The making of *The Horror* was delayed by a situation that's probably no less strange than the story of Beast House, itself. It's been written up . . . many times. There've even been segments about it on such TV shows as *Hard Copy* and *Unsolved Mysteries*.

'As most of you already know, the legendary Marlon Slade came into town to direct *The Horror*. The leading lady was set to be played by Tricia Talbot, a beautiful young actress who would later go on to star in such movies as *Silent Shriek* and *Sunset Nights* before her tragic death in 1988.

'Tricia was supposed to play the role of Janice Crogan in *The Horror*. However, the night before shooting was scheduled to begin, she was brutally beaten and raped by Slade. At the time, it was all kept very hush-hush. She drove off in the middle of the night. The next day, Slade explained her absence by saying that she had quit the film over "creative differences." Tricia later gave her version of the assault to the police, but it wasn't made public until several years later.

'The reason she talked to the police was because – the very next day after raping her – Slade disappeared without a trace. Vanished into thin air.

'According to his assistant, he'd gone off to look for a young lady who called herself Margaret Blume. Margaret had been a guide at Beast House. Apparently, she was a very beautiful young woman, probably no older than sixteen. To this day, she remains a mystery. It's believed that the name she used may have been an alias derived from Judy Blume, the author, and her very popular book, *Are You There, God? It's Me, Margaret*.

'Almost nothing is known about Margaret Blume – just that she'd been guiding tours through Beast House for about a year before the film crew came to town. It's speculated that she was a runaway who wandered into town, went on the Beast House tour, and somehow worked her way into becoming a guide. She would've been hired by Agnes Kutch, but Agnes has never been very communicative. All we really know about Margaret is that she was a young teenager and extremely attractive. Attractive enough to entice Marlon Slade.

'The day after his assault on Tricia Talbot, Slade approached Margaret about taking a role in the movie. Instead of simply turning the offer down, she fled – tailed by Slade's assistant, who later told Slade where to find her. It seems that Margaret lived by herself in an old trailer up in the hills.

'That night, Slade must've gone to pay her a visit. His car was later found abandoned not far from the area where Margaret's trailer was supposed to be. But her trailer was gone. She was gone. Slade was gone. No trace of Marlon Slade or Margaret Blume has ever been discovered.

'Some people say that Slade and Margaret fell madly in love that night, ran off together and changed their identities – and have been living together happily ever after. Personally, I think that's nonsense. It's much more likely that Slade went up to the trailer with the intention of raping Margaret – doing her the same way he'd done Tricia Talbot the night before. Perhaps she got the upper hand, killed him in self-defense, and then went into hiding. More likely, though, it went the other way around: Slade raped and murdered the beautiful teenaged guide. He somehow disposed of her body, and *he* went into hiding.'

'I like it better the other way,' Darke whispered.

'Me, too.'

She squeezed Owen's hand.

'It's one of those mysteries,' Lynn said, 'that piques the imagination but has no answers. We'll probably *never* know what became of Marlon Slade or the girl who called herself Margaret Blume. And we can only wonder how the movie might've been different if Slade *had* directed it, if it *had* starred Tricia Talbot.

'As things turned out, however, *The Horror* launched the career of Ray Cunningham, who has gone on to become one of our major directors. It starred Melinda James in the role of Janice Crogan – originally intended to be played by Tricia Talbot. Melinda went on to reprise the role of Janice in four sequels, and has appeared in numerous other thrillers.'

'Melinda rules!' called out Dennis.

'Bodacious babe,' called out Arnold.

'How about *Pieces of Hate*?'

'How about *Death Cruise*, man?'

'Cool.'

'Way cool.'

'You see her hangin' upside-down?'

'Oh, yeah. Awesome.'

Lynn raised a hand for silence. 'Arnold and Dennis are absolutely right. Melinda starred in *Pieces of Hate*, *Death Cruise*, and quite a few other films. And it was indeed awesome when they hung her upside-down at the climax of *Death Cruise*.'

A few people in the audience laughed.

Darke even laughed.

Dennis said, 'Her shoulders *disappeared*, dude.'

'Let's just say they were temporarily obstructed from view,' said Lynn, grinning.

'I *do* wish they'd get on with the film,' Bixby muttered.

'As if anybody *cares* about any of this,' said Monica. 'It's all so incredibly lame and sophomoric.'

Vein looked back and said, 'Shut your faces, both of you.'

'. . . original "Beast," ' Lynn was saying, 'and continued to play the beast through *The Horror III: Resurrection*.'

'Sligo forever!'

'My man!

'Guys,' Lynn said. 'Chill. Please.'

'Cool,' said one.

'Sorry,' said the other.

'Gunther Sligo then went on to be stunt coordinator for several films. Recently, he has made a name for himself as the director of

Expungement Night, which was a big hit this year at the Sundance Festival.

'*The Horror*, as I'm sure you all know, was a box-office smash. It not only launched several successful careers, but also an epidemic of sequels and prequels. Last time I checked, we were up to *The Horror VII: The Ripper*. Some have been fairly good, but there've been a couple of real clunkers. I'm sure you all have your favorites. For most people, though, the best of the bunch was the first. It's generally considered to be a classic of the genre.

'Tonight, you'll have the very rare opportunity to experience *The Horror* on the big screen, completely uncut, in its original unrated version. This is a version that you won't find at any other movie theater, and you'll never see on television. If you rent or buy *The Horror* at a video store, you'll be getting the one that's rated R. It happens to be missing thirteen minutes – thirteen minutes that you'll be seeing tonight.'

Lynn glanced at her wristwatch. 'We're running a little late, so please save any questions for later. Now, let's start the movie. Clyde?'

The spotlight went out.

Moments later, Lynn was gone from the stage as the movie screen went bright with color.

Black letters on a scarlet background read, MALCASA PICTURES PRESENTS

Jungle drums began to pound.

The black letters faded away, leaving the screen red and empty like a sea of blood.

The drums kept booming.

And a beast lumbered out from the left side of the screen.

The instant it appeared, the small group of tourists scattered through the auditorium of The Haunted Palace erupted with applause and whistles and shouts.

The beast stopped in the middle of the screen, turned toward the audience, and roared.

Chapter Fifty-Three

'Let's Book!'

Entering the auditorium just before the lights went out, Dana had asked Warren, 'Where do you want to sit?'

'Do you think there's room for us?'

Of about two hundred seats, only thirteen were occupied.

'Maybe we'll have to split up,' Dana had said.

'I think there might be a couple of vacant seats over there.' Warren had pointed to the last row, where every seat was empty.

'Well, if we can squeeze in.'

'I'll go first.'

In the middle of the row, they'd eased down into the soft armchairs. 'Is this too far back for you?' Warren had asked.

'I don't mind.'

'I like having the wall behind us.'

'A lot safer that way,' Dana had agreed. 'And we can make out.'

As the lights faded to darkness, Warren had leaned toward Dana and slipped his arm around her back.

He'd been fine during Tuck's presentation, even laughing a few times, mostly at the antics of Dennis and Arnold. But when *The Horror* began, Dana could sense his tension. His back stiffened. His right hand, gently caressing her shoulder and upper arm, stopped moving. During the first beast attack, his thigh muscles flexed rigid under Dana's hand and she heard his breath hissing in and out.

She turned her head slightly to look at him. He was gazing at the screen, eyes wide, mouth open.

'Are you okay?' she whispered.

He didn't respond.

She shook his leg. 'Warren?'

As if dragged out of a trance, he looked at her. 'Huh?'

'Are you all right?'

'Yeah. Sure. I guess so.'

'You've *seen* this before, haven't you?'

'Sure.' Mouth twitching, he added, 'A few times. Like maybe fifty or sixty.'

'You seem awfully upset.'

'Well . . .'

'Is it the movie?'

'I . . . Yeah, I guess so. I haven't . . . this is the first time I've watched it since . . . you know, getting jumped.' Grimacing, he said, 'I didn't think it'd be a problem. But I guess maybe it is.'

'Let's book,' Dana said.

'No, no. I'll manage. It'll be all right.'

'Sure,' Dana said. She gave his leg a squeeze, then let go and stood up. '*I'm* booking. Want to come with me?' Not waiting for an answer, she took his hand and pulled.

Warren rose out of his seat and hurried along behind Dana to the end of the row.

She shoved open the door and towed him into the lobby.

'You can let go, now. I'll be fine.'

She didn't let go.

'You don't want to miss the movie,' he said.

'I've seen it plenty of times.' She pushed open the glass door and towed Warren outside. After a few more strides, she turned around and took him into her arms. He was panting for air. His whole body seemed to be trembling. She hugged him tightly.

Soon, his breathing relaxed and his tremors faded.

Dana eased her hold on him. She gently caressed his back and brushed her lips against his cheek. 'Feeling better?' she whispered.

'Feel like a jerk,' he muttered.

'Nah.'

'Can't even watch a damn movie . . .'

'I don't care about the movie. I just care about *you*.' Then she kissed him on the mouth, moaning, rubbing herself against him, sliding a hand down and squeezing his rump.

She felt Warren's hands on her buttocks.

Against her thigh, she felt his rising hardness.

And she realized they were standing beneath the brightly lighted marquee of The Haunted Palace, in plain view of anyone who might wander by on the sidewalk or drive past them on Front Street.

'Maybe we should go someplace,' she said.

'What've you got in your pocket?'

'What?'

'That *hard* thing,' Warren said.

'Oh, that. It's my rod.'

'Your *what?*'

'Reach in.'

Frowning slightly, Warren slipped a hand down the deep front pocket of her shorts. The pistol swayed, bumping against her thigh. 'It's a *gun?*'

'Eve loaned it to me.'

Saying Eve's name, Dana felt a surge of worry.

Where is she?

If she doesn't show up for the tour, Dana thought, we'd better go looking for her.

She suddenly became aware of Warren's hand, still down there with the pistol, rubbing her thigh through the thin fabric of her pocket lining.

She met his eyes.

He smiled. 'You aren't *really* wearing my skivvies, are you?'

'What do you think?'

'Uh . . . Doesn't feel like you're wearing *anything* under there.'

'Bingo.'

'Oh, man.'

'So. Where would you like to go?'

'Maybe we can find a Bingo game.'

Dana laughed.

Warren removed his hand from her pocket, took a deep breath, and sighed. 'What about . . . should we go back into the theater? It'll at least be warm.'

'No,' she said, and kissed him on the mouth.

'You could go back in without me,' Warren suggested. 'I'll head on back to Beast House and help the gals with the cleanup.'

'No,' Dana said, and kissed him on the mouth again. 'They'd be disappointed. They wanted us to have a nice, romantic time at the movie.'

'I don't think *that's* in the cards.'

'No, it's not.' She kissed him on the mouth again. 'Not at the movie, anyway.' Letting go of Warren's rump, she raised her arm over his shoulder and glanced at her wristwatch. 'We've got an hour and a half before the tour starts. Let's try to use it wisely.'

Warren laughed, his body shaking against her. 'I thought you were worn out from last night.'

'Not *that* worn out. Let's figure out where to go.'

'There's *my* place,' Warren said.

'What's that, about a ten-minute walk from here?'

'About.'

'We'd be killing twenty minutes just going back and forth.'

'There's the snack stand.' He shook his head. 'Only thing is, we'd probably run into Windy and Rhonda.'

'Let's not.'

'I know! The museum!'

'The *Beast House Museum?*'

'Sure.'

Dana could see it from where she stood – on the other side of Front Street and half a block to the north. The neon sign above its door flashed *BEAST HOUSE MUSEUM & SOUVENIRS* in swirling red letters that appeared to be dripping blood. Perched above the words was the blue neon outline of a seven-foot-tall, prowling beast.

A much smaller sign, also blue neon, lit up the middle of the display window. It read *CLOSED*.

'We can be there in a couple of minutes,' Warren said.

'Can we get in?' Dana asked.

'Sure. I've got keys to *everything*.' He pulled her by the hand.

They rushed over to the curb. There was no traffic in sight, so they ran across the street.

As they hurried up the sidewalk, Dana asked, 'Will you be all right in there?'

'Sure.'

'*Are* you sure? I mean, if the movie got to you like that . . . I'd think the museum might be even *worse*.'

'It doesn't bother me.'

'Have you been in it lately?'

'Does last week count?'

Dana nodded.

'Janice normally runs the place, you know. When she's there, I drop in two, three times a week. And I have no troubles.'

'Might be a little different at this hour of the night.'

'Might be. Thanks for mentioning it.'

'You're welcome.'

Approaching the door, Warren dug a key case out of his pocket. 'When I get it unlocked, I'll have to make a run for the alarm.'

'It won't go off, will it?'

'Not if I get there in time. But don't worry. It's no big deal. I just won't be able to dally in the doorway.'

'You don't want me to clutch you to my bosom in a feverish embrace?'

He chuckled. 'Did I say that? Never mind. Screw the alarm.'

At the door, Warren slipped a key into the lock. Dana stood behind him. 'I feel like a lookout for a heist,' she said.

'Anybody coming?'

In both directions, the sidewalks looked deserted. A few cars were parked along the curbs. A van that had already passed them was heading away, its taillights glowing red.

'Coast is clear,' Dana reported.

'Ever been in jail?' Warren asked, and opened the door.

'No.'

Pausing at the threshold, he smiled back at her. 'Always a first time.'

'*Warren!*'

Laughing, he hurried into the darkness.

Dana stepped inside, shut the door, and waited. Compared to the outside chill, the museum felt comfortable. And it *smelled* wonderful, air rich with pleasant scents from the candles and soaps in the gift area.

The neon *CLOSED* sign in the window gave everything nearby an eerie blue glow. It cast a dim shine along the top of the glass counter beside Dana, but it left most of the museum in darkness.

Off in the darkness, she heard footsteps.

'Got it,' Warren said.

'So we won't be going to jail?'

'Hope not.'

Dana made out a vague shape coming toward her. 'That better be you,' she said.

The shape stopped in front of her and reached out. She felt a warm hand drift against the side of her face. 'Maybe we should get away from the windows,' Warren said. 'Might be a slight bit embarrassing if we got caught in here.'

'Maybe we'd better not *be* in here.'

'We aren't breaking any laws. I have a key.' He took Dana by the hand and began leading her into the darkness. 'I also have Janice's permission to come and go whenever I want.'

'Do you really?'

'Yeah. Far as she's concerned, I can do no wrong.'

'Do you think she'd approve of *this?*'

'Oh, yes. When she finds out . . .'

'You're not going to *tell* her?'

'Well . . .'

'You can't tell her we snuck in here in the middle of the night.'

'If you don't want me to, I won't.'

'I'd rather you didn't. Do you tell her *everything?*'

'Pretty much.'

'Wonderful.'

'I can't *wait* to tell her about you. She's been . . . a little worried about me. Since the incident, you know? She's been afraid I might . . . sort of cut myself off.'

They stopped walking.

They seemed to be somewhere near the back of the museum's main room, near a corner. Looking toward the front, Dana glimpsed a few small mists of blue glow. Most of her view was blocked by tall shelving, shrouded by darkness. From where she stood, no windows were in sight.

She turned toward Warren, but could barely see him.

'So anyway,' he said, 'Janice'll be awfully glad to find out that I've . . . uh . . . found someone I really care about.'

'You really care about me?' Dana whispered.

'More than . . . yeah. I sure do.'

'More than what?' she asked, her heart pounding faster.

'More than anyone. Ever.'

She wrapped her arms around him.

Sprawled on top of Warren, breathless and sweaty, Dana pushed herself up to a sitting position.

He stayed in her.

Raising both hands toward her face, she pressed a button to light the numbers of her wristwatch.

11:47

'What's the bad news?' Warren asked.

'Quarter till twelve.'

He groaned.

'I'd better get dressed.'

He took hold of her thighs. 'No, wait.'

'I promised Tuck.'

'I know. But . . . five more minutes?'

Smiling in the darkness, Dana hunkered down over him. She placed her hands on the carpet and eased from side to side. Her breasts swung, nipples brushing across Warren's chest. She felt him move inside her. Felt him grow.

'You *want* me to miss the tour, don't you?' she asked.

'You don't have to miss it. Five or ten more minutes . . .'

He pushed up slightly, sliding himself deeper.

Dana moaned. 'You don't make it easy.'

'Sorry.'

'Sure.'

'You'd better get going,' Warren said.

'Yeah. I'd better.'

She sank down on him, mashing herself against him, sucking his tongue into her mouth. His tongue slurped out as she pushed herself up. Gasping for air, she guided his hands to her breasts, then clutched him by the shoulders. 'I think I can spare a minute or two,' she said.

* * *

By 11:55, they were both dressed and standing just inside the museum's front door.

Dana gave Warren a quick hug and kiss. 'I've got to run,' she said. 'Maybe you'd better stay here, make sure we didn't lose anything in the dark.'

'You didn't lose your pistol, did you?'

She had felt the weight of the .380 in her pocket as she'd pulled up her shorts, had felt it bump against her thigh with each step she took on her way to the door. She could feel it now like a hand trying to tug down her shorts. 'Still there, all right.'

'I hope you don't need it.'

'If I do, should I save the last bullet for myself?'

'Don't even joke about that.'

'I've gotta go.'

'I'll come along.'

She shook her head. 'No, really. You should stay here and clean the place up. We don't want to leave a mess behind.'

'You're probably right.'

'See you tomorrow?'

Warren nodded.

Dana pulled him against herself and gave him one long, hard kiss. Then she eased him away, turned around and opened the door.

'Be careful,' he called after her.

'Bye-bye, honey,' she said, and hurried to the curb.

The fog was much thicker than before.

She could hardly see to the other side of the road. The street lights looked as if they'd been muffled with cotton. A block away, the marquee of The Haunted Palace was a shapeless, fuzzy red blur.

Shivering, Dana rubbed her arms.

She glanced both ways, looking for headlights. Then she dashed across Front Street. At the other side, she leaped the curb, swerved to the right, and sprinted up the sidewalk toward Beast House in a race to beat the midnight deadline.

Chapter Fifty-Four

Warnings

'I know you're all freezing,' Lynn called, walking backwards at the front of the group. 'So I'll spare you my usual twenty-minute speech in front of the porch, and we'll go straight in.'

'Hear hear!' bellowed the professor.

As they hurried along, Vein zipped up her leather jacket.

Darke let go of Owen's hand and huddled against his side. He put an arm around her back. Through the thin silk of her shirt, he felt her shaking.

'Hang on,' he said. He pulled off his Crawford Junior High School windbreaker. 'Here, put this on.' He held it open while Darke slipped her arms into the sleeves.

Though her black blouse was still unbuttoned, exposing bare skin all the way down to her waist, she drew the windbreaker shut and fastened its snaps. Trembling, she smiled up at Owen. 'Thanks,' she said, then once again tucked herself in against his side.

Again, he put his arm around her back.

Turning his head, he pushed his face into her soft hair.

'Oh, how sweet,' came Monica's voice from somewhere behind him. 'Owie's got a boyfriend.'

As she spoke the last word, Darke reached back and slipped a hand down inside the seat pocket of Owen's jeans.

'If you look to your left,' Lynn announced, 'you may note that something seems to be missing.'

Owen looked. Through the iron bars of the front fence, he saw the lawn dissolve into fog. There was no trace at all of Beast House.

'We may have to rethink our plans for the tour,' Lynn said.

'This is *so* cool,' Darke said quietly to Owen.

'Yeah.'

'I just love the fog.'

'Me, too,' he said. 'Do you get much of it where you live?'

'Not much.'

Somewhere in the fog ahead of them, Lynn said, 'Go all the way up to the house.'

'Where *do* you live?' Owen asked.

'Tucson.'

'*Arizona?*'

Darke nodded. 'I'm in grad school at the university.'

'What're you working on?'

'Go on up to the house,' Lynn said, closer now. 'I'll be along in a minute.'

'An M.A. in literature. Vein, too. We're roomies.'

Following those in front of them, they turned to the left just before the ticket booth. They passed Lynn, who was holding the gate open.

'Go all the way up to the house,' she told them. 'I'll be along in a minute.'

As they headed up the walkway, Lynn repeated the instructions to those behind them.

'Is Darke your real name?' Owen asked.

'Of course not,' she said.

Soon, the black shape of Beast House began to emerge through the fog. Somehow, it made Owen think of a ghost ship bearing down on them.

'Look at that,' he said. 'It's like something out of William Hope Hodgson.'

The hand in his back pocket squeezed his rump. 'You been talking to Vein?'

'Huh?'

'I just love Hodgson.'

'You're kidding,' Owen said. 'Most people have never even heard of him.'

'You meet the coolest people on a Beast House tour.' She squeezed his butt again. 'Who else do you like?'

'Herbert.'

'Herbert who?' Darke asked.

'James.'

'Herbert James? Any relation to Henry?'

'I *hate* Henry,' Owen said.

'I *love* Herbert,' said Darke. 'And you're right about Henry. He's a bore. And he don't know shit about rats.'

They climbed the porch stairs. In the midst of the other tourists, they turned around and waited. A few more people, down on the walkway, were materializing out of the fog.

Then Lynn appeared. 'Is everybody ready for the Midnight Tour?' she called.

A few scattered voices replied, 'Ready,' and 'All set,' and 'Any time.'

'It's *terribly* cold out here,' complained the woman in the tennis outfit. Since the last time Owen had noticed her, she'd put her sweater on.

'Colder than a witch's tit,' said Arnold.

'Colder than a zombie's dick,' said Dennis.

'Colder than . . .'

Raising a hand, Lynn said, 'Guys, guys, guys.'

'Morons.' The quiet mutter came from Monica. She sounded as if she were standing directly behind Owen.

'There are ladies present,' Clive proclaimed.

'It's an *unexpurgated* tour, dude,' Dennis said.

'Right on,' said Arnold.

Stopping at the foot of the porch stairs, Lynn said, 'I'm sure everyone would appreciate . . .'

A dark, running shape raced out of the fog behind her.

'Look out!' someone shouted.

She whirled around.

'It's me, it's me!'

Owen recognized the voice *and* the tall, shapely figure.

Dana.

He felt as if an old friend had shown up. Strangely, however, he didn't find himself excited or even very interested in her arrival.

The lack of interest made him feel as if he'd somehow let her down.

That's crazy, he told himself. She never cared about me. We're strangers.

But I wanted her so badly!

He tried to picture how she'd looked last night, naked by the Jacuzzi. But the image that entered his mind and made him start to stiffen was Darke in the men's restroom earlier tonight when she first pulled open her shirt.

'You made it,' Lynn said.

'Hi, everyone!' Dana called out.

'Dana!' Dennis yelled, waving furiously.

'The main babe!' yelled Arnold.

'Lynn's the main babe,' Dana told him. 'I'm just here to help out. I hope I didn't delay things.'

'We were just about to start,' Lynn told her. 'Tell you what. I'll lead the way. Why don't you do me a favor and take up the rear? Keep an eye out for stragglers.' Facing the group, Lynn said, 'We should all stay close together after we enter the house. That way, everyone'll be able to see and hear what's going on. Also, we'll be less likely to lose any of you. Every now and then, stragglers get picked off.'

Owen heard a few quiet laughs.

'I *assume* she's kidding,' Eleanor muttered.

'Anybody has any questions, wait till we're inside. It *is* a little nippy out here.'

With that, Lynn rushed up the porch stairs. Several people moved quickly to let her by. Owen heard keys jangle.

He and Darke turned around to face the door.

Darke pulled her hand out of his pocket. Taking hold of his hand, she looked up at him. 'I've been wanting to do this for *so* long.'

'Me, too,' he said.

'I can't believe I'm finally here.'

Neither can I, Owen thought.

She's here, all right. Here with me. And it's not a dream.

Better not be.

Holding Darke's small, warm hand, he stepped over the threshold.

Lynn must've turned on a light as she entered; a chandelier cast a murky glow through the foyer.

She made her way forward to the main stairway, climbed to the third stair, then turned around. 'Welcome to Beast House,' she said.

Dana shut the door.

'Now, I *know* you've all seen *The Horror*. I'm going to *assume* that you've already taken the self-guided audio tour, and that some of you have read one or both of Janice Crogan's books. If you *haven't*, you've put the cart before the horse. The Midnight Tour is like an *advanced* class. We're really not here to rehash the basic stuff. But it's not exactly a *class*, either. We're here to have a good time, and we hope to give you an experience that you'll always remember and look back on with pleasure.

'During the next two hours, we'll be exploring the entire house. You'll see places that aren't shown during the regular tours. And you'll hear things that aren't said on the tapes. I want to give you a few warnings along those lines. In the course of the tour, we'll be visiting both the attic and the cellar. There are a couple of fairly steep stairways involved. If any of you have problems with climbing stairs, you might want to bow out before we get started. The same with anyone who is easily offended. This tour isn't meant for prudes. I'll be telling you things that any normal person would find shocking and revolting. That's the point of the tour – to give the uncensored truth. You probably knew that before you shelled out your hundred bucks, but in case you weren't paying attention, I'm warning you now. It gets nasty. I don't hold back. So you'd better bow out if you're afraid of what I might say.

'If you do quit the tour now, we'll refund a hundred per cent of your admission price.'

'A *hundred* per cent?' asked the man with the mustache and camel sweater. He sounded surprised.

'I know,' Lynn said. 'You've already had the picnic and seen the movie. But we don't want anyone on the tour who *shouldn't* be here. It can ruin it for everyone.'

'That's certainly generous,' said the man's wife – the one with the great eyes.

'It might *sound* generous. The thing is, nobody has ever taken us up on it. By the time we get this far, nobody can *stand* to back out.'

Tourists chuckled and nodded.

'One final warning. Some people find the tour to be *extremely* stressful. Since you're here, I figure you enjoy being a little frightened. You should prepare yourselves to be *very* frightened. Anybody pregnant?'

Owen saw several of the females shake their heads.

Beside him, Darke's head shook.

He heard a snigger, probably from Monica.

'We're no doubt *all* pregnant with expectation,' said Bixby.

'Oh, duuuude,' Dennis said. It came out like a moan of despair.

'Bail out, Boxboy,' Arnold suggested.

'Bugger off,' Bixby responded.

'Huh huh.'

'*Booger* off.'

Lynn raised her hand. 'Okay,' she said. 'I take it that nobody is pregnant – with child. That's good. We had a gal one time who got so excited on the tour that she went into early labor. We've also had a couple of heart attacks. If you have any history of high blood pressure or heart disease, you'd be better off not taking the tour. Anybody with trouble along those lines?'

She waited. Heads shook. No arms were raised and nobody spoke up.

'Are you sure? I don't want anybody pitching over on us.'

'Looks like we're all fine 'n dandy,' said the stocky guy who was married to the woman in the tennis costume.

'Okay. One last thing before we start. If any of you *do* experience physical or emotional trouble during the course of the tour, please speak up. I'm sure Dana will be happy to escort you outside.'

'What sort of refund then?' asked the man in the camel sweater.

'After the tour has actually started,' Lynn said, 'there will be no refunds at all.'

'When *does* it start?' asked Clive.

'I'll count to five. While I'm counting, you can all decide if you really want to go through with this. One.' She paused for a second, then said, 'Two.' A few moments later, 'Three.' As she said, 'Four,' quick thumps erupted in the darkness behind her.

People gasped.

Owen's heart jumped.

Darke jerked stiff and squeezed his hand.

Then some screamed and others shouted, '*Look out!*' and '*Behind you!*' and a solitary female voice shouted out, '*Duck!*' as a shiny white hairless creature rushed down through the darkness at the top of the stairs.

The beast!

Lynn looked over her shoulder, saw it and shrieked.

Dana plowed through the group, shoving people out of her way.

Someone – Owen didn't see who – flung open the front door to escape.

The beast pounded its way down the stairs, dead white and shiny, all muscle and teeth and claws – and penis. Erect, it tilted up like a broom handle.

Two stairs above Lynn, the creature lurched to a halt and lifted its head off.

Clyde, hair mussed from the full-head mask, smiled down at his audience. 'Welcome to Beast House!' he called out.

Dana abruptly stopped at the foot of the stairs.

Many of those who remained in the foyer began to laugh with relief, clap loudly and mutter.

'Bravo!' Bixby called out.

Darke looked up at Owen, smiled and shook her head.

'Pretty cool,' Owen said to her.

'I almost wet my pants,' Darke said.

'A tough guy like you?'

She grinned.

Several people began to snap photos of Clyde and Lynn on the stairs.

Off to the side, Vein looked around, raised a single black eyebrow at Owen and Darke, then bent down and slid the knife into her boot. Nobody seemed to be watching her. She stepped closer to Owen and Darke. 'I knew it was a fake-out,' she said.

They both laughed.

Lynn was now standing with Clyde on the same stair. Holding the hideous white head under one arm like a football helmet, Clyde nodded, grinned and waved.

Lynn held up both arms. 'Would somebody like to go outside and try to bring back our runaways?'

'I'll take care of it.'

'Thanks, Phil.'

Owen had seen Phil around. A normal-looking guy with a nice-looking wife. Though Owen hadn't spoken to either of them, he'd noticed Phil's unusual hair. Black with a patch of white near the front, it had reminded him of Cotton Hawes, one of Ed McBain's 87th Precinct cops.

'I'll go with you,' Phil's wife said. She was husky and had a pleasant face. Wearing a flannel shirt, jeans and boots, she looked as if she belonged in the woods somewhere. She followed Phil out the door.

'While they're gone,' Lynn said, 'the rest of you can take a couple of minutes to relax.' She grinned. 'Glad to see that you're all still standing.'

'That was a dirty trick,' said the camel sweater man, chuckling and shaking his head. 'I *loved* it.'

'I almost pooped,' announced Arnold.

'You're crude, dude.'

'Huh-huh.'

'Get a load of the *schlong* on that guy.'

'*That's* crude.'

Phil and his wife came back in, followed by the woman in the tennis whites and her husband. With a big smile, the man waved at the group. 'Just stepped out for a breath of fresh air, everyone.' He gave a thumbs-up to Clyde. 'Nice job, fellow. Sure put one over on me.'

'Are you both all right?' Lynn asked.

'Oh, fine,' the man said.

His wife said nothing, but glowered toward Lynn and Clyde.

'All in good fun,' Lynn said. Then she took a deep breath and said, 'Last call for bailing out of the tour and getting a full refund. Any takers?'

A sour look on her face, the tennis woman muttered, 'Biff?'

'*I'm* staying,' he told her. 'If you want to leave, be my guest. You can wait for me in the car.'

'What'll it be, Eleanor?' Lynn asked.

The woman almost snarled. 'I'll stay.'

'Very good,' Lynn said. 'The tour starts now.'

Chapter Fifty-Five

The Strangeness of Beasts

Heart still racing from the scare of what she'd thought was a real attack on Tuck, Dana rubbed her sweaty hands on the sides of her shorts. The pistol had been halfway out of her pocket by the time Clyde had stopped and pulled off his mask.

My God, what if I'd shot him?

Tuck should've warned me, she thought.

Probably didn't want to ruin the surprise.

'This is Clyde,' Tuck announced, slapping him on the back.

'Hi, everyone,' he said.

'He's a regular member of our staff, and our favorite beast. Some of the ladies like to say it's type casting.'

Clyde chuckled, then raised the ugly, snouted mask and pulled it down over his head.

'Behold a beast,' Lynn said. 'This is what they actually look like. Not quite like the ones they show in the movies, is he? The movie beasts are almost *pretty* compared to the real thing. And of course, they never let you see this.'

Tuck gave the jutting shaft a flick with the back of her hand. The gentle blow made it sway from side to side. A few people chuckled. Some made sounds of dismay. An impish smile appeared on Tuck's face.

'Don't worry,' she said, 'it's not real. Like the rest of the suit, it's made of synthetics. But every detail of the suit is accurate. According to people who *know*, its appearance and texture is almost exactly like the actual beasts. Down to the slightest details. Note the sharp claws on its hands and feet. Note its teeth – in *both* mouths.'

As she wrapped her right hand around the shaft, just about everyone in the group either groaned or snickered.

'Go for it,' Dennis said.

'I'm sure that most of you have heard about *this*,' Lynn said. With her left hand, she pointed at the blunt head of the penis. Stretched across it was a mouthlike orifice that seemed to be frozen in a snarl. 'There are passing mentions of it in Janice Crogan's books, but it's one of those things nobody wants to dwell on . . . no pun intended.'

After a pause, there came a mixture of laughs and moans. Dennis and Arnold elbowed each other, chuckling. Eleanor shook her head. Owen and Darke laughed. Monica, standing close behind them, looked as if she might be smelling something sour.

'This . . .' Tuck said, 'is obviously the beast's most unusual feature. But it's something you don't hear much about and you certainly never *see* it in any of the movies. You never hear about it on the day tour, either. This is the beast's deep, dark secret.'

With her left hand, Lynn withdrew an eight-inch long flashlight from a front pocket of her shorts. 'I'll light it up for you.' She thumbed the switch, then shined the bright beam on the mouth. 'Why don't you come over here, one at a time, and take a closer look if you're so inclined?'

Nobody took her up on the offer.

'I *know* you all want to look. Dennis, Arnold, you guys wanta break the ice?'

'Bitchin',' said Arnold.

'Cool,' said Dennis.

As they made their way toward the foot of the stairs, Lynn resumed her talk. 'The beast comes equipped with quite an impressive mouthful of teeth. There is also a forked tongue. On an actual beast, the tongue extends about two to three inches, but our replica doesn't do that. You'll only be able to see the very tips of it.'

Dennis leaned forward for a close look. 'Whoa, dude,' he muttered. He stepped aside. While Arnold inspected the mouth, Andy and Alison Lawrence stepped up behind him to await their turn.

'We're not entirely sure about the *functions* of the second mouth,' Tuck went on. 'We don't know, for instance, whether the creatures are able to consume *food* with it, or *breathe* through it. We do know that they *bite*.'

A few people winced.

'Charming,' muttered Eleanor.

More people lined up to inspect the mouth.

'They bite and suck. And taste. As Lilly Thorn wrote in her diary, "This orifice and tongue enabled him not only to titilate me in the extreme, but also heighten his ardor by the taste of my juices." '

'Awesome,' Arnold muttered.

Dana had read that section of the diary. The portions dealing with the beast had been printed in Janice Crogan's first book, *The Horror at Malcasa Point*, and photographs of the actual diary pages had appeared in the second book, *Savage Times*. Tuck was telling her nothing she didn't already know.

Regardless, Dana found herself pressing her thighs together. Doing that, she felt her soreness and stickiness and stopped thinking about the beast. She was suddenly back in the museum with Warren. In the dark. Wrapped around him, enveloped by him, feeling him everywhere.

After a while, she realized she was missing the show.

Tuck still stood beside Clyde on the third stair, shining her flashlight on the costume's nasty little mouth while people from the tour stepped up for a closer look.

'. . . said to be *great* lovers,' Tuck was explaining. 'Because of their wild ways, their unbridled lust, the staggering size of their penises *and* the mouths, women were known to lose all interest in normal men after having a close encounter with a beast. That's what happened to Lilly Thorn, the woman who built Beast House.'

Dana wondered if she should take a look at Clyde's costume.

Why not? Might as well go whole hog.

She stepped forward.

'As soon as everyone's done,' Tuck said, 'I'll take you downstairs into the cellar and we'll have look at the place where, in a sense, it all began. In the meantime, any questions?'

'What about *female* beasts?' Monica asked, smirking. 'Or *aren't* there any?'

'We know that females existed on Bobo Island when the *Mary Jane* landed there in 1901. In the battle that took place between the ship's crew and the beasts, however, all the females were slaughtered. Only Bobo, an infant male, was brought back to the States. All the subsequent beasts are apparently his descendents.'

'From human mothers?' asked Eleanor, sounding a bit skeptical.

'That's correct.'

'If that were the case,' said Andy, 'it seems that the first offspring should've been half human.'

'Genetically speaking,' added his wife, Alison, nodding in agreement.

'And if *that* one mated with a human female,' Andy continued, 'their child ought to lose about three-quarters of its beast traits.'

'I know,' Tuck said. 'That's generally the way it's *supposed* to be. I completely understand. In *fact*, though, there hasn't been any noticeable change in the physical appearance of the beasts since Bobo came to town almost a hundred years ago. Maybe there've been changes that nobody noticed, but nothing obvious.'

'From a scientific standpoint,' Andy said, 'it seems impossible.'

Tuck grinned. 'And yet, it's *true*.'

'Aren't their *offspring* ever female?' asked Connie.

Next in line, Dana watched Professor Bixby step forward to view the mouth.

Do I *really* want to see this thing? she wondered.

Hell, no.

Then how come I'm standing here?

'. . . in Malcasa Point?' Tuck said. 'Not that we know of. If there have been females . . .' She shrugged. 'In certain present-day *human* cultures, you know, female infants are commonly destroyed at birth. Because they aren't considered socially convenient.'

'That's not so,' blurted Eleanor, sounding distressed. 'I don't believe that for a single minute.'

'I'm afraid it is true,' said Alison, coming to Tuck's defense.

'India, for starters,' Andy pointed out.

'Exactly,' said Tuck. 'In present-day India, there's wholesale slaughter of female infants. Apparently, they're considered a burden on family finances.'

'That's ridiculous,' Eleanor insisted.

'But true,' Tuck said. 'Anyway, I only brought it up to indicate the possibility that the beasts may have practiced something along those lines – killing the females at birth. That could explain why we've never seen any around here. Or maybe something else is going on.'

At last, Bixby moved on.

Dana stepped closer to the stairs. Standing in front of Clyde, she crouched slightly. Tuck still shined her flashlight on the mouthlike orifice. The opening was rimmed by thin, white ridges . . . lips? The teeth looked sharp. The tongue, just inside, was bright red.

What would it be like to . . .?

Dana found herself blushing.

The rigid, half-open mouth suddenly darted at the tip of her nose. She gasped and lurched backward.

'Hey!' Tuck snapped. She gave Clyde a quick jab with her elbow.

'Very funny, Clyde,' Dana said.

Quiet, muffled laughter came out of the beast mask.

As Dana hurried away, Tuck asked the group, 'Any more questions?'

'I understand that the beasts are *bi*-sexual,' boomed Bixby.

'I'd say that's an understatement,' Tuck answered. 'They appear to be *omni*sexual. To be crude about it, they'd screw the crack of dawn. If there isn't a suitable orifice for the purpose, they'll *create* one with their teeth. They've been known to *chew* their way in.'

'Oh, dear God,' blurted Eleanor, sounding appalled.

'Is everybody done inspecting Clyde's anatomy?' Tuck asked. 'He *will* be accompanying us on the tour, so you'll have plenty of other opportunities to observe his peculiarities.'

'The *beast's* peculiarities,' Clyde corrected her.

'Those, too.'

'Lynn's nothing if not amusing,' Clyde announced. 'And she's rarely that.'

Tuck said, 'He only *thinks* I won't fire him.'

Keeping her flashlight on, she stepped to the bottom of the stairs. 'We'll be going down to the cellar, now. I'll lead the way. Everybody stay close behind me. Dana will take up the rear.'

Tuck stepped around the newel post and disappeared into the hallway alongside the staircase. Hanging back, Dana watched the others follow her. Clyde waited on the stairs. His white, hairless head swiveled as he looked from the group to Dana. After all the tourists had crowded into the hallway, he stepped down to the first stair.

Dana motioned for him to go ahead.

He stayed. 'Ladies first.'

'Lynn wants *me* to take up the rear.'

'I *always* go last.'

'Okay,' Dana said. 'Whatever.' She followed the others into the hallway.

Clyde hopped off the bottom stair and came after her.

The hallway was murky with remains of light from the foyer chandelier. The tourists in front of Dana were pressed close together, slowly shuffling along.

Clyde prodded her in the rump.

She jerked her head around. 'Stop that,' she whispered.

'My reputation precedes me.'

'Keep that thing away from me.'

He poked her with it again. 'How would you like it *in* you?'

'Knock it off.'

'If you'd like to just make a little detour into the employee's rest-room . . .'

'No thanks.'

'The next best thing to getting it from a *real* beast.'

She stopped, turned sideways, and shoved her face up close to the twisted snout of his mask. Seething but trying to sound calm, she whispered, 'Listen to me, Clyde. I'm not interested. Okay? So just keep your damn prick to yourself, keep your mouth shut and leave me alone. Please.'

He laughed softly. It sounded strange through the mask. 'What if I don't?' he asked, his voice smirky and taunting. 'You gonna tell on me to Lynn? Think she'll fire me? She wouldn't dare.'

'Just leave me alone.'

'Sue me for sexual harassment?'

'Maybe.'

He lifted a pale hand and clutched her left breast. Through the fabric of her shirt and bra, the points of the claws were sharp against her skin.

She bashed the hand away. 'Touch me again and you'll be sorry.' She whirled around and hurried up the hallway. It was deserted in front of her. The tour had moved on.

She heard Clyde close behind her.

With each stride of her right leg, she felt the pistol bump against her thigh.

Just forget about that, she told herself. I can't shoot him for pawing me.

Eve probably would.

Eve!

Why isn't she here?

Dana found the tour group inside the dark kitchen. They were gathered near the open pantry door, where Tuck stood with her flashlight. Its beam swept toward Dana and lit her.

'Thought maybe the beast had nailed you,' Tuck said.

'Nope. Everything's fine.'

Clyde stepped through the doorway. Tuck shined the flashlight on him. 'Staying out of trouble?' she asked.

He waved. The claws of his beast hand cast long, hooked shadows on the wall to his right.

'Okay,' Tuck said. 'Before we descend into the cellar, let me tell you that the audio tour is loaded with lies and half truths. It's based very closely on the original tours given by Maggie Kutch, and Maggie had a lot to hide. You already know most of this if you've read Janice's books. Have any of you *not* read either book?'

More than half the people in the group raised a hand.

'That's fine. If you're only familiar with the audio tour and haven't read either book, then you've been misled about a lot of things. During the course of tonight's tour, I'll be telling you what *really* happened.

'Let's start at the beginning – with the beast's first foray into the house. On the night of August second, 1903, it supposedly came wandering out of the hills, just happened to stumble upon this house, came in and slaughtered Ethel Hughes in the parlor. Then it ran upstairs and murdered Lilly's kids. Lilly managed to escape by climbing out her bedroom window. That's the way Maggie always told it. But that's not how it happened.

'The *real* story begins more than two months before that bloody night in August. On the night of May eighteenth, Lilly went down into her cellar to bring up a jar of canned fruit – and made a startling discovery. Two of her jars were broken. A third was empty. She'd had a visitor. A hungry visitor.

'To be continued in the cellar,' Tuck said.

Dana heard a few murmurs and moans.

'Nobody's required to come with me,' Tuck said. 'If any of you think you can't deal with the cellar, you're welcome to wait for us here. Of course, you'll be missing a major highlight of the tour.'

'How long will you be down there?' asked Eleanor.

'Ten minutes, maybe a little longer. Would you rather stay here?'

'I'm not sure. Maybe. Would I be the only one?'

'*I'm* not going to miss the cellar,' Biff told her.

'I'm not asking you to.'

'Anyone else want to wait here?' Tuck asked. Nobody responded. 'Looks like you'd be on your own, Eleanor.'

'I can't stay here by *myself*.'

'Well, if you'd rather wait outside the house . . .'

'And miss the tour?'

'If you don't want to miss the tour,' Tuck said, 'you really should stick with the rest of us. It'll be fine. The cellar might *seem* a little creepy, but it's perfectly safe. We haven't lost a tourist yet . . . Except for a few who stayed behind.' Through scattered laughter, Tuck said, 'I was just kidding about that. We haven't lost anyone. You'll be safe whether you wait here or come with us.'

'Come on, honey,' Biff said.

'Well . . . I guess I'll come.'

'Bravo!' said Bixby.

'Thata girl,' said Biff.

'All right,' said Tuck. 'Everybody wait here. I'll go down and turn the light on. As soon as it's on, you can begin coming down the stairs. Be careful, though. They're very steep. I suggest you hold on to a railing.'

Tuck vanished into the pantry.

Dana heard whispers, a few quiet chuckles. Somebody let out a long, ghostly '*Wooooooooo!*'

'Childish,' said a female voice. Dana suspected Monica.

Another female voice crooned, 'Here it comes, the vile beast. It wants to rape you, then to feast. And if it doesn't like your taste, it spits you out like gory paste.'

Laughter and applause.

'Awesome ditty,' said Arnold.

'Rrrrrrrape!'

'Huh-huh.'

Dim light suddenly filled the doorway.

'All right,' Tuck called. 'Come on down. But please, take it carefully.'

Though Clyde stayed close behind Dana, she tried to ignore him as she followed the tourists through the doorway, into the pantry, and down the cellar stairs.

Chapter Fifty-Six

The Cellar

Owen wanted to ask Vein about the poem she'd recited. Where had she found it? Had she made it up? Was there more to it?

But then the cellar light cast its glow into the pantry, Lynn called up from below, and the group started shuffling forward.

'Here we go,' Owen whispered.

Darke squeezed his hand.

Side by side, they stepped through the doorway and began to follow Vein down the stairs.

Owen felt trembly with fear and excitement.

This is it, he thought. We're going down.

Can't believe it.

Owen had often hoped that he would someday find a chance to experience the Midnight Tour. But he'd never really expected it to happen. That he was here now seemed unreal.

And all the more unreal because of Darke.

It seemed impossible that such a strange, beautiful creature had actually sipped his blood, sucked him, taken him into her body, and was now holding hands with him like a cherished lover as they made their way down the stairs.

Best night of my life!

Below them, a woman said quietly, 'I don't liiiike this.' Though Owen didn't recognize the voice, he thought it might belong to Connie, Phil's wife.

'It's all right, honey,' said a guy. Phil?

'This is the hour when the beast *loves* to strike,' said Vein in a voice loud enough for all to hear. 'And this is its lair.'

Nervous chuckles.

'I do hope you're enjoying yourself, Owie,' Monica muttered from behind him.

Eat your heart out, he thought. But he said nothing.

Darke turned her head and looked up at him. Her eyes made him forget all about Monica. They made him want to know every secret of Darke's life.

What if tonight is all we ever have? he thought. Tomorrow, maybe she won't be interested in me anymore. She'll go away with Vein and I'll never see her again. Never hold her hand again, never kiss her again . . .

A terrible sorrow welled up in Owen.

She's with me now, he told himself. I'm in the cellar on the Midnight Tour and I've got Darke holding my hand right now, right at this very second, right here in the present. Here in the present, this is the greatest of all possible nights. Don't ruin it by worrying about tomorrow.

At the bottom of the stairs, they walked over the dry dirt floor of the cellar and joined the semi-circle of tourists in front of Lynn.

Darke let go of Owen's hand. Easing in against his side, she reached across his back and rested a hand on his hip.

He slid his hand across the back of his own windbreaker and curled his hand over Darke's shoulder.

'Awwww,' said Monica. 'What a handsome couple.'

Darke rubbed his hip.

'Did we lose anyone?' Lynn asked.

Heads turned this way and that.

'Beast didn't put the snatch on anyone?' Lynn asked, grinning.

'All accounted for,' announced Bixby.

'Okay, then I guess we'll continue with Lilly's story. As I mentioned in the kitchen, she found that someone had been in the cellar, breaking jars and sampling some of her canned goods. She knew her boys hadn't done it; the empty jar had contained beets. Her kids *hated* beets. So she was sure that a stranger had been down here. She was no coward, Lilly Thorn. Instead of running away, she searched the cellar. And she found a hole in the floor. *This* hole.' Lynn stepped aside and gestured behind her.

Owen couldn't see the hole. People blocked his view. He didn't worry, though; he was certain that everyone would be given a good chance to look at it before leaving the cellar.

'When Lilly found the hole,' Lynn said, 'there was no steel cover. We added that a few years ago – along with the padlock – as a security precaution. This hole is the mouth of a tunnel that leads into the hills behind the house. We used to get occasional woodland visitors before we sealed it.

'When Lilly found the hole, she figured it must've been the way in for her intruder. The next night, she came down with a shovel, planning to fill it in. But her intruder had paid another visit in the meantime, helping himself to a couple of jars of peaches. Suddenly feeling sorry for him, Lilly gave up her notion of filling the hole. In her diary, she wrote, "My heart went out to the luckless, desperate soul who had dug into my cellar for a few mouthfuls of my preserves. I vowed to meet him, and help him if I could."

'Later that night, after her kids were in bed and her lover had gone home, she came back down into the cellar. She was dressed in her nightgown. She sat on the bottom stair to wait in total darkness for the arrival of her hungry visitor.

'Soon, she heard stealthy sounds of movement from the direction of the hole. She was able to make out a dim, pale shape rising out of the darkness. "And I was filled with dread," she wrote, "for this was no man. Nor was he an ape."

'As the creature approached Lilly, she *had* to see it better. So she struck a match.'

Vein and Darke suddenly recited in unison, ' "Whether he was one of God's exotic creatures, or an ill-made perversion vomited forth by the devil, I know not. His ghastly appearance and nudity shocked me. Yet I was drawn, by an irresistible force, to lay my hand upon his misshapen shoulder." '

'Very good!' Lynn said.

Dennis and Arnold clapped wildly and said, 'Far out' and 'Bitchin'.' Several of the other tourists clapped as well, while others nodded in approval.

'For those of you who might not have recognized it,' Lynn said, 'Vein and Darke have just done a very nice rendition from Lilly's diary. Making my job a lot easier. Can you give us more?'

'If you like,' Darke said, squeezing Owen's hand.

'Please. Proceed.'

Again in unison, their voices rose through the silence. ' "I allowed the match to die. In the darkness, totally without sight, I felt the creature turn." '

As they continued, the beast itself – with Clyde inside – made his way through the group. Startled, some people flinched or gasped before stepping aside to let him pass.

' "His warm breath on my face smelled of the earth and wild, uninhabited forests. He lay his hands upon my shoulders. Claws bit into me. I stood before the creature, helpless with fear and wonder, as he split the fabric of my nightgown." '

Clyde in the beast suit climbed onto an old steamer trunk beside Lynn and began to strike muscle-man poses.

' "When I was bare, he nuzzled my body like a dog. He licked my breasts. He sniffed me, even my private areas, which he probed with his snout." '

Lynn seemed delighted. 'Excellent. Can you go on?'

' "He moved behind me. His claws pierced my back, forcing me to my knees." '

Clyde began to pantomime the beast's movements.

' "I felt the slippery warmth of his flesh press down on me, and I knew with certainty what he was about. The thought of it appalled me to the heart, and yet I was somehow thrilled by the touch of him, and strangely eager.

' "He mounted me from behind, a manner as unusual for humans as it is customary among many lower animals. At the first touch of his organ, fear wrenched my vitals, not for the safety of my flesh but for my everlasting soul. And yet I allowed him to continue. I know, now, that no power of mine could have prevented him from having his will with me. I made no attempt to resist, however. On the contrary, I welcomed his entry. I hungered for it as if I somehow presaged its magnificence.

' "Oh Lord, how he plundered me! How his claws tore my flesh! How his teeth bore into me! How his prodigious organ battered my tender womb. How brutal he was in his savagery, how gentle in his heart.

' "I knew, as we lay spent on the earthen cellar floor, that no man could ever stir my passion in such a way. I wept. The creature, disturbed by my outburst, slipped away into his hole and disappeared." '

Simultaneously, Vein and Darke bowed deeply like stage actors. Atop the steamer trunk, Clyde raised both arms in triumph.

The midnight tourists burst into wild applause and cheers. Bixby shouted, 'Bravo!' Others called out, 'Wow!' and 'Well done!' and 'Great!' Through the tumult, Owen heard Dennis and Arnold shouting, 'Awesome!' and 'Dudes!' and 'the Beast *rules!*'

Owen hugged Darke. 'That was fantastic!' he whispered.

When the group settled down, Lynn said, 'Thank you *very* much, Vein and Darke. We've never had anything like that before. Did you prepare it especially for tonight?'

Vein shook her head. 'We performed it for a Halloween show at college.'

'Really?' Lynn seemed amused and delighted.

'But we never got to finish,' Darke explained. 'They stopped us.'

'Escorted us off stage,' Vein added.

'We almost got expelled.'

Laughing softly, Lynn shook her head. 'Why does that not surprise me?' she said.

'This is the only time we've ever been allowed to do the entire piece.'

'I wish we could have you here to do it *every* Saturday night,' Lynn told them. '*I* can't recite all that stuff. I just paraphrase. So thank you again. You've given us all a real treat.'

They received more applause.

'And now,' said Lynn, 'it's time for a treat that *is* a regular feature of the Midnight Tour. I'm about to remove the padlock and open the steel cover so you'll all be able to take a look down the hole itself. This is the beast's *actual* hole. Nobody on the daytime tours ever gets a chance to see it uncovered. It's for the *Midnight* Tourists only.'

Lynn turned her back to the group and squatted down. Owen heard a jingle of keys.

'Do you unlock the other one, too?' asked the man in the camel sweater.

'Afraid not,' Lynn said. 'We never open the door to the Kutch tunnel. Not even for the Midnight Tour. It's totally off limits. But we will be talking about the tunnel a little bit later.'

Owen heard a quiet *snick*. The padlock snapping open, he supposed. A moment later, Lynn stood up and stepped to the side. 'We'll have our own beast do the honors,' she said. 'I'm prettier, but he's stronger.'

Clyde jumped down from the trunk. He sank to a crouch. As he came up, hinges groaned. Then came a heavy metallic clank.

'Thank you, beast,' Lynn said.

He gave her a casual salute, touching the claws of one hand to his brow. Then he stalked away.

'You can come up one at a time, now, and take a good look at the hole. I'll shine my flashlight down there for you. When you look, try to imagine Lilly Thorn's beast crawling out of it on a summer night so long ago. A night very much like this one. Okay, who wants to go first?'

In the silence following her question, a faint, distant voice called, '*Helllllp meeee!*'

People gasped. Others chuckled.

'Cool,' said Arnold.

'You've got someone *in* there?' asked the camel-sweater man, sounding suprised and amused.

'Bully!' proclaimed Bixby.

'Awesome,' said Dennis.

'Probably just a lame recording,' Monica said.

Lynn held up a hand for silence. '*Quiet, everyone.* This isn't part of the show.'

'Oh, sure,' Monica muttered.

Several people went, 'SHHHHHH.'

'. . . *ellllp!*'

It seemed to be coming up through the hole in the cellar floor. A woman's voice.

'Holy shit,' Lynn muttered.

'Let me through.' Dana's voice sounded quiet but urgent. 'Excuse me. Excuse me. Let me through.'

As those in front of Owen stepped out of the way, he saw Lynn drop to her knees beside the hole and bend over it. '*HELLO!*' she yelled.

Dana squatted beside her.

'It's just a big act,' Monica said.

'Shhh.'

'*I'm in the tunnel! I can't get out! My hands are cuffed!*'

'Holy shit,' Lynn muttered.

Dana shouted into the hole, '*EVE! IS THAT YOU!*'

'*Dana? Lynn?*'

'*RIGHT!*' Lynn shouted. '*WHAT THE HELL HAPPENED?*'

'*What the hell took you so long?*' asked the faraway voice.

'*ARE YOU OKAY?*' Dana yelled.

'*Been better. Can you get me out of here?*'

'*ARE YOU ALONE?*' Lynn asked.

'*For now. But he might come back.*'

'Shit,' Lynn said.

Members of the tour began speaking to each other. Owen heard confusion in some voices, alarm in others.

'Is this real or isn't it?' Bixby suddenly demanded.

'It's real,' Lynn said. 'Please be quiet.'

'We've gotta *do* something,' Dennis said.

'Gotta *save* her,' said Arnold.

'Somebody needs to call the cops,' said the camel-sweater man.

'Where's the nearest phone?' asked Biff.

'I'll go call,' said a muffled voice.

Lynn leaped to her feet. 'Clyde! We need cops *and* an ambulance.'

'Got it.'

Looking over his shoulder, Owen saw the shiny white beast spring up the cellar stairs, taking them two at a time.

Behind him, Dana said, 'Give me.'

He jerked his head forward in time to see her grab the shiny aluminum flashlight out of Lynn's hand. 'I'm going in,' she said.

'No, you'd better just . . .'

'See ya later.'

Dana dropped to her knees. She shined her light into the hole and shouted, '*I'M COMING AFTER YOU!*' Then she toppled forward, arms first, and plunged headlong.

In less than a second, she was gone to the ankles.

Her feet kicked.

The soles of her boots vanished into the darkness.

Chapter Fifty-Seven

The Rescue

From the accounts Dana had read, she'd expected the tunnel to be a tight squeeze. Diving in, she'd feared that she would have to squirm through, flat on her belly.

But the accounts must've been wrong. Either that, or the tunnel had been enlarged in recent years.

After a wild downhill skid just below the cellar floor, Dana found that the tunnel had enough room to let her crawl on her hands and knees.

In the lurching beam of her flashlight, she saw only more tunnel ahead of her.

Dark gray clay on all sides.

She felt as if she were crawling through a bowel.

Doesn't smell too good, either.

What *is* that smell? she wondered.

Something's dead in here!

'Eve?' she called.

'I'm here.' She didn't sound very close.

'Where?'

'Just keep coming. You can't miss me.'

'Is there something dead in here?'

'You bet there is.'

Dana grimaced but kept crawling. The ground felt moist and cool under her hands and knees. She was starting to breathe hard from the exertion.

'How did you get in here?' she called.

'Dragged.'

'Jeez. Who did it?'

'Not sure. I went in the house in last night . . . this *is* Saturday?'

'Right.'

'Midnight Tour?'

'That's right.'

'*Told* you I'd make it.'

'Glad you turned up.' Dana stopped crawling and tried to catch her breath.

'Almost didn't,' Eve said. 'But I heard cheers and stuff.'

'That was us. Had an impromptu performance.'

'Good thing. If I hadn't heard the commotion, I would've kept quiet. You get yourself in a place like this, you don't spend much time yelling, I'll tell you that.'

'Scared?'

'Who, me? You bet I am.'

Dana resumed crawling.

'Know why they call me "Eve of Destruction"? 'Cause I'm so scared, I make sure to get *them* before they can get *me*. Only this time I didn't.'

'How'd that happen?'

'I got jumped from behind. Big-time. Up in the attic. Got myself creamed. Don't know who did it. Stronger than shit. Might've been a beast.'

'You're kidding.'

'*Looked* like a beast. *Felt* like a beast.'

'Had a lot of . . . experience along those lines?'

'A matter of fact, yeah.'

Dana panted for air, then asked, 'How's that?'

'My little secret.'

'Shouldn't keep secrets . . . from your rescuer.'

'How come *you're* the one? Where's Lynn?'

'I beat her to the punch. Anyway, I'm bigger and stronger. Is this gonna call for brawn?'

'Might. Aren't there any *guys* up there?'

'I didn't wait around for volunteers.'

'Well, I sure appreciate . . . I can see your light!'

'Great!'

'You're almost here.'

Huffing for breath, Dana crawled faster. 'He *dragged* you all this way?'

'Guess so. I was really out of it.'

'Must've been a job.'

'Yeah. Too bad he didn't have a heart attack.'

'Do beasts *have* heart attacks?' Dana asked.

'Not sure he *was* one.'

Just ahead of Dana, the left-hand wall of the tunnel seemed to vanish.

'You're here,' Eve said.

Dana crawled the final distance. Shining her light to the left, she found herself looking into a hollowed-out area.

Eve was sitting naked on a rag-littered floor. Her raised arms, cuffed together at the wrists, were suspended by a chain that hung down taut from a four-by-four ceiling beam. Her skin was striped with scratches and furrows, some shiny with blood, others crusted over.

'Jeez,' Dana muttered.

Eve smiled. Her lips were torn and puffy. One cheek was badly scratched. Her right eye was swollen almost shut. 'Looks better than it feels,' she said.

Dana turned her head and shouted over her shoulder, '*FOUND HER!*'

A moment later, she heard Tuck's faint voice. '*How is she?*'

'*I'LL LIVE!*' Eve shouted.

Tuck's faint voice called back, '*Dana? Can you get her out okay?*'

'Tell her yes,' Eve said.

'How'll we get you out of the cuffs?'

'We'll manage.'

'*I'LL GET HER OUT!*' Dana yelled.

After a short pause, she heard Tuck call out, '*Holler if you need help.*'

Dana nodded. To Eve, she said, 'We've got an ambulance coming. And cops.'

'Somebody better call the coroner, too.'

Reluctantly, Dana eased her beam of light away from Eve.

Two other people hung by chains from the center beam.

One looked as if it used to be a child. Not enough was left for Dana to tell whether it had been a boy or girl. The other body still retained one breast, though it was missing a mouth-sized chunk where the nipple should've been.

Hunching over, Dana vomited onto the rag-covered floor.

People's clothes.

Wave after wave of painful spasms racked her body as she choked up a burning flood of stomach acid and cheeseburger and beer and maybe even the Red Hot Beastie Weenie that she'd eaten for lunch. Tears ran from her stinging eyes. Her chest hurt so badly she felt as if she might start coughing up her lungs and heart.

At last, the spasms subsided. She gasped for air.

'Are you all right?' Eve asked.

'Those people . . . they're *eaten*.'

'Yeah.'

'*God!* Are *you* okay?'

'I'm not missing any parts. Not yet.'

'What'd it *do* to you?'

'Nothing that hasn't been done before. Let's get me out of here.'

Though Dana still held on to the flashlight, it was half buried in the floor rags. She raised it and shone the beam on Eve. The brightness climbed to her raised arms, to her cuffed wrists. 'Are they *your* cuffs?' she asked.

'Might be. I had 'em with me.'

'Where did you keep the key?'

'Pocket of my jeans.'

Dana began shining her light on the scattered clothes, searching for blue jeans. A couple of times, she accidently glimpsed the ruined bodies but didn't allow herself to focus on them.

She spotted a rumpled pair of jeans on the floor not far behind Eve. To reach them, she crawled between Eve and the body of the woman. She bumped against Eve.

Eve winced.

'I'm sorry.'

'No problem. I'm a little tender here and there.'

'I'll bet. My God.' She got to the jeans. Kneeling, she lifted them with her left hand and shook them open. 'These yours?'

'Wranglers?'

'Yeah.'

Groaning and wincing, Eve turned herself halfway around. She peered at the jeans from beneath an upraised arm. 'They look like mine.'

Dana set down her flashlight. With her right hand, she began to search the pockets. 'What were you doing in Beast House last night, anyway?' she asked.

'Looking for a beast.'

'Guess you found it.'

'It found me. Whatever it was.'

'There's *nothing* in the pockets.'

'Are the pocket linings shredded?'

'No. I don't see *any* tears.'

'Okay. I guess that settles it.'

'Settles what?'

'It wasn't a beast.'

'*What?*'

'I had my doubts.'

'It *had* to be a beast,' Dana said. 'Look what it *did* to you . . . and to *them!*'

'Beasts don't go around emptying people's pockets,' Eve explained. 'If they want something out of a pocket, they don't reach in – they rip the pocket to shreds. But that isn't the only thing. How'd he get through the padlock on the hatch?'

'I don't . . .'

'With a key. I'll bet everything looked normal up there tonight.'

'Yeah.'

'So he *had* to use a key. And that's *not* how a beast would do it.'

'You said it looked and felt like a beast.'

'Didn't smell like one.'

'Huh?'

'Beasts don't smoke cigarettes.'

'You think it was a *guy* in a beast suit?'

'Scoobie-doobie doo.'

'Fuck,' Dana muttered. She dropped the jeans. With her left hand, she picked up the flashlight. She shoved her right hand down the front pocket of her shorts. 'You think it was Clyde?'

'Could've been, I guess.'

Dana pulled out the pistol. 'He's on the tour,' she said. 'He runs around in that *authentic* beast suit. And he smokes cigarettes.'

'Does he?' Pulling downward with her arms, Eve drew the chain taut.

Dana scurried over to her. She stopped very close to Eve's back. In the pale beam of her flashlight, she saw that Eve's shoulders and back were seamed with claw marks.

Just like Warren!

Clyde did it all! Attacked Warren, tearing him up and sodomizing him and making him always afraid. Dragged Eve in here, ripped her . . .

'Might not've been him,' Eve said.

'Did he . . . rape you?'

'I got nailed pretty good,' Eve said.

With that big fake cock with its mouth and teeth?

'I'll kill him,' Dana said.

'Let's leave the killing to me. I'm not really sure who or what did all this.'

'It had to be Clyde,' Dana said. 'He's got the beast suit. He smokes. And he probably has keys. I bet he *does* have a key to the cellar hatch. He's in charge of the whole operation whenever Tuck's away.'

'He's sounding pretty good for it.'

'Oh, God!'

'What?'

'He's the one who went off to call the cops.'

'Or maybe not,' Eve said.

Dana shone her light on the handcuffs. Stretching out her right arm, she pressed the muzzle of her pistol against the thin, shiny chain connecting the handcuff braclets. Blasted apart, it would free Eve from the heavier chain that suspended her from the ceiling beam.

'Wait,' Eve said.

'What?'

'After you fire, we won't be able to hear ourselves think. We've gotta do our talking now. One shot should take care of things. But keep at it till I'm loose. Then give me the gun.'

Dana almost smiled. 'It's your gun, anyway.'

'Yep.'

'Thank God you gave it to me.'

'Soon as I'm free, I want it back. After that, best thing for you to do is get out of my way.'

'What about the flashlight?'

'I'm not gonna leave you down here in the dark. You keep it. If you can stay fairly close behind me, maybe you can light the way.'

'I'll be right on your tail.'

'Good deal.'

'Ready?' Dana asked.

'Do it.'

Thrusting the muzzle hard against the chain, she pulled the trigger. The pistol bucked in her hand, blasting out a tongue of fire. The *BLAM!* smacked her ears and left them ringing.

Eve jerked her arms down.

It worked!

Twisting around, Eve snatched the pistol out of her hand. And dropped it. She snarled out a word that Dana couldn't hear. Then she shook both her arms and Dana realized that they must be numb. As she kept on shaking them, Dana picked up the pistol. Eve flexed the fingers of both hands, shook her arms some more, flexed her fingers again, then nodded and reached out.

Dana put the pistol into her right hand.

'*GIVE HIM HELL!*' Dana shouted into her face.

Eve's head moved up and down. Then she twisted away, lurched forward, fell to her elbows and knees and scurried up the tunnel.

Clutching the flashlight, Dana crawled after her.

Chapter Fifty-Eight

The Attack

After shouting a few questions down the hole to Dana, Lynn stood up and turned to the group. 'I guess we got more than we bargained for. The way things look, we've walked into a brand-new chapter in Beast House history. Apparently, one of our local police officers, Eve Chaney, somehow got abducted and taken down into the tunnel. It sounds as if she'll be okay. Dana will probably have her out of there in a few minutes. If not, I'm sure she'll be safely rescued by the emergency personnel who should be arriving shortly. You're all welcome to stick around. But as for tonight's tour, I don't see much chance of going on with it. You're certainly free to leave. If you can, stop by the ticket booth tomorrow. We'll either give you a full refund, or . . . If I run a special Midnight Tour tomorrow night, how many of you would be able to make it?'

Owen raised a hand. So did Darke, Vein, Dennis, Arnold and Bixby. Among the three couples that appeared to be married, no hands went up. Owen couldn't hear what was being said, but he figured they were probably talking it over.

'That looks pretty good,' Lynn said. 'I'll definitely run a tour tomorrow night for those of you who can make it – assuming that it's not impossible for one reason or another.'

Done conferring with his wife, the camel-sweater man said, 'I believe we'll be able to stay over for it.'

'Great,' Lynn said.

The cellar door banged shut.

Owen looked over his shoulder and saw Clyde bounding down the stairs in the beast suit.

'Couldn't get through,' a voice announced. The muffled sound seemed to be coming from Clyde's mask.

'What do you mean?' Lynn asked him.

'The phone's out.'

'The office phone?'

'Right.'

'You couldn't go someplace and find a phone that *works*?'

The beast shook its head.

'You're a big lot of help.'

The massive white shoulders shrugged.

'I have a cell phone,' said Eleanor, the tennis lady.

'It won't work down here,' Lynn said. A moment later, she said, 'But it's worth a try.' Holding out a hand, she said, 'Here, let me see it.'

'I'll have a go at it myself,' said Bixby. He reached into a pocket of his safari jacket and hauled out a cell phone.

'We might as well try it, too,' said the camel-sweater man. 'Alison?' His wife reached into her purse.

Shaking her head and laughing softly, Lynn said, 'I'll try 911. Somebody else try to get hold of an operator. Shit, just call anyone you can get. Tell 'em where we are, that we need cops and an ambulance.'

The cellar came alive with twitters and beeps.

'I DON'T THINK SO!'

Owen looked around.

Clyde had taken the beast head off. His face was red and twisted, his eyes wild. The hideous mask seemed to be resting on his shoulder. But he suddenly cocked back his arm and hurled the white head forward like an oversized softball.

Owen heard a distant, heavy *blam!* that sounded like a gunshot.

An instant later, the beast head crashed through the dangling light bulb.

The bulb exploded.

The cellar fell dark.

All around Owen, screams erupted.

He swung Darke around to the front and she came up tight against him. He wrapped his arms around her back. He could feel her panting for air as chaos swarmed around them.

From every side came shrieks of terror, cries of pain.

People yelled—

'No!'

'Who's that?'

'Watch out!'

'Connie? Con, is that you? YAHHH!'

Lynn shouted, 'Calm down, everyone! Don't panic! Try to get to the stairs.'

'Oh, my God!'

'Get away!'

'It's the BEAST!'

'This isn't too cool.'

'Dude.'

'Help me! Help!'

Lynn yelled, 'Shit! Get out of here, everyone! Run!'

'Leave me ALONE!'

'*Owie?*' Monica's voice, a terrified whimper, came from directly behind him.

'Monica?'

'*Owie, where are you?*'

'*Phil!*'

'*Get off me!*'

'*The DOOR'S locked!*'

'*Dude, let's haul ass.*'

'*Who locked the fuckin' door!*'

'Right in front of you,' Owen said.

'*NO! PLEASE!*'

'*Dear God!*'

'*Andy? Andy, where are you?*'

Owen felt a hand pat his right shoulder-blade. Darke's arms were hugging him much lower, just above his waist.

'*Is that you, Owie?*'

'It's me. Are you all right?'

'*Fine and dandy, honey.*'

Something punched into his back. He grunted from the impact. As a molten pain flashed through him, he felt the thing slide out. Then it pounded into him again. He squealed.

Darke made a strange grunting sound.

She suddenly jerked in his embrace, twisting him sideways and driving him backward. He bumped into people but kept stumbling backward as if Darke were playing a rough game of football in a strange, pitch-black stadium – a fierce little contender plowing against him, determined to drive him out of bounds.

At last, they fell.

On their way down, Darke turned him. They landed hard on their sides.

Darke pulled away from him. She turned him face-down against the cellar's dirt floor.

Through the roar in his ears and the cries and shouts, he heard Darke say, 'She *stabbed* you.'

'Where . . .?'

'In the back. The knife's still in you.'

'Where is she?' Owen gasped.

'Don't know. Maybe we lost her. She'll never find us in the dark.'

'*Unless I HEAR you!*' Monica blurted, glee in her voice.

Owen squealed with pain as the knife was suddenly jerked out of his back.

Chapter Fifty-Nine

Sandy's Story – June, 1997

Pistol in hand, steel bracelets shaking and rattling around her wrists, Sandy scurried on all fours through the tunnel. Dana seemed be to following her closely; the flashlight cast shadows and patches of light ahead of her.

She hurt everywhere.

But that was nothing new.

Nothing new, but worse. Though she'd been scratched up by Eric when he attacked her in Terry's beach house, that had been child's play compared to what she'd gone through last night.

Child's play.

Literally.

At the time, barely conscious in the tunnel chamber, she'd expected not to live through it. She'd expected to end up like the two devoured bodies already hanging from the beam. And she'd figured that she most likely deserved it.

Payment in full for her many crimes.

Never should've raised Eric in the first place. Should've killed him when he was still a baby, before he could grow up and destroy so many lives.

Never should've killed Slade or Lib or Harry.

Never should've *gotten* Terry killed.

Never should've murdered Eric's baby.

Did Eric know about that, somehow?

After running off, had he come sneaking back from time to time, spied on her during those endless nine months in the woods, maybe even watched through a window of the cabin as she gave birth . . . as she discovered that it was *his* son, not Terry's, and with her pocket knife cut the umbilical cord first, and then the monster's throat?

And this is payback time?

But as the beast tore at her and thrust into her last night, she'd found herself wondering from a faraway place at the edge of consciousness whether this really *was* Eric.

Has to be.

There IS no beast but Eric. He's the last of them.

Should've named him Chingachgook.

And when the hell did he take up smoking?

But now it all made sense. It had been an imposter. A maniac in a beast suit, ripping her with fake claws and teeth, raping her with a rubber cock – or plastic or . . .

But it came!

Impossible, she thought. Must've been my imagination.

Unless maybe he took off the suit.

She had no memory of anything like that, but she supposed that it might've happened. Plenty must've gone on; she only remembered bits and pieces . . .

Bastard could've brought in five buddies for a gang-bang for all I know.

Crawling as fast as she could through the tunnel, Sandy wondered if she would end up pregnant again.

That'd be just what I need.

Don't do it to me, God, please. Are you there, God? It's me, Sandy. Don't do it to me again. Please, please. I swear, if you do, I'll let it live. You can't ask me to kill my own baby more than once per lifetime, okay? It wouldn't be fair. Are you listening?

The earth beneath Sandy's hands and knees began slanting upward.

We're coming out!

And me without a stitch of clothes on, she thought.

So what else is new?

Too bad good old Blaze isn't here to capture it on canvas. He'd love it. Call it 'Last Charge of the Cave Girl,' sell it for thousands. Only I don't look so terrific at the moment. He'd have to clean me up and put me in a nice see-through gown.

She realized the flashlight's beam was no longer reaching past her. Maybe because the slope was too steep.

She churned her way upward.

The top of her head punched into something heavy but yielding.

A body?

Had somebody fallen across the opening?

Sandy reached up with one hand and touched wet fabric. She shoved hard. The barrier rolled away.

She climbed out of the hole and into complete darkness.

Though her ears still rang from the gunshot, she heard wild outcries, shouts and shrieks.

Somebody bumped into her and yelped, almost knocking her off her feet. From the quick feel of fabric against her bare skin, she knew it wasn't Clyde. She shoved the person away. Crouching slightly, she moved through the chaos with her left arm out to feel the way ahead and block assaults. Her right hand kept the pistol close to her side.

All around her, people were weeping, groaning, shouting.

'What was it?'

'You okay?'

'Where'd it go?'

'Oh, my God! Oh, my God!'

From high in front of Sandy came harsh thuds of someone pounding on wood – the cellar door?

'Who ARE you?'

'SOMEBODY GET US OUT OF HERE!'

A brilliant red light suddenly came on, spinning and flinging out crimson as if a fire truck had somehow made its way into the cellar. Sandy glimpsed blood-red bodies rushing about, some sprawled on the floor, others huddled in corners, a few on the stairway.

And a beast inside the Kutch tunnel, running away.

The barred door stood wide open.

Just inside the entrance, mounted on the shoring of the tunnel wall, was the whirling red light.

Sandy raced for the tunnel, dodging and leaping over bodies that blocked her way.

'Look at her!'

'Fuckin' A!'

'She's got a gun!'

'Help us!'

'Let's go with her!'

Sandy shouted, *'EVERYBODY STAY BACK!'* and ran into the tunnel.

Clyde had already vanished around a bend.

Sandy glanced at the spinning red light and saw a motion sensor.

Clyde must've set it off when he ran by.

How'd he get the door unlocked?

Had the key for it, stupid.

As a kid, Sandy had never liked this tunnel. It gave her the creeps, so she'd avoided it whenever possible.

Now, she wished she'd spent more time down here.

Though her memories were vague, she recalled that the tunnel had plenty of twists and bends, nooks, places where it split in two for a short distance, and even a couple of detours that led to dead-ends.

He could jump me so easily.

Slowing down, she jogged around a curve. Up ahead was another spinning red light.

No sign of Clyde.

She slowed to a quick walk.

What's he up to? she wondered. Planning to make his getaway through Agnes's house?

Feeling a strange mixture of longing and dread, Sandy realized that she would very likely be encountering Agnes within the next few minutes.

The woman had once been her best friend, her only friend, almost like a mother – more like a sister, maybe. Sandy hadn't seen her since the summer of 1980, the day before Marlon Slade showed up at the trailer and ruined everything.

Though she had eventually come back to town in search of Eric, she'd eagerly looked forward to a reunion with Agnes.

Her first day back, she'd gone to the door of the Kutch house, knocked, called out, '*Agnes, it's me. Sandy. How are you? I'm back in town. I want to see you.*' But there'd been no response from inside the house.

The next day, she'd tried again.

Still, no response.

After two weeks of secret visits, knocking and identifying herself, she'd finally gotten an answer from the other side of the door.

'*Go away,*' the voice had said.

'*Agnes? It's me, Sandy. You remember me, don't you?*'

'*I remember.*' Agnes sounded sour about it.

'*I want us to be friends again.*'

'*Get lost.*'

'*Agnes? What's wrong?*'

'*Got no use for you. Run off with the child. He was OURS. You hadn't got no RIGHT!*'

'*I had to leave. We were . . .*'

'*Don't wanta hear no excuses. Get lost. Go kill yourself.*'

After that, Sandy had made no more attempts to contact Agnes.

Maybe Clyde and I can finish this in the tunnel, she thought. *Before he gets all the way across to Agnes's place.*

She must really hate me.

I don't want to see her.

But maybe if we meet face to face . . .

'Wait up!' someone called from behind Sandy.

She looked back. Two geeky-looking teenaged boys were hurrying along behind her. Following them was a husky young woman in a flannel shirt and jeans. The woman's face was bleeding.

'Go back,' Sandy said.

'We wanta help you,' said the taller kid.

His chubby friend stared at her and nodded.

'He killed my husband!' blurted the woman.

Two more people rushed into view behind her. A slim, dapper man in a bloody camel sweater and a dazed-looking woman who was clinging to his hand. 'Is this a way out?' asked the man.

'No, it's not,' Sandy said. 'Go back to the cellar. All of you. You're interfering with police business.'

'You a cop?' asked the tall kid.

'I don't see no badge,' said the chubby one, leering at her breasts.

'Want my sweatshirt?' asked the tall one. He started pulling it up.

'Go!' Sandy shouted. Then she whirled away from them and ran deeper into the tunnel.

To make up for the delay, she picked up her pace. Arms pumping, legs flying out, she ran as fast as she could – too fast for the bends in the tunnel.

If he's waiting for me around one of these . . .

She dodged a dirt wall, lurched around a curve, bumped a wall with her shoulder.

And came out of the curve to find a section ahead that was as straight as a school hallway. This was the place, Sandy realized, where the tunnel passed underneath Front Street.

It was awash in scarlet from still another spinning light.

She spotted Clyde in the distance, a human head atop the body of a beast. Running away for all he was worth.

Fifty, sixty feet away and moving fast.

Sandy lurched to a halt and raised her pistol. '*POLICE!*' she shouted. '*STOP OR I'LL SHOOT!*'

Twisting halfway around, Clyde looked back at her.

Then he gasped out, 'Don't!' He raised his arms high, slowed down, turned until he was facing Sandy, and halted completely.

'Keep your hands up,' Sandy ordered. 'Don't move.' Right arm straight out, pistol aimed at his chest, she walked toward him.

'I give,' he gasped. 'You got me.'

From behind Sandy came sounds of footfalls on the dirt floor. Then she heard quick, labored breathing.

She didn't look back.

She walked straight toward Clyde. 'Get down on your knees,' she said.

'Yes, ma'am.'

As he sank to his knees, someone behind Sandy said, 'Whoa!'

Another voice said, 'Duuuude!'

'Shoot his ass!'

She didn't look back, kept walking toward Clyde.

'You *got* him!' a woman blurted.

Still fifteen or twenty feet from Clyde, Sandy halted. Keeping her pistol aimed at him, she spoke sharply. 'I told you people to go back to the cellar. Now do what I say.'

'We wanta help,' said a kid.

'Is there any assistance we can give you?' asked an adult male voice. She supposed it belonged to the man in the bloody sweater.

'Thanks, but no. I want you all to leave. Go back to the cellar immediately.'

'Don't!' Clyde blurted. 'Don't go! She's gonna kill me! She's gonna shoot me down in cold blood!'

'Is that true?' asked the man.

'Do it,' urged one of the teenagers.

'Kill his ass,' said the other.

'Maybe we'd *better* stay,' said a woman. Probably the man's wife.

'*GET THE HELL OUT OF HERE! NOW!*'

'Don't go! Please!'

Sandy heard someone rushing up behind her.

'Look out!' a kid warned.

She looked back. The chubby gal who'd lost her husband was lurching toward her, reaching out. 'Gimme that!' the gal blurted. '*I'll* kill him.'

'Nobody's going to kill . . .'

'Oh, my God!' someone cried out.

'*Shit!*'

'*Look out!*'

'*HIT THE DECK, CLYDE HONEY!*'

Sandy knew *that* voice.

Jerking her head forward, she saw Clyde throw himself flat on the dirt floor.

Beyond where he lay, Agnes Kutch waddled up the middle of the tunnel. Her hair looked rosy in the flashing red light. She had put on a lot of weight over the past seventeen years. As she trudged closer, her massive body flopped and bounced and swung inside her sheer nightgown.

Down low, clutched in both hands with its stock clamped against her bulging right side, Agnes carried something that looked very much like a Thompson submachine gun with a drum magazine.

'*AGNES!*' Sandy shouted. '*DON'T SHOOT! IT'S ME! DROP THE . . .*'

'Gimme!' a woman squealed into Sandy's ear. An arm reached past her face and a body slammed into her back, crashing her forward.

She stumbled, trying to keep her feet.

But it was no use.

As she began to fall, Agnes opened up. The Thompson jumped in her hands, spitting flame and bullets, deafening Sandy with its pounding roar.

On the way down, the gal on Sandy's back tried to grab her wrist.

But suddenly jerked.

Blood exploded over the back of Sandy's head and neck.

The weight of the woman smashed her against the tunnel floor. The impact knocked her breath out, but she kept her head up.

Agnes kept firing, her grin awash in the lightning of her muzzle flashes, her whole body jumping and shuddering as the Thompson jerked in her arms.

Flat on her belly, hurting all over, Sandy blinked her eyes clear of sweat and blood, stretched out her arm and fired a single shot.

It smacked Agnes in the forehead.

She keeled backward on stiff legs, raking the tunnel ceiling with gunfire, and landed flat on her back.

The Thompson went silent, stood erect by her side for a moment, then fell over sideways.

Sandy rolled out from under the body of the woman who'd wanted her pistol. The gal flopped over. She'd caught one in the right eye.

Clyde was still sprawled flat on the floor.

Sandy stood up.

She didn't much want to turn around.

She turned around, anyway.

All of them were down, knocked sprawling by the heavy slugs of Agnes's submachine gun: two teenaged boys, the man in the camel sweater and his wife. She looked at them only long enough to see that they'd been riddled beyond help. They were dead or dying.

She turned to Clyde.

'Get up,' she said.

He pushed himself to his knees.

Sandy saw that the big, fake penis was broken and dangling.

She walked toward him.

He raised his arms.

'I give,' he said, and smiled nervously.

She shot him in the face.

The blowback splashed her belly and breasts.

She watched him topple backwards.

Then she sighed and lowered the pistol.

And stood there.

I'd better go back to the others, she thought. But her body ached everywhere and she felt too weary to move.

Chapter Sixty

A Fight to the Death

Crawling through the narrow tunnel, Dana tried her best to keep up with Eve. Each time she raised her head, however, the naked legs and rear end of her friend were farther away.

She was tempted to call out, 'Slow down.'

But it would be a waste of breath.

Eve wouldn't slow down and wait for her; she was a woman on a mission, out to save the day.

Dana kept on crawling, sweating, huffing for air.

When she raised her head again, Eve was nowhere to be seen.

In front of her, the tunnel slanted upward.

Must be almost to the top.

Eve was probably out already.

On knees and elbows, Dana struggled up the slope. Why wasn't any light coming in from the cellar? Maybe she was farther away than she thought.

Through the ringing in her ears, she heard people shouting.

Suddenly, her head was out of the hole.

What's . . .?

The cellar wasn't dark, after all. It glowed with red, flicking light that came from the Kutch tunnel.

Just as she realized that the barred iron door stood wide open, someone dashed into the tunnel.

Eve?

Dana only caught a glimpse before the woman raced out of sight.

It has to be Eve, she told herself. A naked gal running off with a pistol in her hand. Who else *could* it be?

Besides, nobody else on the tour had a figure like that.

Had Clyde taken off through the tunnel?

She shone her flashlight around, looking for the white costume. Her beam showed people sprawled on the floor, others huddled together, a few hurrying this way and that.

No sign of Clyde.

As Dana crawled out of the hole, someone rushed at her from the left. She flung up an arm, expecting a blow. Her arm was grabbed. 'The shit hit the fan,' Tuck said, pulling to help her up. 'Clyde went nuts.

He busted the light and started clawing everybody. It was fuckin'
pandemonium around here.'

On her feet, Dana said, 'Where is he?'

'Took off through the Kutch tunnel. Eve went after him.'

'*You* okay?'

'Fine.'

Dana shone the light on her.

The left side of Tuck's face looked red and swollen. A path the width
of a large hand had been torn straight down the front of her uniform
shirt from her left shoulder to her waist. Her bra was still intact,
however. She didn't seem to be scratched. The long flap of torn shirt
hung almost to her knee.

'Clyde did that?' Dana asked.

'Sharp claws. It's okay. He pretty much missed. Look, I need you.'
Tuck squeezed her arm. 'We keep some spare bulbs down here.'

'Let's go get 'em.'

'I already did. Come on.' She led Dana over to a steamer trunk.
Bending down, she lifted one end. 'Just light my way.'

Dana raised her flashlight, swept it here and there, and found the
dangling light fixture. 'Here we go.'

Tuck dragged the trunk into position directly beneath the fixture,
then climbed up.

Dana lit the jagged remains of the bulb. 'Careful you don't cut
yourself.'

'Have you got a rag?' Tuck asked.

Dana plucked a handful of fabric out of the left front pocket of her
shorts. Too late, she realized it was Warren's underwear – her souvenir
from last night in his car. She handed it to Tuck, anyway.

Holding the good bulb in her mouth, Tuck balled up the underwear.
She held the fixture with one hand. With the other, she shoved the
bunched briefs up against the sharp remains of the broken bulb.

As she twisted it, Professor Bixby stepped closer to watch.

The base came loose. Tuck tossed it away, handed the underwear
down to Dana, then took the fresh bulb out of her mouth. Twisting it
into the fixture, she said, 'This is how many tour guides it takes to screw
in a light bulb.'

Suddenly, the bulb flared to life, filling the cellar with light.

'Good show!' Bixby proclaimed.

Dana shut off her flashlight and looked around. She saw Phil dead
on the dirt floor just behind the tunnel hole, his throat ripped open. No
sign of his wife, Connie. No sign of Andy or Alison Lawrence, either.
Eleanor was on her knees, stuffing her folded tennis sweater underneath

the head of her husband, Biff. He'd been ripped down the chest. His knit shirt was shredded and bloody, but he was conscious.

Dennis and Arnold seemed to be missing.

Off to the right, Owen lay face-down, bare to the waist. Vein's black leather jacket was spread on the floor underneath him. Darke, on her knees beside him, used both hands to press a cloth against his back – probably his own shirt. She held a red-handled pocket knife in her teeth.

A few feet away from them, Vein had Monica pinned to the floor. In black satin bra, leather short-shorts and boots, Vein sat on top of Monica like a punk Dracula groupie, pressing a knife to her throat.

'Vein?' Dana called. 'What's going on?'

'She stabbed Owen.'

'*Who* stabbed him?'

'Monica.'

Darke met Dana's eyes. Unable to talk because of the knife in her mouth, she nodded her head up and down.

'I did not,' Monica protested. 'They're lying bitches. *She* stabbed him. She was *jealous!*'

'He's hurt pretty badly,' Vein explained. 'We need to get him to a hospital.'

Tuck jumped down from the trunk. 'Whatever the hell Clyde did upstairs – other than locking us in – I'm damn sure he didn't call for an ambulance or cops. If we can't bust the door open, we'd better . . .'

Tuck's voice stopped.

Heads turned.

From somewhere down the Kutch tunnel came a chain of gunfire. Muffled and far away, the shots crashed together so fast they almost sounded like heavy cloth or canvas being ripped down the middle.

'Holy shit,' Tuck said.

'What *is* that?' Dana asked.

Bixby, eyes wide behind his glasses, said, 'Machine gun.'

'That can't be good,' Tuck muttered.

The weapon went silent.

'Could *Eve's* gun sound like that?' Dana asked.

Bixby shook his head. 'If you mean the nude lady with the pistol, I'm afraid not.'

Tuck stared at the entrance to the Kutch tunnel. 'Eve'll be okay,' she said. 'Nothing can stop her.'

Suddenly leaping away from her injured husband, Eleanor blurted, 'We've gotta get out of here!' and raced up the stairs.

'Can't get out that way,' Tuck called to her. 'The door's locked.'

'Maybe we should go see what happened with Eve,' Dana suggested.

'Where'd everybody *else* go?' Tuck asked.

'I don't know.'

'They went chasing after Eve,' Bixby explained. 'Oh, perhaps half a dozen of them. Including those teenagers.'

From the direction of the Kutch tunnel came a single, quick *bam!*

A smile spread across Tuck's face. '*That* was Eve's gun,' she said.

They listened for more shots.

And heard a low grumbling noise that sounded very much like the growl of a vicious dog. But it didn't seem to be coming from the Kutch tunnel.

It came from somewhere in the cellar.

Dana twisted around.

Out of the hole in the floor protruded a hairless, snouted head. It swung from side to side, pale blue eyes darting about.

Tuck yelled, '*SHIT!*'

This can't be happening, Dana thought. *Clyde* was the beast. *Who's THIS?*

The shiny white mouth writhed as it bared its teeth.

And Dana knew this wasn't anyone in a beast suit.

She felt herself shrivel inside.

This had to be the creature that savaged Warren, that snatched Eve and ripped and fucked her and left her handcuffed in its lair – that devoured those other two poor people.

No. Eve's beast was Clyde. It had to be. The cigarette stink, the keys . . .

As if it were in no hurry at all, the creature began to climb out of the hole.

'What's going on down there?' Eleanor called from the stairway.

'We've got a beast,' Tuck said. She sounded strangely calm.

'I *say*,' Bixby muttered.

'A *what*?' asked Eleanor.

In a loud, firm voice, Tuck said, 'Time to scram, everyone! Go for the Kutch tunnel! Run like hell!'

Bixby twisted around and raced for the Kutch tunnel.

Eleanor came rushing down the stairs, tennis skirt flouncing around her thighs.

Darke let the knife fall from her mouth. 'I can't leave Owen.'

'Stay put,' Vein said. 'You, too,' she told Monica as she climbed off. Knife in hand, she turned toward the rising beast.

Suddenly free, Monica scurried up and dashed for the Kutch tunnel.

Vein whirled, flipped her knife and caught it by the blade, then cocked back her arm to throw it.

'No!' Darke yelled. 'Don't! You'll lose your knife!'

Vein lowered her arm.

Monica sprinted into the tunnel, Eleanor racing in close behind her.

The beast now stood on the cellar floor in front of the hole, flexing its claw-tipped fingers as its head turned slowly. It seemed to be studying each of the four women. Its growl sounded like a loud, rumbling purr.

Clyde's suit had been a good replica.

But this was no costume; this was skin. Snow-white skin that rippled with muscles, that gleamed with a sheen of slime. The teeth of this creature were yellow. The mouth drooled.

Unlike Clyde's suit, it had no permanent erection.

The erection grew as the creature stood there, eyeing the women.

Grew longer and longer, thickening and rising.

It had the mouth, all right.

The shaft pointed at Tuck. The mouth bared its teeth and flicked its forked tongue at her.

'Oh, shit,' Tuck murmured.

Dana glanced over at Vein and Darke. 'Get the hell out of here, gals. Carry Owen with you. Or drag him. Just get out of here. Now!'

'Go with 'em,' Tuck said.

'Me?' Dana asked. 'No way.'

'I'll keep the thing busy.'

'Bullshit. *You* go.'

'Not me.'

'Not me, either,' Vein said. 'Three of us, one of it.'

'*Four* of us,' Darke said. She patted Owen's rump, picked up the folding knife, then stood up.

Roaring, the beast suddenly launched itself at Tuck. She held her ground and drew back a fist.

Dana lurched in from the side, swinging her flashlight like a small club. The head of the flashlight bounced off the creature's brow.

Snarling, the beast whirled toward Dana. A paw swept by, knocking the flashlight from her hand. As she backstepped to get away, the thing came at her.

Tuck leaped at it.

A powerful arm bashed Tuck across the chest. She seemed to explode off her feet.

As she soared across the cellar, the beast clutched Dana's shoulders. Claws digging in, it thrust her backward and down. She slammed against the cellar floor. Straddling her, it ripped at her clothes. She punched at it, but her blows seemed to have no effect. Quick claws scratched and furrowed her skin as they tore off her shirt and bra and stripped off her shorts in a matter of seconds.

She glimpsed a blur of motion from her left as someone dived onto the beast.

The running dive snagged it off her.

She rolled onto her side and saw Darke on the floor under the back of the beast, right arm across its throat, left arm across its chest. In her left hand was the pocket knife. She raised the knife and brought it down hard.

Striking the chest of the beast, the short blade folded in and clamped shut on Darke's hand. She squealed in pain, but kept her left arm across the throat of the beast and wrapped her leather-clad legs around its thighs.

It thrashed on top of her, its erection thrusting at the air, mouth snapping.

As Dana struggled to get up, Vein rushed in and dropped to her knees at the heads of Darke and the beast. She raised her knife high, clutching it with both hands. No little pocket knife that might fold on her, this was a dagger with a rigid, eight inch blade. She plunged it down toward the chest of the beast.

The creature slapped it from her hands.

The knife flew at Dana. Before she could move, an inch of its blade entered her just above her left breast.

The creature's next blow ripped off half of Vein's face and knocked her head sideways. Face flapping like a bloody rag, she was suddenly looking behind her back. She tumbled toward the cellar floor.

Dana grabbed the knife and pulled it out of herself.

She stumbled to her feet.

'*Hurry!*' Darke gasped from beneath the beast.

Knife raised overhead, Dana dived between its legs. She expected to land on its penis, but she'd thought it would give way under her weight.

It didn't.

Rigid as a tent pole, it pounded her in the belly and punched her breath out. Folding over it, she tried to drive her knife down into the beast's chest.

Both her wrists were suddenly grabbed.

Instead of mauling her, the beast pulled her arms straight out past its head, stretching her as all of her weight bore down on the stiff, upright shaft.

Though Darke still had an arm across the beast's throat, the thing started to make a hissing sound that seemed like laughter.

The mouth that was shoved so hard against Dana's belly suddenly bit her.

Crying out with pain and horror, she bucked fiercely and flung herself aside.

She fell to the cellar floor, but the beast stayed with her, gripping her wrists. They rolled, and suddenly it was on top of her, Darke somehow still clinging to its back. Seemingly unconcerned by Darke, the beast planted its mouth on Dana's mouth, forced her lips open and thrust its tongue in.

The other mouth no longer bit her belly.

It had moved lower.

Now, she felt it between her legs.

Licking, nibbling.

No! she cried out inside her head.

She chomped down hard on the beast's tongue, but her teeth wouldn't sink in. The tongue was too solid.

Dana suddenly heard a crashing sound – like someone smashing through a door.

The beast jerked its tongue from her mouth and turned its head.

Footfalls began thudding down the wooden stairs.

'What's going on?'

It was a man's voice.

Warren's voice.

'Help us!' Darke yelled.

'Oh, my God!' Warren blurted.

With a roar, the beast sprang off Dana. As it scurried over her body, she reached up with her left hand and caught hold. The shaft was slippery, but she held on tight.

The beast didn't stop, didn't seem to care.

Darke on its back, Dana dragging beneath it, the creature scampered across the cellar floor, roaring, apparently eager to pounce on Warren.

As Dana was dragged between its legs, she pulled at the slippery rod with all the strength in the left arm, raising her head and back out of the cellar dirt, pulling herself higher, higher.

Then she plunged the knife into the creature's belly and ripped downward.

His front opened like a shiny white bag, spilling blood and intestines onto Dana's face.

A woman cried out '*NO!*'

The beast bellowed in agony.

As it fell headlong, Dana let go and dropped against the cool dirt.

'*Oh, God, no!*'

Eve?

Rolling onto her side, Dana wiped some of the mess away from her face and saw Eve rushing forward, naked, a tommy gun in her hands.

Ignoring all else, Eve ran toward the beast.

It was sprawled on the floor, head against the bottom stair. Darke was climbing off its back while Warren stood on the forth stair, his mouth hanging open as he gaped at the carnage.

Eve, sobbing, squatted next to the creature. She set her tommy gun aside, then reached down with both hands, clutched the beast by one shoulder and turned it over.

It flopped onto its back.

Eve hunched over it, weeping as she caressed its hideous face.

'Eve?' Dana said. 'What's wrong?'

One of the sobs suddenly sounded like, 'Huh?'

Eve's back straightened.

'What's wrong?' Dana asked again.

'Nothing.' Eve looked at her with wet red eyes, wiped tears away, and gave her a trembling smile. 'Nothing's wrong,' she said. 'I'm fine.' She gave the beast's face a rough smack with her open hand, then picked up the tommy gun and got to her feet. 'I guess somebody'd better find a telephone.'

Chapter Sixty-One

Sunday Morning

1. Tuck's Long-Distance Call

'Sorry to disturb you, Janice, but I'm afraid we had some trouble last night on the Midnight Tour.'

2. Visiting Hour – Owen

Waking up in a hospital room, Owen found Darke sitting beside his bed. 'Hi,' he said.

She smiled softly at him.

Her clingy, black silk blouse was gone, replaced by a black T-shirt that seemed to be few sizes too small for her. Seeing her in the T-shirt, nobody would mistake her for a guy.

Owen looked at her bandaged hand.

'What happened?' he asked.

'Monica stabbed you.'

'Oh . . . I know that. What happened to *you?*'

'Just a minor cut. I'm fine.' Tears suddenly glistened in her eyes. 'Vein didn't make it, though.'

'Monica stabbed *Vein?*'

'The beast killed her.'

'Oh, my God.'

'She . . . always hoped they were real. Always wanted to meet one face to face. They say you've gotta be careful what you wish for.'

Groggy and confused, Owen shook his head. 'I don't . . . *How* was she killed?'

'We took on the beast. The four of us. Lynn, Dana, me and Vein. And we killed it, too.'

'You mean Clyde? You killed Clyde?'

She shook her head, her pale hair swaying across her brow. 'You really *were* out of it. After Clyde, a *real* beast came along. That's how Monica got away from us. We couldn't keep her prisoner *and* fight the beast, so we let her go. She ran off through the Kutch tunnel and that's the last anyone's seen of her.'

3. Tuck's Long-Distance Call – Part II

'We think Clyde didn't call the police – he called Agnes, instead. So then she came to his rescue with a tommy gun.'

4. Visiting Hour – Sandy

'Okay, honey, quit beating around the bush and tell me who did it.'

'I'm not your honey, Cochran.'

'Oh, excuse *meeee*, Officer Chaney.'

'I'll get out of bed and wreck you.'

Flushing, Cochran said, 'I'm simply trying to determine the truth.'

'The truth is . . . I'm pretty sure it was both of them. Clyde *and* the beast.'

'Which of them abducted you in the attic?'

'I don't know.'

'Which one dragged you into the tunnel?'

'I'm not sure, but Clyde must've been the one who unlocked it.'

'Which one handcuffed you?'

'That must've been Clyde, too.'

'Which one was responsible for your injuries?'

'I smelled the cigarette smoke, but . . . not always. I think it was probably both of them.'

'Taking turns?'

'Something like that. Maybe.'

'Who ate those people?'

'I don't know.'

'Either of 'em eat *you*?'

'Watch it.'

'And which of them do you think committed the sexual assaults on you?'

Eve studied Cochran, her eyes narrow. Finally, she answered, 'Both.'

'Which did you prefer?'

She leaped out of bed. Cochran made it halfway across the hospital room before she got close enough to shove him. Stumbling out of control, he almost made it through the doorway. But his right shoulder collided with the frame and he cried out in pain.

As he flopped on the floor, Sandy called out, 'Is there a doctor in the house?'

5. Tuck's Long-Distance Call – Part III

'Well, we think Clyde must've been having a relationship with Agnes . . . No, I'm not kidding. Just before she opened fire, she yelled out for him to hit the deck. And Eve said she called him "honey" or "darling" or something like that. Sounds like they were lovers . . . I know, I know . . . Well, she *was* filthy rich. Maybe Clyde was hoping for a big inheritance. Or maybe he was just really *into* this whole beast thing. If you ask me, Clyde and the beast and Agnes were probably having a menagerie *à trois* . . . No, not *ménage*, menagerie . . . Well, I don't find it *that* amusing, either. I *know* a lot of people were killed.'

6. Visiting Hour – Owen, Part II

'What're you going to do now?' Owen asked.

Beneath her tight T-shirt, Darke shrugged her shoulders. 'I guess I'll stay right here till they kick me out.'

'What then?'

'Hang around town, I guess, and wait for them to release you. They say it'll probably be a few more days.'

She's going to wait for me!

'Do you have a place to stay?' Owen asked.

'Lynn said I can stay at her house.'

Owen remembered hiding in the bushes with John . . . spying on the three women . . . and he remembered the *third* spy, the one they'd heard but never seen.

What happened to John? Is he still hanging around near the house, or . . .?

'I've got a room at the Welcome Inn,' Owen said. 'That's where my stuff is. And my rental car. If you'd rather stay there, I could call and . . . you know, extend my stay.'

'I have a better idea,' Dark said. 'If you'd like, I'll go to the room and pick up your things. I can take them with me over to Lynn's. That way, you won't have to pay for all those nights at the motel.'

'Well . . . I'm just not sure you should stay at Lynn's house.'

'Why not?'

He couldn't *tell* her about the mysterious prowler hiding in the bushes.

'Maybe it isn't safe,' he said.

'It'll be fine. Dana'll be there, too. I think the three of us can handle just about anything. I mean, we killed the beast, didn't we? With a little help from Vein,' she added, and tears again filled her eyes.

7. *Tuck's Long-Distance Call – Part IV*

'Well, Warren was hanging around outside. You know how he wouldn't set foot in Beast House because of getting jumped that time? Speaking of which, I hear it *wasn't* teenagers. Thanks for the honesty, Janice . . . Oh, little birdies . . . You *should* be . . . Oh, because he was waiting for the tour to end. He and Dana happen to be madly in love. They can't stand to be apart.'

Tuck grinned at Dana and Warren, who were sitting across from each other at the kitchen table. Blushing, Dana watched Warren's face turn scarlet.

'Anyway,' Tuck continued, 'he was out near the street and he heard Agnes's machine gun. Or *felt* it under his feet. So he figured shit was happening down in the tunnel. Fearing for the life of his true love, he cast paranoia to the winds and ran to her rescue . . . No, Dana did, but Warren busted the door open for us.'

'Hey,' Dana protested. 'Warren *distracted* it. That's what saved me. Tell her.'

'Dana says to tell you Warren saved her by distracting the beast.' Tuck listened, nodding, then smiled at Warren. 'Janice says she always knew you were a secret hero.'

Warren blushed again. 'Tell her thanks.'

'He says thanks.'

8. Sandy's Long-Distance Call

Smiling at the sound of his voice, Sandy asked, 'Am I speaking to the one and only Blaze O. Glory? . . . Yep, it's me. How've you been? . . . Yeah, I've been missing you, too . . . A *very* long time . . . Five years . . . Well, I had to go looking for my son . . . No, nothing like that. I'm sure he just ran off on his own. He's always had sort of a wild streak . . . No, I'm afraid not. But I'm sure he's probably getting along just fine, wherever he is . . . The reason I called, I had a little accident. I'm going to be off my job for a couple of weeks, and wondered if you'd like to have a house guest . . . I don't know about *modeling*, I'm pretty banged up . . . Well, we'll see . . . I can probably be there day after tomorrow . . . That'll be great, Blaze.' Her throat tightened, and she felt tears well up in her eyes. 'I'm really looking forward to seeing you again, too.'

9. Visiting Hour – Owen, Part III

Bending over the bed, Darke kissed him gently on the mouth. Then she eased her lips away and whispered, 'See you later, okay?'

'Okay.'

'By the way, I'm Karen.'

'Karen?'

'Karen Marlowe.'

'That's a nice name,' Owen said.

'I don't know how nice it is, but it's mine. Thought you oughta know.'

10. Tuck's Long-Distance Call – Part V

'Hi, Dad. How's the cruise? . . . I'm fine . . . *Really*. Thanks to Dana. She saved my tail when the beast tried to nail me . . . Yeah, I know . . .' Tuck nodded as she listened. Though she was smiling, her chin began to tremble and tears filled her eyes. 'I love you, too, Dad.' She sniffed. She took a deep breath. Then she said, 'So, have you knocked Janice up yet? I'm hoping for a little sister.'

Chapter Sixty-Two

Sunday Night

Sitting with the gift on his lap, he flinched at the sudden brightness as lights came on behind the house and inside the big and little pools. Soon, three women came outside and walked toward the little pool. It was bubbling and steaming.

Last night, nobody at all had shown up.

He'd thought that maybe they stayed away because the one he liked best hadn't been pleased by the gift he'd left in her room.

But she was back, tonight. So was her friend, the smaller woman with the very long yellow hair.

With them was a woman he had never seen before. She was small and thin, with very short yellow hair. She had an injured hand that was wrapped in white.

His mother was not with them.

He felt glad about that.

The one he liked best *looked* a lot like his mother, looked so much like her that he always felt very strange when he saw her. But she *wasn't* his mother.

Mother had been here twice. The first time, he'd felt shocked and happy and frightened, all at once. He'd felt an urge to run up to her and hug her, but was afraid to do that because maybe she was still mad at him. She'd been *very* mad at him the day he hurt her and ran away. Maybe she was *still* mad, and looking for him because she wanted to hurt him back.

He knew that his mother could be very dangerous when she was mad.

He'd felt the danger of her both times when she was here and came hunting for him. If she'd caught him, she would've hurt him. Both times, though, he'd crept away and escaped from her.

Tonight, he wouldn't need to creep away.

Mother was gone, so there was no one to fear.

At the edge of the hot spa, Dana crouched and set down the bottle of wine. And remained in a crouch, aching too much to move. Earlier in the evening, she'd joined Warren for margaritas, then joined him for barbecued ribs, then joined him in bed. They'd compared wounds. They'd laughed and wept and made love. Because of her injuries,

Warren had been very gentle with her. Though she'd wanted to spend the entire night with him, she'd finally asked for a ride home.

There'd been those troubles with the prowler.

Tuck and Darke were likely to use the pool or hot spa, and Eve, laid up in the hospital, wouldn't be around to protect them.

Still crouching, Dana watched Tuck place a stack of folded towels on the concrete within easy reach of the spa. Then Tuck took off her robe and let it fall. Wearing her doe-skin bikini, she stepped down into the bubbly water. 'Ahhh,' she said. 'Nice and hot.'

Darke stood on the edge. Balancing on her left foot, she lowered her right foot into the water and dipped her toes in.

'It's clothing optional, you know,' Tuck told her.

Darke nodded. She wore a skintight black tank suit, cut low in front and high at the hips. 'I think I'll keep mine on for now,' she said. She lowered herself into the water, keeping her bandaged hand high.

'You have a question?' Dana asked her.

Darke laughed.

'Are *you* getting in?' Tuck asked Dana.

Groaning, Dana stood up straight. 'I don't think so. I doubt that hot, dirty water would do my wounds any good.'

'*Dirty* water?' Tuck protested.

'*You're* in it.'

Laughing, Tuck asked, 'How bad *are* you hurt?'

'I'm pretty messed up.'

'We'll be the judges of that,' Tuck said. 'Let's see.'

Dana looked across the pool.

'Give our Peeping Tom a treat,' Tuck urged her.

'What Peeping Tom?' Darke asked.

'Nothing to worry about,' Tuck said.

Dana reached behind her neck, grabbed the Beast House T-shirt with both hands, and pulled it over her head.

Holding the shirt by her side, she asked, 'What do you think?'

Tuck and Darke stared up at her.

She wore nothing.

She knew that she looked as if she'd been been thrown into a pit full of rabid cats. Most of her scratches were shallow. Only a few had been bandaged. In the several places where she'd been bitten, however, she was patched with thick pads of gauze.

'Well,' Tuck said, 'I guess you could soak your *feet*.'

'More than that,' said Darke. 'You look perfectly fine, Dana – all the way up to the knees.'

* * *

Watching from the bushes, he moaned.

The one he liked best was naked.

And *hurt*.

Confused for a moment, he wondered if *he* had done it to her. The other night when he took the gift to her and . . . ? He had touched her while she slept. He had caressed her. But he hadn't *hurt* her.

He hadn't dug his claws into her skin.

Hadn't bit her.

But seeing the wounds and bandages on her body, he thought about how it would feel to have her under him, to put his teeth and claws in her, to taste her and bite her with his big mouth and with his little mouth. He wondered what it would be like to shove up into her . . .

A hulking white shape lurched out of the bushes across the pool, roaring. It carried someone's severed head.

The head swung by its hair. The face looked beaten and chewed. Much was missing.

'*Holy shit!*' Tuck yelled.

As the creature bounded around the far end of the pool, Dana dropped her T-shirt, ducked and grabbed the wine bottle by its neck. She raised the bottle like a club. Wine burbled out, spilling down her arm and splashing the concrete.

Darke sprang out of the spa. Hunched over slightly, she glanced this way and that as if seeking a weapon.

The beast rushed around the pool's corner and came straight at Dana.

'*Get out of the way!*' Tuck yelled.

Dana leaped aside.

The beast dodged and rushed in.

She swung the wine bottle. It exploded against the side of the beast's head.

Growling, the monster swung the severed head at her.

It slammed her in the face.

As she started to fall, she heard the roar of Tuck's .44 magnum.

She crashed against the concrete and flung herself over, hoping to roll clear.

She was face-down when the beast caught her. It thrust a warm, slimy arm under her shoulder and down her chest. As the arm clamped her between her breasts, the beast's other hand clutched her between the legs.

It hoisted her off the concrete. Hugging her sideways, her back tight against its chest, it swung around.

Tuck in the spa with her magnum and Darke running toward Dana whirled by in a blur.

Then the spinning stopped.

The world jerked and bounced as the beast ran along the edge of the pool.

'*SHOOT IT!*' she cried out.

But she didn't hear another gunshot.

Tuck must've missed, that first time. Now, she was probably afraid to try again – afraid of hitting Dana.

Oh, my God, don't let it take me away!

Chapter Sixty-Three

Dream Kiss

In his dream, Karen was kissing him.

A deep, wet kiss, her tongue thrusting into his mouth.

Owen squirmed under the weight of her body. His hands roamed feverishly up and down the smooth bare skin of her back.

Coming up out of the depths of sleep, he realized it was more than a dream.

She was here with him.

Here in the darkness of his hospital room.

Here in his bed.

On top of him.

The mouth eased away, leaving his lips wet.

'Karen,' he whispered.

'Owie.'

Chapter Sixty-Four

Dana

He'll kill me when he gets done.
Kill me, eat me.
Maybe not.
Maybe he likes me too much.
Oh!
Maybe he'll keep me alive.
If I can stay alive, maybe I can escape.
Or they'll rescue me.
Tuck and Darke.
No, no, he lost them.
Long time ago.
Way too fast for 'em.
OH!
Did they give up, go home?
Call the cops?
Call Eve, guys.
Call Eve.
OH!
Get Eve out of the hospital.
She'll find me.
She'll save me.
Eve of Destruction!
OH!
She'll nail him.
Nail him good.
Nail him!
OH!
OH!
YES!!!